Ford Madox Ford's original name was Ford Madox Hueffer. He was born in 1873 of a family prominent in the artistic world of the day. At nineteen he published his first book, a fairy story; by the time he was twenty-two he had written four novels; and in 1898 he began several years of fruitful collaboration with Joseph Conrad. He went on to edit the *English Review* and to write a cycle of successful historical novels, but it was not until 1914 that he created a truly major work, *The Good Soldier*. After serving on active duty in World War I, he settled in France and later in America. As editor of the *transatlantic review*, he published such writers as Joyce and Hemingway while he himself was producing his masterpiece, *Parade's End*, consisting of *Some Do Not . . .* (1924), *No More Parades* (1925), *A Man Could Stand Up—* (1926), and *Last Post* (1928), a tetralogy not to be published in a single edition until after his death. Though he continued to write voluminously, his subsequent work was of markedly inferior quality, with the exception of his autobiographical *It Was the Nightingale*. He spent his last years in obscurity, teaching at Olivet College in Michigan, and it was while on vacation from this post that he died in France in 1939.

PARADE'S END

VOLUME ONE

Some Do Not . . .
No More Parades

FORD MADOX FORD

With an Afterword by
Arthur Mizener

A SIGNET CLASSIC

Published by
THE NEW AMERICAN LIBRARY

"SOME DO NOT . . ." COPYRIGHT 1924 BY THOMAS SELTZER, INC.
"NO MORE PARADES" COPYRIGHT 1925 BY ALBERT & CHARLES BONI, INC.
AFTERWORD COPYRIGHT © 1964 BY THE NEW AMERICAN LIBRARY OF
WORLD LITERATURE, INC.

Published as a SIGNET CLASSIC
by arrangement with Alfred A. Knopf, Inc.,
who have authorized this softcover edition.
A hardcover edition of the text is available from Alfred A. Knopf,
Inc.

First Printing, November, 1964

SIGNET TRADEMARK REG. U.S. PAT. OFF. AND FOREIGN COUNTRIES
REGISTERED TRADEMARK—MARCA REGISTRADA
HECHO EN CHICAGO, U.S.A.

Signet Classics are published by
The New American Library of World Literature, Inc.
501 Madison Avenue, New York, New York 10022

PRINTED IN THE UNITED STATES OF AMERICA

CONTENTS

CONTENTS

Some Do Not . . .

PART ONE

I ~

THE TWO young men—they were of the English public-official class—sat in the perfectly appointed railway carriage. The leather straps to the windows were of virgin newness; the mirrors beneath the new luggage racks immaculate as if they had reflected very little; the bulging upholstery in its luxuriant, regulated curves was scarlet and yellow in an intricate, minute dragon pattern, the design of a geometrician in Cologne. The compartment smelt faintly, hygienically, of admirable varnish; the train ran as smoothly—Tietjens remembered thinking—as British gilt-edged securities. It travelled fast; yet had it swayed or jolted over the rail-joints, except at the curve before Tonbridge or over the points at Ashford where these eccentricities are expected and allowed for, Macmaster, Tietjens felt certain, would have written to the company. Perhaps he would even have written to *The Times*.

Their class administered the world, not merely the newly created Imperial Department of Statistics under Sir Reginald Ingleby. If they saw policemen misbehave, railway porters lack civility, an insufficiency of street lamps, defects in public services or in foreign countries, they saw to it, either with nonchalant Balliol voices or with letters to *The Times,* asking in regretful indignation: "Has the British This or That come to *this!*" Or they wrote, in the serious reviews of which so many still survived, articles taking under their care manners, the arts, diplomacy, interimperial trade or the personal reputations of deceased statesmen and men of letters.

Macmaster, that is to say, would do all that; of himself Tietjens was not so certain. There sat Macmaster: smallish; Whig; with a trimmed, pointed black beard, such as a smallish man might wear to enhance his already germinated distinction; black hair of a stubborn fibre, drilled down with hard

9

metal brushes; a sharp nose; strong, level teeth; a white
butterfly collar of the smoothness of porcelain; a tie confined by a gold ring, steel-blue speckled with black—to match
his eyes, as Tietjens knew.

Tietjens, on the other hand, could not remember what
coloured tie he had on. He had taken a cab from the office
to their rooms, had got himself into a loose, tailored coat
and trousers and a soft shirt, had packed quickly, but still
methodically, a great number of things in an immense two-
handled kit-bag, which you could throw into a guard's van if
need be. He disliked letting that "man" touch his things; he
had disliked letting his wife's maid pack for him. He even
disliked letting porters carry his kit-bag. He was a Tory—and
as he disliked changing his clothes, there he sat, on the journey, already in large, brown, hugely welted and nailed golf
boots, leaning forward on the edge of the cushion, his legs
apart, on each knee an immense white hand, and thinking
vaguely.

Macmaster, on the other hand, was leaning back, reading
some small, unbound printed sheets, rather stiff, frowning
a little. Tietjens knew that this was, for Macmaster, an impressive moment. He was correcting the proofs of his first
book.

To this affair, as Tietjens knew, there attached themselves
many fine shades. If, for instance, you had asked Macmaster
whether he were a writer, he would have replied with the
merest suggestion of a deprecatory shrug.

"No, dear lady!" for of course no man would ask the question of anyone so obviously a man of the world. And he
would continue with a smile: "Nothing so fine! A mere trifler
at odd moments. A critic, perhaps. Yes! A little of a critic."

Nevertheless Macmaster moved in drawing-rooms that, with
long curtains, blue china plates, large-patterned wall-papers
and large, quiet mirrors, sheltered the long-haired of the
arts. And as near as possible to the dear ladies who gave the
At Homes, Macmaster could keep up the talk—a little magis-
terially. He liked to be listened to with respect when he spoke
of Botticelli, Rossetti, and those early Italian artists whom he
called "The Primitives." Tietjens had seen him there. And he
didn't disapprove.

For if they weren't, these gatherings, Society, they formed
a stage on the long and careful road to a career in a first-
class government office. And utterly careless as Tietjens imagined himself of careers or offices, he was, if sardonically,
quite sympathetic towards his friend's ambitiousnesses. It

was an odd friendship, but the oddnesses of friendships are a frequent guarantee of their lasting texture.

The youngest son of a Yorkshire country gentleman, Tietjens himself was entitled to the best—the best that first-class public offices and first-class people could afford. He was without ambition, but these things would come to him as they do in England. So he could afford to be negligent of his attire, of the company he kept, of the opinions he uttered. He had a little private income under his mother's settlement, a little income from the Imperial Department of Statistics; he had married a woman of means, and he was, in the Tory manner, sufficiently a master of flouts and jeers to be listened to when he spoke. He was twenty-six; but, very big, in a fair, untidy, Yorkshire way, he carried more weight than his age warranted. His chief, Sir Reginald Ingleby, when Tietjens chose to talk of public tendencies which influenced statistics, would listen with attention. Sometimes Sir Reginald would say: "You're a perfect encyclopaedia of exact material knowledge, Tietjens," and Tietjens thought that that was his due, and he would accept the tribute in silence.

At a word from Sir Reginald, Macmaster, on the other hand, would murmur: "You're very good, Sir Reginald!" and Tietjens thought that perfectly proper.

Macmaster was a little the senior in the service as he was probably a little the senior in age. For as to his room-mate's years or as to his exact origins, there was a certain blank in Tietjens' knowledge. Macmaster was obviously Scotch by birth, and you accepted him as what was called a son of the manse. No doubt he was really the son of a grocer in Cupar or a railway porter in Edinburgh. It does not matter with the Scotch, and as he was very properly reticent as to his ancestry, having accepted him, you didn't, even mentally, make any inquiries.

Tietjens always had accepted Macmaster—at Clifton, at Cambridge, in Chancery Lane and in their rooms at Gray's Inn. So for Macmaster he had a very deep affection—even a gratitude. And Macmaster might be considered as returning these feelings. Certainly he had always done his best to be of service to Tietjens. Already at the Treasury and attached as private secretary to Sir Reginald Ingleby, whilst Tietjens was still at Cambridge, Macmaster had brought to the notice of Sir Reginald, Tietjens' many great natural gifts, and Sir Reginald, being on the look-out for young men for his ewe lamb, his newly founded department, had very readily accepted Tietjens as his third in command. On the other hand, it had been Tietjens' father who had recommended Macmaster to the notice of Sir Thomas Block at the Treasury itself. And, indeed, the Tietjens family had provided a little money—that was Tietjens' mother, really—to get Macmaster through Cambridge and install him in town. He had repaid the small sum—paying it partly by finding room in his chambers for Tietjens when in turn he came to town.

With a Scots young man such a position had been perfectly possible. Tietjens had been able to go to his fair, ample, saintly mother in her morning-room and say:

"Look here, mother, that fellow Macmaster! He'll need a little money to get through the university," and his mother would answer:

"Yes, my dear. How much?"

With an English young man of the lower orders, that would have left a sense of class obligation. With Macmaster it just didn't.

During Tietjens' late trouble—for four months before, Tietjens' wife had left him to go abroad with another man—Macmaster had filled a place that no other man could have filled. For the basis of Christopher Tietjens' emotional existence was a complete taciturnity—at any rate as to his emotions. As Tietjens saw the world, you didn't "talk." Perhaps you didn't even think about how you felt.

And, indeed, his wife's flight had left him almost completely without emotions that he could realize, and he had not spoken more than twenty words at most about the event. Those had been mostly to his father, who, very tall, very largely built, silver-haired and erect, had drifted, as it were, into Macmaster's drawing-room in Gray's Inn and after five minutes of silence had said:

"You will divorce?"

Christopher had answered:

"No! No one but a blackguard would ever submit a woman to the ordeal of divorce."

Mr. Tietjens had suggested that and after an interval had asked:

"You will permit her to divorce you?"

He had answered:

"If she wishes it. There's the child to be considered."

Mr. Tietjens said:

"You will get her settlement transferred to the child?"

Christopher answered:

"If it can be done without friction."

Mr. Tietjens had commented only:

"Ah!" Some minutes later he had said:

"Your mother's very well." Then: "That motor plough *didn't* answer," and then: "I shall be dining at the club."

Christopher said:

"May I bring Macmaster in, sir? You said you would put him up."

Mr. Tietjens answered:

"Yes, do. Old General Ffolliott will be there. He'll second him. He'd better make his acquaintance." He had gone away.

Tietjens considered that his relationship with his father was an almost perfect one. They were like two men in the club —the *only* club; thinking so alike that there was no need to talk. His father had spent a great deal of time abroad before succeeding to the estate. When, over the moors, he went into the industrial town that he owned, he drove always in a coach-and-four. Tobacco-smoke had never been known inside Groby Hall: Mr. Tietjens had twelve pipes filled every morning by his head gardener and placed in rose-bushes down the drive. These he smoked during the day. He farmed a good deal of his own land, had sat for Holderness from 1876 to 1881, but had not presented himself for election after the redistribution of seats; he was patron of eleven livings, rode to hounds every now and then, and shot fairly regularly. He had three other sons and two daughters, and was now sixty-one.

To his sister Effie, on the day after his wife's elopement, Christopher had said over the telephone:

"Will you take Tommie for an indefinite period? Marchant will come with him. She offers to take charge of your two youngest as well, so you'll save a maid, and I'll pay their board and a bit over."

The voice of his sister—from Yorkshire—had answered:

"Certainly, Christopher." She was the wife of a vicar near Groby, and she had several children.

To Macmaster, Tietjens had said:

"Sylvia has left me with that fellow Perowne."

Macmaster had answered only: "Ah!"

Tietjens had continued:

"I'm letting the house and warehousing the furniture. Tommie is going to my sister Effie. Marchant is going with him."

Macmaster had said:

"Then you'll be wanting your old rooms." Macmaster occupied a very large storey of the Gray's Inn buildings. After Tietjens had left him, on his marriage, he had continued to enjoy solitude, except that his man had moved down from the attic to the bedroom formerly occupied by Tietjens.

Tietjens said:

"I'll come in to-morrow night if I may. That will give Ferens time to get back into his attic."

That morning, at breakfast, four months having passed, Tietjens had received a letter from his wife. She asked, without any contrition at all, to be taken back. She was fed up with Perowne and Brittany.

Tietjens looked up at Macmaster. Macmaster was already half out of his chair, looking at him with enlarged, steel-blue eyes, his beard quivering. By the time Tietjens spoke, Macmaster had his hand on the neck of the cut-glass brandy decanter in the brown wood tantalus.

Tietjens said:

"Sylvia asks me to take her back."

Macmaster said:

"Have a little of this!"

Tietjens was about to say no automatically. He changed that to:

"Yes. Perhaps. A liqueur-glass."

He noticed that the lip of the decanter agitated, tinkling on the glass. Macmaster must be trembling.

Macmaster, with his back still turned, said:

"Shall you take her back?"

Tietjens answered:

"I imagine so." The brandy warmed his chest in its descent.

Macmaster said:

"Better have another."

Tietjens answered:

"Yes. Thanks."

Macmaster went on with his breakfast and his letters. So did Tietjens. Ferens came in, removed the bacon plates and set on the table a silver water-heated dish that contained poached eggs and haddock. A long time afterwards, Tietjens said:

"Yes, in principle I'm determined to. But I shall take three days to think out the details."

He seemed to have no feelings about the matter. Certain insolent phrases in Sylvia's letter hung in his mind. He preferred a letter like that. The brandy made no difference to his mentality, but it seemed to keep him from shivering.

Macmaster said:

"Suppose we go down to Rye by the eleven-forty. We could get a round after tea now the days are long. I want to call on a parson near there. He has helped me with my book."

Tietjens said:

"Did your poet know parsons? But of course he did. Duchemin is the name, isn't it?"

Macmaster said:

"We could call about two-thirty. That will be all right in the country. We stay till four with a cab outside. We can be on the first tee at five. If we like the course we'll stay next day: then Tuesday at Hythe and Wednesday at Sandwich. Or we could stay at Rye all your three days."

"It will probably suit me better to keep moving," Tietjens said. "There are those British Columbia figures of yours. If we took a cab now I could finish them for you in an hour and twelve minutes. Then British North America can go to the printers. It's only eight-thirty now."

Macmaster said, with some concern:

"Oh, but you *couldn't*. I can make our going all right with Sir Reginald."

Tietjens said:

"Oh, yes I can. Ingleby will be pleased if you tell him they're finished. I'll have them ready for you to give him when he comes at ten."

Macmaster said:

"What an extraordinary fellow you are, Chrissie. Almost a genius!"

"Oh," Tietjens answered, "I was looking at your papers yesterday after you'd left and I've got most of the totals in my head. I was thinking about them before I went to sleep. I think you make a mistake in overestimating the pull of Klondike this year on the population. The passes are open, but relatively no one is going through. I'll add a note to that effect."

In the cab he said:

"I'm sorry to bother you with my beastly affairs. But how will it affect you and the office?"

"The office," Macmaster said, "not at all. It is supposed that Sylvia is nursing Mrs. Satterthwaite abroad. As for me, I wish"—he closed his small, strong teeth—"I wish you would drag the woman through the mud. By God I do! Why should she mangle you for the rest of your life? She's done enough!"

Tietjens gazed out over the flap of the cab.

That explained a question. Some days before, a young man, a friend of his wife's rather than of his own, had approached him in the club and had said that he hoped Mrs. Satterthwaite—his wife's mother—was better. He said now:

"I see. Mrs. Satterthwaite has probably gone abroad to

cover up Sylvia's retreat. She's a sensible woman, if a bitch."

The hansom ran through nearly empty streets, it being very early for the public-official quarters. The hoofs of the horse clattered precipitately. Tietjens preferred a hansom, horses being made for gentlefolk. He had known nothing of how his fellows had viewed his affairs. It was breaking up a great, numb inertia to inquire.

During the last few months he had employed himself in tabulating from memory the errors in the *Encyclopaedia Britannica*, of which a new edition had lately appeared. He had even written an article for a dull monthly on the subject. It had been so caustic as to miss its mark, rather. He despised people who used works of reference; but the point of view had been so unfamiliar that his article had galled no one's withers except possibly Macmaster's. Actually it had pleased Sir Reginald Ingleby, who had been glad to think that he had under him a young man with a memory so tenacious and so encyclopaedic a knowledge. . . .

That had been a congenial occupation, like a long drowse. Now he had to make inquiries. He said:

"And my breaking up the establishment at twenty-nine? How's that viewed? I'm not going to have a house again."

"It's considered," Macmaster answered, "that Lowndes Street did not agree with Mrs. Satterthwaite. That accounted for her illness. Drains wrong. I may say that Sir Reginald entirely—expressly—approves. He does not think that young married men in government offices should keep up expensive establishments in the S.W. district."

Tietjens said:

"Damn him." He added: "He's probably right, though." He then said: "Thanks. That's all I want to know. A certain discredit has always attached to cuckolds. Very properly. A man ought to be able to keep his wife."

Macmaster exclaimed anxiously:

"No! No! Chrissie."

Tietjens continued:

"And a first-class public office is very like a public school. It might very well object to having a man whose wife had bolted amongst its members. I remember Clifton hated it when the governors decided to admit the first Jew and the first nigger."

Macmaster said:

"I wish you wouldn't go on."

"There was a fellow," Tietjens continued, "whose land was next to ours. Conder, his name was. His wife was habitually unfaithful to him. She used to retire with some fellow for three months out of every year. Conder never moved a finger. But we felt Groby and the neighbourhood were unsafe. It was awkward introducing him—not to mention her —in your drawing-room. All sorts of awkwardnesses. Everyone knew the younger children weren't Conder's. A fellow married the youngest daughter and took over the hounds. And not a soul called on her. It wasn't rational or just. But that's why society distrusts the cuckold, really. It never knows when it mayn't be driven into something irrational and unjust."

"But you *aren't*," Macmaster said with real anguish, "going to let Sylvia behave like that."

"I don't know," Tietjens said. "How am I to stop it? Mind you, I think Conder was quite right. Such calamities are the will of God. A gentleman accepts them. If the woman won't divorce, he *must* accept them, and it gets talked about. You seem to have made it all right this time. You and, I suppose, Mrs. Satterthwaite between you. But you won't be always there. Or I might come across another woman."

Macmaster said:

"Ah!" and after a moment:

"What then?"

Tietjens said:

"God knows. . . . There's that poor little beggar to be considered. Marchant says he's beginning to talk broad Yorkshire already."

Macmaster said:

"If it wasn't for that . . . That would be a solution."

Tietjens said: "Ah!"

When he paid the cabman, in front of a grey cement portal with a gabled arch, reaching up, he said:

"You've been giving the mare less licorice in her mash. I told you she'd go better."

The cabman, with a scarlet, varnished face, a shiny hat, a drab box-cloth coat and a gardenia in his button-hole, said:

"Ah! Trust you to remember, sir."

In the train, from beneath his pile of polished dressing-and dispatch cases—Tietjens had thrown his immense kit-bag with his own hands into the guard's van—Macmaster looked across at his friend. It was, for him, a great day. Across his face were the proof-sheets of his first, small, delicate-looking volume. . . . A small page, the type black and still odorous! He had the agreeable smell of the printer's ink in his nostrils; the fresh paper was still a little damp. In his white, rather spatulate, always slightly cold fingers was the pressure of the small, flat, gold pencil he had purchased especially for these corrections. He had found none to make.

He had expected a wallowing of pleasure—almost the only sensuous pleasure he had allowed himself for many months. Keeping up the appearances of an English gentleman on an exiguous income was no mean task. But to wallow in your own phrases, to be rejoiced by the savour of your own shrewd pawkinesses, to feel your rhythm balanced and yet sober—that is a pleasure beyond most, and an inexpensive one at that. He had had it from mere "articles"—on the philosophies and domestic lives of such great figures as Carlyle and Mill or on the expansion of intercolonial trade. This was a book.

He relied upon it to consolidate his position. In the office they were mostly "born," and not vastly sympathetic. There was a sprinkling, too—it was beginning to be a large one—of young men who had obtained their entry by merit or by sheer industry. These watched promotions jealously, discerning nepotic increases of increment and clamouring amongst themselves at favouritisms.

To these he had been able to turn a cold shoulder. His intimacy with Tietjens permitted him to be rather on the "born" side of the institution, his agreeableness—he knew he was agreeable and useful!—to Sir Reginald Ingleby protecting him in the main from unpleasantness. His "articles" had given him a certain right to an austerity of demeanour; his book he trusted to let him adopt an almost judicial attitude. He would then be *the* Mr. Macmaster, the critic, the authority. And the first-class departments are not averse from having distinguished men as ornaments to their company; at any rate the promotions of the distinguished are not objected to. So Macmaster saw—almost physically— Sir Reginald Ingleby perceiving the *empressement* with which his valued subordinate was treated in the drawing-rooms of Mrs. Leamington, Mrs. Cressy, the Hon. Mrs. de Limoux; Sir Reginald would perceive that, for he was not a reader himself of much else than government publications, and he would feel fairly safe in making easy the path of his critically gifted and austere young helper. The son of a very poor shipping clerk in an obscure Scotch harbour town, Mac-

master had very early decided on the career that he would
make. As between the heroes of Mr. Smiles, an author
enormously popular in Macmaster's boyhood, and the more
distinctly intellectual achievements open to the very poor
Scot, Macmaster had had no difficulty in choosing. A pit lad
may rise to be a mine owner; a hard, gifted, unsleeping Scots
youth, pursuing unobtrusively and unobjectionably a course
of study and of public usefulness, *will* certainly achieve distinction, security and the quiet admiration of those around
him. It was the difference between the *may* and the *will*,
and Macmaster had had no difficulty in making his choice. He
saw himself by now almost certain of a career that should
give him at fifty a knighthood, and long before that a competence, a drawing-room of his own and a lady who should
contribute to his unobtrusive fame, she moving about, in that
room, amongst the best of the intellects of the day, gracious,
devoted, a tribute at once to his discernment and his
achievements. Without some disaster he was sure of himself.
Disasters come to men through drink, bankruptcy and women.
Against the first two he knew himself immune, though his
expenses had a tendency to outrun his income, and he was
always a little in debt to Tietjens. Tietjens fortunately had
means. As to the third, he was not so certain. His life had
necessarily been starved of women, and, arrived at a stage
when the female element might, even with due respect to
caution, be considered as a legitimate feature of his life, he
had to fear a rashness of choice due to that very starvation.
The type of woman he needed he knew to exactitude: tall,
graceful, dark, loose-gowned, passionate yet circumspect,
oval-featured, deliberative, gracious to everyone around her.
He could almost hear the very rustle of her garments.

And yet . . . He had had passages when a sort of blind
unreason had attracted him almost to speechlessness towards
girls of the most giggling, behind-the-counter order, big-
bosomed, scarlet-cheeked. It was only Tietjens who had saved
him from the most questionable entanglements.

"Hang it," Tietjens would say, "don't get messing round
that trollop. All you could do with her would be to set her
up in a tobacco-shop, and she would be tearing your beard
out inside the quarter. Let alone you can't afford it."

And Macmaster, who would have sentimentalized the
plump girl to the tune of "Highland Mary," would for a
day damn Tietjens up and down for a coarse brute. But at
the moment he thanked God for Tietjens. There he sat,

near to thirty, without an entanglement, a blemish on his
health, or a worry with regard to any woman.

With deep affection and concern he looked across at his
brilliant junior, who hadn't saved himself. Tietjens had fallen
into the most barefaced snare, into the cruellest snare, of the
worst woman that could be imagined.

And Macmaster suddenly realized that he wasn't wallowing, as he had imagined that he would, in the sensuous current of his prose. He had begun spiritedly with the first neat
square of a paragraph. . . . Certainly his publishers had done
well by him in the matter of print:

> "Whether we consider him as the imaginer of mysterious, sen-
> suous and exact plastic beauty; as the manipulator of sonorous,
> rolling and full-mouthed lines; of words as full of colour as
> were his canvases; or whether we regard him as the deep philos-
> opher, elucidating and drawing his illumination from the ar-
> cana of a mystic hardly greater than himself, to Gabriel
> Charles Dante Rossetti, the subject of this little monograph,
> must be accorded the name of one who has profoundly in-
> fluenced the outward aspects, the human contacts, and all those
> things that go to make up the life of our higher civilization as
> we live it to-day. . . ."

Macmaster realized that he had only got thus far with his
prose, and had got thus far without any of the relish that he
had expected, and that then he had turned to the middle paragraph of page three—after the end of his exordium. His eyes
wandered desultorily along the line:

> "The subject of these pages was born in the western-central
> district of the metropolis in the year . . ."

The words conveyed nothing to him at all. He understood
that that was because he hadn't got over that morning. He
had looked up from his coffee-cup—over the rim—and had
taken in a blue-grey sheet of note-paper in Tietjens' fingers,
shaking, inscribed in the large, broad-nibbed writing of that
detestable harridan. And Tietjens had been staring—staring
with the intentness of a maddened horse—at his, Macmaster's, face! And grey! Shapeless! The nose like a pallid tri-
angle on a bladder of lard! That was Tietjens' face. . . .

He could still feel the blow, physical, in the pit of his
stomach! He had thought Tietjens was going mad: that he
was mad. It had passed. Tietjens had assumed the mask of his
indolent, insolent self. At the office, but later, he had deliv-

ered an extraordinarily forceful—and quite rude—lecture to
Sir Reginald on his reasons for differing from the official
figures of population movements in the western territories.
Sir Reginald had been much impressed. The figures were
wanted for a speech of the Colonial Minister—or an answer
to a question—and Sir Reginald had promised to put Tietjens'
views before the great man. That was the sort of thing to do
a young fellow good—because it got kudos for the office.
They had to work on figures provided by the colonial govern-
ments, and if they could correct those fellows by sheer brain
work—that scored.

But there sat Tietjens, in his grey tweeds, his legs apart,
lumpish, clumsy, his tallowy, intelligent-looking hands drooping inert between his legs, his eyes gazing at a coloured
photograph of the port of Boulogne beside the mirror beneath the luggage rack. Blond, high-coloured, vacant, apparently, you couldn't tell what in the world he was thinking
of. The mathematical theory of waves, very likely, or slips in
someone's article on Arminianism. For absurd as it seemed,
Macmaster knew that he knew next to nothing of his friend's
feelings. As to them, practically no confidences had passed
between them. Just two:

On the night before his starting for his wedding in Paris,
Tietjens had said to him:

"Vinny, old fellow, it's a back-door way out of it. She's
bitched *me*."

And once, rather lately, he had said:

"Damn it! I don't even know if the child's my own!"

This last confidence had shocked Macmaster so irreme-
diably—the child had been a seven months' child, rather ail-
ing, and Tietjens' clumsy tenderness towards it had been
so marked that, even without this nightmare, Macmaster had
been affected by the sight of them together—that confidence
then had pained Macmaster so frightfully, it was so appalling,
that Macmaster had regarded it almost as an insult. It was
the sort of confidence a man didn't make to his equal, but
only to solicitors, doctors, or the clergy, who are not quite
men. Or, at any rate, such confidences are not made between
men without appeals for sympathy, and Tietjens had made no
appeal for sympathy. He had just added sardonically:

"She gives me the benefit of the agreeable doubt. And she's
as good as said as much to Marchant"—Marchant had been
Tietjens' old nurse.

Suddenly—and as if in a sort of unconscious losing of his head—Macmaster remarked:

"You can't say the man wasn't a poet!"

The remark had been, as it were, torn from him, because he had observed, in the strong light of the compartment, that half of Tietjens' forelock and a roundish patch behind it was silvery white. That might have been going on for weeks: you live beside a man and notice his changes very little. Yorkshire men of fresh colour and blondish often go speckled with white very young; Tietjens had had a white hair or two at the age of fourteen, very noticeable in the sunlight when he had taken his cap off to bowl.

But Macmaster's mind, taking appalled charge, had felt assured that Tietjens had gone white with the shock of his wife's letter: in four hours! That meant that terrible things must be going on within him; his thoughts, at all costs, must be distracted. The mental process in Macmaster had been quite subconscious. He would not, advisedly, have introduced the painter-poet as a topic.

Tietjens said:

"I haven't said anything at all that I can remember."

The obstinacy of his hard race awakened in Macmaster:
" 'Since,' " he quoted, " 'when we stand side by side

> Only hands may meet,
> Better half this weary world
> Lay between us, sweet!
> Better far tho' hearts may break
> Bid farewell for aye!
> Lest thy sad eyes, meeting mine,
> Tempt my soul away!'

"You can't," he continued, "say that that isn't poetry! Great poetry."

"I can't say," Tietjens answered contemptuously. "I don't read poetry except Byron. But it's a filthy picture. . . ."

Macmaster said uncertainly:

"I don't know that I know the picture. Is it in Chicago?"

"It isn't painted!" Tietjens said. "But it's there!"

He continued with sudden fury:

"Damn it. What's the sense of all these attempts to justify fornication? England's mad about it. Well, you've got your John Stuart Mills and your George Eliots for the high-class thing. Leave the furniture out! Or leave me out, at least. I tell you it revolts me to think of that obese, oily man who never took a bath, in a grease-spotted dressing-gown and the underclothes he's slept in, standing beside a five-shilling model with crimped hair or some Mrs. W. Three Stars, gazing into a mirror that reflects their fetid selves and gilt sunfish and drop chandeliers and plates sickening with cold bacon fat and gurgling about passion."

Macmaster had gone chalk-white, his short beard bristling:

"You daren't . . . you daren't talk like that," he stuttered.

"I *dare!*" Tietjens answered; "but I oughtn't to . . . to you! I admit that. But you oughtn't, almost as much, to talk about that stuff to me, either. It's an insult to my intelligence."

"Certainly," Macmaster said stiffly, "the moment was not opportune."

"I don't understand what you mean," Tietjens answered. "The moment can never be opportune. Let's agree that making a career is a dirty business—for me as for you! But decent augurs grin behind their masks. They never preach to each other."

"You're getting esoteric," Macmaster said faintly.

"I'll underline," Tietjens went on. "I quite understand that the favour of Mrs. Cressy and Mrs. de Limoux is essential to you! They have the ear of that old don Ingleby."

Macmaster said:

"Damn!"

"I quite agree," Tietjens continued, "I quite approve. It's the game as it has always been played. It's the tradition, so it's right. It's been sanctioned since the days of the *Précieuses Ridicules.*"

"You've a way of putting things," Macmaster said.

"I haven't," Tietjens answered. "It's just because I haven't that what I *do* say sticks out in the minds of fellows like you, who are always fiddling about after literary expression. But what I do say is this: I stand for monogamy."

Macmaster uttered a *"You!"* of amazement.

Tietjens answered with a negligent *"I!"* He continued:

"I stand for monogamy and chastity. And for no talking about it. Of course, if a man who's a man wants to have a woman he has her. And again, no talking about it. He'd no doubt be in the end better, and better off, if he didn't. Just as it would probably be better for him if he didn't have the second glass of whisky and soda. . . ."

"You call that monogamy and chastity!" Macmaster interjected.

"I do," Tietjens answered. "And it probably is; at any rate it's clean. What is loathsome is all your fumbling in placket-holes and polysyllabic Justification by Love. You stand for lachrymose polygamy. That's all right if you can get your club to change its rules."

"You're out of my depth," Macmaster said. "And being very disagreeable. You appear to be justifying promiscuity. I don't like it."

"I'm probably being disagreeable," Tietjens said. "Jeremiahs usually are. But there ought to be a twenty years' close time for discussions of sham sexual morality. Your Paolo and Francesca—and Dante's—went, very properly, to Hell, and no bones about it. You don't get Dante justifying them. But your fellow whines about creeping into Heaven."

"He *doesn't*," Macmaster exclaimed. Tietjens continued with equanimity:

"Now, your novelist who writes a book to justify his every tenth or fifth seduction of a commonplace young woman in the name of the rights of shop boys . . ."

"I'll admit," Macmaster coincided, "that Briggs is going too far. I told him only last Thursday at Mrs. de Limoux's . . ."

"I'm not talking of anyone in particular," Tietjens said. "I don't read novels. I'm supposing a case. And it's a cleaner case than that of your Pre-Raphaelite horrors! No! I don't read novels, but I follow tendencies. And if a fellow chooses to justify his seductions of uninteresting and viewy young females along the lines of freedom and the rights of man, it's relatively respectable. It would be better just to boast about his conquests in a straightforward and exultant way. But . . ."

"You carry joking too far sometimes," Macmaster said. "I've warned you about it."

"I'm as solemn as an owl!" Tietjens rejoined. "The lower classes are becoming vocal. Why shouldn't they? They're the only people in this country who are sound in wind and limb. They'll save the country if the country's to be saved."

"And you call yourself a Tory!" Macmaster said.

"The lower classes," Tietjens continued equably, "such of them as get through the secondary schools, want irregular and very transitory unions. During holidays they go together on personally conducted tours to Switzerland and such places. Wet afternoons they pass in their tile bathrooms, slapping each other hilariously on the backs and splashing white enamel paint about."

"You say you don't read novels," Macmaster said, "but I recognize the quotation."

"I don't *read* novels," Tietjens answered. "I know what's in 'em. There has been nothing worth *reading* written in England since the eighteenth century except by a woman. . . . But it's natural for your enamel splashers to want to see themselves in a bright and variegated literature. Why shouldn't they? It's a healthy, human desire, and now that printing and paper are cheap they get it satisfied. It's healthy, I tell you. Infinitely healthier than . . ." He paused.

"Than what?" Macmaster asked.

"I'm thinking," Tietjens said, "thinking how not to be too rude."

"You want to be rude," Macmaster said bitterly, "to people who lead the contemplative . . . the circumspect life."

"It's precisely that," Tietjens said. He quoted:

> " 'She walks, the lady of my delight,
>   A shepherdess of sheep;
>   She is so circumspect and right:
>   She has her thoughts to keep.' "

Macmaster said:

"Confound you, Chrissie. You know everything."

"Well, yes," Tietjens said musingly, "I think I should want to be rude to her. I don't say I should be. Certainly I shouldn't if she were good-looking. Or if she were your soul's affinity. You can rely on that."

Macmaster had a sudden vision of Tietjens' large and clumsy form walking beside the lady of his, Macmaster's, delight, when ultimately she was found—walking along the top of a cliff amongst tall grass and poppies and making himself extremely agreeable with talk of Tasso and Cimabue. All the same, Macmaster imagined, the lady wouldn't like Tietjens. Women didn't, as a rule. His looks and his silences alarmed them. Or they hated him. . . . Or they liked him very much indeed. And Macmaster said conciliatorily:

"Yes, I think I could rely on that!" He added: "All the same, I don't wonder that . . ."

He had been about to say:

"I don't wonder that Sylvia calls you immoral." For Tietjens' wife alleged that Tietjens was detestable. He bored her, she said, by his silences; when he did speak she hated him for the immorality of his views. . . . But he did not finish his sentence, and Tietjens went on:

"All the same, when the war comes it will be these little snobs who will save England, because they've the courage to know what they want and to say so."

Macmaster said loftily:

"You're extraordinarily old-fashioned at times, Chrissie. You ought to know as well as I do that a war is impossible —at any rate with this country in it. Simply because . . ." He hesitated and then emboldened himself: "*We*—the circumspect—yes, the circumspect classes, will pilot the nation through the tight places."

"War, my good fellow," Tietjens said—the train was slowing down preparatorily to running into Ashford—"is inevitable, and with this country plumb centre in the middle of it. Simply because you fellows are such damn hypocrites. There's not a country in the world that trusts us. We're always, as it were, committing adultery—like your fellow!— with the name of Heaven on our lips." He was jibing again at the subject of Macmaster's monograph.

"He never!" Macmaster said in almost a stutter. "He never whined about Heaven."

"He did," Tietjens said: "The beastly poem you quoted ends:

" 'Better far though hearts may break,
        Since we dare not love,
    Part till we once more may meet
        In a Heaven above.' "

And Macmaster, who had been dreading that shot—for he never knew how much or how little of any given poem his friend would have by heart—Macmaster collapsed, as it were, into fussily getting down his dressing-cases and clubs from the rack, a task he usually left to a porter. Tietjens, who, however much a train might be running into a station he was bound for, sat like a rock until it was dead still, said:

"Yes, a war is inevitable. Firstly, there's you fellows who can't be trusted. And then there's the multitude who mean to have bathrooms and white enamel. Millions of them; all over the world. Not merely here. And there aren't enough bathrooms and white enamel in the world to go round. It's like you polygamists with women. There aren't enough women in the world to go round to satisfy your insatiable appetites. And there aren't enough men in the world to give each woman one. And most women want several. So you have divorce cases. I suppose you won't say that because you're so circumspect and right there shall be no more divorce? Well, war is as inevitable as divorce. . . ."

Macmaster had his head out of the carriage window and was calling for a porter.

On the platform a number of women in lovely sable cloaks, with purple or red jewel cases, with diaphanous silky scarves flying from motor-hoods, were drifting towards the branch train for Rye, under the shepherding of erect, burdened footmen. Two of them nodded to Tietjens.

Macmaster considered that he was perfectly right to be tidy in his dress; you never knew whom you mightn't meet on a railway journey. This confirmed him as against Tietjens, who preferred to look like a navvy.

A tall, white-haired, white-moustached, red-cheeked fellow limped after Tietjens, who was getting his immense bag out of the guard's van. He clapped the young man on the shoulder and said:

"Hullo! How's your mother-in-law? Lady Claude wants to know. She says come up and pick a bone to-night if you're going to Rye." He had extraordinarily blue, innocent eyes.

Tietjens said:

"Hullo, general," and added: "I believe she's much better. Quite restored. This is Macmaster. I think I shall be going over to bring my wife back in a day or two. They're both at Lobscheid . . . a German spa."

The general said:

"Quite right. It isn't good for a young man to be alone. Kiss Sylvia's finger-tips for me. She's the real thing, you lucky beggar." He added, a little anxiously: "What about a foursome to-morrow? Paul Sandbach is down. He's as crooked as me. We can't do a full round at singles."

"It's your own fault," Tietjens said. "You ought to have gone to my bone-setter. Settle it with Macmaster, will you?" He jumped into the twilight of the guard's van.

The general looked at Macmaster, a quick, penetrating scrutiny:

"You're *the* Macmaster," he said. "You would be if you're with Chrissie."

A high voice called:

"General! General!"

"I want a word with you," the general said, "about the figures in that article you wrote about Pondoland. Figures are all right. But we shall lose the beastly country if . . . But we'll talk about it after dinner to-night. You'll come up to Lady Claudine's. . . ."

Macmaster congratulated himself again on his appearance. It was all very well for Tietjens to look like a sweep; he was of these people. He, Macmaster, wasn't. He had, if anything, to be an authority, and authorities wear gold tie-rings and broadcloth. General Lord Edward Campion had a son, a permanent head of the Treasury department that regulated increases of salaries and promotions in all the public offices. Tietjens only caught the Rye train by running alongside it, pitching his enormous kit-bag through the carriage window and swinging on the footboard. Macmaster reflected that if he had done that, half the station would have been yelling, "Stand away there."

As it was Tietjens, a stationmaster was galloping after him to open the carriage door and grinningly to part:

"Well caught, sir!" for it was a cricketing county.

"Truly," Macmaster quoted to himself,

> " 'The gods to each ascribe a differing lot:
> Some enter at the portal. Some do not!' "

2 ~

MRS. SATTERTHWAITE with her French maid, her priest, and her disreputable young man, Mr. Bayliss, were at Lobscheid, an unknown and little-frequented air resort amongst the pine-woods of the Taunus. Mrs. Satterthwaite was ultrafashionable and consummately indifferent—she only really lost her temper if at her table and under her nose you consumed her famous black Hamburg grapes without taking their skin and all. Father Consett was out to have an uproarious good time during his three weeks' holiday from the slums of Liverpool; Mr. Bayliss, thin like a skeleton in tight blue serge, golden-haired and pink, was so nearly dead of tuberculosis, was so dead penniless, and of tastes so costly that he was ready to keep stone quiet, drink six pints of milk a day and behave himself. On the face of it he was there to write the letters of Mrs. Satterthwaite, but the lady never let him enter her private rooms for fear of infection. He had to content himself with nursing a growing adoration for Father Consett. This priest, with an enormous mouth, high cheekbones, untidy black hair, a broad face that never looked too clean and waving hands that always looked too dirty, never kept still for a moment and had a brogue such as is seldom

heard outside old-fashioned English novels of Irish life. He
had a perpetual laugh, like the noise made by a steam rounda-
bout. He was, in short, a saint, and Mr. Bayliss knew it,
though he didn't know how. Ultimately, and with the financial
assistance of Mrs. Satterthwaite, Mr. Bayliss became almoner
to Father Consett, adopted the rule of St. Vincent de Paul
and wrote some very admirable, if decorative, devotional
verse.

They proved thus a very happy, innocent party. For Mrs.
Satterthwaite interested herself—it was the only interest she
had—in handsome, thin and horribly disreputable young
men. She would wait for them or send her car to wait for
them at the jail gates. She would bring their usually admirable wardrobes up to date and give them enough money
to have a good time. When, contrary to all expectations—
but it happened more often than not!—they turned out well,
she was lazily pleased. Sometimes she sent them away to a
gay spot with a priest who needed a holiday; sometimes she
had them down to her place in the west of England.

So they were a pleasant company and all very happy. Lobscheid contained one empty hotel with large verandas and
several square farmhouses, white with grey beams, painted
in the gables with bouquets of blue and yellow flowers or
with scarlet huntsmen shooting at purple stags. They were
like gay cardboard boxes set down in fields of long grass;
then the pine-woods commenced and ran, solemn, brown and
geometric, for miles up and downhill. The peasant girls wore
black velvet waistcoats, white bodices, innumerable petticoats
and absurd parti-coloured head-dresses of the shape and size
of halfpenny buns. They walked about in rows of four to six
abreast, with a slow step, protruding white-stockinged feet in
dancing-pumps, their head-dresses nodding solemnly; young
men in blue blouses, knee-breeches and, on Sundays, in three-
cornered hats followed behind singing part-songs.

The French maid—whom Mrs. Satterthwaite had borrowed
from the Duchesse de Carbon Châteaulherault in exchange
for her own maid—was at first inclined to find the place
maussade. But getting up a tremendous love-affair with a
fine, tall, blond young fellow who included a gun, a gold-
mounted hunting-knife as long as his arm, a light, grey-green
uniform with gilt badges and buttons, she was reconciled to
her lot. When the young *Förster* tried to shoot her—*"et pour
cause,"* as she said—she was ravished and Mrs. Satterthwaite
lazily amused.

They were sitting playing bridge in the large, shadowy

dining-hall of the hotel: Mrs. Satterthwaite, Father Consett,
Mr. Bayliss. A young blond sub-lieutenant of great ob-
sequiousness, who was there as a last chance for his right
lung and his career, and the bearded *Kur*-doctor cut in.
Father Consett, breathing heavily and looking frequently at
his watch, played very fast, exclaiming: "Hurry up, now; it's
nearly twelve. Hurry up wid ye." Mr. Bayliss being dummy,
the Father exclaimed: "Three no trumps, I've to make. Get
me a whisky and soda quick, and don't drown it as ye did
the last." He played his hand with extreme rapidity, threw
down his last three cards, exclaimed: "Ach! Botheranouns an'
all; I'm two down and I've revoked on the top av it," swallowed down his whisky and soda, looked at his watch and
exclaimed: "Done it to the minute! Here, doctor, take my
hand and finish the rubber." He was to take the mass next
day for the local priest, and mass must be said fasting from
midnight, and without cards played. Bridge was his only
passion; a fortnight every year was what, in his worn-out
life, he got of it. On his holiday he rose at ten. At eleven
it was: "A four for the Father." From two to four they walked
in the forest. At five it was: "A four for the Father." At nine
it was: "Father, aren't you coming to your bridge?" And
Father Consett grinned all over his face and said: "It's good
ye are to a poor ould soggart. It will be paid back to you in
Heaven."

The other four played on solemnly. The Father sat himself
down behind Mrs. Satterthwaite, his chin in the nape of her
neck. At excruciating moments he gripped her shoulders,
exclaimed: "Play the *queen*, woman!" and breathed hard
down her back. Mrs. Satterthwaite would play the two of
diamonds, and the Father, throwing himself back, would
groan. She said over her shoulder:

"I want to talk to you to-night, Father," took the last trick
of the rubber, collected 17 marks 50 from the doctor and
8 marks from the *unter-leutnant*. The doctor exclaimed:

"You gan't dake that immense sum from us and then ko
off. Now we shall be ropped py Herr Payliss at gutt-
throat!"

She drifted, all shadowy black silk, across the shadows
of the dining-hall, dropping her winnings into her black
satin vanity-bag and attended by the priest. Outside the
door, beneath the antlers of a royal stag, in an atmosphere
of paraffin lamps and varnished pitch-pine, she said:

"Come up to my sitting-room. The prodigal's returned.
Sylvia's here."

The Father said:

"I thought I saw her out of the corner of my eye in the bus after dinner. She'll be going back to her husband. It's a poor world."

"She's a wicked devil!" Mrs. Satterthwaite said.

"I've known her myself since she was nine," Father Consett said, "and it's little I've seen in her to hold up to the commendation of my flock." He added: "But maybe I'm made unjust by the shock of it."

They climbed the stairs slowly.

Mrs. Satterthwaite sat herself on the edge of a cane chair. She said:

"Well!"

She wore a black hat like a cart-wheel, and her dresses appeared always to consist of a great many squares of silk that might have been thrown on to her. Since she considered that her complexion, which was mat white, had gone slightly violet from twenty years of make-up, when she was not made up—as she never was at Lobscheid—she wore bits of puce-coloured satin ribbon stuck here and there, partly to counteract the violet of her complexion, partly to show she was not in mourning. She was very tall and extremely emaciated; her dark eyes, that had beneath them dark brown thumb-marks, were very tired or very indifferent by turns.

Father Consett walked backwards and forwards, his hands behind his back, his head bent, over the not too well polished floor. There were two candles, lit but dim, in imitation pewter *nouvel-art* candlesticks, rather dingy; a sofa of cheap mahogany with red plush cushions and rests, a table covered with a cheap carpet and an American roll-top desk that had thrown into it a great many papers in scrolls or flat. Mrs. Satterthwaite was extremely indifferent to her surroundings, but she insisted on having a piece of furniture for her papers. She liked also to have a profusion of hot-house, not garden, flowers, but as there were none of these at Lobscheid, she did without them. She insisted also, as a rule, on a comfortable chaise-longue, which she rarely, if ever, used; but the German empire of those days did not contain a comfortable chair, so she did without it, lying down on her bed when she was really tired. The walls of the large room were completely covered with pictures of animals in death agonies: capercailzies giving up the ghost with gouts of scarlet blood on the snow; deer dying with their heads back and eyes glazing, gouts of red blood on their necks; foxes dying with scarlet blood on green grass. These pictures were frame to frame, representing sport, the hotel having been a former grand-ducal hunting-box, freshened to suit the taste of the day with varnished pitch-pine, bathrooms, verandas, and excessively modern but noisy lavatory arrangements which had been put in for the delight of possible English guests.

Mrs. Satterthwaite sat on the edge of her chair; she had always the air of being just about to go out somewhere or of having just come in and being on the point of going to take her things off. She said:

"There's been a telegram waiting for her all the afternoon. I knew she was coming."

Father Consett said:

"I saw it in the rack myself. I misdoubted it." He added: "Oh dear, oh dear! After all we've talked about it, now it's come."

Mrs. Satterthwaite said:

"I've been a wicked woman myself, as these things are measured; but . . ."

Father Consett said:

"Ye have! It's no doubt from you she gets it, for your husband was a good man. But one wicked woman is enough for my contemplation at a time. I'm no St. Anthony. . . . The young man says he will take her back?"

"On conditions," Mrs. Satterthwaite said. "He is coming here to have an interview."

The priest said:

"Heaven knows, Mrs. Satterthwaite, there are times when to a poor priest the rule of the Church as regards marriage seems bitter hard and he almost doubts her inscrutable wisdom. He doesn't, mind you. But at times I wish that that young man would take what advantage—it's all there is!— that he can of being a Protestant and divorce Sylvia. For I tell you, there are bitter things to see amongst my flock over there. . . ." He made a vague gesture towards the infinite. . . . "And bitter things I've seen, for the heart of man is a wicked place. But never a bitterer than this young man's lot."

"As you say," Mrs. Satterthwaite said, "my husband was a good man. I hated him, but that was as much my fault as his. More! And the only reason I don't wish Christopher to divorce Sylvia is that it would bring disgrace on my husband's name. At the same time, Father . . ."

The priest said:

"I've heard near enough."

"There's this to be said for Sylvia," Mrs. Satterthwaite went on. "There are times when a woman hates a man—

as Sylvia hates her husband. . . . I tell you I've walked behind
a man's back and nearly screamed because of the desire to
put my nails into the veins of his neck. It was a fascination.
And it's worse with Sylvia. It's a natural antipathy."

"Woman!" Father Consett fulminated, "I've no patience
wid ye! If the woman, as the Church directs, would have
children by her husband and live decent, she would have no
such feelings. It's unnatural living and unnatural practices
that cause these complexes. Don't think I'm an ignoramus,
priest if I am."

Mrs. Satterthwaite said:

"But Sylvia's had a child."

Father Consett swung round like a man that has been shot
at.

"Whose?" he asked, and he pointed a dirty finger at his
interlocutress. "It was that blackguard Drake's, wasn't it?
I've long suspected that."

"It was probably Drake's," Mrs. Satterthwaite said.

"Then," the priest said, "in the face of the pains of the
hereafter, how could you let that decent lad in the hotness
of his sin? . . ."

"Indeed," Mrs. Satterthwaite said, "I shiver sometimes when
I think of it. Don't believe that I had anything to do with
trepanning him. But I couldn't hinder it. Sylvia's my daughter,
and dog doesn't eat dog."

"There are times when it should," Father Consett said contemptuously.

"You don't seriously," Mrs. Satterthwaite said, "say that
I, a mother, if an indifferent one, with my daughter appearing
in trouble, as the kitchen-maids say, by a married man—that
I should step in and stop a marriage that was a Godsend. . . ."

"Don't," the priest said, "introduce the sacred name into
an affair of Piccadilly bad girls. . . ." He stopped. "Heaven
help me," he said again, "don't ask me to answer the question
of what you should or shouldn't have done. You know I
loved your husband like a brother, and you know I've loved
you and Sylvia ever since she was a tiny. And I thank God
that I am not your spiritual adviser, but only your friend
in God. For if I had to answer your question I could answer
it only in one way." He broke off to ask: "Where is that
woman?"

Mrs. Satterthwaite called:

"Sylvia! Sylvia! Come here!"

A door in the shadows opened, and light shone from another room behind a tall figure leaning one hand on the handle of the door. A very deep voice said:

"I can't understand, mother, why you live in rooms like a sergeants' mess." And Sylvia Tietjens wavered into the room. She added: "I suppose it doesn't matter. I'm bored."

Father Consett groaned:

"Heaven help us, she's like a picture of Our Lady by Fra Angelico."

Immensely tall, slight and slow in her movements, Sylvia Tietjens wore her reddish, very fair hair in great bandeaux right down over her ears. Her very oval, regular face had an expression of virginal lack of interest such as used to be worn by fashionable Paris courtesans a decade before that time. Sylvia Tietjens considered that, being privileged to go everywhere where one went and to have all men at her feet, she had no need to change her expression or to infuse into it the greater animation that marked the more common beauties of the early twentieth century. She moved slowly from the door and sat languidly on the sofa against the wall.

"There you are, Father," she said. "I'll not ask you to shake hands with me. You probably wouldn't."

"As I am a priest," Father Consett answered, "I could not refuse. But I'd rather not."

"This," Sylvia repeated, "appears to be a boring place."

"You won't say so to-morrow," the priest said. "There's two young fellows. . . . And a sort of policeman to trepan away from your mother's maid!"

"That," Sylvia answered, "is meant to be bitter. But it doesn't hurt. I am done with men." She added suddenly: "Mother, didn't you one day, while you were still young, say that you had done with men? Firmly! And mean it?"

Mrs. Satterthwaite said:

"I did."

"And did you keep to it?" Sylvia asked.

Mrs. Satterthwaite said:

"I did."

"And shall I, do you imagine?"

Mrs. Satterthwaite said:

"I imagine you will."

Sylvia said:

"Oh, dear!"

The priest said:

"I'd be willing to see your husband's telegram. It makes a difference to see the words on paper."

Sylvia rose effortlessly.

"I don't see why you shouldn't," she said. "It will give you no pleasure." She drifted towards the door.

"If it would give me pleasure," the priest said, "you would not show it me."

"I would not," she said.

A silhouette in the doorway, she halted, drooping, and looked over her shoulder.

"Both you and mother," she said, "sit there scheming to make life bearable for the Ox. I call my husband the Ox. He's repulsive: like a swollen animal. Well . . . you can't do it." The lighted doorway was vacant. Father Consett sighed.

"I told you this was an evil place," he said. "In the deep forests. She'd not have such evil thoughts in another place."

Mrs. Satterthwaite said:

"I'd rather you didn't say that, Father. Sylvia would have evil thoughts in any place."

"Sometimes," the priest said, "at night I think I hear the claws of evil things scratching on the shutters. This was the last place in Europe to be Christianized. Perhaps it wasn't ever even Christianized and they're here yet."

Mrs. Satterthwaite said:

"It's all very well to talk like that in the day-time. It makes the place seem romantic. But it must be near one at night. And things are bad enough as it is."

"They are," Father Consett said. "The devil's at work."

Sylvia drifted back into the room with a telegram of several sheets. Father Consett held it close to one of the candles to read, for he was short-sighted.

"All men are repulsive," Sylvia said; "don't you think so, mother?"

Mrs. Satterthwaite said:

"I do not. Only a heartless woman would say so."

"Mrs. Vanderdecken," Sylvia went on, "says all men are repulsive, and it's woman's disgusting task to live beside them."

"You've been seeing that foul creature?" Mrs. Satterthwaite said. "She's a Russian agent. And worse!"

"She was at Gosingeux all the time we were," Sylvia said. "You needn't groan. She won't split on us. She's the soul of honour."

"It wasn't because of that I groaned, if I did," Mrs. Satterthwaite answered.

The priest, from over his telegram, exclaimed:

"Mrs. Vanderdecken! God forbid."

Sylvia's face, as she sat on the sofa, expressed languid and incredulous amusement.

"What do you know of her?" she asked the Father.

"I know what you know," he answered, "and that's enough."

"Father Consett," Sylvia said to her mother, "has been renewing his social circle."

"It's not," Father Consett said, "amongst the dregs of the people that you must live if you don't want to hear of the dregs of society."

Sylvia stood up. She said:

"You'll keep your tongue off my best friends if you want me to stop and be lectured. But for Mrs. Vanderdecken I should not be here, returned to the fold!"

Father Consett exclaimed:

"Don't say it, child. I'd rather, heaven help me, you had gone on living in open sin."

Sylvia sat down again, her hands listlessly in her lap.

"Have it your own way," she said, and the Father returned to the fourth sheet of the telegram.

"What does this mean?" he asked. He had returned to the first sheet. "This here: *'Accept resumption yoke'?*" he read breathlessly.

"Sylvia," Mrs. Satterthwaite said, "go and light the spirit lamp for some tea. We shall want it."

"You'd think I was a district messenger boy," Sylvia said as she rose. "Why don't you keep your maid up? . . . It's a way we had of referring to our . . . union," she explained to the Father.

"There was sympathy enough between you and him then," he said, "to have by-words for things. It was that I wanted to know. I understood the words."

"They were pretty bitter by-words, as you call them," Sylvia said. "More like curses than kisses."

"It was you that used them, then," Mrs. Satterthwaite said. "Christopher never said a bitter thing to you."

An expression like a grin came slowly over Sylvia's face as she turned back to the priest.

"That's mother's tragedy," she said. "My husband's one of her best boys. She adores him. And he can't bear *her*." She drifted behind the wall of the next room and they heard her tinkling the tea-things as the Father read on again beside the candle. His immense shadow began at the centre and ran along the pitch-pine ceiling, down the wall and across the floor to join his splay feet in their clumsy boots.

"It's bad," he muttered. He made a sound like "Umbleumbleumble. . . . Worse than I feared . . . umbleumble . . . *'Accept resumption yoke but on rigid conditions.'* What's this: *esoecially;* it ought to be a 'p,' *'especially regards child reduce establishment ridiculous our position remake settlements in child's sole interests flat not house entertaining minimum am prepared resign office settle Yorkshire but imagine this not suit you child remain sister Effie open visits both wire if this rough outline provisionally acceptable in that case will express draft general position Monday for you and mother reflect upon follow self Tuesday arrive Thursday Lobscheid go Wiesbaden fortnight on social task discussion Thursday limited solely comma emphasized comma to affairs.' "*

"That means," Mrs. Satterthwaite said, "that he doesn't mean to reproach her. *'Emphasized'* applies to the word *'solely.'* " . . .

"Why d'you take it? . . ." Father Consett asked. "Did he spend an immense lot of money on this telegram? Did he imagine you were in such trepidation? . . ." He broke off. Walking slowly, her long arms extended to carry the tea-tray, over which her wonderfully moving face had a rapt expression of indescribable mystery, Sylvia was coming through the door.

"Oh, child," the Father exclaimed, "whether it's St. Martha or that Mary that made the bitter choice, not one of them ever looked more virtuous than you. Why aren't ye born to be a good man's helpmeet?"

A little tinkle sounded from the tea-tray and three pieces of sugar fell on to the floor. Mrs. Tietjens hissed with vexation.

"I *knew* that damned thing would slide off the tea-cups," she said. She dropped the tray from an inch or so of height on to the carpeted table. "I'd made it a matter of luck between myself and myself," she said. Then she faced the priest.

"I'll tell you," she said, "why he sent the telegram. It's because of that dull display of the English gentleman that I detested. He gives himself the solemn airs of the Foreign Minister, but he's only a youngest son at the best. That is why I loathe him."

Mrs. Satterthwaite said:

"That isn't the reason why he sent the telegram."

Her daughter had a gesture of amused, lazy tolerance.

"Of course it isn't," she said. "He sent it out of consideration: the lordly, full-dress consideration that drives me distracted. As he would say: 'He'd imagine I'd find it convenient to have ample time for reflection.' It's like being addressed as if one were a monument and by a herald according to protocol. And partly because he's the soul of truth like a stiff Dutch doll. He wouldn't write a letter because he couldn't without beginning it 'Dear Sylvia' and ending it 'Yours sincerely' or 'Truly' or 'Affectionately.' . . . He's that sort of precise imbecile. I tell you he's so formal he can't do without all the conventions there are and so truthful he can't use half of them."

"Then," Father Consett said, "if ye know him so well, Sylvia Satterthwaite, how is it ye can't get on with him better? They say: *Tout savoir c'est tout pardonner.*"

"It isn't," Sylvia said. "To know everything about a person is to be bored . . . bored . . . bored!"

"And how are ye going to answer this telegram of his?" the Father asked. "Or have ye answered it already?"

"I shall wait until Monday night to keep him as bothered as I can to know whether he's to start on Tuesday. He fusses like a hen over his packings and the exact hours of his movements. On Monday I shall telegraph: 'Righto' and nothing else."

"And why," the Father asked, "will ye telegraph him a vulgar word that you never use? For your language is the one thing about you that isn't vulgar."

Sylvia said:

"Thanks!" She curled her legs up under her on the sofa and laid her head back against the wall so that her Gothic arch of a chin-bone pointed at the ceiling. She admired her own neck, which was very long and white.

"I know!" Father Consett said. "You're a beautiful woman. Some men would say it was a lucky fellow that lived with you. I don't ignore the fact in my cogitation. He'd imagine all sorts of delights to lurk in the shadow of your beautiful hair. And they wouldn't."

Sylvia brought her gaze down from the ceiling and fixed her brown eyes for a moment on the priest, speculatively.

"It's a great handicap we suffer from," he said.

"I don't know why I selected that word," Sylvia said; "it's one word, so it costs only fifty pfennigs. I couldn't hope really to give a jerk to his pompous self-sufficiency."

"It's great handicaps we priests suffer from," the Father

repeated. "However much a priest may be a man of the world—and he has to be to fight the world . . ."

Mrs. Satterthwaite said:

"Have a cup of tea, Father, while it's just right. I believe Sylvia is the only person in Germany who knows how to make tea."

"There's always behind him the Roman collar and the silk bib, and you don't believe in him," Father Consett went on, "yet he knows ten—a thousand!—times more of human nature than ever you can."

"I don't see," Sylvia said placably, "how you can learn in your slums anything about the nature of Eunice Vanderdecken or Elizabeth B. or Queenie James or any of my set." She was on her feet, pouring cream into the Father's tea. "I'll admit for the moment that you aren't giving me pi-jaw."

"I'm glad," the priest said, "that ye remember enough of yer school-days to use the old term."

Sylvia wavered backwards to her sofa and sank down again.

"There you are," she said, "you can't really get away from preachments. Me for the pyore young girl is always at the back of it."

"It isn't," the Father said. "I'm not one to cry for the moon."

"You don't want me to be a pure young girl," Sylvia asked with lazy incredulity.

"I do not!" the Father said, "but I'd wish that at times ye'd remember you once were."

"I don't believe I ever was," Sylvia said; "if the nuns had known, I'd have been expelled from the Holy Child."

"You would not," the Father said. "Do stop your boasting. The nuns have too much sense. . . . Anyhow, it isn't a pure young girl I'd have you or behaving like a Protestant deaconess for the craven fear of Hell. I'd have ye be a physically healthy, decently honest-with-yourself young devil of a married woman. It's them that are the plague and the salvation of the world."

"You admire mother?" Mrs. Tietjens asked suddenly. She added in parenthesis: "You see you can't get away from salvation."

"I mean keeping bread and butter in their husbands' stomachs," the priest said. "Of course I admire your mother."

Mrs. Satterthwaite moved a hand slightly.

"You're at any rate in league with her against me," Sylvia said. She asked with more interest: "Then, would you have me model myself on her and do good works to escape hell-fire? She wears a hair-shirt in Lent."

Mrs. Satterthwaite started from her doze on the edge of her chair. She had been trusting the Father's wit to give her daughter's insolence a run for its money, and she imagined that if the priest hit hard enough, he might, at least, make Sylvia think a little about some of her ways.

"Hang it, no, Sylvia," she exclaimed more suddenly. "I may not be much, but I'm a sportsman. I'm afraid of hell-fire; horribly, I'll admit. But I don't bargain with the Almighty. I hope He'll let me through; but I'd go on trying to pick men out of the dirt—I suppose that's what you and Father Consett mean—if I were as certain of going to Hell as I am of going to bed to-night. So that's that!"

" 'And lo! Ben Adhem's name led all the rest!' " Sylvia jeered softly. "All the same, I bet you wouldn't bother to reclaim men if you could not find the young, good-looking, interestingly vicious sort."

"I wouldn't," Mrs. Satterthwaite said. "If they didn't interest me, why should I?"

Sylvia looked at Father Consett.

"If you're going to trounce me any more," she said, "get a move on. It's late, I've been travelling for thirty-six hours."

"I will," Father Consett said. "It's a good maxim that if you swat flies enough, some of them stick to the wall. I'm only trying to make a little mark on your common sense. Don't you see what you're going to?"

"What?" Sylvia said indifferently. "Hell?"

"No," the Father said, "I'm talking of this life. Your confessor must talk to you about the next. But I'll not tell you what you're going to. I've changed my mind. I'll tell your mother after you're gone."

"Tell me," Sylvia said.

"I'll not," Father Consett answered. "Go to the fortune-tellers at the Earl's Court exhibition; they'll tell ye all about the fair woman you're to beware of."

"There's some of them said to be rather good," Sylvia said. "Di Wilson's told me about one. She said she was going to have a baby. . . . You don't mean that, Father? For I swear I never will . . ."

"I dare say not," the priest said. "But let's talk about men."

"There's nothing you can tell me I don't know," Sylvia said.

"I dare say not," the priest answered. "But let's rehearse what you do know. Now, suppose you could elope with

a new man every week and no questions asked? Or how
often would you want to?"

Sylvia said:

"Just a moment, Father," and she addressed Mrs. Satterthwaite: "I suppose I shall have to put myself to bed."

"You will," Mrs. Satterthwaite said. "I'll not have any maid
kept up after ten in a holiday resort. What's she to do in a
place like this? Except listen for the bogies it's full of?"

"Always considerate!" Mrs. Tietjens gibed. "And perhaps
it's just as well. I'd probably beat that Marie of yours arms
to pieces with a hairbrush if she came near me." She added:
"You were talking about men, Father. . . ." And then began
with sudden animation to her mother:

"I've changed my mind about that telegram. The first thing
to-morrow I shall wire: *'Agreed entirely but arrange bring
Hullo Central with you.'*"

She addressed the priest again:

"I call my maid Hullo Central because she's got a tinny
voice like a telephone. I say: 'Hullo Central.' When she an-
swers, 'Yes, modd'm,' you'd swear it was the Exchange speaking. . . . But you were telling me about men."

"I was reminding you!" the Father said. "But I needn't
go on. You've caught the drift of my remarks. That is why
you are pretending not to listen."

"I assure you, no," Mrs. Tietjens said. "It is simply that
if a thing comes into my head I have to say it. . . . You
were saying that if one went away with a different man for
every week-end . . ."

"You've shortened the period already," the priest said. "I
gave a full week to every man."

"But, of course, one would have to have a home," Sylvia
said, "an address. One would have to fill one's mid-week engagements. Really it comes to it that one has to have a
husband and a place to store one's maid in. Hullo Central's been on board-wages all the time. But I don't believe
she likes it. . . . Let's agree that if I had a different man every
week I'd be bored with the arrangement. That's what you're
getting at, isn't it?"

"You'd find," the priest said, "that it whittled down until
the only divvy moment was when you stood waiting in the
booking-office for the young man to take the tickets. . . .
And then gradually that wouldn't be divvy any more. . . .
And you'd yawn and long to go back to your husband."

"Look here," Mrs. Tietjens said, "you're abusing the secrets of the confessional. That's exactly what Tottie Charles

said. She tried it for three months while Freddie Charles
was in Madeira. It's *exactly* what she said, down to the yawn
and the booking-office. *And* the 'divvy.' It's only Tottie
Charles who uses it every two words. Most of us prefer
ripping! It *is* more sensible."

"Of course I haven't been abusing the secrets of the confessional," Father Consett said mildly.

"Of course you haven't," Sylvia said with affection.
"You're a good old stick and no end of a mimic, and you
know us all to the bottom of our hearts."

"Not all that much," the priest said; "there's probably a
good deal of good at the bottom of your hearts."

Sylvia said:

"Thanks." She asked suddenly: "Look here. *Was* it what
you saw of us—the future mothers of England, you know,
and all—at Miss Lampeter's—that made you take to the
slums? Out of disgust and despair?"

"Oh, let's not make melodrama out of it," the priest answered. "Let's say I wanted a change. I couldn't see that I
was doing any good."

"You did us all the good there was done," Sylvia said.
"What with Miss Lampeter always drugged to the world, and
all the French mistresses as wicked as hell."

"I've heard you say all this before," Mrs. Satterthwaite
said. "But it was supposed to be the best finishing-school in
England. I know it cost enough!"

"Well, say it was we who were a rotten lot," Sylvia concluded; and then to the Father: "We *were* a lot of rotters,
weren't we?"

The priest answered:

"I don't know. I don't suppose you were—or are—any
worse than your mother or grandmother or the patricianesses
of Rome or the worshippers of Ashtoreth. It seems we have
to have a governing class, and governing classes are subject
to special temptations."

"Who's Ashtoreth?" Sylvia asked. "Astarte?" and then:
"Now, Father, after your experiences would you say the factory girls of Liverpool or any other slum are any better
women than us that you used to look after?"

"Astarte Syriaca," the Father said, "was a very powerful
devil. There's some that hold she's not dead yet. I don't know
that I do myself."

"Well, I've done with her," Sylvia said.

The Father nodded:

"You've had dealings with Mrs. Profumo?" he asked. "And that loathsome fellow . . . What's his name?"

"Does it shock you?" Sylvia asked. "I'll admit it was a bit thick. . . . But I've done with it. I prefer to pin my faith to Mrs. Vanderdecken. And, of course, Freud."

The priest nodded his head and said:

"Of course! Of course . . ."

But Mrs. Satterthwaite exclaimed, with sudden energy:

"Sylvia Tietjens, I don't care what you do or what you read, but if you ever speak another word to that woman, you never do to me!"

Sylvia stretched herself on her sofa. She opened her brown eyes wide and let the lids slowly drop again.

"I've said once," she said, "that I don't like to hear my friends miscalled. Eunice Vanderdecken is a bitterly misjudged woman. She's a real good pal."

"She's a Russian spy," Mrs. Satterthwaite said.

"Russian grandmother," Sylvia answered. "And if she is, who cares? She's welcome for me. . . . Listen now, you two. I said to myself when I came in: 'I dare say I've given them both a rotten time.' I know you're both more nuts on me than I deserve. And I said I'd sit and listen to all the pi-jaw you wanted to give me if I sat till dawn. And I will. As a return. But I'd rather you let my friends alone."

Both the elder people were silent. There came from the shuttered windows of the dark room a low, scratching rustle.

"You hear!" the priest said to Mrs. Satterthwaite.

"It's the branches," Mrs. Satterthwaite answered.

The Father answered: "There's no tree within ten yards! Try bats as an explanation."

"I've said I wish you wouldn't, once," Mrs. Satterthwaite shivered. Sylvia said:

"I don't know what you two are talking about. It sounds like superstition. Mother's rotten with it."

"I don't say that it's devils trying to get in," the Father said. "But it's just as well to remember that devils *are* always trying to get in. And there are especial spots. These deep forests are noted among others." He suddenly turned his back and pointed at the shadowy wall. "Who," he asked, "but a savage possessed by a devil could have conceived of *that* as a decoration?" He was pointing at a life-sized, coarsely daubed picture of a wild boar dying, its throat cut, and gouts of scarlet blood. Other agonies of animals went away into all the shadows.

"*Sport!*" he hissed. "It's deviltry!"

"That's perhaps true," Sylvia said. Mrs. Satterthwaite was crossing herself with great rapidity. The silence remained. Sylvia said:

"Then if you're both done talking I'll say what I have to say. To begin with . . ." She stopped and sat rather erect, listening to the rustling from the shutters.

"To begin with," she began again with impetus, "you spared me the catalogue of the defects of age; I know them. One grows skinny—my sort—the complexion fades, the teeth stick out. And then there is the boredom. I know it; one is bored . . . bored . . . bored! You can't tell me anything I don't know about that. I'm thirty. I know what to expect. You'd like to have told me, Father, only you were afraid of taking away from your famous-man-of-the-world effect—you'd like to have told me that one can insure against the boredom and the long, skinny teeth by love of husband and child. The home stunt! I believe it! I do quite believe it. Only I hate my husband . . . and I hate . . . I hate my child."

She paused, waiting for exclamations of dismay or disapprobation from the priest. These did not come.

"Think," she said, "of all the ruin that child has meant for me; the pain in bearing him and the fear of death."

"Of course," the priest said, "child-bearing is for women a very terrible thing."

"I can't say," Mrs. Tietjens went on, "that this has been a very decent conversation. You get a girl . . . fresh from open sin, and make her talk about it. Of course you're a priest and mother's mother; we're *en famille*. But Sister Mary of the Cross at the convent had a maxim: 'Wear velvet gloves in family life.' We seem to be going at it with the gloves off."

Father Consett still didn't say anything.

"You're trying, of course, to draw me," Sylvia said. "I can see that with half an eye. . . . Very well, then, you shall. . . ."

She drew a breath.

"You want to know why I hate my husband. I'll tell you; it's because of his simple, sheer immorality. I don't mean his actions; his views! Every speech he utters about everything makes me—I swear it makes me—in spite of myself, want to stick a knife into him, and I can't prove he's wrong, not ever, about the simplest thing. But I can pain him. And I will. . . . He sits about in chairs that fit his back, clumsy, like a rock, not moving for hours. . . . And I can make him wince. Oh, without showing it . . . He's what you call . . . oh, loyal. . . . There's an absurd little chit of a fellow . . . oh, Macmaster . . . and his mother . . . whom he persists in a

silly, mystical way in calling a saint . . . a Protestant saint!
. . . And his old nurse, who looks after the child . . . and
the child itself . . . I tell you I've only got to raise an eyelid
. . . yes, cock an eyelid up a little when any one of them is
mentioned . . . and it hurts him dreadfully. His eyes roll in a
sort of mute anguish. . . . Of course he doesn't say anything.
He's an English country gentleman."

Father Consett said:

"This immorality you talk about in your husband . . . I've
never noticed it. I saw a good deal of him when I stayed
with you for the week before your child was born. I talked
with him a great deal. Except in matters of the two communions—and even in these I don't know that we differed so
much—I found him perfectly sound."

"Sound!" Mrs. Satterthwaite said with sudden emphasis; "of
course he's sound. It isn't even the word. He's the best ever.
There was your father, for a good man . . . and him. That's
an end of it."

"Ah," Sylvia said, "you don't know. . . . Look here. Try
and be just. Suppose I'm looking at *The Times* at breakfast
and say, not having spoken to him for a week: 'It's wonderful
what the doctors are doing. Have you seen the latest?' And at
once he'll be on his high horse—he knows everything!—and
he'll prove . . . *prove* . . . that all unhealthy children must be
lethal-chambered or the world will go to pieces. And it's like
being hypnotized; you can't think of what to answer him. Or
he'll reduce you to speechless rage by proving that murderers ought not to be executed. And then I'll ask, casually, if
children ought to be lethal-chambered for being constipated.
Because Marchant—that's the nurse—is always whining that
the child's bowels aren't regular and the dreadful diseases
that leads to. Of course *that* hurts him. For he's perfectly
soppy about that child, though he half knows it isn't his
own. . . . But that's what I mean by immorality. He'll profess
that murderers ought to be preserved in order to breed from
because they're bold fellows, and innocent little children
executed because they're sick. . . . And he'll almost make you
believe it, though you're on the point of retching at the
ideas."

"You wouldn't, now," Father Consett began, and almost
coaxingly, "think of going into retreat for a month or two."

"I wouldn't," Sylvia said. "How could I?"

"There's a convent of female Premonstratensians near
Birkenhead; many ladies go there," the Father went on. "They
cook very well, and you can have your own furniture and

your own maid if ye don't like nuns to wait on you."

"It can't be done," Sylvia said; "you can see for yourself. It would make people smell a rat at once. Christopher wouldn't hear of it. . . ."

"No, I'm afraid it can't be done, Father," Mrs. Satterthwaite interrupted finally. "I've hidden here for four months to cover Sylvia's tracks. I've got Wateman's to look after. My new land steward's coming in next week."

"Still," the Father urged, with a sort of tremulous eagerness, "if only for a month . . . If only for a fortnight . . . So many Catholic ladies do it. . . . Ye might think of it."

"I see what you're aiming at," Sylvia said with sudden anger; "you're revolted at the idea of my going straight from one's man's arms to another."

"I'd be better pleased if there could be an interval," the Father said. "It's what's called bad form."

Sylvia became electrically rigid on her sofa.

"Bad form!" she exclaimed. "You accuse me of bad form."

The Father slightly bowed his head like a man facing a wind.

"I do," he said. "It's disgraceful. It's unnatural. I'd travel a bit at least."

She placed her hand on her long throat.

"I know what you mean," she said; "you want to spare Christopher . . . the humiliation. The . . . the nausea. No doubt he'll feel nauseated. I've reckoned on that. It will give me a little of my own back."

The Father said:

"That's enough, woman. I'll hear no more."

Sylvia said:

"You will, then. Listen here. `. . . I've always got this to look forward to: I'll settle down by that man's side. I'll be as virtuous as any woman. I've made up my mind to it and I'll be it. And I'll be bored stiff for the rest of my life. Except for one thing. I can torment that man. And I'll do it. Do you understand how I'll do it? There are many ways. But if the worst comes to the worst, I can always drive him silly . . . by corrupting the child!" She was panting a little, and round her brown eyes the whites showed. "I'll get even with him. I can. I know how, you see. And with you, through him, for tormenting me. I've come all the way from Brittany without stopping. I haven't slept. . . . But I can . . ."

Father Consett put his hand beneath the tail of his coat.

"Sylvia Tietjens," he said, "in my pistol pocket I've a little bottle of holy water which I carry for such occasions. What if I was to throw two drops of it over you and cry: *Exorciso te Ashtoreth in nomine? . . .*"

She erected her body above her skirts on the sofa, stiffened like a snake's neck above its coils. Her face was quite pallid, her eyes staring out.

"You . . . you *daren't*," she said. "To me . . . an outrage!" Her feet slid slowly to the floor; she measured the distance to the doorway with her eyes. "You *daren't*," she said again; "I'd denounce you to the bishop. . . ."

"It's little the bishop would help you with them burning into your skin," the priest said. "Go away, I bid you, and say a Hail Mary or two. Ye need them. Ye'll not talk of corrupting a little child before me again."

"I won't," Sylvia said. "I shouldn't have. . . ."

Her black figure showed in silhouette against the open doorway.

When the door was closed upon them, Mrs. Satterthwaite said:

"Was it necessary to threaten her with that? You know best, of course. It seems rather strong to me."

"It's a hair from the dog that's bit her," the priest said. "She's a silly girl. She's been playing at black masses along with that Mrs. Profumo and the fellow whose name I can't remember. You could tell that. They cut the throat of a white kid and splash its blood about. . . . That was at the back of her mind. . . . It's not very serious. A parcel of silly, idle girls. It's not much more than palmistry or fortune-telling to them if one has to weigh it, for all its ugliness, as a sin. As far as their volition goes, and it's volition that's the essence of prayer, black or white . . . But it was at the back of her mind, and she won't forget to-night."

"Of course that's your affair, Father," Mrs. Satterthwaite said lazily. "You hit her pretty hard. I don't suppose she's ever been hit so hard. What was it you wouldn't tell her?"

"Only," the priest said, "I wouldn't tell her because the thought's best not put in her head. . . . But her hell on earth will come when her husband goes running, blind, head down, mad after another woman."

Mrs. Satterthwaite looked at nothing; then she nodded. "Yes," she said, "I hadn't thought of it. . . . But will he? He *is* a very sound fellow, isn't he?"

"What's to stop it?" the priest asked. "*What* in the world but the grace of our blessed Lord, which he hasn't got and doesn't ask for? And then . . . He's a young man, full-blooded, and they won't be living . . . *maritalement*. Not if I know him. And then . . . *Then* she'll tear the house down. The world will echo with her wrongs."

"Do you mean to say," Mrs. Satterthwaite said, "that Sylvia would do anything vulgar?"

"Doesn't every woman who's had a man to torture for years when she loses him?" the priest asked. "The more she's made an occupation of torturing him, the less right she thinks she has to lose him."

Mrs. Satterthwaite looked gloomily into the dusk.

"That poor devil . . ." she said. "Will he get any peace anywhere? . . . What's the matter, Father?"

The Father said:

"I've just remembered she gave me tea and cream and I drank it. Now I can't take mass for Father Reinhardt. I'll have to go and knock up his curate, who lives away in the forest."

At the door, holding the candle, he said:

"I'd have you not get up to-day nor yet to-morrow if ye can stand it. Have a headache and let Sylvia nurse you. . . . You'll have to tell how she nursed you when you get back to London. And I'd rather ye didn't lie more out and out than ye need, if it's to please me. . . . Besides, if ye watch Sylvia nursing you, you might hit on a characteristic touch to make it seem more truthful. . . . How her sleeves brushed the medicine bottles and irritated you, maybe . . . or—*you'll* know! If we can save scandal to the congregation, we may as well."

He ran downstairs.

3 ~

AT THE slight creaking made by Macmaster in pushing open his door, Tietjens started violently. He was sitting in a smoking-jacket, playing patience engrossedly in a sort of garret bedroom. It had a sloping roof outlined by black oak beams, which cut into squares the cream-coloured patent distemper of the walls. The room contained also a four-post bedstead, a corner cupboard in black oak, and many rush mats on a polished oak floor of very irregular planking. Tietjens, who hated these disinterred and waxed relics of the past, sat in the centre of the room at a flimsy card-table beneath a white-shaded electric light of a brilliance that, in those sur-

roundings, appeared unreasonable. This was one of those restored old groups of cottages that it was at that date the
fashion to convert into hostelries. To it Macmaster, who was
in search of the inspiration of the past, had preferred to come.
Tietjens, not desiring to interfere with his friend's culture,
had accepted the quarters, though he would have preferred
to go to a comfortable modern hotel as being less affected
and cheaper. Accustomed to what he called the grown old-
nesses of a morose, rambling Yorkshire manor-house, he disliked being among collected and rather pitiful bits, which,
he said, made him feel ridiculous, as if he were trying to behave seriously at a fancy-dress ball. Macmaster, on the other
hand, with gratification and a serious air, would run his
finger-tips along the bevellings of a darkened piece of furniture and would declare it genuine "Chippendale" or "Jaco-
bean oak," as the case might be. And he seemed to gain an
added seriousness and weight of manner with each piece
of ancient furniture that down the years he thus touched. But
Tietjens would declare that you could tell the beastly thing
was a fake by just cocking an eye at it, and if the matter happened to fall under the test of professional dealers in old
furniture, Tietjens was the more often in the right of it, and
Macmaster, sighing slightly, would prepare to proceed still
further along the difficult road to connoisseurship. Eventually,
by conscientious study, he got so far as at times to be called
in by Somerset House to value great properties for probate—
an occupation at once distinguished and highly profitable.

Tietjens swore with the extreme vehemence of a man who
has been made, but who much dislikes being seen, to
start.

Macmaster—in evening dress he looked extremely miniature!—said:

"I'm sorry, old man, I know how much you dislike being
interrupted. But the general is in a terrible temper."

Tietjens rose stiffly, lurched over to an eighteenth-century
rosewood folding wash-stand, took from its top a glass of flat
whisky and soda, and gulped down a large quantity. He
looked about uncertainly, perceived a note-book on a "Chippendale" bureau, made a short calculation in pencil and
looked at his friend momentarily.

Macmaster said again:

"I'm sorry, old man. I must have interrupted one of your
immense calculations."

Tietjens said:

"You haven't. I was only thinking. I'm just as glad you've come. What did you say?"

Macmaster repeated:

"I said the general is in a terrible temper. It's just as well you didn't come up to dinner."

Tietjens said:

"He isn't. . . . He isn't in a temper. He's as pleased as punch at not having to have these women up before him."

Macmaster said:

"He says he's got the police scouring the whole county for them, and that you'd better leave by the first train to-morrow."

Tietjens said:

"I won't. I can't. I've got to wait here for a wire from Sylvia."

Macmaster groaned:

"Oh, dear! Oh, dear!" Then he said hopefully: "But we could have it forwarded to Hythe."

Tietjens said with some vehemence:

"I tell you I won't leave here. I tell you I've settled it with the police and that swine of a Cabinet minister. I've mended the leg of the canary of the wife of the police-constable. Sit down and be reasonable. The police don't touch people like us."

Macmaster said:

"I don't believe you realize the public feeling there is. . . ."

"Of course I do, amongst people like Sandbach," Tietjens said. "Sit down, I tell you. . . . Have some whisky. . . ." He filled himself out another long tumbler and, holding it, dropped into a too-low-seated, reddish wicker arm-chair that had cretonne fixings. Beneath his weight the chair sagged a good deal and his dress-shirt front bulged up to his chin.

Macmaster said:

"What's the matter with you?" Tietjens' eyes were blood-shot.

"I tell you," Tietjens said, "I'm waiting for a wire from Sylvia."

Macmaster said:

"Oh!" And then: "It can't come to-night, it's getting on for one."

"It can," Tietjens said, "I've fixed it up with the postmas-ter—all the way up to town! It probably won't come because Sylvia won't send it until the last moment, to bother me. None the less, I'm waiting for a wire from Sylvia, and this is what I look like."

Macmaster said:

"That woman's the cruellest beast. . . ."

"You might," Tietjens interrupted, "remember that you're talking about my wife."

"I don't see," Macmaster said, "how one can talk about Sylvia without . . ."

"The line is a perfectly simple one to draw," Tietjens said. "You can relate a lady's actions if you know them and are asked to. You mustn't comment. In this case you don't know the lady's actions, even, so you may as well hold your tongue." He sat looking straight in front of him.

Macmaster sighed from deep in his chest. He asked himself if this was what sixteen hours' waiting had done for his friend, what were all the remaining hours going to do?

Tietjens said:

"I shall be fit to talk about Sylvia after two more whiskies. . . . Let's settle your other perturbations first. . . . The fair girl is called Wannop: Valentine Wannop."

"That's the professor's name," Macmaster said.

"She's the late Professor Wannop's daughter," Tietjens said. "She's also the daughter of the novelist."

Macmaster interjected:

"But . . ."

"She supported herself for a year after the professor's death as a domestic servant," Tietjens said. "Now she's housemaid for her mother, the novelist, in an inexpensive cottage. I should imagine the two experiences would make her desire to better the lot of her sex."

Macmaster again interjected a "But . . ."

"I got that information from the policeman whilst I was putting his wife's canary's leg in splints."

Macmaster said:

"The policeman you knocked down?" His eyes expressed unreasoning surprise. He added: "He knew Miss . . . eh . . . Wannop, then!"

"You would not expect much intelligence from the police of Sussex," Tietjens said. "But you would be wrong. P. C. Finn is clever enough to recognize the young lady who for several years past has managed the constabulary's wives' and children's annual tea and sports. He says Miss Wannop holds the quarter-mile, half-mile, high jump, long jump and putting the weight records for East Sussex. That explains how she went over that dike in such tidy style. . . . And precious glad the good, simple man was when I told him he was to leave the girl alone. He didn't know, he said, how he'd ever 'a had the face to serve the warrant on Miss Wannop. The other girl—the one that squeaked—is a stranger, a Londoner probably."

Macmaster said:

"*You* told the policeman . . ."

"I gave him," Tietjens said, "the Rt. Hon. Stephen Fenwick Waterhouse's compliments, and he'd be much obliged if the P. C. would hand in a 'No Can Do' report in the matter of those ladies every morning to his inspector. I gave him also a brand-new fi'-pun' note—from the Cabinet minister— and a couple of quid and the price of a new pair of trousers from myself. So he's the happiest constable in Sussex. A very decent fellow; he told me how to know a dog otter's spoor from a gravid bitch's. . . . But that wouldn't interest you."

He began again:

"Don't look so inexpressibly foolish. I told you I'd been dining with that swine. . . . No, I oughtn't to call him a swine after eating his dinner. Besides, he's a very decent fellow. . . ."

"You didn't tell me you'd been dining with Mr. Waterhouse," Macmaster said. "I hope you remembered that, as he's amongst other things the president of the Funded Debt Commission, he's the power of life and death over the department and us."

"You didn't think," Tietjens answered, "that you are the only one to dine with the great ones of the earth! I wanted to talk to that fellow . . . about those figures their cursed crowd made me fake. I meant to give him a bit of my mind."

"You *didn't!*" Macmaster said with an expression of panic. "Besides, they didn't ask you to fake the calculation. They only asked you to work it out on the basis of given figures."

"Anyhow," Tietjens said, "I gave him a bit of my mind. I told him that, at threepence, it must run the country—and certainly himself as a politician!—to absolute ruin."

Macmaster uttered a deep "Good Lord!" and then: "But won't you ever remember you're a government servant. He could . . ."

"Mr. Waterhouse," Tietjens said, "asked me if I wouldn't consent to be transferred to his secretary's department. And when I said: "Go to hell!" he walked round the streets with me for two hours arguing. . . . I was working out the chances on a four-and-a-half-pence basis for him when you interrupted me. I've promised to let him have the figures when he goes up by the one-thirty on Monday."

Macmaster said:

"You haven't. . . . But by Jove you're the only man in England that could do it."

"That was what Mr. Waterhouse said," Tietjens commented. "He said old Ingleby had told him so."

"I do hope," Macmaster said, "that you answered him politely!"

"I told him," Tietjens answered, "that there were a dozen men who could do it as well as I, and I mentioned your name in particular."

"But I *couldn't*," Macmaster answered. "Of course I could convert a threepence rate into four and a half pence. But these are the actuarial variations; they're infinite. I couldn't touch them."

Tietjens said negligently: "I don't want my name mixed up in the unspeakable affair. When I give him the papers on Monday I shall tell him you did most of the work."

Again Macmaster groaned.

Nor was this distress mere altruism. Immensely ambitious for his brilliant friend, Macmaster's ambition was one ingredient of his strong desire for security. At Cambridge he had been perfectly content with a moderate, quite respectable place on the list of mathematical postulants. He knew that that made him safe, and he had still more satisfaction in the thought that it would warrant him in never being brilliant in after-life. But when Tietjens, two years after, had come out as a mere Second Wrangler, Macmaster had been bitterly and loudly disappointed. He knew perfectly well that Tietjens simply hadn't taken trouble; and, ten chances to one it was on purpose that Tietjens hadn't taken trouble. For the matter of that, for Tietjens it wouldn't have been trouble.

And, indeed, to Macmaster's upbraidings, which Macmaster hadn't spared him, Tietjens had answered that he hadn't been able to think of going through the rest of his life with a beastly placard like Senior Wrangler hung round his neck.

But Macmaster had early made up his mind that life for him would be safest if he could go about not very much observed but still an authority, in the midst of a body of men all labelled. He wanted to walk down Pall Mall on the arm, precisely, of a largely lettered Senior Wrangler; to return eastward on the arm of the youngest lord chancellor England had ever seen; to stroll down Whitehall in familiar converse with a world-famous novelist, saluting on the way a majority of My Lords Commissioners of the Treasury. And, after tea, for an hour at the club, all these, in a little group, should treat him with the courtesy of men who respected him for his soundness. Then he would be safe.

And he had no doubt that Tietjens was the most brilliant man in England of that day, so that nothing caused him more anguish than the thought that Tietjens might not make a brilliant and rapid career towards some illustrious position in the public services. He would very willingly—he desired, indeed, nothing better!—have seen Tietjens pass over his own head! It did not seem to him a condemnation of the public services that this appeared to be unlikely.

Yet Macmaster was still not without hope. He was quite aware that there are other techniques of careers than that which he had prescribed for himself. He could not imagine himself, even in the most deferential way, correcting a superior; yet he could see that though Tietjens treated almost every hierarch as if he were a born fool, no one very much resented it. Of course Tietjens was a Tietjens of Groby; but was that going to be enough to live on forever? Times were changing, and Macmaster imagined this to be a democratic age.

But Tietjens went on, with both hands, as it were, throwing away opportunity and committing outrage. . . .

That day Macmaster could only consider to be one of disaster. He got up from his chair and filled himself another drink; he felt himself to be distressed and to need it. Slouching amongst his cretonnes, Tietjens was gazing in front of him. He said:

"Here!" without looking at Macmaster, and held out his long glass. Into it Macmaster poured whisky with a hesitating hand. Tietjens said: "Go on!"

Macmaster said:

"It's late; we're breakfasting at the Duchemins' at ten." Tietjens answered:

"Don't worry, sonny. We'll be there for your pretty lady." He added: "Wait another quarter of an hour. I want to talk to you."

Macmaster sat down again and deliberately began to review the day. It had begun with disaster, and in disaster it had continued.

And with something like a bitter irony, Macmaster remembered and brought up now for digestion the parting words of General Campion to himself. The general had limped with him to the hall-door up at Mountby and, standing patting him on the shoulder, tall, slightly bent and very friendly, had said:

"Look here. Christopher Tietjens is a splendid fellow. But he needs a good woman to look after him. Get him back to Sylvia as quick as you can. Had a little tiff, haven't they? Nothing serious? Chrissie hasn't been running after the skirts? No? I dare say a little. No? Well, then . . ."

Macmaster had stood like a gate-post, so appalled. He had stuttered:

"No! No!"

"We've known them both so long," the general went on. "Lady Claudine in particular. And believe me, Sylvia is a splendid girl. Straight as a die; the soul of loyalty to her friends. And fearless. She'd face the devil in his rage. You should have seen her out with the Belvoir! Of course you know her. . . . Well, then!"

Macmaster had just managed to say that he knew Sylvia, of course.

"Well, then . . ." the general had continued, "you'll agree with me that if there *is* anything wrong between them, he's to blame. And it will be resented. Very bitterly. He wouldn't set foot in this house again. But he says he's going out to her and Mrs. Satterthwaite. . . ."

"I believe . . ." Macmaster had begun, "I believe he is . . ."

"Well, then!" the general had said: "It's all right. . . . But Christopher Tietjens needs a good woman's backing. . . . He's a splendid fellow. There are few young fellows for whom I have more . . . I could almost say respect. . . . But he needs that. To ballast him."

In the car, running down the hill from Mountby, Macmaster had exhausted himself in the effort to restrain his execrations of the general. He wanted to shout that he was a pigheaded old fool: a meddlesome ass. But he was in the car with the two secretaries of the Cabinet minister: the Rt. Hon. Stephen Fenwick Waterhouse, who, being himself an advanced Liberal down for a week-end of golf, preferred not to dine at the house of the Conservative member. At that date there was in politics a phase of bitter social feud between the parties: a condition that had not till lately been characteristic of English political life. The prohibition had not extended itself to the two younger men.

Macmaster was not unpleasurably aware that these two fellows treated him with a certain deference. They had seen Macmaster being talked to familiarly by General Lord Edward Campion. Indeed, they and the car had been kept waiting whilst the general patted their fellow-guest on the shoulder, held his upper arm and spoke in a low voice into his ear. . . .

But that was the only pleasure that Macmaster got out of it.

Yes, the day had begun disastrously with Sylvia's letter; it ended—if it was ended!—almost more disastrously with the general's eulogy of that woman. During the day he had nerved himself to having an immensely disagreeable scene with Tietjens. Tietjens *must* divorce the woman; it was necessary for the peace of mind of himself, of his friends, of his family; for the sake of his career; in the very name of decency!

In the meantime Tietjens had rather forced his hand. It had been a most disagreeable affair. They had arrived at Rye in time for lunch—at which Tietjens had consumed the best part of a bottle of Burgundy. During lunch Tietjens had given Macmaster Sylvia's letter to read, saying that as he should later consult his friend, his friend had better be made acquainted with the document.

The letter had appeared extraordinary in its effrontery, for it said nothing. Beyond the bare statement, "I am now ready to return to you," it occupied itself simply with the fact that Mrs. Tietjens wanted—could no longer get on without—the services of her maid, whom she called Hullo Central. If Tietjens wanted her, Mrs. Tietjens, to return to him, he was to see that Hullo Central was waiting on the door-step for her, and so on. She added the detail that there was *no one* else, underlined, she could bear round her while she was retiring for the night. On reflection Macmaster could see that this was the best letter the woman could have written if she wanted to be taken back; for had she extended herself into either excuses or explanations, it was ten chances to one Tietjens would have taken the line that he couldn't go on living with a woman capable of such a lapse in taste. But Macmaster had never thought of Sylvia as wanting in *savoir faire*.

It had none the less hardened him in his determination to urge his friend to divorce. He had intended to begin this campaign in the fly, driving to pay his call on the Rev. Mr. Duchemin, who in early life had been a personal disciple of Mr. Ruskin and a patron and acquaintance of the poet-painter, the subject of Macmaster's monograph. On this drive Tietjens preferred not to come. He said that he would loaf about the town and meet Macmaster at the golf-club towards four-thirty. He was not in the mood for making new acquaintances. Macmaster, who knew the pressure under which his friend must be suffering, thought this reasonable enough, and drove off up Iden Hill by himself.

Few women had ever made so much impression on Macmaster as Mrs. Duchemin. He knew himself to be in a mood to be impressed by almost any woman, but he considered that that was not enough to account for the very strong influence she at once exercised over him. There had been two young girls in the drawing-room when he had been ushered in, but they had disappeared almost simultaneously, and although he had noticed them immediately afterwards riding past the window on bicycles, he was aware that he would not have recognized them again. From her first words on rising to greet him: "Not *the* Mr. Macmaster!" he had had eyes for no one else.

It was obvious that the Rev. Mr. Duchemin must be one of those clergymen of considerable wealth and cultured taste who not infrequently adorn the Church of England. The rectory itself, a great, warm-looking manor-house of very old red brick, was abutted on to by one of the largest tithe-barns that Macmaster had ever seen; the church itself, with a primitive roof of oak shingles, nestled in the corner formed by the ends of rectory and tithe-barn, and was by so much the smallest of the three and so undecorated that but for its little belfry it might have been a good cow-byre. All three buildings stood on the very edge of the little row of hills that looks down on the Romney Marsh; they were sheltered from the north wind by a great symmetrical fan of elms and from the south-west by a very tall hedge and shrubbery, all of remarkable yews. It was, in short, an ideal cure of souls for a wealthy clergyman of cultured tastes, for there was not so much as a peasant's cottage within a mile of it.

To Macmaster, in short, this was the ideal English home. Of Mrs. Duchemin's drawing-room itself, contrary to his habit, for he was sensitive and observant in such things, he could afterwards remember little except that it was perfectly sympathetic. Three long windows gave on to a perfect lawn, on which, isolated and grouped, stood standard rose-trees, symmetrical half-globes of green foliage picked out with flowers like bits of carved pink marble. Beyond the lawn was a low stone wall; beyond that the quiet expanse of the marsh shimmered in the sunlight.

The furniture of the room was, as to its woodwork, brown, old, with the rich softnesses of much polishing with beeswax. What pictures there were Macmaster recognized at once as being by Simeon Solomon, one of the weaker and more frail aesthetes—aureoled, palish heads of ladies carrying lilies that were not very like lilies. They were in the tradition—but not the best of the tradition. Macmaster under-

stood—and later Mrs. Duchemin confirmed him in the idea—
that Mr. Duchemin kept his more precious specimens of work
in a sanctum, leaving to the relatively public room, good-
humouredly and with slight contempt, these weaker specimens. That seemed to stamp Mr. Duchemin at once as
being of the elect.

Mr. Duchemin in person was, however, not present; and
there seemed to be a good deal of difficulty in arranging a
meeting between the two men. Mr. Duchemin, his wife said,
was much occupied at the week-ends. She added, with a faint
and rather absent smile, the word "naturally." Macmaster at
once saw that it was natural for a clergyman to be much
occupied during the week-ends. With a little hesitation Mrs.
Duchemin suggested that Mr. Macmaster and his friend might
come to lunch on the next day—Saturday. But Macmaster
had made an engagement to play the foursome with General
Campion—half the round from twelve till one-thirty, half
the round from three to half-past four. And as their then
present arrangements stood, Macmaster and Tietjens were to
take the 6:30 train to Hythe; that ruled out either tea or
dinner next day.

With sufficient, but not too extravagant, regret, Mrs. Duchemin raised her voice to say:

"Oh, dear! Oh, dear! But you must see my husband and the
pictures after you have come so far."

A rather considerable volume of harsh sound was coming
through the end wall of the room—the barking of dogs, apparently the hurried removal of pieces of furniture or perhaps of packing-cases, guttural ejaculations. Mrs. Duchemin
said, with her far-away air and deep voice:

"They are making a good deal of noise. Let us go into
the garden and look at my husband's roses if you've a moment more to give us."

Macmaster quoted to himself:

" 'I looked and saw your eyes in the shadow of your
hair. . . .' "

There was no doubt that Mrs. Duchemin's eyes, which were
of a dark, pebble blue, were actually in the shadow of her
blue-black, very regularly waved hair. The hair came down
on the square, low forehead. It was a phenomenon that
Macmaster had never before really seen, and, he congratulated himself, this was one more confirmation—if confirmation were needed!—of the powers of observation of the subject of his monograph!

Mrs. Duchemin bore the sunlight! Her dark complexion

was clear; there was, over the cheek-bones, a delicate suffusion of light carmine. Her jaw-bone was singularly clear cut to the pointed chin—like an alabaster, mediaeval saint's.

She said:

"Of course you're Scotch. I'm from Auld Reekie myself."

Macmaster would have known it. He said he was from the Port of Leith. He could not imagine hiding anything from Mrs. Duchemin. Mrs. Duchemin said with renewed insistence:

"Oh, but of *course* you must see my husband and the pictures. Let me see. . . . We must think. . . . Would breakfast now? . . ."

Macmaster said that he and his friend were government servants and up to rising early. He had a great desire to breakfast in that house. She said:

"At a quarter to ten, then, our car will be at the bottom of your street. It's a matter of ten minutes only, so you won't go hungry long!"

She said, gradually gaining animation, that of course Macmaster would bring his friend. He could tell Tietjens that he should meet a very charming girl. She stopped and added suddenly: "Probably, at any rate." She said the name which Macmaster caught as "Wanstead." And possibly another girl. And Mr. Horsted or something like it, her husband's junior curate. She said reflectively:

"Yes, we might try quite a party . . ." and added, "quite noisy and gay. I hope your friend's talkative!"

Macmaster said something about trouble.

"Oh, it can't be too much trouble," she said. "Besides, it might do my husband good." She went on: "Mr. Duchemin is apt to brood. It's perhaps too lonely here." And added the rather astonishing words: "After all."

And driving back in the fly, Macmaster said to himself that you couldn't call Mrs. Duchemin ordinary, at least. Yet meeting her was like going into a room that you had long left and never ceased to love. It felt good. It was perhaps partly her Edinburgh-ness. Macmaster allowed himself to coin that word. There was in Edinburgh a society—he himself had never been privileged to move in it, but its annals are part of the literature of Scotland!—where the ladies are all great ladies in tall drawing-rooms; circumspect yet shrewd: still, yet with a sense of the comic: frugal yet warmly hospitable. It was perhaps just Edinburgh-ness that was wanting in the drawing-rooms of his friends in London. Mrs. Cressy, the Hon. Mrs. de Limoux and Mrs. Delawnay were all almost perfection in manner, in speech, in composure. But, then, they were not young, they weren't Edinburgh—and they weren't strikingly elegant!

Mrs. Duchemin was all three! Her assured, tranquil manner she would retain to any age: it betokened the enigmatic soul of her sex, but physically she couldn't be more than thirty. That was unimportant, for she would never want to do anything in which physical youth counted. She would never, for instance, have occasion to run: she would always just "move"—floatingly! He tried to remember the details of her dress.

It had certainly been dark blue—and certainly of silk: that rather coarsely woven, exquisite material that has on its folds as of a silvery shimmer with minute knots. But very dark blue. And it contrived to be at once artistic—absolutely in the tradition! And yet well cut! Very large sleeves, of course, but still with a certain fit. She had worn an immense necklace of yellow polished amber: on the dark blue! And Mrs. Duchemin had said, over her husband's roses, that the blossoms always reminded her of little mouldings of pink cloud come down for the cooling of the earth. . . . A charming thought!

Suddenly he said to himself:

"What a mate for Tietjens!" And his mind added: "Why should she not become an Influence!"

A vista opened before him, in time! He imagined Tietjens in some way proprietarily responsible for Mrs. Duchemin: quite *pour le bon,* tranquilly passionate and accepted, *motif;* and "immensely improved" by the association. And himself, in a year or two, bringing the at-last-found Lady of his Delight to sit at the feet of Mrs. Duchemin—the Lady of his Delight, whilst circumspect, would be also young and impressionable!—to learn the mysterious assuredness of manner, the gift of dressing, the knack of wearing amber and bending over standard roses—and the Edinburgh-ness!

Macmaster was thus not a little excited, and finding Tietjens at tea amid the green-stained furnishings and illustrated papers of the large, corrugated iron golf-house, he could not help exclaiming:

"I've accepted the invitation to breakfast with the Duchemins to-morrow for us both. I hope you won't mind," although Tietjens was sitting at a little table with General Campion and his brother-in-law, the Hon. Paul Sandbach, Conservative member for the division and husband of Lady Claudine. The general said pleasantly to Tietjens:

"Breakfast! With Duchemin! You go, my boy! You'll get the best breakfast you ever had in your life."

He added to his brother-in-law: "Not the eternal mock kedgeree Claudine gives us every morning."

Sandbach grunted:

"It's not for want of trying to steal their cook. Claudine has a shy at it every time we come down here."

The general said pleasantly to Macmaster—he spoke always pleasantly, with a half-smile and a slight sibilance:

"My brother-in-law isn't serious, you understand. My sister wouldn't think of stealing a cook. Let alone from Duchemin. She'd be frightened to."

Sandbach grunted:

"Who wouldn't?"

Both these gentlemen were very lame: Mr. Sandbach from birth and the general as the result of a slight but neglected motor accident. He had practically only one vanity, the belief that he was qualified to act as his own chauffeur, and since he was both inexpert and very careless, he met with frequent accidents. Mr. Sandbach had a dark, round, bull-dog face and a violent manner. He had twice been suspended from his Parliamentary duties for applying to the then Chancellor of the Exchequer the epithet "lying attorney," and he was at that moment still suspended.

Macmaster then became unpleasantly perturbed. With his sensitiveness he was perfectly aware of an unpleasant chill in the air. There was also a stiffness about Tietjens' eyes. He was looking straight before him; there was a silence too. Behind Tietjens' back were two men with bright green coats, red knitted waistcoats, and florid faces. One was bald and blond, the other had black hair, remarkably oiled and shiny; both were forty-fivish. They were regarding the occupants of the Tietjens table with both their mouths slightly open. They were undisguisedly listening. In front of each were three empty sloe-gin glasses and one half-filled tumbler of brandy and soda. Macmaster understood why the general had explained that his sister had not tried to steal Mrs. Duchemin's cook.

Tietjens said:

"Drink up your tea quickly and let's get started." He was drawing from his pocket a number of telegraph forms, which he began arranging. The general said:

"Don't burn your mouth. We can't start off before all . . . all these other gentlemen. We're too slow."

"No, we're beastly well stuck," Sandbach said.

Tietjens handed the telegraph forms over to Macmaster.

"You'd better take a look at these," he said. "I mayn't see you again to-day after the match. You're dining up at Mountby. The general will run you up. Lady Claude will excuse me. I've got work to do."

This was already matter for dismay for Macmaster. He was aware that Tietjens would have disliked dining up at Mountby with the Sandbachs, who would have a crowd, extremely smart but more than usually unintelligent. Tietjens called this crowd, indeed, the plague-spot of the party—meaning of Toryism. But Macmaster couldn't help thinking that a disagreeable dinner would be better for his friend than brooding in solitude in the black shadows of the huddled town. Then Tietjens said:

"I'm going to have a word with that swine!" He pointed his square chin rather rigidly before him, and looking past the two brandy drinkers, Macmaster saw one of those faces that frequent caricature made familiar and yet strange. Macmaster couldn't, at the moment, put a name to it. It must be a politician, probably a minister. But which? His mind was already in a dreadful state. In the glimpse he had caught of the telegraph form now in his hand, he had perceived that it was addressed to Sylvia Tietjens and began with the word "agreed." He said swiftly:

"Has that been sent or is it only a draft?"

Tietjens said:

"That fellow is the Rt. Hon. Stephen Fenwick Waterhouse. He's chairman of the Funded Debt Commission. He's the swine who made us fake that return in the office."

That moment was the worst Macmaster had ever known. A worse came. Tietjens said:

"I'm going to have a word with him. That's why I'm not dining at Mountby. It's a duty to the country."

Macmaster's mind simply stopped. He was in a space, all windows. There was sunlight outside. And clouds. Pink and white. Woolly! Some ships. And two men: one dark and oily, the other rather blotchy on a blond baldness. They were talking, but their words made no impression on Macmaster. The dark, oily man said that he was not going to take Gertie to Budapest. Not half! He winked like a nightmare. Beyond were two young men and a preposterous face. . . . It was all so like a nightmare that the Cabinet minister's features were distorted for Macmaster. Like an enormous mask of pantomime: shiny, with an immense nose and elongated, Chinese eyes.

Yet not unpleasant! Macmaster was a Whig by conviction, by nation, by temperament. He thought that public servants should abstain from political activity. Nevertheless, he couldn't be expected to think a Liberal Cabinet minister ugly. On the contrary, Mr. Waterhouse appeared to have a frank, humorous, kindly expression. He listened deferentially to one of his secretaries, resting his hand on the young man's shoulder, smiling a little, rather sleepily. No doubt he was overworked. And then, letting himself go in a side-shaking laugh. Putting on flesh!

What a pity! What a *pity!* Macmaster was reading a string of incomprehensible words in Tietjens' heavily scored writing. *Not entertain . . . flat not house . . . child remain at sister.* . . . His eyes went backwards and forwards over the phrases. He could not connect the words without stops. The man with the oily hair said in a sickly voice that Gertie was hot stuff, but not the one for Budapest with all the Gitana girls you were telling me of! Why, he'd kept Gertie for five years now. More like the real thing! His friend's voice was like a result of indigestion. Tietjens, Sandbach and the general were stiff, like pokers.

"What a pity!" Macmaster thought.

He ought to have been sitting . . . It would have been pleasant and right to be sitting with the pleasant minister. In the ordinary course he, Macmaster, would have been. The best golfer in the place was usually set to play with distinguished visitors, and there was next to no one in the South of England who ordinarily could beat him. He had begun at four, playing with a miniature cleek and a found shilling ball over the municipal links. Going to the poor school every morning and back to dinner; and back to school and back to bed! Over the cold, rushy, sandy links, beside the grey sea. Both shoes full of sand. The found shilling ball had lasted him three years. . . .

Macmaster exclaimed: "Good God!" He had just gathered from the telegram that Tietjens meant to go to Germany on Tuesday. As if at Macmaster's ejaculation, Tietjens said:

"Yes. It *is* unbearable. If you don't stop those swine, general, I shall."

The general sibilated low, between his teeth:

"Wait a minute. . . . Wait a minute. . . . Perhaps that other fellow will."

The man with the black oily hair said:

"If Budapest's the place for the girls you say it is, old pal, with the Turkish baths and all, we'll paint the old town red, all right, next month," and he winked at Tietjens. His friend, with his head down, seemed to make internal rumblings, looking apprehensively beneath his blotched forehead at the general.

"Not," the other continued argumentatively, "that I don't love my old woman. She's all right. And then there's Gertie. 'Ot stuff, but the real thing. But I say a man wants . . ." He ejaculated, "Oh!"

The general, his hands in his pockets, very tall, thin, red-cheeked, his white hair combed forward in a fringe, sauntered towards the other table. It was not two yards, but it seemed a long saunter. He stood right over them, they looking up, open-eyed, like schoolboys at a balloon. He said:

"I'm glad you're enjoying our links, gentlemen."

The bald man said: "We are! We are! First class. A treat!"

"But," the general said, "it isn't wise to discuss one's . . . eh . . . domestic circumstances . . . at . . . at mess, you know, or in a golf-house. People might hear."

The gentleman with the oily hair half rose and exclaimed: "Oo, the . . ." The other man mumbled: "Shut up, Briggs."

The general said:

"I'm the president of the club, you know. It's my duty to see that the *majority* of the club and its visitors are pleased. I hope you don't mind."

The general came back to his seat. He was trembling with vexation.

"It makes one as beastly a bounder as themselves," he said. "But what the devil else was one to do?" The two city men had ambled hastily into the dressing-rooms; the dire silence fell. Macmaster realized that, for these Tories at least, this was really the end of the world. The last of England! He returned, with panic in his heart, to Tietjens' telegram. . . . Tietjens was going to Germany on Tuesday. He offered to throw over the department. . . . These were unthinkable things. You couldn't imagine them!

He began to read the telegram all over again. A shadow fell upon the flimsy sheets. The Rt. Hon. Mr. Waterhouse was between the head of the table and the windows. He said:

"We're much obliged, general. It was impossible to hear ourselves speak for those obscene fellows' smut. It's fellows like that that make our friends the suffragettes! That warrants them. . . ." He added: "Hullo! Sandbach! Enjoying your rest?"

The general said:

"I was hoping you'd take on the job of telling these fellows off."

Mr. Sandbach, his bull-dog jaw sticking out, the short black hair on his scalp appearing to rise, barked:

"Hullo, Waterslop! Enjoying your plunder?"

Mr. Waterhouse, tall, slouching and untidy-haired, lifted the flaps of his coat. It was so ragged that it appeared as if straws stuck out of the elbows.

"All that the suffragettes have left me," he said laughingly. "Isn't one of you fellows a genius called Tietjens?" He was looking at Macmaster. The general said:

"Tietjens . . . Macmaster . . ." The minister went on, very friendly:

"Oh, it's you? . . . I just wanted to take the opportunity of thanking you."

Tietjens said:

"Good God! What for?"

"*You* know!" the minister said; "we couldn't have got the bill before the House till next session without your figures. . . ." He said slyly: "Could we, Sandbach?" and added to Tietjens: "Ingleby told me. . . ."

Tietjens was chalk-white, and stiffened. He stuttered:

"I can't take any credit. . . . I consider . . ."

Macmaster exclaimed:

"Tietjens . . . you . . ." He didn't know what he was going to say.

"Oh, you're too modest," Mr. Waterhouse overwhelmed Tietjens. "We know whom we've to thank. . . ." His eyes drifted to Sandbach a little absently. Then his face lit up.

"Oh! Look here, Sandbach," he said. . . . "Come here, will you?" He walked a pace or two away, calling to one of his young men: "Oh, Sanderson, give the bobby a drink. A good stiff one." Sandbach jerked himself awkwardly out of his chair and limped to the minister.

Tietjens burst out:

"Me too modest! *Me!* . . . The swine . . . The unspeakable swine!"

The general said:

"What's it all about, Chrissie? You probably are too modest."

Tietjens said:

"Damn it. It's a serious matter. It's driving me out of the unspeakable office I'm in."

Macmaster said:

"No! No! You're wrong. It's a wrong view you take." And

with a good deal of real passion he began to explain to the
general. It was an affair that had already given him a great
deal of pain. The government had asked the statistical department for figures illuminating a number of schedules that
they desired to use in presenting their new bill to the Commons. Mr. Waterhouse was to present it.

Mr. Waterhouse at the moment was slapping Mr. Sandbach
on the back, tossing the hair out of his eyes and laughing
like a hysterical schoolgirl. He looked suddenly tired. A police-constable, his buttons shining, appeared, drinking from
a pewter pot outside the glazed door. The two city men ran
across the angle from the dressing-room to the same door,
buttoning their clothes. The minister said loudly:

"Make it guineas!"

It seemed to Macmaster painfully wrong that Tietjens
should call anyone so genial and unaffected an unspeakable
swine. It was unjust. He went on with his explanation to the
general.

The government had wanted a set of figures based on a
calculation called B 7. Tietjens, who had been working on one
called H 19—for his own instruction—had persuaded himself that H 19 was the lowest figure that was actuarially sound.

The general said pleasantly: "All this is Greek to me."

"Oh no, it needn't be," Macmaster heard himself say. "It
amounts to this. Chrissie was asked by the government—by
Sir Reginald Ingleby—to work out what three times three
comes to: it was that sort of thing in principle. He said that
the only figure that would not ruin the country was nine
times nine. . . ."

"The government wanted to shovel money into the working-man's pockets, in fact," the general said. "Money for
nothing . . . or votes, I suppose."

"But that isn't the point, sir," Macmaster ventured to say.
"All that Chrissie was asked to do was to say what three
times three was."

"Well, he appears to have done it and earned no end of
kudos," the general said. "That's all right. We've all, always, believed in Chrissie's ability. But he's a strong-tempered beggar."

"He was extraordinarily rude to Sir Reginald over it,"
Macmaster went on.

The general said:

"Oh, dear! Oh, dear!" He shook his head at Tietjens and assumed with care the blank, slightly disappointing air of the
regular officer. "I don't like to hear of rudeness to a superior.
In *any* service."

"I don't think," Tietjens said with extreme mildness, "that Macmaster is quite fair to me. Of course he's a right to his opinion as to what the discipline of a service demands. I certainly told Ingleby that I'd rather resign than do that beastly job. . . ."

"You shouldn't have," the general said. "What would become of the services if everyone did as you did?"

Sandbach came back laughing and dropped painfully into his low arm-chair.

"That fellow . . ." he began.

The general slightly raised his hand.

"A minute!" he said. "I was about to tell Chrissie here that if I am offered the job—of course it's an order, really—of suppressing the Ulster Volunteers . . . I'd rather cut my throat than do it. . . ."

Sandbach said:

"Of course you would, old chap. They're our brothers. You'd see the beastly, lying government damned first."

"I was going to say that I should accept," the general said; "I shouldn't resign my commission."

Sandbach said:

"Good *God!*"

Tietjens said:

"Well, I didn't."

Sandbach exclaimed:

"General! You! After all Claudine and I have said . . ."

Tietjens interrupted:

"Excuse me, Sandbach. I'm receiving this reprimand for the moment. I wasn't, then, rude to Ingleby. If I'd expressed contempt for what he said or for himself, that would have been rude. I didn't. He wasn't in the least offended. He looked like a cockatoo, but he wasn't offended. And I let him overpersuade me. He was right, really. He pointed out that if I didn't do the job, those swine would put on one of our little competition-wallah head clerks and get all the schedules faked, as well as starting off with false premises!"

"That's the view I take," the general said; "if I don't take the Ulster job the government will put on a fellow who'll burn all the farmhouses and rape all the women in the three counties. They've got him up their sleeve. He only asks for the Connaught Rangers to go through the North with. And you know what *that* means. All the same . . ." He looked at Tietjens: "One should not be rude to one's superiors."

"I tell you I wasn't rude," Tietjens exclaimed. "Damn your nice, paternal old eyes. Get that into your mind!"

The general shook his head:

"You brilliant fellows!" he said. "The country or the army or anything could not be run by you. It takes stupid fools like me and Sandbach, along with sound, moderate heads like our friend here." He indicated Macmaster and, rising, went on: "Come along. You're playing me, Macmaster. They say you're hot stuff. Chrissie's no good. He can take Sandbach on."

He walked off with Macmaster towards the dressing-room.

Sandbach, wriggling awkwardly out of his chair, shouted:

"Save the country . . . Damn it . . ." He stood on his feet. "I and Campion . . . Look at what the country's come to. . . . What with swine like these two in our club-houses! And policemen to go round the links with ministers to protect them from the wild women . . . By God! I'd like to have the flaying of the skin off some of their backs. I would. By God I would."

He added:

"That fellow Waterslops is a bit of a sportsman. I haven't been able to tell you about our bet, you've been making such a noise. . . . Is your friend really plus one at North Berwick? What are you like?"

"Macmaster is a good plus two anywhere when he's in practice."

Sandbach said:

"Good Lord . . . A stout fellow . . ."

"As for me," Tietjens said, "I loathe the beastly game."

"So do I," Sandbach answered. "We'll just lollop along behind them."

4

THEY CAME out into the bright open, where all the distances under the tall sky showed with distinct prismatic outlines. They made a little group of seven—for Tietjens would not have a caddy—waiting on the flat first teeing ground. Macmaster walked up to Tietjens and said under his voice:

"You've really *sent* that wire? . . ."

Tietjens said:

"It'll be in Germany by now!"

Mr. Sandbach hobbled from one to the other, explaining the terms of his wager with Mr. Waterhouse. Mr. Waterhouse had backed one of the young men playing with him to drive into and hit twice in the eighteen holes the two city men, who would be playing ahead of them. As the minister had taken rather short odds, Mr. Sandbach considered him a good sport.

A long way down the first hole Mr. Waterhouse and his two companions were approaching the first green. They had high sand-hills to the right and, to their left, a road that was fringed with rushes and a narrow dike. Ahead of the Cabinet minister the two city men and their two caddies stood on the edge of the dike or poked downwards into the rushes. Two girls appeared and disappeared on the tops of the sand-hills. The policeman was strolling along the road, level with Mr. Waterhouse. The general said:

"I think we could go now."

Sandbach said:

"Waterslops will get a hit at them from the next tee. They're in the dike."

The general drove a straight, goodish ball. Just as Macmaster was in his swing Sandbach shouted:

"By God! He nearly did it. See that fellow jump!"

Macmaster looked round over his shoulder and hissed with vexation between his teeth:

"Don't you know that you don't shout while a man is driving? Or haven't you played golf?" He hurried fussily after his ball.

Sandbach said to Tietjens:

"Golly! That chap's got a temper!"

Tietjens said:

"Only over this game. You deserved what you got."

Sandbach said:

"I did. . . . But I didn't spoil his shot. He's outdriven the general twenty yards."

Tietjens said:

"It would have been sixty but for you."

They loitered about on the tee, waiting for the others to get their distance. Sandbach said:

"By Jove, your friend is on with his second. . . . You wouldn't believe it of such a *little* beggar!" He added: "He's not much class, is he?"

Tietjens looked down his nose.

"Oh, about *our* class!" he said. "He wouldn't take a bet about driving into the couple ahead."

Sandbach hated Tietjens for being a Tietjens of Groby: Tietjens was enraged by the existence of Sandbach, who was the son of an ennobled mayor of Middlesbrough, seven miles or so from Groby. The feuds between the Cleveland landowners and the Cleveland plutocrats are very bitter. Sandbach said:

"Ah, I suppose he gets you out of scrapes with girls and the Treasury, and you take him about in return. It's a practical combination."

"Like Pottle Mills and Stanton," Tietjens said. The financial operations connected with the amalgamating of these two steelworks had earned Sandbach's father a good deal of odium in the Cleveland district. . . . Sandbach said:

"Look here, Tietjens . . ." But he changed his mind and said:

"We'd better go now." He drove off with an awkward action, but not without skill. He certainly outplayed Tietjens.

Playing very slowly, for both were desultory and Sandbach very lame, they lost sight of the others behind some coastguard cottages and dunes before they had left the third tee. Because of his game leg, Sandbach sliced a good deal. On this occasion he sliced right into the gardens of the cottages and went with his boy to look for his ball among potato-haulms, beyond a low wall. Tietjens patted his own ball lazily up the fairway, and dragging his bag behind him by the strap, he sauntered on.

Although Tietjens hated golf as he hated any occupation that was of a competitive nature, he could engross himself in the mathematics of trajectories when he accompanied Macmaster in one of his expeditions for practice. He accompanied Macmaster because he liked there to be one pursuit at which his friend undisputably excelled himself, for it was a bore always browbeating the fellow. But he stipulated that they should visit three different and, if possible, unknown courses every week-end when they golfed. He interested himself then in the way the courses were laid out, acquiring thus an extraordinary connoisseurship in golf architecture, and he made abstruse calculations as to the flight of balls off sloped club-faces, as to the foot-poundals of energy exercised by one muscle or the other, and as to theories of spin. As often as not, he palmed Macmaster off as a fair, average player on some other unfortunate fair, average stranger. Then he passed the afternoon in the club-house, studying the pedigrees and forms of race-horses, for every club-house contained a copy of *Ruff's Guide*. In the spring he would hunt for and examine the nests of soft-billed birds, for he was interested in the domestic affairs of the cuckoo, though he hated natural history and field botany.

On this occasion he had just examined some notes of other mashie shots, had put the note-book back in his pocket, and had addressed his ball with a niblick that had an unusually roughened face and a head like a hatchet. Meticulously, when he had taken his grip he removed his little and third fingers from the leather of the shaft. He was thanking heaven that Sandbach seemed to be accounted for, for ten minutes at least, for Sandbach was miserly over lost balls and, very slowly, he was raising his mashie to half cock for a sighting shot.

He was aware that someone, breathing a little heavily from small lungs, was standing close to him and watching him: he could, indeed, beneath his cap-rim, perceive the tips of a pair of boy's white sand-shoes. It in no way perturbed him to be watched, since he was avid of no personal glory when making his shots. A voice said:

"I say . . ." He continued to look at his ball.

"Sorry to spoil your shot," the voice said. "But . . ."

Tietjens dropped his club altogether and straightened his back. A fair young woman with a fixed scowl was looking at him intently. She had a short skirt and was panting a little.

"I say," she said, "go and see they don't hurt Gertie. I've lost her . . ." She pointed back to the sand-hills. "There looked to be some beasts among them."

She seemed a perfectly negligible girl except for the frown: her eyes blue, her hair no doubt fair under a white canvas hat. She had a striped cotton blouse, but her fawn tweed skirt was well hung.

Tietjens said:

"You've been demonstrating."

She said:

"Of course we have, and of course you object on principle. But you won't let a girl be man-handled. Don't wait to tell me, I know it. . . ."

Noises existed. Sandbach, from beyond the low garden-wall fifty yards away, was yelping, just like a dog: "Hi! Hi! Hi! Hi!" and gesticulating. His little caddy, entangled in his golf-bag, was trying to scramble over the wall. On top of a high sand-hill stood the policeman: he waved his arms like a windmill and shouted. Beside him and behind, slowly rising, were the heads of the general, Macmaster and their two boys. Further along, in completion, were appearing the figures of Mr. Waterhouse, his two companions and *their* three boys. The minister was waving his driver and shouting. They all shouted.

"A regular rat-hunt," the girl said; she was counting. "Eleven and two more caddies!" She exhibited satisfaction. "I headed them all off except two beasts. They couldn't run. But neither can Gertie . . ."

She said urgently:

"Come along! You aren't going to leave Gertie to those beasts! They're drunk. . . ."

Tietjens said:

"Cut away, then. I'll look after Gertie." He picked up his bag.

"No, I'll come with you," the girl said.

Tietjens answered: "Oh, you don't want to go to jail. Clear out!"

She said:

"Nonsense. I've put up with worse than that. Nine months as a slavey . . . Come *along!*"

Tietjens started to run—rather like a rhinoceros seeing purple. He had been violently spurred, for he had been pierced by a shrill, faint scream. The girl ran beside him.

"You . . . can . . . run!" she panted; "put on a spurt."

Screams protesting against physical violence were at that date rare things in England. Tietjens had never heard the like. It upset him frightfully, though he was aware only of an expanse of open country. The policeman, whose buttons made him noteworthy, was descending his conical sand-hill, diagonally, with caution. There is something grotesque about a town policeman, silvered helmet and all, in the open country. It was so clear and still in the air; Tietjens felt as if he were in a light museum, looking at specimens. . . .

A little young woman, engrossed, like a hunted rat, came round the corner of a green mound. "This is an assaulted female!" the mind of Tietjens said to him. She had a black skirt covered with sand, for she had just rolled down the sand-hill; she had a striped grey and black silk blouse, one shoulder torn completely off, so that a white camisole showed. Over the shoulder of the sand-hill came the two city men, flushed with triumph and panting; their red knitted waistcoats moved like bellows. The black-haired one, his eyes lurid and obscene, brandished aloft a fragment of black and grey stuff. He shouted hilariously:

"Strip the bitch naked! . . . Ugh . . . Strip the bitch stark naked!" and jumped down the little hill. He cannoned into Tietjens, who roared at the top of his voice:

"You infernal swine. I'll knock your head off if you move!"

Behind Tietjens' back the girl said:

"Come along, Gertie. . . . It's only to there. . . ."

A voice panted in answer:

"I . . . can't. . . . My heart . . ."

Tietjens kept his eye upon the city man. His jaw had fallen down, his eyes stared! It was as if the bottom of his assured world, where all men desire in their hearts to bash women, had fallen out. He panted:

"Ergle! Ergle!"

Another scream, a little further than the last voices from behind his back, caused in Tietjens a feeling of intense weariness. What did beastly women want to scream for? He swung round, bag and all. The policeman, his face scarlet like a lobster just boiled, was lumbering unenthusiastically towards the two girls, who were trotting towards the dike. One of his hands, scarlet also, was extended. He was not a yard from Tietjens.

Tietjens was exhausted, beyond thinking or shouting. He slipped his clubs off his shoulder and, as if he were pitching his kit-bag into a luggage van, threw the whole lot between the policeman's running legs. The man, who had no impetus to speak of, pitched forward on to his hands and knees. His helmet over his eyes, he seemed to reflect for a moment; then he removed his helmet and with great deliberation rolled round and sat on the turf. His face was completely without emotion, long, sandy-moustached and rather shrewd. He mopped his brow with a carmine handkerchief that had white spots.

Tietjens walked up to him.

"Clumsy of me!" he said. "I hope you're not hurt." He drew from his breast pocket a curved silver flask. The policeman said nothing. His world, too, contained uncertainties, and he was profoundly glad to be able to sit still without discredit. He muttered:

"Shaken. A bit! Anybody would be!"

That let him out and he fell to examining with attention the bayonet catch of the flask top. Tietjens opened it for him. The two girls, advancing at a fatigued trot, were near the dike side. The fair girl, as they trotted, was trying to adjust her companion's hat; attached by pins to the back of her hair, it flapped on her shoulder.

All the rest of the posse were advancing at a very slow

walk, in a converging semicircle. Two little caddies were
running, but Tietjens saw them check, hesitate and stop.
And there floated to Tietjens' ears the words:

"Stop, you little devils. She'll knock your heads off."

Rt. Hon. Mr. Waterhouse must have found an admirable
voice trainer somewhere. The drab girl was balancing tremulously over a plank on the dike; the other took it at a
jump: up in the air—down on her feet; perfectly business-
like. And, as soon as the other girl was off the plank she
was down on her knees before it, pulling it towards her,
the other girl trotting away over the vast marsh field.

The girl dropped the plank on the grass. Then she looked
up and faced the men and boys who stood in a row on the
road. She called in a shrill, high voice, like a young cock-
erel's:

"Seventeen to two! The usual male odds! You'll *have* to
go round by Camber railway bridge, and we'll be in Folke-
stone by then. We've got bicycles!" She was half going when
she checked and, searching out Tietjens to address, exclaimed: "I'm sorry I said that. Because some of you didn't
want to catch us. But some of you *did*. And you *were* seventeen to two." She addressed Mr. Waterhouse:

"Why *don't* you give women the vote?" she said. "You'll
find it will interfere a good deal with your indispensable
golf if you don't. Then what becomes of the nation's health?"

Mr. Waterhouse said:

"If you'll come and discuss it quietly . . ."

She said:

"Oh, tell that to the marines," and turned away, the men
in a row watching her figure disappear into the distance
of the flatland. Not one of them was inclined to risk that
jump: there was nine foot of mud in the bottom of the dike.
It was quite true that, the plank being removed, to go after
the women they would have had to go several miles round.
It had been a well-thought-out raid. Mr. Waterhouse said
that girl was a ripping girl: the others found her just ordinary. Mr. Sandbach, who had only lately ceased to shout:
"Hi!" wanted to know what they were going to do about
catching the women, but Mr. Waterhouse said: "Oh, chuck
it, Sandy," and went off.

Mr. Sandbach refused to continue his match with Tietjens.
He said that Tietjens was the sort of fellow who was the
ruin of England. He said he had a good mind to issue a
warrant for the arrest of Tietjens—for obstructing the course
of justice. Tietjens pointed out that Sandbach wasn't a

borough magistrate and so couldn't. And Sandbach went off, dot and carry one, and began a furious row with the two city men, who had retreated to a distance. He said they were the sort of men who were the ruin of England. They bleated like rams. . . .

Tietjens wandered slowly up the course, found his ball, made his shot with care and found that the ball deviated several feet less to the right of a straight line than he had expected. He tried the shot again, obtained the same result and tabulated his observations in his note-book. He sauntered slowly back towards the club-house. He was content.

He felt himself to be content for the first time in four months. His pulse beat calmly; the heat of the sun all over him appeared to be a beneficent flood. On the flanks of the older and larger sand-hills he observed the minute herbage, mixed with little purple aromatic plants. To these the constant nibbling of sheep had imparted a protective tininess. He wandered, content, round the sand-hills to the small, silted harbour mouth. After reflecting for some time on the wave-curves in the sloping mud of the watersides, he had a long conversation, mostly in signs, with a Finn who hung over the side of a tarred, stump-masted, battered vessel that had a gaping, splintered hole where the anchor should have hung. She came from Archangel, was of several hundred tons' burthen, was knocked together anyhow, of soft wood, for about ninety pounds, and launched, sink or swim, in the timber trade. Beside her, taut, glistening with brass-work, was a new fishing boat, just built there for the Lowestoft fleet. Ascertaining her price from a man who was finishing her painting, Tietjens reckoned that you could have built three of the Archangel timber ships for the cost of that boat, and that the Archangel vessel would earn about twice as much per hour per ton. . . .

It was in that way his mind worked when he was fit: it picked up little pieces of definite, workman-like information. When it had enough it classified them: not for any purpose, but because to know things was agreeable and gave a feeling of strength, of having in reserve something that the other fellow would not suspect. . . . He passed a long, quiet, abstracted afternoon.

In the dressing-room he found the general, among lockers, old coats, and stoneware, washing-basins set in scrubbed wood. The general leaned back against a row of these things.

"You are the ruddy *limit!*" he exclaimed.

Tietjens said:

"Where's Macmaster?"

The general said he had sent Macmaster off with Sandbach in the two-seater. Macmaster had to dress before going up to Mountby. He added: "The *ruddy* limit!" again.

"Because I knocked the bobby over?" Tietjens asked. "He liked it."

The general said:

"Knocked the bobby over . . . I didn't see that."

"He didn't want to catch the girls," Tietjens said, "you could see him—oh, yearning not to."

"I don't want to know anything about that," the general said. "I shall hear enough about it from Paul Sandbach. Give the bobby a quid and let's hear no more of it. I'm a magistrate."

"Then what have I done?" Tietjens said. "I helped those girls to get off. *You* didn't want to catch them; Waterhouse didn't; the policeman didn't. No one did except the swine. Then what's the matter?"

"Damn it all!" the general said, "don't you remember that you're a young married man?"

With the respect for the general's superior age and achievements, Tietjens stopped himself laughing.

"If you're really serious, sir," he said, "I always remember it very carefully. I don't suppose you're suggesting that I've ever shown want of respect for Sylvia."

The general shook his head.

"I don't know," he said. "And damn it all, I'm worried. I'm . . . Hang it, I'm your father's oldest friend." The general looked indeed worn and saddened in the light of the sand-drifted, ground-glass windows. He said: "Was that skirt a . . . a friend of yours? Had you arranged it with her?"

Tietjens said:

"Wouldn't it be better, sir, if you said what you had on your mind? . . ."

The old general blushed a little.

"I don't like to," he said straightforwardly. "You brilliant fellows . . . I only want, my dear boy, to hint that . . ."

Tietjens said, a little more stiffly:

"I'd prefer you to get it out, sir. . . . I acknowledge your right as my father's oldest friend."

"Then," the general burst out, "who was the skirt you were lolloping up Pall Mall with? On the last day they trooped the colours? . . . I didn't see her myself. . . . Was it this same one? Paul said she looked like a cook-maid."

Tietjens made himself a little more rigid.

"She was, as a matter of fact, a book-maker's secretary," Tietjens said. "I imagine I have the right to walk where I like, with whom I like. And no one has the right to question it. . . . I don't mean you, sir. But no one else."

The general said puzzledly:

"It's you *brilliant* fellows . . . They all say you're brilliant. . . ."

Tietjens said:

"You might let your rooted distrust of intelligence . . . It's natural, of course; but you might let it allow you to be just to me. I assure you there was nothing discreditable."

The general interrupted:

"If you were a stupid young subaltern and told me you were showing your mother's new cook the way to the Piccadilly tube, I'd believe you. . . . But, then, no young subaltern would do such a damn, blasted, tom-fool thing! Paul said you walked beside her like the king in his glory! Through the crush outside the Haymarket, of all places in the world!"

"I'm obliged to Sandbach for his commendation. . . ." Tietjens said. He thought a moment. Then he said:

"I was trying to get that young woman . . . I was taking her out to lunch from her office at the bottom of the Haymarket. . . . To get her off a friend's back. That is, of course, between ourselves."

He said this with great reluctance because he didn't want to cast reflection on Macmaster's taste, for the young lady had been by no means one to be seen walking with a really circumspect public official. But he had said nothing to indicate Macmaster, and he had other friends.

The general choked.

"Upon my soul," he said, "what do you take me for?" He repeated the words as if he were amazed. "If," he said, "my G.S.O. II—who's the stupidest ass I know—told me such a damn-fool lie as that, I'd have him broke to-morrow." He went on expostulatorily: "Damn it all, it's the first duty of a soldier—it's the first duty of all Englishmen—to be able to tell a good lie in answer to a charge. But a lie like that . . ."

He broke off breathless, then he began again:

"Hang it all, I told that lie to my grandmother and my grandfather told it to *his* grandmother. And they call you brilliant! . . ." He paused and then asked reproachfully: "Or do you think I'm in a state of senile decay?"

Tietjens said:

"I know you, sir, to be the smartest general of division in the British Army. I leave you to draw your own conclusions as to why I said what I did. . . ." He had told the exact truth, but he was not sorry to be disbelieved.

The general said:

"Then I'll take it that you tell me a lie meaning me to know that it's a lie. That's quite proper. I take it you mean to keep the woman officially out of it. But look here, Chrissie"—his tone took a deeper seriousness—"if the woman that's come between you and Sylvia—that's broken up your home, damn it, for that's what it is!—is little Miss Wannop . . ."

"Her name was Julia Mandelstein," Tietjens said.

The general said:

"Yes! Yes! Of course! . . . But if it *is* the little Wannop girl and it's not gone too far . . . Put her back. . . . Put her back, as you used to be a good boy! It would be too hard on the mother. . . ."

Tietjens said:

"General! I give you my word . . ."

The general said:

"I'm not asking any questions, my boy; I'm talking now. You've told me the story you want told and it's the story I'll tell for you! But that little piece is . . . she used to be! . . . as straight as a die. I dare say you know better than I. Of course when they get among the wild women, there's no knowing what happens to them. They say they're all whores. . . . I beg your pardon, if you like the girl . . ."

"Is Miss Wannop," Tietjens asked, "the girl who demonstrates?"

"Sandbach said," the general went on, "that he couldn't see from where he was whether that girl was the same as the one in the Haymarket. But he thought it was. . . . He was pretty certain."

"As he's married your sister," Tietjens said, "one can't impugn his taste in women."

"I say again, I'm not asking," the general said. "But I do say again too: put her back. Her father was a great friend of your father's: or your father was a great admirer of his. They say he was the most brilliant brain of the party."

"Of course I know who Professor Wannop was," Tietjens said. "There's nothing you could tell me about him."

"I dare say not," the general said dryly. "Then you know that he didn't leave a farthing when he died, and the rotten Liberal government wouldn't put his wife and children on the

Civil List because he'd sometimes written for a Tory paper. And you know that the mother has had a deuced hard row to hoe and has only just turned the corner. If she can be said to have turned it. I know Claudine takes them all the peaches she can cadge out of Paul's gardener."

Tietjens was about to say that Mrs. Wannop, the mother, had written the only novel worth reading since the eighteenth century. . . . But the general went on:

"Listen to me, my boy. . . . If you can't get on without women . . . I should have thought Sylvia was good enough. But I know what we men are. . . . I don't set up to be a saint. I heard a woman in the promenade of the Empire say once that it was the likes of them that saved the lives and figures of all the virtuous women of the country. And I dare say it's true. . . . But choose a girl that you can set up in a tobacco-shop and do your courting in the back parlour. Not in the Haymarket . . . Heaven knows if you can afford it. That's your affair. You appear to have been sold up. And from what Sylvia's let drop to Claudine . . ."

"I don't believe," Tietjens said, "that Sylvia's said anything to Lady Claudine. . . . She's too straight."

"I didn't say 'said,'" the general exclaimed, "I particularly said 'let drop.' And perhaps I oughtn't to have said as much as that, but you know what devils for ferreting out women are. And Claudine's worse than any woman I ever knew. . . ."

"And of course she's had Sandbach to help," Tietjens said.

"Oh, that fellow's worse than any woman," the general exclaimed.

"Then what does the whole indictment amount to?" Tietjens asked.

"Oh, hang it," the general brought out, "I'm not a beastly detective, I only want a plausible story to tell Claudine. Or not even plausible. An obvious lie as long as it shows you're not flying in the face of society—as walking up the Haymarket with the little Wannop when your wife's left you because of her would be."

"What does it amount to?" Tietjens said patiently. "What Sylvia 'let drop.'"

"Only," the general answered, "that you are—that your views are—immoral. Of course they often puzzle me. And of course if you have views that aren't the same as other people's, and don't keep them to yourself, other people will suspect you of immorality. That's what put Paul Sandbach on your track! . . . and that you're extravagant. . . . Oh, hang it. . . . Eternal hansoms, and taxis and telegrams

. . . You know, my boy, times aren't what they were when your father and I married. We used to say you could do it on five hundred a year as a younger son. . . . And then this girl too . . ." His voice took on a more agitated note of shyness—pain. . . . "It probably hadn't occurred to you . . . But, of course, Sylvia has an income of her own. . . . And, don't you see . . . if you outrun the constable and . . . In short, you're spending Sylvia's money on the other girl, and that's what people can't stand." He added quickly: "I'm bound to say that Mrs. Satterthwaite backs you through thick and thin. Thick and thin! Claudine wrote to her. But you know what women are with a handsome son-in-law that's always polite to them. But I may tell you that but for your mother-in-law, Claudine would have cut you out of her visiting-list months ago. And you'd have been cut out of some others too. . . ."

Tietjens said:

"Thanks. I think that's enough to go on with. . . . Give me a couple of minutes to reflect on what you've said. . . ."

"I'll wash my hands and change my coat," the general said with intense relief.

At the end of two minutes Tietjens said:

"No, I don't see that there is anything I want to say."

The general exclaimed with enthusiasm:

"That's my good lad! Open confession is next to reform. . . . And . . . and try to be more respectful to your superiors. . . . Damn it, they say you're brilliant. But I thank heaven I haven't got you in my command. . . . Though I believe you're a good lad. But you're the sort of fellow to set a whole division by the ears. . . . A regular . . . what's 'is name? A regular Dreyfus!"

"Did you think Dreyfus was guilty?" Tietjens asked.

"Hang it," the general said, "he was worse than guilty— the sort of fellow you couldn't believe in and yet couldn't prove anything against. The curse of the world . . ."

Tietjens said:

"Ah."

"Well, they are," the general said: "fellows like that *unsettle* society. You don't know where you are. You can't judge. They make you uncomfortable. . . . A brilliant fellow too! I believe he's a brigadier-general by now. . . ." He put his arm round Tietjens' shoulders.

"There, there, my dear boy," he said, "come and have a sloe gin. That's the real answer to all beastly problems."

It was some time before Tietjens could get to think of his own problems. The fly that took them back went with the slow pomp of a procession over the winding marsh road in front of the absurdly picturesque red pyramid of the very old town. Tietjens had to listen to the general suggesting that it would be better if he didn't come to the golf-club till Monday. He would get Macmaster some good games. A good, sound fellow that Macmaster now. It was a pity Tietjens hadn't some of his soundness!

The two city men had approached the general on the course and had used some violent invectives against Tietjens: they had objected to being called ruddy swine to their faces: they were going to the police. The general said that he had told them himself, slowly and distinctly, that they *were* ruddy swine and that they would never get another ticket at that club after Monday. But till Monday, apparently, they had the right to be there and the club wouldn't want scenes. Sandbach, too, was infuriated about Tietjens.

Tietjens said that the fault lay with the times that permitted the introduction into gentlemen's company of such social swipes as Sandbach. One acted perfectly correctly, and then a dirty little beggar like that put dirty little constructions on it and ran about and bleated. He added that he knew Sandbach was the general's brother-in-law, but he couldn't help it. That was the truth. . . . The general said: "I know, my boy: I know. . . ." But one had to take society as one found it. Claudine had to be provided for, and Sandbach made a very good husband, careful, sober, and on the right side in politics. A bit of a rip, but they couldn't ask for everything! And Claudine was using all the influence she had with the other side—which was not a little, women are so wonderful!—to get him a diplomatic job in Turkey, so as to get him out of the way of Mrs. Crundall! Mrs. Crundall was the leading anti-suffragette of the little town. That was what made Sandbach so bitter against Tietjens. He told Tietjens so that Tietjens might understand.

Tietjens had hitherto flattered himself that he could examine a subject swiftly and put it away in his mind. To the general he hardly listened. The allegations against himself were beastly; but he could usually ignore allegations against himself, and he imagined that if he said no more about them he would himself hear no more. If there were, in clubs and places where men talk, unpleasant rumours as to himself, he preferred it to be thought that he was the rip, not his wife the strumpet. That was normal, male vanity: the preference of the English gentleman! Had it been a matter of Sylvia spotless and himself as spotless as he was—for in all these things he knew himself to be spotless!—he would certainly have defended himself, at least, to the general. But he had acted practically in not defending himself more vigorously. For he imagined that, had he really tried, he could have made the general believe him. But he had behaved rightly! It was not mere vanity. There was the child up at his sister Effie's. It was better for a boy to have a rip of a father than a whore for a mother!

The general was expatiating on the solidity of a squat castle, like a pile of draughts, away to the left, in the sun, on the flatness. He was saying that we didn't build like that now-a-days.

Tietjens said:

"You're perfectly wrong, general. All the castles that Henry VIII built in 1543 along this coast are mere monuments of jerry-building. . . . 'In 1543 jactat castra Delis, Sandgatto, Reia, Hastingas Henricus Rex' . . . That means he chucked them down. . . ."

The general laughed:

"You are an incorrigible fellow. . . . If ever there's any known, certain fact . . ."

"But go and look at the beastly things," Tietjens said. "You'll see they've got just a facing of Caen-stone that they tide-floated here, and the fillings-up are just rubble, any rubbish. . . . Look here! It's a known, certain fact, isn't it, that your eighteen-pounders are better than the French seventy-fives. They tell us so in the House, on the hustings, in the papers: the public believes it. . . . But would you put one of your tin-pot things firing—what is it?—four shells a minute?—with the little bent pins in their tails to stop the recoil—against their seventy-fives with the compressed-air cylinders? . . ."

The general sat stiffly upon his cushions:

"That's different," he said. "How the devil do you get to know these things?"

"It isn't different," Tietjens said; "it's the same muddle-headed frame of mind that sees good building in Henry VIII as lets us into wars with hopelessly antiquated field-guns and rottenly inferior ammunition. You'd fire any fellow on your staff who said we could stand up for a minute against the French."

"Well, anyhow," the general said, "I thank heaven you're

not on my staff, for you'd talk my hind leg off in a week.
It's perfectly true that the public . . ."

But Tietjens was not listening. He was considering that
it was natural for an unborn fellow like Sandbach to betray
the solidarity that should exist between men. And it was
natural for a childless woman like Lady Claudine Sandbach
with a notoriously, a flagrantly unfaithful, husband to believe in the unfaithfulness of the husbands of other women!

The general was saying:

"Who did you hear that stuff from about the French
field-gun?"

Tietjens said:

"From you. Three weeks ago!"

And all the other society women with unfaithful husbands
. . . They must do their best to down and out a man. They
would cut him off their visiting-lists! Let them. The barren
harlots mated to faithless eunuchs! . . . Suddenly he thought
that he didn't know for certain that he was the father of his
child and he groaned.

"Well, what have I said wrong now?" the general asked.
"Surely you don't maintain that pheasants do eat man-
golds. . . ."

Tietjens proved his reputation for sanity with:

"No! I was just groaning at the thought of the chancellor!
That's sound enough for you, isn't it?" But it gave him a
nasty turn. He hadn't been able to pigeon-hole and padlock
his disagreeable reflections. He had been as good as talking
to himself. . . .

In the bow-window of another hostelry than his own he
caught the eye of Mr. Waterhouse, who was looking at the
view over the marshes. The great man beckoned to him and
he went in. Mr. Waterhouse was anxious that Tietjens—
whom he assumed to be a man of sense—should get any
pursuit of the two girls stopped off. He couldn't move in
the matter himself, but a five-pound note and possibly a
police promotion or so might be handed round if no adver-
tisement were given to the mad women on account of their
raid of that afternoon.

It was not a very difficult matter: for where the great man
was to be found in the club-lounge, there, in the bar, the
mayor, the town clerk, the local head of the police, the
doctors and solicitors would be found drinking together.
And after it was arranged, the great man himself came into
the bar, had a drink and pleased them all immensely by
his affability. . . .

Tietjens himself, dining alone with the minister, to whom he wanted to talk about his Labour Finance Act, didn't find him a disagreeable fellow: not really foolish, not sly except in his humour, tired obviously, but livening up after a couple of whiskies, and certainly not as yet plutocratic; with tastes for apple-pie and cream of a fourteen-year-old boy. And even as regards his famous Act, which was then shaking the country to its political foundations, once you accepted its fundamental unsuitedness to the temperament and needs of the English working-class, you could see that Mr. Waterhouse didn't want to be dishonest. He accepted with gratitude several of Tietjens' emendations in the actuarial schedules. . . . And over their port they agreed on two fundamental legislative ideals: every working-man to have a minimum of four hundred a year and every beastly manufacturer who wanted to pay less to be hung. That, it appeared, was the High Toryism of Tietjens as it was the extreme radicalism of the extreme Left of the Left. . . .

And Tietjens, who hated no man, in face of this simpleminded and agreeable schoolboy type of fellow, fell to wondering why it was that humanity, that was next to always agreeable in its units, was, as a mass, a phenomenon so hideous. You look at a dozen men, each of them not by any means detestable and not uninteresting: for each of them would have technical details of their affairs to impart: you formed them into a government or a club and at once, with oppressions, inaccuracies, gossip, backbiting, lying, corruptions and vileness, you had the combination of wolf, tiger, weasel and louse-covered ape that was human society. And he remembered the words of some Russian: "Cats and monkeys. Monkeys and cats. All humanity is there."

Tietjens and Mr. Waterhouse spent the rest of the evening together.

Whilst Tietjens was interviewing the policeman, the minister sat on the front steps of the cottage and smoked cheap cigarettes, and when Tietjens went to bed Mr. Waterhouse insisted on sending by him kindly messages to Miss Wannop, asking her to come and discuss female suffrage any afternoon she liked in his private room at the House of Commons. Mr. Waterhouse flatly refused to believe that Tietjens hadn't arranged the raid with Miss Wannop. He said it had been too neatly planned for any woman, and he said Tietjens was a lucky fellow, for she was a ripping girl.

Back in his room under the rafters, Tietjens fell, nevertheless, at once a prey to real agitation. For a long time he pounded from wall to wall, and since he could not shake off the train of thought, he got out at last his patience cards, and devoted himself seriously to thinking out the conditions of his life with Sylvia. He wanted to stop scandal if he could; he wanted them to live within his income; he wanted to subtract that child from the influence of its mother. These were all definite but difficult things. . . . Then one-half of his mind lost itself in the rearrangement of schedules, and on his brilliant table his hands set queens on kings and checked their recurrences.

In that way the sudden entrance of Macmaster gave him a really terrible physical shock. He nearly vomited: his brain reeled and the room fell about. He drank a great quantity of whisky in front of Macmaster's goggling eyes; but even at that he couldn't talk, and he dropped into his bed, faintly aware of his friend's efforts to loosen his clothes. He had, he knew, carried the suppression of thought in his conscious mind so far that his unconscious self had taken command and had, for the time, paralysed both his body and his mind.

5

"IT DOESN'T seem quite fair, Valentine," Mrs. Duchemin said. She was rearranging in a glass bowl some minute flowers that floated on water. They made there, on the breakfast-table, a patch, as it were, of mosaic amongst silver chafing-dishes, silver epergnes piled with peaches in pyramids, and great silver rose-bowls filled with roses that drooped to the damask cloth. A congeries of silver largenesses made as if a fortification for the head of the table; two huge silver urns, a great silver kettle on a tripod and a couple of silver vases filled with the extremely tall blue spikes of delphiniums that, spreading out, made as if a fan. The eighteenth-century room was very tall and long; panelled in darkish wood. In the centre of each of four of the panels, facing the light, hung pictures, a mellowed orange in tone, representing mists and the cordage of ships in mists at sunrise. On the bottom of each large gold frame was a tablet bearing the ascription: "J. M. W. Turner." The chairs, arranged along the long table that was set for eight people, had the delicate, spidery, mahogany backs of Chippendale; on the golden mahogany sideboard, that had behind it green silk curtains

on a brass rail, were displayed an immense, crumbed ham,
more peaches on an epergne, a large meat-pie with a varnished crust, another epergne, that supported the large pale
globes of grape-fruit; a galantine, a cube of inlaid meats,
encased in thick jelly.

"Oh, women have to back each other up in these days,"
Valentine Wannop said. "I couldn't let you go through this
alone after breakfasting with you every Saturday since I
don't know when."

"I do feel," Mrs. Duchemin said, "immensely grateful to
you for your moral support. I ought not, perhaps, to have
risked this morning. But I've told Parry to keep him out
till ten-fifteen."

"It's at any rate tremendously sporting of you," the girl
said. "I think it was worth trying."

Mrs. Duchemin, wavering round the table, slightly changed
the position of the delphiniums.

"I think they make a good screen," Mrs. Duchemin said.

"Oh, nobody will be able to see him," the girl answered
reassuringly. She added with a sudden resolution, "Look here,
Edie. Stop worrying about my mind. If you think that anything I hear at your table after nine months as an ash-cat
at Ealing, with three men in the house, an invalid wife and
a drunken cook, can corrupt my mind, you're simply mistaken. You can let your conscience be at rest, and let's say
no more about it."

Mrs. Duchemin said, "Oh, Valentine! How could your
mother let you?"

"She didn't know," the girl said. "She was out of her
mind for grief. She sat for most of the whole nine months
with her hands folded before her in a board-and-lodging
house at twenty-five shillings a week, and it took the five
shillings a week that I earned to make up the money." She
added, "Gilbert had to be kept at school, of course. And in
the holidays, too."

"I don't understand!" Mrs. Duchemin said. "I simply
don't understand."

"Of course you wouldn't," the girl answered. "You're like
the kindly people who subscribed at the sale to buy my
father's library back and present it to my mother. That cost
us five shillings a week for warehousing, and at Ealing they
were always nagging at me for the state of my print
dresses. . . ."

She broke off and said:

"Let's not talk about it any more if you don't mind. You

have me in your house, so I suppose you've a right to references, as the mistresses call them. But you've been very good to me and never asked. Still, it's come up; do you know I told a man on the links yesterday that I'd been a slavey for nine months. I was trying to explain why I was a suffragette; and as I was asking him a favour, I suppose I felt I needed to give *him* references too."

Mrs. Duchemin, beginning to advance towards the girl impulsively, exclaimed:

"You darling!"

Miss Wannop said:

"Wait a minute. I haven't finished. I want to say this: I never talk about that stage of my career because I'm ashamed of it. I'm ashamed of it because I think I did the wrong thing, not for any other reason. I did it on impulse and I stuck to it out of obstinacy. I mean it would probably have been more sensible to go round with the hat to benevolent people, for the keep of mother and to complete my education. But if we've inherited the Wannop ill luck, we've inherited the Wannop pride. And I *couldn't* do it. Besides, I was only seventeen, and I gave out we were going into the country after the sale. I'm not educated at all, as you know, or only half, because father, being a brilliant man, had ideas. And one of them was that I was to be an athletic, not a classical, don at Cambridge, or I might have been, I believe. I don't know why he had that tic. . . . But I'd like you to understand two things. One I've said already: what I hear in this house won't ever shock or corrupt me; that it's said in Latin is neither here nor there. I understand Latin almost as well as English because father used to talk it to me and Gilbert as soon as we talked at all. . . . And, oh yes: I'm a suffragette because I've been a slavey. But I'd like you to understand that though I was a slavey and am a suffragette—you're an old-fashioned woman and queer things are thought about these two things—then I'd like you to understand that in spite of it all I'm pure! Chaste, you know . . . Perfectly virtuous."

Mrs. Duchemin said:

"Oh, Valentine! Did you wear a cap and apron? You! In a cap and apron."

Miss Wannop replied:

"Yes! I wore a cap and apron and sniffled, 'M'm!' to the mistress, and slept under the stairs too. Because I would not sleep with the beast of a cook."

Mrs. Duchemin now ran forward and, catching Miss Wannop by both hands, kissed her first on the left and then on the right cheek.

"Oh, Valentine," she said, "you're a heroine. And you only twenty-two! . . . Isn't that the motor coming?"

But it wasn't the motor coming, and Miss Wannop said:

"Oh, no! I'm not a heroine. When I tried to speak to that minister yesterday, I just couldn't. It was Gertie who went for him. As for me, I just hopped from one leg to the other and stuttered: 'V . . . V . . . Votes for W . . . W . . . W . . . omen!' . . . If I'd been decently brave I shouldn't have been too shy to speak to a strange man. . . . For that was what it really came to."

"But that surely," Mrs. Duchemin said—she continued to hold both the girl's hands—"makes you all the braver. . . . It's the person who does the thing he's afraid of who's the real hero, isn't it?"

"Oh, we used to argue that old thing over with father when we were ten. You can't tell. You've got to define the term brave. I was just abject. . . . I could harangue the whole crowd when I got them together. But speak to one man in cold blood I couldn't. . . . Of course I *did* speak to a fat golfing idiot with bulging eyes, to get him to save Gertie. But that was different."

Mrs. Duchemin moved both the girl's hands up and down in her own.

"As you know, Valentine," she said, "I'm an old-fashioned woman. I believe that woman's true place is at her husband's side. At the same time . . ."

Miss Wannop moved away.

"Now, don't, Edie, don't!" she said. "If you believe that, you're an anti. Don't run with the hare and hunt with the hounds. It's your defect, really. . . . I tell you I'm *not* a heroine. I *dread* prison: I *hate* rows. I'm thankful to goodness that it's my duty to stop and housemaid-typewrite for mother, so that I can't really *do* things. . . . Look at that miserable, adenoidy little Gertie, hiding upstairs in our garret. She was crying all last night—but that's just nerves. Yet she's been in prison five times, stomach-pumped and all. Not a moment of funk about her! . . . But as for me, a girl as hard as a rock that prison wouldn't touch. . . . Why, I'm all of a jump now. That's why I'm talking nonsense like a pert schoolgirl. I just dread that every sound may be the police coming for me."

Mrs. Duchemin stroked the girl's fair hair and tucked a loose strand behind her ear.

"I wish you'd let me show you how to do your hair," she said. "The right man might come along at any moment."

"Oh, the right man!", Miss Wannop said. "Thanks for tactfully changing the subject. The right man for me, when he comes along, will be a married man. That's the Wannop luck!"

Mrs. Duchemin said, with deep concern:

"Don't talk like that. . . . Why should you regard yourself as being less lucky than other people? Surely your mother's done well. She has a position; she makes money. . . ."

"Ah, but mother isn't a Wannop," the girl said, "only by marriage. The real Wannops . . . they've been executed and attaindered and falsely accused and killed in carriage accidents and married adventurers or died penniless like father. Ever since the dawn of history. And then, mother's got her mascot. . . ."

"Oh, what's that?" Mrs. Duchemin asked, almost with animation. "A relic? . . ."

"Don't you know mother's mascot?" the girl asked. "She tells everybody. . . . Don't you know the story of the man with the champagne? How mother was sitting contemplating suicide in her bed-sitting room and there came in a man with a name like Tea-tray; she always calls him the mascot and asks us to remember him as such in our prayers. . . . He was a man who'd been at a German university with father years before and loved him very dearly, but not kept touch with him. And he'd been out of England for nine months when father died and round about it. And he said: 'Now, Mrs. Wannop, what's this?' And she told him. And he said, 'What you want is champagne!' And he sent the slavey out with a sovereign for a bottle of Veuve Cliquot. And he broke the neck of the bottle off against the mantelpiece because they were slow in bringing an opener. And he stood over her while she drank half the bottle out of her tooth-glass. And he took her out to lunch . . . oh . . . oh . . . oh, it's cold! . . . And lectured her . . . And got her a job to write leaders on a paper he had shares in . . ."

Mrs. Duchemin said:

"You're shivering!"

"I know I am," the girl said. She went on very fast. "And of course mother always *wrote* father's articles for him. He found the ideas, but couldn't write, and she's a splendid style. . . . And since then he—the mascot—Tea-tray—has always turned up when she's been in tight places. When the paper blew her up and threatened to dismiss her for inaccuracies! She's frightfully inaccurate. And he wrote her out a table of things every leader writer must know, such as that 'A. Ebor' is the Archbishop of York and that the government is Liberal. And one day he turned up and said: 'Why don't you write a novel on that story you told me?' And he lent her the money to buy the cottage we're in now to be quiet and write in. . . . Oh, I can't go on!"

Miss Wannop burst into tears.

"It's thinking of those beastly days," she said. "And that beastly, *beastly* yesterday!" She ran the knuckles of both her hands fiercely into her eyes and determinedly eluded Mrs. Duchemin's handkerchief and embraces. She said almost contemptuously:

"A nice, considerate person I am. And you with this ordeal hanging over you! Do you suppose I don't appreciate all your silent heroism of the home while we're marching about with flags and shouting? But it's just to stop women like you being tortured, body and soul, week in, week out, that we . . ."

Mrs. Duchemin had sat down on a chair near one of the windows; she had her handkerchief hiding her face.

"Why women in your position don't take lovers . . ." the girl said hotly. "Or that women in your position *do* take lovers . . ."

Mrs. Duchemin looked up; in spite of its tears her white face had an air of serious dignity:

"Oh, *no*, Valentine," she said, using her deeper tones. "There's something beautiful, there's something *thrilling*, about chastity. I'm not narrow-minded. Censorious! I don't *condemn*! But to preserve in word, thought and action a lifelong fidelity . . . It's no mean achievement. . . ."

"You mean like an egg-and-spoon race," Miss Wannop said.

"It isn't," Mrs. Duchemin replied gently, "the way I should have put it. Isn't the real symbol Atalanta, running fast and not turning aside for the golden apple? That always seemed to me the real truth hidden in the beautiful old legend. . . ."

"I don't know," Miss Wannop said, "when I read what Ruskin says about it in *The Crown of Wild Olive*. Or no! It's *The Queen of the Air*. That's his Greek rubbish, isn't it? I always think it seems like an egg-race in which the young woman didn't keep her eyes in the boat. But I suppose it comes to the same thing."

Mrs. Duchemin said:

"My *dear!* Not a word against John Ruskin in *this* house."

Miss Wannop screamed.

An immense voice had shouted:

"This way! This way! . . . The ladies will be here!"

Of Mr. Duchemin's curates—he had three of them, for he had three marshland parishes almost without stipend, so that no one but a very rich clergyman could have held them —it was observed that they were all very large men with the physiques rather of prize-fighters than of clergy. So that when by any chance at dusk Mr. Duchemin, who himself was of exceptional stature, and his three assistants went together along a road, the hearts of any malefactors whom in the mist they chanced to encounter went pit-a-pat.

Mr. Horsley—the number two—had in addition an enormous voice. He shouted four or five words, interjected "tee-hee," shouted four or five words more and again interjected "tee-hee." He had enormous wrist-bones that protruded from his clerical cuffs, an enormous Adam's-apple, a large, thin, close-cropped, colourless face like a skull, with very sunken eyes, and when he was once started speaking it was impossible to stop him, because his own voice in his ears drowned every possible form of interruption.

This morning, as an inmate of the house, introducing to the breakfast-room Messrs. Tietjens and Macmaster, who had driven up to the steps just as he was mounting them, he had a story to tell. The introduction was, therefore, not, as such, a success. . . .

"A STATE OF SIEGE, LADIES! Tee-hee!" he alternately roared and giggled. "We're living in a regular state of siege. . . . What with . . ." It appeared that the night before, after dinner, Mr. Sandbach and rather more than half a dozen of the young bloods who had dined at Mountby had gone scouring the country-lanes, mounted on motor bicycles and armed with loaded canes . . . for suffragettes! Every woman they had come across in the darkness they had stopped, abused, threatened with their loaded canes and subjected to cross-examination. The country-side was up in arms.

As a story this took, with the appropriate reflections and repetitions, a long time in telling and afforded Tietjens and Miss Wannop the opportunity of gazing at each other. Miss Wannop was frankly afraid that this large, clumsy, unusual-looking man, now that he had found her again, might hand her over to the police, whom she imagined to be searching for herself and her friend Gertie, Miss Wilson, at that moment in bed, under the care, as she also imagined, of Mrs. Wannop. On the links he had seemed to her natural and in place; here, with his loosely hung clothes and immense hands, the white patch on the side of his rather cropped head and his masked, rather shapeless features, he affected her queerly as being both in and out of place. He seemed to go with the ham, the meat-pie, the galantine and even at a pinch with the roses; but the Turner pictures, the aesthetic curtain and Mrs. Duchemin's flowing robes, amber and rose in the hair did not go with him at all. Even the Chippendale chairs hardly did. And she felt herself thinking oddly, beneath her perturbations of a criminal and the voice of the Rev. Horsley, that *his* Harris tweeds went all right with her skirt, and she was glad that she had on a clean, cream-coloured silk blouse, not a striped pink cotton.

She was right as to that.

In every man there are two minds that work side by side, the one checking the other; thus emotion stands against reason, intellect corrects passion, and first impressions act a little, but very little, before quick reflection. Yet first impressions have always a bias in their favour, and even quiet reflection has often a job to efface them.

The night before, Tietjens had given several thoughts to this young woman. General Campion had assigned her to him as *maîtresse en titre*. He was said to have ruined himself, broken up his home and spent his wife's money on her. Those were lies. On the other hand they were not inherent impossibilities. Upon occasion and given the right woman, quite sound men have done such things. He might, heaven knows, himself be so caught. But that he should have ruined himself over an unnoticeable young female who had announced herself as having been a domestic servant, and wore a pink cotton blouse . . . that had seemed to go beyond the bounds of even the unreason of club-gossip!

That was the strong, first impression! It was all very well for his surface mind to say that the girl was not by birth a tweeny maid; she was the daughter of Professor Wannop and she could jump! For Tietjens held very strongly the theory that what finally separated the classes was that the upper could lift its feet from the ground whilst common people couldn't. . . . But the strong impression remained.

Miss Wannop was a tweeny maid. Say a lady's help, by nature. She was of good family, for the Wannops were first heard of at Birdlip in Gloucestershire in the year 1417—no doubt enriched after Agincourt. But even brilliant men of good family will now and then throw daughters who are lady helps by nature. That was one of the queernesses of heredity. . . . And though Tietjens had even got as far as to realize that Miss Wannop must be a heroine who had sacrificed her young years to her mother's gifts and, no doubt, to a brother at school—for he had guessed as far as that— even then Tietjens couldn't make her out as more than a lady help. Heroines are all very well; admirable, they may even be saints; but if they let themselves get care-worn in face and go shabby . . . Well, they must wait for the gold that shall be amply stored for them in Heaven. On this earth you could hardly accept them as wives for men of your own set. Certainly you wouldn't spend your own wife's money on them. That was what it really came to.

But, brightened up as he now suddenly saw her, with silk for the pink cotton, shining coiled hair for the white canvas hat, a charming young neck, good shoes beneath neat ankles, a healthy flush taking the place of yesterday's pallor of fear for her comrade; an obvious equal in the surroundings of quite good people; small, but well shaped and healthy; immense blue eyes fixed without embarrassment on his own . . .

"By Jove . . ." he said to himself: "It's true! What a jolly little mistress she'd make!"

He blamed Campion, Sandbach and the club-gossips for the form the thought had taken. For the cruel, bitter and stupid pressure of the world has yet about it something selective; if it couples male and female in its inexorable rings of talk, it will be because there is something harmonious in the union. And there exists then the pressure of suggestion!

He took a look at Mrs. Duchemin and considered her infinitely commonplace and probably a bore. He disliked her large-shouldered, many-yarded style of blue dress and considered that no woman should wear clouded amber, for which the proper function was the provision of cigarette holders for bounders. He looked back at Miss Wannop and considered that she would make a good wife for Macmaster; Macmaster liked bouncing girls and this girl was quite lady enough.

He heard Miss Wannop shout against the gale to Mrs. Duchemin:

"Do I sit beside the head of the table and pour out?"

Mrs. Duchemin answered:

"No! I've asked Miss Fox to pour out. She's nearly stone deaf." Miss Fox was the penniless sister of a curate deceased. "You're to amuse Mr. Tietjens."

Tietjens noticed that Mrs. Duchemin had an agreeable throat-voice; it penetrated the noises of Mr. Horsley as the missel-thrush's note penetrates a gale. It was rather agreeable. He noticed that Miss Wannop made a little grimace.

Mr. Horsley, like a megaphone addressing a crowd, was turning from side to side, addressing his hearers by rotation. At the moment he was bawling at Macmaster; it would be Tietjens' turn again in a moment to hear a description of the heart attacks of old Mrs. Haglen at Nobeys. But Tietjens' turn did not come. . . .

A high-complexioned, round-cheeked, forty-fivish lady, with agreeable eyes, dressed rather well in the black of the not-very-lately widowed, entered the room with precipitation. She patted Mr. Horsley on his declamatory right arm, and since he went on talking, she caught him by the hand and shook it. She exclaimed in high, commanding tones:

"Which is Mr. Macmaster, the critic?" and then, in the dead lull, to Tietjens: "Are you Mr. Macmaster, the critic? No! . . . Then *you* must be."

Her turning to Macmaster and the extinction of her interest in himself had been one of the rudest things Tietjens had ever experienced, but it was an affair so strictly business-like that he took it without any offence. She was remarking to Macmaster:

"Oh, Mr. Macmaster, my new book will be out on Thursday week," and she had begun to lead him towards a window at the other end of the room.

Miss Wannop said:

"What have you done with Gertie?"

"Gertie!" Mrs. Wannop exclaimed with the surprise of one coming out of a dream. "Oh, yes! She's fast asleep. She'll sleep till four. I told Hannah to give a look at her now and then."

Miss Wannop's hands fell open at her side.

"Oh, *mother!*" forced itself from her.

"Oh, yes," Mrs. Wannop said, "we'd agreed to tell old Hannah we didn't want her to-day. So we had!" She said to Macmaster: "Old Hannah is our charwoman," wavered a little and then went on brightly: "Of course it will be of use to you to hear about my new book. To you journalists a little bit of previous explanation . . ." and she dragged off Macmaster. . . .

That had come about because just as she had got into the dog-cart to be driven to the rectory—for she herself could not drive a horse—Miss Wannop had told her mother that there would be two men at breakfast, one whose name she didn't know; the other, a Mr. Macmaster, a celebrated critic. Mrs. Wannop had called up to her:

"A critic? Of what?" her whole sleepy being electrified.

"I don't know," her daughter had answered. "Books, I dare say." . . .

A second or so after, when the horse, a large black animal that wouldn't stand, had made twenty yards at several bounds, the handy-man who drove had said:

"Yer mother's 'owlin' after yer." But Miss Wannop had answered that it didn't matter. She was confident that she had arranged for everything. She was to be back to get lunch; her mother was to give an occasional look at Gertie Wilson in the garret; Hannah, the daily help, was to be told she could go for the day. It was of the highest importance that Hannah should not know that a completely strange young woman was asleep in the garret at eleven in the morning. If she did, the news would be all over the neighbourhood at once, and the police instantly down on them.

But Mrs. Wannop was a woman of business. If she heard of a reviewer within driving distance, she called on him with eggs as a present. The moment the daily help had arrived, she had set out and walked to the rectory. No consideration of danger from the police would have stopped her; besides, she had forgotten all about the police.

Her arrival worried Mrs. Duchemin a good deal, because she wished all her guests to be seated and the breakfast well begun before the entrance of her husband. And this was not easy. Mrs. Wannop, who was uninvited, refused to be separated from Mr. Macmaster. Mr. Macmaster had told her that he never wrote reviews in the daily papers, only articles for the heavy quarterlies, and it had occurred to Mrs. Wannop that an article on her new book in one of the quarterlies was just what was needed. She was, therefore, engaged in telling Mr. Macmaster how to write about herself, and twice after Mrs. Duchemin had succeeded in shepherding Mr. Macmaster nearly to his seat, Mrs. Wannop had conducted him back to the embrasure of the win-

dow. It was only by sitting herself firmly in her chair next
to Macmaster that Mrs. Duchemin was able to retain for
herself this all-essential, strategic position. And it was only
by calling out:

"Mr. Horsley, *do* take Mrs. Wannop to the seat beside
you and feed her," that Mrs. Duchemin got Mrs. Wannop
out of Mr. Duchemin's own seat at the head of the table,
for Mrs. Wannop, having perceived this seat to be vacant
and next to Mr. Macmaster, had pulled out the Chippendale
arm-chair and had prepared to sit down in it. This could
only have spelt disaster, for it would have meant turning
Mrs. Duchemin's husband loose amongst the other guests.

Mr. Horsley, however, accomplished his duty of leading
away this lady with such firmness that Mrs. Wannop conceived of him as a very disagreeable and awkward person.
Mr. Horsley's seat was next to Miss Fox, a grey spinster,
who sat, as it were, within the fortification of silver urns and
deftly occupied herself with the ivory taps of these ma-
chines. This seat, too, Mrs. Wannop tried to occupy, imagining that by moving the silver vases that upheld the tall
delphiniums, she would be able to get a diagonal view of
Macmaster and so to shout to him. She found, however,
that she couldn't, and so resigned herself to taking the chair
that had been reserved for Miss Gertie Wilson, who was
to have been the eighth guest. Once there, she sat in distracted gloom, occasionally saying to her daughter:

"I think it's very bad management. I think this party's
very badly arranged." Mr. Horsley she hardly thanked for
the sole that he placed before her; Tietjens she did not
even look at.

Sitting beside Macmaster, her eyes fixed on a small door
in the corner of a panelled wall, Mrs. Duchemin became a
prey to a sudden and overwhelming fit of apprehension. It
forced her to say to her guest, though she had resolved to
chance it and say nothing:

"It wasn't perhaps fair to ask you to come all this way.
You may get nothing out of my husband. He's apt . . .
especially on Saturdays . . ."

She trailed off into indecision. It was possible that nothing might occur. On two Saturdays out of seven nothing
did occur. Then an admission would be wasted; this sympathetic being would go out of her life with a knowledge
that he needn't have had—to be a slur on her memory in
his mind. . . . But then, overwhelmingly, there came over
her the feeling that if he knew of her sufferings, he might

feel impelled to remain and comfort her. She cast about for words with which to finish her sentence. But Macmaster said:

"Oh, dear lady!" (And it seemed to her to be charming to be addressed thus!) "One understands . . . One is surely trained and adapted to understand . . . that these great scholars, these abstracted *cognoscenti* . . ."

Mrs. Duchemin breathed a great "Ah!" of relief. Macmaster had used the exactly right words.

"And," Macmaster was going on, "merely to spend a short hour, a swallow flight . . . 'As when the swallow gliding from lofty portal to lofty portal . . .' You know the lines . . . in these, your perfect surroundings . . ."

Blissful waves seemed to pass from him to her. It was in this way that men should speak, in that way—steel-blue tie, true-looking gold ring, steel-blue eyes beneath black brows!— that men should look. She was half conscious of warmth; this suggested the bliss of falling asleep, truly, in perfect surroundings. The roses on the table were lovely; their scent came to her.

A voice came to her:

"You *do* do the thing in style, I must say."

The large, clumsy but otherwise unnoticeable being that this fascinating man had brought in his train was setting up pretensions to her notice. He had just placed before her a small blue china plate that contained a little black caviar and a round of lemon; a small Sèvres, pinkish, delicate plate that held the pinkest peach in the room. She had said to him: "Oh . . . a little caviar! A peach!" a long time before, with the vague underfeeling that the names of such comestibles must convey to her person a charm in the eyes of Caliban.

She buckled about her her armour of charm; Tietjens was gazing with large, fishish eyes at the caviar before her.

"How do you get *that,* for instance?" he asked.

"Oh!" she answered: "If it wasn't my husband's doing it would look like ostentation. I'd find it ostentatious for myself." She found a smile, radiant yet muted. "He's trained Simpkins of New Bond Street. For a telephone message overnight special messengers go to Billingsgate at dawn for salmon and red mullet, this, in ice, and great blocks of ice too. It's such pretty stuff . . . and then by seven the car goes to Ashford Junction. . . . All the same, it's difficult to give a breakfast before ten."

She didn't want to waste her careful sentences on this

grey fellow; she couldn't, however, turn back, as she yearned to do, to the kindredly running phrases—as if out of books she had read!—of the smaller man.

"Ah, but it isn't," Tietjens said, "ostentation. It's the great Tradition. You mustn't ever forget that your husband's Breakfast Duchemin of Magdalen."

He seemed to be gazing inscrutably deep into her eyes. But no doubt he meant to be agreeable.

"Sometimes I wish I could," she said. "He doesn't get anything out of it himself. He's ascetic to unreasonableness. On Fridays he eats nothing at all. It makes me quite anxious . . . for Saturdays."

Tietjens said:

"I know."

She exclaimed—and almost with sharpness:

"You *know!*"

He continued to gaze straight into her eyes:

"Oh, of course one knows all about Breakfast Duchemin!" he said. "He was one of Ruskin's road-builders. He was said to be the most Ruskin-like of them all!"

Mrs. Duchemin cried out: "Oh!" Fragments of the worst stories that in his worst moods her husband had told her of his old preceptor went through her mind. She imagined that the shameful parts of her intimate life must be known to this nebulous monster. For Tietjens, turned sideways and facing her, had seemed to grow monstrous, with undefined outlines. He was the male threatening, clumsily odious and external! She felt herself say to herself: "I will do you an injury if ever—" For already she had felt herself swaying the preferences, the thoughts and the future of the man on her other side. He was the male tender, in-fitting; the complement of the harmony, the meat for consumption, like the sweet pulp of figs. . . . It was inevitable; it was essential to the nature of her relationship with her husband that Mrs. Duchemin should have these feelings. . . .

She heard, almost without emotion, so great was her disturbance, from behind her back the dreaded, high, rasping tones:

"*Post coitum tristis!* Ha! Ha! That's what it is?" The voice repeated the words and added sardonically: "You know what *that* means?" But the problem of her husband had become secondary; the real problem was: "What was this monstrous and hateful man going to say of her to his friend when, for long hours, they were away?"

He was still gazing into her eyes. He said nonchalantly, rather low:

"I wouldn't look round if I were you. Vincent Macmaster is quite up to dealing with the situation."

His voice had the familiarity of an elder brother's. And at once Mrs. Duchemin knew—that *he* knew that already close ties were developing between herself and Macmaster. He was speaking as a man speaks in emergencies to the mistress of his dearest friend. He was then one of those formidable and to-be-feared males who possess the gift of right intuitions. . . .

Tietjens said: "You heard!"

To the gloating, cruel tones that had asked:

"You know what that means?" Macmaster had answered clearly, but with the snappy intonation of a reproving don:

"Of course I know what it means. It's no discovery!" That was exactly the right note. Tietjens—and Mrs. Duchemin too—could hear Mr. Duchemin, invisible behind his rampart of blue spikes and silver, give the answering snuffle of a reproved schoolboy. A hard-faced, small man, in grey tweed that buttoned, collar-like, tight round his throat, standing behind the invisible chair, gazed straight forward into infinity.

Tietjens said to himself:

"By God! Parry! The Bermondsey light middle-weight! He's there to carry Duchemin off if he becomes violent!"

During the quick look that Tietjens took round the table Mrs. Duchemin gave, sinking lower in her chair, a short gasp of utter relief. Whatever Macmaster was going to think of her, he thought now. He knew the worst! It was settled, for good or ill. In a minute she would look round at him.

Tietjens said:

"It's all right, Macmaster will be splendid. We had a friend up at Cambridge with your husband's tendencies, and Macmaster could get him through *any* social occasion. . . . Besides, we're all gentlefolk here!"

He had seen the Rev. Horsley and Mrs. Wannop both interested in their plates. Of Miss Wannop he was not so certain. He had caught, bent obviously on himself, from large, blue eyes, an appealing glance. He said to himself: "She must be in the secret. She's appealing to me not to show emotion and upset the apple-cart! It is a shame that she should be here: a girl!" and into his answering glance he threw the message: "It's all right as far as this end of the table is concerned."

But Mrs. Duchemin had felt come into herself a little stiffening of morale. Macmaster by now knew the worst; Duchemin was quoting snuffingly to him the hot licentiousness of the *Trimalchion* of Petronius, snuffling into Macmaster's ear. She caught the phrase: *Festinans, puer calide.* . . . Duchemin, holding her wrist with the painful force of the maniac, had translated it to her over and over again. . . . No doubt that too this hateful man beside her would have guessed!

She said: "Of course we should be all gentlefolk here. One naturally arranges that. . . ."

Tietjens began to say:

"Ah! But it isn't so easy to arrange now-a-days. All sorts of bounders get into all sorts of holies of holies!"

Mrs. Duchemin turned her back on him right in the middle of his sentence. She devoured Macmaster's face with her eyes in an infinite sense of calm.

Macmaster four minutes before had been the only one to see the entrance, from a small panelled door that had behind it another of green baize, of the Rev. Mr. Duchemin, and following him a man whom Macmaster, too, recognized at once as Parry the ex-prize-fighter. It flashed through his mind at once that this was an extraordinary conjunction. It flashed through his mind, too, that it was extraordinary that anyone so ecstatically handsome as Mrs. Duchemin's husband should not have earned high preferment in a church always hungry for male beauty. Mr. Duchemin was extremely tall, with a slight stoop of the proper clerical type. His face was of alabaster; his grey hair, parted in the middle, fell brilliantly on his high brows; his glance was quick, penetrating, austere; his nose very hooked and chiselled. He was the exact man to adorn a lofty and gorgeous fane, as Mrs. Duchemin was the exact woman to consecrate an episcopal drawing-room. With his great wealth, scholarship and tradition . . . "Why, then," went through Macmaster's mind in a swift pinprick of suspicion, "isn't he at least a dean?"

Mr. Duchemin had walked swiftly to his chair, which Parry, as swiftly walking behind him, drew out. His master slipped into it with a graceful, sideways motion. He shook his head at grey Miss Fox, who had moved a hand towards an ivory urn-tap. There was a glass of water beside his plate, and round it his long, very white fingers closed. He stole a quick glance at Macmaster and then looked at him steadily with glittering eyes. He said: "Good morning, doctor," and then, drowning Macmaster's quiet protest: "Yes! Yes! The stethoscope meticulously packed into the top-hat and the shining hat left in the hall."

The prize-fighter, in tight box-cloth leggings, tight whip-cord breeches, and a short tight jacket that buttoned up at the collar to his chin—the exact stud-groom of a man of property—gave a quick glance of recognition of Macmaster and then to Mr. Duchemin's back another quick look, raising his eyebrows. Macmaster, who knew him very well because he had given Tietjens boxing lessons at Cambridge, could almost hear him say: "A queer change this, sir! Keep your eyes on him a second!" and with the quick, light, tiptoe of the pugilist he slipped away to the sideboard. Macmaster stole a quick glance on his own account at Mrs. Duchemin. She had her back to him, being deep in conversation with Tietjens. His heart jumped a little when, looking back again, he saw Mr. Duchemin half raised to his feet, peering round the fortifications of silver. But he sank down again in his chair and, surveying Macmaster with an expression of cunning singular on his ascetic features, exclaimed:

"And your friend? Another medical man! All with stetho-scope complete. It takes, of course, two medical men to certify . . ."

He stopped and with an expression of sudden, distorted rage pushed aside the arm of Parry, who was sliding a plate of sole-fillets on to the table beneath his nose.

"Take away," he was beginning to exclaim thunderously, "these conducements to the filthy lusts of . . ." But with an-other cunning and apprehensive look at Macmaster, he said: "Yes! Yes! Parry! That's right. Yes! Sole! A touch of kidney to follow. Another! Yes! Grape-fruit! With sherry!" He had adopted an old Oxford voice, spread his napkin over his knees and hastily placed in his mouth a morsel of fish.

Macmaster with a patient and distinct intonation said that he must be permitted to introduce himself. He was Mac-master, Mr. Duchemin's correspondent on the subject of his little monograph. Mr. Duchemin looked at him, hard, with an awakened attention that gradually lost suspicion and became gloatingly joyful:

"Ah, yes, Macmaster!" he said. "Macmaster. A budding critic. A little of a hedonist perhaps? And yes . . . you wired that you were coming. Two friends! Not medical men! Friends!" He moved his face closer to Macmaster and said:

"How tired you look! Worn! Worn!"

Macmaster was about to say that he was rather hard-

worked when, in a harsh, high cackle close to his face
there came the Latin words. Mrs. Duchemin—and Tietjens!
—had heard. Macmaster knew then what he was up against.
He took another look at the prize-fighter, moved his head
to one side to catch a momentary view of the gigantic Mr.
Horsley, whose size took on a new meaning. Then he settled down in his chair and ate a kidney. The physical
force present was no doubt enough to suppress Mr. Duchemin
should he become violent. And trained! It was one of the
curious, minor coincidences of life that, at Cambridge,
he had once thought of hiring this very Parry to follow round
his dear friend Sim. Sim, the most brilliant of sardonic
ironists, sane, decent and ordinarily a little prudish on the
surface, had been subject to just such temporary lapses
as Mr. Duchemin. On society occasions he would stand up
and shout or sit down and whisper the most unthinkable
indecencies. Macmaster, who had loved him very much, had
run round with Sim as often as he could and had thus
gained skill in dealing with these manifestations. . . . He
felt suddenly a certain pleasure! He thought he might
gain prestige in the eyes of Mrs. Duchemin if he dealt
quietly and efficiently with this situation. It might even
lead to an intimacy. He asked nothing better!

He knew that Mrs. Duchemin had turned towards him: he
could feel her listening and observing him; it was as if
her glance was warm on his cheek. But he did not look
round; he had to keep his eyes on the gloating face of her
husband. Mr. Duchemin was quoting Petronius, leaning
towards his guest. Macmaster consumed kidneys stiffly.

He said:

"That isn't the amended version of the iambics. Willamo-
vitz Möllendorf that we used . . ."

To interrupt him Mr. Duchemin put his thin hand cour-
teously on Macmaster's arm. It had a great cornelian seal set
in red gold on the third finger. He went on reciting in
ecstasy, his head a little on one side as if he were listening to invisible choristers. Macmaster really disliked the
Oxford intonation of Latin. He looked for a short moment
at Mrs. Duchemin; her eyes were upon him, large, shadowy,
full of gratitude. He saw, too, that they were welling over
with wetness.

He looked quickly back at Duchemin. And suddenly it
came to him; she was suffering! She was probably suffering
intensely. It had not occurred to him that she would suffer
—partly because he was without nerves himself, partly be-

cause he had conceived of Mrs. Duchemin as firstly feeling admiration for himself. Now it seemed to him abominable that she should suffer.

Mrs. Duchemin was in an agony. Macmaster had looked at her intently and looked away! She read into his glance contempt for her situation and anger that she should have been placed in such a position. In her pain she stretched out her hand and touched his arm.

Macmaster was aware of her touch; his mind seemed filled with sweetness. But he kept his head obstinately averted. For her sake he did not dare to look away from the maniacal face. A crisis was coming. Mr. Duchemin had arrived at the English translation. He placed his hands on the table-cloth in preparation for rising; he was going to stand on his feet and shout obscenities wildly to the other guests. It was the exact moment.

Macmaster made his voice dry and penetrating to say:

"'Youth of tepid loves' is a lamentable rendering of *puer calide!* It's lamentably antiquated. . . ."

Duchemin choked and said:

"What? What? What's that?"

"It's just like Oxford to use an eighteenth-century crib. I suppose that's Whiston and Ditton? Something like that . . ." He observed Duchemin, brought out of his impulse, to be wavering—as if he were coming awake in a strange place! He added:

"Anyhow it's wretched schoolboy smut. Fifth form. Or not even that. Have some galantine. I'm going to. Your sole's cold."

Mr. Duchemin looked down at his plate.

"Yes! Yes!" he muttered. "Yes! With sugar and vinegar sauce!" The prize-fighter slipped away to the sideboard, an admirable, quiet fellow, as unobtrusive as a burying beetle. Macmaster said:

"You were about to tell me something for my little monograph. What became of Maggie . . . Maggie Simpson. The Scots girl who was Rossetti's model for *Alla Finestra del Cielo?*"

Mr. Duchemin looked at Macmaster with sane, muddled, rather exhausted eyes:

"*Alla Finestra!*" he exclaimed: "Oh yes! I've got the water-colour. I saw her sitting for it and bought it on the spot. . . ." He looked again at his plate, started at sight of the galantine and began to eat ravenously: "A beautiful girl!" he said: "Very long-necked . . . She wasn't, of course . . . eh

. . . respectable! She's living yet, I think. Very old. I saw her two years ago. She had a lot of pictures. Relics, of course! . . . In the Whitechapel Road she lived. She was naturally of that class. . . ." He went muttering on, his head above his plate. Macmaster considered that the fit was over. He was irresistibly impelled to turn to Mrs. Duchemin; her face was rigid, stiff. He said swiftly:

"If he'll eat a little: get his stomach filled . . . It calls the blood down from the head. . . ."

She said:

"Oh, forgive! It's dreadful for you! Myself I will never forgive!"

He said:

"No! No! . . . Why, it's what I'm *for!*"

A deep emotion brought her whole white face to life:

"Oh, you *good* man!" she said in her profound tones, and they remained gazing at each other.

Suddenly, from behind Macmaster's back, Mr. Duchemin shouted:

"I say he made a settlement on her, *dum casta et sola,* of course. Whilst she remained chaste and alone!"

Mr. Duchemin, suddenly feeling the absence of the powerful will that had seemed to overweigh his own like a great force in the darkness, was on his feet, panting and delighted:

"Chaste!" He shouted. "Chaste, you observe! What a world of suggestion in the word . . ." He surveyed the opulent broadness of his table-cloth; it spread out before his eyes as if it had been a great expanse of meadow in which he could gallop, relaxing his limbs after long captivity. He shouted three obscene words and went on in his Oxford Movement voice: "But chastity . . ."

Mrs. Wannop suddenly said:

"Oh!" and looked at her daughter, whose face grew slowly crimson as she continued to peel a peach. Mrs. Wannop turned to Mr. Horsley beside her and said:

"You write, too, I believe, Mr. Horsley. No doubt something more learned than my poor readers would care for . . ." Mr. Horsley had been preparing, according to his instructions from Mrs. Duchemin, to shout a description of an article he had been writing about the *Mosella* of Ausonius, but as he was slow in starting, the lady got in first. She talked on serenely about the tastes of the large public. Tietjens leaned across to Miss Wannop and, holding in his right hand a half-peeled fig, said to her as loudly as he could:

"I've got a message for you from Mr. Waterhouse. He says if you'll . . ."

The completely deaf Miss Fox—who had had her training by writing—remarked diagonally to Mrs. Duchemin:

"I think we shall have thunder to-day. Have you remarked the number of minute insects? . . ."

"When my revered preceptor," Mr. Duchemin thundered on, "drove away in the carriage on his wedding-day, he said to his bride: 'We will live like the blessed angels!' How sublime! I, too, after my nuptials . . ."

Mrs. Duchemin suddenly screamed:

"Oh . . . *no!*"

As if checked for a moment in their stride, all the others paused—for a breath. Then they continued talking with polite animation and listening with minute attention. To Tietjens that seemed the highest achievement and justification of English manners!

Parry, the prize-fighter, had twice caught his master by the arm and shouted that breakfast was getting cold. He said now to Macmaster that he and the Rev. Horsley could get Mr. Duchemin away, but there'd be a hell of a fight. Macmaster whispered: "Wait!" and turning to Mrs. Duchemin, he said: "I can stop him. Shall I?" She said:

"Yes! Yes! Anything!" He observed tears, isolated upon her cheeks, a thing he had never seen. With caution and with hot rage he whispered into the prize-fighter's hairy ear that was held down to him:

"Punch him in the kidney. With your thumb. As *hard* as you can without breaking your thumb . . ."

Mr. Duchemin had just declaimed:

"I, too, after my nuptials . . ." He began to wave his arms, pausing and looking from unlistening face to unlistening face. Mrs. Duchemin had just screamed.

Mr. Duchemin thought that the arrow of God struck him. He imagined himself an unworthy messenger. In such pain as he had never conceived of, he fell into his chair and sat huddled up, a darkness covering his eyes.

"He won't get up again," Macmaster whispered to the appreciative pugilist. "He'll want to. But he'll be afraid."

He said to Mrs. Duchemin:

"Dearest lady! It's all over. I assure you of that. It's a scientific nerve counter-irritant."

Mrs. Duchemin said:

"Forgive!" with one deep sob: "You can never respect . . ."

She felt her eyes explore his face as the wretch in a cell explores the face of his executioner for a sign of pardon. Her heart stayed still: her breath suspended itself. . . .

Then complete heaven began. Upon her left palm she felt cool fingers beneath the cloth. This man knew always the exact right action! Upon the fingers, cool, like spikenard and ambrosia, her fingers closed themselves.

In complete bliss, in a quiet room, his voice went on talking. At first with great neatness of phrase, but with what refinement! He explained that certain excesses, being merely nervous cravings, can be combated if not, indeed, cured altogether, by the fear of, by the determination not to endure, sharp physical pain—which, of course, is a nervous matter, too! . . .

Parry, at a given moment, had said into his master's ear:

"It's time you prepared your sermon for to-morrow, sir," and Mr. Duchemin had gone as quietly as he had arrived, gliding over the thick carpet to the small door.

Then Macmaster said to her:

"You come from Edinburgh? You'll know the Fifeshire coast, then."

"Do I not?" she said. His hand remained in hers. He began to talk to the whins of the links and the sanderlings along the flats, with such a Scots voice and in phrases so vivid that she saw her childhood again and had in her eyes a wetness of a happier order. She released his cool hand after a long, gentle pressure. But when it was gone it was as if much of her life went. She said: "You'll be knowing Kingussie House, just outside your town. It was there I spent my holidays as a child."

He answered:

"Maybe I played round it a barefoot lad and you in your grandeur within."

She said:

"Oh, no! Hardly! There would be the difference of our ages! And . . . And indeed there are other things I will tell you."

She addressed herself to Tietjens, with all her heroic armour of charm buckled on again:

"Only think! I find Mr. Macmaster and I almost played together in our youths."

He looked at her, she knew, with a commiseration that she hated:

"Then you're an older friend than I," he said, "though

I've known him since I was fourteen, and I don't believe you could be a better. He's a good fellow. . . ."

She hated him for his condescension towards a better man and for his warning—she *knew* it was a warning—to her to spare his friend.

Mrs. Wannop gave a distinct, but not an alarming, scream. Mr. Horsley had been talking to her about an unusual fish that used to inhabit the Moselle in Roman times. The *Mosella* of Ausonius; the subject of the essay he was writing is mostly fish. . . .

"No," he shouted, "it's been said to be the roach. But there are no roach in the river now. '*Vannulis viridis, oculisque.*' No. It's the other way round: *Red* fins . . ."

Mrs. Wannop's scream and her wide gesture—her hand, indeed, was nearly over his mouth and her trailing sleeve across his plate!—were enough to interrupt him.

"*Tietjens!*" she again screamed. "Is it possible? . . ."

She pushed her daughter out of her seat, and moving round beside the young man, she overwhelmed him with vociferous love. As Tietjens had turned to speak to Mrs. Duchemin she had recognized his aquiline half-profile as exactly that of his father at her own wedding-breakfast. To the table that knew it by heart—though Tietjens himself didn't!—she recited the story of how his father had saved her life and was her mascot. And she offered the son—for to the father she had never been allowed to make any return— her house, her purse, her heart, her time, her all. She was so completely sincere that as the party broke up she just nodded to Macmaster and, catching Tietjens forcibly by the arm, said perfunctorily to the critic:

"Sorry I can't help you any more with the article. But my dear Chrissie must have the books he wants. At once! This very minute!"

She moved off, Tietjens grappled to her, her daughter following as a young swan follows its parents. In her gracious manner Mrs. Duchemin had received the thanks of her guests for her wonderful breakfast and had hoped that now that they had found their ways there. . . .

The echoes of the dispersed festival seemed to whisper in the room. Macmaster and Mrs. Duchemin faced each other, their eyes wary—and longing.

He said:

"It's dreadful to have to go now. But I have an engagement."

She said:

"Yes! I know! With your great friends."

He answered:

"Oh, only with Mr. Waterhouse and General Campion . . . and Mr. Sandbach, of course . . ."

She had a moment of fierce pleasure at the thought that Tietjens was not to be of the company: *her* man would be outsoaring the vulgarian of his youth, of his past that she didn't know. . . . Almost harshly she exclaimed:

"I don't want you to be mistaken about Kingussie House. It was just a holiday school. Not a grand place."

"It was very costly," he said, and she seemed to waver on her feet.

"Yes! Yes!" she said, nearly in a whisper. "But you're so grand now! I was only the child of very poor bodies. Johnstons of Midlothian. But very poor bodies. . . . I . . . He bought me, you might say. You know . . . Put me to very rich schools: when I was fourteen . . . my people were glad. . . . But I think if my mother had known when I married . . ." She writhed her whole body. "Oh, dreadful! Dreadful!" she exclaimed. "I want you to know . . ."

His hands were shaking as if he had been in a jolting cart. . . .

Their lips met in a passion of pity and tears. He removed his mouth to say: "I must see you this evening. . . . I shall be mad with anxiety about you." She whispered: "Yes! Yes! . . . In the yew walk." Her eyes were closed; she pressed her body fiercely into his. "You are the . . . first . . . man . . ." she breathed.

"I will be the only one forever," he said.

He began to see himself: in the tall room, with the long curtains: a round, eagle mirror reflected them gleaming: like a bejewelled picture with great depths: the entwined figures.

They drew apart to gaze at each other: holding hands. . . . The voice of Tietjens said:

"Macmaster! You're to dine at Mrs. Wannop's to-night. Don't dress; I shan't." He was looking at them without any expression, as if he had interrupted a game of cards; large, grey, fresh-featured, the white patch glistening on the side of his grizzling hair.

Macmaster said:

"All right. It's near here, isn't it? . . . I've got an engagement just after. . . ." Tietjens said that that would be all right: he would be working himself. All night, probably. For Waterhouse . . .

Mrs. Duchemin said with swift jealousy:

"You let him order you about. . . ." Tietjens was gone.

Macmaster said absently:

"Who? Chrissie? . . . Yes! Sometimes I him, sometimes he me . . . We make engagements. My best friend. The most brilliant man in England, of the best stock too. Tietjens of Groby . . ." Feeling that she didn't appreciate his friend, he was abstractly piling on commendations: "He's making calculations now for the government that no other man in England could make. But he's going . . ."

An extreme languor had settled on him; he felt weakened but yet triumphant with the cessation of her grasp. It occurred to him numbly that he would be seeing less of Tietjens. A grief. He heard himself quote:

" 'Since when we stand side by side!' " His voice trembled.

"Ah! yes!" came in her deep tones: "The beautiful lines . . . They're true. We must part. In this world . . ." They seemed to her lovely and mournful words to say; heavenly to have them to say, vibratingly, arousing all sorts of images. Macmaster, mournfully too, said:

"We must wait." He added fiercely: "But to-night, at dusk!" He imagined the dusk, under the yew hedge. A shining motor drew up in the sunlight under the window.

"Yes! Yes!" she said. "There's a little white gate from the lane." She imagined their interview of passion and mournfulness amongst dim objects half seen. So much of glamour she could allow herself.

Afterwards he must come to the house to ask after her health, and they would walk side by side on the lawn, publicly, in the warm light, talking of indifferent but beautiful poetries, a little wearily, but with what currents electrifying and passing between their flesh. . . . And then: long, circumspect years . . .

Macmaster went down the tall steps to the car that gleamed in the summer sun. The roses shone over the supremely levelled turf. His heel met the stones with the hard tread of a conqueror. He could have shouted aloud!

6 ~

TIETJENS LIT a pipe beside the stile, having first meticulously cleaned out the bowl and the stem with a surgical needle, in his experience the best of all pipe-cleaners, since, made of German silver, it is flexible, won't corrode and is indestructible. He wiped off methodically, with a great dock-leaf, the glutinous brown products of burnt tobacco, the young woman, as he was aware, watching him from behind his back. As soon as he had restored the surgical needle to the note-book in which it lived and had put the note-book into its bulky pocket, Miss Wannop moved off down the path: it was only suited for Indian file, and had on the left hand a ten-foot, untrimmed quicken hedge, the hawthorn blossoms just beginning to blacken at the edges and small green haws to show. On the right the grass was above knee-high and bowed to those that passed. The sun was exactly vertical; the chaffinchs said: "Pink! Pink!": the young woman had an agreeable back.

"This," Tietjens thought, "is England! A man and a maid walk through Kentish grass fields: the grass ripe for the scythe. The man honourable, clean, upright; the maid virtuous, clean, vigorous: he of good birth; she of birth quite as good; each filled with a too good breakfast that each could yet capably digest. Each come just from an admirably appointed establishment: a table surrounded by the best people: their promenade sanctioned, as it were, by the Church: two clergy; the State: two government officials; by mothers, friends, old maids. . . . Each knew the names of birds that piped and grasses that bowed: chaffinch, greenfinch, yellow-ammer (*not,* my dear, hammer! *ammer* from the Middle High German for "finch"), garden-warbler, Dartford-warbler, pied wagtail, known as "dish-washer." (These *charming* local dialect names.) Marguerites over the grass, stretching in an infinite white blaze: grasses purple in a haze to the far distant hedgerow: coltsfoot, wild white clover, sainfoin, Italian rye-grass (all technical names that the best people must know: the best grass mixture for permanent pasture on the Wealden loam). In the hedge: Our Lady's bedstraw: dead-nettle: bachelor's button (but in *Sussex* they call it ragged robin, my dear): So interesting! Cowslip (paigle, you know, from old French pasque, meaning Easter): burr, burdock (farmer that thy wife may thrive, but not burr and burdock wive!); violet leaves, the flowers, of course, over; black briony; wild clematis: later it's old man's beard; purple loosestrife. (That our young maids long purples call and literal shepherds give a grosser name. *So* racy of the soil!) . . . Walk, then, through the field, gallant youth and fair maid, minds cluttered up with all these useless anodynes for thought, quotation, imbecile epithets! Dead silent: unable to talk: from too good breakfast to probably extremely bad lunch. The young woman, so the young man is duly warned, to prepare it: pink india-rubber half-cooked cold beef, no doubt: tepid potatoes, water in the bottom of willow-pattern dish. (*No! Not* genuine willow pattern, of *course*, Mr. Tietjens.) Overgrown lettuce with wood-vinegar to make the mouth scream with pain; pickles, also preserved in wood-vinegar; two bottles of public-house beer that, on opening, squirts to the wall. A glass of invalid port . . . for the *gentleman!* . . . and the jaws hardly able to open after the too enormous breakfast at 10:15. Midday now!

"God's England!" Tietjens exclaimed to himself in high good humour. " 'Land of Hope and Glory!'—F natural descending to tonic, C major: chord of 6–4, suspension over dominant seventh to common chord of C major. . . . All absolutely correct! Double-basses, 'cellos, all violins: all woodwind: all brass. Full grand organ: all stops: special *vox humana* and key-bugle effect. . . . Across the counties came the sound of bugles that his father knew. . . . Pipe exactly right. It must be: pipe of Englishman of good birth: ditto tobacco. Attractive young woman's back. English midday midsummer. Best climate in the world! No day on which man may not go abroad!" Tietjens paused and aimed with his hazel stick an immense blow at a tall spike of yellow mullein with its undecided, furry, glaucous leaves and its undecided, buttony, unripe, lemon-coloured flower. The structure collapsed gracefully, like a woman killed among crinolines!

"Now I'm a bloody murderer!" Tietjens said. "Not gory! Green stained with vital fluid of innocent plant . . . And by God! Not a woman in the country who won't let you rape her after an hour's acquaintance!" He slew two more mulleins and a sow-thistle! A shadow, but not from the sun, a gloom, lay across the sixty acres of purple grass bloom and marguerites, white: like petticoats of lace over the grass!

"By God," he said, "Church! State! Army! H.M. Ministry: H.M. Opposition: H.M. City Man . . . All the governing class! All rotten! Thank God we've got a navy! . . . But perhaps that's rotten too! Who knows! Britannia needs no bulwarks. . . . Then thank God for the upright young man and the virtuous maiden in the summer fields: he Tory of the Tories as he should be: she suffragette of the militants: militant here in earth . . . as she should be! As she should be! In the early decades of the twentieth century, however else can a woman keep clean and wholesome! Ranting from platforms, splendid for the lungs: bashing in policemen's

helmets . . . No! It's I do that: my part, I think, miss!
. . . Carrying heavy banners in twenty-mile processions
through streets of Sodom. All splendid! I bet she's virtuous.
But you don't have to bet. It isn't done on certainties. You
can tell it in the eye. Nice eyes! Attractive back. Virginal
cockiness . . . Yes, better occupation for mothers of empire
than attending on lewd husbands year in year out till you're
as hysterical as a female cat in heat. . . . You could see it
in her: that woman: you can see it in most of 'em! Thank
God, then, for the Tory, upright young married man and
the suffragette kid. . . . Backbone of England! . . ."

He killed another flower.

"But by God! we're both under a cloud! Both! . . . That
kid and I! And General Lord Edward Campion, Lady Claudine Sandbach, and the Hon. Paul, M.P. (suspended), to
spread the tale. . . . And forty toothless fogies in the club
to spread it: and no end visiting-books yawning to have your
names cut out of them, my boy! . . . My dear boy: I so
regret: your father's oldest friend . . . By Jove, the pistachio
nut of that galantine! Repeating! Breakfast gone wrong:
gloomy reflections! Thought I could stand anything: digestion
of an ostrich. . . . But no! Gloomy reflections: I'm hysterical:
like that large-eyed whore! For same reason! Wrong diet
and wrong life: diet meant for partridge shooters over the
turnips consumed by the sedentary. England the land of pills
. . . *Das Pillen-Land*, the Germans call us. Very properly . . .
And, damn it: outdoor diet: boiled mutton, turnips: sedentary life . . . and forced up against the filthiness of the world:
your nose in it all day long! . . . Why, hang it, I'm as badly off as she. Sylvia's as bad as Duchemin! . . . I'd never have
thought that . . . No wonder meat's turned to uric acid . . .
prime cause of neurasthenia. . . . What a beastly muddle!
Poor Macmaster! He's finished. Poor devil: he'd better have
ogled this kid. He could have sung: 'Highland Mary' a better
tune than 'This Is the End of Every Man's Desire' . . .
You can cut it on his tombstone, you can write it on his
card, that a young man tacked on to a paulo-post Pre-
Raphaelite prostitute . . ."

He stopped suddenly in his walk. It had occurred to him
that he ought not to be walking with this girl!

"But damn it all," he said to himself, "she makes a good
screen for Sylvia . . . who cares! She must chance it. She's
probably struck off all their beastly visiting-lists already . . .
as a suffragette!"

Miss Wannop, a cricket pitch or so ahead of him, hopped

over a stile: left foot on the step, right on the top bar, a touch of the left on the other steps, and down on the white, drifted dust of a road they no doubt had to cross. She stood waiting, her back still to him. . . . Her nimble foot-work, her attractive back, seemed to him now infinitely pathetic. To let scandal attach to her was like cutting the wings of a goldfinch: the bright creature, yellow, white, golden and delicate that in the sunlight makes a haze with its wings beside thistle-tops. No, damn it! it was worse; it was worse than putting out, as the bird-fancier does, the eyes of a chaffinch. . . . Infinitely pathetic!

Above the stile, in an elm, a chaffinch said: "Pink! Pink!"

The imbecile sound filled him with rage; he said to the bird:

"Damn your eyes! *Have* them put out, then!" The beastly bird that made the odious noise, when it had its eyes put out, at least squealed like any other skylark or tom-tit. Damn all birds, field-naturalists, botanists! In the same way he addressed the back of Miss Wannop: "Damn your eyes! *Have* your chastity impugned, then! What do you speak to strange men in public for? You know you can't do it in this country. If it were a decent, straight land like Ireland, where people cut each other's throats for clean issues: Papist versus Prot . . . well, you could! You could walk through Ireland from east to west and speak to every man you met. . . . 'Rich and rare were the gems she wore. . . .' To every man you met as long as he wasn't an Englishman of good birth: *that* would deflower you!" He was scrambling clumsily over the stile. "Well! *be* deflowered, then: *lose* your infantile reputation. You've spoken to strange pitch: you're defiled . . . with the benefit of Clergy, Army, Cabinet, Administration, Opposition, mothers and old maids of England. . . . They'd all tell you you can't talk to a strange man, in the sunlight, on the links, without becoming a screen for some Sylvia or other. . . . Then *be* a screen for Sylvia: *get* struck off the visiting-books! The deeper you're implicated, the more bloody villain I am! I'd like the whole lot to see us here: that would settle it. . . ."

Nevertheless, when at the roadside he stood level with Miss Wannop, who did not look at him, and saw the white road running to right and left with no stile opposite, he said gruffly to her:

"Where's the next stile? I hate walking on roads!" She pointed with her chin along the opposite hedgerow. "Fifty yards!" she said.

"Come along!" he exclaimed, and set off at a trot almost. It had come into his head that it would be just the beastly sort of thing that would happen if a car with General Campion and Lady Claudine and Paul Sandbach all aboard should come along that blinding stretch of road: or one alone: perhaps the general driving the dog-cart he affected. He said to himself:

"By God! If they cut this girl I'd break their backs over my knee!" and he hastened. "Just the beastly thing that *would* happen." The road probably led straight in at the front door of Mountby!

Miss Wannop trotted along a little in his rear. She thought him the most extraordinary man: as mad as he was odious. Sane people, if they're going to hurry—but *why* hurry!—do it in the shade of field hedgerows, not in the white blaze of county-council roads. Well, he could go ahead. In the next field she was going to have it out with him: she didn't intend to be hot with running: let him be, his hateful, but certainly noticeable, eyes protruding at her like a lobster's, but she cool and denunciatory in her pretty blouse. . . .

There was a dog-cart coming behind them!

Suddenly it came into her head: that fool had been lying when he had said that the police meant to let them alone: lying over the breakfast-table. . . . The dog-cart contained the police: after them! She didn't waste time looking round: she wasn't a fool like Atalanta in the egg-race. She picked up her heels and sprinted. She beat him by a yard and a half to the kissing-gate, white in the hedge: panicked: breathing hard. He panted into it after her: the fool hadn't the sense to let her through first. They were jammed in together: face to face, panting! An occasion on which sweethearts kiss in Kent: the gate being made in three, the inner flange of the V moving on hinges. It stops cattle getting through: but this great lout of a Yorkshireman didn't know: trying to push through like a mad bullock! Now they were caught. Three weeks in Wandsworth jail . . . Oh, hang . . .

The voice of Mrs. Wannop—of course it was only mother! twenty feet on high or so behind the kicking mare, with a good, round face like a peony—said:

"Ah, you can jam my Val in a gate and hold her . . . but she gave you seven yards in twenty and beat you to the gate. That was her father's ambition!" She thought of them as children running races. She beamed down, round-faced and simple, on Tietjens from beside the driver, who had a black slouch hat and the grey beard of St. Peter.

"My dear boy!" she said, "my dear boy; it's such a satis-faction to have you under my roof!"

The black horse reared on end, the patriarch sawing at its mouth. Mrs. Wannop said unconcernedly: "Stephen Joel! I haven't done talking."

Tietjens was gazing enragedly at the lower part of the horse's sweat-smeared stomach.

"You soon will have," he said, "with the girth in that state. Your neck will be broken."

"Oh, I don't think so," Mrs. Wannop said. "Joel only bought the turn-out yesterday."

Tietjens addressed the driver with some ferocity:

"Here, get down, you," he said. He held, himself, the head of the horse, whose nostrils were wide with emotion: it rubbed its forehead almost immediately against his chest. He said: "Yes! Yes! There! There!" Its limbs lost their taut-ness. The aged driver scrambled down from the high seat, trying to come down at first forward and then backwards. Tietjens fired indignant orders at him:

"Lead the horse into the shade of that tree. Don't touch his bit: his mouth's sore. Where did you get this job lot? Ashford market: thirty pounds: it's worth more. . . . But, blast you, don't you see you've got a thirteen hands' pony's harness for a sixteen and a half hands' horse. Let the bit out: three holes: it's cutting the animal's tongue in half. . . . This animal's a rig. Do you know what a rig is? If you give it corn for a fortnight it will kick you and the cart and the stable to pieces in five minutes one day." He led the con-veyance, Mrs. Wannop triumphantly complacent and all, into a patch of shade beneath elms.

"Loosen that bit, confound you," he said to the driver. "Ah! you're afraid."

He loosened the bit himself, covering his fingers with greasy harness polish, which he hated. Then he said:

"Can you hold his head or are you afraid of that too? You *deserve* to have him bite your hands off." He addressed Miss Wannop: "Can *you?*" She said: "No! I'm afraid of horses. I can drive any sort of car: but I'm afraid of horses." He said: "Very proper!" He stood back and looked at the horse: it had dropped its head and lifted its near hind foot, rest-ing the toe on the ground: an attitude of relaxation.

"He'll stand now!" he said. He undid the girth, bending down uncomfortably, perspiring and greasy: the girth-strap parted in his hand.

"It's true," Mrs. Wannop said. "I'd have been dead in three

minutes if you hadn't seen that. The cart would have gone over backwards . . ."

Tietjens took out a large, complicated, horn-handled knife like a schoolboy's. He selected a punch and pulled it open. He said to the driver:

"Have you got any cobbler's thread? Any string? Any copper wire? A rabbit wire, now? Come, you've got a rabbit wire or you're not a handy-man."

The driver moved his slouch hat circularly in negation. This seemed to be Quality, who summons you for poaching if you own to possessing rabbit wires.

Tietjens laid the girth along the shaft and punched into it with his punch.

"Woman's work!" he said to Mrs. Wannop, "but it'll take you home and last you six months as well. . . . But I'll sell this whole lot for you to-morrow."

Mrs. Wannop sighed:

"I suppose it'll fetch a ten-pound note. . . ." She said: "I ought to have gone to market myself."

"No!" Tietjens answered: "I'll get you fifty for it or I'm no Yorkshireman. This fellow hasn't been swindling you. He's got you deuced good value for money, but he doesn't know what's suited for ladies; a white pony and a basket-work chaise is what you want."

"Oh, I like a bit of spirit," Mrs. Wannop said.

"Of course you do," Tietjens answered: "but this turnout's too much."

He sighed a little and took out his surgical needle.

"I'm going to hold this band together with this," he said. "It's so pliant it will make two stitches and hold forever. . . ."

But the handy-man was beside him, holding out the contents of his pockets: a greasy leather pouch, a ball of beeswax, a knife, a pipe, a bit of cheese and a pale rabbit wire. He had made up his mind that *this* Quality was benevolent, and he made offering of all his possessions.

Tietjens said: "Ah," and then, while he unknotted the wire:

"Well! Listen . . . you bought this turn-out of a higgler at the back door of the Leg of Mutton Inn."

"Saracen's 'Ed!" the driver muttered.

"You got it for thirty pounds because the higgler wanted money bad. *I* know. And dirt cheap . . . But a rig isn't everybody's driving. All right for a vet or a horse-coper. Like the cart that's too tall! . . . But you did damn well.

Only you're not what you were, are you, at thirty? And the horse looked to be a devil and the cart so high you couldn't get out once you were in. And you kept it in the sun for two hours waiting for your mistress."

"There wer' a bit o' lewth 'longside stable wall," the driver muttered.

"Well! He didn't like waiting," Tietjens said placably. "You can be thankful your old neck's not broken. Do this band up, one hole less for the bit I've taken in."

He prepared to climb into the driver's seat, but Mrs. Wannop was there before him, at an improbable altitude on the sloping watch-box with strapped cushions.

"Oh, no, you don't," she said, "no one drives me and my horse but me or my coachman when I'm about. Not even you, dear boy."

"I'll come with you, then," Tietjens said.

"Oh, no, you don't," she answered. "No one's neck's to be broken in this conveyance but mine and Joel's," she added: "perhaps to-night if I'm satisfied the horse is fit to drive."

Miss Wannop suddenly exclaimed:

"Oh, *no*, mother." But the handy-man having climbed in, Mrs. Wannop flirted her whip and started the horse. She pulled up at once and leaned over to Tietjens:

"*What* a life for that poor woman," she said. "We must *all* do all we can for her. She could have her husband put in a lunatic asylum to-morrow. It's sheer self-sacrifice that she doesn't."

The horse went off at a gentle, regular trot.

Tietjens addressed Miss Wannop:

"What hands your mother's got," he said; "it isn't often one sees a woman with hands like that on a horse's mouth. . . . Did you see how she pulled up? . . ."

He was aware that, all this while, from the roadside, the girl had been watching him with shining eyes: intently even: with fascination.

"I suppose you think that a mighty fine performance," she said.

"I didn't make a very good job of the girth," he said. "Let's get off this road."

"Setting poor, weak women in their places," Miss Wannop continued. "Soothing the horse like a man with a charm. I suppose you soothe women like that too. I pity your wife. . . . The English country male! And making a devoted vassal at sight of the handy-man. The feudal system all complete . . ."

Tietjens said:

"Well, you know, it'll make him all the better servant to you if he thinks you've friends in the know. The lower classes are like that. Let's get off this road."

She said:

"You're in a mighty hurry to get behind the hedge. Are the police after us or aren't they? Perhaps you were lying at breakfast: to calm the hysterical nerves of a weak woman."

"I wasn't lying," he said, "but I hate roads when there are field-paths . . ."

"That's a phobia, like any woman's," she exclaimed.

She almost ran through the kissing-gate and stood awaiting him:

"I suppose," she said, "if you've stopped off the police with your high and mighty male ways you think you've destroyed my romantic young dream. You haven't. I don't *want* the police after me. I believe I'd *die* if they put me in Wandsworth. . . . I'm a coward."

"Oh, no, you aren't," he said, but he was following his own train of thought, just as she wasn't in the least listening to him. "I dare say you're a heroine all right. *Not* because you persevere in actions the consequences of which you fear. But I dare say you can touch pitch and not be defiled."

Being too well brought up to interrupt, she waited till he had said all he wanted to say, then she exclaimed:

"Let's settle the preliminaries. It's obvious mother means us to see a great deal of you. *You're* going to be a mascot too, like your father. I suppose you think you are: you saved me from the police yesterday, you appear to have saved mother's neck to-day. You appear, too, to be going to make twenty pounds' profit on a horse deal. You say you will and you seem to be that sort of a person. . . . Twenty pounds is no end in a family like ours. . . . Well, then, you appear to be going to be the regular *bel ami* of the Wannop family. . . ."

Tietjens said:

"I hope not."

"Oh, I don't mean," she said, "that you're going to rise to fame by making love to all the women of the Wannop family. Besides, there's only me. But mother will press you into all sorts of odd jobs: and there will always be a plate for you at the table. Don't shudder! I'm a regular good cook —*cuisine bourgeoise*, of course. I learned under a real professed cook, though a drunkard. That meant I used to do half the cooking, and the family was particular. Ealing people are: county councillors, half of them, and the like. So I know what men are. . . ." She stopped and said good-naturedly: "But do, for goodness' sake, get it over. I'm sorry I was rude to you. But it *is* irritating to have to stand like a stuffed rabbit while a man is acting like a regular Admirable Crichton, and cool and collected, with the English country gentleman air and all."

Tietjens winced. The young woman had come a little too near the knuckle of his wife's frequent denunciations of himself. And she exclaimed:

"No! That's not fair! I'm an ungrateful pig! You didn't show a bit more side really than a capable workman must who's doing his job in the midst of a crowd of incapable duffers. But just get it out, will you? Say once and for all that—you know the proper, pompous manner: you are not without sympathy with our aims: but you disapprove—oh, immensely, strongly—of our methods."

It struck Tietjens that the young woman was a good deal more interested in the cause—of votes for women—than he had given her credit for. He wasn't much in the mood for talking to young women, but it was with considerably more than the surface of his mind that he answered:

"I don't. I approve entirely of your methods: but your aims are idiotic."

She said:

"You don't know, I suppose, that Gertie Wilson, who's in bed at our house, is wanted by the police: not only for yesterday, but for putting explosives in a whole series of letter-boxes?"

He said:

"I didn't . . . but it was a perfectly proper thing to do. She hasn't burned any of my letters or I might be annoyed: but it wouldn't interfere with my approval."

"You don't think," she asked earnestly, "that we . . . mother and I . . . are likely to get heavy sentences for shielding her. It would be beastly bad luck on mother. Because she's an anti . . ."

"I don't know about the sentence," Tietjens said, "but we'd better get the girl off your premises as soon as we can. . . ."

She said:

"Oh, you'll *help*?"

He answered:

"Of course, your mother can't be incommoded. She's writ-

ten the only novel that's been fit to read since the eighteenth
century."

She stopped and said earnestly:

"Look here. *Don't* be one of those ignoble triflers who say
the vote won't do women any good. Women have a rotten
time. They do, really. If you'd seen what I've seen, I'm not
talking through my hat." Her voice became quite deep:
she had tears in her eyes: "*Poor* women *do!*" she said, "little
insignificant creatures. We've *got* to change the divorce laws.
We've *got* to get better conditions. *You* couldn't stand it if
you knew what I know."

Her emotion vexed him, for it seemed to establish a sort of
fraternal intimacy that he didn't at the moment want. Women
do not show emotion except before their familiars. He said
dryly:

"I dare say I shouldn't. But I don't know, so I can!"

She said with deep disappointment:

"Oh, you *are* a beast! And I shall never beg your pardon
for saying that. I don't believe you mean what you say, but
merely to say it is heartless."

This was another of the counts of Sylvia's indictment, and
Tietjens winced again. She explained:

"You don't know the case of the Pimlico army-clothing
factory workers or you wouldn't say the vote would be no
use to women."

"I know the case perfectly well," Tietjens said: "It came
under my official notice, and I remember thinking that there
never was a more signal instance of the uselessness of the
vote to anyone."

"We can't be thinking of the same case," she said.

"We are," he answered. "The Pimlico army-clothing factory is in the constituency of Westminster; the Under-secretary for War is member for Westminster; his majority at
the last election was six hundred. The clothing factory employed seven hundred men at one shilling sixpence an hour,
all these men having votes in Westminster. The seven hundred men wrote to the Under-secretary to say that if their
screw wasn't raised to two bob, they'd vote solid against
him at the next election. . . ."

Miss Wannop said: "Well, then!"

"So," Tietjens said: "The Under-secretary had the seven
hundred men at eighteen pence fired and took on seven hundred women at tenpence. What good did the vote do the
seven hundred men? What good did a vote ever do anyone?"

Miss Wannop checked at that, and Tietjens prevented her exposure of his fallacy by saying quickly:

"Now, if the seven hundred women, backed by all the other ill-used, sweated women of the country, had threatened the Under-secretary, burned the pillar-boxes, and cut up all the golf greens round his country-house, they'd have had their wages raised to half a crown next week. That's the only straight method. It's the feudal system at work."

"Oh, but we couldn't cut up *golf* greens," Miss Wannop said. "At least the W.S.P.U. debated it the other day, and decided that anything so unsporting would make us *too* unpopular. I was for it, personally."

Tietjens groaned:

"It's maddening," he said, "to find women, as soon as they get in council, as muddle-headed and as afraid to face straight issues as men! . . ."

"You won't, by the by," the girl interrupted, "be able to sell our horse to-morrow. You've forgotten that it will be Sunday."

"I shall have to on Monday, then," Tietjens said. "The point about the feudal system . . ."

Just after lunch—and it was an admirable lunch of the cold lamb, new potatoes and mint-sauce variety, the mint-sauce made with white-wine vinegar and as soft as kisses, the claret perfectly drinkable and the port much more than that, Mrs. Wannop having gone back to the late professor's wine merchants—Miss Wannop herself went to answer the telephone. . . .

The cottage had no doubt been a cheap one, for it was old, roomy and comfortable; but effort had no doubt, too, been lavished on its low rooms. The dining-room had windows on each side and a beam across; the dining-silver had been picked up at sales, the tumblers were old cut glass; on each side of the ingle was a grandfather's chair. The garden had red brick paths, sunflowers, hollyhocks and scarlet gladioli. There was nothing to it all, but the garden-gate was well hung.

To Tietjens all this meant effort. Here was a woman who, a few years ago, was penniless, in the most miserable of circumstances, supporting life with the most exiguous of all implements. What effort hadn't it meant! And what effort didn't it mean? There was a boy at Eton . . . a senseless, but a gallant, effort.

Mrs. Wannop sat opposite him in the other grandfather's chair, an admirable hostess, an admirable lady. Full of

spirit in dashes, but tired. As an old horse is tired that, taking
three men to harness it in the stable-yard, starts out like a
stallion, but soon drops to a jog-trot. The face tired, really;
scarlet-cheeked with the good air, but seamed downward.
She could sit there at ease, the plump hands covered with a
black lace shawl, and descending on each side of her lap, as
much at ease as any other Victorian great lady. But at lunch
she had let drop that she had written for eight hours every
day for the last four years—till that day—without missing a
day. To-day being Saturday, she had no leader to write:

"And, my darling boy," she had said to him, "I'm giving it
to you. I'd give it to no other soul but your father's son.
Not even to . . ." And she had named the name that she most
respected. "And that's the truth," she had added. Nevertheless, even over lunch, she had fallen into abstractions, heavily
and deeply, and made fantastic mis-statements, mostly
about public affairs. . . . It all meant a tremendous record. . . .

And there he sat, his coffee and port on a little table beside him, the house belonging to him. . . .

She said:

"My dearest boy . . . you've so much to do. Do you think
you ought really to drive the girls to Plimsoll to-night?
They're young and inconsiderate; work comes first."

Tietjens said:

"It isn't the distance. . . ."

"You'll find that it is," she answered humorously. "It's
twenty miles beyond Tenterden. If you don't start till ten,
when the moon sets, you won't be back till five, even if you've
no accidents. . . . The horse is all right, though. . . ."

Tietjens said:

"Mrs. Wannop, I ought to tell you that your daughter and
I are being talked about. Uglily!"

She turned her head to him, rather stiffly. But she was
only coming out of an abstraction.

"Eh?" she said, and then: "Oh! About the golf-links epi-
sode . . . It must have looked suspicious. I dare say you
made a fuss, too, with the police, to head them off her."
She remained pondering for a moment, heavily, like an old
pope:

"Oh, you'll live it down," she said.

"I ought to tell you," he persisted, "that it's more serious
than you think. I fancy I ought not to be here."

"Not here!" she exclaimed. "Why, where else in the
world should you be? You don't get on with your wife; I

know. She's a regular wrong 'un. Who else could look after you as well as Valentine and I."

In the acuteness of that pang, for, after all, Tietjens cared more for his wife's reputation than for any other factor in a complicated world, Tietjens asked rather sharply why Mrs. Wannop had called Sylvia a wrong 'un. She said in rather a protesting, sleepy way:

"My dear boy, nothing! I've guessed that there are differences between you; give me credit for some perception. Then, as you're perfectly obviously a right 'un, she must be a wrong 'un. That's all, I assure you."

In his relief Tietjens' obstinacy revived. He liked this house; he liked this atmosphere; he liked the frugality, the choice of furniture, the way the light fell from window to window; the weariness after hard work; the affection of mother and daughter; the affection, indeed, that they both had for himself, and he was determined, if he could help it, not to damage the reputation of the daughter of the house.

Decent men, he held, don't do such things, and he recounted with some care the heads of the conversation he had had with General Campion in the dressing-room. He seemed to see the cracked wash-bowls in their scrubbed oak settings. Mrs. Wannop's face seemed to grow greyer, more aquiline, a little resentful! She nodded from time to time, either to denote attention or else in sheer drowsiness:

"My dear boy," she said at last, "it's pretty damnable to have such things said about you. I can see that. But I seem to have lived in a bath of scandal all my life. Every woman who has reached my age has that feeling. . . . Now it doesn't seem to matter. . . ." She really nodded nearly off: then she started. "I don't see . . . I really don't see how I can help you as to your reputation. I'd do it if I could: believe me. . . . But I've other things to think of. . . . I've this house to keep going and the children to keep fed and at school. I can't give all the thought I ought to to other people's troubles. . . ."

She started into wakefulness and right out of her chair.

"But what a beast I am!" she said, with a sudden intonation that was exactly that of her daughter; and drifting with a Victorian majesty of shawl and long skirt behind Tietjens' high-backed chair, she leaned over it and stroked the hair on his right temple:

"My dear boy," she said. "Life's a bitter thing. I'm an old novelist and know it. There you are, working yourself to death to save the nation with a wilderness of cats and monkeys howling and squalling your personal reputation away.

... It was Dizzy himself said these words to me at one of our receptions. 'Here I am, Mrs. Wannop,' he said. And . . ." She drifted for a moment. But she made another effort: "My dear boy," she whispered, bending down her head to get it near his ear: "My dear boy, it doesn't matter; it doesn't really matter. You'll live it down. The only thing that matters is to do good work. Believe an old woman that has lived very hard; 'Hard lying money,' as they call it in the navy. It sounds like cant, but it's the only real truth. . . . You'll find consolation in that. And you'll live it all down. Or perhaps you won't; that's for God in His mercy to settle. But it won't matter; believe me, as thy day so shall thy strength be." She drifted into other thoughts; she was much perturbed over the plot of a new novel and much wanted to get back to the consideration of it. She stood gazing at the photograph, very faded, of her husband in side-whiskers and an immense shirt front, but she continued to stroke Tietjens' temple with a subliminal tenderness.

This kept Tietjens sitting there. He was quite aware that he had tears in his eyes; this was almost too much tenderness to bear, and at bottom his was a perfectly direct, simple and sentimental soul. He always had bedewed eyes at the theatre after tender love-scenes, and so avoided the theatre. He asked himself twice whether he should or shouldn't make another effort, though it was almost beyond him. He wanted to sit still.

The stroking stopped; he scrambled on to his feet:

"Mrs. Wannop," he said, facing her, "it's perfectly true. I oughtn't to care what these swine say about me, but I do. I'll reflect about what you say till I get it into my system. . . ."

She said:

"Yes, yes! My dear," and continued to gaze at the photograph.

"But," Tietjens said; he took her mittened hand and led her back to her chair: "what I'm concerned for at the moment is not my reputation, but your daughter Valentine's."

She sank down into the high chair, balloon-like, and came to rest.

"Val's reputation!" she said. "Oh! you mean they'll be striking her off their visit-lists. It hadn't struck me. So they will!" She remained lost in reflection for a long time.

Valentine was in the room, laughing a little. She had been giving the handy-man his dinner, and was still amused at his commendations of Tietjens.

"You've got one admirer," she said to Tietjens. " 'Punched

that rotten strap,' he goes on saying, 'like a gret ol' yaffle punchin' a 'ollow log!' He's had a pint of beer and said it between each gasp." She continued to narrate the quaintnesses of Joel, which appealed to her; informed Tietjens that "yaffle" was Kentish for great green woodpecker; and then said:

"You haven't got any friends in Germany, have you?" She was beginning to clear the table.

Tietjens said:

"Yes, my wife's in Germany; at a place called Lobscheid."

She placed a pile of plates on a black japanned tray.

"I'm so sorry," she said, without an expression of any deep regret. "It's the ingenious, clever stupidities of the telephone. I've got a telegraph message for you, then. I thought it was the subject for mother's leader. It always comes through with the initials of the paper, which are not unlike Tietjens, and the girl who always sends it is called Hopside. It seemed rather inscrutable, but I took it to have to do with German politics, and I thought mother would understand it. . . . You're not both asleep, are you?"

Tietjens opened his eyes; the girl was standing over him, having approached from the table. She was holding out a slip of paper on which she had transcribed the message. She appeared all out of drawing and the letters of the message ran together. The message was:

"Righto. But arrange for certain Hullo Central travels with you. Sylvia Hopside Germany."

Tietjens leaned back for a long time looking at the words; they seemed meaningless. The girl placed the paper on his knee and went back to the table. He imagined the girl wrestling with these incomprehensibilities on the telephone.

"Of course if I'd had any sense," the girl said, "I should have known it couldn't have been mother's leader note; she never gets one on a Saturday."

Tietjens heard himself announce clearly, loudly and with between each word a pause:

"It means I go to my wife on Tuesday and take her maid with me."

"Lucky you!" the girl said. "I wish I was you. I've never been in the Fatherland of Goethe and Rosa Luxemburg." She went off with her great tray load, the table-cloth over her forearm. He was dimly aware that she had before then removed the crumbs with a crumb-brush. It was extraordinary with what swiftness she worked, talking all the time. That was what domestic service had done for her; an ordinary

young lady would have taken twice the time and would certainly have dropped half her words if she had tried to talk.
Efficiency! He had only just realized that he was going back
to Sylvia and, of course, to Hell! Certainly it was Hell. If a
malignant and skilful devil . . . though the devil, of course, is
stupid and uses toys like fire-works and sulphur; it is probably only God who can, very properly, devise the long ail-
ings of mental oppressions . . . if God, then, desired (and
one couldn't object, but one hoped He would not!) to devise
for him, Christopher Tietjens, a cavernous eternity of weary
hopelessness . . . But He had done it, no doubt as retribution.
What for? Who knows what sins of his own are heavily
punishable in the eyes of God, for God is just? . . . Perhaps
God, then, after all, visits thus heavily sexual offences.

There came back into his mind, burnt in, the image of
their breakfast-room, with all the brass electrical fixings,
poachers, toasters, grillers, kettle-heaters, that he detested
for their imbecile inefficiency; with gross piles of hot-house
flowers—that he detested for their exotic waxennesses!—with
white enamelled panels that he disliked, and framed, weak
prints—quite genuine, of course, my dear, guaranteed so by
Sotheby—pinkish women in sham Gainsborough hats, selling
mackerel or brooms. A wedding-present that he despised. And
Mrs. Satterthwaite, in négligé, but with an immense hat,
reading the *Times* with an eternal rustle of leaves because
she never could settle down to any one page; and Sylvia
walking up and down because she could not sit still, with a
piece of toast in her fingers or her hands behind her back.
Very tall, fair, as graceful, as full of blood and as cruel as
the usual degenerate Derby winner. Inbred for generations
for one purpose: to madden men of one type. . . . Pacing
backwards and forwards, exclaiming: "I'm bored! Bored!";
sometimes even breaking the breakfast-plates . . . And talking!
Forever talking; usually, cleverly, with imbecility; with maddening inaccuracy; with wicked penetration, and clamouring
to be contradicted; a gentleman has to answer his wife's
questions. . . . And in his forehead the continual pressure;
the determination to sit put; the *décor* of the room seeming
to burn into his mind. It was there, shadowy before him now.
And the pressure upon his forehead . . .

Mrs. Wannop was talking to him now; he did not know
what she said; he never knew afterwards what he had answered.

"God!" he said within himself, "if it's sexual sins God
punishes, He indeed is just and inscrutable!" . . . Because he

had had physical contact with this woman before he marrie
her, in a railway carriage, coming down from the Dukeries.
An extravagantly beautiful girl!

Where was the physical attraction of her gone to now?
Irresistible, reclining back as the shires rushed past . . . His
mind said that she had lured him on. His intellect put the
idea from him. No gentleman thinks such things of his wife.

No gentleman thinks . . . By God, she must have been
with child by another man. . . . He had been fighting the conviction down all the last four months. . . . He knew now that
he had been fighting the conviction all the last four months
whilst, anaesthetised, he had bathed in figures and wave-
theories. . . . Her last words had been: her very last words:
late: all in white she had gone up to her dressing-room, and
he had never seen her again; her last words had been about
the child. . . . "Supposing," she had begun. . . . He didn't remember the rest. But he remembered her eyes. And her gesture as she peeled off her long white gloves . . .

He was looking at Mrs. Wannop's ingle; he thought it a
mistake in taste, really, to leave logs in an ingle during the
summer. But then what are you to do with an ingle in
summer. In Yorkshire cottages they shut the ingles up
with painted doors. But that is stuffy, too!

He said to himself:

"By God! I've had a stroke!" and he got out of his chair
to test his legs. . . . But he hadn't had a stroke. It must, then,
he thought, be that the pain of his last consideration must
be too great for his mind to register, as certain great
physical pains go unperceived. Nerves, like weighing ma-
chines, can't register more than a certain amount, then they
go out of action. A tramp who had had his leg cut off by a
train had told him that he had tried to get up, feeling nothing
at all. . . . The pain comes back, though. . . .

He said to Mrs. Wannop, who was still talking:

"I beg your pardon. I really missed what you said."

Mrs. Wannop said:

"I was saying that that's the best thing I can do for you."

He said:

"I'm really very sorry; it was that that I missed. I'm a little in trouble, you know."

She said:

"I know: I know. The mind wanders, but I wish you'd listen. I've got to go to work, so have you. I said: after tea
you and Valentine will walk into Rye to fetch your luggage."

Straining his intelligence, for in his mind he felt a sudden strong pleasure: sunlight on pyramidal red roof in the distance: themselves descending in a long diagonal, a green hill: God, yes, he wanted open air. Tietjens said:

"I see. You take us both under your protection. You'll bluff it out."

Mrs. Wannop said rather coolly:

"I don't know about you both. It's you I'm taking under my protection (it's *your* phrase!). As for Valentine: she's made her bed; she must lie on it. I've told you all that already. I can't go over it again."

She paused, then made another effort:

"It's disagreeable," she said, "to be cut off the Mountby visiting-list. They give amusing parties. But I'm too old to care, and they'll miss my conversation more than I do theirs. Of course I back my daughter against the cats and monkeys. Of course I back Valentine through thick and thin. I'd back her if she lived with a married man or had illegitimate children. But I don't approve, I don't approve of the suffra- gettes: I despise their aims: I detest their methods. I don't think young girls ought to talk to strange men. Valentine spoke to you, and look at the worry it has caused you. I disapprove. I'm a woman: but I've made my own way: other women could do it if they liked or had the energy. I dis- approve! But don't believe that I will ever go back on any suffragette, individual, in gangs, my Valentine or any other. Don't believe that I will ever say a word against them that's to be repeated—*you* won't repeat them. Or that I will ever write a word against them. No, I'm a woman and I stand by my sex!"

She got up energetically:

"I must go and write my novel," she said. "I've Monday's instalment to send off by train to-night. You'll go into my study: Valentine will give you paper, ink, twelve differ- ent kinds of nibs. You'll find Professor Wannop's books all round the room. You'll have to put up with Valentine typing in the alcove. I've got two serials running, one typed, the other in manuscript."

Tietjens said:

"But *you!*"

"I," she exclaimed, "I shall write in my bedroom on my knee. I'm a woman and can. You're a man and have to have a padded chair and sanctuary. . . . You feel fit to work? Then: you've got till five; Valentine will get tea then. At half-past five you'll set off to Rye. You'll be back with your luggage and your friend and your friend's luggage at seven."

She silenced him imperiously with:

"Don't be foolish. Your friend will certainly prefer this house and Valentine's cooking to the pub and the pub's cooking. And he'll save on it. . . . It's *no* extra trouble. I suppose your friend won't inform against that wretched little suffragette girl upstairs." She paused and said: "You're *sure* you can do your work in the time and drive Valentine and her to that place. . . . Why it's necessary is that the girl daren't travel by train, and we've relations there who've never been connected with the suffragettes. The girl can live hid there for a bit. . . . But sooner than you shouldn't finish your work I'd drive them myself. . . ."

She silenced Tietjens again: this time sharply:

"I tell you it's *no* extra trouble. Valentine and I *always* make our own beds. We don't like servants among our intimate things. We can get three times as much help in the neighbourhood as we want. We're liked here. The extra work you give will be met by extra help. We could have servants if we wanted. But Valentine and I like to be alone in the house together at night. We're very fond of each other."

She walked to the door and then drifted back to say:

"You know I can't get out of my head that unfortunate woman and her husband. We must *all* do what we can for them." Then she started and exclaimed: "But, good heavens, I'm keeping you from your work. . . . The study's in there, through that door."

She hurried through the other doorway and no doubt along a passage, calling out:

"Valentine! Valentine! Go to Christopher in the study. At once . . . at . . ." Her voice died away.

7 ~

JUMPING DOWN from the high step of the dog-cart, the girl completely disappeared into the silver: she had on an otter-skin toque, dark, that should have been visible. But she was gone more completely than if she had dropped into deep water, into snow—or through tissue-paper. More suddenly, at least! In darkness or in deep water a moving paleness would have been visible for a second: snow or a paper hoop would have left an opening. Here there had been nothing.

The constatation interested him. He had been watching her intently and with concern, for fear she should miss the hidden lower step, in which case she would certainly bark her shins. But she had jumped clear of the cart: with unreasonable pluckiness, in spite of his: "Look out how you get down." He wouldn't have done it himself: he couldn't have faced jumping down into that white solidity. . . .

He would have asked: "Are you all right?" but to express more concern than the "Look out," which he had expended already, would have detracted from his stolidity. He was Yorkshire and stolid: she South Country and soft: emotional: given to such ejaculations as, "I hope you're not hurt," when the Yorkshireman only grunts. But soft because she was South Country. She was as good as a man—a South Country man. She was ready to acknowledge the superior woodenness of the North. . . . That was their convention: so he did not call down: "I hope you're all right," though he had desired to.

Her voice came, muffled, as if from the back of the top of his head: the ventriloquial effect was startling:

"Make a noise from time to time. It's ghostly down here and the lamp's no good at all. It's almost out."

He returned to his constatation of the concealing effect of water-vapour. He enjoyed the thought of the grotesque appearance he must present in that imbecile landscape. On his right an immense, improbably brilliant horn of a moon, sending a trail as if down the sea, straight to his neck: beside the moon a grotesquely huge star: in an extravagant position above them the Plough, the only constellation that he knew; for, though a mathematician, he despised astronomy. It was not theoretical enough for the pure mathematician and not sufficiently practical for daily life. He had, of course, calculated the movements of abstruse heavenly bodies: but only from given figures: he had never looked for the stars of his calculations. . . . Above his head and all over the sky were other stars: large and weeping with light or, as the dawn increased, so paling that at times you saw them, then missed them. Then the eye picked them up again.

Opposite the moon was a smirch or two of cloud; pink below, dark purple above; on the more pallid, lower blue of the limpid sky.

But the absurd thing was this mist! . . . It appeared to spread from his neck, absolutely level, absolutely silver, to infinity on each side of him. At great distances on his right black tree-shapes, in groups—there were four of them—were exactly like coral islands on a silver sea. He couldn't escape the idiotic comparison: there wasn't any other.

Yet it didn't actually spread from his neck: when he now held his hands, nipple-high, like pallid fish they held black reins which ran downwards into nothingness. If he jerked the rein, the horse threw its head up. Two pricked ears were visible in greyness: the horse being sixteen two and a bit over, the mist might be ten foot high. Thereabouts . . . He wished the girl would come back and jump out of the cart again. Being ready for it, he would watch her disappearance more scientifically. He couldn't, of course, ask her to do it again: that was irritating. The phenomenon would have proved—or it might, of course, disprove—his idea of smoke-screens. The Chinese of the Ming dynasty were said to have approached and overwhelmed their enemies under clouds of—of course, not acrid—vapour. He had read that the Patagonians, hidden by smoke, were accustomed to approach so near to birds or beasts as to be able to take them by hand. The Greeks under Paleologus the . . .

Miss Wannop's voice said—from beneath the bottom board of the cart:

"I wish you'd make some noise. It's lonely down here, besides being possibly dangerous. There might be dicks on each side of the road."

If they were on the marsh there certainly would be dikes —why did they call ditches "dikes," and why did she pronounce it "dicks"?—on each side of the road. He could think of nothing to say that wouldn't express concern and he couldn't do that by the rules of the game. He tried to whistle "John Peel"! But he was no hand at whistling. He sang:

"D'ye ken, John Peel, at the break of day . . ." and felt like a fool. But he kept on at it, the only tune that he knew. It was the Yorkshire Light Infantry quick step: the regiment of his brothers in India. He wished he had been in the army: but his father hadn't approved of having more than two younger sons in the army. He wondered if he would ever run with John Peel's hounds again: he had once or twice. Or with any of the trencher-fed foot packs of the Cleveland district, of which there had been still several when he had been a boy. He had been used to think of himself as being like John Peel with his coat so grey . . . Up through the heather, over Wharton's place; the pack running wild; the heather dripping; the mist rolling up . . . another kind of mist than this South Country silver sheet. Silly stuff! Magical! That was the word. A silly word. . . . South Country . . . In the North the old grey mists rolled together, revealing black hill-sides!

He didn't suppose he'd have the wind now: this rotten

bureaucratic life! . . . If he had been in the army like the two brothers, Ernest and James, next above him . . . But no doubt he would not have liked the army. Discipline! . . . He supposed he would have put up with the discipline: a gentleman had to. Because *noblesse oblige*: not for fear of consequences . . . But army officers seemed to him pathetic. They spluttered and roared: to make men jump smartly: at the end of apoplectic efforts the men jumped smartly. But there was the end of it. . . .

Actually, this mist was not silver or was, perhaps, no longer silver: if you looked at it with the eye of the artist . . . With the exact eye! It was smirched with bars of purple; of red; of orange: delicate reflections: dark blue shadows from the upper sky, where it formed drifts like snow. . . . The exact eye: exact observation: it was a man's work. The only work for a man. Why, then, were artists soft: effeminate: not men at all: whilst the army officer, who had the inexact mind of the schoolteacher, was a manly man? Quite a manly man: until he became an old woman!

And the bureaucrat, then? Growing fat and soft like himself or dry and stringy like Macmaster or old Ingleby? They did men's work: exact observation: return No. 17642 with figures exact. Yet they grew hysterical: they ran about corridors or frantically rang table-bells, asking with high voices of querulous eunuchs why Form ninety thousand and two wasn't ready. Nevertheless men liked the bureaucratic life: his own brother, Mark, head of the family: heir to Groby. . . . Fifteen years older: a quiet stick: wooden: brown: always in a bowler hat, as often as not with his racing-glasses hung around him. Attending his first-class office when he liked: too good a man for any administration to lose by putting on the screw . . . But heir to Groby: what would that stick make of the place? . . . Let it, no doubt, and go on pottering from the Albany to race-meetings—where he never betted—to Whitehall, where he was said to be indispensable. . . . Why indispensable? Why, in heaven's name? That stick who had never hunted, never shot: couldn't tell coulter from plough-handle and lived in his bowler hat! . . . A "sound" man: the archetype of all sound men. Never in his life had anyone shaken his head at Mark and said:

"You're *brilliant!*" Brilliant! That stick! No, he was indispensable!

"Upon my soul!" Tietjens said to himself, "that girl down there is the only intelligent living soul I've met for years. . . ." A little pronounced in manner sometimes; faulty in reasoning naturally, but quite intelligent, with a touch of wrong accent now and then. But if she was wanted anywhere, there she'd be! Of good stock, of course: on both sides! . . . But, positively, she and Sylvia were the only two human beings he had met for years whom he could respect: the one for sheer efficiency in killing: the other for having the constructive desire and knowing how to set about it. Kill or cure! The two functions of man. If you wanted something killed you'd go to Sylvia Tietjens in the sure faith that she would kill it: emotion: hope: ideal: kill it quick and sure. If you wanted something kept alive you'd go to Valentine: she'd find something to do for it. . . . The two types of mind: remorseless enemy: sure screen: dagger . . . sheath!

Perhaps the future of the world, then, was to women? Why not? He hadn't in years met a man that he hadn't to talk down to—as you talk down to a child: as he had talked down to General Campion or to Mr. Waterhouse . . . as he always talked down to Macmaster. All good fellows in their way . . .

But why was he born to be a sort of lonely buffalo: outside the herd? Not artist: not soldier: not bureaucrat: not certainly indispensable anywhere: apparently not even sound in the eyes of these dim-minded specialists . . . An exact observer . . .

Hardly even that for the last six and a half hours:

> *"Die Sommer Nacht hat mir's angethan.*
> *Das war ein schwiegsame Reiten . . ."*

he said aloud.

How could you translate that: you couldn't translate it: no one could translate Heine:

> "It was the summer night came over me:
> That was silent riding . . ."

A voice cut into his warm, drowsy thought:

"Oh, you *do* exist. But you've spoken too late. I've run into the horse." He must have been speaking aloud. He had felt the horse quivering at the end of the reins. The horse, too, was used to her by now. It had hardly stirred. . . . He wondered when he had left off singing "John Peel. . . ." He said:

"Come along, then: have you found anything?"

The answer came:

"Something . . . But you can't talk in this stuff . . . I'll just . . ."

The voice died away as if a door had shut. He waited: consciously waiting: as an occupation! Contritely and to make a noise he rattled the whip-stock in its bucket. The horse started and he had to check in quickly: a damn fool he was. Of course a horse would start if you rattled a whip-stock. He called out:

"Are you all right?" The cart might have knocked her down. He had, however, broken the convention. Her voice came from a great distance:

"I'm all right. Trying the other side . . ."

His last thought came back to him. He had broken their convention: he had exhibited concern: like any other man. . . . He said to himself:

"By God! Why not take a holiday: why not break all conventions?"

They erected themselves intangibly and irrefragably. He had not known this young woman twenty-four hours: not to speak to: and already the convention existed between them that he must play stiff and cold, she warm and clinging. . . . Yet she was obviously as cool a hand as himself: cooler, no doubt, for at bottom he was certainly a sentimentalist.

A convention of the most imbecile type . . . Then break all conventions: with the young woman: with himself above all. For forty-eight hours . . . almost exactly forty-eight hours till he started for Dover . . .

"And I must to the greenwood go,
    Alone: a banished man!"

By the descending moon: it being then just after cock-crow of midsummer night—what sentimentality!—it must be half-past four on Sunday. He had worked out that to catch the morning Ostend boat at Dover he must leave the Wannops' at 5:15 on Tuesday morning, in a motor for the junction. . . . What incredible cross-country train connexions! Five hours for not forty miles.

He had, then, forty-eight and three-quarter hours! Let them be a holiday! A holiday from himself above all: a holiday from his standards: from his convention with himself. From clear observation: from exact thought: from knocking over all the skittles of the exactitudes of others: from the suppression of emotions . . . From all the

wearinesses that made him intolerable to himself . . . He
felt his limbs lengthen, as if they too had relaxed.

Well, already he had had six and a half hours of it.
They had started at 10 and, like any other man, he had
enjoyed the drive, though it had been difficult to keep the
beastly cart balanced, the girl had had to sit behind with
her arm round the other girl, who screamed at every oak
tree. . . .

But he had—if he put himself to the question—mooned
along under the absurd moon that had accompanied them
down the heaven: to the scent of hay: to the sound of
nightingales, hoarse by now, of course—in June he changes
his tune; of corn-crakes, of bats, of a heron twice, overhead. They had passed the blue-black shadows of corn-
stacks, of heavy, rounded oaks, of hop-oasts that are half
church-tower, half finger-post. And the road silver-grey, and
the night warm . . . It was midsummer night that had done
that to him. . . .

Hat mir's angethan.
Das war ein schwiegsame Reiten. . . .

Not absolutely silent, of course: but silentish! Coming
back from the parson's, where they had dropped the little
London sewer-rat, they had talked very little. . . . Not unpleasant people, the parson's: an uncle of the girl's: three
girl cousins, not unpleasant, like the girl but without the
individuality . . . A remarkably good bite of beef: a truly
meritorious Stilton and a drop of whisky that proved the
parson to be a man. All in candlelight. A motherly mother
of the family to take the rat up some stairs . . . a great
deal of laughter of girls . . . then a restart an hour later
than had been scheduled . . . Well, it hadn't mattered: they
had the whole of eternity before them: the good horse—
really it was a good horse!—putting its shoulders into the
work. . . .

They had talked a little at first; about the safeness of the
London girl from the police now; about the brickishness
of the parson in taking her in. She certainly would never
have reached Charing Cross by train. . . .

There had fallen long periods of silences. A bat had
whirled very near their off lamp.

"What a large bat!" she had said. *"Noctilux major. . ."*
He said:

"Where do you get your absurd Latin nomenclature from?
Isn't it *phalaena* . . ." She had answered:

"From White . . . The *Natural History of Selborne* is the only natural history I ever read. . . ."

"He's the last English writer that could write," said Tietjens.

"He calls the downs 'those majestic and amusing mountains,'" she said. "Where do you get your dreadful Latin pronunciation from? Phal . . . i . . . i . . . na! To rhyme with Dinah!"

"It's '*sublime* and amusing mountains,' not 'majestic and amusing,'" Tietjens said. "I got my Latin pronunciation, like all public schoolboys of to-day, from the German."

She answered:

"You would! Father used to say it made him sick."

"Caesar equals Kaiser," Tietjens said.

"Bother your Germans," she said; "they're no ethnologists; they're rotten at philology!" She added: "Father used to say so," to take away from an appearance of pedantry.

A silence then! She had right over her head a rug that her aunt had lent her; a silhouette beside him, with a cocky nose turned up straight out of the descending black mass. But for the square toque she would have had the silhouette of a Manchester cotton-hand: the toque gave it a different line; like the fillet of Diana. It was piquant and agreeable to ride beside a quite silent lady in the darkness of the thick Weald that let next to no moonlight through. The horse's hoofs went clock, clock: a good horse. The near lamp illuminated the russet figure of a man with a sack on his back, pressed into the hedge, a blinking lurcher beside him.

"Keeper between the blankets!" Tietjens said to himself: "All these South Country keepers sleep all night. . . . And then you give them a five-quid tip for the week-end shoot . . ." He determined that, as to that too, he would put his foot down. No more week-ends with Sylvia in the mansions of the Chosen People . . .

The girl said suddenly—they had run into a clearing of the deep underwoods:

"I'm not stuffy with you over that Latin, though you were unnecessarily rude. And I'm not sleepy. I'm loving it all."

He hesitated for a minute. It was a silly-girl thing to say. She didn't usually say silly-girl things. He ought to snub her for her own sake. . . .

He had said:

"I'm rather loving it too!" She was looking at him; her

nose had disappeared from the silhouette. He hadn't been able to help it; the moon had been just above her head; unknown stars all round her; the night was warm. Besides, a really manly man may condescend at times! He rather owes it to himself. . . .

She said:

"That was nice of you! You might have hinted that the rotten drive was taking you away from your so important work. . . ."

"Oh, I can think as I drive," he said. She said:

"Oh!" and then: "The reason why I'm unconcerned over your rudeness about my Latin is that I know I'm a much better Latinist than you. You can't quote a few lines of Ovid without sprinkling howlers in. . . . It's *vastum*, not *longum*. . . . '*Terra tribus scopulis vastum procurrit* . . .' It's *alto*, not *caelo* . . . '*Uvidus exalto desilientis*. . . .' How could Ovid have written *ex caelo*? The 'c' after the 'x' sets your teeth on edge."

Tietjens said:

"*Excogitabo!*"

"That's purely canine!" she said with contempt.

"Besides," Tietjens said, "*longum* is much better than *vastum*. I hate cant adjectives like 'vast.' . . ."

"It's like your modesty to correct Ovid," she exclaimed. "Yet you say Ovid and Catullus were the only two Roman poets to *be* poets. That's because they *were* sentimental and used adjectives like *vastum*. . . . What's 'Sad tears mixed with kisses' but the sheerest sentimentality!"

"It ought, you know," Tietjens said with soft dangerousness, "to be 'Kisses mingled with sad tears. . . .' '*Tristibus et lacrimis oscula mixta dabis.*' . . ."

"I'm hanged if I ever could," she exclaimed explosively. "A man like you could die in a ditch and I'd never come near. You're desiccated even for a man who has learned his Latin from the Germans."

"Oh, well, I'm a mathematician," Tietjens said. "Classics is not my line!"

"It *isn't*," she answered tartly.

A long time afterwards from her black figure came the words:

"You used 'mingled' instead of 'mixed' to translate *mixta*. I shouldn't think you took English at Cambridge, either! Though they're as rotten at that as at everything else, father used to say."

"Your father was Balliol, of course," Tietjens said with

the snuffy contempt of a scholar of Trinity College, Cambridge. But having lived most of her life amongst Balliol people, she took this as a compliment and an olive-branch.

Some time afterwards Tietjens, observing that her silhouette was still between him and the moon, remarked:

"I don't know if you know that for some minutes we've been running nearly due west. We ought to be going southeast by a bit south. I suppose you *do* know this road. . . ."

"Every inch of it," she said, "I've been on it over and over again on my motor bicycle with mother in the sidecar. The next cross-road is called Grandfather's Wantways. We've got eleven miles and a quarter still to do. The road turns back here because of the old Sussex iron pits; it goes in and out amongst them; hundreds of them. You know the exports of the town of Rye in the eighteenth century were hops, cannon, kettles and chimney backs. The railings round St. Paul's are made of Sussex iron."

"I knew that, of course," Tietjens said: "I come of an iron county myself. . . . Why didn't you let me run the girl over in the side-car? It would have been quicker."

"Because," she said, "three weeks ago I smashed up the side-car on the milestone at Hog's Corner: doing forty."

"It must have been a pretty tidy smash!" Tietjens said. "Your mother wasn't aboard?"

"No," the girl said, "suffragette literature. The side-car was full. It *was* a pretty tidy smash. Hadn't you observed I still limp a little?" . . .

A few minutes later she said:

"I haven't the least notion where we really are. I clean forgot to notice the road. And I don't care. . . . Here's a sign-post, though; pull into it. . . ."

The lamps would not, however, shine on the arms of the post; they were burning dim and showing low. A good deal of fog was in the air. Tietjens gave the reins to the girl and got down. He took out the near light and, going back a yard or two to the sign-post, examined its bewildering ghostlinesses. . . .

The girl gave a little squeak that went to his backbone; the hoofs clattered unusually; the cart went on. Tietjens went after it; it was astonishing; it had completely disappeared. Then he ran into it: ghostly, reddish and befogged. It must have got much thicker suddenly. The fog swirled all round the near lamp as he replaced it in its socket.

"Did you do that on purpose?" he asked the girl. "Or can't you hold a horse?"

"I can't drive a horse," the girl said; "I'm afraid of them. I can't drive a motor bike either. I made that up because I *knew* you'd say you'd rather have taken Gertie over in the side-car than driven with me."

"Then do you mind," Tietjens said, "telling me if you know this road at all?"

"Not a bit!" she answered cheerfully. "I never drove it in my life. I looked it up on the map before we started because I'm sick to death of the road we went by. There's a one-horse bus from Rye to Tenterden, and I've walked from Tenterden to my uncle's over and over again. . . ."

"We shall probably be out all night, then," Tietjens said. "Do you mind? The horse may be tired. . . ."

She said:

"Oh, the poor horse! . . . I *meant* us to be out all night. . . . But the poor horse . . . What a brute I was not to think of it."

"We're thirteen miles from a place called Brede; eleven and a quarter from a place whose name I couldn't read; six and three-quarters from somewhere called something like Uddlemere. . . ." Tietjens said. "This is the road to Uddlemere."

"Oh, that was Grandfather's Wantways, all right," she declared. "I know it well. It's called 'Grandfather's' because an old gentleman used to sit there called Gran'fer Finn. Every Tenterden market day he used to sell fleed cakes from a basket to the carts that went by. Tenterden market was abolished in 1845—the effect of the repeal of the Corn Laws, you know. As a Tory you ought to be interested in that."

Tietjens sat patiently: He could sympathize with her mood; she had now a heavy weight off her chest; and if long acquaintance with his wife had not made him able to put up with feminine vagaries, nothing ever would.

"Would you mind," he said then, "telling me . . ."

"If," she interrupted, "that was really Gran'fer's Wantways: Midland English. 'Vent' equals four cross-roads: high French *carrefour* . . . Or perhaps that isn't the right word. But it's the way your mind works. . . ."

"You have, of course, often walked from your uncle's to Gran'fer's Wantways," Tietjens said, "with your cousins, taking brandy to the invalid in the old toll-gate house. That's how you know the story of Grandfer. You said you had never driven it; but you *have* walked it. That's the way *your* mind works, isn't it?"

She said: *"Oh!"*

"Then," Tietjens went on, "would you mind telling me—for the sake of the poor horse—whether Uddlemere is or isn't on our road home. I take it you don't know just this stretch of road, but you know whether it is the right road."

"The touch of pathos," the girl said, "is a wrong note. It's you who're in mental trouble about the road. The horse isn't. . . ."

Tietjens let the cart go on another fifty yards; then he said:

"It *is* the right road. The Uddlemere turning *was* the right one. You wouldn't let the horse go another five steps if it wasn't. You're as soppy about horses as . . . as I am."

"There's at least that bond of sympathy between us," she said dryly. "Gran'fer's Wantways is six and three-quarters miles from Udimore; Udimore is exactly five from us; total, eleven and three-quarters; twelve and a quarter if you add half a mile for Udimore itself. The name is Udimore, not Uddlemere. Local place-name enthusiasts derive this from 'O'er the mere.' Absurd! Legend as follows: Church-builders desiring to put church with relic of St. Rumwold in wrong place, voice wailed: 'O'er the mere.' Obviously absurd! . . . Putrid! *O'er the* by Grimm's Law impossible as *Udi; mere* not a middle Low German word at all. . . ."

"Why," Tietjens said, "are you giving me all this information?"

"Because," the girl said, "it's the way your mind works. . . . It picks up useless facts as silver after you've polished it picks up sulphur vapour; and tarnishes! It arranges the useless facts in obsolescent patterns and makes Toryism out of them. . . . I've never met a Cambridge Tory man before. I thought they were all in museums and you work them up again out of bones. That's what father used to say; he was an Oxford Disraelian Conservative Imperialist. . . ."

"I know, of course," Tietjens said.

"Of course you know," the girl said. "You know everything. . . . And you've worked everything into absurd principles. You think father was unsound because he tried to apply tendencies to life. *You* want to be an English country gentleman and spin principles out of the newspapers and the gossip of horse-fairs. And let the country go to hell, you'll never stir a finger except to say I told you so."

She touched him suddenly on the arm:

"*Don't* mind me!" she said. "It's reaction. I'm so happy. I'm so happy."

He said:

"That's all right! That's all right!" But for a minute or two it wasn't really. All feminine claws, he said to himself, are sheathed in velvet; but they can hurt a good deal if they touch you on the sore places of the defects of your qualities—even merely with the velvet. He added: "Your mother works you very hard."

She exclaimed:

"How you *understand*. You're amazing: for a man who tries to be a sea-anemone!" She said: "Yes, this is the first holiday I've had for four solid months; six hours a day typing; four hours a day work for the movement; three, house-work and gardening; three, mother reading out her day's work for slips of the pen. . . . And on top of it the raid and the anxiety . . . Dreadful anxiety, you know. Suppose mother *had* gone to prison. . . . Oh, I'd have gone mad. . . . Weekdays and Sundays . . ." She stopped: "I'm apologizing, really," she went on. "Of course I ought not to have talked to you like that. You, a great Panjandrum, saving the country with your statistics and all . . . It *did* make you a rather awful figure, you know . . . and the relief to find you're . . . oh, a man like oneself with feet of clay. . . . I'd dreaded this drive. . . . I'd have dreaded it dreadfully if I hadn't been in such a dread about Gertie and the police. And if I hadn't let off steam I should have had to jump out and run beside the cart. . . . I could still . . ."

"You couldn't," Tietjens said. "You couldn't see the cart."

They had just run into a bank of solid fog that seemed to encounter them with a soft, ubiquitous blow. It was blinding; it was deadening to sounds; it was in a sense mournful; but it was happy, too, in its romantic unusualness. They couldn't see the gleam of the lamps; they could hardly hear the step of the horse; the horse had fallen at once to a walk. They agreed that neither of them could be responsible for losing the way; in the circumstances, that was impossible. Fortunately the horse would take them somewhere; it had belonged to a local higgler: a man that used the roads buying poultry for resale. . . . They agreed that they had no responsibilities, and after that went on for unmeasured hours in silence; the mist growing, but very, very gradually, more luminous. . . . Once or twice, at a rise in the road, they saw again the stars and the moon, but mistily. On the fourth occasion they had emerged into the silver lake; like mermen rising to the surface of a tropical sea. . . .

Tietjens had said:

"You'd better get down and take the lamp. See if you can find a milestone; I'd get down myself, but you might not be able to hold the horse. . . ." She had plunged in. . . .

And he had sat, feeling, he didn't know why, like a Guy Fawkes; up in the light, thinking by no means disagreeable thoughts—intent, like Miss Wannop herself, on a complete holiday of forty-eight hours; till Tuesday morning! He had to look forward to a long and luxurious day of figures; a rest after dinner; half a night more of figures; a Monday devoted to a horse-deal in the market town where he happened to know the horse-dealer. The horse-dealer, indeed, was known to every hunting-man in England! A luxurious, long argument in the atmosphere of stable-hartshorn and slow wranglings couched in ostlers' epigrams. You couldn't have a better day; the beer in the pub, probably good, too. Or if not that, the claret . . . The claret in South Country inns was often quite good; there was no sale for it so it got well kept. . . .

On Tuesday it would close in again, beginning with the meeting of his wife's maid at Dover. . . .

He was to have, above all, a holiday from himself and to take it like other men; free of his conventions, his strait waistcoatings. . . .

The girl said:

"I'm coming up now! I've found out something. . . ." He watched intently the place where she must appear; it would give him pointers about the impenetrability of mist to the eye.

Her otter-skin cap had beads of dew: beads of dew were on her hair beneath: she scrambled up, a little awkwardly: her eyes sparkled with fun: panting a little: her cheeks bright. Her hair was darkened by the wetness of the mist, but appeared golden in the sudden moonlight.

Before she was quite up, Tietjens almost kissed her. Almost. An all but irresistible impulse! He exclaimed:

"Steady, the Buffs!" in his surprise.

She said:

"Well, you might as well have given me a hand. I found," she went on, "a stone that had I.R.D.C. on it, and then the lamp went out. We're not on the marsh because we're

between quick hedges. That's all I've found. . . . But I've
worked out what makes me so tart with you. . . ."

He couldn't believe she could be so absolutely calm: the
after-wash of that impulse had been so strong in him that
it was as if he had tried to catch her to him and had been
foiled by her. . . . She ought to be indignant, amused, even
pleased. . . . She ought to show some emotion. . . .

She said:

"It was your silencing me with that absurd *non sequitur*
about the Pimlico clothing factory. It was an insult to my
intelligence."

"You recognized that it was a fallacy!" Tietjens said. He
was looking hard at her. He didn't know what had happened to him. She took a long look at him, cool, but with
immense eyes. It was as if for a moment Destiny, which
usually let him creep past somehow, had looked at him.
"Can't," he argued with Destiny, "a man want to kiss a
schoolgirl in a scuffle? . . ." His own voice, a caricature
of his own voice, seemed to come to him: "Gentlemen
don't. . . ." He exclaimed:

"Don't gentlemen? . . ." and then stopped because he
realized that he had spoken aloud.

She said:

"Oh, *gentlemen* do!" she said, "use fallacies to glide over
tight places in arguments. And they browbeat schoolgirls
with them. It's that, that underneath, has been exasperating
me with you. You regarded me at that date—three-quarters
of a day ago—as a schoolgirl."

Tietjens said:

"I don't now!" He added: "Heaven knows I don't now!"

She said: "No, you don't now!"

He said:

"It didn't need your putting up all that blue-stocking
erudition to convince me. . . ."

"Blue-stocking!" she exclaimed contemptuously. "There's
nothing of the blue-stocking about me. I know Latin because father spoke it with us. It was your pompous blue
socks I was pulling."

Suddenly she began to laugh. Tietjens was feeling sick,
physically sick. She went on laughing. He stuttered:

"What is it?"

"The sun!" she said, pointing. Above the silver horizon
was the sun; not a red sun: shining, burnished.

"I don't see . . ." Tietjens said.

"What there is to laugh at?" she asked. "It's the day!

. . . The longest day's begun . . . and to-morrow's as long.
. . . The summer solstice, you know . . . After to-morrow
the days shorten towards winter. But to-morrow's as
long. . . . I'm so glad. . . ."

"That we've got through the night? . . ." Tietjens asked.

She looked at him for a long time. "You're not so dreadfully ugly, really," she said.

Tietjens said:

"What's that church?"

Rising out of the mist on a fantastically green knoll, a
quarter of a mile away, was an unnoticeable place of wor-
ship: an oak-shingle tower roof that shone grey like lead:
an impossibly bright weathercock, brighter than the sun.
Dark elms all round it, holding wetnesses of mist.

"Icklesham!" she cried softly. "Oh, we're nearly home.
Just above Mountby . . . That's the Mountby drive. . . ."

Trees existed, black and hoary with the dripping mist.
Trees in the hedgerow and the avenue that led to Mountby:
it made a right angle just before coming into the road, and
the road went away at right angles across the gate.

"You'll have to pull to the left before you reach the
avenue," the girl said. "Or as like as not the horse will walk
right up to the house. The higgler who had him used to
buy Lady Claudine's eggs. . . ."

Tietjens exclaimed barbarously:

"Damn Mountby. I wish we'd never come near it," and
he whipped the horse into a sudden trot. The hoofs sounded
suddenly loud. She placed her hand on his gloved driving
hand. Had it been his flesh, she wouldn't have done it.

She said:

"My dear, it couldn't have lasted forever. . . . But you're
a good man. And very clever . . . You will get through.
. . ."

Not ten yards ahead Tietjens saw a tea-tray, the underneath of a black-lacquered tea-tray, gliding towards them:
mathematically straight, just rising from the mist. He
shouted: mad: the blood in his head. His shout was drowned
by the scream of the horse: he had swung it to the left.
The cart turned up: the horse emerged from the mist:
head and shoulders: pawing. A stone sea-horse from the
fountain of Versailles! Exactly that! Hanging in air for an
eternity: the girl looking at it, leaning slightly forward.

The horse didn't come over backwards: he had loosened
the reins. It wasn't there any more. The damnedest thing

that *could* happen! He had known it would happen. He said:

"We're all right now!" There was a crash and scraping: like twenty tea-trays: a prolonged sound. They must be scraping along the mudguard of the invisible car. He had the pressure of the horse's mouth: the horse was away: going hell-for-leather. He increased the pressure. The girl said:

"I know I'm all right with you."

They were suddenly in bright sunlight: cart: horse: commonplace hedgerows. They were going uphill: a steep brae. He wasn't certain she hadn't said: "Dear!" or "My dear!" Was it possible after so short? . . . But it had been a long night. He was, no doubt, saving her life too. He increased his pressure on the horse's mouth gently: up to all his twelve stone: all his strength. The hill told too. Steep, white road between shaven grass banks!

Stop, damn you! Poor beast . . . The girl fell out of the cart. No! jumped clear! Out to the animal's head. It threw its head up. Nearly off her feet: she was holding the bit. . . . She couldn't! Tender mouth . . . afraid of horses . . . He said:

"Horse cut!" Her face like a little white blancmange!

"Come quick," she said.

"I must hold a minute," he said; "might go off if I let go to get down. Badly cut?"

"Blood running down solid! Like an apron," she said.

He was at last at her side. It was true. But not so much like an apron. More like a red, varnished stocking. He said:

"You've a white petticoat on. Get over the hedge; jump it, and take it off. . . ."

"Tear it into strips?" she asked. "Yes!"

He called to her; she was suspended half-way up the bank:

"Tear one-half off first. The rest into strips."

She said: "All right!" She didn't go over the quickset as neatly as he had expected. No take-off. But she was over. . . .

The horse, trembling, was looking down, its nostrils distended, at the blood pooling from its near foot. The cut was just on the shoulder. He put his left arm right over the horse's eyes. The horse stood it, almost with a sigh of relief. . . . A wonderful magnetism with horses. Perhaps with women too? God knew. He was almost certain she had said "Dear."

She said: "Here." He caught a round ball of whitish stuff. He undid it. Thank God: what sense! A long, strong, white band. What the devil was the hissing? A small, closed car

with crumpled mudguards, noiseless nearly, gleaming black
. . . God curse it, it passed them, stopped ten yards
down . . . the horse rearing back: mad! Clean mad . . .
something like a scarlet and white cockatoo, fluttering out
of the small car door . . . a general. In full tog. White
feathers! Ninety medals! Scarlet coat! Black trousers with
red stripe. Spurs too, by God!

Tietjens said:

"God damn you, you bloody swine. Go away!"

The apparition, past the horse's blinkers, said:

"I can, at least, hold the horse for you. I went past to get
you out of Claudine's sight."

"Damn good-natured of you," Tietjens said as rudely as
he could. "You'll have to pay for the horse."

The general exclaimed:

"Damn it all! Why should I? You were driving your
beastly camel right into my drive."

"You never sounded your horn," Tietjens said.

"I was on private ground," the general shouted. "Besides,
I did." An enraged, scarlet scarecrow, very thin, he was
holding the horse's bridle. Tietjens was extending the half-
petticoat, with a measuring eye, before the horse's chest.
The general said:

"Look here! I've got to take the escort for the royal party
at St.-Peter-in-Manor, Dover. They're laying the Buff's colours
on the altar or something."

"You never sounded your horn," Tietjens said. "Why
didn't you bring your chauffeur? He's a capable man. . . .
You talk very big about the widow and child. But when it
comes to robbing them of fifty quid by slaughtering their
horse . . ."

The general said:

"What the devil were you doing coming into our drive at
five in the morning?"

Tietjens, who had applied the half-petticoat to the horse's
chest, exclaimed:

"Pick up that thing and give it me." A thin roll of linen
was at his feet: it had rolled down from the hedge.

"Can I leave the horse?" the general asked.

"Of course you can," Tietjens said. "If I can't quiet a horse
better than you can run a car . . ."

He bound the new linen strips over the petticoat: the horse
dropped its head, smelling his hand. The general, behind
Tietjens, stood back on his heels, grasping his gold-mounted
sword. Tietjens went on twisting and twisting the bandage.

"Look here," the general suddenly bent forward to whisper into Tietjens' ear, "what am I to tell Claudine? I believe she saw the girl."

"Oh, tell her we came to ask what time you cast off your beastly otter hounds," Tietjens said; "that's a matutinal job. . . ."

The general's voice had a really pathetic intonation:

"On a Sunday!" he exclaimed. Then in a tone of relief he added: "I shall tell her you were going to early communion in Duchemin's church at Pett."

"If you want to add blasphemy to horse-slaughtering as a profession, do," Tietjens said. "But you'll have to pay for the horse."

"I'm damned if I will," the general shouted. "I tell you, you were driving into my drive."

"Then I *shall*," Tietjens said, "and you know the construction you'll put on *that*."

He straightened his back to look at the horse.

"Go away," he said, "say what you like. Do what you like! But as you go through Rye send up the horse-ambulance from the vet's. Don't forget that. I'm going to save this horse. . . ."

"You know, Chris," the general said, "you're the most wonderful hand with a horse. . . . There isn't another man in England . . ."

"I know it," Tietjens said. "Go away. And send up that ambulance. . . . There's your sister getting out of your car. . . ."

The general began:

"I've an awful lot to get explained. . . ." But at a thin scream of: "General! General!" he pressed on his sword hilt to keep it from between his long, black, scarlet-striped legs and, running to the car, pushed back into its door a befeathered black bolster. He waved his hand to Tietjens:

"I'll send the ambulance," he called.

The horse, its upper leg swathed with criss-crosses of white through which a purple stain was slowly penetrating, stood motionless, its head hanging down, mulelike, under the blinding sun. To ease it, Tietjens began to undo the trace. The girl hopped over the hedge and, scrambling down, began to help him.

"Well. *My* reputation's gone," she said cheerfully. "I know what Lady Claudine is. . . . Why did you try to quarrel with the general? . . ."

"Oh, you'd better," Tietjens said wretchedly, "have a

lawsuit with him. It'll account for . . . for your not going to Mountby. . . ."

"You think of everything," she said.

They wheeled the cart backwards off the motionless horse. Tietjens moved it two yards forward—to get it out of sight of its own blood. Then they sat down, side by side, on the slope of the bank.

"Tell me about Groby," the girl said at last.

Tietjens began to tell her about his home. . . . There was, in front of it, an avenue that turned into the road at right angles. Just like the one at Mountby.

"My great-great-grandfather made it," Tietjens said. "He liked privacy and didn't want the house visible to vulgar people on the road . . . just like the fellow who planned Mountby, no doubt. . . . But it's beastly dangerous with motors. We shall have to alter it . . . just at the bottom of a dip. We can't have horses hurt. . . . You'll see . . ."

It came suddenly into his head that he wasn't perhaps the father of the child who was actually the heir to that beloved place over which generation after generation had brooded. Ever since Dutch William! A damn Nonconformist swine!

On the bank his knees were almost level with his chin. He felt himself slipping down.

"If I ever take you there . . ." he began.

"Oh, but you never will," she said.

The child wasn't his. The heir to Groby! All his brothers were childless. . . . There was a deep well in the stable-yard. He had meant to teach the child how if you dropped a pebble in, you waited to count twenty-three. And there came up a whispering roar. . . . But not his child! Perhaps he hadn't even the power to beget children. His married brothers hadn't. . . . Clumsy sobs shook him. It was the dreadful injury to the horse which had finished him. He felt as if the responsibility were his. The poor beast had trusted him and he had smashed it up. Miss Wannop had her arm over his shoulder.

"My dear!" she said, "you won't ever take me to Groby. . . . It's perhaps . . . oh . . . short acquaintance; but I feel you're the splendidest . . ."

He thought: "It *is* rather short acquaintance."

He felt a great deal of pain, over which there presided the tall, eel-skin, blonde figure of his wife. . . .

The girl said:

"There's a fly coming!" and removed her arm.

A fly drew up before them with a blear-eyed driver. He

said General Campion had kicked him out of bed, from beside his old woman. He wanted a pound to take them to Mrs. Wannop's, waked out of his beauty-sleep and all. The knacker's cart was following.

"You'll take Miss Wannop home at once," Tietjens said; "she's got her mother's breakfast to see to. . . . I shan't leave the horse till the knacker's van comes."

The fly-driver touched his age-green hat with his whip.

"Aye," he said thickly, putting a sovereign into his waistcoat pocket. "Always the gentleman . . . a merciful man is merciful also to his beast. . . . But I wouldn't leave my little wooden 'ut nor miss my breakfast for no beast. . . . Some do and some . . . do not."

He drove off with the girl in the interior of his antique conveyance.

Tietjens remained on the slope of the bank, in the strong sunlight, beside the drooping horse. It had done nearly forty miles and lost, at last, a lot of blood.

Tietjens said:

"I suppose I could get the governor to pay fifty quid for it. They want the money. . . ."

He said:

"But it wouldn't be playing the game!"

A long time afterwards he said:

"Damn all principles!" And then:

"But one has to keep on going. . . . Principles are like a skeleton map of a country—you know whether you're going east or north."

The knacker's cart lumbered round the corner.

PART TWO

I ~

SYLVIA TIETJENS rose from her end of the lunch-table and swayed along it, carrying her plate. She still wore her hair in bandeaux and her skirts as long as she possibly could: she didn't, she said, with her height, intend to be taken for a Girl Guide. She hadn't, in complexion, in figure or in the languor of her gestures aged by a minute. You couldn't discover in the skin of her face any deadness: in her eyes the shade more of fatigue than she intended to express, but she had purposely increased her air of scornful insolence. That was because she felt that her hold over men increased to the measure of her coldness. Someone, she knew, had once said of a dangerous woman that when she entered the room, every woman kept her husband on the leash. It was Sylvia's pleasure to think that before she went out of that room, all the women in it realized with mortification—that they needn't! For if coolly and distinctly she had said on entering: "Nothing doing!" as barmaids will to the enterprising, she couldn't more plainly have conveyed to the other women that she had no use for their treasured rubbish.

Once, on the edge of a cliff in Yorkshire, where the moors come above the sea, during one of the tiresome shoots that are there the fashion, a man had bidden her observe the demeanour of the herring-gulls below. They were dashing from rock to rock on the cliff face, screaming, with none of the dignity of gulls. Some of them even let fall the herrings that they had caught, and she saw the pieces of silver dropping into the blue motion. The man told her to look up; high, circling and continuing for a long time to circle, illuminated by the sunlight below, like a pale flame against the sky was a bird. The man told her that that was some sort of fish-eagle or hawk. Its normal habit was to chase the gulls, which, in their terror, would drop their booty of

150

herrings, whereupon the eagle would catch the fish before,
it struck the water. At the moment, the eagle was not on
duty, but the gulls were just as terrified as if it had been.

Sylvia stayed for a long time, watching the convolutions
of the eagle. It pleased her to see that though nothing threatened the gulls, they yet screamed and dropped their herrings
. . . The whole affair reminded her of herself in her relationship to the ordinary women of the barn-yard. . . .
Not that there was the breath of a scandal against herself;
that she very well knew, and it was her preoccupation, just
as turning down nice men—the "really nice men" of com-
merce—was her hobby.

She practised every kind of "turning down" on these
creatures: the really nice ones, with the Kitchener moustaches,
the seal's brown eyes, the honest, thrilling voices, the clipped
words, the straight backs and the admirable records—as
long as you didn't inquire *too* closely. Once, in the early days
of the Great Struggle, a young man—she *had* smiled at him
in mistake for someone more trustable—had followed in a
taxi, hard on her motor, and flushed with wine, glory and the
firm conviction that all women in that lurid carnival had become common property, had burst into her door from the
public stairs. . . . She had overtopped him by the forehead,
and before a few minutes were up she seemed to him to have
become ten foot high with a gift of words that scorched his
backbone and the voice of a frozen marble statue: a *chaud-
froid* effect. He had come in like a stallion, red-eyed and all
his legs off the ground: he went down the stairs like a half-
drowned rat, with dim eyes and really looking wet, for some
reason or other.

Yet she hadn't really told him more than the way one
should behave to the wives of one's brother-officers then
actually in the line, a point of view that, with her intimates,
she daily agreed was pure bosh. But it must have seemed
to him like the voice of his mother—when his mother had
been much younger, of course—speaking from paradise, and
his conscience had contrived the rest of his general wetness.
This, however, had been melodrama and war stuff at that:
it hadn't, therefore, interested her. She preferred to inflict
deeper and more quiet pains.

She could, she flattered herself, tell the amount of *empressement* which a man would develop about herself at the
first glance—the amount and the quality too. And from not
vouchsafing a look at all, or a look of the barest and most
incurious, to some poor devil who even on introduction

couldn't conceal his desires, to letting, after dinner, a measured glance travel from the right foot of a late dinner-
partner diagonally up the ironed fold of the right trouser to
the watch pocket, diagonally still, across the shirt front, pausing at the stud and so rather more quickly away over the left
shoulder, while the poor fellow stood appalled, with his
dinner going wrong—from the milder note to the more pronounced, she ran the whole gamut of "turnings-down." The
poor fellows next day would change their bootmakers, their
sock merchants, their tailors, the designers of their
dress-studs and shirts: they would sigh even to change the
cut of their faces, communing seriously with their after-
breakfast mirrors. But they knew in their hearts that calamity
came from the fact that she hadn't deigned to look into their
eyes. . . . Perhaps hadn't dared was the right word!

Sylvia, herself, would have cordially acknowledged that it
might have been. She knew that, like her intimates—all the
Elizabeths, Alixes, and Lady Moiras of the smooth-papered,
be-photographed weekly journals—she was man-mad. It was
the condition, indeed, of their intimacy as of their eligi-
bilities for reproduction on hot-pressed paper. They went
about in bands with, as it were, a corn-field of feather boas
floating above them, though, to be sure, no one *wore* feather
boas; they shortened their hair and their skirts, and flattened, as far as possible, their chest developments, which
does give, oh, you know . . . a *certain* . . . They adopted
demeanours as like as possible—and yet how unlike—to
those of waitresses in tea-shops frequented by city men. And
one reads in police-court reports of raids what *those* are!
Probably they were, in action, as respectable as any body of
women; *more* respectable, probably, than the great middle
class of before the war and certainly spotless by comparison
with their own upper servants, whose morals, merely as recorded in the divorce-court statistics—*that* she had from
Tietjens—would put to shame even those of Welsh or low-
land Scotch villages. Her mother was accustomed to say that
she was sure her butler would get to Heaven simply because
the Recording Angel, being an angel—and, as such, delicately
minded—wouldn't have the face to put down, much less
read out, the least venial of Morgan's offences. . . .

And sceptical as she was by nature, Sylvia Tietjens didn't
really even believe in the capacity for immoralities of her
friends. She didn't believe that any one of them was seriously
what the French would call the *maîtresse en titre* of any
particular man. Passion wasn't, at least, their strong suit: they

left that to more—or to less—august circles. The Duke of
A—— and all the little A's might be the children of the
morose and passion-stricken Duke of B—— instead of the
still more morose but less passionate late Duke of A——.
Mr. C——, the Tory statesman and late foreign minister,
might equally be the father of all the children of the Tory
Lord Chancellor E——. The Whig front benches, the gloomy
and disagreeable Russells and Cavendishes trading off these—
again French—*collages sérieux* against the matrimonial
divagations of their own Lord F—— and Mr. G——. But
those amorous of heavily titled and born front-benchers
were rather of august politics. The hot-pressed weekly
journals never got hold of them: the parties to them didn't,
for one thing, photograph well, being old, uglyish and terribly, badly dressed. They were matter rather for the memoirs of the indiscreet, already written, but not to see the light
for fifty years. . . .

The affairs of her own set, female front-benchers of
one side or other as they were, were more tenuous. If they
ever came to heads, their affairs, they had rather the nature of
promiscuity and took place at the country-houses where bells
rang at five in the morning. Sylvia had heard of such country-
houses, but she didn't know of any. She imagined that they
might be the baronial halls of such barons of the Crown as
had patronymics ending in schen . . . stein . . . and baum.
There were getting to be a good many of these, but Sylvia
did not visit them. She had in her that much of the papist.

Certain of her more brilliant girl friends certainly made
very sudden marriages; but the averages of those were not
markedly higher than in the case of the daughters of doctors, solicitors, the clergy, the lord mayors and common
councilmen. They were the product usually of the more in-
formal type of dance, of inexperience and champagne—of
champagne of unaccustomed strength or of champagne
taken in unusual circumstances—fasting as often as not.
They were, these hasty marriages, hardly ever the result of
either passion or temperamental lewdness.

In her own case—years ago now—she had certainly
been taken advantage of, after champagne, by a married
man called Drake. A bit of a brute she acknowledged him
now to be. But after the event, passion had developed: intense on her side and quite intense enough on his. When, in a
scare that had been as much her mother's as her own, she had
led Tietjens on and married him in Paris to be out of the
way—though it was fortunate that the English Catholic

church of the Avenue Hoche had been the scene of her
mother's marriage also, thus establishing a precedent and an
ostensible reason!—there had been dreadful scenes right up
to the very night of the marriage. She had hardly to close
her eyes in order to see the Paris hotel bedroom, the distorted face of Drake, who was mad with grief and jealousy,
against a background of white things, flowers and the like,
sent in overnight for the wedding. She knew that she had
been very near death. She had wanted death.

And even now she had only to see the name of Drake in
the paper—her mother's influence with the pompous front-
bencher of the Upper House, her cousin, had put Drake in
the way of colonial promotions that were recorded in ga-
zettes—nay, she had only involuntarily to think of that night,
and she would stop dead, speaking or walking, drive her
nails into her palms and groan slightly. . . . She had to invent a chronic stitch in her heart to account for this groan,
which ended in a mumble and seemed to herself to degrade
her. . . .

The miserable memory would come, ghostlike, at any time,
anywhere. She would see Drake's face, dark against the
white things; she would feel the thin night-gown ripping off
her shoulder; but most of all she would seem, in darkness
that excluded the light of any room in which she might be,
to be transfused by the mental agony that there she had
felt: the longing for the brute who had mangled her: the
dreadful pain of the mind. The odd thing was that the sight
of Drake himself, whom she had seen several times since the
outbreak of the war, left her completely without emotion. She had no aversion, but no longing for him. . . . She
had, nevertheless, longing, but she knew it was longing
merely to experience again that dreadful feeling. And not
with Drake . . .

Her "turnings-down," then, of the really nice men, if it
were a sport, was a sport not without a spice of danger.
She imagined that, after a success, she must feel much of
the exhilaration that men told her they felt after bringing
off a clean right and left, and no doubt she felt some of
the emotions that the same young men felt when they were
out shooting with beginners. Her personal chastity she now
cherished much as she cherished her personal cleanliness
and persevered in her Swedish exercises after her baths before an open window, her rides afterwards, and her long
nights of dancing, which she would pursue in any room that
was decently ventilated. Indeed, the two sides of life were,

in her mind, intimately connected: she kept herself attractive by her skilfully selected exercises and cleanlinesses: and the same fatigues, healthful as they were, kept her in the mood for chastity of life. She had done so ever since her return to her husband; and this not because of any attachment to her husband or to virtue as such, as because she had made the pact with herself out of caprice and meant to keep it. She *had* to have men at her feet; that was, as it were, the price of her—purely social—daily bread: as it was the price of the daily bread of her intimates. She was, and had been for many years, absolutely continent. And so very likely were, and had been, all her Moiras and Megs and Lady Marjories—but she was perfectly aware that they had to have, above their assemblies, as it were, a light vapour of the airs and habits of the brothel. The public demanded that . . . a light vapour, like the slight traces of steam that she had seen glutinously adhering to the top of the water in the crocodile-houses of the zoo.

It was, indeed, the price; and she was aware that she had been lucky. Not many of the hastily married young women of her set really kept their heads above water *in* her set: for a season you would read that Lady Marjorie and Captain Hunt, after her presentation at Court on the occasion of her marriage, were to be seen at Roehampton, at Goodwood and the like: photographs of the young couple striding along with the palings of the row behind them, would appear for a month or so. Then the records of their fashionable doings would transfer themselves to the lists of the attendants and attachés of distant vice-regal courts in tropics bad for the complexion. "And then no more of he and she," as Sylvia put it.

In her case it hadn't been so bad, but it had been nearish. She had had the advantage of being an only daughter of a very rich woman: her husband wasn't just any Captain Hunt to stick on a vice-regal staff. He was in a first-class office, and when Angélique wrote notes on the young ménage, she could—Angélique's ideas of these things being hazy—always refer to the husband as the future Lord Chancellor or Ambassador to Vienna. And their little, frightfully expensive establishment—to which her mother, who had lived with them, had very handsomely contributed—had floated them over the first dangerous two years. They had entertained like mad, and two much-canvassed scandals had had their beginnings in Sylvia's small drawing-room. She had been quite established when she had gone off with Perowne. . . .

And coming back had not been so difficult. She had expected it would be, but it hadn't. Tietjens had stipulated for large rooms in Gray's Inn. That hadn't seemed to her to be reasonable; but she imagined that he wanted to be near his friend, and though she had no gratitude to Tietjens for taking her back and nothing but repulsion from the idea of living in his house, as they were making a bargain, she owed it to herself to be fair. She had never swindled a railway company, brought dutiable scent past a custom-house or represented to a second-hand dealer that her clothes were less worn than they were, though with her prestige she could actually have done this. It was fair that Tietjens should live where he wished, and live there they did, their very tall windows looking straight into those of Macmaster across the Georgian quadrangle.

They had two floors of a great building, and that gave them a great deal of space; the breakfast-room, in which during the war they also lunched, was an immense room, completely lined with books that were nearly all calf-backed, with an immense mirror over an immense, carved, yellow and white marble mantelpiece, and three windows that, in their great height, with the spideriness of their divisions and their old, bulging glass—some of the panes were faintly violet in age—gave to the room an eighteenth-century distinction. It suited, she admitted, Tietjens, who was an eighteenth-century figure of the Dr. Johnson type—the only eighteenth-century type of which she knew, except for that of the beau something, who wore white satin and ruffles, went to Bath and must have been indescribably tiresome.

Above she had a great white drawing-room, with fixings that she knew were eighteenth century and to be respected. For Tietjens—again she admitted—had a marvellous gift for old furniture: he despised it as such, but he knew it down to the ground. Once when her friend Lady Moira had been deploring the expense of having her new, little house furnished from top to toe under the advice of Sir John Robertson, the specialist (the Moiras had sold Arlington Street, stock, lock and barrel to some American), Tietjens, who had come in to tea and had been listening without speaking, had said, with the soft good nature, rather sentimental in tone, that once in a blue moon he would bestow on her prettiest friends:

"You had better let me do it for you."

Taking a look round Sylvia's great drawing-room, with the white panels, the Chinese lacquer screens, the red lacquer and ormolu cabinets and the immense blue and pink carpet (and Sylvia knew that if only for the three panels by a fellow called Fragonard, bought just before Fragonards had been boomed by the late king, her drawing-room was something remarkable), Lady Moira had said to Tietjens, rather flutteringly and almost with the voice with which she began one of her affairs:

"Oh, if you only *would*."

He had done it, and he had done it for a quarter of the estimate of Sir John Robertson. He had done it without effort, as if with a roll or two of his elephantine shoulders, for he seemed to know what was in every dealer's and auctioneer's catalogue by looking at the green halfpenny stamp on the wrapper. And still more astonishingly, he had made love to Lady Moira—they had stopped twice with the Moiras in Gloucestershire and the Moiras had three times week-ended with Mrs. Satterthwaite as the Tietjens' *invités*. . . . Tietjens had made love to Lady Moira quite prettily and sufficiently to tide Moira over until she was ready to begin her affair with Sir William Heathly.

For the matter of that, Sir John Robertson, the specialist in old furniture, challenged by Lady Moira to pick holes in her beautiful house, had gone there, poked his large spectacles against cabinets, smelt the varnish of table-tops and bitten the backs of chairs in his ancient and short-sighted way, and had then told Lady Moira that Tietjens had bought her nothing that wasn't worth a bit more than he had given for it. This increased their respect for the old fellow: it explained his several millions. For if the old fellow proposed to make out of a friend like Moira a profit of 300 per cent—limiting it to that out of sheer affection for a pretty woman—what wouldn't he make out of a natural—and national—enemy like a United States senator!

And the old man took a great fancy to Tietjens himself—which Tietjens, to Sylvia's bewilderment, did not resent. The old man would come in to tea and, if Tietjens were present, would stay for hours talking about old furniture. Tietjens would listen without talking. Sir John would expatiate over and over again about this to Mrs. Tietjens. It was extraordinary. Tietjens went purely by instinct: by taking a glance at a thing and chancing its price. According to Sir John, one of the most remarkable feats of the furniture trade had been

Tietjens' purchase of the Hemingway bureau for Lady Moira.
Tietjens, in his dislikeful way, had bought this at a cottage
sale for £3 10s., and had told Lady Moira it was the best
piece she would ever possess: Lady Moira had gone to the
sale with him. Other dealers present had hardly looked at it:
Tietjens certainly hadn't opened it. But at Lady Moira's, poking his spectacles into the upper part of the glazed piece,
Sir John had put his nose straight on the little bit of inserted yellow wood by a hinge, bearing signature, name and
date: "Jno. Hemingway, Bath, 1784." Sylvia remembered
them because Sir John told her so often. It was a lost
"piece" that the furnishing world had been after for many
years.

For that exploit the old man seemed to love Tietjens.
That he loved Sylvia herself, she was quite aware. He fluttered round her tremulously, gave fantastic entertainments
in her honour and was the only man she had never turned
down. He had a harem, so it was said, in an enormous house
at Brighton or somewhere. But it was another sort of love
he bestowed on Tietjens: the rather pathetic love that the
aged bestow on their possible successors in office.

Once Sir John came in to tea and quite formally and with
a sort of portentousness announced that that was his seventy-
first birthday, and that he was a broken man. He seriously
proposed that Tietjens should come into partnership with him
with the reversion of the business—not, of course, of his
private fortune. Tietjens had listened amiably, asking a detail or two of Sir John's proposed arrangement. Then he had
said, with the rather caressing voice that he now and then
bestowed on a pretty woman, that he didn't think it would
do. There would be too much beastly money about it. As a
career it would be more congenial to him than his office . . .
but there was too much beastly money about it.

Once more, a little to Sylvia's surprise—but men are queer
creatures!—Sir John seemed to see this objection as quite
reasonable, though he heard it with regret and combated it
feebly. He went away with a relieved jauntiness; for if he
couldn't have Tietjens, he couldn't; and he invited Sylvia
to dine with him somewhere where they were going to have
something fabulous and very nasty at about two guineas the
ounce on the menu. Something like that! And during dinner Sir John had entertained her by singing the praises of
her husband. He said that Tietjens was much too great a
gentleman to be wasted on the old-furniture trade: that was
why he hadn't persisted. But he sent by Sylvia a message

to the effect that if ever Tietjens *did* come to be in want of money . . .

Occasionally Sylvia was worried to know why people—as they sometimes did—told her that her husband had great gifts. To her he was merely unaccountable. His actions and opinions seemed simply the products of caprice—like her own; and since she knew that most of her own manifestations were a matter of contrariety, she abandoned the habit of thinking much about him.

But gradually and dimly she began to see that Tietjens had, at least, a consistency of character and a rather unusual knowledge of life. This came to her when she had to acknowledge that their move to the Inns of Court had been a social success and had suited herself. When they had discussed the change at Lobscheid—or rather when Sylvia had unconditionally given in to every stipulation of Tietjens!—he had predicted almost exactly what would happen, though it had been the affair of her mother's cousin's opera box that had most impressed her. He had told her, at Lobscheid, that he had no intention of interfering with her social level, and he was convinced that he was not going to. He had thought about it a good deal.

She hadn't much listened to him. She had thought, firstly, that he was a fool and, secondly, that he *did* mean to hurt her. And she acknowledged that he had a certain right. If after she had been off with another man she asked this one still to extend to her the honour of his name and the shelter of his roof, she had no right to object to his terms. Her only decent revenge on him was to live afterwards with such equanimity as to let him know the mortification of failure.

But at Lobscheid he had talked a lot of nonsense, as it had seemed to her: a mixture of prophecy and politics. The Chancellor of the Exchequer of that date had been putting pressure on the great landlords: the great landlords had been replying by cutting down their establishments and closing their town houses—not to any great extent, but enough to make a very effective gesture of it, and so as to raise a considerable clamour from footmen and milliners. The Tietjens—both of them—were of the great landowning class: they could adopt that gesture of shutting up their Mayfair house and going to live in a wilderness. All the more if they made their wilderness a thoroughly comfortable affair!

He had counselled her to present this aspect of the matter to her mother's cousin, the morosely portentous Rugeley. Rugeley was a great landowner—almost the greatest of all;

and he was a landowner obsessed with a sense of his duties both to his dependants and even his remote relatives. Sylvia had only, Tietjens said, to go to the duke and tell him that the Chancellor's exactions had forced them to this move, but that they had done it partly as a protest, and the duke would accept it almost as a personal tribute to himself. *He* couldn't, even as a protest, be expected to shut up Mexborough or reduce his expenses. But if his humbler relatives spiritedly did, he would almost certainly make it up to them. And Rugeley's favours were on the portentous scale of everything about him. "I shouldn't wonder," Tietjens had said, "if he didn't lend you the Rugeley box to entertain in."

And that is exactly what had happened.

The duke—who must have kept a register of his remotest cousins—had, shortly before their return to London, heard that this young couple had parted with every prospect of a large and disagreeable scandal. He had approached Mrs. Satterthwaite—for whom he had a gloomy affection—and he had been pleased to hear that the rumour was a gross libel. So that when the young couple actually turned up again—from Russia!—Rugeley, who perceived that they were not only together but to all appearances quite united, was determined not only to make it up to them but to show, in order to abash their libellers, as signal a mark of his favour as he could without inconvenience to himself. He, therefore, twice—being a widower—invited Mrs. Satterthwaite to entertain for him, Sylvia to invite the guests, and then had Mrs. Tietjens' name placed on the roll of those who could have the Rugeley box at the opera, on application at the Rugeley estate office, when it wasn't wanted. This was a very great privilege, and Sylvia had known how to make the most of it.

On the other hand, on the occasion of their conversation at Lobscheid, Tietjens had prophesied what at the time seemed to her a lot of tosh. It had been two or three years before, but Tietjens had said that about the time grouseshooting began, in 1914, a European conflagration would take place which would shut up half the houses in Mayfair and beggar their inhabitants. He had patiently supported his prophecy with financial statistics as to the approaching bankruptcy of various European powers and the growing acquisitive skill and rapacity of the inhabitants of Great Britain. She had listened to that with some attention: it had seemed to her rather like the usual nonsense talked in countryhouses—where, irritatingly, he never talked. But she liked to be able to have a picturesque fact or two with which to support herself when she too, to hold attention, wanted to issue moving statements as to revolutions, anarchies and strife in the offing. And she had noticed that when she mag-pied Tietjens' conversations, more serious men in responsible positions were apt to argue with her and to pay her more attention than before. . . .

And now, walking along the table with her plate in her hand, she could not but acknowledge that, triumphantly—and very comfortably for her!—Tietjens had been right! In the third year of the war it was very convenient to have a dwelling, cheap, comfortable, almost august and so easy to work that you could have, at a pinch, run it with one maid, though the faithful Hullo Central had not let it come to that yet. . . .

Being near Tietjens, she lifted her plate, which contained two cold cutlets in aspic and several leaves of salad: she wavered a little to one side and, with a circular motion of her hand, let the whole contents fly at Tietjens' head. She placed the plate on the table and drifted slowly towards the enormous mirror over the fire-place.

"I'm bored," she said. "Bored! Bored!"

Tietjens had moved slightly as she had thrown: the cutlets and most of the salad leaves had gone over his shoulder. But one, couched, very green leaf was on his shoulder-strap, and the oil and vinegar from the plate—Sylvia *knew* that she took too much of all condiments—had splashed from the revers of his tunic to his green staff-badges. She was glad that she had hit him as much as that: it meant that her marksmanship had not been quite rotten. She was glad, too, that she had missed him. She was also supremely indifferent. It had occurred to her to do it and she had done it. Of that she was glad!

She looked at herself for some time in the mirror of bluish depths. She pressed her immense bandeaux with both hands on to her ears. She was all right: high-featured: alabaster complexion—but that was mostly the mirror's doing—beautiful, long, cool hands—what man's forehead wouldn't long for them? . . . And that hair! What man wouldn't think of it, unloosed on white shoulders! . . . Well, Tietjens wouldn't! Or, perhaps, he did . . . she hoped he did, curse him, for he never saw that sight. Obviously sometimes, at night, with a little whisky taken, he must want to!

She rang the bell and bade Hullo Central sweep the plateful from the carpet; Hullo Central, tall and dark, looking with wide-open eyes motionlessly at nothing.

Sylvia went along the bookshelves, pausing over a book back, *Vitae Hominum Notiss* . . . in gilt, irregular capitals pressed deep into the old leather. At the first long window she supported herself by the blind-cord. She looked out and back into the room.

"There's that veiled woman!" she said, "going into eleven. . . . It's two o'clock, of course. . . ."

She looked at her husband's back hard, the clumsy khaki back that was getting round-shouldered now. Hard! She wasn't going to miss a motion or a stiffening.

"I've found out who it is!" she said, "and who she goes to. I got it out of the porter." She waited. Then she added:

"It's the woman you travelled down from Bishop's Auckland with. On the day war was declared."

Tietjens turned solidly round in his chair. She knew he would do that out of stiff politeness, so it meant nothing.

His face was whitish in the pale light, but it was always whitish since he had come back from France and passed his day in a tin hut among dust heaps. He said:

"So you saw me!" But that, too, was mere politeness.

She said:

"Of course the whole crowd of us from Claudine's saw you! It was old Campion who said she was a Mrs. . . . I've forgotten the name."

Tietjens said:

"I imagined he would know her. I saw him looking in from the corridor!"

She said:

"Is she your mistress, or only Macmaster's, or the mistress of both of you? It would be like you to have a mistress in common. . . . She's got a mad husband, hasn't she? A clergyman."

Tietjens said:

"She hasn't!"

Sylvia checked suddenly in her next questions, and Tietjens, who in these discussions never manoeuvred for position, said:

"She has been Mrs. Macmaster over six months."

Sylvia said:

"She married him, then, the day after her husband's death."

She drew a long breath and added:

"I don't care. . . . She has been coming here every Friday for three years. . . . I tell you I shall expose her unless that little beast pays you to-morrow the money he owes you. . . . God knows you need it!" She said then hurriedly, for she didn't know how Tietjens might take that proposition:

"Mrs. Wannop rang up this morning to know who was . . . oh! . . . the evil genius of the Congress of Vienna. Who, by the by, is Mrs. Wannop's secretary? She wants to see you this afternoon. About war-babies!"

Tietjens said:

"Mrs. Wannop hasn't got a secretary. It's her daughter who does her ringing up."

"The girl," Sylvia said, "you were so potty about at that horrible afternoon Macmaster gave. Has she had a war-baby by you? They all say she's your mistress."

Tietjens said:

"No, Miss Wannop isn't my mistress. Her mother has had a commission to write an article about war-babies. I told her yesterday there weren't any war-babies to speak of, and she's upset because she won't be able to make a sensational article. She wants to try and make me change my mind."

Sylvia said:

"It *was* Miss Wannop at that beastly affair of your friend's?" Sylvia asked. "And I suppose the woman who received was Mrs. What's-er-name: your other mistress. An unpleasant show. I don't think much of your taste. The one where all the horrible geniuses in London were? There was a man like a rabbit talked to me about how to write poetry."

"That's no good as an identification of the party," Tietjens said. "Macmaster gives a party every Friday, not Saturday. He has for years. Mrs. Macmaster goes there every Friday. To act as hostess. She has for years. Miss Wannop goes there every Friday after she has done work for her mother. To support Mrs. Macmaster . . ."

"She has for years!" Sylvia mocked him. "And you go there every Friday! to croodle over Miss Wannop. Oh, Christopher!"—she adopted a mock-pathetic voice—"I never did have much opinion of your taste . . . but not *that!* Don't let it be that. Put her back. She's too young for you. . . ."

"All the geniuses in London," Tietjens continued equably, "go to Macmaster's every Friday. He has been trusted with the job of giving away Royal Literary Bounty money: that's why they go. They go: that's why he was given his C.B."

"I should not have thought they counted," Sylvia said.

"Of course they count," Tietjens said. "They write for the

press. They can get anybody anything . . . except themselves!"

"Like you!" Sylvia said; "exactly like you! They're a lot of bribed squits."

"Oh, no," Tietjens said. "It isn't done obviously or discreditably. Don't believe that Macmaster distributes forty-pounders yearly of bounty on condition that he gets advancement. He hasn't, himself, the least idea of how it works, except by his atmosphere."

"I never knew a beastlier atmosphere," Sylvia said. "It *reeked* of rabbit's food."

"You're quite mistaken," Tietjens said; "that is the Russian leather of the backs of the specially bound presentation copies in the *large* bookcase."

"I don't know what you're talking about," Sylvia said. "What *are* presentation copies? I should have thought you'd had enough of the beastly Russian smells Kiev stunk of."

Tietjens considered for a moment.

"No! I don't remember it," he said. "Kiev? . . . Oh, it's where we were. . . ."

"You put half your mother's money," Sylvia said, "into the government of Kiev twelve and a half per cent City Tramways. . . ."

At that Tietjens certainly winced, a type of wincing that Sylvia hadn't wanted.

"You're not fit to go out to-morrow," she said. "I shall wire to old Campion."

"Mrs. Duchemin," Tietjens said woodenly, "Mrs. Macmaster, that is, also used to burn a little incense in the room before the parties. . . . Those Chinese stinks . . . what do they call them? Well, it doesn't matter"; he added that resignedly. Then he went on: "Don't you make any mistake. Mrs. Macmaster is a very superior woman. Enormously efficient! Tremendously respected. I shouldn't advise even you to come up against her, now she's in the saddle."

Mrs. Tietjens said:

"*That* sort of woman!"

Tietjens said:

"I don't say you ever will come up against her. Your spheres differ. But if you do, don't. . . . I say it because you seem to have got your knife into her."

"I don't like that sort of thing going on under my windows," Sylvia said.

Tietjens said:

"What sort of thing? . . . I was trying to tell you a little about Mrs. Macmaster . . . she's like the woman who was the mistress of the man who burned the other fellow's horrid book. . . . I can't remember the names."

Sylvia said quickly:

"Don't try!" In a slower tone she added: "I don't in the least want to know. . . ."

"Well, she was an Egeria!" Tietjens said. "An inspiration to the distinguished. Mrs. Macmaster is all that. The geniuses swarm round her, and with the really select ones she corresponds. She writes superior letters, about the Higher Morality, usually; very delicate in feeling. Scotch, naturally. When they go abroad she sends them snatches of London literary happenings; well done, mind you! And then, every now and then, she slips in something she wants Macmaster to have. But with great delicacy . . . Say it's this C.B. . . . she transfuses into the minds of Genius One, Two and Three the idea of a C.B. for Macmaster. . . . Genius No. One lunches with the Deputy Sub-Patronage Secretary, who looks after literary honours and lunches with geniuses to get the gossip. . . ."

"Why," Sylvia said, "did you lend Macmaster all that money?"

"Mind you," Tietjens continued his own speech, "it's perfectly proper. That's the way patronage *is* distributed in this country; it's the way it should be. The only clean way. Mrs. Duchemin backs Macmaster because he's a first-class fellow for his job. And *she* is an influence over the geniuses because she's a first-class person for hers. . . . She represents the higher, nicer morality for really nice Scots. Before long she will be getting tickets stopped from being sent to people for the Academy soirées. She already does it for the Royal Bounty dinners. A little later, when Macmaster is knighted for bashing the French in the eye, she'll have a tiny share in auguster assemblies. . . . Those people have to ask *somebody* for advice. Well, one day you'll want to present some débutante. And you won't get a ticket. . . ."

"Then I'm glad," Sylvia exclaimed, "that I wrote to Brownie's uncle about the woman. I was a little sorry this morning because, from what Glorvina told me, you're in such a devil of a hole. . . ."

"Who's Brownie's uncle?" Tietjens asked. "Lord . . . Lord . . . The banker! I know Brownie's in his uncle's bank."

"Port Scatho!" Sylvia said. "I wish you wouldn't act forgetting people's names. You overdo it."

Tietjens' face went a shade whiter. . . .

"Port Scatho," he said, "is the chairman of the Inn

Billeting Committees, of course. And you wrote to him? . . ."

"I'm sorry," Sylvia said. "I mean I'm sorry I said that about your forgetting. . . . I wrote to him and said that as a resident of the Inn I objected to your mistress—he knows the relationship, of course!—creeping in every Friday under a heavy veil and creeping out every Saturday at four in the morning."

"Lord Port Scatho knows about my relationship," Tietjens began.

"He saw her in your arms in the train," Sylvia said. "It upset Brownie so much he offered to shut down your over-draft and return any cheques you had out marked R.D."

"To please you?" Tietjens asked. "*Do* bankers do that sort of thing? It's a new light on British society. . . ."

"I suppose bankers try to please their women friends, like other men," Sylvia said. "I told him very emphatically it wouldn't please me. . . . But . . ." She hesitated: "I wouldn't give him a chance to get back on you. I don't want to inter-fere in your affairs. But Brownie doesn't like you. . . ."

"He wants you to divorce me and marry him?" Tietjens asked.

"How did you know?" Sylvia asked indifferently. "I let him give me lunch now and then because it's convenient to have him manage my affairs, you being away. . . . But of course he hates you for being in the army. All the men who aren't hate all the men that are. And of course when there's a woman between them, the men who aren't do all they can to do the others in. When they're bankers they have a pretty good pull. . . ."

"I suppose they have," Tietjens said vaguely; "of course they would have. . . ."

Sylvia abandoned the blind-cord on which she had been dragging with one hand. In order that light might fall on her face and give more impressiveness to her words, for, in a minute or two, when she felt brave enough, she meant really to let him have her bad news!—she drifted to the fire-place. He followed her round, turning on his chair to give her his face.

She said:

"Look here, it's all the fault of this beastly war, isn't it? Can you deny it? . . . I mean that decent, gentlemanly fellows like Brownie have turned into beastly squits!"

"I suppose it is," Tietjens said dully. "Yes, certainly it is. You're quite right. It's the incidental degeneration of the heroic impulse: if the heroic impulse has too even a strain put on it the incidental degeneration gets the upper hand. That accounts for the Brownies . . . all the Brownies . . . turning squits. . . ."

"Then why do you go on with it?" Sylvia said. "God knows I could wangle you out if you'd back me in the least little way."

Tietjens said:

"Thanks! I prefer to remain in it. . . . How else am I to get a living? . . ."

"You know, then," Sylvia exclaimed almost shrilly. "You know that they won't have you back in the office if they can find a way of getting you out. . . ."

"Oh, they'll find that!" Tietjens said. He continued his other speech: "When we go to war with France . . ." he said dully. And Sylvia knew he was only now formulating his settled opinion so as not to have his active brain to give to the discussion. He must be thinking hard of the Wannop girl! With her littleness: her tweed-skirtishness . . . A provincial miniature of herself, Sylvia Tietjens . . . If she, then, had been miniature, provincial . . . But Tietjens' words cut her as if she had been lashed with a dog-whip. "We shall behave more creditably," he had said, "because there will be less heroic impulse about it. We shall . . . half of us . . . be ashamed of ourselves. So there will be much less incidental degeneration."

Sylvia, who by that time was listening to him, abandoned the consideration of Miss Wannop and the pretence that obsessed her, of Tietjens talking to the girl, against a background of books at Macmaster's party. She exclaimed:

"Good God! What are you talking about? . . ."

Tietjens went on:

"About our next war with France . . . We're the natural enemies of the French. We have to make our bread either by robbing them or making cat's paws of them. . . ."

Sylvia said:

"We can't! We couldn't. . . ."

"We've got to!" Tietjens said. "It's the condition of our existence. We're a practically bankrupt, overpopulated, northern country: they're rich southerners, with a falling population. Towards 1930 we shall have to do what Prussia did in 1914. Our conditions will be exactly those of Prussia then. It's the . . . what is it called? . . ."

"But . . ." Sylvia cried out. "You're a Francomaniac. . . . You're thought to be a French agent. . . . That's what's bitching your career!"

"I am?" Tietjens asked uninterestedly. He added: "Yes, that probably *would* bitch my career. . . ." He went on, with a little more animation and a little more of his mind:

"Ah! *that* will be a war worth seeing. . . . None of their drunken rat-fighting for imbecile boodlers . . ."

"It would drive mother mad!" Sylvia said.

"Oh, no it wouldn't," Tietjens said. "It will stimulate her if she is still alive. . . . Our heroes won't be drunk with wine and lechery: our squits won't stay at home and stab the heroes in the back. Our Minister for Water-closets won't keep two and a half million men in any base in order to get the votes of their women at a general election—that's been the first evil effects of giving women the vote! With the French holding Ireland and stretching in a solid line from Bristol to Whitehall, we would hang the minister before he had time to sign the papers. And we should be decently loyal to our Prussian allies and brothers. . . . Our Cabinet won't hate them as they hate the French for being frugal and strong in logic and well educated and remorselessly practical. Prussians are the sort of fellows you can be hoggish with when you want to. . . ."

Sylvia interjected violently:

"For God's sake, stop it. You almost make me believe what you say is true. I tell you mother would go mad. Her greatest friend is the Duchesse Tonnerre Châteaulherault. . . ."

"Well!" Tietjens said. "Your greatest friends are the Med . . . Med . . . the Austrian officers you take chocolates and flowers to. That there was all the row about . . . we're at war with *them* and you haven't gone mad!"

"I don't know," Sylvia said. "Sometimes I think I am going mad!" She drooped. Tietjens, his face very strained, was looking at the table-cloth. He muttered: "Med . . . Met . . . Kos . . ." Sylvia said:

"Do you know a poem called *Somewhere?* It begins: 'Somewhere or other there must surely be . . .'"

Tietjens said:

"I'm sorry. No! I haven't been able to get up my poetry again."

Sylvia said:

"*Don't!*" She added: "You've got to be at the War Office at four-fifteen, haven't you? What's the time now?" She extremely wanted to give him her bad news before he went; she extremely wanted to put off giving it as long as she could. She wanted to reflect on the matter first; she wanted also to keep up a desultory conversation, or he might leave the room. She didn't want to have to say to him: "Wait a minute. I've something to say to you!" for she might not, at that moment, be in the mood. He said it was not yet two. He could give her an hour and a half more.

To keep the conversation going, she said:

"I suppose the Wannop girl is making bandages or being a Waac. Something forceful."

Tietjens said:

"No, she's a pacifist. As pacifist as you. Not so impulsive; but, on the other hand, she has more arguments. I should say she'll be in prison before the war's over. . . ."

"A nice time you must have between the two of us," Sylvia said. The memory of her interview with the great lady nick-named Glorvina—though it was not at all a good nickname —was coming over her forcibly.

She said:

"I suppose you're always talking it over with her? You see her every day."

She imagined that that might keep him occupied for a minute or two. He said—she caught the sense of it only— and quite indifferently that he had tea with Mrs. Wannop every day. She had moved to a place called Bedford Park, which was near his office: not three minutes' walk. The War Office had put up a lot of huts on some public green in that neighbourhood. He only saw the daughter once a week, at most. They never talked about the war; it was too dis-agreeable a subject for the young woman. Or, rather, too painful . . . His talk gradually drifted into unfinished sen-tences. . . .

They played that comedy occasionally, for it is impossible for two people to live in the same house and not have some common meeting-ground. So they would each talk: some-times talking at great length and with politeness, each think-ing his or her thoughts till they drifted into silence.

And since she had acquired the habit of going into retreat —with an Anglican sisterhood in order to annoy Tietjens, who hated converts and considered that the communions should not mix—Sylvia had acquired also the habit of losing herself almost completely in reveries. Thus she was now vaguely conscious that a greyish lump, Tietjens, sat at the head of a whitish expanse: the lunch-table. There were also books . . . actually she was seeing a quite different figure and other books—the books of Glorvina's husband, for the great lady had received Sylvia in that statesman's library.

Glorvina, who was the mother of two of Sylvia's absolutely most intimate friends, had sent for Sylvia. She wished,
kindly and even wittily, to remonstrate with Sylvia because
of her complete abstention from any patriotic activity. She
offered Sylvia the address of a place in the city where she
could buy wholesale and ready-made diapers for babies,
which Sylvia could present to some charity or other as being
her own work. Sylvia said she would do nothing of the sort,
and Glorvina said she would present the idea to poor Mrs.
Pilsenhauser. She—Glorvina—said she spent some time every
day thinking out acts of patriotism for the distressed rich
with foreign names, accents or antecedents. . . .

Glorvina was a fiftyish lady with a pointed, grey face
and a hard aspect; but when she was inclined to be witty or
to plead earnestly she had a kind manner. The room in
which they were was over a Belgravia back garden. It was
lit by a skylight, and the shadows from above deepened
the lines of her face, accentuating the rather dusty grey of
the hair as well as both the hardness and the kind manner.
This very much impressed Sylvia, who was used to seeing the
lady by artificial light. . . .

She said, however:

"You don't suggest, Glorvina, that I'm the distressed rich
with a foreign name!"

The great lady had said:

"My dear Sylvia, it isn't so much you as your husband.
Your last exploit with the Esterhazys and Metternichs has
pretty well done for *him*. You forget that the present powers
that be are not logical. . . ."

Sylvia remembered that she had sprung up from her leather
saddleback chair, exclaiming:

"You mean to say that those unspeakable swine think
that *I'm* . . ."

Glorvina said patiently:

"My dear Sylvia, I've already said it's not you. It's your
husband that suffers. He appears to be too good a fellow to
suffer. Mr. Waterhouse says so. I don't know him myself,
well."

Sylvia remembered that she had said:

"And who in the world is Mr. Waterhouse?" and hearing
that Mr. Waterhouse was a late Liberal minister, had lost interest. She couldn't, indeed, remember any of the futher
words of her hostess, as words. The sense of them had too
much overwhelmed her. . . .

She stood now, looking at Tietjens and only occasionally seeing him, her mind completely occupied with the effort to recapture Glorvina's own words in the desire for exactness. Usually she remembered conversations pretty well; but on this occasion her mad fury, her feeling of nausea, the pain of her own nails in her palms, an unrecoverable sequence of emotions, had overwhelmed her.

She looked at Tietjens now with a sort of gloating curiosity. How was it possible that the most honourable man she knew should be so overwhelmed by foul and baseless rumours? It made you suspect that honour had, in itself, a quality of the evil eye. . . .

Tietjens, his face pallid, was fingering a piece of toast. He muttered:

"Met . . . Met . . . It's Met . . ." He wiped his brow with a table-napkin, looked at it with a start, threw it on the floor and pulled out a handkerchief. . . . He muttered: "Mett . . . Metter . . ." His face illuminated itself like the face of a child listening at a shell.

Sylvia screamed with a passion of hatred:

"For God's sake, say *Metternich* . . . you're driving me mad!"

When she looked at him again, his face had cleared and he was walking quickly to the telephone in the corner of the room. He asked her to excuse him and gave a number at Ealing. He said after a moment:

"Mrs. Wannop? Oh! My wife has just reminded me that Metternich was the evil genius of the Congress of Vienna. . . ." He said: "Yes! Yes!" and listened. After a time he said: "Oh, you could put it stronger than that. You could put it that the Tory determination to ruin Napoleon at all costs was one of those pieces of party imbecility that, etc. . . . Yes, Castlereagh. And of course Wellington . . . I'm very sorry I must ring off. . . . Yes, to-morrow at eight-thirty from Waterloo . . . No, I *shan't* be seeing her again. . . . No, she's made a mistake. . . . Yes, give her my love . . . good-bye." He was reversing the ear-piece to hang it up, but a high-pitched series of yelps from the instrument forced it back to his ear: "Oh! *War-babies!*" he exclaimed. "I've already sent the statistics off to you! No! there *isn't* a marked increase of the illegitimacy rate except in patches. The rate's appallingly high in the lowlands of Scotland; but it always *is* appallingly high there. . . ." He laughed and said good-naturedly: "Oh, you're an old journalist: you won't let fifty quid go for that. . . ." He was breaking off. But: *"Or,"* he suddenly exclaimed, "here's another idea for you. The rate's about the same, probably because of this: half the fellows who go out to France are reckless because it's the last chance, as they see it. But the other half are made twice as conscientious. A decent Tommy thinks twice about leaving his girl in trouble just before he's killed. . . . The divorce statistics are up, of course, because people will chance making new starts within the law. . . . Thanks . . . thanks . . ." He hung up the ear-piece. . . .

Listening to that conversation had extraordinarily cleared Sylvia's mind. She said, almost sorrowfully:

"I suppose that that's why you don't seduce that girl." And she knew—she had known at once from the suddenly changed inflection of Tietjens' voice when he had said "A decent Tommy thinks twice before leaving his girl in trouble"!—that Tietjens himself had thought twice.

She looked at him not almost incredulously, but with great coolness. Why *shouldn't* he, she asked herself, give himself a little pleasure with his girl before going to almost certain death. . . . She felt a real, sharp pain at her heart. . . . A poor wretch in such a devil of a hole . . .

She had moved to a chair close beside the fire-place and now sat looking at him, leaning interestedly forward, as if at a garden-party she had been finding—*par impossible!*—a pastoral play not so badly produced. Tietjens was a fabulous monster. . . .

He was a fabulous monster not because he was honourable and virtuous. She had known several very honourable and very virtuous men. If she had never known an honourable or virtuous woman except among her French or Austrian friends, that was, no doubt, because virtuous and honourable women did not amuse her or because, except just for the French and Austrians, they were not Roman Catholics. . . . But the honourable and virtuous men she had known had usually prospered and been respected. They weren't the great fortunes, but they were well-offish: well spoken of: of the country-gentleman type . . . Tietjens . . .

She arranged her thoughts. To get one point settled in her mind, she asked:

"What really happened to you in France? What is really the matter with your memory? Or your brain, is it?"

He said carefully:

"It's half of it, an irregular piece of it, dead. Or rather pale. Without a proper blood supply . . . So a great portion of it, in the shape of memory, has gone."

She said:

"But *you!* . . . without a brain! . . ." As this was not a question, he did not answer.

His going at once to the telephone as soon as he was in the possession of the name "Metternich" had at last convinced her that he had not been, for the last four months, acting hypochondriacal or merely lying to obtain sympathy or extended sick leave. Amongst Sylvia's friends a wangle known as shell-shock was cynically laughed at and quite approved of. Quite decent and, as far as she knew, quite brave men-folk of her women would openly boast that when they had had enough of it over there, they would wangle a little leave or get a little leave extended by simulating this purely nominal disease, and in the general carnival of lying, lechery, drink and howling that this affair was, to pretend to a little shell-shock had seemed to her to be almost virtuous. At any rate, if a man passed his time at garden-parties—or, as for the last months Tietjens had done, passed his time in a tin hut amongst dust heaps, going to tea every afternoon in order to help Mrs. Wannop with her newspaper articles— when men were so engaged, they were, at least, not trying to kill each other.

She said now:

"Do you mind telling me what actually happened to you?"

He said:

"I don't know that I can very well. . . . Something burst —or 'exploded' is probably the right word—near me, in the dark. I expect you'd rather not hear about it? . . ."

"I want to!" Sylvia said.

He said:

"The point about it is that I *don't* know what happened and I don't remember what I did. There are three weeks of my life dead. . . . What I remember is being in a C.C.S. and not being able to remember my own name."

"You *mean* that?" Sylvia asked. "It's not just a way of talking?"

"No, it's not just a way of talking," Tietjens answered. "I lay in bed in the C.C.S. . . . Your friends were dropping bombs on it."

"You might not call them my friends," Sylvia said.

Tietjens said:

"I beg your pardon. One gets into a loose way of speaking. The poor bloody Huns, then, were dropping bombs from aeroplanes on the hospital huts. . . . I'm not suggesting they knew it was a C.C.S.; it was, no doubt, just carelessness. . . ."

"You needn't spare the Germans for me!" Sylvia said. "You needn't spare any man who has killed another man."

"I was, then, dreadfully worried," Tietjens went on. "I was composing a preface for a book on Arminianism. . . ."

"You haven't written a book!" Sylvia exclaimed eagerly, because she thought that if Tietjens took to writing a book there might be a way of his earning a living. Many people had told her that he ought to write a book.

"No, I hadn't written a book," Tietjens said, "and I didn't know what Arminianism was. . . ."

"You know perfectly well what the Arminian heresy is," Sylvia said sharply; "you explained it all to me years ago."

"Yes," Tietjens exclaimed. "Years ago I could have, but I couldn't then. I could now, but I was a little worried about it then. It's a little awkward to write a preface about a subject of which you know nothing. But it didn't seem to me to be discreditable in an army sense. . . . Still, it worried me dreadfully not to know my own name. I lay and worried and worried and thought how discreditable it would appear if a nurse came along and asked me and I didn't know. Of course my name was on a luggage label tied to my collar; but I'd forgotten they did that to casualties. . . . Then a lot of people carried pieces of a nurse down the hut: the Germans' bombs had done that, of course. They were still dropping about the place."

"But good heavens," Sylvia cried out, "do you mean they carried a dead nurse past you? . . ."

"The poor dear wasn't dead," Tietjens said. "I wish she had been. Her name was Beatrice Carmichael . . . the first name I learned after my collapse. She's dead now, of course. . . . That seemed to wake up a fellow on the other side of the room with a lot of blood coming through the bandages on his head. . . . He rolled out of his bed and, without a word, walked across the hut and began to strangle me. . . ."

"But this isn't believable," Sylvia said. "I'm sorry, but I can't believe it. . . . You were an officer: they *couldn't* have carried a wounded nurse under your nose. They must have known your sister Caroline was a nurse and was killed. . . ."

"Carrie!" Tietjens said, "was drowned on a hospital-ship. I thank God I didn't have to connect the other girl with her. . . . But you don't suppose that in addition to one's name, rank, unit, and date of admission they'd put that I'd lost a sister and two brothers in action and a father—of a broken heart, I dare say. . . ."

"But you only lost one brother," Sylvia said. "I went into mourning for him and your sister. . . ."

"No, two," Tietjens said; "but the fellow who was strangling me was what I wanted to tell you about. He let out a number of ear-piercing shrieks and lots of orderlies came and pulled him off me and sat all over him. Then he began to shout *'Faith!'* He shouted: 'Faith! . . . Faith! . . . Faith! . . .' at intervals of two seconds, as far as I could tell by my pulse, until four in the morning, when he died. . . . I don't know whether it was a religious exhortation or a woman's name, but I disliked him a good deal because he started my tortures, such as they were. . . . There had been a girl I knew called Faith. Oh, not a love-affair: the daughter of my father's head gardener, a Scotsman. The point is that every time he said Faith I asked myself 'Faith . . . Faith what?' I couldn't remember the name of my father's head gardener."

Sylvia, who was thinking of other things, asked:

"What *was* the name?"

Tietjens answered:

"I don't know, I don't know to this day. . . . The point is that when I knew that I didn't know *that* name, I was as ignorant, as *uninstructed*, as a new-born babe and much more worried about it. . . . The Koran says—I've got as far as 'K' in my reading of the Encyclopaedia Britannica every afternoon at Mrs. Wannop's—'The strong man when smitten is smitten in his pride!' . . . Of course I got King's Regs. and the M.M.L. and Infantry Field Training and all the A.C.I.s to date by heart very quickly. And that's all a British officer is really encouraged to know. . . ."

"Oh, Christopher!" Sylvia said. "*You* read that encyclopaedia; it's pitiful. You used to despise it so."

"That's what's meant by 'smitten in his pride,'" Tietjens said. "Of course what I read or hear now I remember. . . . But I haven't got to 'M,' much less 'V.' That was why I was worried about Metternich and the Congress of Vienna. I *try* to remember things on my own, but I haven't yet done so. You see it's as if a certain area of my brain had been wiped white. Occasionally one name suggests another. You noticed, when I got Metternich it suggested Castlereagh and Wellington—and even other names. . . . But that's what the Department of Statistics will get me on. When they fire me out. The real reason will be that I've served. But they'll pretend it's because I've no more general knowledge than is to be found in the encyclopaedia: or two-thirds or more or less—

according to the duration of the war. . . . Or, of course, the real reason will be that I won't fake statistics to dish the French with. They asked me to, the other day, as a holiday task. And when I refused you should have seen their faces."

"Have you *really*," Sylvia asked, "lost two brothers in action?"

"Yes," Tietjens answered. "Curly and Longshanks. You never saw them because they were always in India. And they weren't noticeable. . . ."

"Two!" Sylvia said. "I only wrote to your father about one called Edward. And your sister Caroline. In the same letter . . ."

"Carrie wasn't noticeable either," Tietjens said. "She did Charity-Organization-Society work. . . . But I remember: you didn't like her. She was the born old maid. . . ."

"Christopher!" Sylvia asked, "do you still think your mother died of a broken heart because I left you?"

Tietjens said:

"Good God, no. I never thought so and I don't think so. I *know* she didn't."

"Then!" Sylvia exclaimed, "she died of a broken heart because I came back. . . . It's no good protesting that you don't think so. I remember your face when you opened the telegram at Lobscheid. Miss Wannop forwarded it from Rye. I remember the postmark. She was born to do me ill. The moment you got it I could see you thinking that you must conceal from me that you thought it was because of me she died. I could see you wondering if it wouldn't be practicable to conceal from me that she was dead. You couldn't, of course, do that because, you remember, we were to have gone to Wiesbaden and show ourselves; and we couldn't do that because we should have to be in mourning. So you took me to Russia to get out of taking me to the funeral."

"I took you to Russia," Tietjens said. "I remember it all now—because I had an order from Sir Robert Ingleby to assist the British Consul-General in preparing a blue-book statistical table of the government of Kiev. . . . It appeared to be the most industrially promising region in the world in those days. It isn't now, naturally. I shall never see back a penny of the money I put into it. I thought I was clever in those days. . . . And of course, yes, the money was my mother's settlement. It comes back . . . yes, of course. . . ."

"Did you," Sylvia asked, "get out of taking me to your mother's funeral because you thought I should defile your mother's corpse by my presence? Or because you were afraid

that in the presence of your mother's body you wouldn't be
able to conceal from me that you thought I killed her? . . .
Don't deny it. And don't get out of it by saying that you
can't remember those days. You're remembering now: that
I killed your mother: that Miss Wannop sent the telegram—
why don't you score it against her that she sent the news?
. . . Or, good God, why don't you score it against yourself,
as the wrath of the Almighty, that your mother was dying
while you and that girl were croodling over each other? . . .
At Rye! Whilst I was at Lobscheid . . ."

Tietjens wiped his brow with his handkerchief.

"Well, let's drop that," Sylvia said. "God knows I've no
right to put a spoke in that girl's wheel or in yours. If you
love each other you've a right to happiness and I dare say
she'll make you happy. I can't divorce you, being a Catholic;
but I won't make it difficult for you other ways, and self-
contained people like you and her will manage somehow.
You'll have learned the way from Macmaster and his mistress. . . . But, oh, Christopher Tietjens, have you ever considered how foully you've used *me!*"

Tietjens looked at her attentively, as if with magpie anguish.

"If," Sylvia went on with her denunciation, "you had
once in our lives said to me: 'You whore! You bitch! You
killed my mother. May you rot in hell for it. . . .' If you'd
only once said something like it . . . about the child! About
Perowne! . . . you might have done something to bring us
together. . . ."

Tietjens said:

"That's, of course, true!"

"I know," Sylvia said, "you can't help it. . . . But when,
in your famous county-family pride—though a youngest son!
—you say to yourself: And I dare say if . . . oh, Christ!
. . . you're shot in the trenches you'll say it . . . oh, between the saddle and the ground! . . . that you never did
a dishonourable action. . . . And, mind you, I believe that no
other man save one has ever had more right to say it than
you. . . ."

Tietjens said:

"You believe that!"

"As I hope to stand before my Redeemer," Sylvia said, "I
believe it. . . . But, in the name of the Almighty, how
could any woman live beside you . . . and be forever forgiven? Or no: not forgiven: ignored! . . . Well, be proud
when you die, because of your honour. But, God, you be

humble about . . . your errors in judgement. *You* know what it is to ride a horse for miles with too tight a curb-chain and its tongue cut almost in half. . . . You remember the groom your father had who had the trick of turning the hunters out like that. . . . And you horsewhipped him, and you've told me you've almost cried ever so often afterwards for thinking of that mare's mouth. . . . Well! Think of *this* mare's mouth sometimes! You've ridden me like that for seven years. . . ."

She stopped and then went on again:

"Don't you know, Christopher Tietjens, that there is only one man from whom a woman could take *'Neither I condemn thee'* and not hate him more than she hates the fiend! . . ."

Tietjens so looked at her that he contrived to hold her attention.

"I'd like you to let me ask you," he said, "how I could throw stones at you. I have never disapproved of your actions."

Her hands dropped dispiritedly to her sides.

"Oh, Christopher," she said, "don't carry on that old play-acting. I shall never see you again, very likely, to speak to. You'll sleep with the Wannop girl to-night: you're going out to be killed to-morrow. *Let's* be straight for the next ten minutes or so. And give me your attention. The Wannop girl can spare that much if she's to have all the rest. . . ."

She could see that he was giving her his whole mind.

"As you said just now," he exclaimed slowly, "as I hope to meet my Redeemer I believe you to be a good woman. One that never did a dishonourable thing."

She recoiled a little in her chair.

"Then!" she said, "you're the wicked man I've always made believe to think you, though I didn't."

Tietjens said:

"No! . . . Let me try to put it to you as I see it."

She exclaimed:

"No! . . . I've been a wicked woman. I have ruined you. I am not going to listen to you."

He said:

"I dare say you have ruined me. That's nothing to me. I am completely indifferent."

She cried out:

"Oh! Oh! . . . Oh!" on a note of agony.

Tietjens said doggedly:

"I don't care. I can't help it. Those are—those *should* be

—the conditions of life amongst decent people. When our next war comes I hope it will be fought out under those conditions. Let us, for God's sake, talk of the gallant enemy. Always. We have *got* to plunder the French or millions of our people must starve: they have *got* to resist us successfully or be wiped out. . . . It's the same with you and me. . . ."

She exclaimed:

"You mean to say that you don't think I was wicked when I . . . when I trepanned is what mother calls it? . . ."

He said loudly:

"*No!* . . . You had been let in for it by some brute. I have always held that a woman who has been let down by one man has the right—has the duty for the sake of her child—to let down a man. It becomes woman against man: against one man. I happened to be that one man: it was the will of God. But you were within your rights. I will never go back on that. Nothing will make me, ever!"

She said:

"And the others! And Perowne . . . I know you'll say that anyone is justified in doing anything as long as they are open enough about it. . . . But it killed your mother. Do you disapprove of my having killed your mother? Or you consider that I have corrupted the child . . ."

Tietjens said:

"I don't. . . . I want to speak to you about that."

She exclaimed:

"You *don't*. . . ."

He said calmly:

"You know I don't . . . while I was certain that I was going to be here to keep him straight and an Anglican I fought your influence over him. I'm obliged to you for having brought up of yourself the considerations that I may be killed and that I am ruined. I am. I could not raise a hundred pounds between now and to-morrow. I am, therefore, obviously not the man to have sole charge of the heir of Groby."

Sylvia was saying:

"Every penny I have is at your disposal. . . ." when the maid, Hullo Central, marched up to her master and placed a card in his hand. He said:

"Tell him to wait five minutes in the drawing-room."

Sylvia said:

"Who is it?"

Tietjens answered:

"A man . . . Let's get this settled. I've never thought you corrupted the boy. You tried to teach him to tell white lies. On perfectly straight papist lines. I have no objection to papists and no objection to white lies for papists. You told him once to put a frog in Marchant's bath. I've no objection to a boy's putting a frog in his nurse's bath, as such. But Marchant is an old woman, and the heir to Groby should respect old women always and old family servants in particular. . . . It hasn't, perhaps, struck you that the boy is heir to Groby. . . ."

Sylvia said:

"If . . . if your second brother is killed . . . But your eldest brother . . ."

"He," Tietjens said, "has got a Frenchwoman near Euston Station. He's lived with her for over fifteen years, of afternoons, when there were no race-meetings. She'll never let him marry and she's past the child-bearing stage. So there's no one else. . . ."

Sylvia said:

"You mean that I may bring the child up as a Catholic."

Tietjens said:

"A *Roman* Catholic . . . You'll teach him, please, to use that term before myself if I ever see him again. . . ."

Sylvia said:

"Oh, I thank God that he has softened your heart. This will take the curse off this house."

Tietjens shook his head:

"I think not," he said; "off you, perhaps. Off Groby very likely. It was, perhaps, time that there should be a papist owner of Groby again. You've read Spelden on sacrilege about Groby? . . ."

She said:

"Yes! The first Tietjens who came over with Dutch William, the swine, was pretty bad to the papist owners. . . ."

"He was a tough Dutchman," Tietjens said, "but let us get on! There's enough time, but not too much. . . . I've got this man to see."

"Who is he?" Sylvia asked.

Tietjens was collecting his thoughts.

"My dear!" he said. "You'll permit me to call you 'my dear'? We're old enemies enough and we're talking about the future of our child."

Sylvia said:

"You said 'our' child, not 'the' child. . . ."

Tietjens said with a great deal of concern:

"You will forgive me for bringing it up. You might prefer to think he was Drake's child. He can't be. It would be outside the course of nature. . . . I'm as poor as I am because . . . forgive me . . . I've spent a great deal of money on tracing the movements of you and Drake before our marriage. And if it's a relief to you to know . . ."

"It *is*," Sylvia said. "I . . . I've always been too beastly shy to put the matter before a specialist or even before mother. . . . And we women are so ignorant. . . ."

Tietjens said:

"I know . . . I know you were too shy even to think about it yourself, hard." He went into months and days; then he continued: "But it would have made no difference: a child born in wedlock is by law the father's, and if a man who's a gentleman suffers the begetting of his child, he must, in decency, take the consequences: the woman and the child must come before the man, be he who he may. And worse-begotten children than ours have inherited statelier names. And I loved the little beggar with all my heart and with all my soul from the first minute I saw him. That may be the secret clue or it may be sheer sentimentality. . . . So I fought your influence, because it was papist, while I was a whole man. But I'm not a whole man any more, and the evil eye that is on me might transfer itself to him."

He stopped and said:

"For I must to the greenwood go. Alone a banished man. . . . But have him well protected against the evil eye. . . ."

"Oh, Christopher," she said, "it's true I've not been a bad woman to the child. And I never will be. And I will keep Marchant with him till she dies. You'll tell her not to interfere with his religious instruction, and she won't. . . ."

Tietjens said with a friendly weariness:

"That's right . . . and you'll have Father . . . Father . . . the priest that was with us for a fortnight before he was born, to give him his teachings. He was the best man I ever met and one of the most intelligent. It's been a great comfort to me to think of the boy as in his hands. . . ."

Sylvia stood up, her eyes blazing out of a pallid face of stone:

"Father Consett," she said, "was hung on the day they shot Casement. They dare not put it into the papers because he was a priest and all the witnesses Ulster witnesses. . . . And yet I may not say this is an accursed war."

Tietjens shook his head with the slow heaviness of an aged man.

"You may for me. . . ." he said. "You might ring the bell, will you? Don't go away. . . ."

He sat with the blue gloom of that enclosed space all over him, lumped heavily in his chair.

"Spelden on sacrilege," he said, "may be right after all. You'd say so from the Tietjenses. There's not been a Tietjens since the first Lord Justice cheated the papist Loundeses out of Groby, but died of a broken neck or of a broken heart: for all the fifteen thousand acres of good farming land and iron land, and for all the heather on the top of it. . . . What's the quotation: 'Be ye something as something and something and ye shall not escape. . . .' What is it?"

"Calumny!" Sylvia said. She spoke with intense bitterness. "Chaste as ice and cold as . . . as you are. . . ."

Tietjens said:

"Yes! Yes. . . . And mind you, none of the Tietjens were ever soft. Not one! They had reason for their broken hearts. . . . Take my poor father. . . ."

Sylvia said:

"*Don't!*"

"Both my brothers were killed in Indian regiments on the same day and not a mile apart. And my sister in the same week: out at sea, not so far from them . . . Unnoticeable people. But one can be fond of unnoticeable people. . . ."

Hullo Central was at the door. Tietjens told her to ask Lord Port Scatho to step down.

"You must, of course, know these details," Tietjens said, "as the mother to my father's heir. . . . My father got the three notifications on the same day. It was enough to break his heart. He only lived a month. I saw him. . . ."

Sylvia screamed piercingly:

"Stop! Stop! Stop!" She clutched at the mantelpiece to hold herself up. "Your father died of a broken heart," she said, "because your brother's best friend, Ruggles, told him you were a squit who lived on women's money and had got the daughter of his oldest friend with child. . . ."

Tietjens said:

"Oh! Ah! Yes! . . . I suspected that. I knew it, really. I suppose the poor dear knows better now. Or perhaps he doesn't . . . It doesn't matter."

2 ~

IT HAS been remarked that the peculiarly English habit of self-suppression in matters of the emotions puts the Englishman at a great disadvantage in moments of unusual stresses. In the smaller matters of the general run of life he will be impeccable and not to be moved; but in sudden confrontations of anything but physical dangers he is apt—he is, indeed, almost certain—to go to pieces very badly. This, at least, was the view of Christopher Tietjens, and he very much dreaded his interview with Lord Port Scatho—because he feared that he must be near breaking point.

In electing to be peculiarly English in habits and in as much of his temperament as he could control—for though no man can choose the land of his birth or his ancestry, he can, if he have industry and determination, so watch over himself as materially to modify his automatic habits—Tietjens had quite advisedly and of set purpose adopted a habit of behaviour that he considered to be the best in the world for the normal life. If every day and all day long you chatter at high pitch and with the logic and lucidity of the Frenchman; if you shout in self-assertion, with your hat on your stomach, bowing from a stiff spine and by implication threaten all day long to shoot your interlocutor, like the Prussian; if you are as lachrymally emotional as the Italian or as dryly and epigramatically imbecile over unessentials as the American, you will have a noisy, troublesome and thoughtless society without any of the surface calm that should distinguish the atmosphere of men when they are together. You will never have deep arm-chairs in which to sit for hours in clubs, thinking of nothing at all—or of the off-theory in bowling. On the other hand, in the face of death—except at sea, by fire, railway accident or accidental drowning in rivers; in the face of madness, passion, dishonour or—and particularly—prolonged mental strain, you will have all the disadvantage of the beginner at any game and may come off very badly indeed. Fortunately death, love, public dishonour and the like are rare occurrences in the life of the average man, so that the great advantage would seem to have lain with English society; at any rate, before the later months of the year 1914. Death for man came but once: the danger of death so seldom as to be practically negligible:

love of a distracting kind was a disease merely of the weak: public dishonour for persons of position—so great was the hushing-up power of the ruling class and the power of absorption of the remoter colonies—was practically unknown.

Tietjens found himself now faced by all these things, coming upon him cumulatively and rather suddenly, and he had before him an interview that might cover them all and with a man whom he much respected and very much desired not to hurt. He had to face these, moreover, with a brain two-thirds of which felt numb. It was exactly like that.

It was not so much that he couldn't use what brain he had as trenchantly as ever: it was that there were whole regions of fact upon which he could no longer call in support of his argument. His knowledge of history was still practically negligible: he knew nothing whatever of the humaner letters and, what was far worse, nothing at all of the higher and more sensuous phases of mathematics. And the comings-back of these things was much slower than he had confessed to Sylvia. It was with these disadvantages that he had to face Lord Port Scatho.

Lord Port Scatho was the first man of whom Sylvia Tietjens had thought when she had been considering of men who were absolutely honourable, entirely benevolent . . . and rather lacking in constructive intelligence. He had inherited the management of one of the most respected of the great London banks, so that his commercial and social influences were very extended: he was extremely interested in promoting Low Church interests, the reform of the divorce laws and sports for the people, and he had a great affection for Sylvia Tietjens. He was forty-five, beginning to put on weight, but by no means obese; he had a large, quite round head, very high-coloured cheeks that shone as if with frequent ablutions, an uncropped, dark moustache, dark, very cropped, smooth hair, brown eyes, a very new grey tweed suit, a very new grey Trilby hat, a black tie in a gold ring and very new patent-leather boots that had white calf tops. He had a wife almost the spit of himself in face, figure, probity, kindliness and interests except that for his interest in sports for the people, she substituted that for maternity hospitals. His heir was his nephew, Mr. Brownlie, known as Brownie, who would also be physically the exact spit of his uncle except that, not having put on flesh, he appeared to be taller and that his moustache and hair were both a little longer and more fair. This gentleman entertained for Sylvia Tietjens a gloomy and deep passion that he considered to be perfectly honourable because he desired to marry her after she had divorced her husband. Tietjens he desired to ruin because he wished to marry Mrs. Tietjens and partly because he considered Tietjens to be an undesirable person of no great means. Of this passion Lord Port Scatho was ignorant.

He now came into the Tietjens' dining-room, behind the servant, holding an open letter: he walked rather stiffly because he was very much worried. He observed that Sylvia had been crying and was still wiping her eyes. He looked round the room to see if he could see in it anything to account for Sylvia's crying. Tietjens was still sitting at the head of the lunch-table: Sylvia was rising from a chair beside the fire-place.

Lord Port Scatho said:

"I want to see you, Tietjens, for a minute on business."

Tietjens said:

"I can give you ten minutes. . . ."

Lord Port Scatho said:

"Mrs. Tietjens perhaps . . ."

He waved the open letter towards Mrs. Tietjens. Tietjens said:

"No! Mrs. Tietjens will remain." He desired to say something more friendly. He said: "Sit down."

Lord Port Scatho said:

"I shan't be stopping a minute. But really . . ." and he moved the letter, but not with so wide a gesture, towards Sylvia.

"I have no secrets from Mrs. Tietjens," Tietjens said. "Absolutely none . . ."

Lord Port Scatho said:

"No . . . No, of course not . . . But . . ."

Tietjens said:

"Similarly, Mrs. Tietjens has no secrets from me. Again absolutely none."

Sylvia said:

"I don't, of course, tell Tietjens about my maid's love-affairs or what the fish costs every day."

Tietjens said:

"You'd better sit down." He added on an impulse of kindness: "As a matter of fact, I was just clearing up things for Sylvia to take over . . . this command." It was part of the disagreeableness of his mental disadvantages that upon occasion he could not think of other than military phrases. He felt intense annoyance. Lord Port Scatho affected him with some of the slight nausea that in those days you felt at contact with the civilian who knew none of your thoughts, phrases or preoccupations. He added, nevertheless equably:

"One has to clear up. I'm going out."

Lord Port Scatho said hastily:

"Yes, yes. I won't keep you. One has so many engagements in spite of the war. . . ." His eyes wandered in bewilderment. Tietjens could see them at last fixing themselves on the oil stains that Sylvia's salad dressing had left on his collar and green tabs. He said to himself that he must remember to change his tunic before he went to the War Office. He must not forget. Lord Port Scatho's bewilderment at these oil stains was such that he had lost himself in the desire to account for them. . . . You could see the slow thoughts moving inside his square, polished brown forehead. Tietjens wanted very much to help him. He wanted to say: "It's about Sylvia's letter that you've got in your hand, isn't it?" But Lord Port Scatho had entered the room with the stiffness, with the odd, high-collared sort of gait that on formal and unpleasant occasions Englishmen use when they approach each other; braced up, a little like strange dogs meeting in the street. In view of that, Tietjens couldn't say "Sylvia." But it would add to the formality and unpleasantness if he said again "Mrs. Tietjens!" *That* wouldn't help Port Scatho. . . .

Sylvia said suddenly:

"You don't understand, apparently. My husband is going out to the front line. To-morrow morning. It's for the second time."

Lord Port Scatho sat down suddenly on a chair beside the table. With his fresh face and brown eyes suddenly anguished he exclaimed:

"But, my dear fellow! You! Good God!" and then to Sylvia: "I beg your pardon!" To clear his mind he said again to Tietjens: *"You!* going out to-morrow!" And when the idea was really there, his face suddenly cleared. He looked with a swift, averted glance at Sylvia's face and then for a fixed moment at Tietjens' oil-stained tunic. Tietjens could see him explaining to himself with immense enlightenment that *that* explained both Sylvia's tears and the oil on the tunic. For Port Scatho might well imagine that officers went to the conflict in their oldest clothes. . . .

But if his puzzled brain cleared, his distressed mind became suddenly distressed doubly. He had to add to the distress he had felt on entering the room and finding himself in the midst of what he took to be a highly emotional family parting. And Tietjens knew that during the whole war Port Scatho had never witnessed a family parting at all. Those that were not inevitable he would avoid like the plague, and his own nephew and all his wife's nephews were in the bank. That was quite proper, for if the ennobled family of Brownlie were not of the Ruling Class—who had to go!—they were of the Administrative Class, who were privileged to stay. So he had seen no partings.

Of his embarrassed hatred of them he gave immediate evidence. For he first began several sentences of praise of Tietjens' heroism which he was unable to finish, and then, getting quickly out of his chair, exclaimed:

"In the circumstances, then . . . the little matter I came about . . . I couldn't, of course, think . . ."

Tietjens said:

"No, don't go. The matter you came about—I know all about it, of course—had better be settled."

Port Scatho sat down again: his jaw fell slowly: under his bronzed complexion his skin became a shade paler. He said at last:

"You know what I came about? But then . . ."

His ingenuous and kindly mind could be seen to be working with reluctance: his athletic figure drooped. He pushed the letter that he still held along the table-cloth towards Tietjens. He said, in the voice of one awaiting a reprieve:

"But you *can't* be . . . aware. . . . Not of this letter . . ."

Tietjens left the letter on the cloth; from there he could read the large handwriting on the blue-grey paper:

"Mrs. Christopher Tietjens presents her compliments to Lord Port Scatho and the Honourable Court of Benchers of the Inn. . . ." He wondered where Sylvia had got hold of that phraseology: he imagined it to be fantastically wrong. He said:

"I have already told you that I know about this letter, as I have already told you that I know—and I will add that I approve!—of all Mrs. Tietjens' actions. . . ." With his hard blue eyes he looked browbeatingly into Port Scatho's soft brown orbs, knowing that he was sending the message: "Think what you please and be damned to you!"

The gentle brown things remained on his face; then they filled with an expression of deep pain. Port Scatho cried:

"But, good God! Then . . ."

He looked at Tietjens again. His mind, which took refuge

from life in the affairs of the Low Church, of Divorce Law
Reform and of Sports for the People, became a sea of pain
at the contemplation of strong situations. His eyes said:

"For heaven's sake, do not tell me that Mrs. Duchemin, the
mistress of your dearest friend, is the mistress of yourself,
and that you take this means of wreaking a vulgar spite on
them."

Tietjens, leaning heavily forward, made his eyes as enigmatic as he could; he said very slowly and very clearly:

"Mrs. Tietjens is, of course, not aware of *all* the circumstances."

Port Scatho threw himself back in his chair.

"I don't understand!" he said. "I do not understand. How
am I to act? You do not wish me to act on this letter?
You can't!"

Tietjens, who found himself, said:

"You had better talk to Mrs. Tietjens about that. I will
say something myself later. In the meantime let me say that
Mrs. Tietjens would seem to me to be quite within her
rights. A lady, heavily veiled, comes here every Friday and
remains until four of the Saturday morning. . . . If you are
prepared to palliate the proceeding, you had better do so to
Mrs. Tietjens. . . ."

Port Scatho turned agitatedly on Sylvia.

"I can't, of course, palliate," he said. "God forbid. . . .
But, my dear Sylvia . . . my dear Mrs. Tietjens . . . In
the case of two people so much esteemed! . . . We have,
of course, argued the matter of principle. It is a part of a
subject I have very much at heart: the granting of divorce
. . . civil divorce, at least . . . in cases in which one of the
parties to the marriage is in a lunatic asylum. I have sent
you the pamphlets of E. S. P. Haynes that we publish. I
know that as a Roman Catholic you hold strong views. . . .
I do not, I assure you, stand for latitude. . . ." He became
then simply eloquent: he really had the matter at heart, one
of his sisters having been for many years married to a lunatic.
He expatiated on the agonies of this situation all the more
eloquently in that it was the only form of human distress
which he had personally witnessed.

Sylvia took a long look at Tietjens: he imagined for
counsel. He looked at her steadily for a moment, then at
Port Scatho, who was earnestly turned to her, then back at
her. He was trying to say:

"Listen to Port Scatho for a minute. I need time to think
of my course of action!"

He needed, for the first time in his life, time to think of his course of action.

He had been thinking with his undermind ever since Sylvia had told him that she had written her letter to the benchers denouncing Macmaster and his woman; ever since Sylvia had reminded him that Mrs. Duchemin in the Edinburgh to London express of the day before the war had been in his arms, he had seen, with extraordinary clearness, a great many North Country scenes, though he could not affix names to all the places. The forgetfulness of the names was abnormal: he ought to know the names of places from Berwick down to the vale of York—but that he should have forgotten the incidents was normal enough. They had been of little importance: he preferred not to remember the phases of his friend's love-affair; moreover, the events that happened immediately afterwards had been of a nature to make one forget quite normally what had just preceded them. That Mrs. Duchemin should be sobbing on his shoulder in a locked corridor carriage hadn't struck him as in the least important: she was the mistress of his dearest friend: she had had a very trying time for a week or so, ending in a violent, nervous quarrel with her agitated lover. She was, of course, crying off the effects of the quarrel, which had been all the more shaking in that Mrs. Duchemin, like himself, had always been almost too self-contained. As a matter of fact, he did not himself like Mrs. Duchemin, and he was pretty certain that she herself more than a little disliked him; so that nothing but their common feeling for Macmaster had brought them together. General Campion, however, was not to know that. . . . He had looked into the carriage in the way one does in a corridor just after the train had left. . . . He couldn't remember the name. . . . Doncaster . . . No! . . . Darlington; it wasn't that. At Darlington there was a model of the Rocket . . . or perhaps it isn't the Rocket. An immense, clumsy leviathan of a locomotive by . . . by . . . The great gloomy stations of the north-going trains . . . Durham . . . No! Alnwick . . . No! . . . Wooler . . . By God! Wooler! The junction for Bamborough . . .

It had been in one of the castles at Bamborough that he and Sylvia had been staying with the Sandbachs. Then . . . a name had come into his mind spontaneously! . . . Two names! . . . It was, perhaps, the turn of the tide! For the first time . . . To be marked with a red stone . . . after this: some names, sometimes, on the tip of the tongue, might come over! He had, however, to get on. . . .

The Sandbachs, then, and he and Sylvia . . . others too . . . had been in Bamborough since mid-July: Eton and Harrow at Lord's, waiting for the real house-parties that would come with the twelfth. . . . He repeated these names and dates to himself for the personal satisfaction of knowing that, amongst the repairs effected in his mind, these two remained: Eton and Harrow, the end of the London season: twelfth of August, grouse-shooting begins. . . . It was pitiful. . . .

When General Campion had come up to rejoin his sister, he, Tietjens, had stopped only two days. The coolness between the two of them remained; it was the first time they had met, except in court, after the accident. . . . For Mrs. Wannop, with grim determination, had sued the general for the loss of her horse. It had lived, all right—but it was only fit to draw a lawn-mower for cricket pitches. . . . Mrs. Wannop, then, had gone bald-headed for the general, partly because she wanted the money, partly because she wanted a public reason for breaking with the Sandbachs. The general had been equally obstinate and had undoubtedly perjured himself in court: not the best, not the most honourable, the most benevolent man in the world would not turn oppressor of the widow and orphan when his efficiency as a chauffeur was impugned or the fact brought to light that at a very dangerous turning he hadn't sounded his horn. Tietjens had sworn that he hadn't: the general that he had. There *could* not be any question of doubt, for the horn was a beastly thing that made a prolonged noise like that of a terrified peacock. . . . So Tietjens had not, till the end of that July, met the general again. It had been quite a proper thing for gentlemen to quarrel over and was quite convenient, though it had cost the general fifty pounds for the horse and, of course, a good bit over for costs. Lady Claudine had refused to interfere in the matter: she was privately of opinion that the general *hadn't* sounded his horn, but the general was both a passionately devoted and explosive brother. She had remained closely intimate with Sylvia, mildly cordial with Tietjens, and had continued to ask the Wannops to such of her garden-parties as the general did not attend. She was also very friendly with Mrs. Duchemin.

Tietjens and the general had met with the restrained cordiality of English gentlemen who had some years before accused each other of perjury in a motor accident. On the second morning a violent quarrel had broken out between them on the subject of whether the general had or hadn't

sounded his horn. The general had ended up by shouting
. . . really shouting:

"By God! If I ever get you under my command . . ."

Tietjens remembered that he had quoted and given the
number of a succinct paragraph in King's Regs. dealing with
the fate of general or higher field-officers who gave their
subordinates bad confidential reports because of private
quarrels. The general had exploded into noises that ended in
laughter.

"What a rag-bag of a mind you have, Chrissie!" he said.
"What's King's Regs. to you? And how do you know it's paragraph sixty-six or whatever you say it is? I don't." He
added more seriously: *"What* a fellow you are for getting
into obscure rows! What in the world do you do it for?"

That afternoon Tietjens had gone to stop, a long way up in
the moors, with his son, the nurse, his sister Effie and her
children. They were the last days of happiness he was to
know, and he hadn't known so many. He was then content.
He played with his boy, who, thank God, was beginning to
grow healthy at last. He walked about the moors with his
sister Effie, a large, plain, parson's wife, who had no conversation at all, though at times they talked of their mother. The
moors were like enough to those above Groby to make them
happy. They lived in a bare, grim farmhouse, drank great
quantities of buttermilk and ate great quantities of Wensley-
dale. It was the hard, frugal life of his desire and his mind
was at rest.

His mind was at rest because there was going to be a war.
From the first moment of his reading the paragraph about
the assassination of the Archduke Franz Ferdinand, he had
known that, calmly and with assurance. Had he imagined that
this country would come in, he would not have known a
mind at rest. He loved this country for the run of its hills,
the shape of its elm-trees and the way the heather, running
uphill to the sky-line, meets the blue of the heavens. War
for this country could only mean humiliation, spreading
under the sunlight, an almost invisible pall, over the elms,
the hills, the heather, like the vapour that spread from . . .
oh, Middlesbrough! We were fitted neither for defeat nor
for victory: we could be true to neither friend nor foe. Not
even to ourselves!

But of war for us he had no fear. He saw our Ministry
sitting tight till the opportune moment and then grabbing
a French channel port or a few German colonies as the price
of neutrality. And he was thankful to be out of it; for his

back-doorway out—his second!—was the French Foreign
Legion. First Sylvia: then that! Two tremendous disciplines:
for the soul and for the body.

The French he admired: for their tremendous efficiency, for
their frugality of life, for the logic of their minds, for their
admirable achievements in the arts, for their neglect of the
industrial system, for their devotion, above all, to the eighteenth century. It would be restful to serve, if only as a slave,
people who saw clearly, coldly, straight: not obliquely and
with hypocrisy only such things as should deviously conduce
to the standard of comfort of hogs and to lecheries winked
at. . . . He would rather sit for hours on a bench in a
barrack-room polishing a badge in preparation for the cruellest of route marches of immense lengths under the Algerian
sun.

For as to the Foreign Legion, he had had no illusion.
You were treated not as a hero, but as a whipped dog: he
was aware of all the *asticoteries,* the cruelties, the weight of
the rifle, the cells. You would have six months of training in
the desert and then be hurtled into the line to be massacred
without remorse . . . as foreign dirt. But the prospect seemed
to him one of deep peace: he had never asked for soft living
and now was done with it. . . . The boy was healthy; Sylvia,
with the economies they had made, very rich . . . and even
at that date he was sure that if the friction of himself,
Tietjens, were removed, she would make a good mother. . . .

Obviously he might survive; but after that tremendous
physical drilling what survived would not be himself, but
a man with cleaned, sand-dried bones: a clear mind. His
private ambition had always been for saintliness: he must be
able to touch pitch and not be defiled. That, he knew, marked
him off as belonging to the sentimental branch of humanity.
He couldn't help it: Stoic or Epicurean: Caliph in the harem
or Dervish desiccating in the sand: one or the other you must
be. And his desire was to be a saint of the Anglican variety
. . . as his mother had been, without convent, ritual, vows,
or miracles to be performed by your relics! That sainthood,
truly, the Foreign Legion might give you. . . . The desire of
every English gentleman from Colonel Hutchinson upwards
. . . A mysticism . . .

Remembering the clear sunlight of those naïvetés—
though in his blue gloom he had abated no jot of the
ambition—Tietjens sighed deeply as he came back for a moment to regard his dining-room. Really it was to see how
much time he had left in which to think out what to say to

Port Scatho . . . Port Scatho had moved his chair over to
beside Sylvia and, almost touching her, was leaning over and
recounting the griefs of his sister who was married to a lunatic. Tietjens gave himself again for a moment to the luxury of
self-pity. He considered that he was dull-minded, heavy,
ruined, and so calumniated that at times he believed in his
own infamy, for it is impossible to stand up forever against
the obloquy of your kind and remain unhurt in the mind. If
you hunch your shoulders too long against a storm, your
shoulders will grow bowed. . . .

His mind stopped for a moment and his eyes gazed dully
at Sylvia's letter, which lay open on the table-cloth. His
thoughts came together, converging on the loosely written
words:

"For the last nine months a woman . . ."

He wondered swiftly what he had already said to Port
Scatho: only that he had known of his wife's letter; not when!
And that he approved! Well, on principle! He sat up. To
think that one could be brought down to thinking so slowly!

He ran swiftly over what had happened in the train from
Scotland and before. . . .

Macmaster had turned up one morning beside their breakfast-table in the farmhouse, much agitated, looking altogether
too small in a cloth cap and a new grey tweed suit. He had
wanted £50 to pay his bill with: at some place up the line
above . . . above . . . Berwick suddenly flashed into Tietjens'
mind. . . .

That was the geographic position. Sylvia was at Bamborough on the coast (junction Wooler); he, himself, to the
north-west, on the moors. Macmaster to the north-east of him,
just over the border: in some circumspect beauty spot where
you did not meet people. Both Macmaster and Mrs. Duchemin would know that country and gurgle over its beastly
literary associations. . . . The Shirra! Maida! Pet Marjorie . . .
Faugh! Macmaster would, no doubt, turn an honest penny
by writing articles about it, and Mrs. Duchemin would hold
his hand. . . .

She had become Macmaster's mistress, as far as Tietjens
knew, after a dreadful scene in the rectory, Duchemin having
mauled his wife like a savage dog, and Macmaster in the
house. . . . It was natural: a Sadic reaction, as it were. But
Tietjens rather wished they hadn't. Now it appeared they had
been spending a week together . . . or more. Duchemin by
that time was in an asylum. . . .

From what Tietjens had made out, they had got out of

bed early one morning to take a boat and see the sunrise on some lake and had passed an agreeable day together quoting, "Since when we stand side by side only hands may meet" and other poems of Gabriel Charles Dante Rossetti, no doubt to justify their sin. On coming home, they had run their boat's nose into the tea-table of the Port Scathos with Mr. Brownlie, the nephew, just getting out of a motor to join them. The Port Scatho group were spending the night at the Macmasters' hotel, which backed on to the lake. It was the ordinary damn sort of thing that must happen in these islands that are only a few yards across.

The Macmasters appear to have lost their heads frightfully, although Lady Port Scatho had been as motherly as possible to Mrs. Duchemin; so motherly, indeed, that if they had not been unable to observe anything, they might have recognized the Port Scathos as backers rather than spies upon themselves. It was, no doubt, however, Brownlie who had upset them: he wasn't very civil to Macmaster, whom he knew as a friend of Tietjens. He had dashed up from London in his motor to consult his uncle, who was dashing down from the west of Scotland, about the policy of the bank in that moment of crisis. . . .

Macmaster, anyhow, did not spend the night in the hotel, but went to Jedburgh or Melrose or some such place, turning up again almost before it was light to have a frightful interview about five in the morning with Mrs. Duchemin, who, towards three, had come to a disastrous conclusion as to her condition. They had lost their nerves for the first time in their association, and they had lost them very badly indeed, the things that Mrs. Duchemin said to Macmaster seeming almost to have passed belief. . . .

Thus, when Macmaster turned up at Tietjens' breakfast, he was almost out of his mind. He wanted Tietjens to go over in the motor he had brought, pay the bill at the hotel, and travel down to town with Mrs. Duchemin, who was certainly in no condition to travel alone. Tietjens was also to make up the quarrel with Mrs. Duchemin and to lend Macmaster £50 in cash, as it was then impossible to change cheques anywhere. Tietjens got the money from his old nurse, who, because she distrusted banks, carried great sums in £5 notes in a pocket under her underpetticoat.

Macmaster, pocketing the money, had said:

"That makes exactly two thousand guineas that I owe you. I'm making arrangements to repay you next week. . . ."

Tietjens remembered that he had rather stiffened and had

said: "For God's sake, don't. I beg you not to. Have Duchemin properly put under trustee in lunacy, and leave his capital alone. I really beg you. You don't know what you'll be letting yourselves in for. You don't owe me anything and you can always draw on me."

Tietjens never knew what Mrs. Duchemin had done about her husband's estate, over which she had at that date had a power of attorney; but he had imagined that from that time on, Macmaster had felt a certain coldness for himself and that Mrs. Duchemin had hated him. During several years Macmaster had been borrowing hundreds at a time from Tietjens. The affair with Mrs. Duchemin had cost her lover a good deal: he had week-ended almost continuously in Rye at the expensive hostel. Moreover, the famous Friday parties for geniuses had been going on for several years now, and these had meant new furnishings, bindings, carpets, and loans to geniuses—at any rate, before Macmaster had had the ear of the Royal Bounty. So the sum had grown to £2,000, and now to guineas. And from that date, the Macmasters had not offered any repayment.

Macmaster had said that he dare not travel with Mrs. Duchemin because all London would be going south by that train. All London had. It pushed in at every conceivable and inconceivable station all down the line—it was the great route of the 3-8-14. Tietjens had got on board at Berwick, where they were adding extra coaches, and by giving a £5 note to the guard, who hadn't been able to promise isolation for any distance, had got a locked carriage. It hadn't remained locked for long enough to let Mrs. Duchemin have her cry out—but it had apparently served to make some mischief. The Sandbach party had got on, no doubt, at Wooler; the Port Scatho party somewhere else. Their petrol had run out somewhere and sales were stopped, even to bankers. Macmaster, who after all had travelled by the same train, hidden beneath two bluejackets, had picked up Mrs. Duchemin at King's Cross and that had seemed the end of it.

Tietjens, back in his dining-room, felt relief and also anger. He said:

"Port Scatho. Time's getting short. I'd like to deal with this letter if you don't mind."

Port Scatho came as if up out of a dream. He had found the process of attempting to convert Mrs. Tietjens to divorce-law reform very pleasant—as he always did. He said:

"Yes! . . . Oh, yes!"

Tietjens said slowly:

"If you can listen . . . Macmaster had been married to Mrs.
Duchemin exactly nine months. . . . Have you got that? Mrs.
Tietjens did not know this till this afternoon. The period Mrs.
Tietjens complains of in her letter is nine months. She did
perfectly right to write the letter. As such, I approve of it.
If she had known that the Macmasters were married she would
not have written it. I didn't know she was going to write it.
If I had known she was going to write it I should have requested her not to. If I had requested her not to she would,
no doubt, not have done so. I did know of the letter at the
moment of your coming in. I had heard of it at lunch only
ten minutes before. I should, no doubt, have heard of it before, but this is the first time I have lunched at home in four
months. I have to-day had a day's leave as being warned for
foreign service. I have been doing duty at Ealing. To-day is the
first opportunity I have had for serious business conversation with Mrs. Tietjens. . . . Have you got all that? . . ."

Port Scatho was running towards Tietjens, his hand extended, and over his whole shining personage the air of an
enraptured bridegroom. Tietjens moved his right hand a
little to the right, thus eluding the pink, well-fleshed hand of
Port Scatho. He went on frigidly:

"You had better, in addition, know as follows: The late
Mr. Duchemin was a scatological—afterwards a homicidal
—lunatic. He had recurrent fits, usually on a Saturday morning. That was because he fasted—not abstained merely—on
Fridays. On Fridays he also drank. He had acquired the craving for drink when fasting, from finishing the sacramental
wine after communion services. That is a not-unknown oc-
currence. He behaved latterly with great physical violence to
Mrs. Duchemin. Mrs. Duchemin, on the other hand, treated
him with the utmost consideration and concern: she might
have had him certified much earlier, but, considering the pain
that confinement must cause him during his lucid intervals,
she refrained. I have been an eyewitness of the most excruciating heroisms on her part. As for the behaviour of Macmaster and Mrs. Duchemin, I am ready to certify—and I believe society accepts—that it has been most . . . oh, circumspect and right! . . . There has been no secret of their attachment to each other. I believe that their determination to
behave with decency during their period of waiting has not
been questioned. . . ."

Lord Port Scatho said:

"No! No! Never . . . Most . . . as you say . . . circumspect and, yes . . . right!"

"Mrs. Duchemin," Tietjens continued, "has presided at Macmaster's literary Fridays for a long time; of course since long before they were married. But, as you know, Macmaster's Fridays have been perfectly open: you might almost call them celebrated. . . ."

Lord Port Scatho said:

"Yes! Yes! Indeed . . . I sh'd be only too glad to have a ticket for Lady Port Scatho. . . ."

"She's only got to walk in," Tietjens said. "I'll warn them: they'll be pleased. . . . If, perhaps, you would look in to-night! They have a special party. . . . But Mrs. Macmaster was always attended by a young lady who saw her off by the last train to Rye. Or I very frequently saw her off myself, Macmaster being occupied by the weekly article that he wrote for one of the papers on Friday things. . . . They were married on the day after Mr. Duchemin's funeral. . . ."

"You can't blame 'em!" Lord Port Scatho proclaimed.

"I don't propose to," Tietjens said. "The really frightful tortures Mrs. Duchemin had suffered justified—and indeed necessitated—her finding protection and sympathy at the earliest possible moment. They have deferred this announcement of their union partly out of respect for the usual period of mourning, partly because Mrs. Duchemin feels very strongly that, with all the suffering that is now abroad, wedding-feasts and signs of rejoicing on the part of non-participants are eminently to be deprecated. Still, the little party of to-night is by way of being an announcement that they are married. . . ." He paused to reflect for a moment.

"I perfectly understand!" Lord Port Scatho exclaimed. "I perfectly approve. Believe me, I and Lady Port Scatho will do everything. . . . Everything! . . . Most admirable people . . . Tietjens, my dear fellow, your behaviour . . . most handsome . . ."

Tietjens said:

"Wait a minute. . . . There was an occasion in August, '14. In a place on the border. I can't remember the name. . . ."

Lord Port Scatho burst out:

"My dear fellow . . . I beg you won't . . . I beseech you not to . . ."

Tietjens went on:

"Just before then Mr. Duchemin had made an attack of an unparalleled violence on his wife. It was that that caused his final incarceration. She was not only temporarily disfigured, but she suffered serious internal injuries and, of course, great mental disturbance. It was absolutely neces-

sary that she should have change of scene. . . . But I think
you will bear me out that, in that case too, their behaviour
was . . . again, circumspect and right. . . ."

Port Scatho said:

"I know, I know . . . Lady Port Scatho and I agreed—even
without knowing what you have just told me—that the poor
things almost exaggerated it. . . . He slept, of course, at Jedburgh? . . . ."

Tietjens said:

"Yes! They almost exaggerated it. . . . I had to be called in
to take Mrs. Duchemin home. . . . It caused, apparently, mis-
understandings. . . ."

Port Scatho—full of enthusiasm at the thought that at
least two unhappy victims of the hateful divorce laws had,
with decency and circumspectness, found the haven of their
desires—burst out:

"By God, Tietjens, if I ever hear a man say a word against
you . . . Your splendid championship of your friend. . . .
Your . . . your unswerving devotion . . ."

Tietjens said:

"Wait a minute, Port Scatho, will you?" He was unbutton-
ing the flap of his breast pocket.

"A man who can act so splendidly in one instance . . ."
Port Scatho said. "And your going to France . . . If anyone
. . . if *anyone* . . . dares . . ."

At the sight of a vellum-cornered, green-edged book in
Tietjens' hand Sylvia suddenly stood up; as Tietjens took
from an inner flap a cheque that had lost its freshness she
made three great strides over the carpet to him.

"Oh, Chrissie! . . ." she cried out. "He hasn't . . . That
beast hasn't . . ."

Tietjens answered:

"He has. . . ." He handed the soiled cheque to the banker.
Port Scatho looked at it with slow bewilderment.

" 'Account overdrawn,' " he read. "Brownie's . . . my nephew's handwriting . . . To the club . . . It's . . ."

"You aren't going to take it lying down?" Sylvia said. "Oh,
thank goodness, you aren't going to take it lying down."

"No! I'm not going to take it lying down," Tietjens said.
"Why should I?" A look of hard suspicion came over the
banker's face.

"You appear," he said, "to have been overdrawing your
account. People should not overdraw their accounts. For
what sum are you overdrawn?"

Tietjens handed his pass-book to Port Scatho.

"I don't understand on what principle you work," Sylvia said to Tietjens. "There are things you take lying down; this you don't."

Tietjens said:

"It doesn't matter, really. Except for the child."

Sylvia said:

"I guaranteed an overdraft for you up to a thousand pounds last Thursday. You can't be overdrawn over a thousand pounds."

"I'm not overdrawn at all," Tietjens said. "I was for about fifteen pounds yesterday. I didn't know it."

Port Scatho was turning over the pages of the pass-book, his face completely blank.

"I simply don't understand," he said. "You appear to be in credit. . . . You appear always to have been in credit except for a small sum now and then. For a day or two."

"I was overdrawn," Tietjens said, "for fifteen pounds yesterday. I should say for three or four hours: the course of a post, from my army agent to your head office. During these two or three hours your bank selected two out of six of my cheques to dishonour—both being under two pounds. The other one was sent back to my mess at Ealing, who won't, of course, give it back to me. That also is marked 'account overdrawn,' and in the same handwriting."

"But, good God," the banker said. "That means your ruin."

"It certainly means my ruin," Tietjens said. "It was meant to."

"But," the banker said—a look of relief came into his face, which had begun to assume the aspect of a broken man's—"you must have other accounts with the bank . . . a speculative one, perhaps, on which you are heavily down. . . . I don't myself attend to clients' accounts except the very huge ones, which affect the bank's policy."

"You ought to," Tietjens said. "It's the very little ones you ought to attend to, as a gentleman making his fortune out of them. I have no other account with you. I have never speculated in anything in my life. I have lost a great deal in Russian securities—a great deal for me. But so, no doubt, have you."

"Then . . . betting!" Port Scatho said.

"I never put a penny on a horse in my life," Tietjens said. "I know too much about them."

Port Scatho looked at the faces first of Sylvia, then of Tietjens. Sylvia, at least, was his very old friend. She said:

"Christopher never bets and never speculates. His personal

expenses are smaller than those of any man in town. You could say he had *no* personal expenses."

Again the swift look of suspicion came into Port Scatho's open face.

"Oh," Sylvia said, "you couldn't suspect Christopher and me of being in a plot to blackmail you."

"No, I couldn't suspect that," the banker said. "But the other explanation is just as extraordinary. . . . To suspect the bank . . . the *bank* . . . How do *you* account? . . ." He was addressing Tietjens; his round head seemed to become square, below; emotion worked on his jaws.

"I'll tell you simply this," Tietjens said. "You can then repair the matter as you think fit. Ten days ago I got my marching orders. As soon as I had handed over to the officer who relieved me I drew cheques for everything I owed—to my military tailor, the mess—for one pound twelve shillings. I had also to buy a compass and a revolver, the Red Cross orderlies having annexed mine when I was in hospital. . . ."

Port Scatho said: "Good God!"

"Don't you know they annex things?" Tietjens asked. He went on: "The total, in fact, amounted to an overdraft of fifteen pounds, but I did not think of it as such because my army agents ought to have paid my month's army pay over to you on the first. As you perceive, they have only paid it over this morning, the thirteenth. But, as you will see from my pass-book, they have always paid about the thirteenth, not the first. Two days ago I lunched at the club and drew that cheque for one pound fourteen shillings and sixpence: one ten for personal expenses and the four-and-six for lunch. . . ."

"You were, however, actually overdrawn," the banker said sharply.

Tietjens said:

"Yesterday, for two hours."

"But then," Port Scatho said, "what do you want done? We'll do what we can."

Tietjens said:

"I don't know. Do what you like. You'd better make what explanation you can to the military authority. If they courtmartialled me it would hurt you more than me. I assure you of that. There *is* an explanation."

Port Scatho began suddenly to tremble.

"What . . . what . . . what explanation?" he said. "You . . . damn it . . . you draw this out. . . . Do you dare to say my bank . . ." He stopped, drew his hand down his face and said: "But yet . . . you're a sensible, sound man. . . . I've heard things against you. But I don't believe them. . . . Your father always spoke very highly of you. . . . I remember he said if you wanted money you could always draw on him through us for three or four hundred. . . . That's what makes it so incomprehensible. . . . It's . . . it's . . ." His agitation grew on him. "It seems to strike at the very heart . . ."

Tietjens said:

"Look here, Port Scatho. . . . I've always had a respect for you. Settle it how you like. Fix the mess up for both our sakes with any formula that's not humiliating for your bank. I've already resigned from the club. . . ."

Sylvia said: "Oh, *no*, Christopher . . . not from the *club!*"

Port Scatho started back from beside the table.

"But if you're in the right!" he said. "You *couldn't* . . . Not resign from the club . . . I'm on the committee. . . . I'll explain to them, in the fullest, in the most generous . . ."

"You couldn't explain," Tietjens said. "You can't get ahead of rumour. . . . It's half over London at this moment. You know what the toothless old fellows of your committee are. . . . Anderson! Ffolliott . . . And my brother's friend Ruggles . . ."

Port Scatho said:

"Your brother's friend Ruggles . . . But look here. . . . He's something about the Court, isn't he? But look here. . . ." His mind stopped. He said: "People shouldn't overdraw. . . . But if your father said you could draw on him I'm really much concerned. . . . You're a first-rate fellow. . . . I can tell that from your pass-book alone. . . . Nothing but cheques drawn to first-class tradesmen for reasonable amounts. The sort of pass-book I liked to see when I was a junior clerk in the bank . . ." At that early reminiscence feelings of pathos overcame him, and his mind once more stopped.

Sylvia came back into the room; they had not perceived her going. She in turn held in her hand a letter.

Tietjens said:

"Look here, Port Scatho, don't get into this state. Give me your word to do what you can when you've assured yourself the facts are as I say. I wouldn't bother you at all, it's not my line, except for Mrs. Tietjens. A man alone can live that sort of thing down or die. But there's no reason why Mrs. Tietjens should live tied to a bad hat while he's living it down or dying."

"But that's not *right*," Port Scatho said, "it's not the right way to look at it. You can't pocket . . . I'm simply bewildered. . . ."

"You've no right to be bewildered," Sylvia said. "You're worrying your mind for expedients to save the reputation of your bank. We know your bank is more to you than a baby. You should look after it better, then."

Port Scatho, who had already fallen two paces away from the table, now fell two paces back, almost on top of it. Sylvia's nostrils were dilated.

She said:

"Tietjens shall not resign from your beastly club. He shall not! Your committee will request him formally to withdraw his resignation. You understand? He will withdraw it. Then he will resign for good. He is too good to mix with people like you. . . ." She paused, her chest working fast. "Do you understand what you've got to do?" she asked.

An appalling shadow of a thought went through Tietjens' mind: he would not let it come into words.

"I don't know . . ." the banker said. "I don't know that I can get the committee . . ."

"You've got to," Sylvia answered. "I'll tell you why . . . Christopher was never overdrawn. Last Thursday I instructed your people to pay a thousand pounds to my husband's account. I repeated the instruction by letter, and I kept a copy of the letter witnessed by my confidential maid. I also registered the letter and have the receipt for it. . . . You can see them."

Port Scatho mumbled from over the letter:

"It's to Brownlie . . . Yes, a receipt for a letter to Brownlie . . ." She examined the little green slip on both sides. He said: "Last Thursday . . . To-day's Monday. . . . An instruction to sell North-Western stock to the amount of one thousand pounds and place to the account of . . . Then . . ."

Sylvia said:

"That'll do. . . . You can't angle for time any more. . . . Your nephew has been in an affair of this sort before. . . . I'll tell you. Last Thursday at lunch your nephew told me that Christopher's brother's solicitors had withdrawn all the permissions for overdrafts on the books of the Groby estate. There were several to members of the family. Your nephew said that he intended to catch Christopher on the hop—that's his own expression—and dishonour the next cheque of his that came in. He said he had been waiting for the chance ever since the war, and the brother's withdrawal had given it him. I begged him not to. . . ."

"But, good God," the banker said, "this is unheard of. . . ."

"It isn't," Sylvia said. "Christopher has had five snotty,

little, miserable subalterns to defend at court-martials for exactly similar cases. One was an exact reproduction of this. . . ."

"But, good God," the banker exclaimed again, "men giving their lives for their country . . . Do you mean to say Brownlie did this out of revenge for Tietjens' defending at court-martials . . . And then . . . your thousand pounds is not shown in your husband's pass-book. . . ."

"Of course it's not," Sylvia said. "It has never been paid in. On Friday I had a formal letter from your people pointing out that North-Westerns were likely to rise and asking me to reconsider my position. The same day I sent an express telling them explicitly to do as I said. . . . Ever since then your nephew has been on the phone begging me not to save my husband. He was there, just now, when I went out of the room. He was also beseeching me to fly with him."

Tietjens said:

"Isn't that enough, Sylvia? It's rather torturing."

"Let them be tortured," Sylvia said. "But it appears to be enough."

Port Scatho had covered his face with both his pink hands. He had exclaimed:

"Oh, my God! Brownlie again . . ."

Tietjens' brother Mark was in the room. He was smaller, browner and harder than Tietjens, and his blue eyes protruded more. He had in one hand a bowler hat, in the other an umbrella, wore a pepper-and-salt suit and had race-glasses slung across him. He disliked Port Scatho, who detested him. He had lately been knighted. He said:

"Hullo, Port Scatho," neglecting to salute his sister-in-law. His eyes, whilst he stood motionless, rolled a look round the room and rested on a miniature bureau that stood on a writing-table, in a recess, under and between bookshelves.

"I see you've still got that cabinet," he said to Tietjens.

Tietjens said:

"I haven't. I've sold it to Sir John Robertson. He's waiting to take it away till he has room in his collection."

Port Scatho walked, rather unsteadily, round the lunch-table and stood looking down from one of the long windows. Sylvia sat down on her chair beside the fire-place. The two brothers stood facing each other, Christopher suggesting wheat-sacks, Mark, carved wood. All round them, except for the mirror that reflected bluenesses, the gilt backs of books. Hullo Central was clearing the table.

"I hear you're going out again to-morrow," Mark said. "I want to settle some things with you."

"I'm going at nine from Waterloo," Christopher said. "I've not much time. You can walk with me to the War Office if you like."

Mark's eyes followed the black and white of the maid round the table. She went out with the tray. Christopher suddenly was reminded of Valentine Wannop clearing the table in her mother's cottage. Hullo Central was no faster about it. Mark said:

"Port Scatho! As you're there, we may as well finish one point. I have cancelled my father's security for my brother's overdraft."

Port Scatho said, to the window, but loud enough:

"We all know it. To our cost."

"I wish you, however," Mark Tietjens went on, "to make over from my own account a thousand a year to my brother as he needs it. Not more than a thousand in any one year."

Port Scatho said:

"Write a letter to the bank. I don't look after clients' accounts on social occasions."

"I don't see why you don't," Mark Tietjens said. "It's the way you make your bread and butter, isn't it?"

Tietjens said:

"You may save yourself all this trouble, Mark. I am closing my account in any case."

Port Scatho spun round on his heel.

"I beg that you won't," he exclaimed. "I beg that we . . . that we may have the honour of continuing to have you draw upon us." He had the trick of convulsively working jaws: his head against the light was like the top of a rounded gate-post. He said to Mark Tietjens: "You may tell your friend Mr. Ruggles that your brother is empowered by me to draw on my private account . . . on my personal and private account up to any amount he needs. I say that to show my estimate of your brother; because I know he will incur no obligations he cannot discharge."

Mark Tietjens stood motionless; leaning slightly on the crook of his umbrella on the one side; on the other displaying, at arm's length, the white silk lining of his bowler hat, the lining being the brightest object in the room.

"That's your affair," he said to Port Scatho. "All I'm concerned with is to have a thousand a year paid to my brother's account till further notice."

Christopher Tietjens said, with what he knew was a sentimental voice, to Port Scatho. He was very touched; it appeared to him that with the spontaneous appearance of several names in his memory, and with this estimate of himself from the banker, his tide was turning and that this day might indeed be marked by a red stone:

"Of course, Port Scatho, I won't withdraw my wretched little account from you if you want to keep it. It flatters me that you should." He stopped and added: "I only wanted to avoid these . . . these family complications. But I suppose you can stop my brother's money being paid into my account. I don't want his money."

He said to Sylvia:

"You had better settle the other matter with Port Scatho."

To Port Scatho:

"I'm intensely obliged to you, Port Scatho. . . . You'll get Lady Port Scatho round to Macmaster's this evening if only for a minute; before eleven. . . ." And to his brother:

"Come along, Mark. I'm going down to the War Office. We can talk as we walk."

Sylvia said very nearly with timidity—and again a dark thought went over Tietjens' mind:

"Do we meet again, then? . . . I know you're very busy. . . ."

Tietjens said:

"Yes. I'll come and pick you out from Lady Job's if they don't keep me too long at the War Office. I'm dining, as you know, at Macmaster's; I don't suppose I shall stop late."

"I'd come," Sylvia said, "to Macmaster's if you thought it was appropriate. I'd bring Claudine Sandbach and General Wade. We're only going to the Russian dancers. We'd cut off early."

Tietjens could settle that sort of thought very quickly.

"Yes, do," he said hurriedly. "It would be appreciated." He got to the door: he came back: his brother was nearly through. He said to Sylvia, and for him the occasion was a very joyful one:

"I've worried out some of the words of that song. It runs:

'Somewhere or other there must surely be
    The face not seen: the voice not heard . . .'

Probably it's 'the voice not ever heard' to make up the metre. . . . I don't know the writer's name. But I hope I'll worry it all out during the day."

Sylvia had gone absolutely white.

"Don't!" she said. "Oh . . . *don't.*" She added coldly:

"Don't take the trouble," and wiped her tiny handkerchief across her lips as Tietjens went away.

She had heard the song at a charity concert and had cried as she heard it. She had read, afterwards, the words in the program and had almost cried again. But she had lost the program and had never come across the words again. The echo of them remained with her like something terrible and alluring: like a knife she would some day take out and with which she would stab herself.

3 ~

THE TWO brothers walked twenty steps from the door along the empty Inn pavements without speaking. Each was completely expressionless. To Christopher it seemed like Yorkshire. He had a vision of Mark standing on the lawn at Groby, in his bowler hat and with his umbrella, whilst the shooters walked over the lawn and up the hill to the butts. Mark probably never had done that; but it was so that his image always presented itself to his brother. Mark was considering that one of the folds of his umbrella was disarranged. He seriously debated with himself whether he should unfold it at once and refold it—which was a great deal of trouble to take!—or whether he should leave it till he got to his club, where he would tell the porter to have it done at once. That would mean that he would have to walk for a mile and a quarter through London with a disarranged umbrella, which was disagreeable.

He said:

"If I were you I wouldn't let that banker fellow go about giving you testimonials of that sort."

Christopher said:

"Ah!"

He considered that with a third of his brain in action, he was over a match for Mark, but he was tired of discussions. He supposed that some unpleasant construction would be put by his brother's friend Ruggles on the friendship of Port Scatho for himself. But he had no curiosity. Mark felt a vague discomfort. He said:

"You had a cheque dishonoured at the club this morning?"

Christopher said:

"Yes."

Mark waited for explanations. Christopher was pleased at the speed with which the news had travelled: it confirmed what he had said to Port Scatho. He viewed his case from outside. It was like looking at the smooth working of a mechanical model.

Mark was more troubled. Used as he had been for thirty years to the vociferous South, he had forgotten that there were taciturnities still. If at his ministry he laconically accused a transport-clerk of remissness or if he accused his French mistress—just as laconically—of putting too many condiments on his nightly mutton-chop or too much salt in the water in which she boiled his potatoes, he was used to hearing a great many excuses or negations, uttered with energy and continued for long. So he had got into the habit of considering himself almost the only laconic being in the world. He suddenly remembered with discomfort—but also with satisfaction—that his brother was his brother.

He knew nothing about Christopher, for himself. He had seemed to look at his little brother down avenues, from a distance, the child misbehaving himself. Not a true Tietjens: born very late: a mother's child, therefore, rather than a father's. The mother an admirable woman, but from the South Riding. Soft, therefore, and ample. The elder Tietjens children, when they had experienced failures, had been wont to blame their father for not marrying a woman of their own riding. So, for himself, he knew nothing of this boy. He was said to be brilliant: an un-Tietjens-like quality. Akin to talkativeness! . . . Well, he wasn't talkative. Mark said:

"What have you done with all the brass our mother left you? Twenty thousand, wasn't it?"

They were just passing through a narrow way between Georgian houses. In the next quadrangle Tietjens stopped and looked at his brother. Mark stood still to be looked at. Christopher said to himself:

"This man has the right to ask these questions!"

It was as if a queer slip had taken place in a moving picture. This fellow had become the head of the house: he, Christopher, was the heir. At that moment their father, in the grave four months now, was for the first time dead.

Christopher remembered a queer incident. After the funeral, when they had come back from the churchyard and had lunched, Mark—and Tietjens could now see the wooden gesture—had taken out his cigar-case and, selecting one cigar for himself, had passed the rest round the table. It was as if people's hearts had stopped beating. Groby had never, till that day, been smoked in: the father had had his twelve pipes filled and put in the rose-bushes in the drive. . . .

It had been regarded merely as a disagreeable incident: a piece of bad taste. . . . Christopher, himself, only just back from France, would not even have known it as such, his mind was so blank, only the parson had whispered to him: "And Groby never smoked in till this day."

But now! It appeared a symbol, and an absolutely right symbol. Whether they liked it or not, here were the head of the house and the heir. The head of the house must make his arrangements, the heir agree or disagree; but the elder brother had the right to have his inquiries answered.

Christopher said:

"Half the money was settled at once on my child. I lost seven thousand in Russian securities. The rest I spent. . . ."

Mark said:

"Ah!"

They had just passed under the arch that leads into Holborn. Mark, in turn, stopped and looked at his brother, and Christopher stood still to be inspected, looking into his brother's eyes. Mark said to himself:

"The fellow isn't at least afraid to look at you!" He had been convinced that Christopher would be. He said:

"You spent it on women? Or where do you get the money that you spend on women?"

Christopher said:

"I never spent a penny on a woman in my life."

Mark said:

"Ah!"

They crossed Holborn and went by the back-ways towards Fleet Street.

Christopher said:

"When I say 'woman' I'm using the word in the ordinary sense. Of course I've given women of our own class tea or lunch and paid for their cabs. Perhaps I'd better put it that I've never—either before or after marriage—had connexion with any woman other than my wife."

Mark said:

"Ah!"

He said to himself:

"Then Ruggles must be a liar." This neither distressed nor astonished him. For twenty years he and Ruggles had shared a floor of a large and rather gloomy building in Mayfair. They were accustomed to converse whilst shaving in a joint toilet-room, otherwise they did not often meet except at the club. Ruggles was attached to the Royal Court in some capacity, possibly as sub-deputy gold-stick-in-waiting. Or he might have been promoted in the twenty years. Mark Tietjens had never taken the trouble to inquire. Enormously proud and shut in on himself, he was without curiosity of any sort. He lived in London because it was immense, solitary, administrative and apparently without curiosity as to its own citizens. If he could have found, in the North, a city as vast and as distinguished by the other characteristics, he would have preferred it.

Of Ruggles he thought little or nothing. He had once heard the phrase "agreeable rattle," and he regarded Ruggles as an agreeable rattle, though he did not know what the phrase meant. Whilst they shaved, Ruggles gave out the scandal of the day. He never, that is to say, mentioned a woman whose virtue was not purchasable or a man who would not sell his wife for advancement. This matched with Mark's ideas of the South. When Ruggles aspersed the fame of a man of family from the North, Mark would stop him with:

"Oh, no. That's not true. He's a Craister of Wantley Fells," or another name, as the case might be. Half Scotchman, half Jew, Ruggles was very tall and resembled a magpie, having his head almost always on one side. Had he been English, Mark would never have shared his rooms with him: he knew indeed few Englishmen of sufficient birth and position to have that privilege, and on the other hand, few Englishmen of birth and position would have consented to share rooms so grim and uncomfortable, so furnished with horsehair-seated mahogany or so lit with ground-glass skylights. Coming up to town at the age of twenty-five, Mark had taken these rooms with a man called Peebles, long since dead, and he had never troubled to make any change, though Ruggles had taken the place of Peebles. The remote similarity of the names had been less disturbing to Mark Tietjens than would have been the case had the names been more different. It would have been very disagreeable, Mark often thought, to share with a man called, say, Granger. As it was, he still often called Ruggles Peebles, and no harm was done. Mark knew nothing of Ruggles' origins, then—so that, in a remote way, their union resembled that of Christopher with Macmaster. But whereas Christopher would have given his satellite the shirt off his back, Mark would not have lent Ruggles more than a five-pound note, and would have turned him out of their rooms if it had not been returned by the end of the quarter. But since Ruggles never had asked to borrow anything at all, Mark considered him an entirely honourable man. Occasionally Ruggles would talk of his determination to marry some widow or other with money or of his influence with people in exalted stations, but when he talked like that, Mark would not listen to him, and he soon returned to stories of purchasable women and venial men.

About five months ago Mark had said one morning to Ruggles:

"You might pick up what you can about my youngest brother, Christopher, and let me know."

The evening before that, Mark's father had called Mark to him from over the other side of the smoking-room and had said:

"You might find out what you can about Christopher. He may be in want of money. Has it occurred to you that he's the heir to the estate! After you, of course." Mr. Tietjens had aged a good deal after the deaths of his children. He said: "I suppose you won't marry?" and Mark had answered:

"No, I shan't marry. But I suppose I've a better life than Christopher. He appears to have been a good deal knocked about out there."

Armed, then, with this commission, Mr. Ruggles appears to have displayed extraordinary activity in preparing a Christopher Tietjens dossier. It is not often that an inveterate gossip gets a chance at a man whilst being at the same time practically shielded against the law of libel. And Ruggles disliked Christopher Tietjens with the inveterate dislike of the man who revels in gossip for the man who never gossips. And Christopher Tietjens had displayed more than his usual insolence to Ruggles. So Ruggles' coat-tails flashed round an unusual number of doors and his top-hat gleamed before an unusual number of tall portals during the next week.

Amongst others, he had visited the lady known as Glorvina.

There is said to be a book kept in a holy of holies, in which bad marks are set down against men of family and position in England. In this book Mark Tietjens and his father—in common with a great number of hard-headed Englishmen of county rank—implicitly believed. Christopher Tietjens didn't: he imagined that the activities of gentlemen like Ruggles were sufficient to stop the careers of people whom they disliked. On the other hand, Mark and his father looked abroad upon English society and saw fellows apparently with every qualification for successful careers in one service or the other; and these fellows got no advancements, orders, titles or preferments of any kind. Just, rather mysteriously, they didn't make their marks. This they put down to the workings of the book.

Ruggles, too, not only believed in the existence of that compilation of the suspect and doomed, but believed that his hand had a considerable influence over the inscriptions in its pages. He believed that if, with more moderation and with more grounds than usual, he uttered denigrations of certain men before certain personages, it would at least do those men a great deal of harm. And quite steadily, and with, indeed, real belief in much of what he said, Ruggles had denigrated Tietjens before these personages. Ruggles could not see why Christopher had taken Sylvia back after her elopement with Perowne: he could not see why Christopher had, indeed, married Sylvia at all when she was with child by a man called Drake—just as he wasn't going to believe that Christopher could get a testimonial out of Lord Port Scatho except by the sale of Sylvia to the banker. He couldn't see anything but money or jobs at the bottom of these things: he couldn't see how Tietjens otherwise got the money to support Mrs. Wannop, Miss Wannop and her child, and to maintain Mrs. Duchemin and Macmaster in the style they affected, Mrs. Duchemin being the mistress of Christopher. He simply could see no other solution. It is, in fact, asking for trouble if you are more altruist than the society that surrounds you.

Ruggles, however, hadn't any pointers as to whether or no or to what degree he had really damaged his roommate's brother. He had talked in what he considered to be the right quarters, but he hadn't any evidence that what he had said had got through. It was to ascertain that that he had called on the great lady, for if anybody knew, she would.

He hadn't definitely ascertained anything, for the great lady was—and he knew it—a great deal cleverer than himself. The great lady, he was allowed to discover, had a real affection for Sylvia, her daughter's close friend, and she expressed real concern to hear that Christopher Tietjens wasn't getting on. Ruggles had gone to visit her quite openly to ask whether something better couldn't be done for the brother of the man with whom he lived. Christopher had, it was admitted, great abilities; yet neither in his office—in which he would surely have remained had he been satisfied with his prospects—nor in the army did he occupy anything but a very subordinate position. Couldn't, he asked, Glorvina do anything for him? And he added: "It's almost as if he had a bad mark against him. . . ."

The great lady had said, with a great deal of energy, that she could not do anything at all. The energy was meant to show how absolutely her party had been downed, outed and jumped on by the party in power, so that she had no influence of any sort anywhere. That was an exaggeration; but it did Christopher Tietjens no good, since Ruggles chose to take it to mean that Glorvina said she could do nothing because there *was* a black mark against Tietjens in the book of the inner circle, to which—if anyone had—the great lady must have had access.

Glorvina, on the other hand, had been awakened to concern for Tietjens. In the existence of a book she didn't believe: she had never seen it. But that a black mark of a metaphorical nature might have been scored against him she was perfectly ready to believe, and when occasion served, during the next five months, she made inquiries about Tietjens. She came upon a Major Drake, an intelligence officer, who had access to the central depot of confidential reports upon officers, and Major Drake showed her, with a great deal of readiness, as a specimen, the report on Tietjens. It was of a most discouraging sort and peppered over with hieroglyphics, the main point being Tietjens' impecuniosity and his predilection for the French, and apparently for the French Royalists. There being at that date and with that government a great deal of friction with our allies, this characteristic, which earlier had earned him a certain number of soft jobs, had latterly done him a good deal of harm. Glorvina carried away the definite information that Tietjens had been seconded to the French artillery as a liaison officer and had remained with them for some time, but, having been shell-shocked, had been sent back. After that a mark had been added against him: "Not to be employed as liaison officer again."

On the other hand, Sylvia's visits to Austrian officer prisoners had also been noted to Tietjens' account and a final note added: "Not to be entrusted with any confidential work."

To what extent Major Drake himself compiled these records the great lady didn't know and didn't want to know. She was acquainted with the relationships of the parties and was aware that in certain dark, full-blooded men the passion for sexual revenge is very lasting, and she let it go at that. She discovered, however, from Mr. Waterhouse—now also in retreat—that he had a very high opinion of Tietjens' character and abilities, and that just before Waterhouse's retirement he had especially recommended Tietjens for very high promotion. That alone, in the then state of ministerial friendships and enmities, Glorvina knew to be sufficient to ruin any man within range of governmental influence.

She had, therefore, sent for Sylvia and had put all these matters before her, for she had too much wisdom to believe that, even supposing there should be differences between the young people, of which she had no evidence at all, Sylvia could wish to do anything but promote her husband's material interests. Moreover, sincerely benevolent as the great lady was towards this couple, she also saw that here was a possibility of damaging, at least, individuals of the party in power. A person in a relatively unimportant official position can sometimes make a very nasty stink if he is unjustly used, has determination and a small amount of powerful backing. This Sylvia, at least, certainly had.

And Sylvia had received the great lady's news with so much emotion that no one could have doubted that she was utterly devoted to her husband and would tell him all about it. This Sylvia had not as yet managed to do.

Ruggles in the meantime had collected a very full budget of news and inferences to present to Mark Tietjens whilst shaving. Mark had been neither surprised nor indignant. He had been accustomed to call all his father's children except the brother immediately next him "the whelps," and their concerns had been no concerns of his. They would marry, beget unimportant children, who would form collateral lines of Tietjens and disappear as is the fate of sons of younger sons. And the deaths of the intermediate brothers had been so recent that Mark was not yet used to thinking of Christopher as anything but a whelp, a person whose actions might be disagreeable but couldn't matter. He said to Ruggles:

"You had better talk to my father about this. I don't know that I could keep all these particulars accurately in my head."

Ruggles had been only too pleased to, and—with to give him weight his intimacy with the eldest son, who certified to his reliability in money matters and his qualifications for amassing details as to personalities, acts and promotions—that day, at tea at the club, in a tranquil corner, Ruggles had told Mr. Tietjens senior that Christopher's wife had been with child when he had married her; he had hushed up her elopement with Perowne and connived at other love-affairs of hers to his own dishonour, and was suspected in high places of being a French agent, thus being marked down as suspect in the great book. . . . All this in order to obtain money for the support of Miss Wannop, by whom he had had a child, and to maintain Macmaster and Mrs. Duchemin on a scale unsuited to their means, Mrs. Duchemin being his mistress. The story that Tietjens had had a child by Miss Wannop was first suggested, and then supported, by the fact that in Yorkshire he certainly had a son who never appeared in Gray's Inn.

Mr. Tietjens was a reasonable man: not reasonable enough to doubt Ruggles' circumstantial history. He believed implicitly in the great book—which has been believed in by several generations of country gentlemen: he perceived that his brilliant son had made no advancement commensurate with either his brilliance or his influence: he suspected that brilliance was synonymous with reprehensible tendencies. Moreover, his old friend General Ffolliott had definitely told him some days before that he ought to inquire into the goings-on of Christopher. On being pressed, Ffolliott had, also definitely, stated that Christopher was suspected of very dishonourable dealings, both in money and women. Ruggles' allegations came, therefore, as a definite confirmation of suspicions that appeared only too well backed up.

He bitterly regretted that, knowing Christopher to be brilliant, he had turned the boy—as is the usual portion of younger sons—adrift, with what of a competence could be got together, to sink or swim. He had, he said to himself, always wished to keep at home and under his own eyes this boy, for whom he had had especial promptings of tenderness. His wife, to whom he had been absolutely attached by a passionate devotion, had been unusually wrapped up in Christopher, because Christopher had been her youngest son, born very late. And since his wife's death, Christopher had been especially dear to him, as if he had carried about his presence some of the radiance and illumination that had seemed to attach to his mother. Indeed, after his wife's death, Mr. Tietjens had very nearly asked Christopher and his wife to come and keep house for him at Groby, making, of course, special testamentary provision for Christopher in order to atone for his giving up his career at the Department of Statistics. His sense of justice to his other children had prevented him doing this.

What broke his heart was that Christopher should not only have seduced but should have had a child by Valentine Wannop. Very grand-seigneur in his habits, Mr. Tietjens had always believed in his duty to patronize the arts, and if he had actually done little in this direction beyond purchasing some chocolate-coloured pictures of the French historic school, he had for long prided himself on what he had done for the widow and children of his old friend Professor Wannop. He considered, and with justice, that he had made Mrs. Wannop a novelist, and he considered her to be a very great novelist. And his conviction of the guilt of Christopher was strengthened by a slight tinge of jealousy of his son: a feeling that he would not have acknowledged to himself. For since Christopher—he didn't know how, for he had given his son no introduction—had become an intimate of the Wannop household, Mrs. Wannop had completely given up asking him, Mr. Tietjens, clamorously and constantly for advice. In return she had sung the praises of Christopher in almost extravagant terms. She had, indeed, said that if Christopher had not been almost daily in the house or, at any rate, at the end of the phone, she would hardly have been able to keep on working at full pressure. This had not overpleased Mr. Tietjens. Mr. Tietjens entertained for Valentine Wannop an affection of the very deepest, the same qualities appealing to the father as appealed to the son. He had even, in spite of his sixty-odd years, seriously entertained the idea of marrying the girl. She was a lady: she would have managed Groby very well; and although the entail on the property was very strict indeed, he would, at least, have been able to put her beyond the reach of want after his death. He had thus no doubt of his son's guilt, and he had to undergo the additional humiliation of thinking that not only had his son betrayed this radiant personality, but he had done it so clumsily as to give the girl a child and let it be known. That was unpardonable want of management in the son of a gentleman. And now this boy was his heir with a misbegotten brat to follow. Irrevocably!

All his four tall sons, then, were down. His eldest tied for good to a—quite admirable!—trollop: his two next dead: his youngest worse than dead: his wife dead of a broken heart.

A soberly but deeply religious man, Mr. Tietjens' very religion made him believe in Christopher's guilt. He knew that it is as difficult for a rich man to go to Heaven as it is for a camel to go through the gate in Jerusalem called the Needle's Eye. He humbly hoped that his Maker would receive him amongst the pardoned. Then, since he was a rich—an enormously rich—man, his sufferings on this earth must be very great. . . .

From tea-time that day until it was time to catch the midnight train for Bishop's Auckland, he had been occupied with his son Mark in the writing-room of the club. They had made many notes. He had seen his son Christopher, in uniform, looking broken and rather bloated, the result, no doubt, of debauch. Christopher had passed through the other end of the room and Mr. Tietjens had avoided his eye. He had caught the train and reached Groby, travelling alone. Towards dusk he had taken out a gun. He was found dead next morning, a couple of rabbits beside his body, just over the hedge from the little churchyard. He appeared to have crawled through the hedge, dragging his loaded gun, muzzle forwards, after him. Hundreds of men, mostly farmers, die from that cause every year in England. . . .

With these things in his mind—or as much of them as he could keep at once—Mark was now investigating his brother's affairs. He would have let things go on longer, for his father's estate was by no means wound up, but that morning Ruggles had told him that the club had had a cheque of his brother's returned and that his brother was going out to France next day. It was five months exactly since the death of their father. That had happened in March, it was now August: a bright, untidy day in narrow, high courts.

Mark arranged his thoughts.

"How much of an income," he said, "do you need to live in comfort? If a thousand isn't enough, how much? Two?"

Christopher said that he needed no money and didn't intend to live in comfort. Mark said:

"I am to let you have three thousand if you'll live abroad. I'm only carrying out our father's instructions. You could cut a hell of a splash on three thousand in France."

Christopher did not answer.

Mark began again:

"The remaining three thousand, then: that was over from our mother's money. Did you settle it on your girl or just spend it on her?"

Christopher repeated with patience that he hadn't got a girl.

Mark said:

"The girl who had a child by you. I'm instructed, if you haven't settled anything already—but father took it that you would have—I was to let her have enough to live in comfort. How much do you suppose she'll need to live in comfort? I allow Charlotte four hundred. Would four hundred be enough? I suppose you want to go on keeping her? Three thousand isn't a great lot for her to live on with a child."

Christopher said:

"Hadn't you better mention names?"

Mark said:

"No! I never mention names. I mean a woman writer and her daughter. I suppose the girl is father's daughter, isn't she?"

Christopher said:

"No. She couldn't be. I've thought of it. She's twenty-seven. We were all in Dijon for the two years before she was born. Father didn't come into the estate till next year. The Wannops were also in Canada at the time. Professor Wannop was principal of a university there. I forget the name."

Mark said:

"So we were. In Dijon! For my French!" He added: "Then she can't be father's daughter. It's a good thing. I thought, as he wanted to settle money on them, they were very likely his children. There's a son, too. He's to have a thousand. What's he doing?"

"The son," Tietjens said, "is a conscientious objector. He's on a mine-sweeper. A bluejacket. His idea is that picking up mines is saving life, not taking it."

"Then he won't want the brass yet," Mark said; "it's to start him in any business. What's the full name and address of your girl? Where do you keep her?"

They were in an open space, dusty, with half-timber buildings whose demolition had been interrupted. Christopher halted close to a post that had once been a cannon; up against this he felt that his brother could lean in order to assimilate ideas. He said slowly and patiently:

"If you're consulting with me as to how to carry out our father's intentions, and as there's money in it, you had better make an attempt to get hold of the facts. I wouldn't bother you if it wasn't a matter of money. In the first place, no money is wanted at this end. I can live on my pay. My wife is a rich woman, relatively. Her mother is a very rich woman. . . ."

"She's Rugeley's mistress, isn't she?" Mark asked.

Christopher said:

"No, she isn't. I should certainly say she wasn't. Why should she be? She's his cousin."

"Then it's your wife who was Rugeley's mistress?" Mark asked. "Or why should she have the loan of his box?"

"Sylvia also is Rugeley's cousin, of course, a degree further removed," Tietjens said. "She isn't anyone's mistress. You can be certain of that."

"They *say* she is," Mark answered. "They say she's a regular tart. . . . I suppose you think I've insulted you."

Christopher said:

"No, you haven't. . . . It's better to get all this out. We're practically strangers, but you've a right to ask."

Mark said:

"Then you haven't got a girl and don't need money to keep her. . . . You could have what you liked. There's no reason why a man shouldn't have a girl, and if he has he ought to keep her decently. . . ."

Christopher did not answer. Mark leaned against the half-buried cannon and swung his umbrella by its crook.

"But," he said, "if you don't keep a girl, what do you do for? . . ." He was going to say "for the comforts of home," but a new idea had come into his mind. "Of course," he said, "one can see that your wife's soppily in love with you." He added: "Soppily . . . one can see that with half an eye. . . ."

Christopher felt his jaw drop. Not a second before—that very second!—he had made up his mind to ask Valentine Wannop to become his mistress that night. It was no good, any more, he said to himself. She loved him, he knew, with a deep, an unshakable, passion, just as his passion for her was a devouring element that covered his whole mind as the atmosphere envelops the earth. Were they, then, to go down to death separated by years, with no word ever spoken? To what end? For whose benefit? The whole world conspired to force them together! To resist became a weariness!

His brother Mark was talking on. "I know all about women," he had announced. Perhaps he did. He had lived with exemplary fidelity to a quite unpresentable woman for a number of years. Perhaps the complete study of one woman gave you a map of all the rest!

Christopher said:

"Look here, Mark. You had better go through all my

pass-books for the last ten years. Or ever since I had an account. This discussion is no good if you don't believe what I say."

Mark said:

"I don't want to see your pass-books. I believe you."

He added, a second later:

"Why the devil shouldn't I believe you? It's either believing you're a gentleman or Ruggles a liar. It's only common sense to believe Ruggles a liar in that case. I didn't before because I had no grounds to." Christopher said:

"I doubt if liar is the right word. He picked up things that were said against me. No doubt he reported them faithfully enough. Things *are* said against me. I don't know why."

"Because," Mark said with emphasis, "you treat these South Country swine with the contempt that they deserve. They're incapable of understanding the motives of a gentleman. If you live among dogs they'll think you've the motives of a dog. What other motives can they give you?" He added: "I thought you'd been buried so long under their muck that you were as mucky as they!"

Tietjens looked at his brother with the respect one has to give to a man ignorant but shrewd. It was a discovery: that his brother was shrewd.

But of course he would be shrewd. He was the indispensable head of a great department. He had to have some qualities. . . . Not cultivated, not even instructed. A savage! But penetrating!

"We must move on," he said, "or I shall have to take a cab." Mark detached himself from his half-buried cannon.

"What did you do with the other three thousand?" he asked. "Three thousand is a hell of a big sum to chuck away. For a younger son."

"Except for some furniture I bought for my wife's rooms," Christopher said, "it went mostly in loans."

"Loans!" Mark exclaimed. "To that fellow Macmaster?"

"Mostly to him," Christopher answered. "But about seven hundred to Dicky Swipes, of Cullercoats."

"Good God! Why to him?" Mark ejaculated.

"Oh, because he was Swipes, of Cullercoats," Christopher said, "and asked for it. He'd have had more, only that was enough for him to drink himself to death on."

Mark said:

"I suppose you don't give money to every fellow that asks for it?"

Christopher said:

"I do. It's a matter of principle."

"It's lucky," Mark said, "that a lot of fellows don't know that. You wouldn't have much brass left for long."

"I didn't have it for long," Christopher said.

"You know," Mark said, "you couldn't expect to do the princely patron on a youngest son's portion. It's a matter of taste. I never gave a ha'penny to a beggar myself. But a lot of the Tietjens were princely. One generation to addle brass: one to keep: one to spend. That's all right. . . . I suppose Macmaster's wife *is* your mistress? That'll account for it not being the girl. They keep an arm-chair for you."

Christopher said:

"No. I just backed Macmaster for the sake of backing him. Father lent him money to begin with."

"So he did," Mark exclaimed.

"His wife," Christopher said, "was the widow of Breakfast Duchemin. *You* knew Breakfast Duchemin?"

"Oh, *I* knew Breakfast Duchemin," Mark said. "I suppose Macmaster's a pretty warm man now. Done himself proud with Duchemin's money."

"Pretty proud!" Christopher said. "They won't be knowing me long now."

"But damn it all!" Mark said. "You've Groby, to all intents and purposes. *I'm* not going to marry and beget children to hinder you."

Christopher said:

"Thanks. I don't want it."

"Got your knife into me?" Mark asked.

"Yes. I've got my knife into you," Christopher answered. "Into the whole bloody lot of you, and Ruggles and Ffolliott and our father!"

Mark said: "Ah!"

"You don't suppose I wouldn't have?" Christopher asked.

"Oh, *I* don't suppose you wouldn't have," Mark answered. "I thought you were a soft sort of bloke. I see you aren't."

"I'm as North Riding as yourself!" Christopher answered.

They were in the tide of Fleet Street, pushed apart by foot passengers and separated by traffic. With some of the imperiousness of the officer of those days Christopher barged across through motor buses and paper lorries. With the imperiousness of the head of a department Mark said:

"Here, policeman, stop these damn things and let me get over." But Christopher was over much the sooner and waited for his brother in the gateway of the Middle Temple. His mind was completely swallowed up in the endeavour to imagine the embraces of Valentine Wannop. He said to himself that he had burnt his boats.

Mark, coming alongside him, said:

"You'd better know what our father wanted."

Christopher said:

"Be quick, then. I must get on." He had to rush through his War Office interview to get to Valentine Wannop. They would have only a few hours in which to recount the loves of two lifetimes. He saw her golden head and her enraptured face. He wondered how her face would look enraptured. He had seen on it humour, dismay, tenderness, in the eyes— and fierce anger and contempt for his, Christopher's, political opinions. His militarism!

Nevertheless they halted by the Temple fountain. That respect was due to their dead father. Mark had been explaining. Christopher had caught some of his words and divined the links. Mr. Tietjens had left no will, confident that his desires as to the disposal of his immense fortune would be carried out meticulously by his eldest son. He would have left a will, but there was the vague case of Christopher to be considered. Whilst Christopher had been a youngest son you arranged that he had a good lump sum and went, with it, to the devil how he liked. He was no longer a youngest son: by the will of God.

"Our father's idea," Mark said by the fountain, "was that no settled sum could keep you straight. His idea was that if you were a bloody pimp living on women . . . You don't mind?"

"I don't mind your putting it straightforwardly," Christopher said. He considered the base of the fountain that was half full of leaves. This civilization had contrived a state of things in which leaves rotted by August. Well, it was doomed!

"If you were a pimp living on women," Mark repeated, "it was no good making a will. You might need uncounted thousands to keep you straight. You were to have 'em. You were to be as debauched as you wanted, but on clean money. I was to see how much in all probability that would be and arrange the other legacies to scale. . . . Father had crowds of pensioners. . . ."

"How much did father cut up for?" Christopher asked.

Mark said:

"God knows. . . . You saw we proved the estate at a million and a quarter as far as ascertained. But it might be twice that. Or five times! . . . With steel prices what they have been for the last three years it's impossible to say what the Middlesbrough district property won't produce. . . . The death-duties even can't catch it up. And there are all the ways of getting round *them*."

Christopher inspected his brother with curiosity. This brown-complexioned fellow with bulging eyes, shabby on the whole, tightly buttoned into a rather old pepper-and-salt suit, with a badly rolled umbrella, old race-glasses and his bowler hat the only neat thing about him, was, indeed, a prince. With a rigid outline! All real princes must look like that. He said:

"Well! You won't be a penny the poorer by me."

Mark was beginning to believe this. He said:

"You won't forgive father?"

Christopher said:

"I won't forgive father for not making a will. I won't forgive him for calling in Ruggles. I saw him and you in the writing-room the night before he died. He never spoke to me. He could have. It was clumsy stupidity. That's unforgivable."

"The fellow shot himself," Mark said. "You usually forgive a fellow who shoots himself."

"I don't," Christopher said. "Besides, he's probably in Heaven and won't need my forgiveness. Ten to one he's in Heaven. He was a good man."

"One of the best," Mark said. "It was I that called in Ruggles, though."

"I don't forgive you either," Christopher said.

"But you *must*," Mark said—and it was a tremendous concession to sentimentality—"take enough to make you comfortable."

"By God!" Christopher exclaimed. "I loathe your whole beastly buttered-toast, mutton-chopped, carpet-slippered, rum-negused comfort as much as I loathe your beastly Riviera-palaced, chauffeured, hydraulic-lifted, hot-house-aired beastliness of fornication. . . ." He was carried away, as he seldom let himself be, by the idea of his amours with Valentine Wannop, which should take place on the empty boards of a cottage, without draperies, fat meats, gummy aphrodisiacs. . . . "You won't," he repeated, "be a penny the poorer by me."

Mark said:

"Well, you needn't get shirty about it. If you won't, you won't. We'd better move on. You've only just time. We'll say that settles it. . . . Are you or aren't you overdrawn

at your bank? I'll make that up, whatever you damn well do
to stop it."

"I'm not overdrawn," Christopher said. "I'm over thirty
pounds in credit, and I've an immense overdraft guaranteed
by Sylvia. It was a mistake of the bank's."

Mark hesitated for a moment. It was to him almost unbelievable that a bank could make a mistake. One of the great
banks. The props of England.

They were walking down towards the embankment. With
his precious umbrella Mark aimed a violent blow at the
railings above the tennis-lawns, where whitish figures, be-
drabbled by the dim atmosphere, moved like marionettes
practising crucifixions.

"By God!" he said, "this is the last of England. . . .
There's only my department where they never make mistakes. I tell you, if there were any mistakes made there, there
would be some backs broken!" He added: "But don't you
think that I'm going to give up comfort; I'm not. My Charlotte makes better buttered toast than they can at the club.
And she's got a tap of French rum that's saved my life over
and over again after a beastly wet day's racing. And she
does it all on the five hundred I give her and keeps herself
clean and tidy on top of it. Nothing like a Frenchwoman
for managing . . . By God, I'd marry the doxy if she wasn't
a papist. It would please her and it wouldn't hurt me. But I
couldn't stomach marrying a papist. They're not to be
trusted."

"You'll have to stomach a papist coming into Groby,"
Christopher said. "My son's to be brought up as a papist."

Mark stopped and dug his umbrella into the ground.

"Eh, but that's a bitter one," he said. "Whatever made ye
do that? . . . I suppose the mother made you do it. She tricked
you into it before you married her." He added: "I'd not like
to sleep with that wife of yours. She's too athletic. It'd be like
sleeping with a bundle of faggots. I suppose, though, you're
a pair of turtle-doves. . . . Eh, but I'd not have thought ye
would have been so weak."

"I only decided this morning," Christopher said, "when
my cheque was returned from the bank. You won't have
read Spelden on sacrilege, about Groby."

"I can't say I have," Mark answered.

"It's no good trying to explain that side of it, then,"
Christopher said; "there isn't time. But you're wrong in
thinking Sylvia made it a condition of our marriage. Nothing
would have made me consent then. It has made her a happy

woman that I have. The poor thing thought our house was
under a curse for want of a papist heir."

"What made ye consent now?" Mark asked.

"I've told you," Christopher said; "it was getting my
cheque returned to the club; that on the top of the rest of
it. A fellow who can't do better than that had better let
the mother bring up the child. . . . Besides, it won't hurt a
papist boy to have a father with dishonoured cheques as
much as it would a Protestant. They're not quite English."

"That's true too," Mark said.

He stood still by the railings of the public garden near
the Temple station.

"Then," he said, "if I'd let the lawyers write and tell
you the guarantee for your overdraft from the estate was
stopped as they wanted to, the boy wouldn't be a papist?
You wouldn't have overdrawn."

"I didn't overdraw," Christopher said. "But if you had
warned me I should have made inquiries at the bank and the
mistake wouldn't have occurred. Why didn't you?"

"I meant to," Mark said. "I meant to do it myself. But
I hate writing letters. I put it off. I didn't much like having
dealings with the fellow I thought you were. I suppose
that's another thing you won't forgive me for?"

"No. I shan't forgive you for not writing to me," Christopher said. "You ought to write business letters."

"I hate writing 'em," Mark said. Christopher was moving
on. "There's one thing more," Mark said. "I suppose the boy
is your son?"

"Yes, he's my son," Christopher said.

"Then that's all," Mark said. "I suppose if you're killed
you won't mind my keeping an eye on the youngster?"

"I'll be glad," Christopher said.

They strolled along the embankment side by side, walking
rather slowly, their backs erected and their shoulders squared
because of their satisfaction of walking together, desiring to
lengthen the walk by going slow. Once or twice they stopped
to look at the dirty silver of the river, for both liked grim
effects of landscape. They felt very strong, as if they owned
the land!

Once Mark chuckled and said:

"Its too damn funny. To think of our both being . . .
what is it? . . . monogamists? Well, it's a good thing to stick
to one woman . . . you can't say it isn't. It saves trouble.
And you know where you are."

Under the lugubrious arch that leads into the War Office quadrangle Christopher halted.

"No. I'm coming in," Mark said. "I want to speak to Hogarth. I haven't spoken to Hogarth for some time. About the transport-waggon parks in Regent's Park. I manage all those beastly things and a lot more."

"They say you do it damn well," Christopher said. "They say you're indispensable." He was aware that his brother desired to stay with him as long as possible. He desired it himself.

"I damn well am!" Mark said. He added: "I suppose you couldn't do that sort of job in France? Look after transport and horses."

"I could," Christopher said, "but I suppose I shall go back to liaison work."

"I don't think you will," Mark said. "I could put in a word for you with the transport-people."

"I wish you would," Christopher said. "I'm not fit to go back into the front line. Besides, I'm no beastly hero! And I'm a rotten infantry officer. No Tietjens was ever a soldier worth talking of."

They turned the corner of the arch. Like something fitting in, exact and expected, Valentine Wannop stood looking at the lists of casualties that hung beneath a cheaply green-stained deal shelter against the wall, a tribute at once to the weaker art movements of the day and the desire to save the rate-payers' money.

With the same air of finding Christopher Tietjens fit in exactly to an expected landscape she turned on him. Her face was blue-white and distorted. She ran upon him and exclaimed:

"Look at this horror! And you in that foul uniform can support it!"

The sheets of paper beneath the green roof were laterally striped with little serrated lines: each line meant the death of a man, for the day.

Tietjens had fallen a step back off the kerb of the pavement that ran round the quadrangle. He said:

"I support it because I have to. Just as you decry it because you have to. They're two different patterns that we see." He added: "This is my brother Mark."

She turned her head stiffly upon Mark: her face was perfectly waxen. It was as if the head of a shopkeeper's lay-figure had been turned. She said to Mark:

"I didn't know Mr. Tietjens had a brother. Or hardly. I've never heard him speak of you."

Mark grinned feebly, exhibiting to the lady the brilliant lining of his hat.

"I don't suppose anyone has ever heard me speak of *him*," he said, "but he's my brother all right!"

She stepped on to the asphalt carriage-way and caught between her fingers and thumb a fold of Christopher's khaki sleeve.

"I must speak to you," she said; "I'm going then."

She drew Christopher into the centre of the enclosed, hard and ungracious space, holding him still by the stuff of his tunic. She pushed him round until he was facing her. She swallowed hard; it was as if the motion of her throat took an immense time. Christopher looked round the sky-line of the buildings of sordid and besmirched stone. He had often wondered what would happen if an air-bomb of some size dropped into the mean, grey stoniness of that cold heart of an embattled world.

The girl was devouring his face with her eyes: to see him flinch. Her voice was hard between her little teeth. She said:

"Were you the father of the child Ethel was going to have? Your wife says you were."

Christopher considered the dimensions of the quadrangle. He said vaguely:

"Ethel? Who's she?" In pursuance of the habits of the painter-poet, Mr. and Mrs. Macmaster called each other always "Gug Gums!" Christopher had in all probability never heard Mrs. Duchemin's Christian names since his disaster had swept all names out of his head.

He came to the conclusion that the quadrangle was not a space sufficiently confined to afford much bursting resistance to a bomb.

The girl said:

"Edith Ethel Duchemin! Mrs. Macmaster, that is!" She was obviously waiting intensely. Christopher said with vagueness:

"No! Certainly not! . . . What was said?"

Mark Tietjens was leaning forward over the kerb in front of the green-stained shelter, like a child over a brookside. He was obviously waiting, quite patient, swinging his umbrella by the hook. He appeared to have no other means of self-expression. The girl was saying that when she had rung up Christopher that morning, a voice had said, without any preparation at all: the girl repeated, without any preparation at all:

"You'd better keep off the grass if you're the Wannop girl. Mrs. Duchemin is my husband's mistress already. You keep off!"

Christopher said:

"She said that, did she?" He was wondering how Mark kept his balance, really. The girl said nothing more. She was waiting. With an insistence that seemed to draw him: a sort of sucking in of his personality. It was unbearable. He made his last effort of that afternoon.

He said:

"Damn it all. How could you ask such a tom-fool question? *You!* I took you to be an intelligent person. The only intelligent person I know. Don't you *know* me?"

She made an effort to retain her stiffening.

"Isn't Mrs. Tietjens a truthful person?" she asked. "I thought she looked truthful when I saw her at Vincent and Ethel's."

He said:

"What she says she believes. But she only believes what she wants to, for the moment. If you call that truthful, she's truthful. I've nothing against her." He said to himself: "I'm not going to appeal to her by damning my wife."

She seemed to go all of a piece, as the hard outline goes suddenly out of a piece of lump sugar upon which you drop water.

"Oh," she said, "it *isn't* true. I *knew* it wasn't true." She began to cry.

Christopher said:

"Come along. I've been answering tom-fool questions all day. I've got another tom-fool to see here, then I'm through."

She said:

"I can't come with you, crying like this."

He answered:

"Oh, yes you can. This is the place where women cry." He added. "Besides, there's Mark. He's a comforting ass."

He delivered her over to Mark.

"Here, look after Miss Wannop," he said. "You want to talk to her anyhow, don't you?" and he hurried ahead of them like a fussy shop-walker into the lugubrious hall. He felt that if he didn't come soon to an unemotional ass in red, green, blue or pink tabs, who would have fishlike eyes and would ask the sort of questions that fishes ask in tanks, he, too, must break down and cry. With relief! However, that was a place where men cried, too!

He got through at once by sheer weight of personality, down miles of corridors, into the presence of a quite intelligent, thin, dark person with scarlet tabs. That meant a superior staff affair: not dust-bins.

The dark man said to him at once:

"Look here! What's the matter with the command depots? You've been lecturing a lot of them. In economy. What are all these damn mutinies about? Is it the rotten old colonels in command?"

Tietjens said amiably:

"Look here! I'm not a beastly spy, you know? I've had hospitality from the rotten old colonels."

The dark man said:

"I dare say you have. But that's what you were sent round for. General Campion said you were the brainiest chap in his command. He's gone out now, worse luck. . . . What's the matter with the command depots? Is it the men? Or is it the officers? You needn't mention names."

Tietjens said:

"Kind of Campion. It isn't the officers and it isn't the men. It's the foul system. You get men who think they've deserved well of their country—and they damn well have!—and you crop their heads . . ."

"That's the M.O.s," the dark man said. "They don't want lice."

"If they prefer mutinies . . ." Tietjens said. "A man wants to walk with his girl and have a properly oiled quiff. They don't like being regarded as convicts. That's how they are regarded."

The dark man said:

"All right. Go on. Why don't you sit down?"

"I'm a little in a hurry," Tietjens said. "I'm going out to-morrow and I've got a brother and people waiting below."

The dark man said:

"Oh, I'm sorry. . . . But damn. You're the sort of man we want at home. Do you want to go? We can, no doubt, get you stopped if you don't."

Tietjens hesitated for a moment."

"Yes!" he said eventually. "Yes, I want to go."

For the moment he had felt temptation to stay. But it came into his discouraged mind that Mark had said that Sylvia was in love with him. It had been underneath his thoughts all the while: it had struck him at the time like a

kick from the hind leg of a mule in his subliminal consciousness. It was the impossible complication. It might not be true;
but, whether or no, the best thing for him was to go and get
wiped out as soon as possible. He meant, nevertheless, fiercely,
to have his night with the girl who was crying downstairs. . . .

He heard in his ear, perfectly distinctly, the lines:

> "The voice that never yet . . .
> Made answer to my word . . ."

He said to himself:

"That was what Sylvia wanted! I've got that much!"

The dark man had said something. Tietjens repeated:

"I'd take it very unkindly if you stopped my going. . . .
I want to go."

The dark man said:

"Some do. Some do not. I'll make a note of your name
in case you come back. . . . You won't mind going on with
your cinder-sifting if you do? . . . Get on with your story
as quick as you can. And get what fun you can before you
go. They say it's rotten out there. Damn awful! There's a hell
of a strafe on. That's why they want all of you."

For a moment Tietjens saw the grey dawn at rail-head
with the distant sound of a ceaselessly boiling pot, from miles
away! The army feeling redescended upon him. He began to
talk about command depots, at great length and with enthusiasm. He snorted with rage at the way men were treated
in these gloomy places. With ingenious stupidity!

Every now and then the dark man interrupted him with:

"Don't forget that a command depot is a place where sick
and wounded go to get made fit. We've got to get 'em back
as soon as we can."

"And do you?" Tietjens would ask.

"No, we don't," the other would answer. "That's what this
inquiry is about."

"You've got," Tietjens would continue, "on the north
side of a beastly clay hill nine miles from Southampton three
thousand men from the Highlands, north Wales, Cumber-
land. . . . God knows where, as long as it's three hundred
miles from home to make them rather mad with nostalgia
. . . You allow 'em out for an hour a day during the pub's
closing time: you shave their heads to prevent 'em appealing
to local young women who don't exist, and you don't let
'em carry the swagger-canes! God knows why! To prevent
their poking their eyes out if they fall down, I suppose. Nine

miles from anywhere, with chalk down roads to walk on and not a bush for shelter or shade . . . And, damn it, if you get two men, chums, from the Seaforths or the Argylls, you don't let them sleep in the same hut, but shove 'em in with a lot of fat Buffs or Welshmen who stink of leeks and can't speak English. . . ."

"That's the infernal medicals' orders to stop 'em talking all night."

"To make 'em conspire all night not to turn out for parade," Tietjens said. "And there's a beastly mutiny begun. . . . And, damn it, they're fine men. They're first-class fellows. Why don't you—as this is a Christian land—let 'em go home to convalesce with their girls and pubs and friends and a little bit of swank, for heroes? Why, in God's name, don't you? Isn't there suffering enough?"

"I wish you wouldn't say 'you,' " the dark man said. "It isn't me. The only A.C.I. I've drafted was to give every command depot a cinema and a theatre. But the beastly medicals got it stopped . . . for fear of infection. And, of course, the parsons and Nonconformist magistrates . . ."

"Well, you'll have to change it all," Tietjens said, "or you'll just have to say: thank God we've got a navy. You won't have an army. The other day three fellows—Warwicks —asked me at question time, after a lecture, why they were shut up there in Wiltshire whilst Belgian refugees were getting bastards on their wives in Birmingham. And when I asked how many men made that complaint, over fifty stood up. All from Birmingham . . ."

The dark man said:

"I'll make a note of that. . . . Go on."

Tietjens went on; for as long as he stayed there he felt himself a man, doing work that befitted a man, with the bitter contempt for fools that a man should have and express. It was a letting up: a real last leave.

4 ~

MARK TIETJENS, his umbrella swinging sheepishly, his bowler hat pushed firmly down on to his ears to give him a sense of stability, walked beside the weeping girl in the quadrangle.

"I say," he said, "don't give it to old Christopher too

beastly hard about his militarist opinions. . . . Remember, he's going out to-morrow and he's one of the best."

She looked at him quickly, tears remaining upon her cheeks, and then away.

"One of the best," Mark said. "A fellow who never told a lie or did a dishonourable thing in his life. Let him down easy, there's a good girl. You ought to, you know."

The girl, her face turned away, said:

"I'd lay down my life for him!"

Mark said:

"I know you would. I know a good woman when I see one. And think! He probably considers that he *is* . . . offering his life, you know, for you. And me, too, of course! . . . It's a different way of looking at things." He gripped her awkwardly but irresistibly by the upper arm. It was very thin under her blue cloth coat. He said to himself:

"By Jove! Christopher likes them skinny. It's the athletic sort that attracts him. This girl is as clean-run as . . ." He couldn't think of anything as clean-run as Miss Wannop, but he felt a warm satisfaction at having achieved an intimacy with her and his brother. He said:

"You aren't going away? Not without a kinder word to him. You think! He might be killed. . . . Besides. Probably he's never killed a German. He was a liaison officer. Since then he's been in charge of a dump where they sift army dust-bins. To see how they can give the men less to eat. That means that the civilians get more. You don't object to his giving civilians more meat? . . . It isn't even helping to kill Germans. . . ."

He felt her arm press his hand against her warm side.

"What's he going to do now?" she asked. Her voice wavered.

"That's what I'm here about," Mark said. "I'm going in to see old Hogarth. You don't know Hogarth? Old General Hogarth? I think I can get him to give Christopher a job with the transport. A safe job. Safeish! No beastly glory business about it. No killing beastly Germans either. . . . I beg your pardon if you like Germans."

She drew her arm from his hand in order to look him in the face.

"Oh!" she said, "*you* don't want him to have any beastly military glory!" The colour came back into her face: she looked at him open-eyed.

He said:

"No! Why the devil should he?" He said to himself:

"She's got enormous eyes: a good neck: good shoulders: good breasts: clean hips: small hands. She isn't knock-kneed: neat ankles. She stands well on her feet. Feet not too large! Five foot four, say! A real good filly!" He went on aloud: "Why in the world should he want to be a beastly soldier? He's the heir to Groby. That ought to be enough for one man."

Having stood still sufficiently long for what she knew to be his critical inspection, she put her hand in turn, precipitately, under his arm and moved him towards the entrance steps.

"Let's be quick, then," she said. "Let's get him into your transport at once. Before he goes to-morrow. Then we'll know he's safe."

He was puzzled by her dress. It was very business-like, dark blue and very short. A white blouse with a black silk man's tie. A wideawake with, on the front of the band, a cipher.

"You're in uniform yourself," he said. "Does your conscience let you do war work?"

She said:

"No. We're hard up. I'm taking the gym classes in a great big school to turn an honest penny. . . . *Do* be quick!"

Her pressure on his elbow flattered him. He resisted it a little, hanging back, to make her more insistent. He liked being pleaded with by a pretty woman: Christopher's girl at that.

He said:

"Oh, it's not a matter of minutes. They keep 'em weeks at the base before they send 'em up. . . . We'll fix him up all right, I've no doubt. We'll wait in the hall till he comes down."

He told the benevolent commissionaire, one of two in a pulpit in the crowded, grim hall, that he was going up to see General Hogarth in a minute or two. But not to send a bell-boy. He might be some time yet.

He sat himself beside Miss Wannop, clumsily, on a wooden bench, humanity surging over their toes as if they had been on a beach. She moved a little to make room for him and that, too, made him feel good. He said:

"You said just now: 'we' are hard up. Does 'we' mean you and Christopher?"

She said:

"I and Mr. Tietjens. Oh, no! I and mother! The paper she used to write for stopped. When your father died, I believe. He found money for it, I think. And mother isn't suited to free-lancing. She's worked too hard in her life."

He looked at her, his round eyes protruding.

"I don't know what that is, free-lancing," he said. "But you've got to be comfortable. How much do you and your mother need to keep you comfortable? And put in a bit more so that Christopher could have a mutton-chop now and then!"

She hadn't really been listening. He said with some insistence: "Look here! I'm here on business. Not like an elderly admirer forcing himself on you. Though, by God, I do admire you too . . . But my father wanted your mother to be comfortable. . . ."

Her face, turned to him, became rigid.

"You don't mean . . ." she began. He said:

"You won't get it any quicker by interrupting. I have to tell my stories in my own way. My father wanted your mother to be comfortable. He said so that she could write books, not papers. I don't know what the difference is: that's what he said. He wants you to be comfortable too. . . . You've not got any encumbrances? Not . . . oh, say a business: a hat shop that doesn't pay? Some girls have. . . ."

She said: "No. I just teach . . . oh, *do* be quick. . . ."

For the first time in his life he dislocated the course of his thoughts to satisfy a longing in someone else.

"You may take it to go on with," he said, "as if my father had left your mother a nice little plum." He cast about to find his scattered thoughts.

"He has! He *has!* After all!" the girl said. "Oh, thank God!"

"There'll be a bit for you, if you like," Mark said, "or perhaps Christopher won't let you. He's ratty with me. And something for your brother to buy a doctor's business with." He asked: "You haven't fainted, have you?" She said:

"No. I don't faint. I cry."

"That'll be all right," he answered. He went on: "That's your side of it. Now for mine. I want Christopher to have a place where he'll be sure of a mutton-chop and an arm-chair by the fire. And someone to be good for him. *You're* good for him. I can see that. I know women!"

The girl was crying, softly and continuously. It was the first moment of the lifting of strain that she had known since the day before the Germans crossed the Belgian frontier, near a place called Gemmenich.

It had begun with the return of Mrs. Duchemin from

Scotland. She had sent at once for Miss Wannop to the
rectory, late at night. By the light of candles in tall silver
stocks, against oak panelling, she had seemed like a mad
block of marble, with staring, dark eyes and mad hair. She
had exclaimed in a voice as hard as a machine's:

"How do you get rid of a baby? You've been a servant.
You ought to know!"

That had been the great shock, the turning-point, of Valentine Wannop's life. Her last years before that had been
of great tranquillity, tinged of course with melancholy
because she loved Christopher Tietjens. But she had early
learned to do without, and the world as she saw it was a
place of renunciations, of high endeavour and sacrifice.
Tietjens had to be a man who came to see her mother and
talked wonderfully. She had been happy when he had been
in the house—she in the housemaid's pantry, getting the
tea-things. She had, besides, been very hard worked for
her mother; the weather had been, on the whole, good; the
corner of the country in which they lived had continued
to seem fresh and agreeable. She had had excellent health,
got an occasional ride on the *qui-tamer* with which Tietjens
had replaced Joel's rig; and her brother had done admirably
at Eton, taking such a number of exhibitions and things
that, once at Magdalen, he had been nearly off his mother's
hands. An admirable, gay boy, not unlikely to run for, as
well as being a credit to, his university, if he didn't get
sent down for his political extravagances. He was a Communist!

And at the rectory there had been the Duchemins or,
rather, Mrs. Duchemin and, during most week-ends, Macmaster somewhere about.

The passion of Macmaster for Edith Ethel and of Edith
Ethel for Macmaster had seemed to her one of the beautiful things of life. They seemed to swim in a sea of renunciations, of beautiful quotations, and of steadfast waiting. Macmaster did not interest her personally much, but she took
him on trust because of Edith Ethel's romantic passion and
because he was Christopher Tietjens' friend. She had never
heard him say anything original; when he used quotations
they would be apt rather than striking. But she took it for
granted that he was the right man—much as you take it
for granted that the engine of an express train in which
you are is reliable. The right people have chosen it for
you. . . .

With Mrs. Duchemin mad before her, she had the first

intimation that her idolized friend, in whom she had believed as she had believed in the firmness of the great, sunny earth, had been the mistress of her lover—almost since the first day she had seen him. . . . And that Mrs. Duchemin had, stored somewhere, a character of an extreme harshness and great vulgarity of language. She raged up and down in the candlelight, before the dark oak panelling, screaming coarse phrases of the deepest hatred for her lover. Didn't the oaf know his business better than to ? . . . the dirty little Port of Leith fish-handler. . . .

What, then, were tall candles in silver sticks for? And polished panelling in galleries?

Valentine Wannop couldn't have been a little ash-cat in worn cotton dresses, sleeping under the stairs, in an Ealing household with a drunken cook, an invalid mistress and three overfed men without acquiring a considerable knowledge of the sexual necessities and excesses of humanity. But as all the poorer helots of great cities hearten their lives by dreaming of material beauties, elegance, and suave wealth, she had always considered that, far from the world of Ealing and its county councillors who overate and neighed like stallions, there were bright colonies of beings, chaste, beautiful in thought, altruist and circumspect.

And till that moment, she had imagined herself on the skirts of such a colony. She presupposed a society of beautiful intellects centring in London round her friends. Ealing she just put out of her mind. She considered: she had, indeed, once heard Tietjens say that humanity was made up of exact and constructive intellects on the one hand and on the other of stuff to fill graveyards. . . . Now, what had become of the exact and constructive intellects?

Worst of all, what became of her beautiful inclination towards Tietjens? For she couldn't regard it as anything more. Couldn't her heart sing any more whilst she was in the housemaid's pantry and he in her mother's study? And what became, still more, of what she knew to be Tietjens' beautiful inclination towards her? She asked herself the eternal question—and she knew it to be the eternal question—whether no man and woman can ever leave it at the beautiful inclination. And looking at Mrs. Duchemin rushing backwards and forwards in the light of candles, blue-white of face and her hair flying, Valentine Wannop said: "No! No! The tiger lying in the reeds will always raise its head!" But tiger . . . it was more like a peacock. . . .

Tietjens, raising his head from the other side of the tea-table and looking at her with his long, meditative glance from beside her mother: ought he, then, instead of blue and protruding, to have eyes divided longitudinally in the blacks of them—that should divide, closing or dilating, on a yellow ground, with green glowings of furtive light?

She was aware that Edith Ethel had done her an irreparable wrong, for you cannot suffer a great sexual shock and ever be the same. Or not for years. Nevertheless, she stayed with Mrs. Duchemin until far into the small hours, when that lady fell, a mere parcel of bones in a peacock-blue wrapper, into a deep chair and refused to move or speak; nor did she afterwards slacken in her faithful waiting on her friend. . . .

On the next day came the war. That was a nightmare of pure suffering, with never a let-up, day or night. It began on the morning of the fourth with the arrival of her brother from some sort of Oxford Communist Summer School on the Broads. He was wearing a German corps student's cap and was very drunk. He had been seeing German friends off from Harwich. It was the first time she had ever seen a drunken man, so that was a good present to her.

Next day, and sober, he was almost worse. A handsome, dark boy like his father, he had his mother's hooked nose and was always a little unbalanced: not mad, but always overviolent in any views he happened for the moment to hold. At the summer school he had been under very vitriolic teachers of all sorts of notions. That hadn't hitherto mattered. Her mother had written for a Tory paper: her brother, when he had been at home, had edited some sort of Oxford organ of disruption. But her mother had only chuckled.

The war changed that. Both seemed to be filled with a desire for blood and to torture: neither paid the least attention to the other. It was as if—so for the rest of those years the remembrance of that time lived with her—in one corner of the room her mother, ageing and on her knees, from which she only with difficulty rose, shouted hoarse prayers to God, to let her, with her own hands, strangle, torture, and flay off all his skin, a being called the Kaiser, and as if in the other corner of the room her brother, erect, dark, scowling and vitriolic, one hand clenched above his head, called down the curse of heaven on the British soldier, so that in thousands he might die in agony, the blood spouting from his scalded lungs. It appeared that the Communist leader whom Edward Wannop affected had had ill success in his attempts to cause disaffection among some units or other of the British army and had failed rather gallingly, being laughed at or ignored rather than being ducked in a horse-pond, shot or otherwise martyrized. That made it obvious that the British man in the ranks was responsible for the war. If those ignoble hirelings had refused to fight, all the other embattled and terrorized millions would have thrown down their arms!

Across that dreadful phantasmagoria went the figure of Tietjens. He was in doubt. She heard him several times voice his doubts to her mother, who grew every day more vacant. One day Mrs. Wannop had said:

"What does your wife think about it?"

Tietjens had answered:

"Oh, Mrs. Tietjens is a pro-German. . . . Or no, that isn't exact! She has German prisoner friends and looks after them. But she spends nearly all her time in retreat in a convent, reading novels of before the war. She can't bear the thought of physical suffering. I can't blame her."

Mrs. Wannop was no longer listening: her daughter was.

For Valentine Wannop the war had turned Tietjens into far more of a man and far less of an inclination—the war and Mrs. Duchemin between them. He had seemed to grow less infallible. A man with doubts is more of a man, with eyes, hands, the need for food and for buttons to be sewn on. She had actually tightened up a loose glove-button for him.

One Friday afternoon at Macmaster's she had had a long talk with him: the first she had had since the drive and the accident.

Ever since Macmaster had instituted his Friday afternoons—and that had been some time before the war—Valentine Wannop had accompanied Mrs. Duchemin to town by the morning train and back at night to the rectory. Valentine poured out the tea, Mrs. Duchemin drifting about the large book-lined room amongst the geniuses and superior journalists.

On this occasion—a November day of very chilly wet—there had been next to nobody present, the preceding Friday having been unusually full. Macmaster and Mrs. Duchemin had taken a Mr. Spong, an architect, into the dining-room to inspect an unusually fine set of Piranesi's *Views of Rome* that Tietjens had picked up somewhere and had given to Macmaster. A Mr. Jegg and a Mrs. Haviland were sitting close together in the far window-seat. They were talking in low tones. From time to time Mr. Jegg used the word "inhibition." Tietjens rose from the fire-seat on which he had been sitting and came to her. He ordered her to bring her cup of tea over by the fire and talk to him. She obeyed. They sat side by side on the leather fire-seat that stood on polished brass rails, the fire warming their backs. He said:

"Well, Miss Wannop. What have you been doing?" and they drifted into talking of the war. You couldn't not. She was astonished not to find him so loathsome as she had expected, for just at that time, with the facts that were always being driven into her mind by the pacifist friends of her brother and with continual brooding over the morals of Mrs. Duchemin, she had an automatic feeling that all manly men were lust-filled devils, desiring nothing better than to stride over battle-fields, stabbing the wounded with long daggers in frenzies of sadism. She knew that this view of Tietjens was wrong, but she cherished it.

She found him—as subconsciously she knew he was—astonishingly mild. She had too often watched him whilst he listened to her mother's tirades against the Kaiser not to know that. He did not raise his voice; he showed no emotion. He said at last:

"You and I are like two people . . ." He paused and began again more quickly: "Do you know these soap-advertisement signs that read differently from several angles? As you come up to them you read 'Monkey's Soap'; if you look back when you've passed, it's 'Needs No Rinsing. . . .' You and I are standing at different angles, and though we both look at the same thing we read different messages. Perhaps if we stood side by side we should see yet a third. . . . But I hope we respect each other. We're both honest. I, at least, tremendously respect you and I hope you respect me."

She kept silent. Behind their backs the fire rustled. Mr. Jegg, across the room, said: "The failure to co-ordinate . . ." and then dropped his voice.

Tietjens looked at her attentively.

"You don't respect me?" he asked. She kept obstinately silent.

"I'd have liked you to have said it," he repeated.

"Oh," she cried out, "how can I respect you when there is all this suffering? So much pain! Such torture . . . I can't sleep . . . Never . . . I haven't slept a whole night since . . . Think of the immense spaces, stretching out under the night . . . I believe pain and fear must be worse at night. . . ." She knew she was crying out like that because her dread had come true. When he had said: "I'd have liked you to have said it," using the past, he had said his valedictory. Her man, too, was going.

And she knew too: she had always known under her mind and now she confessed it: her agony had been, half of it, because one day he would say farewell to her: like that with the inflexion of a verb. As, just occasionally, using the word "we"—and perhaps without intention—he had let her know that he loved her.

Mr. Jegg drifted across from the window: Mrs. Haviland was already at the door.

"We'll leave you to have your war talk out," Mr. Jegg said. He added: "For myself, I believe it's one's sole duty to preserve the beauty of things that's preservable. I can't help saying that."

She was alone with Tietjens and the quiet day. She said to herself:

"Now he must take me in his arms. He must. He *must!*" The deepest of her instincts came to the surface, from beneath layers of thought hardly known to her. She could feel his arms round her: she had in her nostrils the peculiar scent of his hair—like the scent of the skin of an apple, but very faint. "You must! You *must!*" she said to herself. There came back to her overpoweringly the memory of their drive together and the moment, the overwhelming moment, when, climbing out of the white fog into the blinding air, she had felt the impulse of his whole body towards her and the impulse of her whole body towards him. A sudden lapse: like the momentary dream when you fall . . . She saw the white disk of the sun over the silver mist and behind them was the long, warm night. . . .

Tietjens sat, huddled rather together, dejectedly, the firelight playing on the silver places of his hair. It had grown nearly dark outside: they had a sense of the large room that, almost week by week, had grown, for its gleams of gilding and hand-polished dark woods, more like the great dining-room at the Duchemins. He got down from the fireseat with a weary movement, as if the fire-seat had been very high. He said, with a little bitterness, but as if with more fatigue:

"Well, I've got the business of telling Macmaster that I'm leaving the office. That, too, won't be an agreeable affair! Not that what poor Vinnie thinks matters." He added: "It's queer, dear . . ." In the tumult of her emotions she was almost certain that he had said "dear. . . ." "Not three hours ago my wife used to me almost the exact words you have just used. Almost the exact words. She talked of her inability to sleep at night for thinking of immense spaces full of pain that was worse at night. . . . And she, too, said that she could not respect me. . . ."

She sprang up.

"Oh," she said, "she didn't mean it. *I* didn't mean it. Almost every man who is a man must do as you are doing. But don't you see it's a desperate attempt to get you to stay: an attempt on moral lines? How can we leave any stone unturned that could keep us from losing our men?" She added, and it was another stone that she didn't leave unturned: "Besides, how can you reconcile it with your sense of duty, even from your point of view? You're more useful—you know you're more useful to your country here than . . ."

He stood over her, stooping a little, somehow suggesting great gentleness and concern.

"I can't reconcile it with my conscience," he said. "In this affair there is nothing that any man can reconcile with his conscience. I don't mean that we oughtn't to be in this affair and on the side we're on. We ought. But I'll put to you things I have put to no other soul."

The simplicity of his revelation seemed to her to put to shame any of the glibnesses she had heard. It appeared to her as if a child were speaking. He described the disillusionment it had cost him personally as soon as this country had come into the war. He even described the sunlit heather landscape of the North, where naïvely he had made his tranquil resolution to join the French Foreign Legion as a common soldier and his conviction that that would give him, as he called it, clean bones again.

That, he said, had been straightforward. Now there was nothing straightforward: for him or for any man. One could have fought with a clean heart for a civilization: if you like, for the eighteenth century against the twentieth, since that was what fighting for France against the enemy countries meant. But our coming in had changed the aspect at once. It was one part of the twentieth century using the eighteenth as a cat's-paw to bash the other half of the twentieth. It was true there was nothing else for it. And as long as we did it in a decent spirit it was just bearable. One could keep at one's job—which was faking statistics against

the other fellow—until you were sick and tired of faking
and your brain reeled. And then some!

It was probably impolitic to fake—to overstate!—a case
against enemy nations. The chickens would come home to
roost in one way or another, probably. Perhaps they wouldn't.
That was a matter for one's superiors. Obviously! And the
first gang had been simple, honest fellows. Stupid, but relatively disinterested. But now! . . . What was one to do?
. . . He went on, almost mumbling. . . .

She had suddenly a clear view of him as a man extraordinarily clear-sighted in the affairs of others, in great
affairs, but in his own so simple as to be almost a baby.
And gentle! And extraordinarily unselfish. He didn't betray
one thought of self-interest . . . not one!

He was saying:

"But now! . . . with this crowd of boodlers! . . . Supposing one's asked to manipulate the figures of millions of
pairs of boots in order to force someone else to send some
miserable general and his troops to, say, Salonika—when
they and you and common sense and everyone and everything else know it's disastrous? . . . And from that to
monkeying with our own forces . . . Starving particular
units for political . . ." He was talking to himself, not to
her. And indeed he said:

"I can't, you see, talk really before you. For all I know,
your sympathies, perhaps your activities, are with the enemy
nations."

She said passionately:

"They're not! They're not! How dare you say such a
thing?"

He answered:

"It doesn't matter . . . No! I'm sure you're not . . . But,
anyhow, these things are official. One can't, if one's
scrupulous, even talk about them. . . . And then . . . You
see it means such infinite deaths of men, such an infinite
prolongation . . . all this interference for side-ends! . . .
I seem to see these fellows with clouds of blood over their
heads. . . . And then . . . I'm to carry out their orders
because they're my superiors. . . . But helping them means
unnumbered deaths. . . ."

He looked at her with a faint, almost humorous smile:

"You see!" he said, "we're perhaps not so very far apart!
You mustn't think you're the only one that sees all the
deaths and all the sufferings. All, you see: I, too, am a

conscientious objector. My conscience won't let me continue any longer with these fellows. . . ."

She said:

"But isn't there any other . . ."

He interrupted:

"No! There's no other course. One is either a body or a brain in these affairs. I suppose I'm more brain than body. I suppose so. Perhaps I'm not. But my conscience won't let me use my brain in this service. So I've a great, hulking body! I'll admit I'm probably not much good. But I've nothing to live for: what I stand for isn't any more in this world. What I want, as you know, I can't have. So . . ."

She exclaimed bitterly:

"Oh, say it! Say it! Say that your large, hulking body will stop two bullets in front of two small anaemic fellows. . . . And how can you say you'll have nothing to live for? You'll come back. You'll do your good work again. You know you did good work. . . ."

He said:

"Yes! I believe I did. I used to despise it, but I've come to believe I did. . . . But no! They'll never let me back. They've got me out, with all sorts of bad marks against me. They'll pursue me, systematically. . . . You see, in such a world as this, an idealist—or perhaps it's only a sentimentalist— must be stoned to death. He makes the others so uncomfortable. He haunts them at their golf. . . . No, they'll get me, one way or the other. And some fellow—Macmaster here—will do my jobs. He won't do them so well, but he'll do them more dishonestly. Or no. I oughtn't to say dishonestly. He'll do them with enthusiasm and righteousness. He'll fulfil the order of his superiors with an immense docility and unction. He'll fake figures against our allies with the black enthusiasm of a Calvin, and when *that* war comes, he'll do the requisite faking with the righteous wrath of Jehovah smiting the priests of Baal. And he'll be right. It's all we're fitted for. We ought never to have come into this war. We ought to have snaffled other peoples' colonies as the price of neutrality. . . ."

"Oh!" Valentine Wannop said, "how can you so hate your country?"

He said with great earnestness:

"Don't say it! Don't believe it! Don't even for a moment think it! I love every inch of its fields and every plant in the hedgerows: comfrey, mullein, paigles, long red purples, that liberal shepherds give a grosser name . . . and all the rest of the rubbish—you remember the field between the Duchemins' and your mother's—and we have always been boodlers and robbers and reivers and pirates and cattle-thieves, and so we've built up the great tradition that we love. . . . But, for the moment, it's painful. Our present crowd is not more corrupt than Walpole's. But one's too near them. One sees of Walpole that he consolidated the nation by building up the national debt: one doesn't see his methods. . . . My son or his son will only see the glory of the boodle we make out of this show. Or rather out of the next. He won't know about the methods. They'll teach him at school that across the counties went the sound of bugles that his father knew. . . . Though that was another discreditable affair. . . ."

"But you!" Valentine Wannop exclaimed. "*You!* What will *you* do! After the war!"

"I!" he said rather bewilderedly. "I! . . . Oh, I shall go into the old-furniture business. I've been offered a job. . . ."

She didn't believe he was serious. He hadn't, she knew, ever thought about his future. But suddenly she had a vision of his white head and pale face in the back glooms of a shop full of dusty things. He would come out, get heavily on to a dusty bicycle and ride off to a cottage sale. She cried out:

"Why don't you do it at once? Why don't you take the job at once?" for in the back of the dark shop he would at least be safe.

He said:

"Oh, no! Not at this time! Besides, the old-furniture trade's probably not itself for the minute. . . ." He was obviously thinking of something else.

"I've probably been a low cad," he said, "wringing your heart with my doubts. But I wanted to see where our similarities come in. We've always been—or we've seemed always to me—so alike in our thoughts. I dare say I wanted you to respect me. . . ."

"Oh, I respect you! I respect you!" she said. "You're as innocent as a child."

He went on:

"And I wanted to get some thinking done. It hasn't been often of late that one has had a quiet room and a fire and . . . you! To think in front of. You *do* make one collect one's thoughts. I've been very muddled till to-day . . . till five minutes ago! Do you remember our drive? You analysed my character. I'd never have let another soul . . . But you see . . . Don't you see?"

She said:

"No! What am I to see? I remember . . ."

He said:

"That I'm certainly not an English country gentleman now, picking up the gossip of the horse-markets and saying: let the country go to hell, for me!"

She said:

"Did I say that? . . . Yes, I said that!"

The deep waves of emotion came over her: she trembled. She stretched out her arms. . . . She thought she stretched out her arms. He was hardly visible in the fire-light. But she could see nothing: she was blind for tears. She could hardly be stretching out her arms, for she had both hands to her handkerchief on her eyes. He said something: it was no word of love or she would have held it; it began with: "Well, I must be . . ." He was silent for a long time: she imagined herself to feel great waves coming from him to her. But he wasn't in the room. . . .

The rest, till that moment at the War Office, had been pure agony, and unrelenting. Her mother's paper cut down her money; no orders for serials came in: her mother, obviously, was failing. The eternal diatribes of her brother were like lashes upon her skin. He seemed to be praying Tietjens to death. Of Tietjens she saw and heard nothing. At the Macmasters she heard, once, that he had just gone out. It added to her desire to scream when she saw a newspaper. Poverty invaded them. The police raided the house in search of her brother and his friends. Then her brother went to prison: somewhere in the Midlands. The friendliness of their former neighbours turned to surly suspicion. They could get no milk. Food became almost unprocurable without going to long distances. For three days Mrs. Wannop was clean out of her mind. Then she grew better and began to write a new book. It promised to be rather good. But there was no publisher. Edward came out of prison, full of good humour and boisterousness. They seemed to have had a great deal to drink in prison. But, hearing that his mother had gone mad over that disgrace, after a terrible scene with Valentine, in which he accused her of being the mistress of Tietjens and therefore militarist, he consented to let his mother use her influence—of which she had still some— to get him appointed as an A.B. on a mine-sweeper. Great winds became an agony to Valentine Wannop in addition to the unbearable sounds of firing that came continuously over the sea. Her mother grew much better: she took pride in having a son in a service. She was then the more able to appreciate the fact that her paper stopped payment altogether.

A small mob on the fifth of November burned Mrs. Wannop in effigy in front of their cottage and broke their lower windows. Mrs. Wannop ran out and in the illumination of the fire knocked down two farm-labourer hobbledehoys. It was terrible to see Mrs. Wannop's grey hair in the fire-light. After that the butcher refused them meat altogether, ration card or no ration card. It was imperative that they should move to London.

The marsh horizon became obscured with giant stilts: the air above it filled with aeroplanes: the roads covered with military cars. There was then no getting away from the sounds of the war.

Just as they had decided to move, Tietjens came back. It was for a moment heaven to have him in this country. But when, a month later, Valentine Wannop saw him for a minute, he seemed very heavy, aged and dull. It was then almost as bad as before, for it seemed to Valentine as if he hardly had his reason.

On hearing that Tietjens was to be quartered—or, at any rate, occupied—in the neighbourhood of Ealing, Mrs. Wannop at once took a small house in Bedford Park, whilst, to make ends meet—for her mother made terribly little—Valentine Wannop took a post as athletic mistress in a great school in a not very near suburb. Thus, though Tietjens came in for a cup of tea almost every afternoon with Mrs. Wannop in the dilapidated little suburban house, Valentine Wannop hardly ever saw him. The only free afternoon she had was the Friday, and on that day she still regularly chaperoned Mrs. Duchemin: meeting her at Charing Cross towards noon and taking her back to the same station in time to catch the last train to Rye. On Saturdays and Sundays she was occupied all day in typing her mother's manuscript.

Of Tietjens, then, she saw almost nothing. She knew that his poor mind was empty of facts and of names; but her mother said he was a great help to her. Once provided with facts, his mind worked out sound Tory conclusions—or quite startling and attractive theories—with extreme rapidity. This Mrs. Wannop found of the greatest use to her whenever—though it wasn't now very often—she had an article to write for an excitable newspaper. She still, however, contributed to her failing organ of opinion, though it paid her nothing. . . .

Mrs. Duchemin, then, Valentine Wannop still chaperoned, though there was no bond any more between them. Valentine knew, for instance, perfectly well that Mrs. Duchemin, after

she had been seen off by train from Charing Cross, got out at
Clapham Junction, took a taxi-cab back to Gray's Inn after
dark and spent the night with Macmaster, and Mrs. Duchemin
knew quite well that Valentine knew. It was a sort of parade
of circumspection and rightness, and they kept it up even
after, at a sinister registry office, the wedding had taken
place, Valentine being the one witness and an obscure-looking
substitute for the usual pew opener another. There seemed
to be, by then, no very obvious reason why Valentine should
support Mrs. Macmaster any more on the rather dreary occasions, but Mrs. Macmaster said she might just as well until
they saw fit to make the marriage public. There were, Mrs.
Macmaster said, censorious tongues, and even if these were
confuted afterwards it is difficult, if not impossible, to outrun
scandal. Besides, Mrs. Macmaster was of opinion that the
Macmaster afternoons with these geniuses must be a liberal
education for Valentine. But as Valentine sat most of the time
at the tea-table near the door, it was the backs and side-
faces of the distinguished rather than their intellects with
which she was most acquainted. Occasionally, however, Mrs.
Duchemin would show Valentine, as an enormous privilege,
one of the letters to herself from men of genius: usually north
British, written, as a rule, from the Continent or more distant
and peaceful climates, for most of them believed it their
duty in these hideous times to keep alive in the world the
only glimmering spark of beauty. Couched in terms so eulo-
gistic as to resemble those used in passionate love-letters
by men more profane, these epistles recounted or consulted Mrs. Duchemin as to their love-affairs with foreign
princesses, the progress of their ailments or the progress
of their souls towards those higher regions of morality
in which floated their so beautiful-souled correspondence.

The letters entertained Valentine and, indeed, she was entertained by that whole mirage. It was only the Macmasters'
treatment of her mother that finally decided Valentine
that this friendship had died; for the friendships of women
are very tenacious things, surviving astonishing disillusion-
ments, and Valentine Wannop was a woman of more than
usual loyalty. Indeed, if she couldn't respect Mrs. Duchemin on the old grounds, she could very really respect her
for her tenacity of purpose, her determination to advance
Macmaster and for the sort of ruthlessness that she put into
these pursuits.

Valentine's affection had, indeed, survived even Edith
Ethel's continued denigrations of Tietjens—for Edith Ethel

regarded Tietjens as a clog round her husband's neck if only because he was a very unpopular man, grown personally rather unpresentable and always extremely rude to the geniuses on Fridays. Edith Ethel, however, never made these complaints, that grew more and more frequent as more and more the distinguished flocked to the Fridays, before Macmaster. And they ceased very suddenly and in a way that struck Valentine as odd.

Mrs. Duchemin's grievance against Tietjens was that, Macmaster being a weak man, Tietjens had acted as his banker until, what with interest and the rest of it, Macmaster owed Tietjens a great sum: several thousand pounds. And there had been no real reason: Macmaster had spent most of the money either on costly furnishings for his rooms or on his costly journeys to Rye. On the one hand Mrs. Duchemin could have found Macmaster all the bric-à-brac he could possibly have wanted from amongst the things at the rectory, where no one would have missed them and, on the other, she, Mrs. Duchemin, would have paid all Macmaster's travelling expenses. She had had unlimited money from her husband, who never asked for accounts. But, whilst Tietjens still had influence with Macmaster, he had used it uncompromisingly against this course, giving him the delusion—it enraged Mrs. Duchemin to think!—that it would have been dishonourable. So that Macmaster had continued to draw upon him.

And, most enraging of all, at a period when she had had a power of attorney over all Mr. Duchemin's fortune and could, perfectly easily, have sold out something that no one would have missed for the couple of thousand or so that Macmaster owed, Tietjens had very forcibly refused to allow Macmaster to agree to anything of the sort. He had again put into Macmaster's weak head that it would be dishonourable. But Mrs. Duchemin—and she closed her lips determinedly after she had said it—knew perfectly well Tietjens' motive. So long as Macmaster owed him money he imagined that they couldn't close their doors upon him. And their establishment was beginning to be a place where you meet people of great influence who might well get for a person as lazy as Tietjens a sinecure that would suit him. Tietjens, in fact, knew which side his bread was buttered.

For what, Mrs. Duchemin asked, could there have been dishonourable about the arrangement she had proposed? Practically the whole of Mr. Duchemin's money was to come to her: he was by then insane; it was therefore, morally, her own. But immediately after that, Mr. Duchemin having been

certified, the estate had fallen into the hands of the Lunacy
Commissioners and there had been no further hope of taking
the capital. Now, her husband being dead, it was in the hands
of trustees, Mr. Duchemin having left the whole of his
property to Magdalen College and merely the income to his
widow. The income was very large; but where, with their
expenses, with the death-duties and taxation, which were by
then merciless, was Mrs. Duchemin to find the money? She
was to be allowed, under her husband's will, enough capital
to buy a pleasant little place in Surrey, with rather a nice lot
of land—enough to let Macmaster know some of the leisures
of a country gentleman's lot. They were going in for short-
horns, and there was enough land to give them a small golf-
course and, in the autumn, a little—oh, mostly rough!—
shooting for Macmaster to bring his friends down to. It would
just run to that. Oh, no ostentation. Merely a nice little
place. As an amusing detail the villagers there already
called Macmaster "squire" and the women curtsied to him.
But Valentine Wannop would understand that, with all these
expenses, they couldn't find the money to pay off Tietjens.
Besides, Mrs. Macmaster said she wasn't going to pay off
Tietjens. He had had his chance once: now he could go
without, for her. Macmaster would have to pay it himself
and he would never be able to, his contribution to their
housekeeping being what it was. And there were going to be
complications. Macmaster wondered about their little place
in Surrey, saying that he would consult Tietjens about this
and that alteration. But over the door-sill of that place the
foot of Tietjens was never going to go! Never! It would
mean a good deal of unpleasantness; or rather it would mean
one sharp: "C-r-r-unch!" And then: Napoo finny! Mrs. Duchemin sometimes, and with great effect, condescended to use
one of the more picturesque phrases of the day.

To all these diatribes Valentine Wannop answered hardly
anything. It was no particular concern of hers; even if, for
a moment, she felt proprietarily towards Christopher, as she
did now and then, she felt no particular desire that his intimacy with the Macmasters should be prolonged, because
she knew he could have no particular desire for its prolongation. She imagined him turning them down with an un-
spoken and good-humoured gibe. And, indeed, she agreed on
the whole with Edith Ethel. It *was* demoralizing for a weak
little man like Vincent to have a friend with an ever-open
purse beside him. Tietjens ought not to have been princely:
it was a defect, a quality that she did not personally admire

in him. As to whether it would or wouldn't have been dishonourable for Mrs. Duchemin to take her husband's money
and give it to Macmaster, she kept an open mind. To all intents and purposes the money *was* Mrs. Duchemin's, and if
Mrs. Duchemin had then paid Christopher off it would have
been sensible. She could see that later it had become very
inconvenient. There were, however, male standards to be
considered, and Macmaster, at least, passed for a man. Tietjens, who was wise enough in the affairs of others, had, in
that, probably been wise; for there might have been great
disagreeablenesses with trustees and heirs-at-law had Mrs.
Duchemin's subtraction of a couple of thousand pounds from
the Duchemin estate afterwards come to light. The Wannops
had never been large property owners as a family, but Valentine had heard enough of collateral wranglings over small
family dishonesties to know how very disagreeable these
could be.

So she had made little or no comment; sometimes she had
even faintly agreed as to the demoralization of Macmaster
and that had sufficed. For Mrs. Duchemin had been certain
of her rightness and cared nothing at all for the opinion of
Valentine Wannop or else took it for granted.

And when Tietjens had been gone to France for a little
time, Mrs. Duchemin seemed to forget the matter, contenting
herself with saying that he might very likely not come back.
He was the sort of clumsy man who generally got killed. In
that case, since no I.O.U.s or paper had passed, Mrs. Tietjens
would have no claim. So that would be all right.

But two days after the return of Christopher—and that
was how Valentine knew he had come back!—Mrs. Duchemin
with a lowering brow exclaimed:

"That oaf, Tietjens, is in England, perfectly safe and
sound. And now the whole miserable business of Vincent's
indebtedness . . . Oh!"

She had stopped so suddenly and so markedly that even
the stoppage of Valentine's own heart couldn't conceal the
oddness from her. Indeed it was as if there were an interval
before she completely realized what the news was and as
if, during that interval, she said to herself:

"It's very queer. It's exactly as if Edith Ethel has stopped
abusing him on my account. . . . As if she *knew!*" But how
could Edith Ethel know that she loved the man who had returned? It was impossible! She hardly knew herself. Then the
great wave of relief rolled over her: he was in England. One
day she would see him, there: in the great room. For these

colloquies with Edith Ethel always took place in the great
room where she had last seen Tietjens. It looked suddenly
beautiful and she was resigned to sitting there, waiting for
the distinguished.

It was indeed a beautiful room: it had become so during
the years. It was long and high—matching the Tietjens'. A
great cut-glass chandelier from the rectory hung dimly corus-
cating in the centre, reflected and rereflected in convex gilt
mirrors, topped by eagles. A great number of books had
gone to make place on the white panelled walls for the mirrors and for the fair orange and brown pictures by Turner,
also from the rectory. From the rectory had come the immense scarlet and lapis lazuli carpet, the great brass fire-
basket and appendages, the great curtains that, in the three
long windows, on their peacock-blue Chinese silk showed
parti-coloured cranes ascending in long flights—and all the
polished Chippendale arm-chairs. Amongst all these, gracious,
trailing, stopping with a tender gesture to rearrange very
slightly the crimson roses in the famous silver bowls, still in
dark blue silks, with an amber necklace and her elaborate
black hair, waved exactly like that of Julia Domna of the
Musée Lapidaire at Arles, moved Mrs. Macmaster—also from
the rectory. Macmaster had achieved his desire: even to the
short-bread cakes and the peculiarly scented tea that came
every Friday morning from Princes Street. And if Mrs.
Macmaster hadn't the pawky, relishing humour of the great
Scots ladies of past days, she had in exchange her deep
aspect of comprehension and tenderness. An astonishingly beautiful and impressive woman: dark hair; dark,
straight eyebrows; a straight nose; dark blue eyes in the shadows of her hair and bowed, pomegranate lips in a chin
curved like the bow of a Greek boat . . .

The etiquette of the place on Fridays was regulated as if
by a royal protocol. The most distinguished and, if possible,
titled person was led to a great walnut-wood fluted chair that
stood askew by the fire-place, its back and seat of blue velvet,
heaven knows how old. Over him would hover Mrs. Duchemin:
or, if he were *very* distinguished, both Mr. and Mrs. Macmaster. The not so distinguished were led up by turns to be
presented to the celebrity and would then arrange themselves in a half-circle in the beautiful arm-chairs; the less
distinguished still, in outer groups in chairs that had no arms:
the almost undistinguished stood, also in groups, or lan-
guished, awe-struck, on the scarlet leather window-seats.
When all were there Macmaster would establish himself on

the incredibly unique hearth-rug and would address wise sayings to the celebrity, occasionally, however, saying a kind
thing to the youngest man present—to give him a chance
of distinguishing himself. Macmaster's hair, at that date, was
still black, but not quite so stiff or so well brushed; his beard
had in it greyish streaks, and his teeth, not being quite so
white, looked less strong. He wore also a single eye-glass, the
retaining of which in his right eye gave him a slightly
agonized expression. It gave him, however, the privilege of
putting his face very close to the face of anyone upon whom
he wished to make a deep impression. He had lately become
much interested in the drama, so that there were usually
several large—and, of course, very reputable and serious—
actresses in the room. On rare occasions Mrs. Duchemin
would say across the room in her deep voice:

"Valentine, a cup of tea for His Highness" or "Sir
Thomas," as the case might be, and when Valentine had
threaded her way through the chairs with a cup of tea,
Mrs. Duchemin, with a kind, aloof smile, would say: "Your
Highness, this is my little brown bird." But as a rule Valentine sat alone at the tea-table, the guests fetching from her
what they wanted.

Tietjens came to the Fridays twice during the five months
of his stay at Ealing. On each occasion he accompanied Mrs.
Wannop.

In earlier days—during the earliest Fridays—Mrs. Wannop, if she ever came, had always been installed, with her
flowing black, in the throne, and like an enlarged Queen
Victoria, had sat there whilst suppliants were led up to this
great writer. But now: on the first occasion Mrs. Wannop got
a chair without arms in the outer ring, whilst a general officer commanding lately in chief somewhere in the East,
whose military success had not been considerable, but whose
dispatches were considered very literary, occupied, rather
blazingly, the throne. But Mrs. Wannop had chatted very con-
tentedly all the afternoon with Tietjens, and it had been
comforting to Valentine to see Tietjens' large, uncouth, but
quite collected figure and to observe the affection that these
two had for each other.

But, on the second occasion, the throne was occupied by a
very young woman who talked a great deal and with great
assurance. Valentine didn't know who she was. Mrs. Wannop,
very gay and distracted, stood nearly the whole afternoon by
a window. And even at that, Valentine was contented, quite a

number of young men crowding round the old lady and
leaving the younger one's circle rather bare.

There came in a very tall, clean-run and beautiful, fair
woman, dressed in nothing in particular. She stood with
extreme—with noticeable—unconcern near the doorway. She
let her eyes rest on Valentine, but looked away before Valentine could speak. She must have had an enormous quantity
of fair, tawny hair, for it was coiled in a great surface over
her ears. She had in her hand several visiting-cards, which
she looked at with a puzzled expression and then laid on a
card-table. She was no one who had ever been there before.

Edith Ethel—it was for the second time!—had just broken
up the ring that surrounded Mrs. Wannop, bearing the
young men tributary to the young woman in the walnut
chair and leaving Tietjens and the older woman high and
dry in a window: thus Tietjens saw the stranger, and there
was no doubt left in Valentine's mind. He came, diagonally,
right down the room to his wife and marched her straight
up to Edith Ethel. His face was perfectly without expression.

Macmaster, perched on the centre of the hearth-rug, had
an emotion that was extraordinarily comic to witness, but
that Valentine was quite unable to analyse. He jumped
two paces forward to meet Mrs. Tietjens, held out a little
hand, half withdrew it, retreated half a step. The eye-glass
fell from his perturbed eye: this gave him actually an expression less perturbed, but, in revenge, the hairs on the back of
his scalp grew suddenly untidy. Sylvia, wavering along beside her husband, held out her long arm and careless hand.
Macmaster winced almost at the contact, as if his fingers
had been pinched in a vice. Sylvia wavered desultorily towards Edith Ethel, who was suddenly small, insignificant and
relatively coarse. As for the young woman celebrity in the
arm-chair, she appeared to be about the size of a white rabbit.

A complete silence had fallen on the room. Every woman
in it was counting the pleats of Sylvia's skirt and the
amount of material in it. Valentine Wannop knew that because she was doing it herself. If one had that amount of
material and that number of pleats one's skirt might hang
like that. . . . For it was extraordinary: it fitted close round
the hips, and gave an effect of length and swing—yet it did
not descend as low as the ankles. It was, no doubt, the
amount of material that did that, like the Highlander's kilt,
that takes twelve yards to make. And from the silence Valentine could tell that every woman and most of the men—if
they didn't know that this was Mrs. Christopher Tietjens—

knew that this was a personage of *Illustrated Weekly*, as
who should say of county family, rank. Little Mrs. Swan,
lately married, actually got up, crossed the room and sat
down beside her bridegroom. It was a movement with which
Valentine could sympathize.

And Sylvia, having just faintly greeted Mrs. Duchemin
and completely ignored the celebrity in the arm-chair—in
spite of the fact that Mrs. Duchemin had tried half-heartedly
to effect an introduction—stood still, looking round her.
She gave the effect of a lady in a nurseryman's hot-house,
considering what flower should interest her, collectedly
ignoring the nurserymen who bowed round her. She had
just dropped her eye-lashes, twice, in recognition of two
staff officers with a good deal of scarlet streak about them
who were tentatively rising from their chairs. The staff officers who came to the Macmasters' were not of the first
vintages; still, they had the labels and passed as such.

Valentine was by that time beside her mother, who had
been standing all alone between two windows. She had
dispossessed, in hot indignation, a stout musical critic of his
chair and had sat her mother in it. And just as Mrs. Duchemin's deep voice sounded, yet a little waveringly:

"Valentine . . . a cup of tea for . . ." Valentine was
carrying a cup of tea to her mother.

Her indignation had conquered her despairing jealousy,
if you could call it jealousy. For what was the good of
living or loving when Tietjens had beside him, forever, the
radiant, kind and gracious perfection. On the other hand, of
her two deep passions, the second was for her mother.

Rightly or wrongly, Valentine regarded Mrs. Wannop as a
great, an august, figure: a great brain, a high and generous
intelligence. She had written, at least, one great book, and if
the rest of her time had been frittered away in the desperate
struggle to live that had taken both their lives, that could
not detract from that one achievement that should last and
forever take her mother's name down time. That this
greatness should not weigh with the Macmasters had hitherto neither astonished nor irritated Valentine. The Macmasters
had their game to play and, for the matter of that, they had
their predilections. Their game kept them amongst the
officially influential, the semi-official and the officially ac-
credited. They moved with such C.B.s, knights, presidents
and the rest as dabbled in writing or the arts: they went
upwards with such reviewers, art critics, musical writers
and archaeologists as had posts in, if possible, first-class

public officies or permanent positions on the more august periodicals. If an imaginative author seemed assured of position and lasting popularity, Macmaster would send out feelers towards him, would make himself dumbly useful, and sooner or later either Mrs. Duchemin would be carrying on with him one of her high-souled correspondences—or she wouldn't.

Mrs. Wannop they had formerly accepted as permanent leader writer and chief critic of a great organ, but the great organ having dwindled and now disappeared, the Macmasters no longer wanted her at their parties. That was the game—and Valentine accepted it. But that it should have been with such insolence, so obviously meant to be noted—for in twice breaking up Mrs. Wannop's little circle Mrs. Duchemin had not even once so much as said: "How d'ye do?" to the elder lady!—that was almost more than Valentine could, for the moment, bear, and she would have taken her mother away at once and would never have re-entered the house but for the compensations.

Her mother had lately written and even found a publisher for a book—and the book had showed no signs of failing powers. On the contrary, having been perforce stopped off the perpetual journalism that had dissipated her energies, Mrs. Wannop had turned out something that Valentine knew was sound, sane and well done. Abstractions of failing attention to the outside world are not necessarily in a writer signs of failing, as a writer. It may mean merely that she is giving so much thought to her work that her outside contacts suffer. If that is the case her work will gain. That this might be the case with her mother was Valentine's great and secret hope. Her mother was barely sixty: many great works have been written by writers aged between sixty and seventy. . . .

And the crowding of the youngish men round the old lady had given Valentine a little confirmation of that hope. The book naturally, in the maelstrom flux and reflux of the time, had attracted no attention, and poor Mrs. Wannop had not succeeded in extracting a penny for it from her adamantine publisher: she hadn't, indeed, made a penny for several months, and they existed almost at starvation point in their little den of a villa—on Valentine's earnings as athletic teacher. . . . But that little bit of attention in that semi-public place had seemed, at least, as a confirmation to Valentine: there probably was something sound, sane and well done in her mother's work. That was almost all she asked of life.

And, indeed, while she stood by her mother's chair, thinking with a little bitter pathos that if Edith Ethel had left the three or four young men to her mother, the three or four might have done her poor mother a little good, with innocent puffs and the like—and heaven knew they needed that little good badly enough!—a very thin and untidy young man *did* drift back to Mrs. Wannop and asked, precisely, if he might make a note or two for publication as to what Mrs. Wannop was doing. "Her book," he said, "had attracted so much attention. They hadn't known that they had still writers among them. . . ."

A singular, triangular drive had begun through the chairs from the fire-place. That was how it had seemed to Valentine! Mrs. Tietjens had looked at them, had asked Christopher a question and, immediately, as if she were coming through waist-high surf, had borne down Macmaster and Mrs. Duchemin, flanking her obsequiously, setting aside chairs and their occupants, Tietjens and the two rather bashfully following staff officers broadening out the wedge.

Sylvia, her long arm held out from a yard or so away, was stretching out her hand to Valentine's mother. With her clear, high, unembarrassed voice she exclaimed, also from a yard or so away, so as to be heard by everyone in the room:

"You're Mrs. Wannop. The great writer! I'm Christopher Tietjens' wife."

The old lady, with her dim eyes, looked up at the younger woman towering above her.

"You're Christopher's wife!" she said. "I must kiss you for all the kindness he has shown me."

Valentine felt her eyes filling with tears. She saw her mother stand up, place both her hands on the other woman's shoulders. She heard her mother say:

"You're a most beautiful creature. I'm sure you're good!"

Sylvia stood, smiling faintly, bending a little to accept the embrace. Behind the Macmasters, Tietjens and the staff officers, a little crowd of goggle eyes had ranged itself.

Valentine was crying. She slipped back behind the tea-urns, though she could hardly feel the way. Beautiful! The most beautiful woman she had ever seen! And good! Kind! You could see it in the lovely way she had given her cheek to that poor old woman's lips. . . . And to live all day, forever, beside him . . . she, Valentine, ought to be ready to lay down her life for Sylvia Tietjens. . . .

The voice of Tietjens said, just above her head:

"Your mother seems to be having a regular triumph," and, with his good-natured cynicism, he added, "it seems to have upset some apple-carts!" They were confronted with the spectacle of Macmaster conducting the young celebrity from her deserted arm-chair across the room to be lost in the horseshoe of crowd that surrounded Mrs. Wannop.

Valentine said:

"You're quite gay to-day. Your voice is different. I suppose you're better?" She did not look at him. His voice came:

"Yes! I'm relatively gay!" It went on: "I thought you might like to know. A little of my mathematical brain seems to have come to life again. I've worked out two or three silly problems. . . ."

She said:

"Mrs. Tietjens will be pleased."

"Oh!" the answer came. "Mathematics don't interest her any more than cock-fighting." With immense swiftness, between word and word, Valentine read into that a hope! This splendid creature did not sympathize with her husband's activities. But he crushed it heavily by saying: "Why should she? She's so many occupations of her own that she's unrivalled at!"

He began to tell her, rather minutely, of a calculation he had made only that day at lunch. He had gone into the Department of Statistics and had had rather a row with Lord Ingleby of Lincoln. A pretty title the fellow had taken! They had wanted him to ask to be seconded to his old department for a certain job. But he had said he'd be damned if he would. He detested and despised the work they were doing.

Valentine, for the first time in her life, hardly listened to what he said. Did the fact that Sylvia Tietjens had so many occupations of her own mean that Tietjens found her unsympathetic? Of their relationships she knew nothing. Sylvia had been so much of a mystery as hardly to exist as a problem hitherto. Macmaster, Valentine knew, hated her. She knew that through Mrs. Duchemin; she had heard it ages ago, but she didn't know why. Sylvia had never come to the Macmaster afternoons; but that was natural. Macmaster passed for a bachelor, and it was excusable for a young woman of the highest fashion not to come to bachelor teas of literary and artistic people. On the other hand, Macmaster dined at the Tietjens' quite often enough to make it public that he was a friend of that family. Sylvia, too, had never come down to see Mrs. Wannop. But, then, it would, in the old days, have been a long way to come for a lady of fashion with no especial literary interests. And no one, in mercy, could have been expected to call on poor them in their dog-kennel in an outer suburb. They had had to sell almost all their pretty things.

Tietjens was saying that after his tempestuous interview with Lord Ingleby of Lincoln—she wished he would not be so rude to powerful people!—he had dropped in on Macmaster in his private room and, finding him puzzled over a lot of figures, had, in the merest spirit of bravado, taken Macmaster and his papers out to lunch. And, he said, chancing to look, without any hope at all, at the figures, he had suddenly worked out an ingenious mystification. It had just come!

His voice had been so gay and triumphant that she hadn't been able to resist looking up at him. His cheeks were fresh-coloured, his hair shining; his blue eyes had a little of their old arrogance—and tenderness! Her heart seemed to sing with joy! He was, she felt, her man. She imagined the arms of his mind stretching out to enfold her.

He went on explaining. He had rather, in his recovered self-confidence, gibed at Macmaster. Between themselves, wasn't it easy to do what the department, under orders, wanted done? They had wanted to rub into our allies that their losses by devastation had been nothing to write home about—so as to avoid sending reinforcements to their lines! Well, if you took just the bricks and mortar of the devastated districts, you could prove that the loss in bricks, tiles, woodwork and the rest didn't—and the figures with a little manipulation would prove it!—amount to more than a normal year's dilapidations spread over the whole country in peace-time. . . . House repairs in a normal year had cost several million sterling. The enemy had only destroyed just about so many million sterling in bricks and mortar. And what was a mere year's dilapidations in house property! You just neglected to do them and did them next year.

So if you ignored the lost harvests of three years, the lost industrial output of the richest industrial region of the country, the smashed machinery, the barked fruit-trees, the three years' loss of four and a half tenths of the coal output for three years—and the loss of life!—we could go to our allies and say:

"All your yappings about losses are the merest bulls. You can perfectly well afford to reinforce the weak places of

your own lines. We intend to send our new troops to the
Near East, where lies our true interest!" And though they
might sooner or later point out the fallacy, you would by
so much have put off the abhorrent expedient of a single
command.

Valentine, though it took her away from her own thoughts,
couldn't help saying:

"But weren't you arguing against your own convictions?"

He said:

"Yes, of course I was. In the lightness of my heart! It's
always a good thing to formulate the other fellow's objections."

She had turned half round in her chair. They were gazing into each other's eyes, he from above, she from below.
She had no doubt of his love: he, she knew, could have
no doubt of hers. She said:

"But isn't it dangerous? To show these people how to do
it?"

He said:

"Oh, no, no. No! You don't know what a good soul
little Vinnie is. I don't think you've ever been quite just
to Vincent Macmaster! He'd as soon think of picking my pockets as of picking my brains. The soul of honour!"

Valentine had felt a queer, queer sensation. She was not
sure afterwards whether she had felt it before she had
realized that Sylvia Tietjens was looking at them. She stood
there, very erect, a queer smile on her face. Valentine could
not be sure whether it was kind, cruel, or merely distantly
ironic; but she was perfectly sure it showed, whatever was
behind it, that its wearer knew all that there was to know
of her, Valentine's, feelings for Tietjens and for Tietjens' feelings for her. . . . It was like being a woman and man in
adultery in Trafalgar Square.

Behind Sylvia's back, their mouths agape, were the two
staff officers. Their dark hairs were too untidy for them to
amount to much, but, such as they were, they were the
two most presentable males of the assembly—and Sylvia had
snaffled them.

Mrs. Tietjens said:

"Oh, Christopher! I'm going on to the Basils'."

Tietjens said:

"All right. I'll pop Mrs. Wannop into the tube as soon as
she's had enough of it, and come along and pick you up!"

Sylvia had just dropped her long eye-lashes, in sign of
salutation, to Valentine Wannop, and had drifted through the

door, followed by her rather unmilitary military escort in khaki and scarlet.

From that moment Valentine Wannop never had any doubt. She knew that Sylvia Tietjens knew that her husband loved her, Valentine Wannop, and that she, Valentine Wannop, loved her husband—with a passion absolute and ineffable. The one thing she, Valentine, didn't know, the one mystery that remained impenetrable, was whether Sylvia Tietjens was good to her husband!

A long time afterwards Edith Ethel had come to her beside the tea-cups and had apologized for not having known, earlier than Sylvia's demonstration, that Mrs. Wannop was in the room. She hoped that they might see Mrs. Wannop much more often. She added after a moment that she hoped Mrs. Wannop wouldn't, in future, find it necessary to come under the escort of Mr. Tietjens. They were too old friends for that, surely.

Valentine said:

"Look here, Ethel, if you think that you can keep friends with mother and turn on Mr. Tietjens after all he's done for you, you're mistaken. You are really. And mother's a great deal of influence. I don't want to see you making any mistakes: just at this juncture. It's a mistake to make nasty rows. And you'd make a very nasty one if you said anything against Mr. Tietjens to mother. She knows a great deal. Remember. She lived next door to the rectory for a number of years. And she's got a dreadfully incisive tongue. . . ."

Edith Ethel coiled back on her feet as if her whole body were threaded by a steel spring. Her mouth opened, but she bit her lower lip and then wiped it with a very white handkerchief. She said:

"I hate that man! I detest that man! I shudder when he comes near me."

"I know you do!" Valentine Wannop answered. "But I wouldn't let other people know it if I were you. It doesn't do you any real credit. He's a good man."

Edith Ethel looked at her with a long, calculating glance. Then she went to stand before the fire-place.

That had been five—or at most six—Fridays before Valentine sat with Mark Tietjens in the War Office waiting-hall, and on the Friday immediately before that again, all the guests being gone, Edith Ethel had come to the tea-table and, with her velvet kindness, had placed her right hand on

Valentine's left. Admiring the gesture with a deep fervour, Valentine knew that that was the end.

Three days before, on the Monday, Valentine, in her school uniform, in a great store to which she had gone to buy athletic paraphernalia, had run into Mrs. Duchemin, who was buying flowers. Mrs. Duchemin had been horribly distressed to observe the costume. She had said:

"But do you go *about* in that? It's really dreadful."

Valentine had answered:

"Oh, yes. When I'm doing business for the school in school hours I'm expected to wear it. And I wear it if I'm going anywhere in a hurry after school hours. It saves my dresses. I haven't got too many."

"But *any*one might meet you," Edith Ethel said in a note of agony. "It's very inconsiderate. Don't you *think* you've been very inconsiderate? You might meet any of the people who come to our Fridays!"

"I frequently do," Valentine said. "But they don't seem to mind. Perhaps they think I'm a Waac officer. That would be quite respectable. . . ."

Mrs. Duchemin drifted away, her arms full of flowers and real agony upon her face.

Now, beside the tea-table, she said, very softly:

"My dear, we've decided not to have our usual Friday afternoon next week." Valentine wondered whether this was merely a lie to get rid of her. But Edith Ethel went on: "We've decided to have a little evening festivity. After a great deal of thought we've come to the conclusion that we ought, now, to make our union public." She paused to await comment, but Valentine making none, she went on: "It coincides very happily—I can't help feeling it coincides very happily!—with another event. Not that *we* set much store by these things . . . But it has been whispered to Vincent that next Friday . . . Perhaps, my dear Valentine, you, too, will have heard. . . ."

Valentine said:

"No, I haven't. I suppose he's got the O.B.E. I'm very glad."

"The Sovereign," Mrs. Duchemin said, "is seeing fit to confer the honour of knighthood on him."

"Well!" Valentine said. "He's had a quick career. I've no doubt he deserves it. He's worked very hard. I do sincerely congratulate you. It'll be a great help to you."

"It's," Mrs. Duchemin said, "not for mere plodding. That's what makes it so gratifying. It's for a special piece of bril-

liance that has marked him out. It's, of course, a secret.
But . . ."

"Oh, I know!" Valentine said. "He's worked out some
calculations to prove that losses in the devastated districts,
if you ignore machinery, coal output, orchard-trees, harvests,
industrial products and so on, don't amount to more than a
year's household dilapidations for the . . ."

Mrs. Duchemin said with real horror:

"But how did you know? How on *earth* did you know? . . ."
She paused. "It's such a *dead* secret. . . . That fellow must
have told you. . . . But how on earth could *he* know?"

"I haven't seen Mr. Tietjens to speak to since the last
time he was here," Valentine said. She saw, from Edith
Ethel's bewilderment, the whole situation. The miserable
Macmaster hadn't even confided to his wife that the practically stolen figures weren't his own. He desired to have a
little prestige in the family circle; for once a little prestige!
Well! Why shouldn't he have it? Tietjens, she knew, would
wish him to have all he could get. She said, therefore:

"Oh, it's probably in the air. . . . It's known the government want to break their claims to the higher command.
And anyone who could help them to that would get a
knighthood. . . ."

Mrs. Duchemin was more calm.

"It's certainly," she said, "Burke'd, as you call it, those
beastly people." She reflected for a moment. "It's probably
that," she went on. "It's in the air. Anything that can help to
influence public opinion against those horrible people is to
be welcomed. That's known pretty widely. . . . No! It could
hardly be Christopher Tietjens who thought of it and told
you. It wouldn't enter his head. He's their friend! He would
be . . ."

"He's certainly," Valentine said, "not a friend of his
country's enemies. I'm not, myself."

Mrs. Duchemin exclaimed sharply, her eyes dilated.

"What do you mean? What on earth do you dare to mean?
I thought you were a pro-German!"

Valentine said:

"I'm not! I'm not! . . . I hate men's deaths. . . . I
hate any men's deaths. . . . Any men . . ." She calmed herself by main force. "Mr. Tietjens says that the more we
hinder our allies, the more we drag the war on and the
more lives are lost. . . . More lives, do you understand? . . ."

Mrs. Duchemin assumed her most aloof, tender and high
air: "My poor child," she said, "what possible concern can

the opinions of that broken fellow cause anyone? You can warn him from me that he does himself no good by going on uttering these discredited opinions. He's a marked man. Finished! It's no good Guggums, my husband, trying to stand up for him."

"He *does* stand up for him?" Valentine asked. "Though I don't see why it's needed. Mr. Tietjens is surely able to take care of himself."

"My good child," Edith Ethel said, "you may as well know the worst. There's not a more discredited man in London than Christopher Tietjens, and my husband does himself infinite harm in standing up for him. It's our one quarrel."

She went on again:

"It was all very well whilst that fellow had brains. He was said to have some intellect, though I could never see it. But now that, with his drunkenness and debaucheries, he has got himself into the state he is in; for there's no other way of accounting for his condition! They're striking him, I don't mind telling you, off the roll of his office. . ."

It was there that, for the first time, the thought went through Valentine Wannop's mind, like a mad inspiration: this woman must at one time have been in love with Tietjens. It was possible, men being what they were, that she had even once been Tietjens' mistress. For it was impossible otherwise to account for this spite, which to Valentine seemed almost meaningless. She had, on the other hand, no impulse to defend Tietjens against accusations that could not have any possible grounds.

Mrs. Duchemin was going on with her kind loftiness:

"Of course a fellow like that—in that condition!—could not understand matters of high policy. It is imperative that these fellows should not have the higher command. It would pander to their insane spirit of militarism. They *must* be hindered. I'm talking, of course, between ourselves, but my husband says that that is the conviction in the very highest circles. To let them have their way, even if it led to earlier success, would be to establish a precedent—so my husband says!—compared with which the loss of a few lives . . ."

Valentine sprang up, her face distorted.

"For the sake of Christ," she cried out, "as you believe that Christ died for you, try to understand that millions of men's lives are at stake. . . ."

Mrs. Duchemin smiled.

"My poor child," she said, "if you moved in the higher

circles you would look at these things with more aloof-
ness. . . ."

Valentine leant on the back of a high chair for support.

"You don't move in the higher circles," she said. "For
heaven's sake—for your own—remember that you are a
woman, not forever and for always a snob. You were a
good woman once. You stuck to your husband for quite
a long time. . . ."

Mrs. Duchemin, in her chair, had thrown herself back.

"My good girl," she said, "have you gone mad?"

Valentine said:

"Yes, very nearly. I've got a brother at sea; I've had a
man I loved out there for an infinite time. You can understand that, I suppose, even if you can't understand how
one can go mad merely at the thoughts of suffering at all.
. . . And I know, Edith Ethel, that you are afraid of my
opinion of you or you wouldn't have put up all the
subterfuges and concealments of all these years. . . ."

Mrs. Duchemin said quickly:

"Oh, my good girl . . . If you've got personal interests
at stake you can't be expected to take abstract views of the
higher matters. We had better change the subject."

Valentine said:

"Yes, do. Get on with your excuses for not asking me
and mother to your knighthood party."

Mrs. Duchemin, too, rose at that. She felt at her amber
beads with long fingers that turned very slightly at the tips.
She had behind her all her mirrors, the drops of her lustres,
shining points of gilt and of the polish of dark woods.
Valentine thought that she had never seen anyone so absolutely impersonate kindness, tenderness and dignity. She
said:

"My dear, I was going to suggest that it was the sort of
party to which you might not care to come. . . . The people will be stiff and formal and you probably haven't got a
frock."

Valentine said:

"Oh, I've got a frock all right. But there's a Jacob's ladder
in my party stockings and that's the sort of ladder you
can't kick down." She couldn't help saying that.

Mrs. Duchemin stood motionless, and very slowly red-
ness mounted into her face. It was most curious to see
against that scarlet background the vivid white of the eyes
and the dark, straight eyebrows that nearly met. And slowly
again her face went perfectly white; then her dark blue eyes

became marked. She seemed to wipe her long, white hands one in the other, inserting her right hand into her left and drawing it out again.

"I'm sorry," she said in a dead voice. "We had hoped that if that man went to France—or if other things happened —we might have continued on the old friendly footing. But you yourself must see that with our official position, we can't be expected to connive . . ."

Valentine said:

"I don't understand!"

"Perhaps you'd rather I didn't go on!" Mrs. Duchemin retorted. "I'd much rather not go on."

"You'd probably better," Valentine answered.

"We had meant," the elder woman said, "to have a quiet little dinner—we two and you, before the party—for auld lang syne. But that fellow has forced himself in, and you see for yourself that we can't have you as well."

Valentine said:

"I don't see why not. I always like to see Mr. Tietjens!"

Mrs. Duchemin looked hard at her.

"I don't see the use," she said, "of your keeping on that mask. It is surely bad enough that your mother should go about with that man and that terrible scenes like that of the other Friday should occur. Mrs. Tietjens was heroic, nothing less than heroic. But you have no right to subject us, your friends, to such ordeals."

Valentine said:

"You mean . . . Mrs. Christopher Tietjens . . ."

Mrs. Duchemin went on:

"My husband insists that I should ask you. But I will not. I simply will not. I invented for you the excuse of the frock. Of course we could have given you a frock if that man is so mean or so penniless as not to keep you decent. But I repeat, with our official position we cannot—we cannot; it would be madness!—connive at this intrigue. And all the more as the wife appears likely to be friendly with us. She has been once: she may well come again." She paused and went on solemnly: "And I warn you, if the split comes—as it must, for what woman could stand it!—it is Mrs. Tietjens we shall support. She will always find a home here."

An extraordinary picture of Sylvia Tietjens standing beside Edith Ethel and dwarfing her as a giraffe dwarfs an emu came into Valentine's head. She said:

"Ethel! Have I gone mad? Or is it you? Upon my word I can't understand . . ."

Mrs. Duchemin exclaimed:

"For God's sake, hold your tongue, you shameless thing! You've had a child by the man, haven't you?"

Valentine saw suddenly the tall silver candlesticks, the dark polished panels of the rectory and Edith Ethel's mad face and mad hair whirling before them.

She said:

"No! I certainly haven't. Can you get that into your head? I certainly haven't." She made a further effort over immense fatigue. "I assure you—I beg you to believe if it will give you any ease—that Mr. Tietjens has never addressed a word of love to me in his life. Nor have I to him. We have hardly talked to each other in all the time we have known each other."

Mrs. Duchemin said in a harsh voice:

"Seven people in the last five weeks have told me you have had a child by that brute beast: he's ruined because he has to keep you and your mother and the child. You won't deny that he has a child somewhere hidden away? . . ."

Valentine exclaimed suddenly:

"Oh, Ethel, you mustn't . . . you *mustn't* be jealous of me! If you only knew, you wouldn't be jealous of me. . . . I suppose the child you were going to have was by Christopher? Men are like that. . . . But not of me! You need never, never. I've been the best friend you can ever have had. . . ."

Mrs. Duchemin exclaimed harshly, as if she were being strangled:

"A sort of blackmail! I knew it would come to that! It always does with your sort. Then do your damnedest, you harlot. You never set foot in this house again! Go, you, and rot. . . ." Her face suddenly expressed extreme fear, and with great swiftness she ran up the room. Immediately afterwards she was tenderly bending over a great bowl of roses beneath the lustre. The voice of Vincent Macmaster from the door had said:

"Come in, old man. Of course I've got ten minutes. The book's in here somewhere. . . ."

Macmaster was beside her, rubbing his hands, bending with his curious, rather abject manner, and surveying her agonizedly with his eye-glass, which enormously magnified his lashes, his red lower lid and the veins on his cornea.

"Valentine!" he said, "my dear Valentine . . . You've heard? We've decided to make it public. . . . Guggums will have

invited you to our little feast. And there will be a surprise, I
believe. . . ."

Edith Ethel looked, as she bent, lamentably and sharply,
over her shoulder at Valentine.

"Yes," she said bravely, aiming her voice at Edith Ethel,
"Ethel has invited me. I'll try to come. . . ."

"Oh, but you must," Macmaster said, "just you and
Christopher, who've been so kind to us. For old time's sake.
You could not . . ."

Christopher Tietjens was ballooning slowly from the door,
his hand tentatively held out to her. As they practically
never shook hands at home, it was easy to avoid his hand.
She said to herself: "Oh! How is it possible! How could he
have . . ." And the terrible situation poured itself over her
mind: the miserable little husband, the desperately nonchalant lover—and Edith Ethel mad with jealousy! A doomed
household. She hoped Edith Ethel had seen her refuse her
hand to Christopher.

But Edith Ethel, bent over her rose-bowl, was burying her
beautiful face in flower after flower. She was accustomed to
do this for many minutes on end: she thought that, so, she
resembled a picture by the subject of her husband's first
little monograph. And so, Valentine thought, she did. She was
trying to tell Macmaster that Friday evenings were difficult
times for her to get away. But her throat ached too much.
That, she knew, was her last sight of Edith Ethel, whom she
had loved very much. That also, she hoped, would be her last
sight of Christopher Tietjens—whom also she had loved very
much. . . . He was browsing along a bookshelf, very big and
very clumsy.

Macmaster pursued her into the stony hall with clamorous repetitions of his invitation. She couldn't speak. At the
great iron-lined door he held her hand for an eternity,
gazing lamentably, his face close up against hers. He exclaimed in accents of great fear:

"Has Guggums? . . . She *hasn't* . . ." His face, which when
you saw it so closely was a little blotched, distorted itself
with anxiety: he glanced aside with panic at the drawing-
room door.

Valentine burst a voice through her agonized throat.

"Ethel," she said, "has told me she's to be Lady Macmaster.
I'm so glad. I'm so truly glad for you. You've got what you
wanted, haven't you?"

His relief let him get out distractedly, yet as if he were
too tired to be any more agitated:

"Yes! Yes! . . . It's, of course, a secret. . . . I don't want *him* told till Friday next . . . so as to be a sort of *bonne bouche* . . . He's practically certain to go out again on Saturday. . . . They're sending out a great batch of them . . . for the big push. . . ." At that she tried to draw her hand from his: she missed what he was saying. It was something to the effect that he would give it all for a happy little party. She caught the rather astonishing words: *"Wie der alten schoenen Zeit."* She couldn't tell whether it was his or her eyes that were full of tears. She said:

"I believe . . . I believe you're a kind man!"

In the great stone hall, hung with long Japanese paintings on silk, the electric light suddenly jumped; it was at best a sad, brown place.

He exclaimed:

"I, too, beg you to believe that I will never abandon . . ." He glanced again at the inner door and added: "You both . . . I will never abandon . . . you both!" he repeated.

He let go her hand: she was on the stone stairs in the damp air. The great door closed irresistibly behind her, sending a whisper of air downwards.

5 ~

MARK TIETJENS' announcement—that his father had after all carried out his long-standing promise to provide for Mrs. Wannop in such a way as to allow her to write for the rest of her life only the more lasting kind of work—delivered Valentine Wannop of all her problems except one. That one loomed, naturally and immediately, immensely large.

She had passed a queer, unnatural week, the feeling dominating its numbness having been, oddly, that she would have nothing to do on Friday! This feeling recurred to her whilst she was casting her eyes over a hundred girls all in their cloth jumpers and men's black ties, aligned upon asphalt; whilst she was jumping on trams; whilst she was purchasing the tinned or dried fish that formed the staple diet of herself and her mother; whilst she was washing up the dinner-things, upbraiding the house agent for the state of the bath or bending closely over the large but merciless handwriting of the novel of her mother's that she was typing. It came, half as a joy, half mournfully across her familiar businesses; she felt as a man might feel who, luxuriating in the anticipation

of leisure, knew that it was obtained by being compulsorily retired from some laborious but engrossing job. There would be
nothing to do on Fridays!

It was, too, as if a novel had been snatched out of her
hand so that she would never know the end. Of the
fairy-tale she knew the end: the fortunate and adventurous
tailor had married his beautiful and be-princessed goose girl,
and was well on the way to burial in Westminster Abbey—or
at any rate to a memorial service, the squire being actually
buried amongst his faithful villagers. But she would never
know whether they, in the end, got together all the blue
Dutch tiles they wanted to line their bathroom. . . . She
would never know. Yet witnessing similar ambitions had
made up a great deal of her life.

And, she said to herself, there was another tale ended. On
the surface the story of her love for Tietjens had been
static enough. It had begun in nothing and in nothing it had
ended. But, deep down in her being—ah! It had progressed
enough. Through the agency of two women! Before the scene
with Mrs. Duchemin there could, she thought, have been few
young women less preoccupied than she with the sexual sub-
strata, either of passion or of life. Her months as a domestic
servant had accounted for that, sex, as she had seen it from
a back kitchen, having been a repulsive affair, whilst the
knowledge of its manifestations that she had thus attained
had robbed it of the mystery which caused most of the young
women whom she knew to brood upon these subjects.

Her convictions as to the moral incidence of sex were, she
knew, quite opportunist. Brought up amongst rather "advanced" young people, had she been publicly challenged to
pronounce her views, she would probably, out of loyalty to
her comrades, have declared that neither morality nor any
ethical aspects were concerned in the matter. Like most of
her young friends, influenced by the advanced teachers and
tendential novelists of the day, she would have stated herself
to advocate an—of course, enlightened!—promiscuity. That,
before the revelations of Mrs. Duchemin! Actually she had
thought very little about the matter.

Nevertheless, even before that date, had her deeper feelings
been questioned, she would have reacted with the idea that
sexual incontinence was extremely ugly and chastity to be
prized in the egg-and-spoon race that life was. She had been
brought up by her father—who, perhaps, was wiser than appeared on the surface—to admire athleticism, and she was
aware that proficiency of the body calls for chastity, sobriety,

cleanliness and the various qualities that group themselves
under the heading of abnegation. She couldn't have lived
amongst the Ealing servant-class—the eldest son of the house
in which she had been employed had been the defendant
in a peculiarly scabrous breach-of-promise case, and the
comments of the drunken cook on this and similar affairs had
run the whole gamut from the sentimentally reticent to the
extreme of coarseness according to the state of her alcoholic
barometer—she couldn't, then, have lived among the Ealing
servant-class and come to any other subliminal conclusion.
So that, dividing the world into bright beings on the one
hand and, on the other, into the mere stuff to fill graveyards,
whose actions during life couldn't matter, she had considered
that the bright beings must be people whose public ad-
vocating of enlightened promiscuity went along with an absolute continence. She was aware that enlightened beings
occasionally fell away from these standards in order to become portentous Egerias; but the Mary Wollstonecrafts,
the Mrs. Taylors, and the George Eliots of the last century
she had regarded humorously as rather priggish nuisances.
Indeed, being very healthy and very hard worked, she had
been in the habit of regarding the whole matter, if not
humorously, then at least good-humouredly, as a nuisance.

But being brought right up against the sexual necessities of
a first-class Egeria had been for her a horrible affair. For
Mrs. Duchemin had revealed the fact that her circumspect,
continent and suavely aesthetic personality was doubled by
another at least as coarse as, and infinitely more incisive
in expression than, that of the drunken cook. The language
that she had used about her lover—calling him always "that
oaf" or "that beast"!—had seemed literally to pain the girl in-
ternally, as if it had caused so many fallings-away of internal supports at each two or three words. She had hardly
been able to walk home through the darkness from the rectory.

And she had never heard what had become of Mrs. Duchemin's baby. Next day Mrs. Duchemin had been as suave,
as circumspect, and as collected as ever. Never a word
more had passed between them on the subject. This left in
Valentine Wannop's mind a dark patch, as it were, of
murder—at which she must never look. And across the darkened world of her sexual tumult there flitted continually the
quick suspicion that Tietjens might have been the lover of her
friend. It was a matter of the simplest analogy. Mrs. Duchemin had appeared a bright being: so had Tietjens. But Mrs.

Duchemin was a foul whore. . . . How much more, then, must Tietjens, who was a man, with the larger sexual necessities of the male . . . Her mind always refused to complete the thought.

Its suggestion wasn't to be combated by the idea of Vincent Macmaster himself: he was, she felt, the sort of man that it was almost a necessity for either mistress or comrade to betray. He seemed to ask for it. Besides, she once put it to herself, how could any woman, given the choice and the opportunity—and God knows there was opportunity enough —choose that shadowy, dried leaf if there were the splendid masculinity of Tietjens in whose arms to lie. She so regarded these two men. And that shadowy conviction was at once fortified and appeased when, a little later, Mrs. Duchemin herself began to apply to Tietjens the epithets of "oaf" and "beast"—the very ones that she had used to designate the father of her putative child!

But, then, Tietjens must have abandoned Mrs. Duchemin; and if he had abandoned Mrs. Duchemin, he must be available for her, Valentine Wannop! The feeling, she considered, made her ignoble; but it came from depths of her being that she could not control and, existing, it soothed her. Then, with the coming of the war, the whole problem died out, and between the opening of hostilities and what she had known to be the inevitable departure of her lover, she had surrendered herself to what she thought to be the pure physical desire for him. Amongst the terrible, crashing anguishes of that time, there had been nothing for it but surrender! With the unceasing—the never-ceasing—thought of suffering; with the never-ceasing idea that her lover, too, must soon be so suffering, there was in the world no other refuge. No other!

She surrendered. She waited for him to speak the word or look the look that should unite them. She was finished. Chastity: napoo finny! Like everything else!

Of the physical side of love she had neither image nor conception. In the old days when she had been with him, if he had come into the room in which she was or if he had merely been known to be coming down to the village, she had hummed all day under her breath and had felt warmer, little currents passing along her skin. She had read somewhere that to take alcohol was to send the blood into the surface vessels of the body, thus engendering a feeling of warmth. She had never taken alcohol, or not enough to produce recognizably that effect; but she imagined that it was thus love worked upon the body—and that it would stop forever at that!

But, in these later days, much greater convulsions had over-whelmed her. It sufficed for Tietjens to approach her to make her feel as if her whole body was drawn towards him as, being near a terrible height, you are drawn towards it. Great waves of blood rushed across her being as if physical forces as yet undiscovered or invented attracted the very fluid itself. The moon so draws the tides.

Once before, for a fraction of a second, after the long, warm night of their drive, she had felt that impulsion. Now, years after, she was to know it all the time, waking or half waking; and it would drive her from her bed. She would stand all night at the open window till the stars paled above a world turned grey. It could convulse her with joy; it could shake her with sobs and cut through her breast like a knife.

The day of her long interview with Tietjens, amongst the amassed beauties of Macmaster furnishings, she marked in the calendar of her mind as her great love-scene. That had been two years ago: he had been going into the army. Now he was going out again. From that she knew what a love-scene was. It passed without any mention of the word "love"; it passed in impulses, warmths, rigors of the skin. Yet with every word they had said to each other they had confessed their love; in that way, when you listen to the nightingale you hear the expressed craving of your lover beating upon your heart.

Every word that he had spoken amongst the amassed beauties of Macmaster furnishings had been a link in a love-speech. It was not merely that he had confessed to her as he would have to no other soul in the world—"To no other soul in the world," he had said!—his doubts, his mis-givings and his fears: it was that every word he uttered and that came to her, during the lasting of that magic, had sung of passion. If he had uttered the word "come" she would have followed him to the bitter ends of the earth; if he had said, "There is no hope," she would have known the finality of despair. Having said neither, he said, she knew: "This is our condition; so we must continue!" And she knew, too, that he was telling her that he, like her, was . . . oh, say on the side of the angels. She was, then, she knew, so nicely balanced that, had he said, "Will you to-night be my mistress?" she would have said yes; for it was as if they had been, really, at the end of the world.

But his abstention not only strengthened her in her pre-

dilection for chastity; it restored to her her image of the
world as a place of virtues and endeavours. For a time, at
least, she again hummed beneath her breath upon occasion,
for it seemed as if her heart sang within her. And there was
restored to her her image of her lover as a beautiful spirit.
She had been able to look at him across the tea-table of their
dog-kennel in Bedford Park, during the last months, almost
as she had looked across the more shining table of the
cottage near the rectory. The deterioration that she knew
Mrs. Duchemin to have worked in her mind was assuaged. It
could even occur to her that Mrs. Duchemin's madness had
been no more than a scare to be followed by no necessary
crime. Valentine Wannop had rebecome her confident self
in a world of at least straight problems.

But Mrs. Duchemin's outbreak of a week ago had driven
the old phantoms across her mind. For Mrs. Duchemin she
had still had a great respect. She could not regard her Edith
Ethel as merely a hypocrite or, indeed, as a hypocrite at
all. There was her great achievement of making something
like a man of that miserable little creature—as there had been
her other great achievement of keeping her unfortunate husband for so long out of a lunatic asylum. That had been no
mean feat; neither feat had been mean. And Valentine knew
that Edith Ethel really loved beauty, circumspection, urban-
ity. It was no hypocrisy that made her advocate the Atalanta
race of chastity. But, also, as Valentine Wannop saw it, humanity has these doublings of strong natures; just as the
urbane and grave Spanish nation must find its outlet in the
shrieking lusts of the bull-ring or the circumspect, laborious
and admirable city typist must find her derivative in the
cruder lusts of certain novelists, so Edith Ethel must break
down into physical sexualities—and into shrieked coarseness
of fishwives. How else, indeed, do we have saints? Surely,
alone, by the ultimate victory of the one tendency over the
other!

But now after her farewell scene with Edith Ethel a simple
rearrangement of the pattern had brought many of the old
doubts at least temporarily back. Valentine said to herself that
just because of the very strength of her character, Edith
Ethel couldn't have been brought down to uttering her
fantastic denunciation of Tietjens, the merely mad charges
of debauchery and excesses and finally the sexually lunatic
charge against herself except under the sting of some such
passion as jealousy. She, Valentine, couldn't arrive at any
other conclusion. And viewing the matter as she believed she

now did, more composedly, she considered with seriousness that men being what they are, her lover, respecting or despairing of herself, had relieved the grosser necessities of his being—at the expense of Mrs. Duchemin, who had, no doubt, been only too ready.

And in certain moods during the past week she had accepted this suspicion; in certain other moods she had put it from her. Towards the Thursday it had no longer seemed to matter. Her lover was going from her; the long pull of the war was on; the hard necessities of life stretched out; what could an infidelity more or less matter in the long, hard thing that life is. And on the Thursday two minor or major worries came to disturb her level. Her brother announced himself as coming home for several days' leave, and she had the trouble of thinking that she would have forced upon her a companionship and a point of view that would be coarsely and uproariously opposed to anything that Tietjens stood for —or for which he was ready to sacrifice himself. Moreover, she would have to accompany her brother to a number of riotous festivities whilst all the time she would have to think of Tietjens as getting hour by hour nearer to the horrible circumstances of troops in contact with enemy forces. In addition her mother had received an enviably paid-for commission from one of the more excitable Sunday papers to write a series of articles on extravagant matters connected with the hostilities. They had wanted the money so dreadfully— more particularly as Edward was coming home—that Valentine Wannop had conquered her natural aversion from the waste of time of her mother. . . . It would have meant very little waste of time, and the £60 that it would have brought in would have made all the difference to them for months and months.

But Tietjens, whom Mrs. Wannop had come to rely on as her right-hand man in these matters, had, it appeared, shown an unexpected recalcitrancy. He had, Mrs. Wannop said, hardly seemed himself and had gibed at the two first subjects proposed—that of "war-babies" and the fact that the Germans were reduced to eating their own corpses— as being below the treatment of any decent pen. The illegitimacy rate, he had said, had shown very little increase; the French-derived German word "*Kadaver*" meant bodies of horses or cattle; *Leichnan* being the German for the word "corpse." He had practically refused to have anything to do with the affair.

As to the *Kadaver* business, Valentine agreed with him;

as to the "war-babies," she kept a more open mind. If there weren't any war-babies it couldn't, as far as she could see, matter whether one wrote about them; it couldn't certainly matter as much as to write about them supposing the poor little things to exist. She was aware that this was immoral, but her mother needed the money desperately and her mother came first.

There was nothing for it, therefore, but to plead with Tietjens, for Valentine knew that without so much of moral support from him as would be implied by a good-natured or an enforced sanction of the article, Mrs. Wannop would drop the matter and so would lose her connexion with the excitable paper which paid well. It happened that on the Friday morning, Mrs. Wannop received a request that she would write for a Swiss review a propaganda article about some historical matter connected with the peace after Waterloo. The pay would be practically nothing, but the employment was at least relatively dignified, and Mrs. Wannop—which was quite in the ordinary course of things!— told Valentine to ring Tietjens up and ask him for some details about the Congress of Vienna, at which, before and after Waterloo, the peace terms had been wrangled out.

Valentine rang up—as she had done hundreds of times; it was to her a great satisfaction that she was going to hear Tietjens speak once more at least. The telephone was answered from the other end, and Valentine gave her two messages, the one as to the Congress of Vienna, the other as to war-babies. The appalling speech came back:

"Young woman! You'd better keep off the grass. Mrs. Duchemin is already my husband's mistress. You keep off." There was about the voice no human quality; it was as if from an immense darkness the immense machine had spoken words that dealt blows. She answered; and it was as if a substratum of her mind of which she knew nothing must have been prepared for that every speech; so that it was not her own "she" that answered levelly and coolly:

"You have probably mistaken the person you are speaking to. Perhaps you will ask Mr. Tietjens to ring up Mrs. Wannop when he is at liberty."

The voice said:

"My husband will be at the War Office at four-fifteen. He will speak to you there—about your war-babies. But I'd keep off the grass if I were you!" The receiver at the other end was hung up.

She went about her daily duties. She had heard of a kind

of pine kernel that was very cheap and very nourishing or at least very filling. They had come to it that it was a matter of pennies balanced against the feeling of satiety, and she visited several shops in search of this food. When she had found it she returned to the dog-kennel; her brother Edward had arrived. He was rather subdued. He brought with him a piece of meat, which was part of his leave ration. He occupied himself with polishing up his sailor's uniform for a rag-time party to which they were to go that evening. They were to meet plenty of conchies, he said. Valentine put the meat—it was a Godsend, though very stringy!—on to stew with a number of chopped vegetables. She went up to her room to do some typing for her mother.

The nature of Tietjens' wife occupied her mind. Before, she had barely thought about her: she had seemed unreal; so mysterious as to be a myth! Radiant and high-stepping: like a great stag! But she must be cruel! She must be vindictively cruel to Tietjens himself or she could not have revealed his private affairs! Just broadcast; for she could not, bluff it how she might, have been certain of to whom she was speaking! A thing that wasn't done! But she had delivered her cheek to Mrs. Wannop; a thing, too, that wasn't done! Yet so kindly! The telephone bell rang several times during the morning. She let her mother answer it.

She had to get the dinner, which took three-quarters of an hour. It was a pleasure to see her mother eat so well; a good stew, rich and heavy with haricot beans. She herself couldn't eat, but no one noticed, which was a good thing. Her mother said that Tietjens had not yet telephoned, which was very inconsiderate. Edward said: "What! The Huns haven't killed old Feather Bolster yet? But of course he's been found a safe job." The telephone on the sideboard became a terror to Valentine; at any moment his voice might . . . Edward went on telling anecdotes of how they bamboozled petty officers on mine-sweepers. Mrs. Wannop listened to him with the courteous, distant interest of the great listening to commercial travellers. Edward desired draught ale and produced a two-shilling piece. He seemed very much coarsened; it was, no doubt, only on the surface. In these days everyone was very much coarsened on the surface.

She went with a quart-jug to the jug and bottle department of the nearest public-house—a thing she had never done before. Even at Ealing the mistress hadn't allowed her to be sent to a public-house; the cook had had to fetch her dinner beer herself or have it send in. Perhaps the Ealing

mistress had exercised more surveillance than Valentine had
believed; a kind woman, but an invalid. Nearly all day in bed.
Blind passion overcame Valentine at the thought of Edith
Ethel in Tietjens' arms. Hadn't she got her own eunuch?
Mrs. Tietjens had said: "Mrs. Duchemin is his mistress!" *Is!*
Then he might be there now!

In the contemplation of that image she missed the
thrills of buying beer in a bottle and jug department. Apparently it was like buying anything else, except for the
smell of beer on the sawdust. You said: "A quart of the best
bitter!" and a fat, quite polite man, with an oily head and
a white apron, took your money and filled your jug. . . . But
Edith Ethel had abused Tietjens so foully! The more foully,
the more certain it made it! . . . Draught beer in a jug had
little marblings of burst foam on its brown surface. It
mustn't be spilt at the kerbs of crossings!—the more certain
it made it! Some women did so abuse their lovers after
sleeping with them, and the more violent the transports, the
more frantic the abuse. It was the *"post-dash-tristis"* of the
Rev. Duchemin! Poor devil! Tristis! Tristis!

Terra tribus scopulis vastum . . . Not longum!

Brother Edward began communing with himself, long and
unintelligibly, as to where he should meet his sister at
19:30 and give her a blow-out! The names of restaurants fell
from his lips into her panic. He decided hilariously and
not quite steadily—a quart is a lot to a fellow from a mine-
sweeper carrying no booze at all!—on meeting her at 7:20 at
High Street and going to a pub he knew; they would go on
to the dance afterwards. In a studio. "Oh, God!" her heart
said, "if Tietjens should want her then!" To be his; on his last
night. He might! Everybody was coarsened then; on the
surface. Her brother rolled out of the house, slamming the
door so that every tile on the jerry-built dog-kennel rose
and sat down again.

She went upstairs and began to look over her frocks.
She couldn't tell what frocks she looked over; they lay like
aligned rags on the bed, the telephone bell ringing madly.
She heard her mother's voice, suddenly assuaged: "Oh! Oh!
. . . It's you!" She shut her door and began to pull open and
to close drawer after drawer. As soon as she ceased that
exercise her mother's voice became half audible; quite audible
when she raised it to ask a question. She heard her say;
"Not get her into trouble . . . Of *course!*" then it died away
into mere high sounds.

She heard her mother calling:

"Valentine! Valentine! Come down. . . . Don't you want
to speak to Christopher? . . . Valentine! Valentine! . . ."
And then another burst: "Valentine . . . Valentine . . .
Valentine . . ." As if she had been a puppy dog! Mrs.
Wannop, thank God, was on the lowest step of the creaky
stairs. She had left the telephone. She called up:

"Come down. I want to tell you! The dear boy has saved
me! He always saves me! What shall I do now he's gone?"

"He saved others: himself he could not save!" Valentine
quoted bitterly. She caught up her wideawake. She wasn't
going to prink herself for him. He must take her as she
was. . . . Himself he could not save! But he did himself
proud! With women! . . . Coarsened! But perhaps only on
the surface! She herself! . . . She was running downstairs.

Her mother had retreated into the little parlour: nine feet
by nine; in consequence, at ten feet it was too tall for its
size. But there was in it a sofa with cushions. . . . With her
head upon those cushions, perhaps . . . If he came home with
her! Late! . . .

Her mother was saying: He's a splendid fellow. . . . A
root idea for a war-baby article . . . If a Tommy was a decent
fellow he abstained because he didn't want to leave his girl
in trouble. . . If he wasn't he chanced it because it might
be his last chance. . . .

"A message to me!" Valentine said to herself. "But *which*
sentence? . . ." She moved, absently, all the cushions to one
end of the sofa. Her mother exclaimed:

"He sent his love! His mother was lucky to have such a
son!" and turned into her tiny hole of a study.

Valentine ran down over the broken tiles of the garden-
path, pulling her wideawake firmly on. She had looked at
her wrist-watch; it was two and twelve: 14:45. If she was to
walk to the War Office by 4:15—16:15—a sensible innova-
tion!—she must step out. Five miles to Whitehall. God
knows what then! Five miles back! Two and a half, diagonally, to High Street Station by half-past 19! Twelve and a half
miles in five hours or less. And three hours dancing on the
top of it. And to dress! . . . She needed to be fit. . . . And,
with violent bitterness, she said:

"Well! I'm fit. . . ." She had an image of the aligned hundred of girls in blue jumpers and men's ties keeping whom
fit had kept her super-fit. She wondered how many of them
would be men's mistresses before the year was out. It was
August then. But perhaps none! Because she had kept them
fit . . .

"Ah!" she said, "if I had been a loose woman, with flaccid breasts and a softy body. All perfumed!" . . . But neither Sylvia Tietjens nor Ethel Duchemin were soft. They might be scented on occasion! But they could not contemplate with equanimity doing a twelve-mile walk to save a few pence and dancing all night on top of it! She could! And perhaps the price she paid was just that; she was in such hard condition she hadn't moved him to . . . She perhaps exhaled such an aura of sobriety, chastity and abstinence as to suggest to him that . . . that a decent fellow didn't get his girl into trouble before going to be killed. . . . Yet if he were such a town bull! . . . She wondered how she knew such phrases. . . .

The sordid and aligned houses seemed to rush past her in the mean August sunshine. That was because if you thought hard, time went quicker; or because after you noticed the paper-shop at this corner you would be up to the boxes of onions outside the shop of the next corner before you noticed anything else.

She was in Kensington Gardens, on the north side; she had left the poor shops behind. . . . In sham country, with sham lawns, sham avenues, sham streams. Sham people pursuing their ways across the sham grass. Or no! Not sham! In a vacuum! No! "Pasteurized" was the word! Like dead milk. Robbed of their vitamins . . .

If she saved a few coppers by walking, it would make a larger pile to put into the leering—or compassionate—taxicabman's hand after he had helped her support her brother into the dog-kennel door. Edward would be dead drunk. She had fifteen shillings for the taxi. . . . If she gave a few coppers more, it seemed generous. . . . What a day to look forward to still! Some days were lifetimes!

She would rather die than let Tietjens pay for the cab!

Why? Once a taxi-man had refused payment for driving her and Edward all the way to Chiswick, and she hadn't felt insulted. She had paid him; but she hadn't felt insulted! A sentimental fellow; touched at the heart by the pretty sister—or perhaps he didn't really believe it was a sister—and her incapable bluejacket brother! Tietjens was a sentimental fellow too. . . . What was the difference? . . . And then! The mother a dead, heavy sleeper; the brother dead drunk. One in the morning! He couldn't refuse her! Blackness: cushions! She had arranged the cushions, she remembered. Arranged them subconsciously! Blackness! Heavy sleep; dead drunkenness! . . . Horrible! . . . A disgusting affair! An affair of Ealing . . . It shall make her one with all the stuff to fill graveyards. . . . Well, what else was she, Valentine Wannop: daughter of her father? And of her mother? Yes! But she herself . . . Just a little nobody!

They were no doubt wirelessing from the Admiralty. . . . But her brother was at home or getting a little more intoxicated and talking treason. At any rate, the flickering intermittences over the bitter seas couldn't for the moment concern him. . . . That bus touched her skirt as she ran for the island. . . . It might have been better. . . . But one hadn't the courage!

She was looking at patterned deaths under a little green roof, such as they put over bird-shelters. Her heart stopped! Before, she had been breathless! She was going mad. She was dying. . . . All these deaths! And not merely the deaths . . . The waiting for the approach of death; the contemplation of the parting from life! This minute you were; that, and you weren't! What was it like? Oh, heaven, she knew. . . . She stood there contemplating parting from . . . One minute you were; the next . . . Her breath fluttered in her chest. . . . Perhaps he wouldn't come. . . .

He was immediately framed by the sordid stones. She ran upon him and said something; with a mad hatred. All these deaths and he and his like responsible! . . . He had apparently a brother, a responsible one too! Browner complexioned! . . . But he! He! He! He! Completely calm; with direct eyes . . . It wasn't possible. *"Holde Lippen: klaare Augen: heller Sinn. . . ."* Oh, a little bit wilted, the clear intellect! And the lips? No doubt too. But he couldn't look at you so, unless . . .

She caught him fiercely by the arm; for the moment he belonged—more than to any browner, mere civilian brother! —to her! She was going to ask him! If he answered: "Yes! I am such a man!" she was going to say: "Then you must take me too! If them, why not me? I must have a child. I too!" She desired a child. She would overwhelm these hateful lodestones with a flood of argument; she imagined—she felt—the words going between her lips. . . . She imagined her fainting mind, her consenting limbs . . .

His looks were wandering round the cornice of these stone buildings. Immediately she was Valentine Wannop again; it needed no word from him. Words passed, but words could no more prove an established innocence than words can enhance a love that exists. He might as well have recited the names of railway stations. His eyes, his unconcerned face, his tranquil shoulders; they were what acquitted him. The

greatest love-speech he had ever and could ever make her
was when, harshly and angrily, he said something like:

"Certainly not. I imagined you knew me better"—brushing her aside as if she had been a midge. And, thank God,
he had hardly listened to her!

She was Valentine Wannop again; in the sunlight the chaf-
finches said "Pink! Pink!" The seed-heads of the tall grasses
were brushing against her skirt. She was clean-limbed, clear-
headed. . . . It was just a problem whether Sylvia Tietjens
was good to him. . . . Good *for* him was, perhaps, the more
exact way of putting it. Her mind cleared, like water that
goes off the boil. . . . "Waters stilled at even." Nonsense. It
was sunlight, and he had an adorable brother! He could
save *his* brother. . . . Transport! There was another meaning
to the word. A warm feeling settled down upon her; this was
her brother; the next to the best ever! It was as if you had
matched a piece of stuff so nearly with another piece of stuff
as to make no odds. Yet just not the real stuff! She must be
grateful to this relative for all he did for her; yet, ah, never
so grateful as to the other—who had done nothing!

Providence is kind in great batches! She heard, mounting
the steps, the blessed word "transport"! "They," so Mark
said: he and she—the family feeling again—were going to
get Christopher into the Transport. . . . By the kindness of
God the First Line Transport was the only branch of the
services of which Valentine knew anything. Their charwoman, who could not read and write, had a son, a sergeant
in a line regiment. "Hooray!" he had written to his mother.
"I've been off my feed; recommended for the D.C.M. too.
So they're putting me senior N.C.O. of First Line Transport
for a rest; the safest soft job of the whole bally front line
caboodle!" Valentine had had to read this letter in the scul-
lery amongst black beetles. Aloud! She had hated reading it
as she had hated reading anything that gave details of the
front line. But charity begins surely with the char! She had
had to. Now she could thank God. The sergeant, in direct,
perfectly sincere language, to comfort his mother, had described his daily work, detailing horses and G.S. lumber wag-
gons for jobs and superintending the horse-standings. "Why,"
one sentence ran, "our O.C. Transport is one of those fishing
lunatics. Wherever we go he has a space of grass cleared out
and pegged and b——y hell to the man who walks across
it!" There the O.C. practised casting with trout and salmon
rods by the hour together. "That'll show you what a soft job
it is!" the sergeant had finished triumphantly. . . .

So that there she, Valentine Wannop, sat on a hard bench against a wall; downright, healthy middle class—or perhaps upper middle class—for the Wannops were, if impoverished, yet of ancient family! Over her sensible, moccasined shoes the tide of humanity flowed before her hard bench. There were two commissionaires, the one always benevolent, the other perpetually querulous, in a pulpit on one side of her; on the other, a brown-visaged sort of brother-in-law with bulging eyes, who in his shy efforts to conciliate her was continually trying to thrust into his mouth the crook of his umbrella. As if it had been a knob. She could not, at the moment, imagine why he should want to conciliate her; but she knew she would know in a minute.

For just then she was occupied with a curious pattern; almost mathematically symmetrical. *Now* she was an English middle-class girl—whose mother had a sufficient income—in blue cloth, a wideawake hat, a black silk tie; without a thought in her head that she shouldn't have. And with a man who loved her: of crystal purity. Not ten, not five, minutes ago, she had been . . . She could not even remember what she had been! And he had been, he had assuredly appeared a town . . . No, she could not think the words. . . . A raging stallion, then! If now he should approach her, by the mere movement of a hand along the table, she would retreat.

It was a Godsend; yet it was absurd. Like the weather machine of the old man and the old woman on opposite ends of the stick . . . When the old man came out, the old woman went in and it would rain; when the old woman came out . . . It was exactly like that! She hadn't time to work out the analogy. But it was like that. . . . In rainy weather the whole world altered. Darkened! . . . The catgut that turned them slackened . . . slackened. . . . But, always, they remained at opposite ends of the stick!

Mark was saying, the umbrella crook hindering his utterance:

"We buy, then, an annuity of five hundred for your mother. . . ."

It was astonishing, though it spread tranquillity through her, how little this astonished her. It was the merely retarded expected. Mr. Tietjens senior, an honourable man, had promised as much years ago. Her mother, an august genius, was to wear herself out putting, Mr. Tietjens alive, his political views in his paper. He was to make it up to her. He was making it up. In no princely fashion, but adequately, as a gentleman.

Mark Tietjens, bending over, held a piece of paper. A bell-boy came up to him and said: "Mr. Riccardo!" Mark Tietjens said: "No! He's gone!" He continued:

"Your brother . . . Shelved for the moment. But enough to buy a practice, a good practice! When he's a full-fledged sawbones." He stopped; he directed upon her his atrabilarian eyes, biting his umbrella handle; he was extremely nervous.

"Now you!" he said. "Two or three hundred. A year, of course! The capital absolutely your own . . ." He paused: "But I warn you! Christopher won't like it. He's got his knife into me. I wouldn't grudge you . . . oh, any sum! . . ." He waved his hand to indicate an amount boundless in its figures. "I know you keep Christopher straight," he said. "The only person that could!" He added: "Poor devil!"

She said:

"He's got his knife into you? Why?"

He answered vaguely:

"Oh, there's been all this talk. . . . Untrue, of course."

She said:

"People have been saying things against you? To him? Perhaps because there's been delay in settling the estate."

He said:

"Oh, no! The other way round, in fact!"

"Then they have been saying," she exclaimed, "things against . . . against me. And him!"

He exclaimed in anguish:

"Oh, but I ask you to believe . . . I beg you to believe that I believe . . . *you!* Miss Wannop!" He added grotesquely: "As pure as dew that lies within Aurora's sun-tipped . . ." His eyes stuck out like those of a suffocating fish. He said: "I beg you not on that account to hand the giddy mitten to . . ." He writhed in his tight double collar. "His wife! . . ." he said "She's no good to . . . *for* him! . . . She's soppily in love with him. But no *good* . . ." He very nearly sobbed. "You're the only . . ." he said, "I *know* . . ."

It came into her head that she was losing too much time in this Salle des Pas Perdus! She would have to take the train home! Fivepence! But what did it matter. Her mother had five hundred a year. . . . Two hundred and forty times five . . .

Mark said brightly:

"If now we bought your mother an annuity of five hundred . . . You say that's ample to give Christopher his chop. . . . And settled on her three . . . four . . . I like to be exact . . . hundred a year . . . The capital of it: with remainder to you . . ." His interrogative face beamed.

She saw now the whole situation with perfect plainness. She understood Mrs. Duchemin's:

"You couldn't expect us, with our official position . . . to connive . . ." Edith Ethel had been perfectly right. She *couldn't* be expected. . . . She had worked too hard to appear circumspect and right! You can't ask people to lay down their whole lives for their friends! . . . It was only of Tietjens you could ask that! She said—to Mark:

"It's as if the whole world had conspired . . . like a carpenter's vice—to force us . . ." She was going to say "together. . . ." But he burst in, astonishingly:

"He must have his buttered toast . . . and his mutton-chop . . . and Rhum St. James!" He said: "Damn it all. . . . You were made for him. . . . You can't blame people for coupling you. . . . They're forced to it. . . . If you hadn't existed they'd have had to invent you. . . . Like Dante for . . . who was it? . . . Beatrice? There *are* couples like that."

She said:

"Like a carpenter's vice . . . Pushed together. Irresistibly. Haven't we resisted?"

His face became panic-stricken; his bulging eyes pushed away towards the pulpit of the two commissionaires. He whispered:

"You won't . . . because of my ox's hoof . . . desert . . ."

She said—she heard Macmaster whispering it hoarsely—

"I ask you to believe that I will never . . . abandon . . ."

It was what Macmaster had said. He must have got it from Mrs. Micawber!

Christopher Tietjens—in his shabby khaki, for his wife had spoilt his best uniform—spoke suddenly from behind her back. He had approached her from beyond the pulpit of the two commissionaires, and she had been turned towards Mark on his bench:

"Come along! Let's get out of this!" He was, she asked herself, getting out of this! Towards what?

Like mutes from a funeral—or as if she had been, between the brothers, a prisoner under escort—they walked down steps; half righted towards the exit arch; one and a half righted to face Whitehall. The brothers grunted inaudible but satisfied sounds over her head. They crossed, by the islands, Whitehall, where the bus had brushed her skirt. Under an archway—

In a stony, gravelled, majestic space the brothers faced each other. Mark said:

"I suppose you won't shake hands!"

Christopher said:

"No! Why should I?" She herself had cried out to Christopher:

"Oh, *do!*" (The wireless squares overhead no longer concerned her. Her brother was, no doubt, getting drunk in a bar in Piccadilly. . . . A surface coarseness!)

Mark said:

"Hadn't you better? You might get killed! A fellow just getting killed would not like to think he had refused to shake his brother by the hand!"

Christopher had said: "Oh . . . well!"

During her happiness over this hyperborean sentimentality he had gripped her thin upper arm. He had led her past swans—or possibly huts; she never remembered which —to a seat that had over it or near it a weeping willow. He had said, gasping, too, like a fish:

"Will you be my mistress to-night? I am going out tomorrow at eight-thirty from Waterloo."

She had answered:

"Yes! Be at such and such a studio just before twelve. . . . I have to see my brother home. . . . He will be drunk. . . ." She meant to say: "Oh, my darling, I have wanted you so much. . . ."

She said instead:

"I have arranged the cushions. . . ."

She said to herself:

"Now whatever made me say that? It's as if I had said: 'You'll find the ham in the larder under a plate. . . .' No tenderness about it . . ."

She went away, up a cockle-shelled path, between ankle-high railings, crying bitterly. An old tramp, with red, weeping eyes and a thin white beard, regarded her curiously from where he lay on the grass. He imagined himself the monarch of that landscape.

"That's women!" he said with the apparently imbecile enigmaticality of the old and the hardened. "Some do!" He spat into the grass, said: "Ah!" then added: "Some do not!"

6 ~

HE LET himself in at the heavy door; when he closed it behind him, in the darkness, the heaviness of the door sent long surreptitious whisperings up the great stone stairs. These sounds irritated him. If you shut a heavy door on an enclosed space it will push air in front of it and there will be whisperings; the atmosphere of mystery was absurd. He was just a man, returning after a night out. . . . Two-thirds, say, of a night out! It must be half-past three. But what the night had lacked in length it had made up in fantastic aspects. . . .

He laid his cane down on the invisible oak chest, and through the tangible and velvety darkness that had always in it the chill of the stone of walls and stairs, he felt for the handle of the breakfast-room door.

Three long parallelograms existed: pale glimmerings above, cut two-thirds of the way down by the serrations of chimney-pot and roof shadows! Nine full paces across the heavy piled carpet; then he ought to reach his round-backed chair, by the left-hand window. He reached his round-backed chair by the left-hand window. He sank into it; it fitted exactly his back. He imagined that no man had ever been so tired and that no man had ever been so alone! A small, alive sound existed at the other end of the room; in front of him existed one and a half pale parallelograms. They were the reflection of the windows of the mirror; the sound was no doubt Calton, the cat. Something alive, at any rate! Possibly Sylvia at the other end of the room, waiting for him, to see what he looked like. Mostly likely! It didn't matter!

His mind stopped! Sheer weariness!

When it went on again it was saying:

"Naked shingles and surges drear . . ." and, "On these debatable borders of the world!" He said sharply: "Nonsense!" The one was either *Calais beach* or *Dover sands* of the whiskered man: Arnold. . . . He would be seeing them both within the twenty-four hours. . . . But, no! He was going from Waterloo. Southampton, Havre, therefore! . . . The other was by that detestable fellow: "The subject of our little monograph!" . . . What a long time ago! . . . He saw a pile of shining dispatch cases: the inscription *"This*

rack is reserved for . . .": a coloured—pink and blue!—
photograph of Boulogne sands and the held-up squares, the
proofs of "our little . . ." What a long time ago! He heard
his own voice saying in the new railway carriage, proudly,
clearly and with male hardness:

*"I stand for monogamy and chastity. And for no talking
about it. Of course, if a man who's a man wants to have a
woman he has her. And again, no talking about it . . ."*
His voice—his own voice—came to him as if from the other
end of a long-distance telephone. A damn long-distance
one! Ten years . . .

If, then, a man who's a man wants to have a woman . . .
Damn it, he doesn't! In ten years he had learnt that a Tommy
who's a decent fellow . . . His mind said at one and the
same moment, the two lines running one over the other like
the two subjects of a fugue:

"Some beguiling virgins with the broken seals of perjury," and:

"Since when we stand side by side, only hands may
meet!"

He said:

"But damn it; damn it again! The beastly fellow was
wrong! Our hands didn't meet. . . . I don't believe I've shaken
hands. . . . I don't believe I've touched the girl . . . in my
life. . . . Never once! . . . Not the hand-shaking sort. . . . A
nod! . . . A meeting and parting! . . . English, you know . . .
But yes, she put her arm over my shoulders. . . . On the
bank! . . . *'On such short acquaintance!'* I said to myself
then. . . . Well, we've made up for it since then. Or no!
Not made up! . . . Atoned . . . As Sylvia so aptly put it at that
moment mother was dying . . ."

He, his conscious self, said:

"But it was probably the drunken brother. . . . You don't
beguile virgins with the broken seals of perjury in Kensington High Street at two at night supporting, one on each side,
a drunken bluejacket with intermittent legs. . . ."

"Intermittent!" was the word. "Intermittently function-
ing!"

At one point the boy had broken from them and run with
astonishing velocity along the dull wood paving of an immense empty street. When they had caught him up he had
been haranguing under black hanging trees, with an Oxford
voice, an immobile policeman:

"You're the fellows!" he'd been exclaiming, "who make

old England what she is! You keep the peace in our homes!
You save us from the vile excesses. . . ."

Tietjens himself he had always addressed with the voice
and accent of a common seaman; with his coarsened surface
voice!

He had the two personalities. Two or three times he had
said:

"Why don't you kiss the girl? She's a *nice* girl, isn't she?
You're a poor b——y Tommy, ain't cher? Well, the poor
b——y Tommies ought to have all the nice girls they want!
That's straight, isn't it? . . ."

And even at that time they hadn't known what was going
to happen. . . . There are certain cruelties. . . . They had
got a four-wheel cab at last. The drunken boy had sat beside the driver; he had insisted. . . . Her little, pale, shrunken
face had gazed straight before her. . . . It hadn't been possible
to speak; the cab, rattling all over the road, had pulled up
with frightful jerks when the boy had grabbed at the reins.
. . . The old driver hadn't seemed to mind; but they had
had to subscribe all the money in their pockets to pay him
after they had carried the boy into the black house. . . .

Tietjens' mind said to him:

"Now when they came to her father's house so nimbly
she slipped in and said: 'There is a fool without and there is a
maid within. . . .'"

He answered dully:

"Perhaps that's what it really amounts to. . . ." He had
stood at the hall-door, she looking out at him with a pitiful
face. Then from the sofa within, the brother had begun to
snore; enormous, grotesque sounds, like the laughter of unknown races from darkness. He had turned and walked
down the path, she following him. He had exclaimed:

"It's perhaps too . . . untidy. . . ."

She had said:

"Yes! Yes . . . Ugly . . . Too . . . oh . . . *private!*"

He said, he remembered:

"But . . . forever . . ."

She said, in a great hurry:

"But when you come back . . . Permanently. And . . . oh,
as if it were in public . . . I don't know," she had added.
"Ought we? . . . I'd be ready. . . ." She added: "I will be
ready for anything you ask."

He had said at some time: "But obviously . . . Not under
this roof . . ." And he had added: "We're the sort that . . .
do not!"

She had answered, quickly too:

"Yes—that's it. We're that sort!" And then she had asked: "And Ethel's party? Was it a great success?" It hadn't, she knew, been an inconsequence. He had answered:

"Ah . . . *That's* permanent. . . . *That's* public. . . . There was Rugeley. The duke . . . Sylvia brought him. She'll be a great friend! . . . And the President of the . . . Local Government Board, I think . . . And a Belgian . . . equivalent to Lord Chief Justice . . . and, of course, Claudine Sandbach . . . Two hundred and seventy; all of the best, the modestly elated Guggumses said as I left! And Mr. Ruggles . . . Yes! . . . They're established. . . No place for me!"

"Nor for *me!*" She had answered. She added: "But I'm glad!"

Patches of silence ran between them: they hadn't yet got out of the habit of thinking they had to hold up the drunken brother. That had seemed to last for a thousand painful months. . . . Long enough to acquire a habit. The brother seemed to roar: "Haw—Haw—Kuryasch . . ." And after two minutes: "Haw—Haw—Kuryasch . . ." Hungarian, no doubt!

He said:

"It was splendid to see Vincent standing beside the duke. Showing him a first edition! Not, of course, *quite* the thing for a, after all, wedding-party! But how was Rugeley to know that? . . . And Vincent not in the least servile! He even corrected cousin Rugeley over the meaning of the word *"colophon"!* The first time he ever corrected a superior! . . . Established, you see! . . . And *practically* cousin Rugeley . . . Dear Sylvia Tietjens' cousin, so the next to nearest thing! Wife of Lady Macmaster's *oldest* friend . . . Sylvia going to them in their—quite modest!—little place in Surrey . . . As for us," he had concluded, " 'they also serve who only stand and wait. . . .' "

She said:

"I suppose the rooms looked lovely."

He had answered:

"Lovely . . . They'd got all the pictures by that beastly fellow up from the rectory study in the dining-room on dark oak panelling. . . . A fair blaze of bosoms and nipples and lips and pomegranates . . . The tallest silver candlesticks, of course . . . You remember, silver candlesticks and dark oak. . . ."

She said:

"Oh, my dear . . . Don't. . . . *Don't!*"

He had just touched the rim of his helmet with his folded gloves.

"So we just wash out!" he had said.

She said:

"Would you take this bit of parchment. . . . I got a little Jew girl to write on it in Hebrew: It's 'God bless you and keep you: God watch over you at your goings-out and at . . .' "

He tucked it into his breast pocket.

"The talismanic passage," he said. "Of course I'll wear it. . . ."

She said:

"If we *could* wash out this afternoon . . . It would make it easier to bear. . . . Your poor mother, you know, she was dying when we last . . ."

He said:

"You remember *that.* . . . Even, then, you . . . And if I hadn't gone to Lobscheid . . ."

She said:

"From the first moment I set eyes on you . . ."

He said:

"And I . . . from the first moment . . . I'll tell you . . . If I looked out of a door . . . It was all like sand. . . . But to the half-left a little bubbling up of water. That could be trusted. To keep on forever . . . You, perhaps, won't understand."

She said:

"Yes! I know!"

They were seeing landscapes. . . . Sand-dunes, close-cropped . . . Some negligible shipping; a stump-masted brig from Archangel . . .

"From the first moment," he repeated.

She said:

"If we *could* wash out . . ."

He said, and for the first moment felt grand, tender, protective:

"Yes, you *can,*" he said. "You cut out from this afternoon, just before 4:58 it was when I said that to you and you consented . . . I heard the Horse Guards clock . . . to now. . . . Cut it out; and join time up. . . . It *can* be done. . . . You know they do it surgically; for some illness; cut out a great length of the bowel and join the tube up. . . . For colitis I think . . ."

She said:

"But I *wouldn't* cut it out. . . . It was the first spoken sign."

He said:

"No, it wasn't. . . . From the very beginning . . . with every word . . ."

She exclaimed:

"You felt that. . . . Too! . . . We've been pushed, as in a carpenter's vice. . . . We couldn't have got away. . . ."

He said: "By God! That's it. . . ."

He suddenly saw a weeping willow in St. James's Park; 4:59! He had just said: "Will you be my mistress to-night?" She had gone away, half left; her hands to her face. . . . A small fountain; half left. That could be trusted to keep on forever. . . .

Along the lake-side, sauntering, swinging his crooked stick, his incredibly shiny top-hat perched sideways, his claw-hammer coat-tails very long, flapping out behind, in dusty sunlight, his magpie pince-nez gleaming, had come, naturally, Mr. Ruggles. He had looked at the girl, then down at Tietjens, sprawled on his bench. He had just touched the brim of his shiny hat. He said:

"Dining at the club to-night? . . ."

Tietjens said: "No, I've resigned."

With the aspect of a long-billed bird chewing a bit of putridity, Ruggles said:

"Oh, but we've had an emergency meeting of the committee . . . the committee was sitting . . . and sent you a letter asking you to reconsider. . . ."

Tietjens said:

"I know. . . . I shall withdraw my resignation to-night . . . And resign again to-morrow morning."

Ruggles' muscles had relaxed for a quick second, then they stiffened.

"Oh, I say!" he had said. "Not that . . . You couldn't do that. . . . Not to the *club!* . . . It's never been done . . . It's an insult. . . ."

"It's meant to be," Tietjens said. "Gentlemen shouldn't be expected to belong to a club that has certain members on its committee."

Ruggles' deepish voice suddenly grew very high.

"Eh, I say, you know!" he squeaked.

Tietjens had said:

"I'm not vindictive. . . . But I *am* deadly tired: of all old women and their chatter."

Ruggles had said:

"I don't . . ." His face had become suddenly dark brown, scarlet and then brownish-purple. He stood droopingly looking at Tietjens' boots.

"Oh! Ah! Well!" he said at last. "See you at Macmaster's to-night. . . . A great thing, his knighthood. First-class man . . ."

That had been the first Tietjens had heard of Macmaster's knighthood; he had missed looking at the honours' list of that morning. Afterwards, dining alone with Sir Vincent and Lady Macmaster, he had seen, pinned up, a back view of the Sovereign doing something to Vincent; a photo for next morning's papers. From Macmaster's embarrassed hushings of Edith Ethel's explanation that the honour was for special services of a specific kind Tietjens guessed both the nature of Macmaster's service and the fact that the little man hadn't told Edith Ethel who, originally, had done the work. And—just like his girl—Tietjens had let it go at that. He didn't see why poor Vincent shouldn't have that little bit of prestige at home—under all the monuments! But he hadn't—though through all the evening Macmaster, with the solicitude and affection of a cringing Italian greyhound, had hastened from celebrity to celebrity to hang over Tietjens, and although Tietjens knew that his friend was grieved and appalled, like any woman, at his, Tietjens', going out again to France—Tietjens hadn't been able to look Macmaster again in the face. . . . He had felt ashamed. He had felt, for the first time in his life, ashamed!

Even when he, Tietjens, had slipped away from the party—to go to his good fortune!—Macmaster had come panting down the stairs, running after him, through guests coming up. He had said:

"Wait . . . You're not going . . . I want to . . ." With a miserable and appalled glance he had looked up the stairs; Lady Macmaster might have come out too. His black, short beard quivering and his wretched eyes turned down, he had said:

"I wanted to explain. . . . This miserable knighthood . . ."

Tietjens patted him on the shoulder, Macmaster being on the stairs above him.

"It's all right, old man," he had said—and with real affection: "We've powlered up and down enough for a little thing like that not to . . . I'm very glad. . . ."

Macmaster had whispered:

"And Valentine . . . She's not here to-night. . . ."

He had exclaimed:

"By God! . . . If I thought . . ." Tietjens had said: "It's all right. It's all right. She's at another party . . . I'm going on . . ."

Macmaster had looked at him doubtingly and with misery, leaning over and clutching the clammy banisters.

"Tell her . . ." he said. "Good God! You may be killed . . . I beg you . . . I beg you to believe . . . I will . . . Like the apple of my eye . . ." In the swift glance that Tietjens took of his face he could see that Macmaster's eyes were full of tears.

They both stood looking down at the stone stairs for a long time.

Then Macmaster had said: "Well . . ."

Tietjens had said: "Well . . ." But he hadn't been able to look at Macmaster's eyes, though he had felt his friend's eyes pitiably exploring his own face. . . . "A back-stairs way out of it," he had thought; a queer thing that you couldn't look in the face a man you were never going to see again!

"But, by God," he said to himself fiercely when his mind came back again to the girl in front of him, "this isn't going to be another back-stairs exit. . . . I must tell her. . . . I'm damned if I don't make an effort. . . ."

She had her handkerchief to her face.

"I'm always crying," she said. "A little bubbling spring that can be trusted to keep on . . ."

He looked to the right and to the left. Ruggles or General Someone with false teeth that didn't fit *must* be coming along. The street with its sooty boskage was clean, empty and silent. She was looking at him. He didn't know how long he had been silent; he didn't know where he had been; intolerable waves urged him towards her.

After a long time he said:

"Well . . ."

She moved back. She said:

"I won't watch you out of sight. . . . It is unlucky to watch anyone out of sight. . . . But I will never . . . I will never cut what you said then out of my memory. . . ." She was gone; the door shut. He had wondered what she would never cut out of her memory. That he had asked her that afternoon to be his mistress? . . .

He had caught, outside the gates of his old office, a transport-lorry that had given him a lift to Holborn. . . .

No More Parades

For two things my heart is grieved: A man
of war that suffereth from poverty and men
of intelligence that are counted as refuse.

PROVERBS

PART ONE

I ~

WHEN YOU came in, the space was desultory, rectangular,
warm after the drip of the winter night, and transfused with
a brown-orange dust that was light. It was shaped like the
house a child draws. Three groups of brown limbs spotted
with brass took dim high-lights from shafts that came from
a bucket pierced with holes, filled with incandescent coke
and covered in with a sheet of iron in the shape of a tunnel.
Two men, as if hierarchically smaller, crouched on the floor
beside the brazier; four, two at each end of the hut, drooped
over tables in attitudes of extreme indifference. From the
eaves above the parallelogram of black that was the doorway
fell intermittent drippings of collected moisture, persistent,
with glasslike intervals of musical sound. The two men squat-
ting on their heels over the brazier—they had been miners—
began to talk in a low sing-song of dialect, hardly audible.
It went on and on, monotonously, without animation. It was
as if one told the other long, long stories to which his companion manifested his comprehension or sympathy with
animal grunts. . . .

An immense tea-tray, august, its voice filling the black
circle of the horizon, thundered to the ground. Numerous
pieces of sheet-iron said, "Pack. Pack. Pack." In a minute the
clay floor of the hut shook, the drums of ears were pressed
inwards, solid noise showered about the universe, enormous
echoes pushed these men—to the right, to the left, or down
towards the tables—and crackling like that of flames among
vast underwood became the settled condition of the night.
Catching the light from the brazier as the head leaned over,
the lips of one of the two men on the floor were incredibly
red and full and went on talking and talking. . . .

The two men on the floor were Welsh miners, of whom
the one came from the Rhondda Valley and was unmarried;

the other, from Pontardulais, had a wife who kept a laundry, he having given up going underground just before the war. The two men at the table to the right of the door were sergeants-major; the one came from Suffolk and was a time-serving man of sixteen years' seniority as a sergeant in a line regiment. The other was Canadian of English origin. The two officers at the other end of the hut were captains, the one a young regular officer born in Scotland but educated at Oxford; the other, nearly middle-aged and heavy, came from Yorkshire and was in a militia battalion. The one runner on the floor was filled with a passionate rage because the elder officer had refused him leave to go home and see why his wife, who had sold their laundry, had not yet received the purchase money from the buyer; the other was thinking about a cow. His girl, who worked on a mountainy farm above Caerphilly, had written to him about a queer cow: a black-and-white Holstein—surely to goodness a queer cow. The English sergeant-major was almost tearfully worried about the enforced lateness of the draft. It would be twelve midnight before they could march them off. It was not right to keep men hanging about like that. The men did not like to be kept waiting, hanging about. It made them discontented. They did not like it. He could not see why the depot quartermaster could not keep up his stock of candles for the hooded lamps. The men had no call to be kept waiting, hanging about. Soon they would have to be having some supper. Quarter would not like that. He would grumble fair. Having to indent for suppers. Put his accounts out fair, it would. Two thousand nine hundred and thirty-four suppers at a penny halfpenny. But it was not right to keep the men hanging about till midnight and no suppers. It made them discontented, and them going up the line for the first time, poor devils.

The Canadian sergeant-major was worried about a pigskin leather pocket-book. He had bought it at the ordnance depot in the town. He imagined himself bringing it out on parade to read out some return or other to the adjutant. Very smart it would look on parade, himself standing up straight and tall. But he could not remember whether he had put it in his kit-bag. On himself it was not. He felt in his right and left breast pockets, his right and left skirt pockets, in all the pockets of his overcoat, that hung from a nail within reach of his chair. He did not feel at all certain that the man who acted as his batman had packed that pocket-book with his kit, though he declared he had. It was very annoying. His present wallet, bought in Ontario, was bulging and split. He did not like to bring it out when imperial officers asked for something out of a return. It gave them a false idea of Canadian troops. Very annoying. He was an auctioneer. He agreed that at this rate it would be half-past one before they had the draft down to the station and entrained. But it was very annoying to be uncertain whether that pocket-book was packed or not. He had imagined himself making a good impression on parade, standing up straight and tall, taking out that pocket-book when the adjutant asked for a figure from one return or the other. He understood their adjutants were to be imperial officers now they were in France. It was very annoying.

An enormous crashing sound said things of an intolerable intimacy to each of those men and to all of them as a body. After its mortal vomiting, all the other sounds appeared a rushing silence, painful to ears in which the blood audibly coursed. The young officer stood violently up on his feet and caught at the complications of his belt hung from a nail. The elder, across the table, lounging sideways, stretched out one hand with a downwards movement. He was aware that the younger man, who was the senior officer, was just upon out of his mind. The younger man, intolerably fatigued, spoke sharp, injurious, inaudible words to his companion. The elder spoke sharp, short words, inaudible too, and continued to motion downwards with his hand over the table. The old English sergeant-major said to his junior that Captain Mackenzie had one of his mad fits again, but what he said was inaudible and he knew it. He felt arising in his motherly heart, that yearned at the moment over his two thousand nine hundred and thirty-four nurslings, a necessity, like a fatigue, to extend the motherliness of his functions to the orfcer. He said to the Canadian that Captain Mackenzie there going temporary off his nut was the best orfcer in His Majesty's army. And going to make a bleedin' fool of hisself. The best orfcer in His Majesty's army. Not a better. Careful, smart, brave as an 'ero. And considerate of his men in the line. You wouldn't believe . . . He felt vaguely that it was a fatigue to have to mother an officer. To a lance-corporal or a young sergeant beginning to go wrong you could mutter wheezy suggestions through your moustache. But to an officer you had to say things slantways. Difficult it was. Thank God they had a trustworthy, cool hand in the other captain. Old and good, the proverb said.

Dead silence fell.

"Lost the ——, they 'ave"; the runner from the Rhondda made his voice startlingly heard. Brilliant illuminations flickered on hut-gables visible through the doorway.

"No reason," his mate from Pontardulais rather whined in his native sing-song, "why the bleedin' searchlights, surely to goodness, should light us up for all the —— 'Un planes to see. I want to see my bleedin' little 'ut on the bleedin' Mumbles again, if they don't."

"Not so much swear-words, O Nine Morgan," the ser-geant-major said.

"Now, Dai Morgan, I'm telling you," 09 Morgan's mate continued. "A queer cow it must have been, whatever. Black-and-white Holstein it wass. . . ."

It was as if the younger captain gave up listening to the conversation. He leant both hands on the blanket that cov-ered the table. He exclaimed:

"Who the hell are you to give me orders? I'm your senior. Who the hell . . . Oh, by God, who the hell . . . Nobody gives me orders . . ." His voice collapsed weakly in his chest. He felt his nostrils to be inordinately dilated so that the air pouring into them was cold. He felt that there was an entangled conspiracy against him and all round him. He exclaimed: "You and your —— pimp of a general! . . ." He desired to cut certain throats with a sharp trench-knife that he had. That would take the weight off his chest. The "Sit *down*" of the heavy figure lumping opposite him para-lysed his limbs. He felt an unbelievable hatred. If he could move his hand to get at his trench-knife . . .

09 Morgan said:

"The ——'s name who's bought my bleedin' laundry is Williams. . . . If I thought it was Evans Williams of Castell Goch, I'd desert."

"Took a hatred for its cawve," the Rhondda man said. "And look you, before you could say . . ." The conversation of orfcers was a thing to which they neither listened. Officers talked of things that had no interest. Whatever could possess a cow to take a hatred of its calf? Up behind Caerphilly on the mountains? On an autumny morning the whole hill-side was covered with spider-webs. They shone down the sun like spun glass. Overlooked the cow must be.

The young captain leaning over the table began a long argument as to relative seniority. He argued with himself, taking both sides in an extraordinarily rapid gabble. He him-self had been gazetted after Gheluvelt. The other not till a year later. It was true the other was in permanent command of that depot, and he himself attached to the unit only for rations and discipline. But that did not include orders to sit down. What the hell, he wanted to know, did the other mean by it? He began to talk, faster than ever, about a circle. When its circumference came whole by the disintegration of the atom, the world would come to an end. In the millennium there would be no giving or taking orders. Of course he obeyed orders till then.

To the elder officer, burdened with the command of a unit of unreasonable size, with a scratch headquarters of useless subalterns who were continually being changed, with N.C.O.s all unwilling to work, with rank and file nearly all colonials and unused to doing without things, and with a depot to draw on that, being old established, felt that it belonged exclusively to a regular British unit and resented his drawing anything at all, the practical difficulties of his everyday life were already sufficient, and he had troublesome private affairs. He was lately out of hospital; the sackcloth hut in which he lived, borrowed from the depot medical officer, who had gone to England on leave, was suffocatingly hot with the paraffin heater going and intolerably cold and damp without it; the batman whom the M.O. had left in charge of the hut appeared to be half-witted. These German air raids had lately become continuous. The base was packed with men, tighter than sardines. Down in the town you could not move in the streets. Draft-finding units were commanded to keep their men out of sight as much as possible. Drafts were to be sent off only at night. But how could you send off a draft at night when every ten minutes you had two hours of lights out for an air raid? Every man had nine sets of papers and tags that had to be signed by an officer. It was quite proper that the poor devils should be properly documented. But how was it to be done? He had two thousand nine hundred and ninety-four men to send off that night, and nine times two thousand nine hundred and ninety-four is twenty-six thousand nine hundred and forty-six. They would not or could not let him have a disk-punching machine of his own, but how was the depot armourer to be expected to punch five thousand nine hundred and eighty-eight extra identity disks in addition to his regular jobs?

The other captain rambled on in front of him. Tietjens did not like his talk of the circle and the millennium. You get alarmed, if you have any sense, when you hear that. It may prove the beginnings of definite, dangerous lunacy. . . . But he knew nothing about the fellow. He was too dark and good-looking, too passionate, probably, to be a good regular officer on the face of him. But he *must* be a good officer: he had the D.S.O. with a clasp, the M.C., and some foreign ribbon up. And the general said he was: with the additional odd piece of information that he was a vice-chancellor's Latin Prize man. . . . He wondered if General Campion knew what a vice-chancellor's Latin Prize man was. Probably he did not, but had just stuck the piece of information into his note as a barbaric ornament is used by a savage chief. Wanted to show that he, General Lord Edward Campion, was a man of culture. There was no knowing where vanity would not break out.

So this fellow was too dark and good-looking to be a good officer: yet he *was* a good officer. That explained it. The repressions of the passionate drive them mad. He must have been being sober, disciplined, patient, absolutely repressed ever since 1914—against a background of hell-fire, row, blood, mud, old tins. . . . And indeed the elder officer had a vision of the younger as if in a design for a full-length portrait—for some reason with his legs astride—against a background of tapestry scarlet with fire and more scarlet with blood. . . . He sighed a little: that was the life of all those several millions. . . .

He seemed to see his draft: two thousand nine hundred and ninety-four men he had had command of for over a couple of months—a long space of time, as that life went—men he and Sergeant-Major Cowley had looked after with a great deal of tenderness, superintending their morale, their morals, their feet, their digestions, their impatiences, their desires for women. . . . He seemed to see them winding away over a great stretch of country, the head slowly settling down, as in the zoo you will see an enormous serpent slowly sliding down into its water-tank. . . . Settling down out there, a long way away, up against that impassable barrier that stretched from the depths of the ground to the peak of heaven . . .

Intense dejection: endless muddles: endless follies: endless villainies. All these men given into the hands of the most cynically carefree intriguers in long corridors who made plots that harrowed the hearts of the world. All these men toys: all these agonies mere occasions for picturesque phrases to be put into politicians' speeches without heart or even intelligence. Hundreds of thousands of men tossed here and there in that sordid and gigantic mud-brownness of mid-winter . . . by God, exactly as if they were nuts wilfully

picked up and thrown over the shoulder by magpies. . . .
But men. Not just populations. Men you worried over there.
Each man a man with a backbone, knees, breeches, braces,
a rifle, a home, passions, fornications, drunks, pals, some
scheme of the universe, corns, inherited diseases, a green-
grocer's business, a milk-walk, a paper-stall, brats, a slut of
a wife . . . The Men: the Other Ranks! And the poor —— little
officers. God help them. Vice-chancellor's Latin Prize men . . .

This particular poor —— Prize man seemed to object to
noise. They ought to keep the place quiet for him. . . .

By God, he was perfectly right. That place was meant
for the quiet and orderly preparation of meat for the
shambles. Drafts! A base is a place where you meditate:
perhaps you should pray: a place where in peace the
Tommies should write their last letters home and describe
'ow the guns are 'owling 'orribly.

But to pack a million and a half of men into and round
that small town was like baiting a trap for rats with a great
chunk of rotten meat. The Hun planes could smell them
from a hundred miles away. They could do more harm
there than if they bombed a quarter of London to pieces.
And the air defences there were a joke: a mad joke. They
pooped off, thousands of rounds, from any sort of pieces
of ordnance, like schoolboys bombarding swimming rats
with stones. Obviously your best-trained air-defence men
would be round your metropolis. But this was no joke for
the sufferers.

Heavy depression settled down more heavily upon him.
The distrust of the home Cabinet, felt by then by the
greater part of that army, became like physical pain. These
immense sacrifices, this ocean of mental sufferings, were all
undergone to further the private vanities of men who amidst
these hugenesses of landscapes and forces appeared pygmies!
It was the worries of all these wet millions in mud-brown
that worried him. They could die, they could be massacred,
by the quarter million, in shambles. But that they should
be massacred without jauntiness, without confidence, with
depressed brows: without parade . . .

He knew really nothing about the officer in front of him.
Apparently the fellow had stopped for an answer to some
question. What question? Tietjens had no idea. He had not
been listening. Heavy silence settled down on the hut. They
just waited. The fellow said with an intonation of hatred:

"Well, what about it? That's what I want to know!"

Tietjens went on reflecting. . . . There were a great many

kinds of madness. What kind was this? The fellow was not drunk. He talked like a drunkard, but he was not drunk. In ordering him to sit down, Tietjens had just chanced it. There are madmen whose momentarily subconscious selves will respond to a military command as if it were magic. Tietjens remembered having barked: "About . . . turn," to a poor little lunatic fellow in some camp at home, and the fellow, who had been galloping hot-foot past his tent, waving a naked bayonet, with his pursuers fifty yards behind, had stopped dead and faced about with a military stamp like a guardsman. He had tried it on this lunatic for want of any better expedient. It had apparently functioned intermittently. He risked saying:

"What about what?"

The man said as if ironically:

"It seems as if I were not worth listening to by your high and mightiness. I said: 'What about my foul squit of an uncle?' Your filthy, best friend."

Tietjens said:

"The general's your uncle? General Campion? What's he done to you?"

The general had sent this fellow down to him with a note asking him, Tietjens, to keep an eye in his unit on a very good fellow and an admirable officer. The chit was in the general's own writing and contained the additional information as to Captain Mackenzie's scholastic prowess. . . . It had struck Tietjens as queer that the general should take so much trouble about a casual infantry company commander. How could the fellow have been brought markedly to his notice? Of course, Campion was good-natured, like another man. If a fellow, half dotty, whose record showed that he was a very good man, was brought to his notice, Campion would do what he could for him. And Tietjens knew that the general regarded himself, Tietjens, as a heavy, bookish fellow, able reliably to look after one of his protégés. . . . Probably Campion imagined that they had no work to do in that unit: they might become an acting lunatic ward. But if Mackenzie was Campion's nephew, the thing was explained.

The lunatic exclaimed:

"Campion, *my* uncle? Why, he's *yours!*"

Tietjens said:

"Oh, no, he isn't." The general was not even a connexion of his, but he did happen to be Tietjens' godfather and his father's oldest friend.

The other fellow answered:

"Then it's damn funny. *Damn* suspicious . . . Why should he be interested in you if he's not your filthy uncle? You're no soldier. . . . You're no sort of a soldier. . . . A meal-sack, that's what you look like. . . ." He paused and then went on very quickly: "They say up at H.Q. that your wife has got hold of the disgusting general. I didn't believe it was true. I didn't believe you were that sort of fellow. I've heard a lot about you!"

Tietjens laughed at this madness. Then, in the dark brownness, an intolerable pang went all through his heavy frame —the intolerable pang of home news to these desperately occupied men, the pain caused by disasters happening in the darkness and at a distance. You could do nothing to mitigate them! . . . The extraordinary beauty of the wife from whom he was separated—for she was extraordinarily beautiful!— might well have caused scandals about her to have penetrated to the general's headquarters, which was a sort of family party! Hitherto there had, by the grace of God, been no scandals. Sylvia Tietjens had been excruciatingly unfaithful, in the most painful manner. He could not be certain that the child he adored was his own. . . . That was not unusual with extraordinarily beautiful—and cruel!—women. But she had been haughtily circumspect.

Nevertheless, three months ago, they had parted. . . . Or he thought they had parted. Almost complete blankness had descended upon his home life. She appeared before him so extraordinarily bright and clear in the brown darkness that he shuddered: very tall, very fair, extraordinarily fit and clean, even. Thoroughbred! In a sheath gown of gold tissue, all illuminated, and her mass of hair, like gold tissue too, coiled round and round in plaits over her ears. The features very clean-cut and thinnish; the teeth white and small; the breasts small; the arms thin, long and at attention at her sides. . . . His eyes, when they were tired, had that trick of reproducing images on their retinas with that extreme clearness, images sometimes of things he thought of, sometimes of things merely at the back of the mind. Well, to-night his eyes were very tired! She was looking straight before her, with a little inimical disturbance of the corners of her lips. She had just thought of a way to hurt terribly his silent personality. . . . The semi-clearness became a luminous blur, like a tiny Gothic arch, and passed out of his vision to the right. . . .

He knew nothing of where Sylvia was. He had given up

looking at the illustrated papers. She had said she was going into a convent at Birkenhead—but twice he had seen photographs of her. The first showed her merely with Lady Fiona Grant, daughter of the Earl and Countess of Ulleswater—and a Lord Swindon, talked of as next minister for international finance—a new Business Peer. . . . All three walking straight into the camera in the court-yard of Lord Swindon's castle . . . all three smiling! . . . It announced Mrs. Christopher Tietjens as having a husband at the front.

The sting had, however, been in the second picture—in the description of it supplied by the journal! It showed Sylvia standing in front of a bench in the park. On the bench in profile there extended himself, in a guffaw of laughter, a young man in a top-hat jammed well on to his head, which was thrown back, his prognathous jaw pointing upwards. The description stated that the picture showed Mrs. Christopher Tietjens, whose husband was in hospital at the front, telling a good story to the son and heir of Lord Brigham! . . . Another of these pestilential, crooked, newspaper-owning financial peers . . .

It had struck him for a painful moment whilst looking at the picture in a dilapidated mess ante-room after he had come out of hospital—that, considering the description, the journal had got its knife into Sylvia. . . . But the illustrated papers do not get their knives into society beauties. They are too precious to the photographers. . . . Then Sylvia must have supplied the information; she desired to cause comment by the contrast of her hilarious companions and the statement that her husband was in hospital at the front. . . . It had occurred to him that she was on the war-path. But he had put it out of his mind. . . . Nevertheless, brilliant mixture as she was of the perfectly straight, perfectly fearless, perfectly reckless, of the generous, the kind, even—and the atrociously cruel—nothing might suit her better than positively to show contempt—no, not contempt! cynical hatred —for her husband, for the war, for public opinion . . . even for the interest of their child! . . . Yet, it came to him, the image of her that he had just seen had been the image of Sylvia standing at attention, her mouth working a little, whilst she read out the figures beside the bright filament of mercury in a thermometer. . . . The child had had, with measles, a temperature that, even then, he did not dare think of. And—it was at his sister's in Yorkshire, and the local doctor hadn't cared to take the responsibility—he could still feel the warmth of the little mummy-like body; he had covered the head and face with a flannel, for he didn't care for the sight, and lowered the warm, terrible, fragile weight into a shining surface of crushed ice in water. . . . She had stood at attention, the corners of her mouth moving a little: the thermometer going down as you watched it. . . . So that she mightn't want, in damaging the father, atrociously to damage the child. . . . For there could not be anything worse for a child than to have a mother known as a whore. . . .

Sergeant-Major Cowley was standing beside the table. He said:

"Wouldn't it be a good thing, sir, to send a runner to the depot sergeant cook and tell him we're going to indent for suppers for the draft? We could send the other with the one-twenty-eights to Quarter. They're neither wanted here for the moment."

The other captain went on incessantly talking—but about his fabulous uncle, not about Sylvia. It was difficult for Tietjens to get what he wanted said. He wanted the second runner sent to the depot quartermaster with a message to the effect that if G.S. candles for hooded lamps were not provided for the use of his orderly room by return of bearer, he, Captain Tietjens, commanding Number XVI Casual Battalion, would bring the whole matter of supplies for his battalion that same night before base headquarters. They were all three talking at once: heavy fatalism overwhelmed Tietjens at the thought of the stubbornness showed by the depot quartermaster. The big unit beside his camp was a weary obstinacy of obstruction. You would have thought they would have displayed some eagerness to get his men up into the line. Let alone that the men were urgently needed, the more of his men went, the more of *them* stayed behind. Yet they tried to stop his meat, his groceries, his braces, his identification disks, his soldiers' small books. . . . Every imaginable hindrance, and not even self-interested common sense! . . . He managed also to convey to Sergeant-Major Cowley that as everything seemed to have quieted down, the Canadian sergeant-major had better go and see if everything was ready for falling his draft in. . . . If things remained quiet for another ten minutes, the "all clear" might then be expected. . . . He knew that Sergeant-Major Cowley wanted to get the Other Ranks out of the hut with that captain carrying on like that, and he did not see why the old N.C.O. should not have what he wanted.

It was as if a tender and masculine butler withdrew himself. Cowley's grey walrus moustache and scarlet cheeks showed for a moment beside the brazier, whispering at the ears of the runners, a hand kindly on each of their shoulders. The runners went; the Canadian went. Sergeant-Major Cowley, his form blocking the doorway, surveyed the stars. He found it difficult to realize that the same pin-pricks of light through black manifolding paper as he looked at looked down also on his villa and his elderly wife at Isleworth beside the Thames above London. He knew it to be the fact, yet it was difficult to realize. He imagined the trams going along the High Street, his missis in one of them with her supper in a string bag on her stout knees. The trams lit up and shining. He imagined her having kippers for supper: ten to one it would be kippers. Her favourites. His daughter was in the Waacs by now. She had been cashier to Parks's, the big butchers in Brentford, and pretty she had used to look in the glass case. Like as if it might have been the British Museum, where they had pharaohs and others in glass cases . . . There were threshing-machines droning away all over the night. He always said they were like threshing-machines. . . . Crikey, if only they were! . . . But they might be our own planes, of course. A good Welsh rarebit he had had for tea.

In the hut, the light from the brazier having fewer limbs on which to fall, a sort of intimacy seemed to descend, and Tietjens felt himself gain in ability to deal with his mad friend. Captain Mackenzie—Tietjens was not sure that the name was Mackenzie: it had looked something like it in the general's hand—Captain Mackenzie was going on about the wrongs he had suffered at the hands of some fabulous uncle. Apparently at some important juncture the uncle had refused to acknowledge acquaintanceship with the nephew. From that all the misfortunes of the nephew had arisen. . . . Suddenly Tietjens said:

"Look here, pull yourself together. Are you mad? Stark, staring? . . . Or only just play-acting?"

The man suddenly sank down on to the bully-beef case that served for a chair. He stammered a question as to what —what—what Tietjens meant.

"If you let yourself go," Tietjens said, "you may let yourself go a tidy sight farther than you want to."

"You're not a mad-doctor," the other said. "It's no good your trying to come it over me. I know all about you. I've got an uncle who's done the dirty on me—the dirtiest dirty ever was done on a man. If it hadn't been for him I shouldn't be here now."

"You talk as if the fellow had sold you into slavery," Tietjens said.

"He's your closest friend," Mackenzie seemed to advance as a motive for revenge on Tietjens. "He's a friend of the general's, too. Of your wife's as well. He's in with everyone."

A few desultory, pleasurable "pop-op-ops" sounded from far overhead to the left.

"They imagine they've found the Hun again," Tietjens said. "That's all right; you concentrate on your uncle. Only don't exaggerate his importance to the world. I assure you you are mistaken if you call him a friend of mine. I have not got a friend in the world." He added: "Are you going to mind the noise? If it is going to get on your nerves you can walk in a dignified manner to a dug-out, now, before it gets bad. . . ." He called out to Cowley to go and tell the Canadian sergeant-major to get his men back into their shelters if they had come out. Until the "all clear" went.

Captain Mackenzie sat himself gloomily down at table.

"Damn it all," he said, "don't think I'm afraid of a little shrapnel. I've had two periods solid of fourteen and nine months in the line. I could have got out on to the rotten staff. . . . It's, damn it: it's the beastly row. . . . Why isn't one a beastly girl and privileged to shriek? By God, I'll get even with some of them one of these days. . . ."

"Why not shriek?" Tietjens asked. "You can, for me. No one's going to doubt your courage here."

Loud drops as of rain spattered down all round the hut; there was a familiar thud on the ground a yard or so away, a sharp tearing sound above, a sharper knock on the table between them. Mackenzie took the shrapnel bullet that had fallen and turned it round and round between finger and thumb.

"You think you caught me on the hop just now," he said injuriously. "You're damn clever."

Two stories down below someone let two hundred-pound dumb-bells drop on the drawing-room carpet; all the windows of the house slammed in a race to get it over; the "pop-op-ops" of the shrapnel went in wafts all over the air. There was again sudden silence that was painful, after you had braced yourself up to bear noise. The runner from the Rhondda came in with a light step, bearing two fat candles. He took the hooded lamps from Tietjens and began to press the candles up against the inner springs, snorting sedulously through his nostrils. . . .

"Nearly got me, one of those candlesticks did," he said. "Touched my foot as it fell, it did. I did run. Surely to goodness I did run, cahptn."

Inside the shrapnel shell was an iron bar with a flattened, broad nose. When the shell burst in the air this iron object fell to the ground, and since it came often from a great height, its fall was dangerous. The men called these candle-sticks, which they much resembled.

A little ring of light now existed on the puce colour of the blanket-covered table. Tietjens showed, silver-headed, fresh-coloured and bulky; Mackenzie, dark, revengeful eyes above a prognathous jaw. A very thin man; thirtyish.

"You can go into the shelter with the colonial troops if you like," Tietjens said to the runner. The man answered after a pause, being very slow thinking, that he preferred to wait for his mate, 09 Morgan, whatever.

"They ought to let my orderly room have tin hats," Tietjens said to Mackenzie. "I'm damned if they didn't take these fellows' tin hats into store again when they attached to me for service, and I'm equally damned if they did not tell me that if I wanted tin hats for my own headquarters, I had to write to H.Q. Canadians, Aldershot, or some such place in order to get the issue sanctioned."

"Our headquarters are full of Huns doing the Huns' work," Mackenzie said hatefully. "I'd like to get among them one of these days."

Tietjens looked with some attention at that young man with the Rembrandt shadows over his dark face. He said:

"Do you believe that tripe?"

The young man said:

"No . . . I don't know that I do. . . . I don't know what to think. . . . The world's rotten. . . ."

"Oh, the world's pretty rotten, all right," Tietjens answered. And, in his fatigue of mind caused by having to attend to innumerable concrete facts like the providing of households for a thousand men every few days, arranging parade states for an extraordinarily mixed set of troops of all arms with very mixed drills, and fighting the Assistant Provost Marshal to keep his own men out of the clutches of the beastly garrison Military Police, who had got a down on all Canadians, he felt he had not any curiosity at all left. . . . Yet he felt vaguely that at the back of his mind, there was some reason for trying to cure this young member of the lower-middle classes.

He repeated:

"Yes, the world's certainly pretty rotten. But that's not its particular line of rottenness as far as we are concerned. . . . We're tangled up, not because we've got Huns in our orderly rooms, but just because we've got English. That's the bat in our belfry. . . . That Hun plane is presumably coming back. Half a dozen of them . . ."

The young man, his mind eased by having got off his chest a confounded lot of semi-nonsensical ravings, considered the return of the Hun planes with gloomy indifference. His problem really was: could he stand the —— noise that would probably accompany their return? He had to get really into his head that this was an open space to all intents and purposes. There would not be splinters of stone flying about. He was ready to be hit by iron, steel, lead, copper, or brass shell rims, but not by beastly splinters of stone knocked off house-fronts. That consideration had come to him during his beastly, his beastly, his infernal, damnable leave in London, when just such a filthy row had been going on. . . . Divorce leave! . . . Captain McKechnie, second attached Ninth Glamorganshires, is granted leave from the 14/11 to the 29/11 for the purpose of obtaining a divorce. . . . The memory seemed to burst inside him with the noise of one of those beastly, enormous tin-pot crashes—and it always came when guns made that particular kind of tin-pot crash: the two came together, the internal one and the crash outside. He felt that chimney-pots were going to crash on to his head. You protected yourself by shouting at damned, infernal idiots: if you could outshout the row you were safe. . . . That was not sensible, but you got ease that way! . . .

"In matters of information they're not a patch on us." Tietjens tried the speech on cautiously and concluded: "We know what the enemy rulers read in the sealed envelopes beside their breakfast bacon-and-egg plates."

It had occurred to him that it was a military duty to bother himself about the mental equilibrium of this member of the lower classes. So he talked . . . *any* old talk, wearisomely, to keep his mind employed! Captain Mackenzie was an officer of His Majesty the King: the property, body and soul, of His Majesty and His Majesty's War Office. It was Tietjens' duty to preserve this fellow as it was his duty to prevent deterioration in any other piece of the King's property. That was implicit in the oath of allegiance. He went on talking:

The curse of the army, as far as the organization is concerned, was our imbecile national belief that the game is more than the player. That was our ruin, mentally, as a nation. We were taught that cricket is more than clearness of mind, so the blasted quartermaster, O.C. Depot Ordnance Stores next door, thought he had taken a wicket if he refused to serve out tin hats to their crowd. That's the game! And if any of his, Tietjens', men were killed, he grinned and said the game was more than the players of the game. . . . And of course if he got his bowling average down low enough he got promotion. There was a quartermaster in a West Country cathedral city who'd got more D.S.O.s and combatant medals than anyone on active service in France, from the sea to Peronne, or wherever our lines ended. His achievement was to have robbed almost every wretched Tommy in the Western command of several weeks' separation allowance . . . for the good of the taxpayer, of course. The poor —— Tommies' kids went without proper food and clothing, and the Tommies themselves had been in a state of exasperation and resentment. And nothing in the world was worse for discipline and the army as a fighting machine. But there that quartermaster sat in his office, playing the romantic game over his A.F.B.s till the broad buff sheets fairly glowed in the light of the incandescent gas. "And," Tietjens concluded, "for every quarter of a million sterling for which he bowls out the wretched fighting men, he gets a new clasp on his fourth D.S.O. ribbon. . . . The game, in short, is more than the players of the game."

"Oh, damn it!" Captain Mackenzie said. "That's what's made us what we are, isn't it?"

"It is," Tietjens answered. "It's got us into the hole and it keeps us there."

Mackenzie remained dispiritedly looking down at his fingers.

"You may be wrong or you may be right," he said. "It's contrary to everything that I ever heard. But I see what you mean."

"At the beginning of the war," Tietjens said, "I had to look in on the War Office, and in a room I found a fellow. . . . What do you think he was doing . . . what the hell do you think he was doing? He was devising the ceremonial for the disbanding of a Kitchener battalion. You can't say we were not prepared in one matter at least. . . . Well, the end of the show was to be: the adjutant would stand the battalion at ease: the band would play 'Land of Hope and Glory,' and then the adjutant would say: *There will be no more parades.* . . . Don't you see how symbolical it was: the band playing 'Land of Hope and Glory,' and then the adjutant saying *There will be no more parades?* . . . For there won't. There won't, there damn well won't. . . . No more Hope, no more Glory, no more parades for you and me any more. Nor for the country . . . Nor for the world, I dare say . . . None . . . Gone . . . Napoo finny! No . . . more . . . parades!"

"I dare say you're right," the other said slowly. "But, all the same, what am I doing in this show? I hate soldiering. I hate this whole beastly business. . . ."

"Then why didn't you go on the gaudy staff?" Tietjens asked. "The gaudy staff apparently was yearning to have you. I bet God intended you for intelligence: not for the foot-slogging department."

The other said wearily:

"I don't know. I was with the battalion. I wanted to stop with the battalion. I was intended for the Foreign Office. My miserable uncle got me hoofed out of that. I was with the battalion. The C.O. wasn't up to much. *Someone* had to stay with the battalion. I was not going to do the dirty on it, taking any soft job. . . ."

"I suppose you speak seven languages and all?" Tietjens asked.

"Five," the other said patiently, "and read two more. And Latin and Greek, of course."

A man, brown, stiff, with a haughty parade step, burst into the light. He said with a high wooden voice:

"'Ere's another bloomin' casualty." In the shadow he appeared to have draped half his face and the right side of his breast with crape. He gave a high, rattling laugh. He bent, as if in a stiff bow, woodenly at his thighs. He pitched, still bent, onto the iron sheet that covered the brazier, rolled off that and lay on his back across the legs of the other runner, who had been crouched beside the brazier. In the bright light it was as if a whole pail of scarlet paint had been dashed across the man's face on the left and his chest. It glistened in the fire-light—just like fresh paint, moving! The runner from the Rhondda, pinned down by the body across his knees, sat with his jaw fallen, resembling one girl that should be combing the hair of another, recumbent before her. The red viscousness welled across the floor; you some-

times so see fresh water bubbling up in sand. It astonished
Tietjens to see that a human body could be so lavish of blood.
He was thinking it was a queer mania that that fellow should
have, that his uncle was a friend of his, Tietjens. He had
no friend in trade, uncle of a fellow who in ordinary times
would probably bring you pairs of boots on approval. . . .
He felt as he did when you patch up a horse that has been
badly hurt. He remembered a horse from a cut on whose
chest the blood had streamed down over the off foreleg like
a stocking. A girl had lent him her petticoat to bandage it.
Nevertheless his legs moved slowly and heavily across the
floor.

The heat from the brazier was overpowering on his bent
face. He hoped he would not get his hands all over blood,
because blood is very sticky. It makes your fingers stick
together impotently. But there might not be any blood in
the darkness under the fellow's back where he was putting
his hand. There was, however: it was very wet.

The voice of Sergeant-Major Cowley said from outside:

"Bugler, call two sanitary lance-corporals and four men.
Two sanitary corporals and four men." A prolonged wailing
with interruptions transfused the night, mournful, resigned,
and prolonged.

Tietjens thought that, thank God, someone would come
and relieve him of that job. It was a breathless affair,
holding up the corpse with the fire burning his face. He said
to the other runner:

"Get out from under him, damn you! Are you hurt?"
Mackenzie could not get at the body from the other side
because of the brazier. The runner from under the corpse
moved with short, sitting shuffles as if he were getting his
legs out from under a sofa. He was saying:

"Poor —— O Nine Morgan! Surely to goodness I did
not recognice the pore —— . . . Surely to goodness I did not
recognice the pore ——"

Tietjens let the trunk of the body sink slowly to the floor.
He was more gentle than if the man had been alive. All
hell in the way of noise burst about the world. Tietjens'
thoughts seemed to have to shout to him between earthquake
shocks. He was thinking it was absurd of that fellow Mackenzie to imagine that he could know any uncle of his. He
saw very vividly also the face of his girl, who was a pacifist.
It worried him not to know what expression her face would
have if she heard of his occupation now. Disgust? . . . He
was standing with his greasy, sticky hands held out from the

flaps of his tunic. . . . Perhaps disgust! . . . It was impossible
to think in this row. . . . His very thick soles moved gluily
and came up after suction. . . . He remembered he had not
sent a runner along to I.B.D. orderly room to see how many
of his crowd would be wanted for garrison fatigue next day,
and this annoyed him acutely. He would have no end of a
job warning the officers he detailed. They would all be in
brothels down in the town by now. . . . He could not work out
what the girl's expression would be. He was never to see her
again, so what the hell did it matter? . . . Disgust, probably!
. . . He remembered that he had not looked to see how
Mackenzie was getting on in the noise. He did not want to
see Mackenzie. He was a bore. . . . How would her face
express disgust? He had never seen her express disgust. She
had a perfectly undistinguished face. Fair . . . Oh, God,
how suddenly his bowels turned over! . . . Thinking of the
girl . . . The face below him grinned at the roof—the half-
face! The nose was there, half the mouth with the teeth
showing in the fire-light. . . . It was extraordinary how de-
fined the peaked nose and the serrated teeth were in that
mess. . . . The eye looked jauntily at the peak of the canvas
hut-roof. . . . Gone with a grin. Singular the fellow should
have spoken! After he was dead. He must have been dead
when he spoke. It had been done with the last air automatically going out of the lungs. A reflex action, probably, in the
dead . . . If he, Tietjens, had given the fellow the leave he
wanted, he would be alive now! . . . Well, he was quite right
not to have given the poor devil his leave. He was, anyhow,
better where he was. And so was he, Tietjens. He had not
had a single letter from home since he had been out this
time! Not a single letter. Not even gossip. Not a bill. Some
circulars of old-furniture dealers. They never neglected him!
They had got beyond the sentimental stage at home. Obviously so . . . He wondered if his bowels would turn over
again if he thought of the girl. He was gratified that they
had. It showed that he had strong feelings. . . . He thought
about her deliberately. Hard. Nothing happened. He thought
of her fair, undistinguished, fresh face that made your heart
miss a beat when you thought about it. His heart missed a
beat. Obedient heart! Like the first primrose. Not *any* primrose. The *first* primrose. Under a bank with the hounds
breaking through the underwood . . . It was sentimental to
say *Du bist wie eine blume.* . . . Damn the German language! But that fellow was a Jew. . . . One should not say
that one's young woman was like *a* flower, *any* flower. Not

even to oneself. That was sentimental. But one might say one special flower. A *man* could say that. A man's job. She smelt like a primrose when you kissed her. But, damn it, he had never kissed her. So how did he know how she smelt! She was a little tranquil, golden spot. He himself must be a —— eunuch. By temperament. That dead fellow down there must be one, physically. It was probably indecent to think of a corpse as impotent. But he was, very likely. That would be why his wife had taken up with the prize-fighter Red Evans Williams of Castell Goch. If he had given the fellow leave the prize-fighter would have smashed him to bits. The police of Pontardulais had asked that he should not be let come home—because of the prize-fighter. So he was better dead. Or perhaps not. Is death better than discovering that your wife is a whore and being done in by her cully? *Gwell angau na gwillth*—their own regimental badge bore the words. *"Death is better than dishonour. . . ."* No, not death, *angau* means pain. Anguish! Anguish is better than dishonour. The devil it is! Well, that fellow would have got both. Anguish and dishonour. Dishonour from his wife and anguish when the prize-fighter hit him . . . That was, no doubt, why his half-face grinned at the roof. The gory side of it had turned brown. Already! Like a mummy of a pharaoh, *that* half looked. . . . He was born to be a blooming casualty. Either by shell-fire or by the fist of the prize-fighter . . . Pontardulais! Somewhere in mid-Wales. He had been through it once in a car, on duty. A long, dull village. Why should anyone want to go back to it? . . .

A tender butler's voice said beside him: "This ain't your job, sir. Sorry you had to do it . . . Lucky it wasn't you, sir . . . This was what done it, I should say."

Sergeant-Major Cowley was standing beside him holding a bit of metal that was heavy in his hand and like a candlestick. He was aware that a moment before, he had seen the fellow, Mackenzie, bending over the brazier, putting the sheet of iron back. Careful officer, Mackenzie. The Huns must not be allowed to see the light from the brazier. The edge of the sheet had gone down on the dead man's tunic, nipping a bit by the shoulder. The face had disappeared in shadow. There were several men's faces in the doorway.

Tietjens said: "No: I don't believe that did it. Something bigger . . . Say, a prize-fighter's fist . . ."

Sergeant Cowley said:

"No, no prize-fighter's fist would have done that, sir. . . ."

And then he added, "Oh, I take your meaning, sir. . . . O Nine Morgan's wife, sir . . ."

Tietjens moved, his feet sticking, towards the sergeant-major's table. The other runner had placed a tin basin with water on it. There was a hooded candle there now, alight; the water shone innocently, a half-moon of translucence wavering over the white bottom of the basin. The runner from Pontardulais said:

"Wash your hands first, sir!"

He said:

"Move a little out of it, cahptn." He had a rag in his black hands. Tietjens moved out of the blood that had run in a thin stream under the table. The man was on his knees, his hands rubbing Tietjens' boot-welts heavily, with the rags. Tietjens placed his hands in the innocent water and watched light purple-scarlet mist diffuse itself over the pale half-moon. The man below him breathed heavily, sniffing. Tietjens said:

"Thomas, O Nine Morgan was your mate?"

The man's face, wrinkled, dark and apelike, looked up.

"He was a good pal, pore old ——," he said. "You would not like, surely to goodness, to go to mess with your shoes all bloody."

"If I had given him leave," Tietjens said, "he would not be dead now."

"No, surely not," One Seven Thomas answered. "But it is all one. Evans of Castell Goch would surely to goodness have killed him."

"So you knew, too, about his wife!" Tietjens said.

"We thocht it wass that," One Seven Thomas answered, "or you would have given him leave, cahptn. You are a good cahptn."

A sudden sense of the publicity that that life was came over Tietjens.

"You knew that," he said. "I wonder what the hell you fellows don't know and all!" he thought. "If anything went wrong with one it would be all over the command in two days. Thank God Sylvia can't get here!"

The man had risen to his feet. He fetched a towel of the sergeant-major's, very white with a red border.

"We know," he said, "that your honour is a very goot cahptn. And Captain McKechnie is a *fery* goot cahptn. And Captain Prentiss and Le'tenant Jonce of Merthyr . . ."

Tietjens said:

"That'll do. Tell the sergeant-major to give you a pass to

go with your mate to the hospital. Get someone to wash this floor."

Two men were carrying the remains of 09 Morgan, the trunk wrapped in a ground sheet. They carried him in a bandy chair out of the hut. His arms over their shoulders waved a jocular farewell. There would be an ambulance stretcher on bicycle wheels outside.

2 ~

THE "all clear" went at once after that. Its suddenness was something surprising, the mournful-cheerful, long notes dying regretfully on a night that had only just gone quiet after the perfectly astonishing row. The moon had taken it into its head to rise; begumboiled, jocular and grotesque, it came from behind the shoulder of one of the hut-covered hills and sent down the lines of Tietjens' huts long, sentimental rays that converted the place into a slumbering, pastoral settlement. There was no sound that did not contribute to the silence; little dim lights shone through the celluloid casements. Of Sergeant-Major Cowley, his numerals gilded by the moon in the lines of A Company, Tietjens, who was easing his lungs of coke-vapours for a minute, asked in a voice that hushed itself in tribute to the moonlight and the now keen frost:

"Where the deuce is the draft?"

The sergeant-major looked poetically down a ribbon of whitewashed stones that descended the black downside. Over the next shoulder of hill was the blur of a hidden conflagration.

"There's a Hun plane burning down there. In Twenty-seven's parade-ground. The draft's round that, sir," he said.

Tietjens said:

"Good God!" in a voice of caustic tolerance. He added, "I did think we had drilled some discipline into these blighters in the seven weeks we have had them. . . . You remember the first time when we had them on parade and that acting lance-corporal left the ranks to heave a rock at a sea-gull. . . . And called you Ol' Hunkey! . . . Conduct prejudicial to good order and military discipline? Where's that Canadian sergeant-major? Where's the officer in charge of the draft?"

Sergeant-Major Cowley said:

"Sergeant-Major Ledoux said it was like a cattle-stampede on the . . . some river where they come from. You *couldn't* stop them, sir. It was their first German plane. . . . And they going up the line to-night, sir."

"To-night!" Tietjens exclaimed. "Next Christmas!"

The sergeant-major said:

"Poor boys!" and continued to gaze into the distance. "I heard another good one, sir," he said. "The answer to the one about the King saluting a private soldier and he not taking any notice is: when he's dead. . . . But if you marched a company into a field through a gateway and you wanted to get it out again but you did not know any command in the drill-book for change of direction, what would you do, sir? . . . You have to get that company out, but you must not use about turn, or right or left wheel. . . . There's another one, too, about saluting. . . . The officer in charge of draft is Second-Lieutenant Hotchkiss. . . . But he's an A.S.C. officer and turned of sixty. A farrier he is, sir, in civil life. An A.S.C. major was asking me, sir, very civil, if you could not detail someone else. He says he doubts if Second-Lieutenant Hitchcock . . . Hotchkiss could walk as far as the station, let alone march the men, him not knowing anything but cavalry words of command, if he knows them. He's only been in the army a fortnight. . . ."

Tietjens turned from the idyllic scene with the words:

"I suppose the Canadian sergeant-major and Lieutenant Hotchkiss are doing what they can to get their men to come back."

He re-entered the hut.

Captain Mackenzie in the light of a fantastically brilliant hurricane-lamp appeared to be bathing dejectedly in a surf of coiling papers spread on the table before him.

"There's all this bumph," he said, "just come from all the headquarters in the bally world."

Tietjens said cheerfully:

"What's it all about?" There were, the other answered, garrison headquarter orders, divisional orders, lines of communication orders, half a dozen A.F.B.W. two-four-twos. A terrific strafe from First Army forwarded from garrison H.Q. about the draft's not having reached Hazebrouck the day before yesterday. Tietjens said:

"Answer them politely to the effect that we had orders not to send off the draft without its complement of four hundred Canadian Railway Service men—the fellows in furred hoods. They only reached us from Étaples at five this afternoon without blankets or ring papers. Or any other papers, for the matter of that."

Mackenzie was studying with increased gloom a small buff memorandum slip:

"This appears to be meant for you privately," he said. "I can't make head or tail of it otherwise. It isn't *marked* private."

He tossed the buff slip across the table.

Tietjens sank down bulkily on to his bully-beef case. He read on the buff at first the initials of the signature, "E. C. Genl.," and then: "For God's sake keep your wife off me. I *will* not have skirts round my H.Q. You are more trouble to me than all the rest of my command put together."

Tietjens groaned and sank more deeply on to his beef case. It was as if an unseen and unsuspected wild beast had jumped on his neck from an overhanging branch. The sergeant-major at his side said in his most admirable butler manner:

"Colour-Sergeant Morgan and Lance-Corporal Trench are obliging us by coming from depot orderly room to help with the draft's papers. Why don't you and the other officer go and get a bit of dinner, sir? The colonel and the padre have only just come in to mess, and I've warned the mess orderlies to keep your foods 'ot. . . . Both good men with papers, Morgan and Trench. We can send the soldiers' small books to you at table to sign. . . ."

His feminine solicitude enraged and overwhelmed Tietjens with blackness. He told the sergeant-major that he was to go to hell, for he himself was not going to leave that hut till the draft was moved off. Captain Mackenzie could do as he pleased. The sergeant-major told Captain Mackenzie that Captain Tietjens took as much trouble with his rag-time detachments as if he had been the Coldstream adjutant at Chelsea sending off a draft of guards. Captain Mackenzie said that that was why they damn well got their details off four days faster than any other I.B.D. in that camp. He *would* say that much, he added grudgingly, and dropped his head over his papers again. The hut was moving slowly up and down before the eyes of Tietjens. He might have just been kicked in the stomach. That was how shocks took him. He said to himself that by God he must take himself in hand. He grabbed with his heavy hands at a piece of buff paper and wrote on it in a column of fat, wet letters

a
b
b
a
a
b
b
a

and so on.

He said opprobriously to Captain Mackenzie:

"Do you know what a sonnet is? Give me the rhymes for a sonnet. That's the plan of it."

Mackenzie grumbled:

"Of course I know what a sonnet is. What's your game?"

Tietjens said:

"Give me the fourteen end-rhymes of a sonnet and I'll write the lines. In under two minutes and a half."

Mackenzie said injuriously:

"If you do I'll turn it into Latin hexameters in three. In *under* three minutes."

They were like men uttering deadly insults the one to the other. To Tietjens it was as if an immense cat were parading, fascinated and fatal, round that hut. He had imagined himself parted from his wife. He had not heard from his wife since her four-in-the-morning departure from their flat, months and eternities ago, with the dawn just showing up the chimney-pots of the Georgian roof-trees opposite. In the complete stillness of dawn he had heard her voice say very clearly "Paddington" to the chauffeur, and then all the sparrows in the inn waking up in chorus. . . . Suddenly and appallingly it came into his head that it might not have been his wife's voice that had said "Paddington," but her maid's. . . . He was a man who lived very much by rules of conduct. He had a rule: *Never think on the subject of a shock at a moment of shock.* The mind was then too sensitized. Subjects of shock require to be thought all round. If your mind thinks when it is too sensitized its then conclusions will be too strong. So he exclaimed to Mackenzie:

"Haven't you got your rhymes yet? Damn it *all!*"

Mackenzie grumbled offensively:

"No, I haven't. It's more difficult to get rhymes than to

write sonnets . . . death, moil, coil, breath. . . ." He paused.

"Heath, soil, toil, staggereth," Tietjens said contemptuously. "That's your sort of Oxford young woman's rhyme. . . . Go on . . . *What is it?*"

An extremely age-faded and unmilitary officer was beside the blanketed table. Tietjens regretted having spoken to him with ferocity. He had a grotesquely thin white beard. Positively, white whiskers! He must have gone through as much of the army as he had gone through, with those whiskers, because no superior officer—not even a field-marshal—would have the heart to tell him to take them off! It was the measure of his pathos. This ghostlike object was apologizing for not having been able to keep the draft in hand: he was requesting his superior to observe that these colonial troops were without any instincts of discipline. None at all. Tietjens observed that he had a blue cross on his right arm where the vaccination marks are as a rule. He imagined the Canadians talking to this hero. . . . The hero began to talk of Major Cornwallis of the R.A.S.C.

Tietjens said, apropos of nothing:

"Is there a Major Cornwallis in the A.S.C.? Good God!"

The hero protested faintly:

"The *R.A.S.C.*"

Tietjens said kindly:

"Yes. Yes. The *Royal* Army Service Corps."

Obviously his mind until now had regarded his wife's *"Paddington"* as the definite farewell between his life and hers. . . . He had imagined her, like Eurydice, tall, but faint and pale, sinking back into the shades. . . . *"Che faro senz' Eurydice? . . ."* he hummed. Absurd! And of course it might have been only the maid that had spoken. . . . She too had a remarkably clear voice. So that the mystic word "Paddington" might perfectly well be no symbol at all, and Mrs. Sylvia Tietjens, far from being faint and pale, might perfectly well be playing the very devil with half the general officers commanding-in-chief from Whitehall to Alaska.

Mackenzie—he *was* like a damned clerk—was transferring the rhymes that he had no doubt at last found on to another sheet of paper. Probably he had a round, copy-book hand. Positively, his tongue followed his pen round, inside his lips. These were what His Majesty's regular officers of to-day were. Good God! A damned intelligent, dark-looking fellow. Of the type that is starved in its youth and takes all the scholarships that the board-schools have to offer. Eyes

too big and black. Like a Malay's . . . Any blasted member
of any subject race.

The A.S.C. fellow had been talking positively about
horses. He had offered his services in order to study
the variation of pink-eye that was decimating all the service
horses in the lines. He had been a professor—positively a
professor—in some farriery college or other. Tietjens said
that in that case, he ought to be in the A.V.C.—the *Royal
Army Veterinary Corps*, perhaps it was. The old man
said he didn't know. He imagined that the R.A.S.C. had
wanted his services for their own horses. . . .

Tietjens said:

"I'll tell you what to do, Lieutenant Hitchcock. . . . For,
damn it, you're a stout fellow . . ." The poor old fellow,
pushing out at that age from the cloisters of some provincial
university . . . He certainly did not look a horsy sportsman. . . .

The old lieutenant said:

"Hotchkiss . . ." And Tietjens exclaimed:

"Of course it's Hotchkiss. . . . I've seen your name signing a testimonial to Pigg's Horse Embrocation. . . . Then
if you don't want to take this draft up the line . . . Though
I'd advise you to . . . It's merely a Cook's tour to Hazebrouck. . . . No, Bailleul . . . And the sergeant-major will
march the men for you. . . . And you will have been in the
First Army lines and able to tell all your friends you've been
on active service at the real front. . . ."

His mind said to himself while his words went on:

"Then, good God, if Sylvia is actively paying attention
to my career I shall be the laughing-stock of the whole
army. I was thinking that ten minutes ago! . . . What's to be
done? What in God's name is to be done?" A black crape
veil seemed to drop across his vision. . . . Liver . . .

Lieutenant Hotchkiss said with dignity:

"I'm *going* to the front. I'm going to the real front. I
was passed A-one this morning. I am going to study the
blood reactions of the service horse under fire."

"Well, you're a damn good chap," Tietjens said. There
was nothing to be done. The amazing activities of which
Sylvia would be capable were just the thing to send laughter
raging like fire through a cachinnating army. She could not,
thank God, get into France: to that place. But she could
make scandals in the papers that every Tommy read. There
was no game of which she was not capable. That sort
of pursuit was called "pulling the strings of shower-baths"

in her circle of friends. Nothing. Nothing to be done. . . .
the beastly hurricane-lamp was smoking.

"I'll tell you what to do," he said to Lieutenant Hotchkiss.

Mackenzie had tossed his sheet of rhymes under his nose.
Tietjens read: *Death, moil, coil, breath* . . . *saith*—"The dirty
Cockney!" *Oil, soil, wraith* . . .

"I'd be blowed," Mackenzie said with a vicious grin, "if
I was going to give you rhymes you had suggested yourself . . ."

The officer said:

"I don't, of course, want to be a nuisance if you're busy."

"It's no nuisance," Tietjens said. "It's what we're for. But
I'd suggest that now and then you say 'sir' to the officer
commanding your unit. It sounds well before the men. . . .
Now, you go to Number Sixteen I.B.D. mess ante-room. . . .
The place where they've got the broken bagatelle-table. . ."

The voice of Sergeant-Major Cowley exclaimed tranquilly
from outside:

"Fall in, now. Men who've got their ring papers and
identity disks—three of them—on the left. Men who haven't,
on the right. Any man who has not been able to draw
his blankets, tell Colour-Sergeant Morgan. Don't forget. You
won't get anywhere you're going. Any man who hasn't made
his will in his soldier's small book or elsewhere and wants to,
to consult Captain Tietjens. Any man who wants to draw
money, ask Captain Mackenzie. Any R.C. who wants to go to
confession after he has got his papers signed can find the
R.C. padre in the fourth hut from the left in the main
line from here. . . . And damn kind it is of his reverence
to put himself out for a set of damn blinking mustard-
faced red herrings like you who can't keep from running
away to the first baby's bonfire you sees. You'll be running
the other way before you're a week older, though what
good they as asks for you thinks you'll be out there God
knows. You *look* like a squad of infants' companions from
a Wesleyan Sunday-school. That's what you look like, and
thank God we've got a navy."

Under cover of his voice Tietjens had been writing:

"Now we affront the grinning chops of *Death*," and saying to Lieutenant Hotchkiss: "In the I.B.D. ante-room you'll
find any number of dirty little squits of Glamorganshires
drinking themselves blind over *La Vie Parisienne*. . . . Ask
any one of them you like. . . ." He wrote:

"And in between our carcass and the *moil*
  Of marts and cities, toil and moil and *coil*. . ."

"You think this difficult!" he said to Mackenzie. "Why,
you've written a whole undertaker's mortuary ode in the
rhymes alone," and went on to Hotchkiss: "Ask anyone
you like as long as he's a P.B. officer. . . . Do you know what
'P.B.' means? No, not Poor B——y, Permanent Base. Unfit
. . . If he'd like to take a draft to Bailleul."

The hut was filling with devious, slow, ungainly men in
yellow-brown. Their feet shuffled desultorily; they lumped
dull canvas bags along the floor and held in unliterary
hands small open books that they dropped from time to
time. From outside came a continuing, swelling and descending chant of voices; at times it would seem to be all
one laugh, at times one menace, then the motives mingled
fugally, like the sea on a beach of large stones. It seemed
to Tietjens suddenly extraordinary how shut in on oneself
one was in this life. . . . He sat scribbling fast: "Old Spectre
blows a cold protecting *breath*. . . . Vanity of vanities, the
preacher *saith*. . . . No more parades, not any more, no
oil . . ." He was telling Hotchkiss, who was obviously shy
of approaching the Glamorganshires in their ante-room . . .
"Unambergris'd our limbs in the naked *soil*" . . . that he
did not suppose any P.B. officer would object. They would
go on a bean-feast up into the giddy line in a first-class
carriage and get draft leave and command pay too, probably. . . . "No funeral struments cast before our wraiths . . ."
If any fellow does object, you just send his name to
me and I will damn well shove it into extra orders. . . .

The advanced wave of the brown tide of men was already at his feet. The extraordinary complications of even
the simplest lives! . . . A fellow was beside him . . . Private
Logan, formerly, of all queer things for a Canadian private,
a trooper of the Inniskillings: owner, of all queer things,
of a milk-walk or a dairy-farm outside Sydney, which is
in Australia . . . A man of sentimental complications,
jauntiness as became an Inniskilling, a Cockney accent such
as ornaments the inhabitants of Sydney, and a complete
distrust of lawyers. On the other hand, with the completest
trust in Tietjens. Over his shoulder—he was blond, upright,
with his numerals shining like gold—looked a lumpish, *café-
au-lait*, eagle-nosed countenance: a half-caste member of
one of the Six Nations, who had been a doctor's errand boy
in Quebec. . . . He had his troubles, but was difficult to un-

derstand. Behind him, very black-avised with a high colour, truculent eyes and an Irish accent, was a graduate of Mc-Gill University who had been a teacher of languages in Tokyo and had some sort of claim against the Japanese government. . . . And faces, two and two, in a coil round the hut . . . Like dust: like a cloud of dust that would approach and overwhelm a landscape: every one with preposterous troubles and anxieties, even if they did not overwhelm you personally with them . . . Brown dust . . .

He kept the Inniskilling waiting while he scribbled the rapid sestet to his sonnet, which ought to make a little plainer what it all meant. Of course the general idea was that when you got into the line or near it, there was no room for swank: typified by expensive funerals. As you might say: No flowers by compulsion . . . No more parades! . . . He had also to explain, while he did it, to the heroic veterinary sexagenarian that he need not feel shy about going into the Glamorganshire mess on a man-catching expedition. The Glamorganshires were bound to lend him, Tietjens, P.B. officers if they had not got other jobs. Lieutenant Hotchkiss could speak to Colonel Johnson, whom he would find in the mess and quite good-natured over his dinner. A pleasant and sympathetic old gentleman who would appreciate Hotchkiss's desire not to go superfluously into the line. Hotchkiss could offer to take a look at the colonel's charger: a Hun horse, captured on the Marne and called Schomburg, that was off its feed. . . . He added: "But don't do anything professional to Schomburg. I ride him myself!"

He threw his sonnet across to Mackenzie, who with a background of huddled khaki limbs and anxious faces was himself anxiously counting out French currency notes and dubious-looking tokens. . . . What the deuce did men want to draw money—sometimes quite large sums of money, the Canadians being paid in dollars converted into local coins —when in an hour or so they would be going up? But they always did and their accounts were always in an incredibly entangled state. Mackenzie might well look worried. As like as not, he might find himself a fiver or more down at the end of the evening for unauthorized payments. If he had only his pay and an extravagant wife to keep, that might well put the wind up him. But that was *his* funeral. He told Lieutenant Hotchkiss to come and have a chat with him in his hut, the one next the mess. About horses. He

knew a little about horse-illnesses himself. Only empirically, of course.

Mackenzie was looking at his watch.

"You took two minutes and eleven seconds," he said.
"I'll take it for granted it's a sonnet. . . . I have not read it
because I can't turn it into Latin here. . . . I haven't got
your knack of doing eleven things at once. . . ."

A man with a worried face, encumbered by a bundle
and a small book, was studying figures at Mackenzie's elbow.
He interrupted Mackenzie in a high American voice to say
that he had never drawn fourteen dollars seventy-five cents
in Thrasna Barracks, Aldershot.

Mackenzie said to Tietjens:

"You understand. I have not read your sonnet. I shall
turn it into Latin in the mess: in the time stipulated. I don't
want you to think I've read it and taken time to think about
it."

The man beside him said:

"When I went to the Canadian agent, Strand, London, his
office was shut up. . . ."

Mackenzie said with white fury:

"How much service have you got? Don't you know better
than to interrupt an officer when he is talking. You must
settle your own figures with your own confounded colonial
paymaster. I've sixteen dollars thirty cents here for you.
Will you take them or leave them?"

Tietjens said:

"I know that man's case. Turn him over to me. It isn't
complicated. He's got his paymaster's cheque, but doesn't
know how to cash it, and of course they won't give him
another. . . ."

The man with slow, broad, brown features looked from
one to the other officer's face and back again with a keen,
black-eyed scrutiny as if he were looking into a wind and
dazed by the light. He began a long story of how he owed
Fat-Eared Bill fifty dollars lost at house. He was perhaps half-
Chinese, half-Finn. He continued to talk, being in a state of
great anxiety about his money. Tietjens addressed himself
to the cases of the Sydney Inniskilling ex-trooper and the
McGill graduate who had suffered at the hands of the
Japanese educational ministry. It made altogether a complicated effect. "You would say," Tietjens said to himself,
"that, all together, it ought to be enough to take my mind
up."

The upright trooper had a very complicated sentimental

history. It was difficult to advise him before his fellows. He, however, felt no diffidence. He discussed the points of the girl called Rosie whom he had followed from Sydney to British Columbia, of the girl called Gwen with whom he had taken up in Aberystwyth, of the woman called Mrs. Hosier with whom he had lived maritally, on a sleeping-out pass, at Berwick St. James, near Salisbury Plain. Through the continuing voice of the half-caste Chinaman he discussed them with a large tolerance, explaining that he wanted them all to have a bit, as a souvenir, if he happened to stop one out there. Tietjens handed him the draft of a will he had had written out for him, asked him to read it attentively and copy it with his own hand into his soldier's small book. Then Tietjens would witness it for him. He said:

"Do you think this will make my old woman in Sydney part? I guess it won't. She's a sticker, sir. A regular July burr, God bless her." The McGill graduate was beginning already to introduce a further complication into his story of complications with the Japanese government. It appeared that in addition to his scholastic performances he had invested a little money in a mineral-water spring near Kobe, the water, bottled, being exported to San Francisco. Apparently his company had been indulging in irregularities according to Japanese law, but a pure French Canadian, who had experienced some difficulties in obtaining his baptismal certificate from a mission somewhere in the direction of the Klondike, was allowed by Tietjens to interrupt the story of the graduate; and several men without complications, but anxious to get their papers signed so as to write last letters home before the draft moved, overflowed across Tietjens' table. . . .

The tobacco-smoke from the pipes of the N.C.O.s at the other end of the room hung, opalescent, beneath the wire cages of the brilliant hurricane-lamps hung over each table; buttons and numerals gleamed in the air that the universal khaki tinge of the limbs seemed to turn brown, as if into a gas of dust. Nasal voices, throat voices, drawling voices, melted into a rustle so that the occasional high, sing-song profanity of a Welsh N.C.O.—"Why the *hell* haffn't you got your one-twenty-four? Why the —— hell haffn't you got your one-twenty-four? Don't you *know* you haff to haff your bleedin' one-twenty-fours?"—seemed to wail tragically through a silence. . . . The evening wore on and on. It astounded Tietjens, looking at one time at his watch, to discover that it was only 21 hrs. 19. He seemed to have been thinking drowsily of his own affairs for ten hours. . . . For, in the end, these were his own affairs. . . . Money, women, testamentary bothers. Each of these complications from over the Atlantic and round the world were his own troubles: a world in labour: an army being moved off in the night. Shoved off. Anyhow. And over the top. A lateral section of the world . . .

He had happened to glance at the medical history of a man beside him and noticed that he had been described as C1. . . . It was obviously a slip of the pen on the part of the medical board or one of their orderlies. He had written "C" instead of "A." The man was Pte. 197394 Thomas Johnson, a shining-faced lump of beef, an agricultural odd jobman from British Columbia, where he had worked on the immense estates of Sylvia Tietjens' portentous ducal second cousin Rugeley. It was a double annoyance. Tietjens had not wanted to be reminded of his wife's second cousin, because he had not wanted to be reminded of his wife. He had determined to give his thoughts a field-day on that subject when he got warm into his flea-bag in his hut that smelt of paraffin whilst the canvas walls crackled with frost and the moon shone. . . . He would think of Sylvia beneath the moon. He was determined not to now! But 197394 Pte. Johnson, Thomas, was otherwise a nuisance, and Tietjens cursed himself for having glanced at the man's medical history. If this preposterous yokel was C3 he could not go on a draft . . . C1 rather! It was all the same. That would mean finding another man to make up the strength, and that would drive Sergeant-Major Cowley out of his mind. He looked up towards the ingenuous, protruding, shining, liquid, bottle-blue eyes of Thomas Johnson. . . . The fellow had never had an illness. He could not have had an illness except from a surfeit of cold, fat, boiled pork—and for that you would give him a horse's blue ball and drench, which, ten to one, would not remove the cause of the belly-ache. . . .

His eyes met the non-committal glance of a dark, gentlemanly, thin fellow with a strikingly scarlet hatband, a lot of gilt about his khaki and little strips of steel chain-armour on his shoulders. . . . Levin . . . Colonel Levin, G.S.O. II or something, attached to General Lord Edward Campion . . . How the hell did fellows get into these intimacies of commanders of units and their men? Swimming in like fishes into the brown air of a tank and there at your elbow —— spies! . . . The men had all been called to attention, and stood like gasping cod-fish. The ever-watchful Sergeant-Major Cowley had drifted to his, Tietjens', elbow. You protect your orfcers from the gaudy staff as you protect your infant daughters in lamb's-wool from draughts. The dark, bright, cheerful staff-wallah said with a slight lisp:

"Busy, I see." He might have been standing there for a century and have a century of the battalion headquarters' time to waste like that. "What draft is this?"

Sergeant-Major Cowley, always ready in case his orfcer should not know the name of his unit or his own name, said:

"Number Sixteen I.B.D. Canadian First Division Casual Number Four Draft, sir."

Colonel Levin let air lispingly out between his teeth.

"Number Sixteen Draft not off yet . . . Dear, dear! Dear, dear! . . . We shall be strafed to hell by First Army. . . ." He used the word "hell" as if he had first wrapped it in eau-de-cologned cotton wadding.

Tietjens, on his feet, knew this fellow very well: a fellow who had been a very bad Society water-colour painter of good family on the mother's side: hence the cavalry gadgets on his shoulders. Would it then be good . . . say, good taste, to explode? He let the sergeant-major do it. Sergeant-Major Cowley was of the type of N.C.O. who carried weight because he knew ten times as much about his job as any staff officer. The sergeant-major explained that it had been impossible to get off the draft earlier. The colonel said:

"But surely, sergeant-majah . . ."

The sergeant-major, now a deferential shop-walker in a ladies' store, pointed out that they had had urgent instructions not to send up the draft without the four hundred Canadian Railway Service men who were to come from Étaples. These men had only arrived that evening at 5:30 . . . at the railway station. Marching them up had taken three-quarters of an hour. The colonel said:

"But surely, sergeant-majah . . ."

Old Cowley might as well have said "madam" as "sir" to the red hatband. . . . The four hundred had come with only what they stood up in. The unit had had to wangle everything: boots, blankets, tooth-brushes, braces, rifles, iron rations, identity disks out of the depot store. And it was now only twenty-one twenty. . . . Cowley permitted his commanding officer at this point to say:

"You must understand that we work in circumstances of extreme difficulty, sir. . . ."

The graceful colonel was lost in an absent contemplation of his perfectly elegant knees.

"I know, of course. . . ." he lisped. "Very difficult . . ." He brightened up to add: "But you must admit you're unfortunate. . . . You must admit that. . . ." The weight settled, however, again on his mind.

Tietjens said:

"Not, I suppose, sir, any more unfortunate than any other unit working under a dual control for supplies . . ."

The colonel said:

"What's that? Dual . . . Ah, I see you're there, Mackenzie. . . . Feeling well . . . feeling fit, eh?"

The whole hut stood silent. His anger at the waste of time made Tietjens say:

"If you understand, sir, we are a unit whose principal purpose is drawing things to equip drafts with . . ." This fellow was delaying them atrociously. He was brushing his knees with a handkerchief! "I've had," Tietjens said, "a man killed on my hands this afternoon because we have to draw tin hats for my orderly room from Dublin on an A.F.B. Canadian from Aldershot. . . . Killed here . . . We've only just mopped up the blood from where you're standing. . . ."

The cavalry colonel exclaimed:

"Oh, good gracious me! . . ." jumped a little and examined his beautiful, shining, knee-high aircraft boots. "Killed! . . . Here! . . . But there'll have to be a Court of Inquiry. . . . You certainly are *most* unfortunate, Captain Tietjens. . . . Always these mysterious . . . Why wasn't your man in a dug-out? . . . Most unfortunate . . . We cannot have casualties among the colonial troops. . . . Troops from the dominions, I mean . . ."

Tietjens said grimly:

"The man was from Pontardulais . . . not from any dominion. . . . One of my orderly room . . . We are forbidden on pain of court martial to let any but Dominion Expeditionary Force men go into the dug-outs. . . . My Canadians were all there. . . . It's an A.C.I. local of the eleventh of November. . . ."

The staff officer said:

"It makes, of course, a difference! . . . Only a Glamorganshire? You say . . . Oh, well . . . But these mysterious . . ."

He exclaimed, with the force of an explosion, and the relief:

"Look here . . . can you spare, possibly, ten . . . twenty . . . eh . . . minutes? . . . It's not exactly a service matter . . . so per . . ."

Tietjens exclaimed:

"You see how we're situated, colonel. . . ." and, like one sowing grass seed on a lawn, extended both hands over his papers and towards his men. . . . He was choking with rage. Colonel Levin had, under the chaperonage of an English dowager who ran a chocolate store down on the quays in Rouen, a little French piece to whom he was quite seriously engaged. In the most naïve manner. And the young woman, fantastically jealous, managed to make endless insults to herself out of her almost too handsome colonel's barbaric French. It was an idyll, but it drove the colonel frantic. At such times Levin would consult Tietjens, who passed for a man of brains and a French scholar, as to really nicely turned compliments in a difficult language. . . . And as to how you explained that it was necessary for a G.S.O. II, or whatever the colonel was, to be seen quite frequently in the company of very handsome V.A.D.s and female organizers of all arms . . . It was the sort of silliness as to which no gentleman ought to be consulted. . . . And here was Levin with the familiar feminine-agonized wrinkle on his bronzed-alabaster brow. . . . Like a beastly soldier-man out of a revue. Why didn't the ass burst into gesture and a throaty tenor? . . .

Sergeant-Major Cowley naturally saved the situation. Just as Tietjens was as near saying *Go to hell* as you can be to your remarkably senior officer on parade, the sergeant-major, now a very important solicitor's most confidential clerk, began whispering to the colonel. . . .

"The captain might as well take a spell as not. . . . We're through with all the men except the Canadian Railway batch, and they can't be issued with blankets not for half an hour . . . not for three-quarters. If then! It depends if our runner can find where Quarter's lance-corporal is having his supper, to issue them. . . ." The sergeant-major had inserted that last speech deftly. The staff officer, with a vague reminiscence of his regimental days, exclaimed:

"Damn it! . . . I wonder you don't break into the depot blanket store and take what you want. . . ."

The sergeant-major, becoming Simon Pure, exclaimed:

"Oh, no, sir, we could never do that, sir. . . ."

"But the confounded men are urgently needed in the line," Colonel Levin said. "Damn it, it's touch and go! . . . We're rushing. . . ." He appreciated the fact again that he was on the gaudy staff and that the sergeant-major and Tietjens, playing like left backs into each other's hands, had trickily let him in.

"We can only pray, sir," the sergeant-major said, "that these 'ere bloomin' 'Uns has got quartermasters and depots and issuing departments same as ourselves." He lowered his voice into a husky whisper. "Besides, sir, there's a rumour . . . round the telephone in depot orderly room . . . that there's a W.O. order at 'edquarters . . . countermanding this and other drafts. . . ."

Colonel Levin said: "Oh, my God!" and consternation rushed upon both him and Tietjens. The frozen ditches, in the night, out there; the agonized waiting for men; the weight upon the mind like a weight upon the brows; the imminent sense of approaching unthinkableness on the right or the left, according as you looked up or down the trench; the solid, protecting earth of the parapet then turns into pierced mist . . . and no reliefs coming from here. . . . The men up there thinking naïvely that they were coming, and they not coming. Why not? Good God, why not?

Mackenzie said:

"Poor ——— old Bird . . . His crowd had been in eleven weeks last Wednesday. . . . About all they could stick . . ."

"They'll have to stick a damn lot more," Colonel Levin said. "I'd like to get at some of the brutes. . . ." It was at that date the settled conviction of His Majesty's Expeditionary Force that the army in the field was the tool of politicians and civilians. In moments of routine that cloud dissipated itself lightly: when news of ill omen arrived it settled down again heavily like a cloud of black gas. You hung your head impotently. . . .

"So that," the sergeant-major said cheerfully, "the captain could very well spare half an hour to get his dinner. Or for anything else . . ." Apart from the domestic desire that Tietjens' digestion should not suffer from irregular meals, he had the professional conviction that for his captain to be in intimate private converse with a member of the gaudy staff was good for the unit. . . . "I suppose, sir," he added valedictorily to Tietjens, "I'd better arrange to put this draft, and the nine hundred men that came in this afternoon to replace them, twenty in a tent. . . . It's lucky we didn't strike them. . . ."

Tietjens and the colonel began to push men out of their way, going towards the door. The Inniskilling Canadian, a small, open brown book extended deprecatingly, stood, modestly obtrusive, just beside the door-post. Catching avidly at Tietjens' "Eh?" he said:

"You'd got the names of the girls wrong in your copy, sir. It was Gwen Lewis I had a child by in Aberystwyth that I wanted to have the lease of the cottage and the ten bob a week. Mrs. Hosier that I lived with in Berwick St. James, she was only to have five guineas for a soovneer. . . . I've took the liberty of changing the names back again. . . ."

Tietjens grabbed the book from him and, bending down at the sergeant-major's table, scrawled his signature on the bluish page. He thrust the book back at the man and said:

"There . . . fall out." The man's face shone. He exclaimed:

"Thank you, sir. Thank you kindly, captain. . . . I wanted to get off and go to confession. I did bad. . . ." The McGill graduate with his arrogant black moustache put himself in the way as Tietjens struggled into his British warm.

"You won't forget, sir . . ." he began.

Tietjens said:

"Damn you, I've told you I won't forget. I never forget. You instructed the ignorant Jap in Asaki, but the educational authority is in Tokyo. And your flagitious mineral-water company had their headquarters at the Tan Sen spring near Kobe. . . . Is that right? Well, I'll do my best for you."

They walked in silence through the groups of men that hung round the orderly-room door and gleamed in the moonlight. In the broad country street of the main line of the camp Colonel Levin began to mutter between his teeth:

"You take enough trouble with your beastly crowd . . . a whole lot of trouble. . . . Yet . . ."

"Well, what's the matter with us?" Tietjens said. "We get our drafts ready in thirty-six hours less than any other unit in this command."

"I know you do," the other conceded. "It's only all these mysterious rows. Now . . ."

Tietjens said quickly:

"Do you mind my asking: Are we still on parade? Is this a strafe from General Campion as to the way I command my unit?"

The other conceded quite as quickly and much more worriedly:

"God forbid." He added more quickly still: "Old bean!" and prepared to tuck his wrist under Tietjens' elbow.

Tietjens, however, continued to face the fellow. He was really in a temper.

"Then tell me," he said, "how the deuce you can manage to do without an overcoat in this weather?" If only he could get the chap off the topics of his mysterious rows, they might drift to the matter that had brought him up there on that bitter night when he should be sitting over a good wood fire philandering with Mlle. Nanette de Bailly. He sank his neck deeper into the sheepskin collar of his British warm. The other, slim, was with all his badges, ribbons and mail shining darkly in a cold that set all Tietjens' teeth chattering like porcelain. Levin became momentarily animated:

"You should do as I do. . . . Regular hours . . . lots of exercise . . . horse exercise . . . I do P.T. every morning at the open window of my room . . . hardening. . . ."

"It must be very gratifying to the ladies in the rooms facing yours," Tietjens said grimly. "Is that what's the matter with Mlle. Nanette now? . . . I haven't got time for proper exercise. . . ."

"Good gracious, no," the colonel said. He now tucked his hand firmly under Tietjens' arm and began to work him towards the left hand of the road: in the direction leading out of the camp. Tietjens worked their steps as firmly towards the right and they leant one against the other. "In fact, old bean," the colonel said, "Campy is working so hard to get the command of a fighting army—though he's indispensable here—that we might pack up bag and baggage any day. . . . That is what has made Nanette see reason. . . ."

"Then what am I doing in this show?" Tietjens asked. But Colonel Levin continued blissfully:

"In fact, I've got her almost practically for certain to promise that next week . . . or the week after next at latest . . . she'll . . . damn it, she'll name the happy day."

Tietjens said:

"Good hunting! . . . How splendidly Victorian!"

"That's, damn it," the colonel exclaimed manfully, "what I say myself. . . . Victorian is what it is. . . . All these marriage settlements . . . And what is it . . . *droits du seigneur?* . . . And *notaires* . . . And the Count, having his say . . . And the Marchioness . . . And two old grand-aunts . . . But . . . Hoopla! . . ." He executed with his gloved right thumb in the moonlight a rapid pirouette. . . . "Next week . . . or at least the week after . . ." His voice suddenly drooped.

"At least," he wavered, "that was what it was at lunchtime. . . . Since then . . . something happened. . . ."

"You've not been caught in bed with a V.A.D.?" Tietjens asked.

The colonel mumbled:

"No . . . not in bed . . . Not with a V.A.D. . . . Oh, damn it, at the railway station . . . With . . . The general sent me down to meet her . . . and Nanny of course was seeing off her grandmother, the Duchesse. . . . The giddy cut she handed me out . . ."

Tietjens became coldly furious.

"Then it *was* over one of your beastly imbecile rows with Miss de Bailly that you got me out here," he exclaimed. "Do you mind going down with me towards the I.B.D. head-quarters? Your final orders may have come in there. The sappers won't let me have a telephone, so I have to look in there the last thing. . . ." He felt a yearning towards rooms in huts warmed by coke-stoves and electrically lit, with acting lance-corporals bending over A.F.B.s on a background of deal pigeon-holes filled with returns on buff and blue paper. You got quiet and engrossment there. It was a queer thing: the only place where he, Christopher Tietjens of Groby, could be absently satisfied was in some orderly room or other. The only place in the world . . . And why? It was a queer thing. . . .

But not queer, really. It was a matter of inevitable selection if you came to think it out. An acting orderly-room lance-corporal was selected for his penmanship, his power of elementary figuring, his trustworthiness amongst innumerable figures and messages, his dependability. For this he differed a hair's-breadth in rank from the rank and file. A hairbreadth that was to him the difference between life and death. For if he proved not to be dependable, back he went —returned to duty! As long as he was dependable he slept under a table in a warm room, his toilet arrangements and washing in a bully-beef case near his head, a billy full of tea always stewing for him on an always burning stove. . . . A paradise! . . . No! Not a paradise: *the* paradise of the Other Ranks! . . . He might be awakened at one in the morning. Miles away the enemy might be beginning a strafe. . . . He would roll out from among the blankets under the table amongst the legs of hurrying N.C.O.s and officers, the telephone going like hell. . . . He would have to manifold innumerable short orders on buff slips on a typewriter. . . . A bore to be awakened at one in the morning, but not unexciting: the enemy putting up a tremendous barrage in front of the village of Dranoutre: the whole Nineteenth Division to be moved into support along the Bailleul-Nieppe road. In case . . .

Tietjens considered the sleeping army. . . . That country village under the white moon, all of sackcloth sides, celluloid windows, forty men to a hut . . . That slumbering Arcadia was one of . . . how many? Thirty-seven thousand five hundred, say for a million and a half of men. . . . But there were probably more than a million and a half in that base. . . . Well, round the slumbering Arcadias were the fringes of virginly glimmering tents. . . . Fourteen men to a tent . . . For a million . . . Seventy-one thousand four hundred and twenty-one tents round, say, one hundred and fifty I.B.D.s, C.B.D.s, R.E.B.D.s. . . . Base depots for infantry, cavalry, sappers, gunners, anti-airmen, telephone-men, vets, chiropodists, Royal Army Service Corps men, Pigeon Service men, Sanitary Service men, Women's Auxiliary Army Corps women, V.A.D. women—what in the world did V.A.D. stand for?—canteens, rest-tent attendants, barrack-damage superintendents, parsons, priests, rabbis, Mormon bishops, Brahmans, lamas, imams, Fantee men, no doubt, for African troops. And all really dependent on the acting orderly-room lance-corporals for their temporal and spiritual salvation . . . For if by a slip of the pen a lance-corporal sent a papist priest to an Ulster regiment, the Ulster men would lynch him, and all go to hell. Or if by a slip of the tongue at the telephone or a slip of the typewriter he sent a division to Westoutre instead of to Dranoutre at one in the morning, the six or seven thousand poor devils in front of Dranoutre might all be massacred and nothing but His Majesty's Navy could save us. . . .

Yet, in the end, all this tangle was satisfactorily unravelled; the drafts moved off, unknotting themselves like snakes, coiling out of inextricable bunches, sliding vertebrately over the mud to dip into their bowls—the rabbis found Jews dying to whom to administer; the vets, spavined mules; the V.A.D.s, men without jaws and shoulders in C.C.S.s; the camp-cookers, frozen beef; the chiropodists, ingrowing toenails; the dentists, decayed molars; the naval howitzers, camouflaged emplacements in picturesquely wooded dingles. . . . Somehow they got there—even to the pots of strawberry jam by the ten dozen!

For if the acting lance-corporal, whose life hung by a hair, made a slip of the pen over a dozen pots of jam, back he went, *Returned to duty* . . . back to the frozen rifle, the ground sheet on the liquid mud, the desperate suction on

the ankle as the foot was advanced, the landscapes sil-
houetted with broken church-towers, the continual drone
of the planes, the mazes of duckboards in vast plains of
slime, the unending Cockney humour, the great shells labelled
Love to Little Willie. . . . Back to the Angel with the
Flaming Sword. The wrong side of him! . . . So, on the
whole, things moved satisfactorily. . . .

He was walking Colonel Levin imperiously between the
huts towards the mess quarters, their feet crunching on the
freezing gravel, the colonel hanging back a little; but a mere
light-weight and without nails in his elegant boot-soles, so
he had no grip on the ground. He was remarkably silent.
Whatever he wanted to get out he was reluctant to come to.
He brought out, however:

"I wonder you don't apply to be returned to duty . . . to
your battalion. I jolly well should if I were you. . . ."

Tietjens said:

"Why? Because I've had a man killed on me? . . . There
must have been a dozen killed to-night."

"Oh, more, very likely," the other answered. "It was one
of our own planes that was brought down. . . . But it isn't
that. . . . Oh, damn it! . . . Would you mind walking the
other way? . . . I've the greatest respect . . . oh, almost . . .
for you personally. . . . You're a man of intellect. . . ."

Tietjens was reflecting on a nice point of military etiquette.

This lisping, ineffectual fellow—he was a very careful
staff officer or Campion would not have had him about the
place!—was given to moulding himself exactly on his general.
Physically, in costume as far as possible, in voice—for his
lisp was not his own so much as an adaptation of the
general's slight stutter—and above all in his uncompleted
sentences and point of view. . . . Now, if he said:

"Look here, colonel . . ." or "Look here, Colonel Levin . . ."
or "Look here, Stanley, my boy . . ." For the one thing
an officer may not say to a superior whatever their intimacy
was: "Look here, Levin . . ." If he said then:

"Look here, Stanley, you're a silly ass. It's all very well
for Campion to say that I am unsound because I've some
brains. He's my godfather and has been saying it to me since
I was twelve and had more brain in my left heel than he
had in the whole of his beautifully barbered skull. . . . But
when you say it you are just a parrot. You did not think
that out for yourself. You do not even think it. You know
I'm heavy, short in the wind, and self-assertive . . . but you
know perfectly well that I'm as good on detail as yourself.

And a damned sight more. You've never caught me tripping over a return. Your sergeant in charge of returns may have. But not you . . ."

If Tietjens should say that to this popinjay, would that be going farther than an officer in charge of detachment should go with a member of the staff set above him, though not on parade and in a conversation of intimacy? Off parade and in intimate conversation, all His Majesty's poor —— officers are equals . . . gentlemen having His Majesty's commission: there can be no higher rank and all that! Bilge! . . . For how off parade could this descendant of an old-clo' man from Frankfurt be the equal of him, Tietjens of Groby? He wasn't his equal in any way—let alone socially. If Tietjens hit him he would drop dead; if he addressed a little sneering remark to Levin, the fellow would melt so that you would see the old spluttering Jew swimming up through his carefully arranged Gentile features. He couldn't shoot as well as Tietjens, or ride, or play a hand at auction. Why, damn it, he, Tietjens, hadn't the least doubt that he could paint better water-colour pictures. . . . And as for returns . . . he would undertake to tear the guts out of half a dozen new and contradictory A.C.I.s—Army Council Instructions —and write twelve correct command orders founded on them before Levin had lisped out the date and serial number of the first one. . . . He had done it several times up in the room, arranged like a French blue-stocking's salon, where Levin worked at garrison headquarters. . . . He had written Levin's blessed command orders while Levin fussed and fumed about their being delayed for tea with Mlle. de Bailly . . . and curled his delicate moustache. . . . Mlle. de Bailly, chaperoned by old Lady Sachse, had tea by a clear wood fire in an eighteenth-century octagonal room, with blue-grey tapestried walls and powdering closets, out of priceless porcelain cups without handles. Pale tea that tasted faintly of cinnamon!

Mlle. de Bailly was a long, dark, high-coloured Provençale. Not heavy, but precisely long, slow, and cruel; coiled in a deep arm-chair, saying the most wounding, slow things to Levin, she resembled a white Persian cat luxuriating, sticking out a tentative pawful of expanding claws. With eyes slanting pronouncedly upwards and a very thin hooked nose . . . Almost Japanese . . . And with a terrific *cortège* of relatives, swell in a French way. One brother a chauffeur to a marshal of France . . . An aristocratic way of shirking!

With all that, obviously even off parade, you might well

be the social equal of a staff colonel: but you jolly well had
to keep from showing that you were his superior. Especially
intellectually. If you let yourself show a staff officer that he
was a silly ass—you could say it as often as you liked as
long as you didn't prove it!—you could be certain that you
would be for it before long. And quite properly. It was not
English to be intellectually adroit. Nay, it was positively
un-English. And the duty of field-officers is to keep messes as
English as possible. . . . So a staff officer would take it out
of such a regimental inferior. In a perfectly creditable way.
You would never imagine the hash headquarters warrant
officers would make of your returns. Until you were worried
and badgered, and in the end either you were ejected into,
or prayed to be transferred to . . . any other command in
the whole service. . . .

And that was beastly. The process, not the effect. On the
whole, Tietjens did not care where he was or what he did as
long as he kept out of England, the thought of that country,
at night, slumbering across the channel, being sentimentally
unbearable to him. . . . Still, he was fond of old Campion and
would rather be in his command than any other. He had
attached to his staff a very decent set of fellows, as decent
as you could be in contact with . . . if you had to be in
contact with your kind. . . . So he just said:

"Look here, Stanley, you are a silly ass," and left it at
that, without demonstrating the truth of the assertion.

The colonel said:

"Why, what have I been doing now? . . . I *wish* you
would walk the other way. . . ."

Tietjens said:

"No, I can't afford to go out of camp. . . . I've got to
come to witness your fantastic wedding-contract to-morrow
afternoon, haven't I? . . . I can't leave camp twice in one
week. . . ."

"You've got to come down to the camp-guard," Levin
said. "I hate to keep a woman waiting in the cold . . .
though she *is* in the general's car. . . ."

Tietjens exclaimed:

"You've not been . . . oh, extraordinary enough to bring
Miss de Bailly out here? To talk to me?"

Colonel Levin mumbled, so low Tietjens almost imagined
that he was not meant to hear:

"It isn't Miss de Bailly!" Then he exclaimed quite aloud:
"Damn it all, Tietjens, haven't you had hints enough? . . ."

For a lunatic moment it went through Tietjens' mind that

it must be Miss Wannop in the general's car, at the gate, down the hill beside the camp guard-room. But he knew folly when it presented itself to his mind. He had nevertheless turned and they were going very slowly back along the broad way between the huts. Levin was certainly in no hurry. The broad way would come to an end of the hutments; about two acres of slope would descend blackly before them, white stones to mark a sort of coastguard track glimmering out of sight beneath a moon gone dark with the frost. And, down there in the dark frost, at the end of that track, in a terrific Rolls-Royce, was waiting something of which Levin was certainly deucedly afraid. . . .

For a minute Tietjens' backbone stiffened. He didn't intend to interfere between Mlle. de Bailly and any married woman Levin had had as a mistress. . . . Somehow he was convinced that what was in that car was a married woman. . . . He did not dare to think otherwise. If it was not a married woman it might be Miss Wannop. If it was, it couldn't be. . . . An immense waft of calm, sentimental happiness had descended upon him. Merely because he had imagined her! He imagined her little, fair, rather pug-nosed face: under a fur cap, he did not know why. Leaning forward she would be, on the seat of the general's illuminated car: glazed in: a regular raree-show! Peering out, shortsightedly on account of the reflections on the inside of the glass . . .

He was saying to Levin:

"Look here, Stanley . . . why I said you are a silly ass is because Miss de Bailly has one chief luxury. It's exhibiting jealousy. Not feeling it. Exhibiting it."

"Ought you," Levin asked ironically, "to discuss my fiancée before me? As an English gentleman. Tietjens of Groby and all."

"Why, of course," Tietjens said. He continued feeling happy. "As a sort of swollen best man, it's my duty to instruct you. Mothers tell their daughters things before marriage. Best men do it for the innocent Benedict. . . . And you're always consulting me about the young woman. . . ."

"I'm not doing it now," Levin grumbled direly.

"Then what, in God's name, are you doing? You've got a cast mistress, haven't you, down there in old Campion's car? . . ." They were beside the alley that led down to his orderly room. Knots of men, dim and desultory, still half filled it a little way down.

"I *haven't*," Levin exclaimed almost tearfully. "I never *had* a mistress. . . ."

"And you're not married?" Tietjens asked. He used on purpose the schoolboy's ejaculation "Lummy!" to soften the jibe. "If you'll excuse me," he said, "I must just go and take a look at my crown. To see if your orders have come down."

He found no orders in a hut as full as ever of the dull mists and odours of khaki, but he found in revenge a fine, upstanding, blond, Canadian-born lance-corporal of old colonial lineage, with a moving story as related by Sergeant-Major Cowley:

"This man, sir, of the Canadian Railway lot—'is mother's just turned up in the town, come on from Eetarpels. Come all the way from Toronto, where she was bedridden."

Tietjens said:

"Well, what about it? Get a move on."

The man wanted leave to go to his mother, who was waiting in a decent *estaminet* at the end of the tram-line, just outside the camp where the houses of the town began.

Tietjens said:

"It's impossible. It's absolutely impossible. You know that."

The man stood erect and expressionless; his blue eyes looked confoundedly honest to Tietjens, who was cursing himself. He said to the man:

"You can see for yourself that it's impossible, can't you?"

The man said slowly:

"Not knowing the regulations in these circumstances, I can't say, sir. But my mother's is a very special case. . . . She's lost two sons already."

Tietjens said:

"A great many people have. . . . Do you understand, if you went absent off my pass I might—I quite possibly might—lose my commission? I'm responsible for you fellows getting up the line."

The man looked down at his feet. Tietjens said to himself that it was Valentine Wannop doing this to him. He ought to turn the man down at once. He was pervaded by a sense of her being. It was imbecile. Yet it was so. He said to the man:

"You said good-bye to your mother, didn't you, in Toronto, before you left?"

The man said:

"No, sir." He had not seen his mother in seven years. He had been up in the Chilkoot when war broke out and had not heard of it for ten months. Then he had at once joined up in British Columbia, and had been sent straight through for railway work, on to Aldershot, where the Canadians had a camp in building. He had not known that his brothers were killed till he got there, and his mother, being bedridden at the news, had not been able to get down to Toronto when his batch had passed through. She lived about sixty miles from Toronto. Now she had risen from her bed like a miracle and come all the way. A widow: sixty-two years of age. Very feeble.

It occurred to Tietjens as it occurred to him ten times a day that it was idiotic of him to figure Valentine Wannop to himself. He had not the slightest idea where she was: in what circumstances or even in what house. He did not suppose she and her mother had stayed on in that dog-kennel of a place in Bedford Park. They would be fairly comfortable. His father had left them money. "It is preposterous," he said to himself, "to persist in figuring a person to yourself when you have no idea of where they are." He said to the man:

"Wouldn't it do if you saw your mother at the camp-gate, by the guard-room?"

"Not much of a leave-taking, sir," the man said; "she not allowed in the camp and I not allowed out. Talking under a sentry's nose, very likely."

Tietjens said to himself:

"What a monstrous absurdity this is of seeing and talking, for a minute or so! You meet and talk. . . ." And next day at the same hour. Nothing . . . As well not to meet or talk . . . Yet the mere fantastic idea of seeing Valentine Wannop for a minute . . . She not allowed in the camp and he not going out. Talking under a sentry's nose, very likely . . . It had made him smell primroses. Primroses, like Miss Wannop. He said to the sergeant-major:

"What sort of a fellow is this?" Cowley, in open-mouthed suspense, gasped like a fish. Tietjens said:

"I suppose your mother is fairly feeble to stand in the cold?"

"A very decent man, sir," the sergeant-major got out, "one of the best. No trouble. A perfectly clean conduct sheet. Very good education. A railway engineer in civil life . . . Volunteered, of course, sir."

"That's the odd thing," Tietjens said to the man, "that the percentages of absentees is as great amongst the volunteers as the Derby men or the compulsorily enlisted. . . . Do you understand what will happen to you if you miss the draft?"

The man said soberly:

"Yes, sir. Perfectly well."

"You understand that you will be shot? As certainly as that you stand there. And that you haven't a chance of escape."

He wondered what Valentine Wannop, hot pacifist, would think of him if she heard him. Yet it was his duty to talk like that: his human, not merely his military, duty. As much his duty as that of a doctor to warn a man that if he drank of typhoid-contaminated water he would get typhoid. But people are unreasonable. Valentine too was unreasonable. She would consider it brutal to speak to a man of the possibility of his being shot by a firing-party. A groan burst from him. At the thought that there was no sense in bothering about what Valentine Wannop would or would not think of him. No sense. No sense. No sense . . .

The man, fortunately, was assuring him that he knew, very soberly, all about the penalty for going absent off a draft. The sergeant-major, catching a sound from Tietjens, said with admirable fussiness to the man:

"There, there! Don't you hear the officer's speaking? Never interrupt an officer."

"You'll be shot," Tietjens said, "at dawn. . . . Literally at dawn." Why did they shoot them at dawn? To rub it in that they were never going to see another sunrise. But they drugged the fellows so that they wouldn't know the sun if they saw it: all roped in a chair. . . . It was really the worse for the firing-party. He added to the man:

"Don't think I'm insulting you. You appear to be a very decent fellow. But very decent fellows have gone absent. . . ." He said to the sergeant-major:

"Give this man a two hours' pass to go to the . . . whatever's the name of the *estaminet*. . . . The draft won't move off for two hours, will it?" He added to the man: "If you see your draft passing the pub, you run out and fall in. Like mad, you understand. You'd never get another chance."

There was a mumble like applause and envy of a mate's good luck from a packed audience that had hung on the lips of simple melodrama . . . an audience that seemed to be all enlarged eyes, the khaki was so colourless. . . . They came as near applause as they dared, but there was no sense in worrying about whether Valentine Wannop would have applauded or not. . . . And there was no knowing whether the fellow would not go absent, either. As likely as not, there was no mother. A girl, very likely. And very likely the man would desert. . . . The man looked you straight in the eyes. But a strong passion, like that for escape —or a girl—will give you control over the muscles of the eyes. A little thing, that, before a strong passion! One would look God in the face on the day of judgement and lie, in that case.

Because what the devil did he want of Valentine Wannop? Why could he not stall off the thought of her? He could stall off the thought of his wife . . . or his not-wife. But Valentine Wannop came wriggling in. At all hours of the day and night. It was an obsession. A madness . . . What those fools called "a complex"! . . . Due, no doubt, to something your nurse had done or your parents said to you. At birth . . . A strong passion . . . or no doubt not strong enough. Otherwise he, too, would have gone absent. At any rate, from Sylvia . . . Which he hadn't done. Which he hadn't. Or hadn't he? There was no saying. . . .

It was undoubtedly colder in the alley between the huts. A man was saying: "Hoo . . . Hooo . . . Hoo . . ." A sound like that, and flapping his arms and hopping . . . "Hand and foot, mark time! . . ." Somebody ought to fall these poor devils in and give them that to keep their circulations going. But they might not know the command. . . . It was a guards' trick, really. . . . What the devil were these fellows kept hanging about here for? he asked.

One or two voices said that they did not know. The majority said gutturally:

"Waiting for our mates, sir . . ."

"I should have thought you could have waited under cover," Tietjens said caustically. "But never mind; it's your funeral, if you like it. . . ." This getting together . . . a strong passion. There was a warmed recreation-hut for waiting drafts not fifty yards away. . . . But they stood, teeth chattering, and mumbling "Hoo . . . Hooo . . ." rather than miss thirty seconds of gabble. . . . About what the English sergeant-major said and about what the officer said and how many dollars did they give you . . . And of course about what you answered back . . . Or perhaps not that. These Canadian troops were husky, serious fellows, without the swank of the Cockney or the Lincolnshire Moonrakers. They wanted, apparently, to learn the rules of war. They discussed anxiously information that they received in orderly

rooms and looked at you as if you were expounding the
gospels. . . .

But, damn it, he, he himself, would make a pact with
Destiny, at that moment, willingly, to pass thirty months
in the frozen circle of Hell, for the chance of thirty seconds
in which to tell Valentine Wannop what he had answered
back . . . to Destiny! . . . What was the fellow in the
Inferno who was buried to the neck in ice and begged
Dante to clear the icicles out of his eyelids so that he could
see out of them? And Dante kicked him in the face because
he was a Ghibelline. . . . Always a bit of a swine, Dante . . .
Rather like . . . like whom? . . . Oh, Sylvia Tietjens . . . A
good hater! . . . He imagined hatred coming to him in
waves from the convent in which Sylvia had immured herself . . . Gone into retreat . . . He imagined she had gone
into retreat. She had said she was going. For the rest of the
war . . . For the duration of hostilities or life, whichever
were the longer . . . He imagined Sylvia coiled up on a convent bed. . . . Hating . . . Her certainly glorious hair all
round her . . . Hating . . . Slowly and coldly . . . Like the
head of a snake when you examined it . . . Eyes motionless:
mouth closed tight . . . Looking away into the distance and
hating . . . She was presumably in Birkenhead. . . . A long
way to send your hatred . . . Across a country and a sea
in an icy night! . . . Over all that black land and water . . .
with the lights out because of air raids and U-boats . . .
Well, he did not have to think of Sylvia at the moment.
She was well out of it. . . .

It was certainly getting no warmer as the night drew on. . . .
Even that ass Levin was pacing swiftly up and down in the
dusky moon-shadow of the last hutments that looked over
the slope and the vanishing trail of white stones. . . . In
spite of his boasting about not wearing an overcoat: to
catch women's eyes with his pretty staff gadgets he was
carrying on like a leopard at feeding time. . . .

Tietjens said:

"Sorry to keep you waiting, old man. . . . Or rather your
lady . . . But there were some men to see to. . . . And, you
know . . . 'The comfort and—what is it?—of the men comes
before every—is it "consideration"?—except the exigencies
of actual warfare. . . .' My memory's gone phut these days.
. . . And you want me to slide down this hill and wheeze
back again. . . . To see a woman! . . ."

Levin screeched:

"Damn you, you ass! It's your wife who's waiting for you at the bottom there."

3 ~

THE ONE thing that stood out sharply in Tietjens' mind when at last, with a stiff glass of rum punch, his officer's pocket-book complete with pencil because he had to draft before eleven a report as to the desirability for giving his unit special lectures on the causes of the war, and a cheap French novel on a camp-chair beside him, he sat in his flea-bag with six army blankets over him—the one thing that stood out as sharply as staff tabs was that that ass Levin was rather pathetic. His unnailed boot-soles very much cramping his action on the frozen hill-side, he had alternately hobbled a step or two and, reduced to inaction, had grabbed at Tietjens' elbow while he brought out breathlessly puzzled sentences. . . .

There resulted a singular mosaic of extraordinary, bright-coloured and melodramatic statements, for Levin, who first hobbled down the hill with Tietjens and then hobbled back up, clinging to his arm, brought out monstrosities of news about Sylvia's activities, without any sequence, and indeed without any apparent aim except for the great affection he had for Tietjens himself. . . . All sorts of singular things seemed to have been going on round him in the vague zone outside all this engrossed and dust-coloured world—in the vague zone that held . . . oh, the civilian population, tea-parties short of butter! . . .

And as Tietjens, seated on his hams, his knees up, pulled the soft woolliness of his flea-bag under his chin and damned the paraffin heater for letting out a new and singular stink it seemed to him that this affair was like coming back after two months and trying to get the hang of battalion orders. . . . You come back to the familiar, slightly battered mess ante-room. You tell the mess orderly to bring you the last two months' orders, for it is as much as your life is worth not to know what is or is not in them. . . . There might be an A.C.I. ordering you to wear your helmet back to the front or a battalion order that Mills bombs must always be worn in the left breast pocket. Or there might be the detail for putting on a new gas-helmet! . . . The orderly hands you a dishevelled mass of faintly typewritten matter, thumbed out of all chance of legibility, with the orders for November 16 fastened inextricably into the middle of those for the 1st of December, and those for the 10th, 15th and 29th missing altogether. . . . And all that you gather is that headquarters has some exceedingly insulting things to say about A Company; that a fellow called Hartopp, whom you don't know, has been deprived of his commission; that at a Court of Inquiry held to ascertain deficiencies in C Company Captain Wells—poor Wells!—has been assessed at £27 11s. 4d., which he is requested to pay forthwith to the adjutant. . . .

So, on that black hill-side, going and returning, what stuck out for Tietjens was that Levin had been taught by the general to consider that he, Tietjens, was an extraordinarily violent chap who would certainly knock Levin down when he told him that his wife was at the camp-gates; that Levin considered himself to be the descendant of an ancient Quaker family. . . . (Tietjens had said *Good God!* at that); that the mysterious "rows" to which in his fear Levin had been continually referring had been successive letters from Sylvia to the harried general . . . and that Sylvia had accused him, Tietjens, of stealing two pairs of her best sheets. . . . There was a great deal more. But, having faced what he considered to be the worst of the situation, Tietjens set himself coolly to recapitulate every aspect of his separation from his wife. He had meant to face every aspect, not that merely social one upon which, hitherto, he had automatically imagined their disunion to rest. For as he saw it, English people of good position consider that the basis of all marital unions or disunions is the maxim: No scenes. Obviously for the sake of the servants—who are the same thing as the public. No scenes, then, for the sake of the public. And indeed, with him, the instinct for privacy—as to his relationships, his passions, or even as to his most unimportant motives—was as strong as the instinct of life itself. He would, literally, rather be dead than an open book.

And until that afternoon he had imagined that his wife, too, would rather be dead than have her affairs canvassed by the Other Ranks. . . . But that assumption had to be gone over. Revised . . . Of course he might say she had gone mad. But if he said she had gone mad, he would have to revise a great deal of their relationships, so it would be as broad as it was long. . . .

The doctor's batman, from the other end of the hut, said:

"Poor —— O Nine Morgan! . . ." in a sing-song, mocking voice. . . .

For though, hours before, Tietjens had appointed this moment of physical ease that usually followed on his splurging heavily down on to his creaking camp-bed in the doctor's lent hut, for the cool consideration of his relations with his wife, it was not turning out a very easy matter. The hut was unreasonably warm: he had invited Mackenzie—whose real name turned out to be McKechnie, James Grant McKechnie—to occupy the other end of it. The other end of it was divided from him by a partition of canvas and a striped Indian curtain. And McKechnie, who was unable to sleep, had elected to carry on a long—an interminable—conversation with the doctor's batman.

The doctor's batman also could not sleep and, like McKechnie, was more than a little barmy on the crumpet—an almost non-English-speaking Welshman from God knows what up-country valley. He had shaggy hair like a Caribbean savage and two dark, resentful wall eyes; being a miner, he sat on his heels more comfortably than on a chair, and his almost incomprehensible voice went on in a low sort of ululation, with an occasionally and startlingly comprehensible phrase sticking out now and then.

It was troublesome, but orthodox enough. The batman had been blown literally out of most of his senses and the VIth Battalion of the Glamorganshire Regiment by some German high explosive or other, more than a year ago. But before then, it appeared, he had been in McKechnie's own company in that battalion. It was perfectly in order that an officer should gossip with a private formerly of his own platoon or company, especially on first meeting him after long separation caused by a casualty to one or the other. And McKechnie had first remet this scoundrel Jonce, or Evans, at eleven that night—two and a half hours before. So there, in the light of a single candle stuck in a stout bottle, they were tranquilly at it: the batman sitting on his heel by the officer's head; the officer, in his pyjamas, sprawling half out of bed over his pillows, stretching his arms abroad, occasionally yawning, occasionally asking: "What became of Company-Sergeant-Major Hoyt? . . ." They might talk till half-past three.

But that was troublesome to a gentleman seeking to recapture what exactly were his relations with his wife.

Before the doctor's batman had interrupted him by speaking startlingly of 09 Morgan, Tietjens had got as far as what follows with his recapitulation: The lady, Mrs. Tietjens, was certainly without mitigation a whore; he himself, equally certainly and without qualification, had been physically faithful to the lady and their marriage tie. In law, then, he was absolutely in the right of it. But that fact had less weight than a cobweb. For after the last of her highhanded divagations from fidelity he had accorded to the lady the shelter of his roof and of his name. She had lived for years beside him, apparently on terms of hatred and miscomprehension. But certainly in conditions of chastity. Then, during the tenuous and lugubrious small hours, before his coming out there again to France, she had given evidence of a madly vindictive passion for his person. A physical passion at any rate.

Well, those were times of mad, fugitive emotions. But even in the calmest times a man could not expect to have a woman live with him as the mistress of his house and mother of his heir without establishing some sort of claim upon him. They hadn't slept together. But was it not possible that a constant measuring together of your minds was as proper to give you a proprietary right as the measuring together of the limbs? It was perfectly possible. Well, then . . .

What, in the eyes of God, severed a union? . . . Certainly he had imagined—until that very afternoon—that their union had been cut, as the tendon of Achilles is cut in a hamstringing, by Sylvia's clear voice, outside his house, saying in the dawn to a cabman, "Paddington!" . . . He tried to go with extreme care through every detail of their last interview in his still nearly dark drawing-room, at the other end of which she had seemed a mere white phosphorescence. . . .

They had, then, parted for good on that day. He was going out to France; she into retreat in a convent near Birkenhead—to which place you go from Paddington. Well, then, that was one parting. That, surely, set him free for the girl!

He took a sip from the glass of rum and water on the canvas chair beside him. It was tepid and therefore beastly. He had ordered the batman to bring it him hot, strong and sweet, because he had been certain of an incipient cold. He had refrained from drinking it because he had remembered that he was to think cold-bloodedly of Sylvia, and he made a practice of never touching alcohol when about to engage in protracted reflection. That had always been his theory: it had been immensely and empirically strengthened by his warlike experience. On the Somme, in the summer, when stand-to had been at four in the morning, you would come out of your dug-out and survey, with a complete outfit of pessimistic thoughts, a dim, grey, repulsive landscape over a dull and much too thin parapet. There would be repellent posts, altogether too fragile entanglements of barbed wire, broken wheels, detritus, coils of mist over the positions of revolting Germans. Grey stillness, grey horrors, in front and behind, amongst the civilian populations! And clear, hard outlines to every thought. . . . Then your batman brought you a cup of tea with a little—quite a little—rum in it. In three or four minutes the whole world changed beneath your eyes. The wire aprons became jolly, efficient protections that your skill had devised and for which you might thank God; the broken wheels were convenient landmarks for raiding at night in no man's land. You had to confess that when you had re-erected that parapet, after it had last been jammed in, your company had made a pretty good job of it. And even as far as the Germans were concerned, you were there to kill the swine; but you didn't feel that the thought of them would make you sick beforehand. . . . You were, in fact, a changed man. With a mind of a different specific gravity. You could not even tell that the roseate touches of dawn on the mists were not really the effects of rum. . . .

Therefore he had determined not to touch his grog. But his throat had gone completely dry; so, mechanically, he had reached out for something to drink, checking himself when he had realized what he was doing. But why should his throat be dry? He hadn't been on the drink. He had not even had any dinner. And why was he in this extraordinary state? . . . For he was in an extraordinary state. It was because the idea had suddenly occurred to him that his parting from his wife set him free for his girl. . . . The idea had till then never entered his head.

He said to himself: "We must go methodically into this!" Methodically into the history of his last day on earth. . . .

Because he swore that when he had come out to France this time he had imagined that he was cutting loose from this earth. And during the months that he had been there he had seemed to have no connexion with any earthly things. He had imagined Sylvia in her convent and done with; Miss

Wannop he had not been able to imagine at all. But she had seemed to be done with.

It was difficult to get his mind back to that night. You cannot force your mind to a deliberate, consecutive recollection unless you are in the mood; then it will do it whether you want it to or not. . . . He had had, then, three months or so ago, a very painful morning with his wife, the pain coming from a suddenly growing conviction that his wife was forcing herself into an attitude of caring for him. Only an attitude probably, because, in the end, Sylvia was a lady and would not allow herself really to care for the person in the world for whom it would be least decent of her to care. . . . But she would be perfectly capable of forcing herself to take that attitude if she thought that it would enormously inconvenience himself. . . .

But that wasn't the way, wasn't the way, wasn't the way, his excited mind said to himself. He was excited because it was possible that Miss Wannop, too, might not have meant their parting to be a permanency. That opened up an immense perspective. Nevertheless, the contemplation of that immense perspective was not the way to set about a calm analysis of his relations with his wife. The facts of the story *must* be stated before the moral. He said to himself that he must put, in exact language, as if he were making a report for the use of garrison headquarters, the history of himself in his relationship to his wife. . . . And to Miss Wannop, of course. "Better put it into writing," he said.

Well, then. He clutched at his pocket-book and wrote in large pencilled characters:

"When I married Miss Satterthwaite"—he was attempting exactly to imitate a report to general headquarters—"unknown to myself, she imagined herself to be with child by a fellow called Drake. I think she was not. The matter is debatable. I am passionately attached to the child, who is my heir and the heir of a family of considerable position. The lady was subsequently, on several occasions, though I do not know how many, unfaithful to me. She left me with a fellow called Perowne, whom she had met constantly at the house of my godfather, General Lord Edward Campion, on whose staff Perowne was. That was long before the war. This intimacy was, of course, certainly unsuspected by the general. Perowne is again on the staff of General Campion, who has the quality of attachment to his old subordinates, but as Perowne is an inefficient officer, he is used only for more decorative jobs. Otherwise, obviously, as he is an old regular, his seniority should make him a general, and he is only a major. I make this diversion about Perowne because his presence in this garrison causes me natural personal annoyance.

"My wife, after an absence of several months with Perowne, wrote and told me that she wished to be taken back into my household. I allowed this. My principles prevent me from divorcing any woman, in particular any woman who is the mother of a child. As I had taken no steps to ensure publicity for the escapade of Mrs. Tietjens, no one, as far as I know, was aware of her absence. Mrs. Tietjens, being a Roman Catholic, is prevented from divorcing me.

"During this absence of Mrs. Tietjens with the man Perowne, I made the acquaintance of a young woman, Miss Wannop, the daughter of my father's oldest friend, who was also an old friend of General Campion's. Our station in society naturally forms rather a close ring. I was immediately aware that I had formed a sympathetic but not violent attachment for Miss Wannop and fairly confident that my feeling was returned. Neither Miss Wannop nor myself being persons to talk about the state of our feelings, we exchanged no confidences. . . . A disadvantage of being English of a certain station.

"The position continued thus for several years. Six or seven. After her return from her excursion with Perowne, Mrs. Tietjens remained, I believe, perfectly chaste. I saw Miss Wannop sometimes frequently, for a period, in her mother's house or on social occasions, sometimes not for long intervals. No expression of affection on the part of either of us ever passed. Not one. Ever.

"On the day before my second going out to France I had a very painful scene with my wife, during which, for the first time, we went into the question of the parentage of my child and other matters. In the afternoon I met Miss Wannop by appointment outside the War Office. The appointment had been made by my wife, not by me. I knew nothing about it. My wife must have been more aware of my feelings for Miss Wannop than I was myself.

"In St. James's Park I invited Miss Wannop to become my mistress that evening. She consented and made an assignation. It is to be presumed that that was evidence of her affection for me. We have never exchanged words of affection. Presumably a young lady does not consent to go to bed with a married man without feeling affection for him. But I have no proof. It was, of course, only a few hours before my going out to France. Those are emotional sorts of moments for young women. No doubt they consent more easily.

"But we didn't. We were together at one-thirty in the morning, leaning over her suburban garden-gate. And nothing happened. We agreed that we were the sort of persons who didn't. I do not know how we agreed. We never finished a sentence. Yet it was a passionate scene. So I touched the brim of my cap and said: 'So long! . . .' Or she . . . I don't remember. I remember the thoughts I thought and the thoughts I gave her credit for thinking. But perhaps she did not think them. There is no knowing. It is no good going into them . . . except that I gave her credit for thinking that we were parting for good. Perhaps she did not mean that. Perhaps I could write letters to her. And live . . ."

He exclaimed:

"God, what a sweat I am in! . . ."

The sweat, indeed, was pouring down his temples. He became instinct with a sort of passion to let his thoughts wander into epithets and go about where they would. But he stuck at it. He was determined to get it expressed. He wrote on again:

"I got home towards two in the morning and went into the dining-room in the dark. I did not need a light. I sat thinking for a long time. Then Sylvia spoke from the other end of the room. There was thus an abominable situation. I have never been spoken to with such hatred. She went, perhaps, mad. She had apparently been banking on the idea that if I had physical contact with Miss Wannop I might satisfy my affection for the girl. . . . And feel physical desires for *her* . . . But she knew, without my speaking, that I had not had physical contact with the girl. She threatened to ruin me; to ruin me in the army; to drag my name through the mud. . . . I never spoke. I am damn good at not speaking. She struck me in the face. And went away. Afterwards she threw into the room, through the half-open doorway, a gold medallion of St. Michael, the R.C. patron of soldiers in action, that she had worn between her breasts. I took it to mean the final act of parting. As if by no longer wearing it she abandoned all prayer for my safety . . . It might just as well mean that she wished me to wear it myself for my personal protection. . . . I heard her go down the stairs with her maid. The dawn was just showing through the chimney-pots opposite. I heard her say: *Paddington.* Clear, high syllables! And a motor drove off.

"I got my things together and went to Waterloo. Mrs. Satterthwaite, her mother, was waiting to see me off. She was very distressed that her daughter had not come, too. She was of opinion that it meant we had parted for good. I was astonished to find that Sylvia had told her mother about Miss Wannop because Sylvia had always been extremely reticent, even to her mother. . . . Mrs. Satterthwaite, who was *very* distressed—she likes me!—expressed the most gloomy forebodings as to what Sylvia might not be up to. I laughed at her. She began to tell me a long anecdote about what a Father Consett, Sylvia's confessor, had said about Sylvia years before. He had said that if I ever came to care for another woman, Sylvia would tear the world to pieces to get at me. . . . Meaning, to disturb my equanimity! . . . It was difficult to follow Mrs. Satterthwaite. The side of an officer's train, going off, is not a good place for confidences. So the interview ended rather untidily."

At this point Tietjens groaned so audibly that Mc-Kechnie, from the other end of the hut, asked if he had not said anything. Tietjens saved himself with:

"That candle looks from here to be too near the side of the hut. Perhaps it isn't. These buildings are very inflammable."

It was no good going on writing. He was no writer, and this writing gave no sort of psychological pointers. He wasn't, himself, ever much the man for psychology, but one ought to be as efficient at it as at anything else. . . . Well, then . . . What was at the bottom of all the madness and cruelty that had distinguished both himself and Sylvia on his last day and night in his native country? . . . For, mark! it was Sylvia who had made, unknown to him, the appointment through which the girl had met him. Sylvia had wanted to force him and Miss Wannop into each other's arms. Quite definitely. She had said as much. But she had only said that afterwards. When the game had not come off. She had had too much knowledge of amatory manœuvres to show her hand before. . . .

Why, then, had she done it? Partly, undoubtedly, out of pity for him. She had given him a rotten time; she had undoubtedly, at one moment, wanted to give him the consolation of his girl's arms. . . . Why, damn it, she, Sylvia, and no one else, had forced out of him the invitation to the girl to become his mistress. Nothing but the infernal cruelty of their interview of the morning could have forced him to the pitch of sexual excitement that would make him make a proposal of illicit intercourse to a young lady to whom hitherto he had spoken not even one word of affection. It was an effect of a Sadic kind. That was the only way to look at it scientifically. And without doubt Sylvia had known what she was doing. The whole morning, at intervals, like a person directing the whip-lash to a cruel spot of pain, reiteratedly, she had gone on and on. She had accused him of having Valentine Wannop for his mistress. She had accused him of having Valentine Wannop for his mistress. She had accused him of having Valentine Wannop for his mistress. . . . With maddening reiteration, like that. They had disposed of an estate; they had settled up a number of business matters; they had decided that his heir was to be brought up as a papist—the mother's religion! They had gone, agonizedly enough, into their own relationships and past history. Into the very paternity of his child. . . . But always, at moments when his mind was like a blind octopus, squirming in an agony of knife-cuts, she would drop in that accusation. She had accused him of having Valentine Wannop for his mistress. . . .

He swore by the living God. . . . He had never realized that he had a passion for the girl till that morning; that he had a passion deep and boundless like the sea, shaking like a tremor of the whole world, an unquenchable thirst, a thing the thought of which made your bowels turn over. . . . But he had not been the sort of fellow who goes into his emotions. . . . Why, damn it, even at that moment when he thought of the girl, there, in that beastly camp, in that Rembrandt-beshadowed hut, when he thought of the girl, he named her to himself Miss Wannop. . . .

It wasn't in that way that a man thought of a young woman whom he was aware of passionately loving. He wasn't aware. He hadn't been aware. Until that morning. . . .

Then . . , that let him out. . . . Undoubtedly that let him out. . . . A woman cannot throw her man, her official husband, into the arms of the first girl that comes along and consider herself as having any further claims upon him. Especially if on the same day you part with him, he is going out to France! *Did* it let him out? Obviously it did.

He caught with such rapidity at his glass of rum and water that a little of it ran over on to his thumb. He swallowed the lot, being instantly warmed. . . .

What in the world was he doing? Now? With all this

introspection? . . . Hang it all, he was not justifying himself.
. . . He had acted perfectly correctly as far as Sylvia was
concerned. Not perhaps to Miss Wannop . . . Why, if he,
Christopher Tietjens of Groby, had the need to justify him-
self, what did it stand for to be Christopher Tietjens of
Groby? That was the unthinkable thought.

Obviously he was not immune from the seven deadly
sins. In the way of a man. One might lie, yet not bear
false witness against a neighbour; one might kill, yet not
without fitting provocation or for self-interest; one might
conceive of theft as reiving cattle from the false Scots,
which was the Yorkshireman's duty; one might fornicate,
obviously, as long as you did not fuss about it unhealthily.
That was the right of the Seigneur in a world of Other
Ranks. He hadn't personally committed any of these sins
to any great extent. One reserved the right so to do and
to take the consequences. . . .

But what in the world had gone wrong with Sylvia? She
was giving away her own game, and that he had never
known her to do. But she could not have made more certain, if she had wanted to, of returning him to his allegiance
to Miss Wannop than by forcing herself there into his private life and doing it with such blatant vulgarity. For what
she had done had been to make scenes before the servants!
All the while he had been in France she had been working
up to it. Now she had done it. Before the Tommies of his
own unit. But Sylvia did not make mistakes like that. It
was a game. What game? He didn't even attempt to con-
jecture! She could not expect that he would in the future
even extend to her the shelter of his roof. . . . What, then,
was the game? He could not believe that she could be
capable of vulgarity except with a purpose. . . .

She was a thoroughbred. He had always credited her
with being that. And now she was behaving as if she had
every mean vice that a mare could have. Or it looked like
it. Was that, then, because she had been in his stable? But
how in the world otherwise could he have run their lives?
She had been unfaithful to him. She had never been anything but unfaithful to him, before or after marriage. In a
high-handed way so that he could not condemn her, though
it was disagreeable enough to himself. He took her back
into his house after she had been off with the fellow
Perowne. What more could she ask? . . . He could find
no answer. And it was not his business!

But even if he did not bother about the motives of the

poor beast of a woman, she was the mother of his heir. And now she was running about the world declaiming about her wrongs. What sort of a thing was that for a boy to have happen to him? A mother who made scenes before the servants! That was enough to ruin any boy's life. . . .

There was no getting away from it that that was what Sylvia had been doing. She had deluged the general with letters for the last two months or so, at first merely contenting herself with asking where he, Tietjens, was and in what state of health, conditions of danger, and the like. Very decently, for some time the old fellow had said nothing about the matter to him. He had probably taken the letters to be the naturally anxious inquiries of a wife with a husband at the front; he had considered that Tietjens' letters to her must have been insufficiently communicative or concealed what she imagined to be wounds or a position of desperate danger. That would not have been very pleasant in any case; women should not worry superior officers about the vicissitudes of their men-folk. It was not done. Still, Sylvia was very intimate with Campion and his family—more intimate than he himself was, though Campion was his godfather. But quite obviously her letters had got worse and worse.

It was difficult for Tietjens to make out exactly what she had said. His channel of information had been Levin, who was too gentlemanly ever to say anything direct at all. Too gentlemanly, too implicitly trustful of Tietjens' honour . . . and too bewildered by the charms of Sylvia, who had obviously laid herself out to bewilder the poor staff-wallah. . . . But she had gone pretty far, either in her letters or in her conversation since she had been in that city, to which—it was characteristic—she had come without any sort of passports or papers, just walking past gentlemen in their wooden boxes at pierheads and the like, in conversation with —of all people in the world!—with Perowne, who had been returning from leave with King's dispatches or something glorified of the staff sort! In a special train, very likely. That was Sylvia all over.

Levin said that Campion had given Perowne the most frightful dressing down he had ever heard mortal man receive. And it really was *damn* hard on the poor general, who, after happenings to one of his predecessors, had been perfectly rabid to keep skirts out of his headquarters. Indeed it was one of the crosses of Levin's worried life that the general had absolutely refused him, Levin, leave to marry

Miss de Bailly if he would not undertake that that young woman should leave France by the first boat after the ceremony. Levin, of course, was to go with her, but the young woman was not to return to France for the duration of hostilities. And a fine row all her noble relatives had raised over that. It had cost Levin another hundred and fifty thousand francs in the marriage settlements. The married wives of officers in any case were not allowed in France, though you could not keep out their unmarried ones. . . .

Campion, anyhow, had dispatched his furious note to Tietjens after receiving, firstly, in the early morning, a letter from Sylvia in which she said that her ducal second cousin, the lugubrious Rugeley, highly disapproved of the fact that Tietjens was in France at all, and after later receiving, towards four in the afternoon, a telegram, dispatched by Sylvia herself from Havre, to say that she would be arriving by a noon train. The general had been almost as much upset at the thought that his car would not be there to meet Sylvia as by the thought that she was coming at all. But a strike of French railway civilians had delayed Sylvia's arrival. Campion had dispatched, within five minutes, his snorter to Tietjens, who he was convinced knew all about Sylvia's coming, and his car to Rouen Station with Levin in it.

The general, in fact, was in a fine confusion. He was convinced that Tietjens, as Man of Intellect, had treated Sylvia badly, even to the extent of stealing two pair of her best sheets, and he was also convinced that Tietjens was in close collusion with Sylvia. As Man of Intellect, Campion was convinced, Tietjens was dissatisfied with his lowly job of draft-forwarding officer and wanted a place of an extravagantly cooshy kind in the general's own entourage. . . . And Levin had said that it made it all the worse that Campion in his bothered heart thought that Tietjens really ought to have more exalted employment. He had said to Levin:

"Damn it all, the fellow ought to be in command of my intelligence instead of you. But he's unsound. That's what he is: unsound. He's too brilliant. . . . And he'd talk both the hind legs off Sweedlepumpkins." Sweedlepumpkins was the general's favourite charger. The general was afraid of talk. He practically never talked with anyone except about his job—certainly never with Tietjens—without being proved to be in the wrong, and that undermined his belief in himself.

So that altogether he was in a fine fume. And confusion.

He was almost ready to believe that Tietjens was at the bottom of every trouble that occurred in his immense command.

But when all that was gathered, Tietjens was not much farther forward in knowing what his wife's errand in France was.

"She complains," Levin had bleated painfully at some point on the slippery coastguard path, "about your taking her sheets. And about a Miss . . . a Miss Wanostrocht, is it? . . . The general is not inclined to attach much importance to the sheets. . . ."

It appeared that a sort of conference on Tietjens' case had taken place in the immense tapestried salon in which Campion lived with the more intimate members of his headquarters, and which was, for the moment, presided over by Sylvia, who had exposed various wrongs to the general and Levin. Major Perowne had excused himself on the ground that he was hardly competent to express an opinion. Really, Levin said, he was sulking because Campion had accused him of running the risk of getting himself and Mrs. Tietjens "talked about." Levin thought it was a bit thick of the general. Were none of the members of his staff ever to escort a lady anywhere? As if they were sixth-form schoolboys. . . .

"But you . . . you . . . you . . ." he stuttered and shivered together, "certainly *do* seem to have been remiss in not writing to Mrs. Tietjens. The poor lady—excuse me!—really appears to have been out of her mind with anxiety. . . ." That was why she had been waiting in the general's car at the bottom of the hill. To get a glimpse of Tietjens' living body. For they had been utterly unable, up at H.Q., to convince her that Tietjens was even alive, much less in that town.

She hadn't, in fact, waited even so long. Having apparently convinced herself by conversation with the sentries outside the guard-room that Tietjens actually still existed, she had told the chauffeur orderly to drive her back to the Hôtel de la Poste, leaving the wretched Levin to make his way back into the town by tram or as best he might. They had seen the lights of the car below them, turning, with its gaily lit interior, and disappearing among the trees along the road farther down. . . . The sentry, rather monosyllabically and gruffly—you can tell, all right, when a Tommy has something at the back of his mind!—informed them that the sergeant had turned out the guard so that all his men together could

assure the lady that the captain was alive and well. The obliging sergeant said that he had adopted that manœuvre which
generally should attend only the visits of general officers
and, once a day, that of the C.O., because the lady had
seemed so distressed at having received no letters from the
captain. The guard-room itself, which was unprovided with
cells, was decorated by the presence of two drunks, who,
having taken it into their heads to destroy their clothing,
were in a state of complete nudity. The sergeant hoped,
therefore, that he had done no wrong. Rightly the garrison
Military Police ought to take drunks picked up outside camp
to the A.P.M.'s guard-room, but seeing the state of undress
and the violent behaviour of these two, the sergeant had
thought right to oblige the redcaps. The voices of the
drunks singing the martial anthem of the "Men of Harlech"
could be heard corroborating the sergeant's opinion as to
their states. He added that he would not have turned out the
guard if it had not been for its being the captain's lady.

"A damn smart fellow, that sergeant," Colonel Levin had
said. "There couldn't have been any better way of convincing
Mrs. Tietjens."

Tietjens had said—and even whilst he was saying it he
tremendously wished he hadn't:

"Oh, a *damned* smart fellow"; for the bitter irony of his
tone had given Levin the chance to remonstrate with him as
to his attitude towards Sylvia. Not at all as to his actions—
for Levin conscientiously stuck to his thesis that Tietjens was
the soul of honour—but just as to his tone of voice in talking of the sergeant who had been kind to Sylvia and, just
precisely, because Tietjens' not writing to his wife had given
rise to the incident. Tietjens had thought of saying that
considering the terms on which they had parted, he would
have considered himself as molesting the lady if he had
addressed to her any letter at all. But he said nothing, and
for a quarter of an hour the incident resolved itself into a
soliloquy on the slippery hill-side, delivered by Levin on the
subject of matrimony. It was a matter which, naturally, at
that moment very much occupied his thoughts. He considered
that a man should so live with his wife that she should be
able to open all his letters. That was his idea of the idyllic.
And when Tietjens remarked with irony that he had never
in his life either written or received a letter that his wife
might not have read, Levin exclaimed with such enthusiasm
as almost to lose his balance in the mist:

"I was sure of it, old fellow. But it enormously cheers

me up to hear you say so." He added that he desired as
far as possible to model his ideas of life and his behaviour
on those of this his friend. For, naturally, about, as he was,
to unite his fortunes with those of Miss de Bailly, that could
be considered a turning-point of his career.

4 ~

THEY HAD gone back up the hill so that Levin might telephone to headquarters for his own car in case the general's
chauffeur should not have the sense to return for him. But
that was as far as Tietjens got in uninterrupted reminiscence
of that scene. . . . He was sitting in his flea-bag, digging
idly with his pencil into the squared page of his note-book,
which had remained open on his knees, his eyes going over
and over again over the words with which his report on his
own case had concluded—the words: "So the interview ended
rather untidily." Over the words went the image of the dark
hill-side with the lights of the town, now that the air raid
was finished, spreading high up into the sky below them. . . .

But at that point the doctor's batman had uttered, as if
with a jocular, hoarse irony, the name:

"Poor —— O Nine Morgan! . . ." and over the whitish
sheet of paper on a level with his nose Tietjens perceived
thin films of reddish-purple to be wavering, then a glutinous
surface of gummy scarlet pigment. Moving! It was once more
an effect of fatigue, operating on the retina, that was perfectly familiar to Tietjens. But it filled him with indignation
against his own weakness. He said to himself: Wasn't the
name of the wretched O9 Morgan to be mentioned in his
hearing without his retina presenting him with the glowing
image of the fellow's blood? He watched the phenomenon,
growing fainter, moving to the right-hand top corner of the
paper and turning a faintly luminous green. He watched it
with a grim irony.

Was he, he said to himself, to regard himself as responsible for the fellow's death? Was his inner mentality
going to present that claim upon him? That would be absurd.
The end of the earth! The absurd end of the earth . . . Yet
that insignificant ass Levin had that evening asserted the
claim to go into his, Tietjens of Groby's, relations with his
wife. That was an end of the earth as absurd! It was the unthinkable thing, as unthinkable as the theory that the officer

can be responsible for the death of the man. . . . But the idea
had certainly presented itself to him. How could he be responsible for the death? In fact—in literalness—he was. It
had depended absolutely upon his discretion whether the
man should go home or not. The man's life or death had
been in his hands. He had followed the perfectly correct
course. He had written to the police of the man's home town,
and the police had urged him not to let the man come home.
. . . Extraordinary morality on the part of a police force!
The man, they begged, should not be sent home because a
prize-fighter was occupying his bed and laundry. . . . Extraordinary common sense, very likely . . . They probably
did not want to get drawn into a scrap with Red Evans of
the Red Castle. . . .

For a moment he seemed to see . . . he actually saw . . .
O9 Morgan's eyes looking at him with a sort of wonder, as
they had looked when he had refused the fellow his leave.
. . . A sort of wonder! Without resentment, but with incredulity. As you might look at God, you being very small and
ten feet or so below His throne when He pronounced some
inscrutable judgement! . . . The Lord giveth home-leave,
and the Lord refuseth. . . . Probably not blessed, but queer,
be the name of God-Tietjens!

And at the thought of the man as he was alive and of
him now, dead, an immense blackness descended all over
Tietjens. He said to himself: "I am very tired." Yet he was
not ashamed. . . . It was the blackness that descends on
you when you think of your dead. . . . It comes, at any time,
over the brightness of sunlight, in the grey of evening, in
the grey of the dawn, at mess, on parade; it comes at the
thought of one man or at the thought of half a battalion that
you have seen stretched out, under sheeting, the noses making little pimples: or not stretched out, lying face downwards, half buried. Or at the thought of dead that you have
never seen dead at all . . . Suddenly the light goes out. . . .
In this case it was because of one fellow, a dirty enough
man, not even very willing, not in the least endearing, certainly contemplating desertion. . . . But your dead . . . *Yours*
. . . Your own. As if joined to your own identity by a black
cord . . .

In the darkness outside, the brushing, swift, rhythmic pacing of an immense number of men went past, as if they
had been phantoms. A great number of men in fours, carried forward, irresistibly, by the overwhelming will of man-
kind in ruled motion. The sides of the hut were so thin that

it was peopled by an innumerable throng. A sodden voice, just at Tietjens' head, chuckled:

"For God's sake, sergeant-major, stop these———. I'm too —— drunk to halt them. . . ."

It made, for the moment, no impression on Tietjens' conscious mind. Men were going past. Cries went up in the camp. Not orders, the men were still marching. Cries.

Tietjens' lips—his mind was still with the dead—said:

"That obscene Pitkins! . . . I'll have him cashiered for this. . . ." He saw an obscene subaltern, small, with one eyelid that drooped.

He came awake at that. Pitkins was the subaltern he had detailed to march the draft to the station and go on to Bailleul under a boozy field-officer of sorts.

McKechnie said from the other bed:

"That's the draft back."

Tietjens said:

"Good God! . . ."

McKechnie said to the batman:

"For God's sake, go and see if it is. Come back at once. . . ."

The intolerable vision of the line, starving beneath the moon, of grey crowds murderously elbowing back a thin crowd in brown, zigzagged across the bronze light in the hut. The intolerable depression that, in those days, we felt—that all those millions were the playthings of ants busy in the miles of corridors beneath the domes and spires that rise up over the central heart of our comity—that intolerable weight upon the brain and the limbs descended once more on those two men lying upon their elbows. As they listened their jaws fell open. The long, polyphonic babble, rushing in from an extended line of men stood easy, alone rewarded their ears.

Tietjens said:

"That fellow won't come back. . . . He can never do an errand and come back. . . ." He thrust one of his legs cumbrously out of the top of his flea-bag. He said:

"By God, the Germans will be all over here in a week's time!"

He said to himself:

"If they so betray us from Whitehall, that fellow Levin has no right to pry into my matrimonial affairs. It is proper that one's individual feelings should be sacrificed to the necessities of a collective entity. But not if that entity is to be betrayed from above. Not if it hasn't the ten-millionth of a chance . . ." He regarded Levin's late incursion on his privacy as inquiries set afoot by the general. . . . Incredibly painful to him: like a medical examination into nudities, but perfectly proper. Old Campion had to assure himself that the Other Ranks were not demoralized by the spectacle of officers' matrimonial infidelities. . . . But such inquiries were not to be submitted to if the whole show were one gigantic demoralization!

McKechnie said, in reference to Tietjens' protruded foot: "There's no good your going out. . . . Cowley will get the men into their lines. He was prepared." He added: "If the fellows in Whitehall are determined to do old Puffles in, why don't they recall him?"

The legend was that an eminent personage in the government had a great personal dislike for the general in command of one army—the general being nicknamed Puffles. The government, therefore, were said to be starving his command of men so that disaster should fall upon his command.

"They can recall generals easy enough," McKechnie went on, "or anyone else!"

A heavy dislike that this member of the lower-middle classes should have opinions on public affairs overcame Tietjens. He exclaimed: "Oh, that's all tripe!"

He was himself outside all contact with affairs by now. But the other rumour in that troubled host had it that as a political manœuvre, the heads round Whitehall—the civilian heads—were starving the army of troops in order to hold over the allies of Great Britain the threat of abandoning altogether the Western Front. They were credited with threatening a strategic manœuvre on an immense scale in the Near East, perhaps really intending it or perhaps to force the hands of their allies over some political intrigue. These atrocious rumours reverberated backwards and forwards in the ears of all those millions under the black vault of heaven. All their comrades in the line were to be sacrificed as a rear-guard to their departing host. That whole land was to be annihilated as a sacrifice to one vanity. Now the draft had been called back. That seemed proof that the government meant to starve the line! McKechnie groaned:

"Poor —— old Bird! . . . He's booked. Eleven months in the front line, he's been. . . . Eleven *months!* . . . I was nine this stretch. With him."

He added:

"Get back into bed, old bean. . . . I'll go and look after the men if it's necessary. . . ."

Tietjens said:

"You don't so much as know where their lines are. . . ." And sat listening. Nothing but the long roll of tongues came to him. He said:

"Damn it! The men ought not to be kept standing in the cold like that. . . ." Fury filled him beneath despair. His eyes filled with tears. "God," he said to himself, "the fellow Levin presumes to interfere in my private affairs. . . . Damn it," he said again, "it's like doing a little impertinence in a world that's foundering. . . ."

The world was foundering.

"I'd go out," he said, "but I don't want to have to put that filthy little Pitkins under arrest. He only drinks because he's shell-shocked. He's not man enough else, the unclean little Nonconformist. . . ."

McKechnie said:

"Hold on! . . . I'm a Presbyterian myself. . . ."

Tietjens answered:

"You would be! . . ." He said: "I beg your pardon. . . . There will be no more parades. . . . The British Army is dishonoured forever. . . ."

McKechnie said:

"That's all right, old bean. . . ."

Tietjens exclaimed with sudden violence:

"What the hell are you doing in the officers' lines? . . . Don't you know it's a court-martial offence?"

He was confronted with the broad, mealy face of his regimental quartermaster-sergeant, the sort of fellow who wore an officer's cap against the regulations, with a Tommy's silver-plated badge. A man determined to get Sergeant-Major Cowley's job. The man had come in unheard under the roll of voices outside. He said:

"Excuse me, sir, I took the liberty of knocking. . . . The sergeant-major is in an epileptic fit. . . . I wanted your directions before putting the draft into the tents with the other men. . . ." Having said that tentatively, he hazarded cautiously: "The sergeant-major throws these fits, sir, if he is suddenly woke up. . . . And Second-Lieutenant Pitkins woke him very suddenly. . . ."

Tietjens said:

"So you took on you the job of a beastly informer against both of them. . . . I shan't forget it." He said to himself:

"I'll get this fellow one day. . . ." and he seemed to hear with pleasure the clicking and tearing of the scissors as, inside three parts of a hollow square, they cut off his stripes and badges.

McKechnie exclaimed:

"Good God, man, you aren't going out in nothing but your pyjamas. Put your slacks on under your British warm. . . ."

Tietjens said:

"Send the Canadian sergeant-major to me at the double. . . ." to the quarter. "My slacks are at the tailor's, being pressed." His slacks were being pressed for the ceremony of the signing of the marriage contract of Levin, the fellow who had interfered in his private affairs. He continued into the mealy broad face and vague eyes of the quartermaster: "You know as well as I do that it was the Canadian sergeant-major's job to report to me. . . . I'll let you off this time, but, by God, if I catch you spying round the officers' lines again, you are for a D.C.M. . . ."

He wrapped a coarse, Red Cross, grey-wool muffler under the turned-up collar of his British warm.

"That swine," he said to McKechnie, "spies on the officers' lines in the hope of getting a commission by catching out —— little squits like Pitkins when they're drunk. . . . I'm seven hundred braces down. Morgan does not know that I know that I'm that much down. But you can bet he knows where they have gone. . . ."

McKechnie said:

"I wish you would not go out like that. . . . I'll make you some cocoa. . . ."

Tietjens said:

"I can't keep the men waiting while I dress. . . . I'm as strong as a horse. . . ."

He was out amongst the bitterness, the mist, and the moon-gleams on three thousand rifle barrels, and the voices. . . . He was seeing the Germans pour through a thin line, and his heart was leaden. . . . A tall, graceful man swam up against him and said, through his nose, like any American:

"There has been a railway accident, due to the French strikers. The draft is put back till three pip emma the day after to-morrow, sir."

Tietjens exclaimed:

"It isn't countermanded?" breathlessly.

The Canadian sergeant-major said:

"No, sir. . . . A railway accident . . . Sabotage by the French, they say . . . Four Glamorganshire sergeants, all

nineteen-fourteen men, killed, sir, going home on leave. But
the draft is not cancelled. . . ."

Tietjens said:

"Thank God!"

The slim Canadian with his educated voice said:

"You're thanking God, sir, for what's very much to our
detriment. Our draft was ordered for Salonika till this morning. The sergeant in charge of draft returns showed me the
name "Salonika" scored off in his draft roster. Sergeant-
Major Cowley had got hold of the wrong story. Now it's
going up the line. The other would have been a full two
months' more life for us."

The man's rather slow voice seemed to continue for a
long time. As it went on Tietjens felt the sunlight dwelling
on his nearly coverless limbs and the tide of youth returning
to his veins. It was like champagne. He said:

"You sergeants get a great deal too much information.
The sergeant in charge of returns had no business to show
you his roster. It's not your fault, of course. But you are
an intelligent man. You can see how useful that news might
be to certain people: people that it's not to your own interest should know these things. . . ." He said to himself: "A
landmark in history . . ." And then: "Where the devil did
my mind get hold of that expression at this moment?" They
were walking in mist, down an immense lane, one hedge
of which was topped by the serrated heads and irregularly
held rifles that showed here and there. He said to the
sergeant-major: "Call 'em to attention. Never mind their
dressing; we've got to get 'em into bed. Roll-call will be at
nine to-morrow."

His mind said:

"If this means the single command . . . And it's bound
to mean the single command, it's the turning-point. . . . Why
the hell am I so extraordinarily glad? What's it to me?"

He was shouting in a round voice:

"Now, then, men, you've got to go six extra in a tent. See
if you can fall out six at a time at each tent. It's not in the
drill-book, but see if you can do it for yourselves. You're
smart men: use your intelligences. The sooner you get to
bed, the sooner you'll be warm. I wish I was. Don't disturb
the men who're already in the tents. They've got to be up
for fatigues to-morrow at five, poor devils. You can lie soft
till three hours after that. . . . The draft will move to the
left in fours. . . . Form fours. . . . Left . . ." Whilst the
voices of the sergeants in charge of companies yelped vary-

ingly to a distance in the quick-march order he said to himself:

"Extraordinarily glad . . . A strong passion . . . How damn well these fellows move! . . . Cannon fodder . . . Cannon fodder . . . That's what their steps say. . . ." His whole body shook in the grip of the cold that beneath his loose overcoat gnawed his pyjamaed limbs. He could not leave the men, but cantered beside them with the sergeant-major till he came to the head of the column in the open in time to wheel the first double company into a line of ghosts that were tents, silent and austere in the moon's very shadowy light. . . . It appeared to him a magic spectacle. He said to the sergeant-major: "Move the second company to B line, and so on," and stood at the side of the men as they wheeled, stamping, like a wall in motion. He thrust his stick half-way down between the second and third files. "Now, then, a four and half a four to the right; remaining half-four and next four to the left. Fall out into first tents to right and left. . . ." He continued saying: "First four and half, this four to the right . . . Damn you, by the left! How can you tell which beastly four you belong to if you don't march by the left? . . . Remember you're soldiers, not new-chum lumber-men. . . ."

It was sheer exhilaration to freeze there on the downside in the extraordinarily pure air with the extraordinarily fine men. They came round, marking time with the stamp of guardsmen. He said, with tears in his voice:

"Damn it all, I gave them that extra bit of smartness. . . . Damn it all, there's something I've done. . . ." Getting cattle into condition for the slaughter-house. . . . They were as eager as bullocks running down by Camden Town to Smithfield Market. . . . Seventy per cent of them would never come back. . . . But it's better to go to Heaven with your skin shining and master of your limbs than as a hulking lout. . . . The Almighty's orderly room will welcome you better, in all probability. . . . He continued exclaiming monotonously: "Remaining half-four and next four to the left. . . . Hold your beastly tongues when you fall out. I can't hear myself give orders. . . ." It lasted a long time. Then they were all swallowed up.

He staggered, his knees wooden-stiff with the cold, and the cold more intense now the wall of men no longer sheltered him from the wind, out along the brink of the plateau to the other lines. It gave him satisfaction to observe that he had got his men into their lines seventy-five per cent quicker than the best of the N.C.O.s who had had charge

of the other lines. Nevertheless, he swore bitingly at the
sergeants: their men were in knots round the entrance to the
alleys of ghost-pyramids. . . . Then there were no more, and
he drifted with regret across the plain towards his country
street of huts. One of them had a coarse evergreen rose
growing over it. He picked a leaf, pressed it to his lips and
threw it up into the wind. . . . "That's for Valentine," he said
meditatively. "Why did I do that? . . . Or perhaps it's for
England. . . ." He said: "Damn it all, this is patriotism! . . .
This is patriotism. . . ." It wasn't what you took patriotism
as a rule to be. There were supposed to be more parades
about that job! . . . But this was just a broke to the wide,
wheezy, half-frozen Yorkshireman, who despised everyone in
England not a Yorkshireman or from more to the North, at
two in the morning picking a leaf from a rose-tree and slob-
bering over it, without knowing what he was doing. And
then discovering that it was half for a pug-nosed girl whom
he presumed, but didn't know, to smell like a primrose;
and half for . . . England! . . . At two in the morning with
the thermometer ten degrees below zero . . . Damn, it was
cold! . . .

And why these emotions? . . . Because England, not before it was time, had been allowed to decide not to do the
dirty on her associates! . . . He said to himself: "It is probably because a hundred thousand sentimentalists like myself
commit similar excesses of the subconscious that we persevere
in this glorious but atrocious undertaking. All the same, I
didn't know I had it in me!" A strong passion! . . . For his
girl and his country! . . . Nevertheless, his girl was a pro-
German. . . . It was a queer mix-up! . . . Not of course a pro-
German, but disapproving of the preparation of men, like
bullocks, with sleek, healthy skins, for the abattoirs in
Smithfield . . . Agreeing, presumably, with the squits who
had been hitherto starving the B.E.F. of men . . . A queer
mix-up . . .

At half-past one the next day, in chastened winter sunlight, he mounted Schomburg, a coffin-headed, bright chestnut, captured from the Germans on the Marne, by the Second
Battalion of the Glamorganshires. He had not been on the
back of the animal two minutes before he remembered that
he had forgotten to look it over. It was the first time in his
life that he had ever forgotten to look at an animal's hoofs,
fetlocks, knees, nostrils and eyes and to take a pull at the
girth before climbing into the saddle. But he had ordered the

horse for a quarter to one, and even though he had bolted
his cold lunch like a cannibal in haste, there he was three-
quarters of an hour late and with his head still full of teasing
problems. He had meant to clear his head by a long canter
over the be-hutted downs, dropping down into the city by a
bypath.

But the ride did not clear his head—rather, the sleeplessness of the night began for the first time then to tell on him
after a morning of fatigues, during which he had managed
to keep the thought of Sylvia at arm's length. He had to
wait to see Sylvia before he could see what Sylvia wanted.
And morning had brought the common-sense idea that probably she wanted to do nothing more than pull the string of
the shower-bath—which meant committing herself to the first
extravagant action that came into her head and exulting in
the consequences.

He had not managed to get to bed at all the night before.
Captain McKechnie, who had had some cocoa—a beverage
Tietjens had never before tasted—hot and ready for him
on his return from the lines, had kept him till past half-
past four, relating with a male fury his really very painful
story. It appeared that he had obtained leave to go home
and divorce his wife, who, during his absence in France, had
been living with an Egyptologist in government service. Then,
acting under conscientious scruples of the younger school of
the day, he had refrained from divorcing her. Campion had
in consequence threatened to deprive him of his commission.
. . . The poor devil—who had actually consented to contribute to the costs of the household of his wife and the
Egyptologist—had gone raving mad and had showered an
extraordinary torrent of abuse at the decent old fellow that
Campion was. . . . A decent old fellow, really. For the interview, being delicate, had taken place in the general's
bedroom, and the general had not felt it necessary, there
being no orderlies or junior officers present, to take any official notice of McKechnie's outburst. McKechnie was a fellow with an excellent military record; you could, in fact,
hardly have found a regimental officer with a better record.
So Campion had decided to deal with the man as suffering
from a temporary brain-storm and had sent him to Tietjens'
unit for rest and recuperation. It was an irregularity, but the
general was of a rank to risk what irregularities he considered to be of use to the service.

It had turned out that McKechnie was actually the nephew
of Tietjens' very old intimate, Sir Vincent Macmaster, of the

Department of Statistics, being the son of his sister who had married the assistant to the elder Macmaster, a small grocer in the Port of Leith in Scotland. . . . That indeed had been why Campion had been interested in him. Determined as he was to show his godson no unreasonable military favours, the general was perfectly ready to do a kindness that he thought would please Tietjens. All these pieces of information Tietjens had packed away in his mind for future consideration, and it being after four-thirty before McKechnie had calmed himself down, Tietjens had taken the opportunity to inspect the breakfasts of the various fatigues ordered for duty in the town, these being detailed for various hours from a quarter to five to seven. It was a matter of satisfaction to Tietjens to have seen to the breakfasts and inspected his cook-houses, since he did not often manage to make the opportunity and he could by no means trust his orderly officers.

At breakfast in the depot mess hut he was detained by the colonel in command of the depot, the Anglican padre and McKechnie; the colonel, very old, so frail that you would have thought that a shudder or a cough would have shaken his bones one from another, had yet a passionate belief that the Greek Church should exchange communicants with the Anglican: the padre, a stout, militant churchman, had a gloomy contempt for Orthodox theology. McKechnie from time to time essayed to define the communion according to the Presbyterian rite. They all listened to Tietjens whilst he dilated on the historic aspects of the various schisms of Christianity and accepted his rough definition to the effect that in transubstantiation, the host actually became the divine presence, whereas in consubstantiation, the substance of the host, as if miraculously become porous, was suffused with the presence as a sponge is with water. . . . They all agreed that the breakfast-bacon supplied from store was uneatable and agreed to put up half a crown a week apiece to get better for their table.

Tietjens had walked in the sunlight down the lines, past the hut with the evergreen-climbing rose, in the sunlight, thinking in an interval good-humouredly about his official religion: about the Almighty as, on a colossal scale, a great English Landowner, benevolently awful, a colossal duke who never left his study and was thus invisible, but knowing all about the estate down to the last hind at the home farm and the last oak: Christ an almost too benevolent Land Steward, son of the Owner, knowing all about the estate down to the last child at the porter's lodge, apt to be got round by the more detrimental tenants: the Third Person of the Trinity, the spirit of the estate, the Game, as it were, as distinct from the players of the Game: the atmosphere of the estate that of the interior of Winchester Cathedral just after a Handel anthem has been finished, a perpetual Sunday, with, probably, a little cricket for the young men. Like Yorkshire of a Saturday afternoon; if you looked down on the whole broad county you would not see a single village green without its white flannels. That was why Yorkshire always leads the averages. . . . Probably by the time you got to Heaven you would be so worn out by work on this planet that you would accept the English Sunday, forever, with extreme relief!

With his belief that all that was good in English literature ended with the seventeenth century, his imaginations of Heaven must be materialist—like Bunyan's. He laughed goodhumouredly at his projection of a hereafter. It was probably done with. Along with cricket. There would be no more parades of that sort. Probably they would play some beastly yelping game. . . . Like base-ball or association football . . . And Heaven? . . . Oh, it would be a revival meeting on a Welsh hill-side. Or Chatauqua, wherever that was . . . And God? A Real Estate Agent, with Marxist views . . . He hoped to be out of it before the cessation of hostilities, in which case he might be just in time for the last train to the old Heaven. . . .

In his orderly hut he found an immense number of papers. On the top an envelope marked "Urgent." "Private" with a huge rubber stamp. From Levin. Levin, too, must have been up pretty late. It was not about Mrs. Tietjens or even Miss de Bailly. It was a private warning that Tietjens would probably have his draft on his hands another week or ten days and very likely another couple of thousand men extra as well. He warned Tietjens to draw all the tents he could get hold of as soon as possible. . . . Tietjens called to a subaltern with pimples who was picking his teeth with a pen-nib at the other end of the hut: "Here, you! . . . Take two companies of the Canadians to the depot store and draw all the tents you can get up to two hundred and fifty. . . . Have 'em put alongside my D lines. . . . Do you know how to look after putting up tents? . . . Well, then, get Thompson . . . no, Pitkins, to help you. . . ." The subaltern drifted out sulkily. Levin said that the French railway strikers, for some political reason, had sabotaged a mile of railway, the accident of the night before had completely blocked up all the lines, and the French civilians would not let their own break-down gangs make any repairs. German prisoners had been detailed for that fatigue, but probably Tietjens' Canadian Railway corps would be wanted. He had better hold them in readiness. The strike was said to be a manœuvre for forcing our hands—to get us to take over more of the line. In that case they had jolly well dished themselves, for how could we take over more of the line without more men, and how could we send up more men without the railway to send them by? We had half a dozen army corps all ready to go. Now they were all jammed. Fortunately the weather at the front was so beastly that the Germans could not move. He finished up: "Four in the morning, old bean; *à tantôt!*" the last phrase having been learned from Mlle. de Bailly. Tietjens grumbled that if they went on piling up the work on him like this he would never get down to the signing of that marriage contract.

He called the Canadian sergeant-major to him.

"See," he said, "that you keep the Railway Service Corps in camp with their arms ready, whatever their arms are. Tools, I suppose. Are their tools all complete? And their muster-roll."

"Girtin has gone absent, sir," the slim, dark fellow said, with an air of destiny. Girtin was the respectable man with the mother to whom Tietjens had given the two hours' leave the night before.

Tietjens answered:

"He would have!" with a sour grin. It enhanced his views of strictly respectable humanity. They black-mailed you with lamentable and pathetic tales and then did the dirty on you. He said to the sergeant-major:

"You will be here for another week or ten days. See that you get your tents up all right and the men comfortable. I will inspect them as soon as I have taken my orderly room. Full marching order. Captain McKechnie will inspect their kits at two."

The sergeant-major, stiff but graceful, had something at the back of his mind. It came out:

"I have my marching orders for two-thirty this afternoon. The notice for inserting my commission in depot orders is on your table. I leave for the O.T.C. by the three train. . . ."

Tietjens said:

"Your commission! . . ." It was a confounded nuisance.

The sergeant-major said:

"Sergeant-Major Cowley and I applied for our commissions

three months ago. The communications granting them are both on your table together. . . ."

Tietjens said:

"Sergeant-Major Cowley . . . Good God! Who recommended you?"

The whole organization of his confounded battalion fell to pieces. It appeared that a circular had come round three months before—before Tietjens had been given command of that unit—asking for experienced first-class warrant-officers capable of serving as instructors in Officers' Training Corps, with commissions. Sergeant-Major Cowley had been recommended by the colonel of the depot, Sergeant-Major Ledoux by his own colonel. Tietjens felt as if he had been let down—but of course he had not been. It was just the way of the army, all the time. You got a platoon or a battalion or, for the matter of that, a dug-out or a tent by herculean labours into good fettle. It ran all right for a day or two, then it all fell to pieces, the personnel scattered to the four winds by what appeared merely wanton orders, coming from the most unexpected headquarters, or the premises were smashed up by a chance shell that might just as well have fallen somewhere else. . . . The finger of Fate! . . .

But it put a confounded lot more work on him. . . . He said to Sergeant-Major Cowley, whom he found in the next hut, where all the paper-work of the unit was done:

"I should have thought you would have been enormously better off as regimental sergeant-major than with a commission. I know I would rather have the job." Cowley answered—he was very pallid and shaken—that with his unfortunate infirmity coming on at any moment of shock, he would be better in a job where he could slack off, like an O.T.C. He had always been subject to small fits, over in a minute or couple of seconds even. . . . But getting too near an H.E. shell—after Noircourt, which had knocked out Tietjens himself—had brought them on, violent. There was also, he finished, the gentility to be considered. Tietjens said:

"Oh, the gentility! . . . That's not worth a flea's jump. . . . There won't be any more parades after this war. There aren't any now. Look at who your companions will be in an officer's quarters; you'd be in a great deal better society in any self-respecting sergeants' mess." Cowley answered that he knew the service had gone to the dogs. All the same, his missis liked it. And there was his daughter Winnie to be considered. She had always been a bit wild, and his

missis wrote that she had gone wilder than ever, all due to
the war. Cowley thought that the bad boys would be a
little more careful how they monkeyed with her if she was
an officer's daughter. . . . There was probably something in
that!

Coming out into the open, confidentially, with Tietjens,
Cowley dropped his voice huskily to say:

"Take Quartermaster-Sergeant Morgan for R.S.M., sir."

Tietjens said explosively:

"I'm damned if I will." Then he asked: "Why?" The
wisdom of old N.C.O.s is a thing no prudent officer neg-
lects.

"He can do the work, sir," Cowley said. "He's out for
a commission, and he'll do his best. . . ." He dropped his
husky voice to a still greater depth of mystery:

"You're over two hundred—I should say nearer three
hundred—pounds down in your battalion stores. I don't suppose you want to lose a sum of money like that?"

Tietjens said:

"I'm damned if I do. . . . But I don't see . . . Oh, yes, I do.
. . . If I make him sergeant-major he has to hand over the
stores all complete. . . . To-day . . . Can he do it?"

Cowley said that Morgan could have till the day after
to-morrow. He would look after things till then.

"But you'll want to have a flutter before you go," Tietjens
said. "Don't stop for me."

Cowley said that he would stop and see the job through.
He had thought of going down into the town and having
a flutter. But the girls down there were a common sort, and
it was bad for his complaint. . . . He would stop and see
what could be done with Morgan. Of course it was possible
that Morgan might decide to face things out. He might
prefer to stick to the money he'd got by disposing of Tietjens' stores to other battalions that were down or to civilian
contractors. And stand a court martial! But it wasn't likely.
He was a Nonconformist deacon or pew-opener or even a
minister possibly, at home in Wales. . . . From near Denbigh!
And Cowley had got a very good man, a first-class man, an
Oxford professor, now a lance-corporal at the depot, for
Morgan's place. The colonel would lend him to Tietjens and
would get him rated acting quartermaster-sergeant unpaid.
. . . Cowley had it all arranged. . . . Lance-Corporal Caldi-
cott was a first-class man, only he could not tell his right
hand from his left on parade. Literally could not tell
them . . .

So the battalion settled itself down. . . . Whilst Cowley and he were at the colonel's orderly room arranging for the transfer of the professor—he was really only a fellow of his college—who did not know his right hand from his left, Tietjens was engaged in the remains of the colonel's furious argument as to the union of the Anglican and Eastern rites. The colonel—he was a full colonel—sat in his lovely private office, a light, gay compartment of a tin hutment, the walls being papered in scarlet, with, on the purplish, thick, soft baize of his table-cover, a tall glass vase from which sprayed out pale Riviera roses, the gift of young lady admirers amongst the V.A.D.s in the town because he was a darling, and an open, very gilt and leather-bound volume of a biblical encyclopaedia beneath his delicate septuagenarian features. He was confirming his opinion that a union between the Church of England and the Greek Orthodox Church was the only thing that could save civilization. The whole war turned on that. The Central Empires represented Roman Catholicism, the Allies Protestantism and Orthodoxy. Let them unite. The papacy was a traitor to the cause of civilization. Why had the Vatican not protested with no uncertain voice about the abominations practised on the Belgian Catholics? . . .

Tietjens pointed out languidly objections to this theory. The first thing our ambassador to the Vatican had found out on arriving in Rome and protesting about massacres of Catholic laymen in Belgium was that the Russians before they had been a day in Austrian Poland had hanged twelve Roman Catholic bishops in front of their palaces.

Cowley was engaged with the adjutant at another table. The colonel ended his theologico-political tirade by saying:

"I shall be very sorry to lose you, Tietjens. I don't know what we shall do without you. I never had a moment's peace with your unit until you came."

Tietjens said:

"Well, you aren't losing me, sir, as far as I know."

The colonel said:

"Oh, yes, we are. You are going up the line next week. . . ." He added: "Now, don't get angry with me. . . . I've protested very strongly to old Campion—General Campion—that I cannot do without you." And he made, with his delicate, thin, hairy-backed, white hands a motion as of washing.

The ground moved under Tietjens' feet. He felt himself

clambering over slopes of mud with his heavy legs and labouring chest. He said:

"Damn it all! . . . I'm not fit. . . . I'm C3. . . . I was ordered to live in an hotel in the town. . . . I only mess here to be near the battalion."

The colonel said with some eagerness:

"Then you can protest to garrison. . . . I hope you will. . . . But I suppose you are the sort of fellow that won't."

Tietjens said:

"No, sir . . . Of course I cannot protest. . . . Though it's probably a mistake of some clerk . . . I could not stand a week in the line. . . ." The profound misery of brooding apprehension in the line was less on his mind than, precisely, the appalling labour of the lower limbs when you live in mud to the neck. . . . Besides, whilst he had been in hospital practically the whole of his equipment had disappeared from his kit-bag—including Sylvia's two pair of sheets!—and he had no money with which to get more. He had not even any trench-boots. Fantastic financial troubles settled on his mind.

The colonel said to the adjutant at the other purple baize-covered table:

"Show Captain Tietjens those marching orders of his. . . . They're from Whitehall, aren't they? . . . You never know where these things come from now-a-days. I call them the arrow that flieth by night!"

The adjutant, a diminutive, a positively miniature, gentleman with Coldstream badges up and a dreadfully worried brow, drifted a quarto sheet of paper out of a pile, across his table-cloth towards Tietjens. His tiny hands seemed about to fall off at the wrists; his temples shuddered with neuralgia. He said:

"For God's sake, do protest to garrison if you feel you can. . . . We *can't* have more work shoved on us. . . . Major Lawrence and Major Halkett left the whole of the work of your unit to us. . . ."

The sumptuous paper, with the royal arms embossed at the top, informed Tietjens that he would report to his VIth Battalion on the Wednesday of next week in preparation for taking up the duties of divisional transport-officer to the XIXth Division. The order came from room G 14 R at the War Office. He asked what the deuce G 14 R was, of the adjutant, who, in an access of neuralgic agony, shook his head miserably between his two hands, his elbows on the table-cloth.

Sergeant-Major Cowley, with his air of a solicitor's clerk, said the room G 14 R was the department that dealt with civilian requests for the services of officers. To the adjutant who asked what the devil a civilian request for the employment of officers could have to do with sending Captain Tietjens to the XIXth Division, Sergeant-Major Cowley presumed that it was because of the activities of the Earl of Beichan. The Earl of Beichan, a Levantine financier and race-horse owner, was interesting himself in army horses after a short visit to the lines of communication. He also owned several newspapers. So they had been waking up the army transport-animals department to please him. The adjutant would no doubt have observed a Veterinary-Lieutenant Hotchkiss or Hitchcock. He had come to them through G 14 R. At the request of Lord Beichan, who was personally interested in Lieutenant Hotchkiss's theories. He was to make experiments on the horses of the Fourth Army—in which the XIXth Division was then to be found. . . . "So," Cowley said, "you'll be under him as far as your horse lines go. If you go up." Perhaps Lord Beichan was a friend of Captain Tietjens and had asked for him, too: Captain Tietjens was known to be wonderful with horses.

Tietjens, his breath rushing through his nostrils, swore he would not go up the line at the bidding of a hog like Beichan, whose real name was Stavropolides, formerly Nathan.

He said the army was reeling to its base because of the continual interference of civilians. He said it was absolutely impossible to get through his programs of parades because of the perpetual extra drills that were forced on them at the biddings of civilians. Any fool who owned a newspaper, nay, any fool who could write to a newspaper or any beastly little squit of a novelist could frighten the government and the War Office into taking up one more hour of the men's parade time for patent manoeuvres with jam-pots or fancy underclothing. Now he was asked if his men wanted lecturing on the causes of the war and whether he—he, good God!—would not like to give the men cosy chats on the nature of the enemy nations. . . .

The colonel said:

"There, there, Tietjens! . . . There, there! . . . We all suffer alike. *We've* got to lecture our men on the uses of a new patent sawdust stove. If you don't want that job, you can easily get the general to take you off it. They say you can turn him round your little finger. . . ."

"He's my godfather," Tietjens thought it wise to say. "I never asked him for a job, but I'm damned if it isn't his duty as a Christian to keep me out of the clutches of this Greek-'Ebrew pagan peer. . . . He's not even Orthodox, colonel. . . ."

The adjutant here said that Colour-Sergeant Morgan of their orderly room wanted a word with Tietjens. Tietjens said he hoped to goodness that Morgan had some money for him! The adjutant said he understood that Morgan had unearthed quite a little money that ought to have been paid to Tietjens by his agents and hadn't.

Colour-Sergeant Morgan was the regimental magician with figures. Inordinately tall and thin, his body, whilst his eyes peered into distant columns of ciphers, appeared to be always parallel with the surface of his table, and as he always answered the several officers whom he benefited without raising his head, his face was very little known to his superiors. He was, however, in appearance a very ordinary, thin N.C.O., whose spidery legs, when very rarely he appeared on a parade, had the air of running away with him as a race-horse might do. He told Tietjens that, pursuant to his instructions and the A.C.P. i 96 b that Tietjens had signed, he had ascertained that command pay at the rate of two guineas a day and supplementary fuel and light allowance at the rate of 6s. 8d. was being paid weekly by the Paymaster-General's department to his, Tietjens', account at his agents'. He suggested that Tietjens should write to his agents that if they did not immediately pay to his account the sum of £194 13s. 4d., by them received from the paymaster's department, he would proceed against the Crown by petition of right. And he strongly recommended Tietjens to draw a cheque on his own bank for the whole of the money because, if by any chance the agents had not paid the money in, he could sue them for damages and get them cast in several thousand pounds. And serve the devils right. They must have a million or so in hand in unpaid command and detention allowances due to officers. He only wished he could advertise in the papers offering to recover unpaid sums due by agents. He added that he had a nice little computation as to variations in the course of Gunter's Second Comet that he would like to ask Tietjens' advice about one of these days. The colour-sergeant was an impassioned amateur astronomer.

So Tietjens' morning went up and down. . . . The money at the moment, Sylvia being in that town, was of tremendous importance to him and came like an answer to prayer. It was not so agreeable, however, even in a world in which, never, never, never for ten minutes did you know whether you stood on your head or your heels, for Tietjens, on going back to the colonel's private office, to find Sergeant-Major Cowley coming out of the next room, in which, on account of the adjutant's neuralgia, the telephone was kept. Cowley announced to the three of them that the general had the day before ordered his correspondence-corporal to send a very emphatic note to Colonel Gillum to the effect that he was informing the competent authority that he had no intention whatever of parting with Captain Tietjens, who was invaluable in his command. The correspondence-corporal had informed Cowley that neither he nor the general knew who was the competent authority for telling Room G 14 R at the War Office to go to hell, but the matter would be looked up and put all right before the chit was sent off. . . .

That was good as far as it went. Tietjens was really interested in his present job, and although he would have liked well enough to have the job of looking after the horses of a division or even an army, he felt that he would rather it was put off till the spring, given the weather they were having and the state of his chest. And the complication of possible troubles with Lieutenant Hotchkiss, who, being a professor, had never really seen a horse—or not for ten years!—was something to be thought about very seriously. But all this appeared quite another matter when Cowley announced that the civilian authority who had asked for Tietjens' transfer was the permanent secretary to the Ministry of Transport. . . .

Colonel Gillum said:

"That's your brother, Mark. . . ." And indeed the permanent secretary to the Ministry of Transport was Tietjens' brother, Mark, known as the Indispensable Official. Tietjens felt a real instant of dismay. He considered that his violent protest against the job would appear rather a smack in the face for poor old wooden-featured Mark, who had probably taken a good deal of trouble to get him the job. Even if Mark should never hear of it, a man should not slap his brother in the face! Moreover, when he came to think of his last day in London, he remembered that Valentine Wannop, who had exaggerated ideas as to the safety of First Line Transport, had begged Mark to get him a job as divisional officer. . . . And he imagined Valentine's despair if she heard that he—Tietjens—had moved heaven and earth to get out of it.

He saw her lower lip quivering and the tears in her eyes.
. . . But he probably had got that from some novel, because
he had never seen her lower lip quiver. He had seen tears in
her eyes!

He hurried back to his lines to take his orderly room. In
the long hut McKechnie was taking that miniature court of
drunks and defaulters for him, and just as Tietjens reached
it he was taking the case of Girtin and two other Canadian
privates. . . . The case of Girtin interested him, and when
McKechnie slid out of his seat Tietjens occupied it. The
prisoners were only just being marched in by a Sergeant
Davis, an admirable N.C.O. whose rifle appeared to be part
of his rigid body and who executed an amazing number of
stamps in seriously turning in front of the C.O.'s table. It
gave the impression of an Indian war-dance. . . .

Tietjens glanced at the charge sheet, which was marked
as coming from the provost-marshal's office. Instead of the
charge of absence from draft, he read that of conduct
prejudicial to good order and military discipline in that . . .
The charge was written in a very illiterate hand; an immense,
beery lance-corporal of garrison Military Police, with a red
hatband, attended to give evidence. . . . It was a tenuous
and disagreeable affair. Girtin had not gone absent, so
Tietjens had to revise his views of the respectable. At any
rate, of the respectable colonial private soldier with
mother complete. For there really had been a mother, and
Girtin had been seeing her into the last tram down into
the town. A frail old lady. Apparently, trying to annoy the
Canadian, the beery lance-corporal of the garrison Military
Police had hustled the mother. Girtin had remonstrated;
very moderately, he said. The lance-corporal had shouted
at him. Two other Canadians returning to camp had inter-
vened and two more police. The police had called the
Canadians —— conscripts, which was almost more than the
Canadians could stand, they being voluntarily enlisted 1914
or 1915 men. The police—it was an old trick—had kept
the men talking until two minutes after the last post had
sounded and then had run them in for being absent off
pass—and for disrespect to their red hatbands.

Tietjens, with a carefully measured fury, first cross-ex-
amined and then damned the police witness to hell. Then
he marked the charge sheets with the words "Case explained," and told the Canadians to go and get ready for
his parade. It meant, he was aware, a frightful row with the
provost-marshal, who was a port-winey old general called

O'Hara and loved his police as if they had been ewe-lambs.

He took his parade, the Canadian troops looking like real soldiers in the sunlight, went round his lines with the new Canadian sergeant-major, who had his appointment, thank goodness, from his own authorities, wrote a report on the extreme undesirability of lecturing his men on the causes of the war, since his men were either graduates of one or other Canadian university and thus knew twice as much about the causes of the war as any lecturer the civilian authorities could provide, or else they were half-breed Micmac Indians, Eskimo, Japanese, or Alaskan Russians, none of whom could understand any English lecturer. . . . He was aware that he would have to rewrite his report so as to make it more respectful to the newspaper-proprietor peer, who, at that time, was urging on the home government the necessity of lecturing all the subjects of His Majesty on the causes of the war. But he wanted to get that grouse off his chest, and its disrespect would pain Levin, who would have to deal with these reports if he did not get married first. Then he lunched off army sausage-meat and potatoes, mashed with their skins complete, watered with an admirable 1906 *brut* champagne, which they bought themselves, and an appalling Canadian cheese—at the headquarters table to which the colonel had invited all the subalterns who that day were going up the line for the first time. They had some *h*'s in their compositions, but in revenge they must have boasted of a pint of adenoid growths between them. There was, however, a charming young half-caste Goa second-lieutenant, who afterwards proved of an heroic bravery. He gave Tietjens a lot of amusing information as to the working of the purdah in Portuguese India.

So, at half-past one Tietjens sat on Schomburg, the coffin-headed, bright chestnut from the Prussian horse-raising establishment near Celle. Almost a pure thoroughbred, this animal had usually the paces of a dining-room table, its legs being fully as stiff. But to-day its legs might have been made of cotton-wool; it lumbered over frosty ground, breathing stertorously, and at the jumping ground of the Deccan Horse, a mile above and behind Rouen, it did not so much refuse a very moderate jump as come together in a lugubrious crumple. It was, in the light of a red, jocular sun, like being mounted on a broken-hearted camel. In addition, the fatigues of the morning beginning to tell, Tietjens was troubled by an obsession of O9 Morgan which he found tiresome to have to stall off.

"What the hell," he asked of the orderly, a very silent private on a roan beside him, "what the hell is the matter with this horse? . . . Have you been keeping him warm?" He imagined that the clumsy paces of the animal beneath him added to his gloomy obsessions.

The orderly looked straight in front of him over a valley full of hutments. He said:

"No, sir." The 'oss 'ad been put in the 'oss-standings of G Depot. By the orders of Lieutenant 'Itchcock. 'Osses, Lieutenant 'Itchcock said, 'ad to be 'ardened.

Tietjens said:

"Did you tell him that it was my orders that Schomburg was to be kept warm? In the stables of the farm behind Number Sixteen I.B.D."

"The lieutenant," the orderly explained woodenly, "said as 'ow henny departure f'm 'is orders would be visited by the extreme displeasure of Lord Breechem, K.C.V.O., K.C.B., et cetera." The orderly was quivering with rage.

"You will," Tietjens said very carefully, "when you fall out with the horses at the Hôtel de la Poste, take Schomburg and the roan to the stables of La Volonté Farm, behind Number Sixteen I.B.D." The orderly was to close all the windows of the stable, stopping up any chinks with wadding. He would procure, if possible, a sawdust stove, new pattern, from Colonel Gillum's store and light it in the stables. He was also to give Schomburg and the roan oatmeal and water warmed as hot as the horses would take it. . . . And Tietjens finished sharply, "If Lieutenant Hotchkiss makes any comments, you will refer him to me. As his C.O."

The orderly seeking information as to horse-ailments, Tietjens said:

"The school of horse-copers to which Lord Beichan belongs believes in the hardening of all horse-flesh other than racing-cattle." They bred racing-cattle. Under six blankets apiece! Personally Tietjens did not believe in the hardening process and would not permit any animal over which he had control to be submitted to it. . . . It had been observed that if any animal was kept at a lower temperature than that of its normal climatic condition, it would contract diseases to which ordinarily it was not susceptible. . . . If you keep a chicken for two days in a pail of water, it will contract human scarlet fever or mumps if injected with either bacillus. If you remove the chicken from the water, dry it, and restore it to its normal conditions, the scarlet fever or the mumps will die out of the animal. . . . He said to the orderly: "You are an intelligent man. What deduction do you draw?"

The orderly looked away over the valley of the Seine.

"I suppose, sir," he said, "that our 'osses, being kept alwise cold in their standings, 'as hillnesses they wouldn't otherwise 'ave."

"Well, then," Tietjens said, "keep the poor animals warm."

He considered that here was the makings of a very nasty row for himself if, by any means, his sayings came round to the ears of Lord Beichan. But that he had to chance. He could not let a horse for which he was responsible be martyred. . . . There was too much to think about . . . so that nothing at all stood out to be thought of. The sun was glowing. The valley of the Seine was blue-grey, like a Gobelins tapestry. Over it all hung the shadow of a deceased Welsh soldier. An odd skylark was declaiming over an empty field behind the incinerators headquarters. . . . An odd lark. For as a rule larks do not sing in December. Larks sing only when courting or over the nest. . . . The bird must be oversexed. O9 Morgan was the other thing, that accounting for the prize-fighter!

They dropped down a mud lane between brick walls into the town. . . .

PART TWO

I ~

IN THE admirably appointed, white-enamelled, wicker-worked, bemirrored lounge of the best hotel of that town Sylvia Tietjens sat in a wickerwork chair, not listening rather abstractedly to a staff-major who was lachrymosely and continuously begging her to leave her bedroom door unlocked that night. She said:

"I don't know. . . . Yes, perhaps . . . I don't know. . . ." And looked distantly into a bluish wall-mirror that, like all the rest, was framed with white-painted cork bark. She stiffened a little and said:

"There's Christopher!"

The staff-major dropped his hat, his stick and his gloves. His black hair, which was without parting and heavy with some preparation of a glutinous kind, moved agitatedly on his scalp. He had been saying that Sylvia had ruined his life. Didn't Sylvia know that she had ruined his life? But for her, he might have married some pure young thing. Now he exclaimed:

"But what does he want? . . . Good God! . . . What does he want?"

"He wants," Sylvia said, "to play the part of Jesus Christ." Major Perowne exclaimed:

"Jesus Christ! . . . But he's the most foul-mouthed officer in the general's command. . . ."

"Well," Sylvia said, "if you had married your pure young thing she'd have . . . what is it? . . . cuckolded you within nine months. . . ."

Perowne shuddered a little at the word. He mumbled:

"I don't see . . . It seems to be the other way. . . ."

"Oh, no, it isn't," Sylvia said. "Think it over. . . . Morally, *you're* the husband. . . . *Im*morally, I should say . . . Because he's the man I want. . . . He looks ill. . . . Do hospital authorities always tell wives what is the matter with their husbands?"

From his angle in the chair from which he had half emerged Sylvia seemed to him to be looking at a blank wall.

"I don't see him," Perowne said.

"I can see him in the glass," Sylvia said. "Look! From here you can see him."

Perowne shuddered a little more.

"I don't want to see him. . . . I have to see him sometimes in the course of duty. . . . I don't like to. . . ."

Sylvia said:

"*You*," in a tone of very deep contempt. "You only carry chocolate boxes to flappers. . . . How can he come across you in the course of duty? . . . You're not a *soldier!*"

Perowne said:

"But what are we going to do? What will *he* do?"

"I," Sylvia answered, "shall tell the page-boy, when he comes with his card, to say that I'm engaged. . . . I don't know what *he'll* do. Hit you, very likely . . . He's looking at your back now. . . ."

Perowne became rigid, sunk into his deep chair.

"But he *couldn't!*" he exclaimed agitatedly. "You said that he was playing the part of Jesus Christ. Our Lord wouldn't hit people in an hotel lounge. . . ."

"Our Lord!" Sylvia said contemptuously. "What do you know about Our Lord? . . . Our Lord was a gentleman. . . . Christopher is playing at being Our Lord calling on the woman taken in adultery. . . . He's giving me the social backing that his being my husband seems to him to call for."

A one-armed, bearded maître d'hôtel approached them through groups of arm-chairs arranged for tête-à-tête. He said:

"Pardon . . . I did not see madame at first. . . ." And displayed a card on a salver. Without looking at it Sylvia said:

"*Dites à ce monsieur* . . . that I am occupied." The maître d'hôtel moved austerely away.

"But he'll smash me to pieces. . . ." Perowne exclaimed. "What am I to do? . . . What the deuce am I to do?" There would have been no way of exit for him except across Tietjens' face.

With her spine very rigid and the expression of a snake

that fixes a bird, Sylvia gazed straight in front of her and said nothing until she exclaimed:

"For God's sake, leave off trembling. . . . He would not do anything to a girl like you. . . . He's a man. . . ." The wickerwork of Perowne's chair had been crepitating as if it had been in a railway car. The sound ceased with a jerk. . . . Suddenly she clenched both her hands and let out a hateful little breath of air between her teeth.

"By the immortal saints," she exclaimed, "I swear I'll make his wooden face wince yet."

In the bluish looking-glass, a few minutes before, she had seen the agate-blue eyes of her husband, thirty feet away, over arm-chairs and between the fans of palms. He was standing, holding a riding-whip, looking rather clumsy in the uniform that did not suit him. Rather clumsy and worn out, but completely expressionless! He had looked straight into the reflection of her eyes and then looked away. He moved so that his profile was towards her, and continued gazing motionless at an elk's head that decorated the space of wall above glazed doors giving into the interior of the hotel. The hotel servant approaching him, he had produced a card and had given it to the servant, uttering three words. She saw his lips move in the three words: Mrs. Christopher Tietjens. She said, beneath her breath:

"Damn his chivalry! . . . Oh, God damn his chivalry!" She knew what was going on in his mind. He had seen her with Perowne, so he had neither come towards her nor directed the servant to where she sat. For fear of embarrassing her! He would leave it to her to come to him if she wished.

The servant, visible in the mirror, had come and gone deviously back, Tietjens still gazing at the elk's head. He had taken the card and restored it to his pocket-book and then had spoken to the servant. The servant had shrugged his shoulders with the formal hospitality of his class and, with his shoulders still shrugged and his one hand pointing towards the inner door, had preceded Tietjens into the hotel. Not one line of Tietjens' face had moved when he had received back his card. It had been then that Sylvia had sworn that she would yet make his wooden face wince. . . .

His face was intolerable. Heavy, fixed. Not insolent, but simply gazing over the heads of all things and created beings into a world too distant for them to enter . . . And yet it seemed to her, since he was so clumsy and worn out, almost not sporting to persecute him. It was like whipping a dying bull-dog. . . .

She sank back into her chair with a movement almost of discouragement. She said:

"He's gone into the hotel. . . ."

Perowne lurched agitatedly forward in his chair. He exclaimed that he was going. Then he sank discouragedly back again:

"No, I'm not," he said, "I'm probably much safer here. I might run against him going out."

"You've realized that my petticoats protect you," Sylvia said contemptuously. "Of course Christopher would never hit anyone in my presence."

Major Perowne was interrupting her by asking:

"What's he going to do? What's he doing in the hotel?"

Mrs. Tietjens said:

"Guess!" She added: "What would you do in similar circumstances?"

"Go and wreck your bedroom," Perowne answered with promptitude. "It's what I did when I found you had left Yssingueux."

Sylvia said:

"Ah, that was what the place was called."

Perowne groaned.

"You're callous," he said. "There's no other word for it. Callous. That's what you are."

Sylvia asked absently why he called her callous at just that juncture. She was imagining Christopher stumping clumsily along the hotel corridor looking at bedrooms and then giving the hotel servant a handsome tip to ensure that he should be put on the same floor as herself. She could almost hear his not-disagreeable male voice that vibrated a little from the chest and made her vibrate.

Perowne was grumbling on. Sylvia was callous because she had forgotten the name of the Brittany hamlet in which they had spent three blissful weeks together, though she had left it so suddenly that all her outfit remained in the hotel.

"Well, it wasn't any kind of a bean-feast for me," Sylvia went on when she again gave him her attention. "Good heavens! . . . Do you think it *would* be any kind of a bean-feast with you, *pour tout potage*? Why should I remember the name of the hateful place?"

Perowne said:

"Yssingueux-les-Pervenches—such a pretty name," re-proachfully.

"It's no good," Sylvia answered, "your trying to awaken sentimental memories in me. You will have to make me forget what you were like if you want to carry on with me. . . . I'm stopping here and listening to your corn-crake of a voice because I want to wait until Christopher goes out of the hotel. . . . Then I am going to my room to tidy up for Lady Sachse's party and you will sit here and wait for me."

"I'm *not*," Perowne said, "going to Lady Sachse's. Why, *he* is going to be one of the principal witnesses to sign the marriage contract. And old Campion and all the rest of the staff are going to be there. . . . You don't catch *me*. . . . An unexpected prior engagement is my line. No fear."

"You'll come with me, my little man," Sylvia said, "if you ever want to bask in my smile again. . . . I'm not going to Lady Sachse's alone, looking as if I couldn't catch a man to escort me, under the eyes of half the French house of peers. . . . If they've got a house of peers! . . . You don't catch *me*. . . . No fear!" she mimicked his creaky voice. "You can go away as soon as you've shown yourself as my escort. . . ."

"But, good God!" Perowne cried out, "that's just what I mustn't do. Campion said that if he heard any more of my being seen about with you, he would have me sent back to my beastly regiment. And my beastly regiment is in the trenches. . . . You don't see *me* in the trenches, do you?"

"I'd rather see you there than in my own room," Sylvia said. "Any day!"

"Ah, there you are!" Perowne exclaimed with animation. "What guarantee have I that if I do what you want I shall bask in your smile, as you call it? I've got myself into a most awful hole, bringing you here without any papers. You never told me you hadn't any papers. General O'Hara, the P.M., has raised a most awful strafe about it. . . . And what have I got for it? . . . Not the ghost of a smile . . . And you should see old O'Hara's purple face! . . . Someone woke him from his afternoon nap to report to him about your heinous case and he hasn't recovered from the indigestion yet. . . . Besides, he hates Tietjens. . . . Tietjens is always chipping away at his Military Police. . . . O'Hara's lambs . . ."

Sylvia was not listening, but she was smiling a slow smile at an inward thought. It maddened him.

"What's your game?" he exclaimed. "Hell and hounds,

what's your game? . . . You can't have come here to see
. . . *him*. You don't come here to see me, as far as I can see.
Well, then . . ."

Sylvia looked round at him with her eyes wide open
as if she had just awakened from a deep sleep.

"I didn't know I was coming," she said. "It came into my
head to come suddenly. Ten minutes before I started. And
I came. I didn't know papers were wanted. I suppose I could
have got them if I had wanted them. . . . You never asked
me if I had any papers. You just froze on to me and had
me into your special carriage. . . . I didn't know you were
coming."

That seemed to Perowne the last insult. He exclaimed:

"Oh, damn it, Sylvia! you *must* have known. . . . You
were at the Quirks' squash on Wednesday evening. And
they knew. My best friends."

"Since you ask for it," she said, "I didn't know. . . . And
I would not have come by that train if I had known
you would be going by it. You force me to say rude things
to you." She added: "Why can't you be more conciliatory?" to keep him quiet for a little. His jaw dropped
down.

She was wondering where Christopher had got the money
to pay for a bed at the hotel. Only a very short time before she had drawn all the balance of his banking account
except for a shilling. It was the middle of the month and
he could not have drawn any more pay. . . . That, of
course, was a try-on on her part. He might be forced into
remonstrating. In the same way she had tried on the accusation that he had carried off her sheets. It was sheer
wilfulness, and when she looked again at his motionless
features she knew that she had been rather stupid. . . . But
she was at the end of her tether: she had before now tried
making accusations against her husband, but she had never
tried inconveniencing him. . . . Now she suddenly realized
the full stupidity of which she had been guilty. He would
know perfectly well that those petty frightfulnesses of hers
were not in the least in her note; so he would know, too,
that each of them was just a try-on. He would say: "She
is trying to make me squeal. I'm damned if I will!"

She would have to adopt much more formidable methods.
She said: "He shall . . . he shall . . . he *shall* come to heel."

Major Perowne had now closed his jaw. He was reflecting. Once he mumbled: "More *conciliatory!* Holy
smoke!"

She was feeling suddenly in spirits: it was the sight of Christopher had done it: the perfect assurance that they were going to live under the same roof again. She would have betted all she possessed and her immortal soul on the chance that he would not take up with the Wannop girl. And it would have been betting on a certainty! . . . But she had had no idea what their relations were to be after the war. At first she had thought that they had parted for good when she had gone off from their flat at four o'clock in the morning. It had seemed logical. But, gradually, in retreat at Birkenhead, in the still, white, nun's room, doubt had come upon her. It was one of the disadvantages of living as they did that they seldom spoke their thoughts. But that was also at times an advantage. She had certainly meant their parting to be for good. She had certainly raised her voice in giving the name of her station to the taxi-man with the pretty firm conviction that he would hear her; and she had been pretty well certain that he would take it as a sign that the breath had gone out of their union. . . . Pretty certain. But not quite! . . .

She would have died rather than write to him; she would die now rather than give any inkling that she wanted them to live under the same roof again. . . . She said to herself:

"Is he writing to that girl?" And then: "No! . . . I'm certain that he isn't. . . ." She had had all his letters stopped at the flat except for a few circulars that she let dribble through to him, so that he might imagine that all his correspondence was coming through. From the letters to him that she did read she was pretty sure that he had given no other address than the flat in Gray's Inn. . . . But there had been no letters from Valentine Wannop. . . . Two from Mrs. Wannop, two from his brother, Mark, one from Port Scatho, one or two from brother-officers and some official chits . . . She said to herself that if there *had* been any letters from that girl, she would have let all his letters go through, including the girl's. . . . Now she was not so certain she would have.

In the glass she saw Christopher marching woodenly out of the hotel, along the path that led from door to door behind her. . . . It came to her with extraordinary gladness —the absolute conviction that he was not corresponding with Miss Wannop. The absolute conviction . . . If he had come alive enough to do that, he would have looked different. She did not know how he would have looked. But different . . . Alive! Perhaps self-conscious: perhaps . . . satisfied . . .

For some time the major had been grumbling about his wrongs. He said that he followed her about all day, like a lap-dog, and got nothing for it. Now she wanted him to be conciliatory. She said she wanted to have a man on show as escort. Well, then, an escort got something. . . . At just this moment he was beginning again with:

"Look here . . . will you let me come to your room to-night or will you not?"

She burst into high, loud laughter. He said:

"Damn it all, it isn't any laughing matter! . . . Look here! You don't know what I risk. . . . There are A.P.M.s and P.M.s and deputy subacting A.P.M.s walking about the corridors of all the hotels in this town all night long. . . . It's as much as my job is worth. . . ."

She put her handkerchief to her lips to hide a smile that she knew would be too cruel for him not to notice. And even when she took it away, he said:

"Hang it all, what a cruel-looking fiend you are! . . . Why the devil do I hang around you? . . . There's a picture that my mother's got, by Burne-Jones . . . A cruel-looking woman with a distant smile . . . Some vampire . . . La belle dame sans merci . . . That's what you're like."

She looked at him suddenly with considerable seriousness. . . .

"See here, Potty . . ." she began. He groaned:

"I believe you'd like me to be sent to the beastly trenches. . . . Yet a big, distinguished-looking chap like me wouldn't have a chance. . . . At the first volley the Germans fired, they'd pick me off. . . ."

"Oh, Potty," she exclaimed, "try to be serious for a minute. . . . I tell you I'm a woman who's trying . . . who's desperately wanting . . . to be reconciled to her husband! . . . I would not tell that to another soul. . . . I would not tell it to myself. . . . But one owes something . . . a parting scene, if nothing else. . . . Well, something . . . to a man one's been in bed with . . . I didn't give you a parting scene at . . . ah, Yssingueux-les-Pervenches . . . so I give you this tip instead. . . ."

He said:

"Will you leave your bedroom door unlocked or won't you?"

She said:

"If that man would throw his handkerchief to me, I would

follow him round the world in my shift! . . . Look here . . .
see me shake when I think of it. . . ." She held out her hand
at the end of her long arm: hand and arm trembled together, minutely, then very much. . . . "Well," she finished,
"if you see that and still want to come to my room . . .
your blood be on your own head. . . ." She paused for a
breath or two and then said:

"You can come. . . . I won't lock my door. . . . But I don't
say that you'll get anything . . . or that you'll like what you
get. . . . That's a fair tip. . . ." She added suddenly: "You
sale fat . . . take what you get and be damned to you! . . ."

Major Perowne had suddenly taken to twirling his
moustaches; he said:

"Oh, I'll chance the A.P.M.s. . . ."

She suddenly coiled her legs into her chair.

"I know now what I came here for," she said.

Major Wilfrid Fosbrooke Eddicker Perowne of Perowne,
the son of his mother, was one of those individuals who
have no history, no strong proclivities, and no, or almost no,
characteristics. He had done nothing, his knowledge seemed
to be bounded by the contents of his newspaper for the immediate day; at any rate, his conversation never went any
farther. He was not bold, he was not shy: he was neither
markedly courageous nor markedly cowardly. His mother
was immoderately wealthy, owned an immense castle that
hung over crags, above a western sea, much as a bird-cage
hangs from a window of a high tenement building, but she
received few or no visitors, her cuisine being indifferent and
her wine atrocious. She had strong temperance opinions, and
immediately after the death of her husband, she had emptied
the contents of his cellar, which were almost as historic as
his castle, into the sea, a shudder going through county-
family England. But even this was not enough to make
Perowne himself notorious.

His mother allowed him—after an eye-opener in early
youth—the income of a junior royalty, but he did nothing
with it. He lived in a great house in Palace Gardens, Kensington, and he lived all alone with rather a large staff of servants who had been selected by his mother, but they did nothing at all, for he ate all his meals, and even took his bath
and dressed for dinner, at the Bath Club. He was otherwise
parsimonious.

He had, after the fashion of his day, passed a year or two
in the army when young. He had been first gazetted to His

Majesty's Forty-second Regiment, but on the Black Watch proceeding to India he had exchanged into the Glamorganshires, at that time commanded by General Campion and recruiting in and around Lincolnshire. The general had been an old friend of Perowne's mother and, on being promoted to brigadier, had taken Perowne on to his staff as his galloper, for although Perowne rode rather indifferently, he had a certain social knowledge and could be counted on to know how correctly to address a regimental invitation to a dowager countess who had married a viscount's third son. . . . As a military figure otherwise he had a very indifferent word of command, a very poor drill and next to no control of his men, but he was popular with his batmen, and in a rather stiff way was presentable in the old scarlet uniform or the blue mess jacket. He was exactly six foot, to a hairbreadth, in his stockings, had very dark eyes and a rather grating voice; the fact that his limbs were a shade too bulky for his trunk, which was not at all corpulent, made him appear a little clumsy. If in a club you asked what sort of a fellow he was, your interlocutor would tell you, most probably, that he had or was supposed to have warts on his head, this to account for his hair, which all his life he had combed back, unparted, from his forehead. But as a matter of fact he had no warts on his head.

He had once started out on an expedition to shoot big game in Portuguese East Africa. But on its arrival his expedition was met with the news that the natives of the interior were in revolt, so Perowne had returned to Kensington Palace Gardens. He had had several mild successes with women, but owing to his habits of economy and fear of imbroglios, until the age of thirty-four he had limited the field of his amours to young women of the lower social orders. . . .

His affair with Sylvia Tietjens might have been something to boast about, but he was not boastful, and indeed he had been too hard hit when she had left him even to bear to account lyingly for the employment of the time he had spent with her in Brittany. Fortunately no one took sufficient interest in his movements to wait for his answer to their indifferent questions as to where he had spent the summer. When his mind reverted to her desertion of him, moisture would come out of his eyes, undemonstratively, as water leaves the surface of a sponge. . . .

Sylvia had left him by the simple expedient of stepping without so much as a reticule on to the little French tramway that took you to the main railway line. From there she

had written to him in pencil on a closed correspondence
card that she had left him because she simply could not bear
either his dullness or his craking voice. She said they would
probably run up against each other in the course of the
autumn season in town and, after purchase of some night
things, had made straight for the German spa to which her
mother had retreated.

At the later date Sylvia had no difficulty in accounting
to herself for her having gone off with such an oaf: she had
simply reacted in a violent fit of sexual hatred, from her
husband's mind. And she could not have found a mind more
utterly dissimilar than Perowne's in any decently groomed
man to be found in London. She could recall, even in the
French hotel lounge, years after, the almost painful emotion of joyful hatred that had visited her when she had first
thought of going off with him. It was the self-applause of
one who has just hit upon an excruciatingly inspiring intellectual discovery. In her previous transitory infidelities to
Christopher she had discovered that however presentable the
man with whom she might have been having an affair, and
however short the affair, even if it were only a matter of a
week-end . . . Christopher had spoilt her for the other man.
It was the most damnable of his qualities that to hear any
other man talk of any subject—any, any subject—from stable
form to the balance of power or from the voice of a given
opera singer to the recurrence of a comet—to have to pass
a week-end with any other man and hear his talk after having spent the inside of the week with Christopher, hate his
ideas how you might, was the difference between listening to
a grown man and, with an intense boredom, trying to entertain an inarticulate schoolboy. As beside him, other men
simply did not seem ever to have grown up. . . .

Just before, with an extreme suddenness, consenting to
go away with Perowne, the illuminating idea had struck her:
"If I did go away with him it would be the most humiliating
thing I could do to Christopher. . . ." And just when the idea
had struck her, beside her chair in the conservatory at a
dance given by the general's sister, Lady Claudine Sandbach,
Perowne, his voice rendered more throaty and less disagreeable than usual by emotion, had been going on and on and begging her to elope with him. . . . She had suddenly said:

"Very well . . . let's. . . ."

His emotion had been so unbridled in its astonishment
that she had, even at that, almost been inclined to treat her
own speech as a joke and to give up the revenge. . . . But

the idea of the humiliation that Christopher must feel proved too much for her. For, for your wife to throw you over for an attractive man is naturally humiliating, but that she should leave you publicly for a man of hardly any intelligence at all, you priding yourself on your brains, must be nearly as mortifying a thing as can happen to you.

But she had hardly set out upon her escapade before two very serious defects in her plan occurred to her with extreme force: the one that however humiliated Christopher might feel, she would not be with him to witness his humiliation; the other that, oaf as she had taken Perowne to be in casual society, in close daily relationship he was such an oaf as to be almost insufferable. She had imagined that he would prove a person out of whom it might be possible to make *something* by a judicious course of alternated mothering and scorn: she discovered that his mother had already done for him almost all that woman could do. For when he had been an already rather backward boy at a private school, his mother had kept him so extremely short of pocket-money that he had robbed other boys' desks of a few shillings here and there—in order to subscribe towards a birthday present for the head master's wife. His mother, to give him a salutary lesson, had given so much publicity to the affair that he had become afflicted with a permanent bent towards shyness that rendered him by turns very mistrustful of himself or very boastful, and although he repressed manifestations of either tendency towards the outside world, the continual repression rendered him almost incapable of any vigorous thought or action. . . .

That discovery did not soften Sylvia towards him: it was, as she expressed it, *his* funeral, and although she would have been ready for any normal job of smartening up a roughish man, she was by no means prepared to readjust other women's hopeless maternal misfits.

So she had got no farther than Ostend, where they had proposed to spend a week or so at the tables, before she found herself explaining to some acquaintances whom she met that she was in that gay city merely for an hour or two, between trains, on the way to join her mother in a German health-resort. The impulse to say that had come upon her by surprise, for until that moment, being completely indifferent to criticism, she had intended to cast no veil at all over her proceedings. But, quite suddenly, on seeing some well-known English faces in the casino, it had come over her to think that however much she imagined

Christopher to be humiliated by her going off with an oaf like Perowne, that humiliation must be as nothing compared with that which she might be expected to feel at having found no one better than an oaf like Perowne to go off with. Moreover . . . she began to miss Christopher.

These feelings did not grow any less intense in the rather stuffy but inconspicuous hotel in the Rue St. Roque in Paris to which she immediately transported the bewildered but uncomplaining Perowne, who had imagined that he was to be taken to Wiesbaden for a course of light gaieties. And Paris when you avoid the more conspicuous resorts, and when you are unprovided with congenial companionship, can prove nearly as overwhelming as is, say, Birmingham on a Sunday.

So that Sylvia waited for only just long enough to convince herself that her husband had no apparent intention of applying for an immediate divorce and had, indeed, no apparent intention of doing anything at all. She sent him, that is to say, a postcard saying that letters and other communications would reach her at her inconspicuous hotel—and it mortified her not a little to have to reveal the fact that her hotel was so inconspicuous. But except that her own correspondence was forwarded to her with regularity, no communications at all came from Tietjens.

In an air-resort in the centre of France, to which she next removed Perowne, she found herself considering rather seriously what it might be expected that Tietjens *would* do. Through indirect and unsuspecting allusions in letters from her personal friends she found that if Tietjens did not put up, he certainly did not deny, the story that she had gone to nurse or be with her mother, who was supposed to be seriously ill. . . . That is to say, her friends said how rotten it was that her mother, Mrs. Satterthwaite, should be so seriously ill; how rotten it must be for her to be shut up in a potty little German *kur-ort* when the world could be so otherwise amusing: and how well Christopher, whom they saw from time to time, seemed to be getting on, considering how rotten it must be for him to be left all alone. . . .

At about this time Perowne began to become, if possible, more irritating than ever. In their air-resort, although the guests were almost entirely French, there was a newly opened golf-course, and at the game of golf Perowne displayed an inefficiency and at the same time a morbid conceit that were surprising in one naturally lymphatic. He would sulk for a whole evening if either Sylvia or any Frenchman beat him in a round, and though Sylvia was by then completely indifferent to his sulking, what was very much worse was that he became gloomily and loud-voicedly quarrelsome over his games with foreign opponents.

Three events, falling within ten minutes of each other, made her determined to get as far away from that air-resort as was feasible. In the first place she observed at the end of the street some English people called Thurston, whose faces she faintly knew, and the emotion she suddenly felt let her know how extremely anxious she was that she should let it remain feasible for Tietjens to take her back. Then, in the golf club-house, to which she found herself fiercely hurrying in order to pay her bill and get her clubs, she overheard the conversation of two players that left no doubt in her mind that Perowne had been detected in little meannesses of moving his ball at golf or juggling with his score. . . . This was almost more than she could stand. And at the same moment, her mind, as it were, condescended to let her remember Christopher's voice as it had once uttered the haughty opinion that no man one could speak to would ever think of divorcing any woman. If he could not defend the sanctity of his hearth, he must lump it unless the woman wanted to divorce him. . . .

At the time when he had said it, her mind—she had been just then hating him a good deal—had seemed to take no notice of the utterance. But now that it presented itself forcibly to her again it brought with it the thought: Supposing he wasn't really only talking through his hat!

. . . She dragged the wretched Perowne off his bed, where he had been lost in an after-lunch slumber, and told him that they must both leave that place at once, and that as soon as they reached Paris or some larger town where he could find waiters and people to understand his French, she herself was going to leave him for good. They did not, in consequence, get away from the air-resort until the six-o'clock train next morning. Perowne's passion of rage and despair at the news that she wished to leave him took an inconvenient form, for instead of announcing any intention of committing suicide, as might have been expected, he became gloomily and fantastically murderous. He said that unless Sylvia swore on a little relic of St. Anthony she carried that she had no intention of leaving him, he would incontinently kill her. He said, as he said for the rest of his days, that she had ruined his life and caused great moral deterioration in himself. But for her, he might have married some pure young thing. Moreover, influencing him against his mother's doctrines, she had forced him to drink wine, by an effect of pure scorn. Thus he had done harm, he was convinced, both to his health and to his manly proportions. . . . It was indeed for Sylvia one of the most unbearable things about this man —the way he took wine. With every glass he put to his lips he would exclaim with an unbearable titter some such imbecility as: Here is another nail in my coffin. And he had taken to wine, and even to stronger liquor, very well.

Sylvia had refused to swear by St. Anthony. She definitely was not going to introduce the saint into her amorous affairs, and she definitely was not going to take on any relic an oath that she meant to break at an early opportunity. There was such a thing as playing it too low down: there are dishonours to which death is preferable. So, getting hold of his revolver at a time when he was wringing his hands, she dropped it into the water-jug and then felt reasonably safe.

Perowne knew no French and next to nothing about France, but he had discovered that the French did nothing to you for killing a woman who intended to leave you. Sylvia, on the other hand, was pretty certain that without a weapon he could not do much to her. If she had had no other training at her very expensive school, she had had so much drilling in callisthenics as to be singularly mistress of her limbs, and in the interests of her beauty she had always kept herself very fit. . . .

She said at last:

"Very well. We will go to Yssingueux-les-Pervenches. . . ."

A rather pleasant French couple in the hotel had spoken of this little place in the extreme west of France as a lonely paradise, they having spent their honeymoon there. . . . And Sylvia wanted a lonely paradise if there was going to be any scrapping before she got away from Perowne. . . .

She had no hesitation as to what she was going to do: the long journey across half France by miserable trains had caused her an agony of home-sickness! Nothing less! . . . It was a humiliating disease from which to suffer. But it was unavoidable, like mumps. You had to put up with it. Besides, she even found herself wanting to see her child, whom she imagined herself to hate, as having been the cause of all her misfortunes. . . .

She therefore prepared, after great thought, a letter telling Tietjens that she intended to return to him. She made the letter as nearly as possible like one she would write announcing her return from a country-house to which she should have been invited for an indefinite period, and she added some rather hard instructions about her maid, these being intended to remove from the letter any possible trace of emotion. She was certain that if she showed any emotion at all, Christopher would never take her under his roof again. . . . She was pretty certain that no gossip had been caused by her escapade. Major Thurston had been at the railway station when they had left, but they had not spoken—and Thurston was a very decentish, brown-moustached fellow, of the sort that does not gossip.

It had proved a little difficult to get away, for Perowne during several weeks watched her like an attendant in a lunatic asylum. But at last the idea presented itself to him that she would never go without her frocks, and one day, in a fit of intense somnolence after a lunch washed down with rather a large quantity of the local and fiery cordial, he let her take a walk alone. . . .

She was by that time tired of men . . . or she imagined that she was; for she was not prepared to be certain, considering the muckers she saw women coming all round her over the most unpresentable individuals. Men, at any rate, never fulfilled expectations. They might, upon acquaintance, turn out more entertaining than they appeared; but almost always, taking up with a man was like reading a book you had read when you had forgotten that you had read it. You had not been for ten minutes in any sort of intimacy with any man before you said: "But I've read all this before. . . ." You knew the opening, you were already bored by the middle, and, especially, you knew the end. . . .

She remembered, years ago, trying to shock her mother's spiritual adviser, Father Consett, whom they had lately murdered in Ireland, along with Casement. . . . The poor saint had not in the least been shocked. He had gone her one better. For when she had said something like that her idea of a divvy life—they used in those days to say divvy—would be to go off with a different man every week-end, he had told her that after a short time she would be bored already by the time the poor dear fellow was buying the railway tickets. . . .

And, by heavens, he had been right. . . . For when she came to think of it, from the day that poor saint had said that thing in her mother's sitting-room in the little German spa—Lobscheid, it must have been called—in the candle-light, his shadow denouncing her from all over the walls, to now, when she sat in the palmish wickerwork of that hotel that had been new-whitely decorated to celebrate hostilities, never once had she sat in a train with a man who had any right to look upon himself as justified in mauling her about. . . . She wondered if, from where he sat in Heaven, Father Consett would be satisfied with her as he looked down into that lounge. . . . Perhaps it was really he that had pulled off that change in her. . . .

Never once till yesterday . . . For perhaps the unfortunate Perowne might just faintly have had the right yesterday to make himself for about two minutes—before she froze him into a choking, pallid snow-man with goggle eyes—the perfectly loathsome thing that a man in a railway train becomes. . . . Much too bold and yet stupidly awkward with the fear of the guard looking in at the window, the train doing over sixty, without corridors . . . "No, never again for *me*, Father," she addressed her voice towards the ceiling. . . .

Why in the world couldn't you get a man to go away with you and be just—oh, light comedy for a whole, a whole blessed week-end. For a whole blessed life . . . Why not? . . . Think of it. . . . A whole blessed life with a man who was a good sort and yet didn't go all gurgly in the voice, and cod-fish-eyed and all-overish—to the extent of not being able to find the tickets when asked for them. . . . "Father, dear," she said again upwards, "if I could find men like that, that would be just heaven . . . where there is no marrying. . . . But, of course," she went on almost resignedly, "he would not be faithful to you. . . ." And then: "One would have to stand it. . . ."

She sat up so suddenly in her chair that beside her, too, Major Perowne nearly jumped out of his wickerwork and asked if *he* had come back. . . . She explained:

"No, I'd be damned if I would. . . . I'd be damned, I'd be damned, I'd be damned if I would. . . . Never. Never. By the living God!"

She asked fiercely of the agitated major:

"Has Christopher got a girl in this town? . . . You'd better tell me the truth!"

The major mumbled:

"He . . . No . . . He's too much of a stick. . . . He never even goes to Suzette's. . . . Except once to fetch out some miserable little squit of a subaltern who was smashing up Mother Hardelot's furniture. . . ."

He grumbled:

"But you shouldn't give a man the jumps like that! . . . Be conciliatory, you said. . . ." He went on to grumble that her manners had not improved since she had been at Yssingueux-les-Pervenches . . . and then went on to tell her that in French the words *yeux de pervenches* meant eyes of periwinkle blue. And that was the only French he knew, because a Frenchman he had met in the train had told him so and he had always thought that if *her* eyes had been periwinkle blue . . . "But you're not listening. . . . Hardly polite, I call it," he had mumbled to a conclusion.

She was sitting forward in her chair, still clenching her hand under her chin at the thought that perhaps Christopher had Valentine Wannop in that town. That was perhaps why he elected to remain there. She asked:

"Why does Christopher stay on in this God-forsaken hole? . . . The inglorious base, they call it . . ."

"Because he's jolly well got to. . . ." Major Perowne said. "He's got to do what he's told. . . ."

She said:

"Christopher! . . . You mean to say they'd keep a man like *Christopher* anywhere he didn't want to be. . . ."

"They'd jolly well knock spots off him if he went away," Major Perowne exclaimed. "What the deuce do you think your blessed fellow is? . . . The King of England? . . ." He added with a sudden sombre ferocity: "They'd shoot him like anybody else if he bolted. . . . What do *you* think?"

She said:

"But all that wouldn't prevent his having a girl in this town?"

"Well, he hasn't got one," Perowne said. "He sticks up in that blessed old camp of his like a blessed she-chicken sitting on addled eggs. . . . That's what they say of him. . . . I don't know anything about the fellow. . . ."

Listening vindictively and indolently, she thought she caught in his droning tones a touch of the homicidal lunacy that had used to underlie his voice in the bedroom at Yssingueux. The fellow had undoubtedly about him a touch of the dull, mad murderer of the police courts. With a sudden animation she thought:

"Suppose he tried to murder Christopher. . . ." And she imagined her husband breaking the fellow's back across his knee, the idea going across her mind as fire traverses the opal. Then, with a dry throat, she said to herself:

"I've got to find out whether he has that girl in Rouen. . . ." Men stuck together. The fellow Perowne might well be protecting Tietjens. It would be unthinkable that any rules of the service could keep Christopher in that place. They could not shut up the upper classes. If Perowne had any sense he would know that to shield Tietjens was the way not to get her. . . . But he had no sense. . . . Besides, sexual solidarity was a terribly strong thing. . . . She knew that she herself would not give a woman's secrets away in order to get her man. Then . . . how was she to ascertain whether the girl was not in that town? How? . . . She imagined Tietjens going home every night to her. . . . But he was going to spend that night with herself. . . . She knew that. . . . Under that roof . . . Fresh from the other . . .

She imagined him there, now. . . . In the parlour of one of the little villas you see from the tram on the top of the town . . . They were undoubtedly, now, discussing her. . . . Her whole body writhed, muscle on muscle, in her chair. . . . She must discover. . . . But how do you discover? Against a universal conspiracy . . . This whole war was an Agapemone. . . . You went to war when you desired to rape innumerable women. . . . It was what war was for. . . . All these men, crowded in this narrow space . . .

She stood up:

"I'm going," she said, "to put on a little powder for Lady Sachse's feast. . . . You needn't stay if you don't want to. . . ." She was going to watch every face she saw until it gave up the secret of where in that town Christopher had the Wannop girl hidden. . . . She imagined her freckled, snub-nosed face pressed—"squashed" was the word—against his cheek. . . . She was going to investigate. . . .

2 ~

SHE FOUND an early opportunity to carry on her investigations. For at dinner that night she found herself, Tietjens having gone to the telephone with a lance-corporal, opposite what she took to be a small tradesman, with fresh-coloured cheeks and a great, grey, forward-sprouting moustache, in a uniform so creased that the creases resembled the veins of a leaf. . . . A very trustworthy small tradesman: the grocer from round the corner whom, sometimes, you allow to supply you with paraffin. . . . He was saying to her:

"If, ma'am, you multiply two thousand nine hundred and something by ten, you arrive at twenty-nine thousand odd. . . ."

And she had exclaimed:

"You really mean that my husband, Captain Tietjens, spent yesterday afternoon in examining twenty-nine thousand toe-nails. . . . And two thousand nine hundred tooth-brushes . . ."

"I told him," her interlocutor answered with deep seriousness, "that these being colonial troops, it was not so necessary to examine their tooth-brushes. . . . Imperial troops *will* use the brush they clean their buttons with for their teeth so as to have a clean tooth-brush to show the medical officer. . . ."

"It sounds," she said with a little shudder, "as if you were all schoolboys playing a game. . . . And you say my husband really occupies his mind with such things. . . ."

Second-Lieutenant Cowley, dreadfully conscious that the shoulder-strap of his Sam Browne belt, purchased that afternoon at the ordnance and therefore brand-new, did not match the abdominal part of the belt that he had had for nearly ten years—a splendid bit of leather, that!—answered nevertheless stoutly:

"Madam! If the brains of an army aren't, the life of an army *is* . . . in its feet. . . . And now-a-days, the medical officers say, in its teeth . . . Your husband, ma'am, is an admirable officer. . . . He says that no draft he turns out shall . . ."

She said:

"He spent three hours in . . . You say, foot and kit inspection. . . ."

Second-Lieutenant Cowley said:

"Of course he had other officers to help him with the kit . . . but he looked at every foot himself. . . ."

She said:

"That took him from two till five. . . . Then he had tea, I suppose. . . . And went to . . . what is it? . . . the papers of the draft . . ."

Second-Lieutenant Cowley said, muffledly through his moustache:

"If the captain is a little remiss in writing letters . . . I *have* heard . . . You might, madam . . . I'm a married man myself . . . with a daughter. . . . And the army is not very good at writing letters. . . . You might say, in that respect, that thank God we have got a navy, ma'am. . . ."

She let him stagger on for a sentence or two, imagining that in his confusion, she might come upon traces of Miss Wannop in Rouen. Then she said handsomely:

"Of course you have explained everything, Mr. Cowley, and I am very much obliged. . . . Of course my husband would not have time to write very full letters. . . . He is not like the giddy young subalterns who run after . . ."

He exclaimed in a great roar of laughter:

"The captain run after skirts . . . Why, I can number on my hands the times he's been out of my sight since he's had the battalion!"

A deep wave of depression went over Sylvia.

"Why," Lieutenant Cowley laughed on, "if we *had* a laugh against him it was that he mothered the lot of us as if he was a hen sitting on addled eggs. . . . For it's only a rag-time army, as the saying is, when you've said the best for it that you can. . . . And look at the other commanding officers we've had before we had him. . . . There was Major Brooks. . . . Never up before noon, if then, and out of camp by two-thirty. Get your returns ready for signing before then or never get 'em signed. . . . And Colonel Potter . . . Bless my soul . . 'e wouldn't sign any blessed papers at all. . . . He lived down here in this hotel, and we never saw him up at the camp at all. . . . But the captain . . . We always say that . . . if 'e was a Chelsea adjutant getting off a draft of the Second Coldstreams. . . ."

With her indolent and gracious beauty—Sylvia knew that she was displaying indolent and gracious beauty—Sylvia leaned over the table-cloth, listening for items in the terrible indictment that, presently, she was going to bring against Tietjens. . . . For the morality of these matters is this: If you have an incomparably beautiful woman on your hands, you must occupy yourself solely with her. . . . Nature exacts that of you . . . until you are unfaithful to her with a snub-nosed girl with freckles: that, of course, being a reaction, is still in a way occupying yourself with your woman! . . . But to betray her with a battalion . . . That is against decency, against Nature. . . . And for him, Christopher Tietjens, to come down to the level of the men you met here! . . .

Tietjens, mooning down the room between tables, had more than his usually aloof air since he had just come out of a telephone box. He slipped, a weary mass, into the polished chair between her and the lieutenant. He said:

"I've got the washing arranged for . . ." and Sylvia gave to herself a little hiss between the teeth, of vindictive pleasure! This was indeed betrayal to a battalion. He added: "I shall have to be up in camp before four-thirty to-morrow morning. . . ."

Sylvia could not resist saying:

"Isn't there a poem—'Ah me, the dawn, the dawn, it comes too soon!'—said, of course, by lovers in bed? . . . Who was the poet?"

Cowley went visibly red to the roots of his hair and evidently beyond. Tietjens finished his speech to Cowley, who had remonstrated against his going up to the camp so early by saying that he had not been able to get hold of an officer to march the draft. He then said in his leisurely way:

"There were a great many poems with that refrain in the Middle Ages. . . . You are probably thinking of an aubade by Arnaut Daniel which someone translated lately. . . . An aubade was a song to be sung at dawn, when, presumably, no one but lovers would be likely to sing. . . ."

"Will there," Sylvia asked, "be anyone but you singing up in your camp to-morrow at four?"

She could not help it. . . . She knew that Tietjens had adopted his slow pomposity in order to give the grotesque object at the table with them time to recover from his confusion. She hated him for it. What right had he to make himself appear a pompous ass in order to shield the confusion of anybody?

The second-lieutenant came out of his confusion to exclaim, actually slapping his thigh:

"There you are, madam. . . . Trust the captain to know everything! . . . I don't believe there's a question under the sun you could ask him that he couldn't answer. . . . They say up at the camp . . ." He went on with long stories of all the questions Tietjens *had* answered up at the camp. . . .

Emotion was going all over Sylvia . . . at the proximity of Tietjens. She said to herself: "Is this to go on forever?" Her hands were ice-cold. She touched the back of her left hand with the fingers of her right. It *was* ice-cold. She looked at her hands. They were bloodless. . . . She said to herself: "It's pure sexual passion . . . it's pure sexual passion. . . . God! Can't I get over this?" She said: "Father! . . . You used to be fond of Christopher. . . . *Get* Our Lady to get me over this. . . . It's the ruin of him and the ruin of me. But, oh *damn*, don't! . . . For it's all I have to live for . . ." She said: "When he came mooning back from the telephone I thought it was all right. . . . I thought what a heavy wooden horse he looked. . . . For two minutes . . . Then it's all over me again. . . . I want to swallow my saliva and I can't. My throat won't work. . . ."

She leaned one of her white bare arms on the tablecloth towards the walrus-moustache that was still snuffling gloriously:

"They used to call him Old Sol at school," she said. "But there's one question of Solomon's he could not answer. . . . The one about the way of a man with . . . oh, a maid! . . . Ask him what happened before the dawn ninety-six—no, ninety-eight—days ago. . . ."

She said to herself: "I can't help it. . . . Oh, I *can't* help it. . . ."

The ex-sergeant-major was exclaiming happily:

"Oh, no one ever said the captain was one of these thought-readers. . . . It's real solid knowledge of men and things he has. . . . Wonderful how he knows the men, considering he was not born in the service. . . . But there, your born gentleman mixes with men all his days and knows them. Down to the ground and inside their puttees. . . ."

Tietjens was looking straight in front of him, his face perfectly expressionless.

"But I bet I got him. . . ." she said to herself, and then to the sergeant-major:

"I suppose, now, an army officer—one of your born gentlemen—when a back-from-leave train goes out from any of the great stations—Paddington, say—to the front . . . He knows how all the men are feeling. . . . But not what the married women think . . . or the . . . the girl . . ."

She said to herself: "Damn it, how clumsy I am getting! . . . I used to be able to take his hide off with a word. Now I take sentences at a time. . . ."

She went on with her uninterrupted sentence to Cowley:

"Of course he may never be going to see his only son again, so it makes him sensitive. . . . The officer at Paddington, I mean . . ."

She said to herself: "By God, if that beast does not give in to me to-night he never *shall* see Michael again. . . . Ah, but I got him. . . ." Tietjens had his eyes closed; round each of his high-coloured nostrils a crescent of whiteness was beginning. And increasing . . . She felt a sudden alarm and held the edge of the table with her extended arm to steady herself. . . . Men went white at the nose like that when they were going to faint. . . . She did not want him to faint. . . . But he *had* noticed the word "Paddington. . . ."

Ninety-eight days before . . . She had counted every day
since. . . . She had got that much information. . . . She had
said *Paddington* outside the house at dawn and he had taken
it as a farewell. He *had*. . . . He had imagined himself free
to do what he liked with the girl. . . . Well, he wasn't. . . .
That was why he was white about the gills. . . .

Cowley exclaimed loudly:

"Paddington! . . . It isn't from there that back-from-leave
trains go. Not for the front: the B.E.F. . . . Not from Paddington . . . The Glamorganshires go from there to the
depot. . . . And the Liverpools . . . They've got a depot at
Birkenhead. . . . Or is that the Cheshires? . . ." He asked
of Tietjens: "Is it the Liverpools or the Cheshires that have a
depot at Birkenhead, sir? . . . You remember we recruited a
draft from there when we were at Penhally. . . . At any
rate, you go to Birkenhead from Paddington. . . . I was
never there myself. . . . They say it's a nice place. . . ."

Sylvia said—she did not want to say it:

"It's quite a nice place . . . but I should not think of
staying there forever. . . ."

Tietjens said:

"The Cheshires have a training-camp—not a depot—near
Birkenhead. And of course there are R.G.A.s there. . . ."
She had been looking away from him. . . . Cowley ex-
claimed:

"You were nearly off, sir," hilariously. "You had your
peepers shut. . . ." Lifting a champagne glass, he inclined
himself towards her. "You must excuse the captain, ma'am,"
he said. "He had no sleep last night. . . . Largely owing to
my fault . . . Which is what makes it so kind of him . . .
I tell you, ma'am, there are few things I would not do for
the captain. . . ." He drank his champagne and began an
explanation: "You may not know, ma'am, this is a great day
for me. . . . And you and the captain are making it the
greatest day of my life. . . ." Why, at four this morning
there hadn't been a wretcheder man in Ruin town. . . .
And now . . . He must tell her that he suffered from an unfortunate—a miserable—complaint. . . . One that makes
one have to be careful of celebrations . . . And to-day was a
day that he had to celebrate. . . . But he dare not have
done it where Sergeant-Major Ledoux is along with a lot of
their old mates. . . . "I dare not . . . I dussn't!" he finished.
"So I might have been sitting, now, at this very moment, up
in the cold camp. . . . But for you and the captain . . . Up
in the cold camp . . . You'll excuse me, ma'am. . . ."

Sylvia felt that her lids were suddenly wavering:

"I might have been, myself," she said, "in a cold camp, too . . . if I hadn't thrown myself on the captain's mercy! . . . At Birkenhead, you know . . . I happened to be there till three weeks ago. . . . It's strange that you mentioned it. . . . There *are* things like signs . . . but you're not a Catholic! They could hardly be coincidences. . . ."

She was trembling. . . . She looked, fumblingly opening it, into the little mirror of her powder-box—of chased, very thin gold with a small blue stone, like a forget-me-not in the centre of the concentric engravings. . . . Drake—the possible father of Michael—had given it to her. . . . The first thing he had ever given her. She had brought it down tonight out of defiance. She imagined that Tietjens disliked it. . . . She said breathlessly to herself: "Perhaps the damn thing is an ill omen. . . ." Drake had been the first man who had ever . . . A hot-breathed brute! . . . In the little glass her features were chalk-white. . . . She looked like . . . She looked like . . . She had a dress of golden tissue. . . . The breath was short between her white set teeth. . . . Her face was as white as her teeth. . . . And . . . Yes! Nearly! Her lips . . . What was her face like? . . . In the chapel of the convent of Birkenhead there was a tomb all of alabaster. . . . She said to herself:

"He was near fainting. . . . I'm near fainting. . . . What's this beastly thing that's between us? . . . If I let myself faint . . . But it would not make that beast's face any less wooden! . . ."

She leaned across the table and patted the ex-sergeant-major's black-haired hand:

"I'm sure," she said, "you're a very good man. . . ." She did not try to keep the tears out of her eyes, remembering his words: "Up in the cold camp." . . . "I'm glad the captain, as you call him, did not leave you in the cold camp. . . . You're devoted to him, aren't you? . . . There are others he does leave . . . up in . . . the cold camp. . . . For punishment, you know . . ."

The ex-sergeant-major, the tears in his eyes too, said:

"Well, there *is* men you 'as to give the C.B. to. . . . 'C.B.' means confined to barracks. . . ."

"Oh, there are!" she exclaimed. "There are! . . . And women, too . . . Surely there are women, too? . . ."

The sergeant-major said:

"Waacs, per'aps . . . I don't know. . . . They say women's discipline is much like ours. . . . Founded on ours!"

She said:

"Do you know what they used to say of the captain? . . ." She said to herself: "I pray to God the stiff, fatuous beast likes sitting here listening to this stuff. . . . Blessed Virgin, Mother of God, make him take me. . . . Before midnight. Before eleven . . . As soon as we get rid of this . . . this . . . No, he's a decent little man. . . . Blessed Virgin!" . . . "Do you know what they used to say of the captain? . . . I heard the warmest banker in England say it of him. . . ."

The sergeant-major, his eyes enormously opened, said:

"Did you know the warmest banker in England? . . . But there, we always knew the captain was well connected. . . ." She went on:

"They said of him . . . He was always helping people." . . . "Holy Mary, Mother of God! . . . He's my *husband*. . . . It's not a sin. . . . Before midnight . . . Oh, give me a sign. . . . Or before . . . the termination of hostilities. . . . If you give me a sign I could wait." . . . "He helped virtuous Scotch students and broken-down gentry. . . . And women taken in adultery . . . All of them . . . Like . . . You know Who. . . . That is his model. . . ." She said to herself: "Curse him! . . . I hope he likes it. . . . You'd think the only thing he thinks about is the beastly duck he's wolfing down. . . ." And then aloud: "They used to say: 'He saved others: himself he could not save. . . .'"

The ex-sergeant-major looked at her gravely:

"Ma'am," he said, "we couldn't say exactly that of the captain. . . . For I fancy it was said of Our Redeemer. . . . But we *'ave* said that if ever there was a poor bloke the captain could 'elp, 'elp 'im 'e would. . . . Yet the unit was always getting 'ellish strafs from headquarters. . . ."

Suddenly Sylvia began to laugh. . . . As she began to laugh she had remembered. . . . The alabaster image in the nun's chapel at Birkenhead, the vision of which had just presented itself to her, had been the recumbent tomb of an honourable Mrs. Tremayne-Warlock. . . . She was said to have sinned in her youth. . . . And her husband had never forgiven her. . . . That was what the nuns said. . . . She said aloud:

"A sign . . ." Then to herself: "Blessed Mary! . . . You've given it me in the neck. . . . Yet you could not name a father for your child, and I can name two. . . . I'm going mad. . . . Both I and he are going to go mad. . . ."

She thought of dashing an enormous patch of red upon

either cheek. Then she thought it would be rather melodramatic. . . .

She made in the smoking-room, whilst she was waiting
for both Tietjens and Cowley to come back from the telephone, another pact. . . . This time with Father Consett in
Heaven! She was fairly sure that Father Consett—and quite
possibly other of the Heavenly powers—wanted Christopher
not to be worried, so that he could get on with the war—or
because he was a good sort of dullish man such as the
Heavenly authorities are apt to like. . . . Something like
that . . .

She was by that time fairly calm again. You cannot keep
up fits of emotion by the hour: at any rate, with her the
fits of emotion were periodical and unexpected, though her
colder passion remained always the same. . . . Thus when
Christopher had come into Lady Sachse's that afternoon, she
had been perfectly calm. He had mooned through a number
of officers, both French and English, in a great octagonal,
bluish salon, where Lady Sachse gave her teas, and had come
to her side with just a nod—the merest inflexion of the head!
. . . Perowne had melted away somewhere behind the disagreeable duchess. The general, very splendid and white-
headed and scarlet-tipped and gilt, had also borne down
upon her at that. . . . At the sight of Perowne with her, he
had been sniffing and snorting whilst he talked to the young
nobleman—a dark fellow in blue with a new belt who seemed
just a shade too theatrical, he being chauffeur to a marshal
of France and first cousin and nearest relative except for
parents and grandparents of the prospective bride. . . .

The general had told her that he was running the show
pretty strong on purpose because he thought it might do
something to cement the *entente cordiale*. But it did not
seem to be doing it. The French—officers, soldiers and women
—kept pretty well all on the one side of the room—the
English on the other. The French were as a rule more
gloomy than men and women are expected to be. A marquis of sorts—she understood that these were all Bona-
partist nobility—having been introduced to her, had distinguished himself no more than by saying that for his part
he thought the duchess was right, and by saying that to
Perowne, who, knowing no French, had choked exactly as
if his tongue had suddenly got too big for his mouth. . . .

She had not heard what the duchess—a very disagreeable
duchess, who sat on a sofa and appeared savagely care-worn

—had been saying, so that she had inclined herself, in the courtly manner that at school she had been taught to reserve for the French legitimist nobility, but that she thought she might expend upon a rather state function even for the Bonapartists, and had replied that without the least doubt the duchess had the right of the matter. . . . The marquis had given her from dark eyes one long glance, and she had returned it with a long cold glance that certainly told him she was meat for his masters. It extinguished him. . . .

Tietjens had staged his meeting with herself remarkably well. It was the sort of lymphatic thing he *could* do, so that, for the fifth of a minute, she wondered if he had any feelings or emotions at all. But she knew that he had. . . . The general, at any rate, bearing down upon them with satisfaction, had remarked:

"Ah, I see you've seen each other before to-day. . . . I thought perhaps you wouldn't have found time before, Tietjens. . . . Your draft must be a great nuisance. . . ."

Tietjens said without expression:

"Yes, we have seen each other before. . . . I made time to call at Sylvia's hotel, sir."

It was at Tietjens' terrifying expressionlessness, at that completely being up to a situation, that the first wave of emotion had come over her. . . . For till that very moment she had been merely sardonically making the constatation that there was not a single presentable man in the room. . . . There was not even one that you could call a gentleman . . . for you cannot size up the French . . . ever! . . . But, suddenly, she was despairing! . . . How, she said to herself, could she ever move, put emotion into, this lump! It was like trying to move an immense mattress filled with feathers. You pulled at one end, but the whole mass sagged down and remained immobile until you seemed to have no strength at all. . . . Until virtue went out from you . . .

It was as if he had the evil eye: or some special protector. He was so appallingly competent, so appallingly always in the centre of his own picture. . . .

The general said, rather joyfully:

"Then you can spare a minute, Tietjens, to talk to the duchess! About coal! . . . For goodness' sake, man, save the situation! I'm worn out. . . ."

Sylvia bit the inside of her lower lip—she never bit her lip itself!—to keep herself from exclaiming aloud. It was just exactly what should not happen to Tietjens at that juncture. . . . She heard the general explaining to her, in his courtly

manner, that the duchess was holding up the whole ceremony because of the price of coal. The general loved her
desperately. Her, Sylvia! In quite a proper manner for an
elderly general . . . But he would go to no small extremes
in her interests! So would his sister!

She looked hard at the room to get her senses into order
again. She said:

"It's like a Hogarth picture. . . ."

The undissolvable air of the eighteenth century that the
French contrive to retain in all their effects kept the scene
singularly together. On a sofa sat the duchess, relatives leaning over her. She was a duchess with one of those impossible names: Beauchain-Radigutz or something like it. The
bluish room was octagonal and vaulted, up to a rosette in
the centre of the ceiling. English officers and V.A.D.s of
some evident presence opened out to the left; French military and very black-clothed women of all ages, but all apparently widows, opened out to the right, as if the duchess
shone down a sea at sunset. Beside her on the sofa you did
not see Lady Sachse; leaning over her you did not see the
prospective bride. This stoutish, unpresentable, coldly ven-
omous woman, in black clothes so shabby that they might
have been grey tweed, extinguished other personalities as
the sun conceals planets. A fattish, brilliantined personality
in mufti, with a scarlet rosette, stood sideways to the
duchess's right, his hands extended forward as if in an invitation to a dance; an extremely squat lady, also apparently a widow, extended, on the left of the duchess, both her
black-gloved hands, as if she too were giving an invitation
to the dance. . . .

The general, with Sylvia beside him, stood glorious in
the centre of the clearing that led to the open doorway of
a much smaller room. Through the doorway you could see
a table with a white damask cloth; a silver-gilt inkpot, fretted,
like a porcupine with pens; a fat, flat leather case for the
transportation of documents; and two *notaires:* one in black,
fat, and bald-headed; one in blue uniform, with a shining
monocle and a brown moustache that he continued to
twirl. . . .

Looking round that scene Sylvia's humour calmed her
and she heard the general say:

"She's supposed to walk on my arm to that table and
sign the settlement. . . . We're supposed to be the first to
sign it together. . . . But she won't. Because of the price
of coal. It appears that she has hot-houses in miles. And she

thinks the English have put up the price of coal as if . . . damn it, you'd think we did it just to keep her hot-house stoves out."

The duchess had delivered, apparently, a vindictive, cold, calm and uninterruptible oration on the wickedness of her country's allies as people who should have allowed France to be devastated and the flower of her youth slain, in order that they might put up the price of a comestible that was absolutely needed in her life. There was no arguing with her. There was no British soul there who both knew anything about economics and spoke French. And there she sat, apparently immovable. She did not refuse to sign the marriage contract. She just made no motion to go to it, and, apparently, the resulting marriage would be illegal if that document were brought to her! . . .

The general said:

"Now, what the deuce will Christopher find to say to her? He'll find something because he could talk the hind legs off anything. But what the deuce will it be? . . ."

It almost broke Sylvia's heart to see how exactly Christopher did the right thing. He walked up that path to the sun and made in front of the duchess a little awkward nick with his head and shoulders that was rather more like a curtsy than a bow. It appeared that he knew the duchess quite well . . . as he knew everybody in the world quite well. He smiled at her and then became just suitably grave. Then he began to speak an admirable, very old-fashioned French with an atrocious English accent. Sylvia had no idea that he knew a word of the language—that she herself knew very well indeed. She said to herself that upon her word it was like hearing Chateaubriand talk—if Chateaubriand had been brought up in an English hunting-country. . . . Of course Christopher *would* cultivate an English accent: to show that he was an English country gentleman. And he would speak correctly—to show that an English Tory can do anything in the world if he wants to. . . .

The British faces in the room looked blank: the French faces turned electrically upon him. Sylvia said:

"Who would have thought? . . ." The duchess jumped to her feet and took Christopher's arm. She sailed with him imperiously past the general and past Sylvia. She was saying that that was just what she would have expected of a *milor anglais . . . avec un spleen tel que vous l'avez!*

Christopher, in short, had told the duchess that as his family owned almost the largest stretch of hot-house coal-bearing land in England and her family the largest stretch of hot-houses in the sister-country of France, what could they do better than make an alliance? He would instruct his brother's manager to see that the duchess was supplied for the duration of hostilities and as long after as she pleased with all the coal needed for her glass at the pit-head prices of the Middlesbrough–Cleveland district as the prices were on the 3rd of August, nineteen-fourteen. . . . He repeated: "The pit-head price . . . *livrable au prix de l'houille-maigre dans l'enceinte des puits de ma campagne*" . . . Much to the satisfaction of the duchess, who knew all about prices.

. . . A triumph for Christopher was at that moment so exactly what Sylvia thought she did not want that she decided to tell the general that Christopher was a socialist. That might well take him down a peg or two in the general's esteem . . . for the general's arm-patting admiration for Tietjens, the man who did not argue, but acted, over the price of coal, was as much as she could bear. . . . But, thinking it over in the smoking-room after dinner, by which time she was a good deal more aware of what she did want, she was not so certain that she *had* done what she wanted. . . . Indeed, even in the octagonal room during the economical festivities that followed the signatures, she had been far from certain that she had not done almost exactly what she did not want. . . .

It had begun with the general's exclaiming to her:

"You know your man's the most unaccountable fellow. . . . He wears the damn-shabbiest uniform of any officer I ever have to talk to. He's said to be unholily hard up. . . . I even heard he had a cheque sent back to the club. . . . Then he goes and makes a princely gift like that—just to get Levin out of ten minutes' awkwardness. . . . I wish to goodness I could understand the fellow. . . . He's got a positive genius for getting all sorts of things out of the most beastly muddles . . . Why, he's even been useful to me. . . . And then he's got a positive genius for getting into the most disgusting messes. . . . You're too young to have heard of Dreyfus. . . . But I always say that Christopher is a regular Dreyfus. . . . I shouldn't be astonished if he didn't end by being drummed out of the army . . . which heaven forfend!"

It had been then that Sylvia had said:

"Hasn't it ever occurred to you that Christopher was a socialist?"

For the first time in her life Sylvia saw her husband's godfather look grotesque. . . . His jaw dropped down, his white hair became disarrayed and he dropped his pretty cap with all the gold oak-leaves and the scarlet. When he rose from picking it up, his thin old face was purple and distorted. She wished she hadn't said it: she wished she hadn't said it. He exclaimed:

"Christopher! . . . A so . . ." He gasped as if he could not pronounce the word. He said: "Damn it all! . . . I've loved that boy. . . . He's my only godson. . . . His father was my best friend. . . . I've watched over him. . . . I'd have married his mother if she would have had me. . . . Damn it all, he's down in my will as residuary legatee after a few small things left to my sister and my collection of horns to the regiment I commanded. . . ."

Sylvia—they were sitting on the sofa the duchess had left —patted him on the forearm and said:

"But, general . . . godfather . . ."

"It explains everything," he said with a mortification that was painful. His white moustache drooped and trembled. "And what makes it all the worse—he's never had the courage to tell me his opinions." He stopped, snorted and exclaimed: "By God, I *will* have him drummed out of the service. . . . By God, I will. I can do that much. . . ."

His grief so shut him in on himself that she could say nothing to him. . . .

"You tell me he seduced the little Wannop girl. . . . The last person in the world he should have seduced . . . Ain't there millions of other women? . . . He got you sold up, didn't he? . . . Along with keeping a girl in a tobacco-shop . . . By Jove, I almost lent him . . . offered to lend him money on that occasion. . . . You can forgive a young man for going wrong with women. . . . We all do. . . . We've all set up girls in tobacco-shops in our time. . . . But damn it all, if the fellow's a socialist it puts a different complexion. . . . I could forgive him even for the little Wannop girl if he wasn't . . . But . . . Good God, isn't it just the thing that a dirty-minded socialist would do? . . . To seduce the daughter of his father's oldest friend next to me . . . Or perhaps Wannop was an older friend than me. . . ."

He had calmed himself a little—and he was not such a fool. He looked at her now with a certain keenness in his blue eyes that showed no sign of age. He said:

"See here, Sylvia. . . . You aren't on terms with Christopher, for all the good game you put up here this afternoon. . . . I shall have to go into this. It's a serious charge to bring against one of His Majesty's officers. . . . Women do say things against their husbands when they are not on good terms with them. . . ." He went on to say that he did not say she wasn't justified. If Christopher had seduced the little Wannop girl it was enough to make her wish to harm him. He had always found her the soul of honour, straight as a die, straight as she rode to hounds. And if she wished to nag against her husband, even if in little things it wasn't quite the truth, she was perhaps within her rights as a woman. She had said, for instance, that Tietjens had taken two pairs of her best sheets. Well, his own sister, her friend, raised Cain if he took anything out of the house they lived in. She had made an atrocious row because he had taken his own shaving-glass out of his own bedroom at Mountby. Women liked to have sets of things. Perhaps she, Sylvia, had sets of pairs of sheets. His sister had linen sheets with the date of the Battle of Waterloo on them. . . . Naturally you would not want a set spoiled. . . . But this was another matter. He ended up very seriously:

"I have not got time to go into this now. . . . I ought not to be another minute away from my office. These are very serious days. . . ." He broke off to utter against the Prime Minister and the Cabinet at home a series of violent imprecations. He went on:

"But this will have to be gone into. . . . It's heart-breaking that my time should be taken up by matters like this in my own family. . . . But these fellows aim at sapping the heart of the army. . . . They say they distribute thousands of pamphlets recommending the rank and file to shoot their officers and go over to the Germans. . . . Do you seriously mean that Christopher belongs to an organization? What is it you are going on? What evidence have you? . . ."

She said:

"Only that he is heir to one of the biggest fortunes in England, for a commoner, and he refuses to touch a penny. . . . His brother, Mark, tells me Christopher could have . . . oh, a fabulous sum a year. . . . But he has made over Groby to me. . . ."

The general nodded his head as if he were ticking off ideas.

"Of course, refusing property is a sign of being one of these fellows. By Jove, I must go. . . . But as for his not going to live at Groby: If he is setting up house with Miss Wannop . . . Well, he could not flaunt her in the face of the county. . . . And, of course, those sheets! . . . As you put it, it looked as if he'd beggared himself with his dissipations. . . . But, of course, if he is refusing money from Mark, it's another matter. . . . Mark would make up a couple of hundred dozen pairs of sheets without turning a hair. . . . Of course there are the extraordinary things Christopher says. . . . I've often heard you complain of the immoral way he looks at the serious affairs of life. . . . You said he once talked of lethal-chambering unfit children."

He exclaimed:

"I must go. There's Thurston looking at me. . . . But what, then, is it that Christopher has said? . . . Hang it all: what *is* at the bottom of that fellow's mind? . . ."

"He desires," Sylvia said, and she had no idea when she said it, "to model himself upon Our Lord. . . ."

The general leant back in the sofa. He said almost indulgently:

"Who's that . . . Our *Lord?*"

Sylvia said:

"Upon Our Lord Jesus Christ . . ."

He sprang to his feet as if she had stabbed him with a hat-pin.

"Our . . ." he exclaimed. "Good God! . . . I always knew he had a screw loose. . . . But . . ." He said briskly: "Give all his goods to the poor! . . . But He wasn't a . . . not a socialist! What was it He said: Render unto Caesar . . . It wouldn't be necessary to drum Him out of the army. . . ." He said: "Good Lord! . . . Good Lord! . . . Of course his poor dear mother was a little . . . But, hang it! . . . The Wannop girl! . . ." Extreme discomfort overcame him. . . . Tietjens was half-way across from the inner room, coming towards them.

He said:

"Major Thurston is looking for you, sir. Very urgently . . ." The general regarded him as if he had been the unicorn of the royal arms come alive. He exclaimed:

"Major Thurston! . . . Yes! Yes! . . ." and, Tietjens saying to him:

"I wanted to ask you, sir . . ." He pushed Tietjens away as if he dreaded an assault and went off with short, agitated steps.

So, sitting there in the smoking-lounge of the hotel, which was cram-jam full of officers and, no doubt, perfectly respectable, but overgiggling, women—the sort of place and environment which she had certainly never expected to be called upon to sit in—and waiting for the return of Tietjens

and the ex-sergeant-major, who again was certainly not the
sort of person that she had ever expected to be asked to
wait for, though for long years she had put up with Tietjens' protégé, the odious Sir Vincent Macmaster, at all
sorts of meals and all sorts of places . . . but of course that
was only Christopher's rights . . . to have in his own house,
which, in the circumstances, wasn't morally hers, any snuffling, nervous, walrus-moustached or orientally obsequious
protégé that he chose to patronize. . . . And she quite believed that Tietjens, when he had invited the sergeant-major
to celebrate his commission with himself at dinner, hadn't
expected to dine with her. . . . It was the sort of obtuseness
of which he was disconcertingly capable, though at other
times he was much more disconcertingly capable of reading
your thoughts to the last hair's-breadth. . . . And, as a matter of fact, she objected much less to dining with the absolute lower classes than with merely snuffly little official
critics like Macmaster, and the sergeant-major had served
her turn very well when it had come to flaying the hide
off Christopher. . . . So, sitting there, she made a new pact,
this time with Father Consett in Heaven. . . .

Father Consett was very much in her mind, for she was
very much in the midst of the British military authorities
who had hung him. . . . She had never seemed before to
be so in the midst of these negligible, odious, unpresentable,
horse-laughing schoolboys. It antagonized her, and it was a
weight upon her, for hitherto she had completely ignored
them: in this place they seemed to have a coherence, a mass
. . . almost a life. . . . They rushed in and out of rooms
occupied, as incomprehensibly, as unpresentably, with things
like boots, washing, vaccination certificates. . . . Even with
old tins! . . . A man with prematurely white hair and a
pasty face, with a tunic that bulged both above and below
his belt, would walk into the drawing-room of a lady who
superintended all the acid-drop and cigarette stalls of that
city and remark to a thin-haired, deaf man with an amaz-
ingly red nose—a nose that had a perfectly definite purple
and scarlet diagonal demarcation running from the bridge
to the upper side of the nostrils—that he had got his old tins
off his hands at last. He would have to repeat it in a shout
because the red-nosed man, his head hanging down, would
have heard nothing at all. The deaf man would say Humph!
Humph! Snuffle. The woman giving the tea—a Mrs. Hem-
merdine, of Tarbolton, whom you might have met at home—
would be saying that at last she had got twelve reams of

note-paper with forget-me-nots in the top corners, when the deaf-faced man would begin, gruffly and uninterruptedly, a monologue on his urgent need for twenty thousand tons of sawdust for the new slow-burning stoves in the men's huts. . . .

It was undeniably like something moving. . . . All these things going in one direction . . . A disagreeable force set in motion by gawky schoolboys—but schoolboys of the sixth form, sinister, hobbledehoy, waiting in the corners of playgrounds to torture someone weak and unfortunate. . . . In one or other corner of their world-wide playground they had come upon Father Consett and hanged him. No doubt they tortured him first. And if he made an offering of his sufferings then and there to Heaven, no doubt he was already in paradise. . . . Or if he was not yet in Heaven, certain of the souls in Purgatory were yet listened to in the midst of their torments. . . .

So she said:

"Blessed and martyred Father, I know that you loved Christopher and wish to save him from trouble. I will make this pact with you. Since I have been in this room I have kept my eyes in the boat—almost in my lap. I will agree to leave off torturing Christopher and I will go into retreat in a convent of Ursuline *dames nobles*—for I can't stand the nuns of that other convent—for the rest of my life. . . . And I know that will please you, too, for you were always anxious for the good of my soul. . . ." She was going to do that if, when she raised her eyes and really looked round the room, she saw in it one man that looked presentable. She did not ask that he should more than look presentable, for she wanted nothing to do with the creature. He was to be a sign: not a prey!

She explained to the dead priest that she could not go all the world over to see if it contained a presentable man, but she could not bear to be in a convent forever and have the thought that there wasn't, for other women, one presentable man in the world. . . . For Christopher would be no good to them. He would be mooning forever over the Wannop girl. Or her memory. That was all one. . . . He was content with LOVE. . . . If he knew that the Wannop girl was loving him in Bedford Park, and he in the Khyber states with the Himalayas between them, he would be quite content. . . . That would be correct in its way, but not very helpful for other women. . . . Besides, if he were the only presentable man in the world, half the women would be in love with him. . . . And that would be disastrous because he was no more responsive than a bullock in a fatting pen.

"So, Father," she said, "work a miracle. . . . It's not very much of a little miracle. . . . Even if a presentable man doesn't exist, you could put him there. . . . I'll give you ten minutes before I look. . . ."

She thought it was pretty sporting of her, for, she said to herself, she was perfectly in earnest. If in that long, dim, green-lamp-shaded, and of course bepalm-leaved, badly proportioned, glazed, ignoble public room, there appeared one decentish man, as decentish men went before this bean-feast began, she would go into retreat for the rest of her life. . . .

She fell into a sort of dim trance after she had looked at her watch. Often she went into these dim trances . . . ever since she had been a girl at school with Father Consett for her spiritual adviser! . . . She seemed to be aware of the Father moving about the room, lifting up a book and putting it down. . . . Her ghostly friend! . . . Goodness, he was unpresentable enough, with his broad, open face that always looked dirtyish, his great dark eyes, and his great mouth. . . . But a saint and a martyr . . . She felt him there. . . . What had they murdered him for? Hung at the word of a half-mad, half-drunk subaltern because he had heard the confession of some of the rebels the night before they were taken. . . . He was over in the far corner of the room. . . . She heard him say: they had not understood, the men that had hanged him. "That is what you would say, Father . . . Have mercy on them, for they know not what they do. . . .

"Then have mercy on me, for half the time I don't know what I'm doing! . . . It was like a spell you put on me. At Lobscheid. Where my mother was when I came back from that place without my clothes . . . You said, didn't you, to mother, but she told me afterwards: 'The real hell for that poor boy,' meaning Christopher, 'will come when he falls in love with some young girl—as, mark me, he will. . . . For she,' meaning me, 'will tear the world down to get at him. . . .' And when mother said she was certain I would never do anything vulgar you obstinately did not agree. . . . You knew me. . . ."

She tried to rouse herself and said: "He *knew* me. . . . Damn it, he knew me! . . . What's vulgarity to me, Sylvia Tietjens, born Satterthwaite? I do what I want and that's good enough for anyone. Except a priest. Vulgarity! I wonder mother could be so obtuse. If I am vulgar I'm vulgar with a purpose. Then it's not vulgarity. It may be vice. Or vicious-ness . . . But if you commit a mortal sin with your eyes open it's not vulgarity. . . . You chance hell-fire forever. . . . Good enough!"

The weariness sank over her again and the sense of the Father's presence. . . . She was back again in Lobscheid, thirty-six hours free of Perowne, with the Father and her mother in the dim sitting-room, all antlers, candlelit, with the Father's shadow waving over the pitch-pine walls and ceilings. . . . It was a bewitched place, in the deep forests of Germany. The Father himself said it was the last place in Europe to be Christianized. Or perhaps it was never Chris-tianized. . . . That was perhaps why these people, the Ger-mans, coming from those deep, devil-infested woods, did all these wickednesses. Or maybe they were not wicked. . . . One would never know properly. . . . But maybe the Father had put a spell on her. . . . His words had never been out of her mind much. . . . At the back of her brain, as the saying was . . .

Some man drifted near her and said:

"How do you do, Mrs. Tietjens? Who would have thought of seeing you here?"

She answered:

"I have to look after Christopher now and then." He re-mained hanging over her with a schoolboy grin for a minute, then he drifted away as an object sinks into deep water. . . . Father Consett again hovered near her. She exclaimed:

"But the real point is, Father . . . is it sporting? . . . Sporting or whatever it is?" And Father Consett breathed:

"Ah! . . ." with his terrible power of arousing doubts. . . . She said:

"When I saw Christopher . . . Last night? . . . Yes, it *was* last night. . . . Turning back to go up that hill . . . And I had been talking about him to a lot of grinning private soldiers. . . . To *madden* him . . . You *mustn't* make scenes before the servants. . . . A heavy man, tired . . . come down the hill and lumbering up again . . . There was a searchlight turned on him just as he turned. . . . I remembered the white bull-dog I thrashed on the night before it died. . . . A tired, silent beast . . . with a fat white behind . . . Tired out . . . You couldn't see its tail because it was turned down, the stump. . . . A great, silent beast . . . The vet said it had been poisoned with red lead by burglars. . . . It's beastly to die of red lead. . . . It eats up the liver. . . . And you think you're getting better for a fortnight. And you're

always cold . . . freezing in the blood-vessels. . . . And the
poor beast had left its kennel to try and be let into the
fire. . . . And I found it at the door when I came in from a
dance without Christopher. . . . And got the rhinoceros
whip and lashed into it . . . There's a pleasure in lashing
into a naked white beast. . . . Obese and silent . . . Like
Christopher . . . I thought Christopher might. . . . That
night . . . It went through my head. . . . It hung down its
head. . . . A great head, room for a whole British encyclopaedia of misinformation, as Christopher used to put it. . . .
It said: 'What a hope!' . . . As I hope to be saved, though
I never shall be, the dog said: 'What a hope!' . . . Snow-
white in quite black bushes . . . And it went under a
bush. . . . They found it dead there in the morning. . . . You
can't imagine what it looked like, with its head over its
shoulder, as it looked back and said: 'What a hope!' to me.
. . . Under a dark bush. An eu . . . eu . . . euonymus,
isn't it? . . . In thirty degrees of frost with all the blood-
vessels exposed on the naked surface of the skin . . . It's
the seventh circle of Hell, isn't it? The frozen one . . . The
last stud-white bull-dog of that breed . . . As Christopher
is the last stud-white hope of the Groby Tory breed . . .
Modelling himself on Our Lord. . . . But Our Lord was
never married. He never touched on topics of sex. Good for
Him . . ."

She said: "The ten minutes is up, Father. . . ." and
looked at the round, starred surface between the diamonds
of her wrist-watch. She said: "Good God! . . . Only one
minute . . . I've thought all that in only one minute. . . .
I understand how Hell can be an eternity. . . ."

Christopher, very weary, and ex-Sergeant-Major Cowley,
very talkative by now, loomed down between palms.
Cowley was saying: "It's infamous! . . . It's past bearing. . . .
To reorder the draft at eleven . . ." They sank into chairs.
. . . Sylvia extended towards Tietjens a small packet of
letters. She said: "You had better look at these. . . . I had
your letters sent to me from the flat, as there was so much
uncertainty about your movements. . . ." She found that she
did not dare, under Father Consett's eyes, to look at Tietjens
as she said that. She said to Cowley: "We might be quiet for
a minute or two while the captain reads his letters. . . . Have
another liqueur? . . ."

She then observed that Tietjens just bent open the top of
the letter from Mrs. Wannop and then opened that from his
brother, Mark.

"Curse it," she said, "I've given him what he wants! . . .
He knows . . . he's seen the address . . . that they're still
in Bedford Park. . . . He can think of the Wannop girl as
there. . . . He has not been able to know, till now, where she
is. . . . He'll be imagining himself in bed with her there. . . ."

Father Consett, his broad, unmodelled dark face full of
intelligence and with the blissful unction of the saint and
martyr, was leaning over Tietjens' shoulder. . . . He must
be breathing down Christopher's back as, her mother said,
he always did when she held a hand at auction and he could
not play because it was between midnight and his celebrating
the holy mass. . . .

She said:

"No, I am not going mad. . . . This is an effect of fatigue
on the optic nerves. . . . Christopher has explained that to
me. . . . He says that when his eyes have been very tired
with making one of his Senior Wrangler's calculations he
has often seen a woman in an eighteenth-century dress looking into a drawer in his bureau. . . . Thank God I've had
Christopher to explain things to me. . . . I'll never let him
go. . . . Never, never let him go . . ."

It was not, however, until several hours later that the
significance of the Father's apparition came to her, and
those intervening hours were extraordinarily occupied—with
emotions, and even with action. To begin with, before he
had read the fewest possible words of his brother's letter,
Tietjens looked up over it and said:

"Of course you will occupy Groby. . . . With Michael
. . . Naturally the proper business arrangements will be
made. . . ." He went on reading the letter, sunk in his chair
under the green shade of a lamp. . . .

The letter, Sylvia knew, began with the words: "Your
—— of a wife has been to see me with the idea of getting
any allowance I might be minded to make you transferred
to herself. Of course she can have Groby, for I shan't let
it, and could not be bothered with it myself. On the other
hand, you may want to live at Groby with that girl and
chance the racket. I should if I were you. You would probably find the place worth the . . . what is it? ostracism, if
there was any. . . . But I'm forgetting that the girl is not
your mistress unless anything has happened since I saw you.
. . . And you probably would want Michael to be brought
up at Groby, in which case you couldn't keep the girl there,
even if you camouflaged her as governess. At least I think
that kind of arrangement always turns out badly: there's

bound to be a stink, though Crosby of Ulick did it and nobody much minded. . . . But it was mucky for the Crosby
children. Of course if you want your wife to have Groby
she must have enough to run it with credit, and expenses
are rising damnably. Still, our incomings rise not a little, too,
which is not the case with some. The only thing I insist on
is that you make plain to that baggage that whatever I allow
her, even if it's no end of a hot income, not one penny
of it comes out of what I wish you would allow me to allow
you. I mean I want you to make plain to that rouged piece—
or perhaps it's really natural, my eyes are not what they
were—that what you have is absolutely independent of what
she sucks up as the mother of our father's heir and to keep
our father's heir in the state of life that is his due. . . . I
hope you feel satisfied that the boy is your son, for it's
more than I should be, looking at the party. . . . But
even if he is not, he is our father's heir, all right, and must
be so treated. . . .

"But be plain about that, for the trollop came to me, if you
please, with the proposal that I should dock you of any
income I might propose to allow you—and to which, of
course, you are absolutely entitled under our father's will,
though it is no good reminding you of that!—as a token
from me that I disapproved of your behaviour when, damn
it, there is not an action of yours that I would not be proud
to have to my credit. At any rate, in this affair, for I cannot
help thinking that you could be of more service to the country
if you were anywhere else but where you are. But you know
what your conscience demands of you better than I, and I
dare say these hell-cats have so mauled you that you are glad
to be able to get away into any hole. But don't let yourself
die in your hole. Groby will have to be looked after, and
even if you do not live there you can keep a strong hand on
Sanders or whoever you elect to have as manager. That
monstrosity you honour with your name—which is also
mine, thank you!—suggested that if I consented to let her live
at Groby she would have her mother to live with her, in
which case her mother would be good to look after the estate.
I dare say she would, though she has had to let her own
place. But, then, almost everyone else has. She seems, anyhow, a notable woman, with her head screwed on the right
way. I did not tell the discreditable daughter that she—her
mother—had come to see me at breakfast immediately after
seeing you off, she was so upset. And she *keawert ho down
i' th' ingle and had a gradely pow*. You remember how

Gobbles the gardener used to say that. A good chap, though he came from Lancashire. . . . The mother has no illusions about the daughter and is heart and soul for you. She was dreadfully upset at your going, the more so as she believes that it's her offspring has driven you out of the country and that you purpose . . . Isn't 'stopping one' the phrase? Don't do that.

"I saw your girl yesterday. . . . She looked peaky. But of course I have seen her several times, and she always looks peaky. I do not understand why you do not write to them. The mother is clamorous because you have not answered several letters and have not sent her military information she wants for some article she is writing for a Swiss magazine. . . ."

Sylvia knew the letter almost by heart as far as that because in the unbearable white room of the convent near Birkenhead she had twice begun to copy it out, with the idea of keeping the copies for use in some sort of publicity. But, at that point, she had twice been overcome by the idea that it was not a very sporting thing to do if you really think about it. Besides, the letter after that—she *had* glanced through it—occupied itself almost entirely with the affairs of Mrs. Wannop. Mark, in his naïve way, was concerned that the old lady, although now enjoying the income from the legacy left her by their father, had not immediately settled down to write a deathless novel; although, as he added, he knew nothing about novels. . . .

Christopher was reading away at his letters beneath the green-shaded lamp; the ex-quartermaster had begun several sentences and dropped into demonstrative silence at the reminder that Tietjens was reading. Christopher's face was completely without expression; he might have been reading a return from the office of statistics in the old days at breakfast. She wondered, vaguely, if he would see fit to apologize for the epithets that his brother had applied to her. Probably he would not. He would consider that she, having opened the letter, must take the responsibility of the contents. Something like that. Thumps and rumbles began to exist in the relative silence. Cowley said: "They're coming again, then!" Several couples passed them on the way out of the room. Amongst them there was certainly no presentable man; they were all either too old or too hobbledehoy, with disproportionate noses and vacant, half-opened mouths.

Accompanying Christopher's mind, as it were, whilst he read his letter had induced in her a rather different mood.

The pictures in her own mind were rather of Mark's dingy breakfast-room in which she had had her interview with him —and of the outside of the dingy house in which the Wannops lived, at Bedford Park. . . . But she was still conscious of her pact with the Father and, looking at her wrist-watch, saw that by now six minutes had passed. . . . It was astonishing that Mark, who was a millionaire at least, and probably a good deal more, should live in such a dingy apartment—it had for its chief decoration the hoofs of several deceased race-winners, mounted as inkstands, as pen-racks, as paper-weights—and afford himself only such a lugubrious breakfast of fat slabs of ham over which bled pallid eggs. . . . For she too, like her mother, had looked in on Mark at breakfast-time—her mother because she had just seen Christopher off to France, and she because, after a sleepless night—the third of a series—she had been walking about St. James's Park, and passing under Mark's windows, it had occurred to her that she might do Christopher some damage by putting his brother wise about the entanglement with Miss Wannop. So, on the spur of the moment, she had invented a desire to live at Groby with the accompanying necessity for additional means. For, although she was a pretty wealthy woman, she was not wealthy enough to live at Groby and keep it up. The immense old place was not so immense because of its room-space, though as far as she could remember there must be anything between forty and sixty rooms, but because of the vast old grounds, the warren of stabling, wells, rose-walks and fencing. . . . A man's place, really, the furniture very grim and the corridors on the ground floor all slabbed with great stones. So she had looked in on Mark, reading his correspondence with his copy of *The Times* airing on a chair-back before the fire—for he was just the man to retain the eighteen-forty idea that you can catch cold by reading a damp newspaper. His grim, tight, brown-wooden features that might have been carved out of an old chair had expressed no emotion at all during the interview. He had offered to have up some more ham and eggs for her and had asked one or two questions as to how she meant to live at Groby if she went there. Otherwise he had said nothing about the information she had given him as to the Wannop girl having had a baby by Christopher—for for purposes of conversation she had adhered to that old story, at any rate till that interview. He had said nothing at all. Not one word . . . At the end of the interview, when he had risen and produced from an adjoining room a bowler hat and an umbrella, saying that he must now go to his office, he had put to her without any expression pretty well what stood in the letter, as far as business was concerned. He said that she could have Groby, but she must understand that, his father being now dead and he a public official, without children and occupied in London with work that suited him, Groby was practically Christopher's property to do what he liked with as long as—which he certainly would—he kept it in proper style. So that if she wished to live there, she must produce Christopher's authorization to that effect. And he added, with an equableness so masking the proposition that it was not until she was well out of the house and down the street that its true amazingness took her breath away:

"Of course Christopher, if what you say is true, might want to live at Groby with Miss Wannop. In that case he would have to." And he had offered her an expressionless hand and shepherded her, rather fussily, through his dingy and awkward front passages that were lit only from ground-glass windows giving apparently on to his bathroom. . . .

It wasn't until that moment, really, that, at once with exhilaration and also with a sinking at the heart, she realized what she was up against in the way of a combination. For when she had gone to Mark's, she had been more than half maddened by the news that Christopher at Rouen was in hospital, and although the hospital authorities had assured her, at first by telegram and then by letter, that it was nothing more than his chest, she had not had any knowledge of to what extent Red Cross authorities did or did not mislead the relatives of casualties.

So it had seemed natural that she should want to inflict on him all the injuries that she could at the moment, the thought that he was probably in pain making her wish to add all she could to that pain. . . . Otherwise, of course, she would not have gone to Mark's. . . . For it was a mistake in strategy. But then she said to herself: "Confound it! . . . What strategy was it a mistake in? What do I care about strategy? What am I out for? . . ." She did what she wanted to, on the spur of the moment! . . .

Now she certainly realized. How Christopher had got round Mark she did not know or much care, but there Christopher certainly was, although his father had certainly died of a broken heart at the rumours that were going round about his son—rumours she, almost as efficiently as the man called Ruggles and more irresponsible gossips, had set going about Christopher. They had been meant to smash Christopher: they had smashed his father instead. . . . But Christopher had got round Mark, whom he had not seen for ten years. . . . Well, he probably would. Christopher was perfectly immaculate, that was a fact, and Mark, though he appeared half-witted in a North Country way, was no fool. He could not be a fool. He was a really august public official. And although as a rule Sylvia gave nothing at all for any public official, if a man like Mark had the position by birth amongst presentable men that he certainly ought to have and was also the head of a department and reputed absolutely indispensable—you could not ignore him. . . . He said, indeed, in the later, more gossipy, parts of his letter that he had been offered a baronetcy, but he wanted Christopher to agree with his refusing it. Christopher would not want the beastly title after his death, and for himself, he would be rather struck with the pip than let that harlot—meaning herself—become Lady T. by any means of his. He had added, with his queer solicitude, "Of course if you thought of divorcing—which I wish to God you would, though I agree that you are right not to—and the title would go to the girl after my decease, I'd take it gladly, for a title is a bit of a help after a divorce. But as it is, I propose to refuse it and ask for a knighthood if it won't too sicken you to have me a Sir. . . . For I hold no man ought to refuse an honour in times like these, as has been done by certain sickening intellectuals, because it is like slapping the sovereign in the face and bound to hearten the other side, which no doubt was what was meant by those fellows."

There was no doubt that Mark—with the possible addition of the Wannops—made a very strong backing for Christopher if she decided to make a public scandal about him. . . . As for the Wannops . . . the girl was negligible. Or possibly not, if she turned nasty and twisted Christopher round her fingers. But the old mother was a formidable figure—with a bad tongue—and viewed with a certain respect in places where people talked . . . both on account of her late husband's position and of the solid sort of articles she wrote. . . . She, Sylvia, had gone to take a look at the place where these people lived . . . a dreary street in an outer suburb, the houses—she knew enough about estates to know—what is called tile-healed: the upper parts of tile, the lower, flimsy brick, and the tiles in bad condition. Oldish houses, really, in spite of their sham artistic aspect, and very much shadowed

by old trees that must have been left to add to the pictur-
esqueness. . . . The rooms poky, and they must be very dark.
. . . The residence of extreme indigence or of absolute
poverty. . . . She understood that the old lady's income had
so fallen off during the war that they had nothing to live on
but what the girl made as a school-teacher or a teacher of
athletics in a girls' school. . . . She had walked two or three
times up and down the street with the idea that the girl
might come out: then it had struck her that that was rather
an ignoble proceeding, really. . . . It was, for the matter of
that, ignoble that she should have a rival who starved in an
ash-bin. . . . But that was what men were like: she might
think herself lucky that the girl did not inhabit a sweet shop.
. . . And the man Macmaster said that the girl had a good
head and talked well, though the woman Macmaster said
that she was a shallow ignoramus. . . . That last probably
was not true; at any rate, the girl had been the Macmaster
woman's most intimate friend for many years—as long as
they were sponging on Christopher and until, lower-middle-
class snobs as they were, they began to think they could get
into Society by carnying to herself. . . . Still, the girl probably
was a good talker, and if little, yet physically uncommonly
fit. . . . A good, homespun article . . . She wished her no ill!

What was incredible was that Christopher should let her
go on starving in such a poverty-stricken place when he had
something like the wealth of the Indies at his disposal. . . .
But the Tietjens were hard people! You could see that in
Mark's rooms . . . and Christopher would lie on the floor as
lief as in a goose-feather bed. And probably the girl would
not take his money. She was quite right. That was the way to
keep him. . . . She herself had no want of comprehension of
the stimulation to be got out of parsimonious living. . . . In
retreat at her convent, she lay as hard and as cold as
any anchorite and rose to the nuns' matins at four.

It was not, in fact, their fittings or food that she objected
to—it was that the lay-sisters and some of the nuns were altogether too much of the lower classes for her to like to have
always about her. . . . That was why it was to the *dames
nobles* that she would go if she had to go into retreat for the
rest of her life, according to contract. . . .

A gun manned by exhilarated anti-aircraft fellows, and so
close that it must have been in the hotel garden, shook her
physically at almost the same moment as an immense maroon
pooped off on the quay at the bottom of the street in which
the hotel was. She was filled with annoyance at these school-

boy exercises. A tall, purple-faced, white-moustached general of the more odious type appeared in the doorway and said that all the lights but two must be extinguished, and if they took his advice, they would go somewhere else. There were good cellars in the hotel. He loafed about the room extinguishing the lights, couples and groups passing him on the way to the door. . . . Tietjens looked up from his letter—he was now reading one of Mrs. Wannop's—but seeing that Sylvia made no motion, he remained sunk in his chair. . . .

The old general said:

"Don't get up, Tietjens. . . . Sit down, lieutenant. . . . Mrs. Tietjens, I presume . . . But of course I know you are Mrs. Tietjens. . . . There's a portrait of you in this week's . . . I forget the name. . . ." He sat down on the arm of a great leather chair and told her of all the trouble her escapade to that city had caused him. . . . He had been awakened immediately after a good lunch by some young officer on his staff who was scared to death by her having arrived without papers. His digestion had been deranged ever since. . . . Sylvia said she was very sorry. He should drink hot water and no alcohol with his lunch. She had had very important business to discuss with Tietjens, and she had really not understood that they wanted papers of grown-up people. The general began to expatiate on the importance of his office and the number of enemy agents his perspicacity caused to be arrested every day in that city and the lines of communication. . . .

Sylvia was overwhelmed at the ingenuity of Father Consett. She looked at her watch. The ten minutes were up, but there did not appear to be a soul in the dim place. . . . The Father had—and no doubt as a Sign that there could be no mistaking!—completely emptied that room. It was like his humour!

To make certain, she stood up. At the far end of the room, in the dimness of the one other reading lamp that the general had not extinguished, two figures were rather indistinguishable. She walked towards them, the general at her side extending civilities all over her. He said that she need not be under any apprehension there. He adopted that device of clearing the room in order to get rid of the beastly young subalterns, who would use the place to spoon in when the lights were turned down. She said she was only going to get a time-table from the far end of the room. . . .

The stab of hope that she had that one of the two figures would turn out to be the presentable man died. . . . They were a young mournful subaltern, with an incipient moustache and practically tears in his eyes, and an elderly, violently indignant bald-headed man in evening civilian clothes that must have been made by a country tailor. He was smacking his hands together to emphasize what, with great agitation, he was saying.

The general said that it was one of the young cubs on his own staff getting a dressing down from his dad for spending too much money. The young devils would get amongst the girls—and the old ones too. There was no stopping it. The place was a hotbed of . . . He left the sentence unfinished. She would not believe the trouble it gave him. . . . That hotel itself . . . The scandals . . .

He said he would excuse him if he took a little nap in one of the arm-chairs too far away to interfere with their business talk. He would have to be up half the night. He seemed to Sylvia a blazingly contemptible personage—too contemptible really for Father Consett to employ as an agent in clearing the room. . . . But the omen was given. She had to consider her position. It meant—or did it?—that she had to be at war with the heavenly powers! . . . She clenched her hands. . . .

In passing by Tietjens in his chair, the general boomed out the words:

"I got your chit of this morning, Tietjens. . . . I must say . . ."

Tietjens lumbered out of his chair and stood at attention, his leg-of-mutton hands stiffly on the seams of his breeches.

"It's pretty strong," the general said, "marking a charge-sheet sent down from *my* department 'Case explained.' We don't lay charges without due thought. And Lance-Corporal Berry is a particularly reliable N.C.O. I have difficulty enough to get them. Particularly after the late riots. It takes courage, I can tell you."

"If," Tietjens said, "you would see fit, sir, to instruct the G.M.P. not to call colonial troops damned conscripts, the trouble would be over. . . . We're instructed to use special discretion, as officers, in dealing with troops from the dominions. They are said to be very susceptible of insult. . . ."

The general suddenly became a boiling pot from which fragments of sentences came away: *damned* insolence; Court of Inquiry: damned conscripts they were too. He calmed enough to say:

"They *are* conscripts, your men, aren't they? They give me

more trouble. . . . I should have thought you would have wanted . . ."

Tietjens said:

"No, sir. I have not a man in my unit, as far as it's Canadian or British Columbian, that is not voluntarily enlisted. . . ."

The general exploded to the effect that he was bringing the whole matter before the G.O.C.I.C.'s department. Campion could deal with it how he wished: it was beyond himself. He began to bluster away from them; stopped; directed a frigid bow to Sylvia, who was not looking at him; shrugged his shoulders and stormed off.

It was difficult for Sylvia to get hold again of her thoughts in the smoking-room, for the evening was entirely pervaded with military effects that seemed to her the pranks of school-boys. Indeed, after Cowley, who had by now quite a good skinful of liquor, had said to Tietjens:

"By Jove, I would not like to be you and a little bit on if Old Blazes caught sight of you to-night," she said to Tietjens with real wonder:

"You don't mean to say that a gaga old fool like that could have any possible influence over you. . . . *You!*"

Tietjens said:

"Well, it's a troublesome business, all this. . . ."

She said that it so appeared to be, for before he could finish his sentence, an orderly was at his elbow extending, along with a pencil, a number of dilapidated papers. Tietjens looked rapidly through them, signing one after the other and saying intermittently:

"It's a trying time." "We're massing troops up the line as fast as we can go." "And with an endlessly changing personnel . . ." He gave a snort of exasperation and said to Cowley: "That horrible little Pitkins has got a job as bombing instructor. He can't march the draft. . . . Who the deuce am I to detail? Who the deuce is there? . . . You know all the little . . ." He stopped because the orderly could hear. A smart boy. Almost the only smart boy left him.

Cowley barged out of his seat and said he would telephone to the mess to see who was there. . . . Tietjens said to the boy:

"Sergeant-Major Morgan made out these returns of religions in the draft?"

The boy answered: "No, sir, I did. They're all right."

He pulled a slip of paper out of his tunic pocket and said shyly:

"If you would not mind signing this, sir . . . I can get a lift on an A.S.C. trolley that's going to Boulogne to-morrow at six. . . ."

Tietjens said:

"No, you can't have leave. I can't spare you. What's it for?"

The boy said almost inaudibly that he wanted to get married.

Tietjens, still signing, said: "Don't. . . . Ask your married pals what it's like!"

The boy, scarlet in his khaki, rubbed the sole of one foot on the instep of the other. He said that, saving madam's presence, it was urgent. It was expected any day now. She was a real good gel. Tietjens signed the boy's slip and handed it to him without looking up. The boy stood with his eyes on the ground. A diversion came from the tele-phone, which was at the far end of the room. Cowley had not been able to get on to the camp because an urgent mes-sage with regard to German espionage was coming through to the sleeping general.

Cowley began to shout: "For goodness' sake, hold the line. . . . For goodness' sake, hold the line. . . . I'm not the general. . . . I'm *not* the general. . . ." Tietjens told the orderly to awaken the sleeping warrior. A violent scene at the mouth of the quiescent instrument took place. The general roared to know who was the officer speaking. . . . Captain Bubbleyjocks . . . Captain Cuddlestocks . . . what in hell's name! And who was he speaking for? . . . Who? Himself? . . . Urgent, was it? . . . Didn't he know the proper procedure was by writing? . . . Urgent, damnation! . . . Did he not know where he was? . . . In the First Army by the Cassell Canal . . . Well, then . . . But the spy was in L. of C. territory, across the canal. . . . The French civilian authorities were very concerned. . . . They were, damn them! . . . And damn the officer. And damn the French *maire*. And damn the horse the supposed spy rode upon. . . . And when the officer was damned, let him write to First Army Headquarters about it and attach the horse and the bandoliers as an exhibit. . . .

There was a great deal more of it. Tietjens, reading his papers still, intermittently explained the story as it came in fragments over the telephone in the general's repetitions. . . . Apparently the French civilian authorities of a place called Warendonck had been alarmed by a solitary horseman in English uniform who had been wandering desultorily about their neighbourhood for several days, seeming to want to cross the canal bridges, but finding them guarded. . . . There was an immense artillery-dump in the neighbourhood, said to be the largest in the world, and the Germans dropped bombs as thick as peas all over those parts in the hopes of hitting it. . . . Apparently the officer speaking was in charge of the canal bridge-head guards: but, as he was in First Army country, it was obviously an act of the utmost impropriety to awaken a general in charge of the spy-catching apparatus on the other side of the canal. . . . The general, returning past them to an arm-chair farther from the telephone, emphasized this point of view with great vigour.

The orderly had returned; Cowley went once more to the telephone, having consumed another liqueur brandy. Tietjens finished his papers and went through them rapidly again. He said to the boy: "Got anything saved up?" The boy said: "A fiver and a few bob." Tietjens said: "How many bob?" The boy: "Seven, sir." Tietjens, fumbling clumsily in an inner pocket and a little pocket beneath his belt, held out one leg-of-mutton fist and said: "There! That will double it. Ten pounds fourteen! But it's very improvident of you. See that you save up a deuced lot more against the next one. Accouchements are confoundedly expensive things, as you'll learn, and ring money doesn't stretch forever! . . ." He called out to the retreating boy: "Here, orderly, come back. . . ." He added: "Don't let it get all over camp. . . . I can't afford to subsidize all the seven months' children in the battalion. . . . I'll recommend you for paid lance-corporal when you return from leave if you go on as well as you have done." He called the boy back again to ask him why Captain McKechnie had not signed the papers. The boy stuttered and stammered that Captain McKechnie was . . . He was . . .

Tietjens muttered: "Good God!" beneath his breath. He said:

"The captain has had another nervous break-down. . . ." The orderly accepted the phrase with gratitude. That was it. A nervous break-down. They say he had been very queer at mess. About divorce. Or the captain's uncle. A barrow-night! Tietjens said: "Yes, yes!" He half rose in his chair and looked at Sylvia. She exclaimed painfully:

"You can't go. I insist that you can't go." He sank down

again and muttered wearily that it was very worrying. He had been put in charge of this officer by General Campion. He ought not to have left the camp at all perhaps. But McKechnie had seemed better. A great deal of the calmness of her insolence had left her. She had expected to have the whole night in which luxuriously to torment the lump opposite her. To torment him and to allure him. She said:

"You have settlements to come to now and here that will affect your whole life. Our whole lives! You propose to abandon them because a miserable little nephew of your miserable little friend . . ." She added in French: "Even as it is you cannot pay any attention to these serious matters because of these childish preoccupations of yours. That is to be intolerably insulting to me!" She was breathless.

Tietjens asked the orderly where Captain McKechnie was now. The orderly said he had left the camp. The colonel of the depot had sent a couple of officers as a search-party. Tietjens told the orderly to go and find a taxi. He could have a ride himself up to camp. The orderly said taxis would not be running on account of the air raid. Could he order the G.M.P. to requisition one on urgent military service? The exhilarated air-gun pooped off thereupon three times from the garden. For the next hour it went off every two or three minutes. Tietjens said: "Yes! Yes!" to the orderly. The noises of the air raid became more formidable. A blue express letter of French-civilian make was handed to Tietjens. It was from the duchess to inform him that coal for the use of green-houses was forbidden by the French government. She did not need to say that she relied on his honour to ensure her receiving her coal through the British military authority, and she asked for an immediate reply. Tietjens expressed real annoyance while he read this. Distracted by the noise, Sylvia cried out that the letter must be from Valentine Wannop in Rouen. Did not the girl intend to let him have an hour in which to settle the whole business of his life? Tietjens moved to the chair next to hers. He handed her the duchess's letter.

He began a long, slow, serious explanation with a long, slow, serious apology. He said he regretted very much that when she should have taken the trouble to come so far in order to do him the honour to consult him about a matter which she would have been perfectly at liberty to settle for herself, the extremely serious military position should render him so liable to interruption. As far as he was concerned,

Groby was entirely at her disposal with all that it contained. And of course a sufficient income for the upkeep.

She exclaimed in an access of sudden and complete despair:

"That means that you do not intend to live there." He said that that must settle itself later. The war would no doubt last a good deal longer. While it lasted there could be no question of his coming back. She said that that meant that he intended to get killed. She warned him that if he got killed, she should cut down the great cedar at the southwest corner of Groby. It kept all the light out of the principal drawing-room and the bedrooms above it. . . . He winced: he certainly winced at that. She regretted that she had said it. It was along other lines that she desired to make him wince.

He said that apart from his having no intention of getting himself killed, the matter was absolutely out of his hands. He had to go where he was ordered to go and do what he was told to do.

She exclaimed:

"You! *You!* Isn't it ignoble? That you should be at the beck and call of these ignoramuses. You!"

He went on explaining seriously that he was in no great danger—in no danger at all unless he was sent back to his battalion. And he was not likely to be sent back to his battalion unless he disgraced himself or showed himself negligent where he was. That was unlikely. Besides, his category was so low that he was not eligible for his battalion, which, of course, was in the line. She ought to understand that everyone that she saw employed there was physically unfit for the line. She said:

"That's why they're such an awful lot. . . . It is not to this place that one should come to look for a presentable man. . . . Diogenes with his lantern was nothing to it."

He said:

"There's that way of looking at it. . . . It is quite true that most of . . . let's say *your* friends . . . were killed off during the early days, or if they're still going they're in more active employments." What she called presentableness was very largely a matter of physical fitness. . . . The horse, for instance, that he rode was rather a crock. . . . But though it was German and not thoroughbred, it contrived to be up to his weight. . . . Her friends, more or less, of before the war were professional soldiers or of the type. Well, they were gone: dead or snowed under. But on the other hand, this vast town full of crocks did keep the thing going if it could be made to go. It was not they that hindered the show: if it was hindered, that was done by her much less presentable friends, the ministry, who, if they were professionals at all, were professional boodlers.

She exclaimed with bitterness:

"Then why didn't you stay at home to check them if they *are* boodlers?" She added that the only people at home who kept social matters going at all with any life were precisely the more successful political professionals. When you were with them you would not know there was any war. And wasn't that what was wanted? Was the *whole* of life to be given up to ignoble horse-play? . . . She spoke with increased rancour because of the increasing thump and rumble of the air raid. . . . Of course the politicians were ignoble beings that before the war you would not have thought of having in your house. . . . But whose fault was that, if not that of the better classes, who had gone away, leaving England a dreary wilderness of fellows without consciences or traditions or manners? And she added some details of the habits at a country-house of a member of the government whom she disliked. "And," she finished up, "it's your fault. Why aren't *you* Lord Chancellor or Chancellor of the Exchequer instead of whoever is, for I am sure I don't know? You could have been, with your abilities and your interests. Then things would have been efficiently and honestly conducted. If your brother, Mark, with not a tithe of your abilities can be a permanent head of a department, what could you not have risen to with your gifts and your influence . . . and your integrity?" And she ended up: "Oh, Christopher!" on almost a sob.

Ex-Sergeant-Major Cowley, who had come back from the telephone and, during an interval in the thunderings, had heard some of Sylvia's light cast on the habits of members of the home government, so that his jaw had really hung down, now, in another interval, exclaimed:

"Hear, hear! Madam! . . . There is nothing the captain might not have risen to. . . . He is doing the work of a brigadier now on the pay of an acting captain. . . . And the treatment he gets is scandalous. . . . Well, the treatment we all get is scandalous, tricked and defrauded as we are all at every turn. . . . And look at this new start with the draft. . . ." They had ordered the draft to be ready and countermanded it, and ordered it to be ready and

countermanded it, until no one knew whether he stood on
'is 'ed or 'is 'eels. . . . It was to have gone off last night:
when they'd 'ad it marched down to the station, they 'ad
it marched back and told them all it would not be wanted
for six weeks. . . . Now it was to be got ready to go before
daylight to-morrow morning in motor lorries to the rail
Ondekoeter way, the rail here 'aving been sabotaged! . . .
Before daylight so that the enemy aeroplanes should not
see it on the road . . . Wasn't that a thing to break the
'arts of men *and* horderly rooms? It was outrageous. Did
they suppose the 'Uns did things like that?

He broke off to say with husky enthusiasm of affection
to Tietjens: "Look 'ere, old . . . I mean sir. . . . There's
no way of getting hold of an officer to march the draft.
Them as are eligible gets to 'ear of what drafts is going
and they've all bolted into their burries. Not a man of 'em
will be back in camp before five to-morrow morning. Not
when they 'ears there's a draft to go at four of mornings
like this. . . . Now . . ." His voice became husky with
emotion as he offered to take the draft hisself to oblige
Captain Tietjens. And the captain knew he could get a
draft off pretty near as good as himself: or very near. As
for the draft-conducting major, he lived in that hotel and
he, Cowley, 'ad seen 'im. No four in the morning for 'im.
He was going to motor to Ondekoeter Station about seven.
So there was no sense in getting the draft off before five,
and it was still dark then: too dark for the 'Un planes
to see what was moving. He'd be glad if the captain would
be up at the camp by five to take a final look and to sign
any papers that only the commanding officer could sign.
But he knew the captain had had no sleep the night before
because of his, Cowley's, infirmity, mostly, so he couldn't
do less than give up a day and a half of his leave to taking
the draft. Besides, he was going home for the duration and he
would not mind getting a look at the old places they'd seen in
'fourteen, for the last time as a Cook's tourist. . . .

Tietjens, who was looking noticeably white, said:

"Do you remember O Nine Morgan at Noircourt?"

Cowley said:

"No. . . . Was 'e there? In your company, I suppose?
. . . The man you mean that was killed yesterday. Died
in your arms owing to my oversight. I ought to have been
there." He said to Sylvia with the gloating idea N.C.O.s had
that wives liked to hear of their husband's near escapes:
"Killed within a foot of the captain, 'e was. An 'orrible

shock it must 'ave been for the captain." A horrible mess
. . . The captain held him in his arms while he died. . . .
As if he'd been a baby. Wonderful tender, the captain was!
Well, you're apt to be when it's one of your own men.
. . . No rank then! "Do you know the only time the King
must salute a private soldier and the private takes no
notice . . . When 'e's dead . . ."

Both Sylvia and Tietjens were silent—and silvery white
in the greenish light from the lamp. Tietjens indeed had
shut his eyes. The old N.C.O. went on rejoicing to have
the floor to himself. He had got on his feet preparatory
to going up to camp, and he swayed a little. . . .

"No," he said, and he waved his cigar gloriously, "I don't
remember O Nine Morgan at Noircourt. . . . But I remember . . ."

Tietjens, with his eyes still shut, said:

"I only thought he might have been a man. . . ."

"No," the old fellow went on imperiously, "I don't remember 'im. . . . But, Lord, I remember what happened
to *you!*" He looked down gloriously upon Sylvia: "The
captain caught 'is foot in . . . You'd never believe what
'e caught 'is foot in! Never! . . . A pretty quiet affair it
was, with a bit of moonlight. . . . Nothing much in the
way of artillery . . . Perhaps we surprised the 'Uns proper,
perhaps they were wanting to give up their front-line
trenches for a purpose. . . . There was next to no one in
'em. . . . I know it made me nervous. . . . My heart was
fair in my boots because there was so little doing! . . .
It was when there was little doing that the 'Uns could be
expected to do their worst. . . . Of course there was some
machine-gunning. . . . There was one in particular away
to the right of us. . . . And the moon, it was shining in
the early morning. Wonderful peaceful. And a little mist
. . . And frozen hard . . . Hard as you wouldn't believe
. . . Enough to make the shells dangerous."

Sylvia said:

"It's not always mud, then?" and Tietjens, to her: "He'll
stop if you don't like it." She said monotonously: "No . . .
I want to hear."

Cowley drew himself for his considerable effect:

"Mud!" he said. "Not then . . . Not by half . . . I tell
you, ma'am, we trod on the frozen faces of dead Germans
as we doubled. . . . A terrible lot of Germans we'd killed
a day or so before. . . . That was no doubt the reason
they give up the trenches so easy: difficult to attack from,

they was. . . . Anyhow, they left the dead for us to bury,
knowing probably they were going, with a better 'art! . . . But
it fair put the wind up me anyhow to think of what their
counter-attack was going to be. . . . The counter-attack
is always ten times as bad as the preliminary resistance.
They 'as you with the rear of their trenches—the parados,
we call it—as your front to boot. So I was precious glad
when the moppers-up and supports come and went through
us. . . . Laughing, they was . . . Wiltshires . . . My missis
comes from that county. . . . Mrs. Cowley, I mean . . .
So I'd seen the captain go down earlier on and I'd said:
'There's another of the best stopped one. . . .' " He dropped
his voice a little: he was one of the noted yarners of the
regiment: "Caught 'is foot, 'e 'ad, between two 'ands. . . .
Sticking up out of the frozen ground . . . As it might be
in prayer . . . Like this!" He elevated his two hands, the
cigar between the fingers, the wrists close together and the
fingers slightly curled inwards: "Sticking up in the moonlight . . . Poor devil!"

Tietjens said:

"I thought perhaps it was O Nine Morgan I saw that
night. . . . Naturally I looked dead. . . . I hadn't a breath
in my body. . . . And I saw a Tommy put his rifle to his
pal's upper arm and fire. . . . As I lay on the ground . . ."

Cowley said:

"Ah, you saw that . . . I heard the men talking of it.
. . . But they naturally did not say who and where!"

Tietjens said with a negligence that did not ring true:

"The wounded man's name was Stilicho. . . . A queer
name . . . I suppose it's Cornish. . . . It was B Company in
front of us."

"You didn't bring 'em to a court martial?" Cowley asked.
Tietjens said: No. He could not be quite certain. Though
he *was* certain. But he had been worrying about a private
matter. He had been worrying about it while he lay on
the ground, and that rather obscured his sense of what
he saw. Besides, he said faintly, an officer must use his
judgement. He had judged it better in this case not to have
seen the . . . His voice had nearly faded away: it was
clear to Sylvia that he was coming to a climax of some
mental torture. Suddenly he exclaimed to Cowley:

"Supposing I let him off one life to get him killed two
years after. My God! That would be too beastly!"

Cowley snuffled in Tietjens' ear something that Sylvia
did not catch—consolatory and affectionate. That intimacy

was more than she could bear. She adopted her most negligent tone to ask:

"I suppose the one man had been trifling with the other's girl. Or wife!"

Cowley exploded: God bless you, no! They'd agreed upon it between them. To get one of them sent 'ome and the other, at any rate, out of *that* 'ell, leading him back to the dressing-station. She said:

"You mean to say that a man would do *that* to get out of it? . . ."

Cowley said:

"God bless you, ma'am, with the *'ell* the Tommies 'as of it . . . For it's in the line that the difference between the Other Ranks' life and the officers' comes in. . . . I tell you, ma'am, old soldier as I am, and I've been in seven wars one with another . . . there were times in this war when I could have shrieked, holding my right hand down. . . ."

He paused and said: "It was my idea. . . . And it's been a good many others', that if I 'eld my 'and up over the parapet with perhaps my hat on it, in two minutes there would be a German sharpshooter's bullet through it. And then me for Blighty, as the soldiers say. . . . And if that could happen to me, a regimental sergeant-major, with twenty-three years in the service . . ."

The bright orderly came in, said he had found a taxi, and melted into the dimness.

"A man," the sergeant-major said, "would take the risk of being shot for wounding his pal. . . . They get to love their pals, passing the love of women. . . ." Sylvia exclaimed: "Oh!" as if at a pang of toothache. "They do, ma'am," he said; "it's downright touching. . . ."

He was by now very unsteady as he stood, but his voice was quite clear. That was the way it took him. He said to Tietjens:

"It's queer, what you say about home worries taking up your mind. . . . I remember in the Afghan campaign, when we were in the devil of a hot corner, I got a letter from my wife, Mrs. Cowley, to say that our Winnie had the measles. . . . And there was only one difference between me and Mrs. Cowley: I said that a child must have flannel next its skin, and she said flannelette was good enough. Wiltshire doesn't hold by wool as Lincolnshire does. Long fleeces, the Lincolnshire sheep have. . . . And dodging the Afghan bullets all day among the boulders as we was, all

I could think of . . . For you know, ma'am, being a mother
yourself, that the great thing with measles is to keep a
child warm. . . . I kep' saying to myself—'arf crying I
was—'If she only keeps wool next Winnie's skin! If she only
keeps wool next Winnie's skin!' . . . But you know that,
being a mother yourself. I've seen your son's photo on the
captain's dressing-table. Michael, 'is name is. . . . So you
see, the captain doesn't forget you and 'im."

Sylvia said in a clear voice:

"Perhaps you would not go on!"

Distracted as she was by the anti-air-gun in the garden,
though it was on the other side of the hotel and permitted you to get in a sentence or two before splitting
your head with a couple of irregular explosions, she was
still more distracted by a sudden vision—a remembrance
of Christopher's face when their boy had had a temperature of 105° with the measles, up at his sister's house
in Yorkshire. He had taken the responsibility, which the
village doctor would not face, of himself placing the child
in a bath full of split ice. . . . She saw him bending, expressionless in the strong lamplight, with the child in his
clumsy arms over the glittering, rubbled surface of the
bath. . . . He was just as expressionless then as now. . . .
He reminded her now of how he had been then: some
strain in the lines of the face perhaps that she could not
analyse. . . . Rather as if he had a cold in the head—a
little suffocating, with suppressing his emotions, of course:
his eyes looking at nothing. You would not have said that
he even saw the child—heir to Groby and all that! . . .
Something had said to her, just in between two crashes
of the gun: "It's his own child. He went, as you might say,
down to Hell to bring it back to life. . . ." She knew it was
Father Consett saying that. She knew it was true: Christopher had been down to Hell to bring the child back. . . .
Fancy facing its pain in that dreadful bath! . . . The thermometer had dropped, running down under their eyes. . . .
Christopher had said: "A good heart he's got! A good
plucked one!" and then held his breath, watching the thin
filament of bright mercury drop to normal. . . . She said
now, between her teeth: "The child is his property as much
as the damned estate. . . . Well, I've got them both. . . ."

But it wasn't at this juncture that she wanted him tortured over that. So, when the second gun had done its
crash, she had said to the bibulous old man:

"I wish you would not go on!" And Christopher had been prompt to the rescue of the *convenances* with:

"Mrs. Tietjens does not see eye to eye with us in some matters!"

She said to herself: "Eye to eye! My God! . . ." The whole of this affair, the more she saw of it, overwhelmed her with a sense of hatred. . . . And of depression! . . . She saw Christopher buried in this welter of fools, playing a schoolboy's game of make-believe. But of a make-believe that was infinitely formidable and infinitely sinister . . . The crashings of the gun and of all the instruments for making noise seemed to her so atrocious and odious because they were, for her, the silly pomp of a schoolboy-man's game. . . . Campion or some similar schoolboy said: "Hullo! Some German aeroplanes about. . . . That lets us out on the air-gun! Let's have some pops!" . . . As they fire guns in the park on the King's birthday. It was sheer insolence to have a gun in the garden of an hotel where people of quality might be sleeping or wishing to converse!

At home she had been able to sustain the conviction that it was such a game. . . . Anywhere: at the house of a minister of the Crown, at dinner, she had only to say: "Do let us leave off talking of these odious things. . . ." And immediately there would be ten or a dozen voices, the minister's included, to agree with Mrs. Tietjens of Groby that they had altogether too much of it. . . .

But here! . . . She seemed to be in the very belly of the ugly affair. . . . It moved and moved, under your eyes dissolving, yet always there. As if you should try to follow one diamond of pattern in the coil of an immense snake that was in irrevocable motion. . . . It gave her a sense of despair: the engrossment of Tietjens, in common with the engrossment of this disreputable toper. She had never seen Tietjens put his head together with any soul before: he was the lonely buffalo. . . . Now! Anyone: any fatuous staff officer, whom at home he would never so much as have spoken to: any trustworthy, beer-sodden sergeant, any street-urchin dressed up as orderly . . . They had only to appear and all his mind went into a close-headed conference over some ignoble point in the child's game: The laundry, the chiropody, the religions, the bastards . . . of millions of the indistinguishable . . . Or their deaths as well! But, in heaven's name, what hypocrisy or what inconceivable chicken-heartedness was this? They promoted this bean-feast of carnage for their own ends: they caused the deaths of men in inconceivable holocausts of pain and terror. Then they had crises of agony over the death of one single man. For it was plain to her that Tietjens was in the middle of a full nervous break-down. Over one man's death! She had never seen him so suffer; she had never seen him so appeal for sympathy: him, a cold fiend of reticence! Yet he was now in an agony! *Now!* . . . And she began to have a sense of the infinitely spreading welter of pain, going away to an eternal horizon of night. . . . 'Ell for the Other Ranks! Apparently it was hell for the officers as well.

The real compassion in the voice of that snuffling, half-drunken old man had given her a sense of that enormous wickedness. . . . These horrors, these infinities of pain, this atrocious condition of the world, had been brought about in order that men should indulge themselves in orgies of promiscuity. . . . That in the end was at the bottom of male honour, of male virtue, observance of treaties, upholding of the flag. . . . An immense warlock's carnival of appetites, lusts, ebrieties . . . And once set in motion, there was no stopping it. . . . This state of things would never cease. . . . Because once they had tasted of the joy—the blood—of this game, who would let it end? . . . These men talked of these things that occupied them there with the lust of men telling dirty stories in smoking-rooms. . . . That was the only parallel!

There was no stopping it, any more than there was any stopping the by now all but intoxicated ex-sergeant-major. He was off! With, as might be expected, advice to a young couple with differences of opinion! The wine had made him bold!

In the depth of her pictures of these horrors, snatches of his wisdom penetrated to her intelligence. . . . Queer snatches . . . She was getting it certainly in the neck! . . . Someone, to add to the noise, had started some mechanical musical instrument in an adjacent hall.

> "Corn an' lasses
> Served by Ras'us!"

a throaty voice proclaimed.

> "I'd be tickled to death to know that I could go
> And stay right there . . ."

The ex-sergeant-major was adding to her knowledge the odd detail that when he, Sergeant-Major Cowley, went to the wars—seven of them—his missis, Mrs. Cowley, spent the first three days and nights unpicking and re-hem-stitching every sheet and pillow-slip in the 'ouse. To keep 'erself f'm thinking . . . This was apparently meant as a reproof or an exhortation to her, Sylvia Tietjens. . . . Well, he was all right! Of the same class as Father Consett, and with the same sort of wisdom.

The gramophone howled: a new note of rumbling added itself to the exterior tumult and continued through six mitigated thumps of the gun in the garden. . . . In the next interval, Cowley was in the midst of a valedictory address to her. He was asking her to remember that the captain had had a sleepless night the night before.

There occurred to her irreverent mind a sentence of one of the Duchess of Marlborough's letters to Queen Anne. The duchess had visited the general during one of his campaigns in Flanders. "My Lord," she wrote, "did me the honour three times in his boots!" . . . The sort of thing she would remember . . . She would—she *would*—have tried it on the sergeant-major, just to see Tietjens' face, for the sergeant-major would not have understood. . . . And who cared if he did! . . . He was bibulously skirting round the same idea. . . .

But the tumult increased to an incredible volume: even the thrillings of the near-by gramophone of two hundred horsepower, or whatever it was, became mere shimmerings of gold thread in a drab fabric of sound. She screamed blasphemies that she was hardly aware of knowing. She had to scream against the noise: she was no more responsible for the blasphemy than if she had lost her identity under an anaesthetic. She *had* lost her identity. . . . She was one of this crowd!

The general woke in his chair and gazed malevolently at their group as if they alone were responsible for the noise. It dropped. Dead! You only knew it because you caught the tail-end of a belated woman's scream from the hall and the general shouting: "For God's sake, don't start that damned gramophone again!" In the blessed silence, after preliminary wheezings and guitar noises, an astonishing voice burst out:

> "Less than the dust . . .
> Before thy char . . ."

And then, stopping after a murmur of voices, began:

> "Pale hands I loved . . ."

The general sprang from his chair and rushed to the hall.
. . . He came back crestfallenly.

"It's some damned civilian bigwig. . . . A novelist, they say
. . . I can't stop *him*. . . ." He added with disgust: "The
hall's full of young beasts and harlots. . . . *Dancing!*" . . . The
melody had indeed, after a buzz, changed to a languorous
and interrupted variation of a waltz. "Dancing in the dark!"
the general said with enhanced disgust. . . . "And the Germans may be here at any moment. . . . If they knew what I
know! . . ."

Sylvia called across to him:

"Wouldn't it be fun to see the blue uniform with the silver
buttons again and some decently set-up men? . . ."

The general shouted:

"*I'd* be glad to see them. . . . I'm sick to death of
these. . . ."

Tietjens took up something he had been saying to Cowley:
what it was Sylvia did not hear, but Cowley answered, still
droning on with an idea Sylvia thought they had got past:

"I remember when I was sergeant in Quetta, I detailed a
man—called Herring—for watering the company horses
after he begged off it because he had a fear of horses. . . . A
horse got him down in the river and drowned 'im. . . . Fell
with him and put its foot on his face . . . A fair sight he
was. . . . It wasn't any good my saying anything about military exigencies. . . . Fair put me off my feed, it did. . . .
Cost me a fortune in Epsom-salts. . . ."

Sylvia was about to scream out that if Tietjens did not
like men being killed it ought to sober him in his war-lust,
but Cowley continued meditatively:

"Epsom-salts, they say, is the cure for it. . . . For seeing
your dead . . . And of course you should keep off women for
a fortnight. . . . I know I did. Kept seeing Herring's face with
the hoof-mark. And . . . there was a piece: a decent bit of
goods in what we called the Government Compound. . . ."

He suddenly exclaimed:

"Saving your . . . Ma'am, I'm . . ." He stuck the stump of
the cigar into his teeth and began assuring Tietjens that he
could be trusted with the draft next morning if only Tietjens
would put him into the taxi.

He went away, leaning on Tietjens' arm, his legs at an
angle of sixty degrees with the carpet. . . .

"He can't . . ." Sylvia said to herself, "he can't, not . . . if
he's a gentleman. . . . After all that old fellow's hints . . .
he'd be a damn coward if he kept off. . . . For a fortnight . . .

And who else is there not a public. . ." She said: "Oh, God! . . ."

The old general, lying in his chair, turned his face aside to say:

"I wouldn't, madam, not if I were you, talk about the blue uniform with silver buttons here. . . . *We*, of course, understand. . . ."

She said: "You see . . . even that extinct volcano . . . He's undressing me with his eyes full of blood-veins. . . . Then why can't *he?* . . ."

She said aloud:

"Oh, but even you, general, said you were sick of your companions!"

She said to herself:

"Hang it! . . . I will have the courage of my convictions. . . . No man shall say I am a coward. . . ."

She said:

"Isn't it saying the same thing as you, general, to say that I'd rather be made love to by a well-set-up man in blue and silver—or anything else!—than by most of the people one sees here! . . ."

The general said:

"Of course, if you put it that way, madam . . ."

She said:

"What other way should a woman put it?" . . . She reached to the table and filled herself a lot of brandy. The old general was leering towards her:

"Bless me," he said, "a lady who takes liquor like that . . ."

She said:

"You're a papist, aren't you? With the name of O'Hara and the touch of the brogue you have . . . And the devil you, no doubt, are with . . . You know what. . . . Well, then . . . It's with a special intention! . . . As you say your Hail Marys. . . ."

With the liquor burning inside her she saw Tietjens loom in the dim light.

The general, to her bitter amusement, said to him:

"Your friend was more than a bit on. . . . Not the society surely for madam!"

Tietjens said:

"I never expected to have the pleasure of dining with Mrs. Tietjens to-night. . . . That officer was celebrating his commission and I could not put him off. . . ." The general said: "Oh, ah! . . . Of course not . . . I dare say . . ." and settled himself again in his chair. . . .

Tietjens was overwhelming her with his great bulk. She had still lost her breath. . . . He stooped over and said: It was the luck of the half-drunk; he said:

"They're dancing in the lounge. . . ."

She coiled herself passionately into her wickerwork. It had dull blue cushions. She said:

"Not with anyone else . . . I don't want any introductions. . . ." Fiercely! . . . He said:

"There's no one there that I could introduce you to. . . ."

She said:

"Not if it's a charity!"

He said:

"I thought it might be rather dull. . . . It's six months since I danced. . . ." She felt beauty flowing over all her limbs. She had a gown of gold tissue. Her matchless hair was coiled over her ears. . . She was humming Venusberg music: she knew music if she knew nothing else. . . .

She said: "You call the compounds where you keep the Waacs Venusbergs, don't you? Isn't it queer that Venus should be your own? . . . Think of poor Elisabeth!"

The room where they were dancing was very dark. . . . It was queer to be in his arms. . . . She had known better dancers. . . . He had looked ill. . . . Perhaps he was . . . Oh, poor Valentine-Elisabeth . . . What a funny position! . . . The good gramophone played. . . . *Destiny!* . . . You see, Father! . . . In his arms! . . . Of course, dancing is not really . . . But so near the real thing! So near! . . . "Good luck to the special intention! . . ." She had almost kissed him on the lips. . . . All but! . . . *Effleurer,* the French called it. . . . But she was not as humble. . . . He had pressed her tighter. . . . All these months without . . . My Lord did me honour . . . Good for Malbrouck *s'en va-t-en guerre.* . . . He *knew* she had almost kissed him on the lips. . . . And that his lips had almost responded. . . The civilian, the novelist, had turned out the last light. . . . Tietjens said, "Hadn't we better talk? . . ." She said: "In my room, then! I'm dog-tired. . . . I haven't slept for six nights. . . . In spite of drugs . . ." He said: "Yes. Of course! Where else? . . ." Astonishingly. . . . Her gown of gold tissue was like the *colobium sidonis* the King wore at the coronation. . . . As they mounted the stairs she thought what a fat tenor Tannhäuser always was! . . . The Venusberg music was dinning in her ears. . . . She said: "Sixty-six inexpressibles! I'm as sober as a judge. . . . I need to be!"

PART THREE

I ∼

A SHADOW—the shadow of the General Officer Commanding-in-Chief—falling across the bar of light that the sunlight
threw in at his open door seemed providentially to awaken
Christopher Tietjens, who would have thought it extremely
disagreeable to be found asleep by that officer. Very thin,
graceful and gay with his scarlet gilt oak-leaves, and ribbons, of which he had many, the general was stepping at-
tractively over the sill of the door, talking backwards over
his shoulder, to someone outside. So, in the old days, gods
had descended! It was, no doubt, really the voices from without that had awakened Tietjens, but he preferred to think
the matter a slight intervention of Providence, because he
felt in need of a sign of some sort! Immediately upon awak-
ening, he was not perfectly certain of where he was, but he
had sense enough to answer with coherence the first question that the general put to him and to stand stiffly on his
legs. The general had said:

"Will you be good enough to inform me, Captain Tietjens, why you have no fire-extinguishers in your unit? You
are aware of the extremely disastrous consequences that
would follow a conflagration in your lines?"

Tietjens said stiffly:

"It seems impossible to obtain them, sir."

The general said:

"How is this? You have indented for them in the proper
quarter. Perhaps you do not know what the proper quarter
is?"

Tietjens said:

"If this were a British unit, sir, the proper quarter would
be the Royal Engineers." When he had sent his indent in
for them to the Royal Engineers they informed him that this
being a unit of troops from the dominions, the quarter to

which to apply was the Ordnance. On applying to the Ordnance, he was informed that no provision was made of fire-extinguishers for troops from the dominions under imperial officers, and that the proper course was to obtain them from a civilian firm in Great Britain, charging them against barrack damages. . . . He had applied to several firms of manufacturers, who all replied that they were forbidden to sell these articles to anyone but to the War Office direct. . . . "I am still applying to civilian firms," he finished.

The officer accompanying the general was Colonel Levin, to whom, over his shoulder, the general said: "Make a note of that, Levin, will you? And get the matter looked into." He said again to Tietjens:

"In walking across your parade-ground, I noticed that your officer in charge of your physical training knew conspicuously nothing about it. You had better put him on to cleaning out your drains. He was unreasonably dirty."

Tietjens said:

"The sergeant instructor, sir, is quite competent. The officer is an R.A.S.C. officer. I have at the moment hardly any infantry officers in the unit. But officers have to be on these parades—by A.C.I. They give no orders."

The general said dryly:

"I was aware from the officer's uniform of what arm he belonged to. I am not saying you do not do your best with the material at your command." From Campion on parade this was an extraordinary graciousness. Behind the general's back Levin was making signs with his eyes, which he meaningly closed and opened. The general, however, remained extraordinarily dry in manner, his face having its perfectly expressionless air of studied politeness which allowed no muscle of its polished-cherry surface to move. The extreme politeness of the extremely great to the supremely unimportant!

He glanced round the hut markedly. It was Tietjens' own office and contained nothing but the blanket-covered tables and, hanging from a strut, an immense calendar on which days were roughly crossed out in red ink and blue pencil. He said:

"Go and get your belt. You will go round your cook-houses with me in a quarter of an hour. You can tell your sergeant cook. What sort of cooking arrangements have you?"

Tietjens said:

"Very good cook-houses, sir."

The general said:

"You're extremely lucky, then. Extremely lucky! . . . Half the units like yours in this camp haven't anything but company cookers and field-ovens in the open. . . ." He pointed with his crop at the open door. He repeated with extreme distinctness: "Go and get your belt!" Tietjens wavered a very little on his feet. He said:

"You are aware, sir, that I am under arrest."

Campion imported a threat into his voice:

"I gave you," he said, "an order. To perform a duty!"

The terrific force of the command from above to below took Tietjens staggering through the door. He heard the general's voice say: "I'm perfectly aware he's not drunk." When he had gone four paces, Colonel Levin was beside him.

Levin was supporting him by the elbow. He whispered:

"The general wishes me to go with you if you are feeling unwell. You understand you are released from arrest!" He exclaimed with a sort of rapture: "You're doing splendidly. . . . It's amazing. Everything I've ever told him about you . . . Yours is the only draft that got off this morning. . . ."

Tietjens grunted:

"Of course I understand that if I'm given an order to perform a duty, it means I am released from arrest." He had next to no voice. He managed to say that he would prefer to go alone. He said: ". . . He's forced my hand. . . . The last thing I want is to be released from arrest. . . ."

Levin said breathlessly:

"You *can't* refuse. . . . You can't upset him. . . . Why, you *can't*. . . . Besides, an officer cannot demand a court martial."

"You look," Tietjens said, "like a slightly faded bunch of wallflowers. . . . I'm sure I beg your pardon. . . . It came into my head!" The colonel drooped intangibly, his moustache a little ragged, his eyes a little rimmed, his shaving a little ridged. He exclaimed:

"Damn it! . . . Do you suppose I don't *care* what happens to you? . . . O'Hara came storming into my quarters at half-past three. . . . I'm not going to tell you what he said. . . ."

Tietjens said gruffly:

"No, don't! I've all I can stand for the moment. . . ."

Levin exclaimed desperately:

"I want you to understand. . . . It's impossible to believe anything against . . ."

Tietjens faced him, his teeth showing like a badger's. He said:

"Whom? . . . Against whom? Curse you!"

Levin said pallidly:

"Against . . . against . . . either of you . . ."

"Then leave it at that!" Tietjens said. He staggered a little until he reached the main lines. Then he marched. It was purgatory. They peeped at him from the corners of huts and withdrew. . . . But they always did peep at him from the corners of huts and withdraw! That is the habit of the Other Ranks on perceiving officers. The fellow called McKechnie also looked out of a hut-door. He too withdrew. . . . There was no mistaking that! He had the news. . . . On the other hand, McKechnie too was under a cloud. It might be his, Tietjens', duty to strafe McKechnie to hell for having left camp last night. So he might be avoiding him. . . . There was no knowing. . . . He lurched infinitesimally to the right. The road was rough. His legs felt like detached and swollen objects that he dragged after him. He must master his legs. He mastered his legs. A batman carrying a cup of tea ran against him. Tietjens said: "Put that down and fetch me the sergeant cook at the double. Tell him the general's going round the cook-houses in a quarter of an hour." The batman ran, spilling the tea in the sunlight.

In his hut, which was dim and profusely decorated with the doctor's ideals of female beauty in every known form of pictorial reproduction, so that it might have been lined with peach-blossom, Tietjens had the greatest difficulty in getting into his belt. He had at first forgotten to remove his hat, then he put his head through the wrong opening; his fingers on the buckles operated like sausages. He inspected himself in the doctor's cracked shaving-glass: he was exceptionally well shaved.

He had shaved that morning at six-thirty: five minutes after the draft had got off. Naturally the lorries had been an hour late. It was providential that he had shaved with extra care. An insolently calm man was looking at him, the face divided in two by the crack in the glass: a naturally white-complexioned double half of a face: a patch of high colour on each cheek-bone; the pepper-and-salt hair ruffled, the white streaks extremely silver. He had gone very silver lately. But he swore he did not look worn. Not care-worn. McKechnie said from behind his back:

"By Jove, what's this all about? The general's been strafing me to hell for not having my table tidy!"

Tietjens, still looking in the glass, said:

"You should keep your table tidy. It's the only strafe the battalion's had."

The general, then, must have been in the orderly room of which he had put McKechnie in charge. McKechnie went on, breathlessly:

"They say you knocked the general. . . ."

Tietjens said:

"Don't you know enough to discount what they say in this town?" He said to himself: "That was all right!" He had spoken with a cool edge on a contemptuous voice.

He said to the sergeant cook, who was panting—another heavy, grey-moustached, very senior N.C.O.:

"The general's going round the cook-houses. . . . You be damn certain there's no dirty cook's clothing in the lockers!" He was fairly sure that otherwise his cook-houses would be all right. He had gone round them himself the morning of the day before yesterday. Or was it yesterday? . . .

It was the day after he had been up all night because the draft had been countermanded. . . . It didn't matter. He said:

"I wouldn't serve out white clothing to the cooks. . . . I bet you've got some hidden away, though it's against orders."

The sergeant looked away into the distance, smiled all-knowingly over his walrus moustache.

"The general likes to see 'em in white," he said, "and he won't know the white clothing has been countermanded."

Tietjens said:

"The snag is that the beastly cooks always will tuck some piece of beastly dirty clothing away in a locker rather than take the trouble to take it round to their quarters when they've changed."

Levin said with great distinctness:

"The general has sent me to you with this, Tietjens. Take a sniff of it if you're feeling dicky. You've been up all night on end two nights running." He extended in the palm of his hand a bottle of smelling-salts in a silver section of tubing. He said the general suffered from vertigo now and then. Really he himself carried that restorative for the benefit of Miss de Bailly.

Tietjens asked himself why the devil the sight of that smelling-salts container reminded him of the brass handle of the bedroom door moving almost imperceptibly . . . and incredibly. It was, of course, because Sylvia had on her illuminated dressing-table, reflected by the glass, just such another smooth, silver segment of tubing. . . . Was everything he saw going to remind him of the minute movement of that handle?

"You can do what you please," the sergeant cook said, "but there will always be one piece of clothing in a locker for a G.O.C.I.C.'s inspection. And the general always walks straight up to that locker and has it opened. I've seen General Campion do it three times."

"If there's any found this time, the man it belongs to goes for a D.C.M.," Tietjens said. "See that there's a clean diet-sheet on the messing board."

"The generals really like to find dirty clothing," the sergeant cook said; "it gives them something to talk about if they don't know anything else about cook-houses. . . . I'll put up my own diet-sheet, sir. . . . I suppose you can keep the general back for twenty minutes or so? It's all I ask."

Levin said towards his rolling, departing back:

"That's a damn smart man. Fancy being as confident as that about an inspection. . . . Ugh! . . ." and Levin shuddered in remembrance of inspections through which in his time he had passed.

"He's a damn smart man!" Tietjens said. He added to McKechnie:

"You might take a look at dinners in case the general takes it into his head to go round them."

McKechnie said darkly:

"Look here, Tietjens, are you in command of this unit or am I?"

Levin exclaimed sharply, for him:

"What's that? What the . . ."

Tietjens said:

"Captain McKechnie complains that he is the senior officer and should command this unit."

Levin ejaculated:

"Of all the . . ." He addressed McKechnie with vigour: "My man, the command of these units is an appointment at disposition of headquarters. Don't let there be any mistake about that!"

McKechnie said doggedly:

"Captain Tietjens asked me to take the battalion this morning. I understood he was under . . ."

"You," Levin said, "are attached to this unit for discipline and rations. You damn well understand that if some uncle or other of yours were not, to the general's knowledge, a protégé of Captain Tietjens', you'd be in a lunatic asylum at this moment. . . ."

McKechnie's face worked convulsively; he swallowed as men are said to swallow who suffer from hydrophobia. He lifted his fist and cried out:

"My un . . ."

Levin said:

"If you say another word you go under medical care the moment it's said. I've the order in my pocket. Now, fall out. At the double!"

McKechnie wavered on the way to the door. Levin added:

"You can take your choice of going up the line to-night. Or a Court of Inquiry for obtaining divorce leave and then not getting a divorce. Or the other thing. And you can thank Captain Tietjens for the clemency the general has shown you!"

The hut now reeling a little, Tietjens put the opened smelling-bottle to his nostrils. At the sharp pang of the odour the hut came to attention. He said:

"We can't keep the general waiting."

"He told me," Levin said, "to give you ten minutes. He's sitting in your hut. He's tired. This affair has worried him dreadfully. O'Hara is the first C.O. he ever served under. A useful man, too, at his job."

Tietjens leaned against his dressing-table of meat-cases.

"You told that fellow McKechnie off, all right," he said. "I did not know you had it in you. . . ."

"Oh," Levin said, "it's just being with *him*. . . . I get his manner and it does all right. . . . Of course I don't often hear him have to strafe anybody in that manner. There's nobody really to stand up to him. Naturally . . . But just this morning I was in his cabinet doing private secretary, and he was talking to Pe . . . talking while he shaved. And he said exactly that: 'You can take your choice of going up the line to-night or a court martial!' . . . So naturally I said as near the same as I could to your little friend. . . ."

Tietjens said:

"We'd better go now."

In the winter sunlight Levin tucked his arm under Tietjens', leaning towards him gaily and not hurrying. The display was insufferable to Tietjens, but he recognized that it was indispensable. The bright day seemed full of things with hard edges—a rather cruel definiteness. . . . Liver! . . .

The little depot adjutant passed them, going very fast, as if before a wind. Levin just waved his hand in acknowledgement of his salute and went on, being enraptured in Tietjens' conversation. He said:

"You and . . . and Mrs. Tietjens are dining at the general's to-night. To meet the G.O.C.I.C. Western Division. And General O'Hara . . . We understand that you have definitely separated from Mrs. Tietjens. . . ." Tietjens forced his left arm to violence to restrain it from tearing itself from the colonel's grasp.

His mind had become a coffin-headed, leather-jawed charger, like Schomburg. Sitting on his mind was like sitting on Schomburg at a dull water-jump. His lips said: "Bub-bub-bub-bub!" He could not feel his hands. He said:

"I recognize the necessity. If the general sees it in that way. I saw it in another way myself." His voice was intensely weary. "No doubt," he said, "the general knows best!"

Levin's face exhibited real enthusiasm. He said:

"You decent fellow! You awfully decent fellow! We're all in the same boat. . . . Now, will you tell me? For *him*. Was O'Hara drunk last night or wasn't he?"

Tietjens said:

"I think he was not drunk when he burst into the room with Major Perowne. . . . I've been thinking about it! I think he became drunk. . . . When I first requested and then ordered him to leave the room he leant against the door-post. . . . He was certainly then—in disorder! . . . I then told him that I should order him under arrest if he didn't go. . . ."

Levin said:

"Mm! Mm! Mm!"

Tietjens said:

"It was my obvious duty. . . . I assure you that I was perfectly collected. . . . I beg to assure you that I was perfectly collected. . . ."

Levin said: "I am not questioning the correctness. . . . But . . . we are all one family. . . . I admit the atrocious . . . the unbearable . . . nature. . . . But you understand that O'Hara had the right to enter your room. . . . As P.M.! . . ."

Tietjens said:

"I am not questioning that it was his right. I was assuring you that I was perfectly collected because the general had honoured me by asking my opinion on the condition of General O'Hara. . . ."

They had by now walked far beyond the line leading to Tietjens' office and, close together, were looking down upon the great tapestry of the French landscape.

"*He*," Levin said, "is anxious for your opinion. It really amounts to as to whether O'Hara drinks too much to con-

tinue in his job! . . . And he says he will take your word.
. . . You could not have a greater testimonial. . . ."

"He could not," Tietjens said studiedly, "do anything less.
Knowing me."

Levin said:

"Good heavens, old man, you rub it in!" He added quickly: "He wishes me to dispose of this side of the matter.
He will take my word and yours. You will forgive . . ."

The mind of Tietjens had completely failed: the Seine below looked like an *S* on fire in an opal. He said: "Eh?" And
then: "Oh, yes! I forgive. . . . It's painful. . . . You probably
don't know what you are doing."

He broke off suddenly:

"By God! . . . Were the Canadian Railway Service to go
with my draft? They were detailed to mend the line here
to-day. Also to go . . . I kept them back. . . . Both orders
were dated the same day and hour. I could not get on to
headquarters either from the hotel or from here. . . ."

Levin said:

"Yes, that's all right. He'll be immensely pleased. He's
going to speak to you about *that!*" Tietjens gave an immense
sigh of relief.

"I remembered that my orders were conflicting just before. . . . It was a terrible shock to remember. . . . If I
sent them up in the lorries, the repairs to the railway might
be delayed. . . . If I didn't, you might get strafed to hell.
. . . It was an intolerable worry. . . ."

Levin said:

"You remembered it just as you saw the handle of your
door moving. . . ."

Tietjens said from a sort of a mist:

"Yes. You know how beastly it is when you suddenly remember you have forgotten something in orders. As if the
pit of your stomach had . . ."

Levin said:

"All I ever thought about if I'd forgotten anything was what
would be a good excuse to put up to the adjutant. . . . When
I was a regimental officer . . ."

Suddenly Tietjens said insistently:

"How did you know that? . . . About the door-handle?
Sylvia could not have seen it. . . ." He added: "And she
could not have known what I was thinking. . . . She had her
back to the door. . . . And to me . . . Looking at me in
the glass . . . She was not even aware of what had happened. . . . So she could not have seen the handle move!"

Levin hesitated:

"I . . ." he said. "Perhaps I ought not to have said that. . . . You've told us. . . . That is to say, you've told . . ." He was pale in the sunlight. He said: "Old man . . . Perhaps you don't know. . . . Didn't you perhaps ever, in your childhood? . . ."

Tietjens said:

"Well . . . what is it?"

"That you talk . . . when you're sleeping!" Levin said.

Astonishingly, Tietjens said:

"What of that? . . . It's nothing to write home about! With the overwork I've had and the sleeplessness . . ."

Levin said, with a pathetic appeal to Tietjens' omniscience:

"But doesn't it mean . . . We used to say when we were boys . . . that if you talk in your sleep . . . you're . . . in fact a bit dotty?"

Tietjens said without passion:

"Not necessarily. It means that one has been under mental pressure, but all mental pressure does not drive you over the edge. Not by any means. . . . Besides, what does it matter?"

Levin said:

"You mean you don't care. . . . Good God!" He remained looking at the view, drooping, in intense dejection. He said: "This *beastly* war! This *beastly* war! . . . Look at all that view. . . ."

Tietjens said:

"It's an encouraging spectacle, really. The beastliness of human nature is always pretty normal. We lie and betray and are wanting in imagination and deceive ourselves, always, at about the same rate. In peace and in war! But somewhere in that view there are enormous bodies of men. . . . If you got a still more extended range of view over this whole front, you'd have still more enormous bodies of men. . . . Seven to ten million . . . All moving towards places towards which they desperately don't want to go. Desperately! Every one of them is desperately afraid. But they go on. An immense blind will forces them in the effort to consummate the one decent action that humanity has to its credit in the whole of recorded history. The one we are engaged in. That effort is the one certain creditable fact in all their lives. . . . But the *other* lives of all those men are dirty, potty and discreditable little affairs. . . . Like yours . . . Like mine . . ."

Levin exclaimed:

"Just heavens! *What* a pessimist you are!"

Tietjens said, "Can't you see that that is optimism?"

"But," Levin said, "we're being beaten out of the field. . . . You don't know how desperate things are."

Tietjens said:

"Oh, I know pretty well. As soon as this weather really breaks we're probably done."

"We can't," Levin said, "possibly hold them. Not possibly."

"But success or failure," Tietjens said, "have nothing to do with the credit of a story. And a consideration of the virtues of humanity does not omit the other side. If we lose they win. If success is necessary to your idea of virtue —*virtus*—they then provide the success instead of ourselves. But the thing is to be able to stick to the integrity of your character, whatever earthquake sets the house tumbling over your head. . . . That, thank God, we're doing. . . ."

Levin said:

"I don't know. . . . If you knew what is going on at home . . ."

Tietjens said:

"Oh, I know. . . . I know that ground as I know the palm of my hand. I could invent that life if I knew nothing at all about the facts."

Levin said:

"I believe you could." He added: "Of course you could. . . . And yet the only use we can make of you is to martyrize you because two drunken brutes break into your wife's bedroom. . . ."

Tietjens said:

"You betray your non-Anglo-Saxon origin by being so vocal. . . . And by your illuminative exaggerations!"

Levin suddenly exclaimed:

"What the devil were we talking about?"

Tietjens said grimly:

"I am here at the disposal of the competent military authority—you!—that is inquiring into my antecedents. I am ready to go on belching platitudes till you stop me."

Levin answered:

"For goodness' sake, help me. This is horribly painful. *He* —the general—has given me the job of finding out what happened last night. He won't face it himself. He's attached to you both."

Tietjens said:

"It's asking too much to ask me to help you. . . . What did I say in my sleep? What has Mrs. Tietjens told the general?"

"The general," Levin said, "has not seen Mrs. Tietjens.

He could not trust himself. He knew she would twist him round her little finger."

Tietjens said:

"He's beginning to learn. He was sixty last July, but he's beginning."

"So that," Levin said, "what we do know we learnt in the way I have told you. And from O'Hara, of course. The general would not let Pe . . . the other fellow, speak a word while he was shaving. He just said: 'I won't hear you. I won't hear you. You can take your choice of going up the line as soon as there are trains running or being broke on my personal application to the King in Council.' "

"I didn't know," Tietjens said, "that he could talk as straight as that."

"He's dreadfully hard hit," Levin answered; "if you and Mrs. Tietjens separate—and still more if there's anything real against either of you—it's going to shatter all his illusions. And . . ." He paused: "Do you know Major Thurston? A gunner? Attached to our anti-air-gun crowd? . . . The general is very thick with him. . . ."

Tietjens said:

"He's one of the Thurstons of Lobden Moorside. . . . I don't know him personally. . . ."

Levin said:

"He's upset the general a good deal. . . . With something he told him . . ."

Tietjens said:

"Good God!" And then: "He can't have told the general anything against me. . . . Then it must be against . . ."

Levin said:

"Do you want the general always to be told things against you in contradistinction to things about . . . another person?"

Tietjens said:

"We shall be keeping the fellows in my cook-house a confoundedly long time waiting for inspections. . . . I'm in your hands as regards the general. . . ."

Levin said:

"The general's in your hut: thankful to goodness to be alone. He never is. He said he was going to write a private memorandum for the Secretary of State, and I could keep you any time I liked as long as I got everything out of you. . . ."

Tietjens said:

"Did what Major Thurston allege take place . . . Thurston

has lived most of his life in France. . . . But you had better
not tell me. . . ."

Levin said:

"He's our anti-aircraft liaison officer with the French civilian authorities. Those sort of fellows generally have lived in
France a good deal. A very decentish, quiet man. He plays
chess with the general and they talk over the chess. . . . But
the general is going to talk about what he said, to you, himself. . . ."

Tietjens said:

"Good God! . . . He going to talk as well as you . . .
You'd say the coils were closing in. . . ."

Levin said:

"We can't go on like this. . . . It's my own fault for not
being more direct. But this can't last all day. We could
neither of us stand it. . . . I'm pretty nearly done. . . ."

Tietjens said:

"Where *did* your father come from, really? Not from
Frankfurt? . . ."

Levin said:

"Constantinople . . . His father was financial agent to the
Sultan; my father was his son by an Armenian presented to
him by the Selamlik along with the Order of the Medjidje,
first class."

"It accounts for your very decent manner and for your
common sense. If you had been English, I should have
broken your neck before now."

Levin said:

"Thank you! I hope I always behave like an English
gentleman. But I am going to be brutally direct now. . ." He
went on: "The really queer thing is that you should always
address Miss Wannop in the language of the Victorian *Correct Letter-Writer*. You must excuse my mentioning the
name: it shortens things. You said 'Miss Wannop' every two
or three half-minutes. It convinced the general more than
any possible assertions that your relations were perfectly . . ."

Tietjens, his eyes shut, said:

"I talked to Miss Wannop in my sleep. . . ."

Levin, who was shaking a little, said:

"It was very queer. . . . Almost ghostlike . . . There you
sat, your arms on the table. Talking away. You appeared to
be writing a letter to her. And the sunlight streaming in at
the hut. I was going to wake you, but he stopped me. He took
the view that he was on detective work and that he might as

well detect. He had got it into his mind that you were a socialist."

"He would," Tietjens commented. "Didn't I tell you he was beginning to learn things? . . ."

Levin exclaimed:

"But you aren't a so . . ."

Tietjens said:

"Of course if your father came from Constantinople and his mother was a Georgian, it accounts for your attractiveness. You *are* a most handsome fellow. And intelligent . . . If the general has put you on to inquire whether I am a socialist, I will answer your questions."

Levin said:

"No. . . . That's one of the questions he's reserving for himself to ask. It appears that if you answer that you are a socialist, he intends to cut you out of his will. . . ."

Tietjens said:

"His will! . . . Oh, yes, of course, he might very well leave me something. But doesn't that supply rather a motive for me to say that I *am?* I don't want his money."

Levin positively jumped a step backwards. Money, and particularly money that came by way of inheritance, being one of the sacred things of life for him, he exclaimed:

"I don't see that you *can* joke about such a subject!"

Tietjens answered good-humouredly:

"Well, you don't expect me to play up to the old gentleman in order to get his poor old shekels." He added: "Hadn't we better get it over?"

Levin said:

"You've got hold of yourself?"

Tietjens answered:

"Pretty well . . . You'll excuse my having been emotional so far. You aren't English, so it won't have embarrassed you."

Levin exclaimed in an outraged manner:

"Hang it, I'm English to the backbone! What's the matter with me?"

Tietjens said:

"Nothing . . . Nothing in the world. That's just what makes you un-English. We're all . . . well, it doesn't matter what's wrong with *us*. . . . What did you gather about my relations with Miss Wannop?"

The question was so unemotionally put and Levin was still so concerned as to his origins that he did not at first grasp what Tietjens had said. He began to protest that he had been educated at Winchester and Magdalen. Then he exclaimed, *"Oh!"* And took time for reflection.

"If," he said finally, "the general had not let out that she was young and attractive . . . at least, I suppose attractive . . . I should have thought that you regarded her as an old maid. . . . You know, of course, that it came to me as a shock, the thought that there was anyone. . . . That you had allowed yourself . . . Anyhow . . . I suppose I'm simple. . . ."

Tietjens said:

"What did the general gather?"

"He . . ." Levin said, "he stood over you with his head held to one side, looking rather cunning . . . like a magpie listening at a hole it's dropped a nut into. . . . First he looked disappointed: then quite glad. A simple kind of gladness. Just glad, you know . . . When we got outside the hut he said: 'I suppose in *vino veritas*,' and then he asked me the Latin for 'sleep.' . . . But I had forgotten it too. . . ."

Tietjens said:

"What did I say?"

"It's . . ." Levin hesitated, "extraordinarily difficult to say what you *did* say. . . I don't profess to remember long speeches to the letter. . . . Naturally it was a good deal broken up. . . . I tell you, you were talking to a young lady about matters you don't generally talk to young ladies about. . . . And obviously you were trying to let your . . . Mrs. Tietjens, down easily. . . . You were trying to explain also why you had definitely decided to separate from Mrs. Tietjens. . . . And you took it that the young lady might be troubled . . . at the separation. . . ."

Tietjens said carelessly:

"This is rather painful. Perhaps you would let me tell you exactly what *did* happen last night. . . ."

Levin said:

"If you only would!" He added rather diffidently: "If you would not mind remembering that I am a military court of inquiry. It makes it easier for me to report to the general if you say things dully and in the order they happened."

Tietjens said:

"Thank you . . ." and after a short interval, "I retired to rest with my wife last night at . . . I cannot say the hour exactly. Say half-past one. I reached this camp at half-past four, taking rather over half an hour to walk. What happened, as I am about to relate, took place therefore before four."

"The hour," Levin said, "is not material. We know the incident occurred in the small hours. General O'Hara made his complaint to me at three-thirty-five. He probably took five minutes to reach my quarters."

Tietjens asked:

"The exact charge was . . ."

"The complaints," Levin answered, "were very numerous indeed. . . . I could not catch them all. The succinct charge was at first being drunk and striking a superior officer, then merely that of conduct prejudicial in that you struck. . . . There is also a subsidiary charge of conduct prejudicial in that you improperly marked a charge-sheet in your orderly room. . . . I did not catch what all that was about. . . . You appear to have had a quarrel with him about his redcaps. . . ."

"That," Tietjens said, "is what it is really all about." He asked: "The officer I was said to have struck was? . . ."

Levin said:

"Perowne . . ." dryly.

Tietjens said:

"You are sure it was not himself. I am prepared to plead guilty to striking General O'Hara."

"It is not," Levin said, "a question of pleading guilty. There is no charge to that effect against you, and you are perfectly aware that you are not under arrest. . . . An order to perform any duty after you have been placed under arrest in itself releases you and dissolves the arrest."

Tietjens said coolly:

"I am perfectly aware of that. And that that was General Campion's intention in ordering me to accompany him round my cook-houses . . . But I doubt . . . I put it to you for your serious attention whether that is the best way to hush this matter up. . . . I think it would be more expedient that I should plead guilty to a charge of striking General O'Hara. And naturally to being drunk. An officer does not strike a general when he is sober. That would be a quite inconspicuous affair. Subordinate officers are broken every day for being drunk."

Levin had said "Wait a minute" twice. He now exclaimed with a certain horror:

"Your mania for sacrificing yourself makes you lose all . . . all sense of proportion. You forget that General Campion is a gentleman. Things cannot be done in a hole-and-corner manner in this command. . . ."

Tietjens said:

"They're done unbearably. . . . It would be nothing to me to be broke for being drunk, but raking up all this is hell."

Levin said:

"The general is anxious to know exactly what has happened. You will kindly accept an order to relate exactly what happened."

Tietjens said:

"That is what is perfectly damnable. . . ." He remained silent for nearly a minute, Levin slapping his leggings with his riding-crop in a nervously passionate rhythm. Tietjens stiffened himself and began:

"General O'Hara came to my wife's room and burst in the door. I was there. I took him to be drunk. But from what he exclaimed I have since imagined that he was not so much drunk as misled. There was another man lying in the corridor, where I had thrown him. General O'Hara exclaimed that this was Major Perowne. I had not realized that this was Major Perowne. I do not know Major Perowne very well and he was not in uniform. I had imagined him to be a French waiter coming to call me to the telephone. I had seen only his face round the door: he was looking round the door. My wife was in a state . . . bordering on nudity. I had put my hand under his chin and thrown him through the doorway. I am physically very strong and I exercised all my strength. I am aware of that. I was excited, but not more excited than the circumstances seemed to call for. . . ."

Levin exclaimed:

"But . . . at three in the morning! The telephone!"

"I was ringing up my headquarters and yours. All through the night. The O.I.C. draft, Lieutenant Cowley, was also ringing me up. I was anxious to know what was to be done about the Canadian Railway men. I had three times been called to the telephone since I had been in Mrs. Tietjens' room, and once an orderly had come down from the camp. I was also conducting a very difficult conversation with my wife as to the disposal of my family's estates, which are large, so that the details were complicated. I occupied the room next door to Mrs. Tietjens, and till that moment, the communicating door between the rooms being open, I had heard when a waiter or an orderly had knocked at my own door in the corridor. The night-porter of the hotel was a dark, untidy, surly sort of fellow. . . . Not unlike Perowne."

Levin said:

"Is it necessary to go into all this? We . . ."

Tietjens said:

"If I am to make a statement it seems necessary. I would prefer you to question me. . . ."

Levin said:

"Please go on. . . . We accept the statement that Major Perowne was not in uniform. He states that he was in his pyjamas and dressing-gown. Looking for the bathroom."

Tietjens said: "Ah!" and stood reflecting. He said:

"May I hear the . . . the purport of Major Perowne's statement?"

"He states," Levin said, "what I have just said. He was looking for the bathroom. He had not slept in the hotel before. He opened a door and looked round it, and was immediately thrown with great violence down into the passage with his head against the wall. He says that this dazed him so that, not really appreciating what had happened, he shouted various accusations against the person who had assaulted him. . . . General O'Hara then came out of his room. . . ."

Tietjens said:

"What accusations did Major Perowne shout?"

"He doesn't"—Levin hesitated—"eh! . . . elaborate them in his statement."

Tietjens said:

"It is, I imagine, material that I should know what they are. . . ."

Levin said:

"I don't know that. . . . If you'll forgive me . . . Major Perowne came to see me, reaching me half an hour after General O'Hara. He was very . . . extremely nervous and concerned. I am bound to say . . . for Mrs. Tietjens. . . . And also very concerned to spare yourself! . . . It appears that he had shouted out just anything. . . . And it might be 'Thieves!' or 'Fire!' . . . But when General O'Hara came out he told him, being out of himself, that he had been invited to your wife's room and that—oh, excuse me . . . I'm under great obligations to you . . . the very greatest—that you had attempted to black-mail him!"

Tietjens said:

"Well! . . ."

"You understand," Levin said, and he was pleading, "that that is what he said to General O'Hara in the corridor. He even confessed it was madness. . . . He did not maintain the accusation to me. . . ."

Tietjens said:

"Not that Mrs. Tietjens had given him leave? . . ."

Levin said with tears in his eyes:

"I'll not go on with this. . . . I will rather resign my commission than go on tormenting you. . . ."

"You can't resign your commission," Tietjens said.

"I can resign my appointment," Levin answered. He went on sniffling: "This beastly war! . . . This beastly war! . . ."

Tietjens said:

"If what is distressing you is having to tell me that you believe Major Perowne came with my wife's permission, I know it's true. It's also true that my wife expected me to be there. She wanted some fun: not adultery. But I am also aware—as Major Thurston appears to have told General Campion—that Mrs. Tietjens was with Major Perowne. In France. At a place called Yssingueux-les-Pervenches . . ."

"That wasn't the name," Levin blubbered. "It was Saint . . . Saint . . . Saint something. In the Cévennes. . . ."

Tietjens said:

"Don't, there! . . . Don't distress yourself. . . ."

"But I'm . . ." Levin went on, "under great obligations to you. . . ."

"I'd better," Tietjens said, "finish off this matter myself."

Levin said:

"It will break the general's heart. He believes so absolutely in Mrs. Tietjens. Who wouldn't? . . . How the devil could you guess what Major Thurston told him?"

"He's the sort of brown, trustworthy man who always does know that sort of thing," Tietjens answered. "As for the general's belief in Mrs. Tietjens, he's perfectly justified. . . . Only there will be no more parades. Sooner or later it has to come to that for us all. . . ." He added with a little bitterness: "Only not for you. Being a Turk or a Jew, you are a simple, Oriental, monogamous, faithful soul. . . ." He added again: "I hope to goodness the sergeant cook has the sense not to keep the men's dinners back for the general's inspection. . . . But of course he will not. . . ."

Levin said:

"What in the world would that matter?" fiercely. "He keeps men waiting as much as three hours. On parade."

"Of course," Tietjens said, "if that is what Major Perowne told General O'Hara, it removes a good deal of my suspicions of the latter's sobriety. Try to get the position. General O'Hara positively burst in the little sneck of the door that I had put down and came in shouting: 'Where is the ——

black-mailer?' And it was a full three minutes before I could get rid of him. I had had the presence of mind to switch off the light, and he persisted in asking for another look at Mrs. Tietjens. You see, if you consider it, he is a very heavy sleeper. He is suddenly awakened after, no doubt, not a few pegs. He hears Major Perowne shouting about black-mail and thieves. . . . I dare say this town has its quota of black-mailers. O'Hara might well be anxious to catch one in the act. He hates me, anyhow, because of his redcaps. I'm a shabby-looking chap he doesn't know much about. Perowne passes for being a millionaire. I dare say he is: he's said to be very stingy. That would be how he got hold of the idea of black-mail and hypnotized the general with it. . . ."

He went on again:

"But I wasn't to know that. . . . I had shut the door on Perowne and didn't even know he was Perowne. I really thought he was the night-porter coming to call me to the telephone. I only saw a roaring satyr. I mean that was what I thought O'Hara was. . . . And I assure you I kept my head. . . . When he persisted in leaning against the door-post and asking for another look at Mrs. Tietjens, he kept on saying: 'The woman' and 'The hussy.' Not 'Mrs. Tiet-jens . . .' I thought then that there was something queer. I said: 'This is my wife's room,' several times. He said something to the effect of how could he know she was my wife and . . . that she had made eyes at himself in the lounge, so it might have been himself as well as Perowne. . . . I dare say he had got it into his head that I had im-ported some tart to black-mail someone. . . . But you know . . . I grew exhausted after a time. . . . I saw outside in the corridor one of the little subalterns he has on his staff, and I said: 'If you do not take General O'Hara away I shall order you to put him under arrest for drunkenness.' That seemed to drive the general crazy. I had gone closer to him, being determined to push him out of the door, and he decidedly smelt of whisky. Strongly . . . But I dare say he was thinking himself outraged, really. And perhaps also coming to his senses. As there was nothing else for it, I pushed him gently out of the room. In going, he shouted that I was to consider myself under arrest. I so considered myself. . . . That is to say that, as soon as I had settled certain details with Mrs. Tietjens, I walked up to the camp, which I took to be my quarters, though I am actually under the M.O.'s orders to reside in this hotel, owing to the state of my lungs. I saw the draft off, that not necessitating my giving any orders. I went to my sleeping quarters, it being then about six-thirty, and towards seven awakened McKechnie, whom I asked to take my adjutant's and battalion parade and orderly room. I had breakfast in my hut and then went into my private office to await developments. I think I have now told you everything material. . . ."

2 ～

General Lord Edward Campion, G.C.B., K.C.M.G. (military), D.S.O., etc., sat, radiating glory and composing a confidential memorandum to the Secretary of State for War, on a bully-beef case, leaning forward over a military blanket that covered a deal table. He was for the moment in high good humour on the surface, though his subordinate minds were puzzled and depressed. At the end of each sentence that he wrote—and he wrote with increasing satisfaction!— a mind that he was not using said: "What the devil am I going to do with that fellow?" Or: "How the devil is that girl's name to be kept out of this mess?"

Having been asked to write a confidential memorandum for the information of the home authorities as to what, in his opinion, was the cause of the French railway strike, he had hit on the ingenious device of reporting what was the opinion of the greater part of the forces under his command. This was a dangerous line to take, for he might well come into conflict with the home government. But he was pretty certain that any inquiries that the home government could cause to be made amongst the local civilian population would confirm what he was writing—which he was careful to state was not to be taken as a communication of his own opinion. In addition, he did not care what the government did to him.

He was satisfied with his military career. In the early part of the war, after materially helping mobilization, he had served with great distinction in the East, in command mostly of mounted infantry. He had subsequently so distinguished himself in the organizing and transporting of troops coming and going overseas that, on the part of the lines of communication where he now commanded becoming of great importance, he knew that he had seemed the

only general that could be given that command. It had become of enormous importance—these were open secrets!—
because, owing to divided opinions in the Cabinet, it might
at any moment be decided to move the bulk of H.M. forces
to somewhere in the East. The idea underlying this—as General Campion saw it—had at least some relation to the necessities of the British empire and strategy embracing world
politics as well as military movements—a fact which is often
forgotten—there was this much to be said for it: The pre-
ponderance of British imperial interests might be advanced
as lying in the Middle and Far Easts—to the east, that is to
say, of Constantinople. This might be denied, but it was a
feasible proposition. The present operations on the Western
Front, arduous and even creditable as they might have been
until relatively lately, were very remote from our Far Eastern
possessions and mitigated from, rather than added to, our
prestige. In addition, the unfortunate display in front of
Constantinople in the beginning of the war had almost elimi-
nated our prestige with the Mohammedan races. Thus a demonstration in enormous force in any region between European Turkey and the north-western frontiers of India might
point out to Mohammedans, Hindus, and other Eastern races
what overwhelming forces Great Britain, were she so minded,
could put into the field. It is true that that would mean the
certain loss of the war on the Western Front, with corresponding loss of prestige in the West. But the wiping out
of the French republic would convey little to the Eastern
races, whereas we could no doubt make terms with the
enemy nations, as a price for abandoning our allies, that
might well leave the empire not only intact, but actually
increased in colonial extent, since it was unlikely that the
enemy empires would wish to be burdened with colonies for
some time.

General Campion was not overpoweringly sentimental over
the idea of the abandonment of our allies. They had won
his respect as fighting organizations and that, to the professional soldier, is a great deal; but still he *was* a professional soldier, and the prospect of widening the bounds
of the British empire could not be contemptuously dismissed
at the price of rather sentimental dishonour. Such bargains
had been struck before during wars involving many nations, and doubtless such bargains would be struck again.
In addition, votes might be gained by the government from
the small but relatively noisy and menacing part of the
British population that favoured the enemy nations.

But when it came to tactics—which, it should be remembered, concerns itself with the movement of troops actually in contact with enemy forces—General Campion had no doubt that that plan was the conception of the brain of a madman. The dishonour of such a proceeding must of course be considered—and its impracticability was hopeless. The dreadful nature of what would be our debacle, did we attempt to evacuate the Western Front, might well be unknown to or might be deliberately ignored by the civilian mind. But the general could almost see the horrors as a picture—and, professional soldier as he was, his mind shuddered at the picture. They had by now in the country enormous bodies of troops who had hitherto not come into contact with the enemy forces. Did they attempt to withdraw these, in the first place the native population would at once turn from a friendly into a bitterly hostile factor, and moving troops through hostile country is to the nth power a more lengthy matter than moving them through territory where the native populations lend a helping hand or are at least not obstructive. They had in addition this enormous force to ration, and they would doubtless have to supply them with ammunition on the almost certain breaking through of the enemy forces. It would be impossible to do this without the use of the local railways—and the use of these would at once be prohibited. If, on the other hand, they attempted to begin the evacuation by shortening the front, the operation would be very difficult with troops who, by now, were almost solely men trained only in trench warfare, with officers totally unused to that keeping up of communications between units which is the life and breath of a retreating army. Training, in fact, in that element had been almost abandoned in the training-camps, where instruction was almost limited to bomb-throwing, the use of machine-guns, and other departments which had been forced on the War Office by eloquent civilians—to the almost complete neglect of the rifle. Thus at the mere hint of a retreat the enemy forces must break through and come upon the vast unorganized or semi-organized bodies of troops in the rear. . . .

The temptation for the professional soldier was to regard such a state of things with equanimity. Generals have not infrequently enormously distinguished themselves by holding up retreats from the rear when vanguard commanders have disastrously failed. But General Campion resisted the temptation of even hoping that this chance of distinguishing himself might offer itself. He could not contemplate with equanimity the slaughter of great bodies of men under his command, and not even a successful retreating action of that description could be carried out without horrible slaughter. And he would have little hope of conducting necessarily delicate and very hurried movements with an army that, except for its rough training in trench warfare, was practically civilian in texture. So that although, naturally, he had made his plans for such an eventuality, having indeed in his private quarters four enormous paper-covered black boards upon which he had changed daily the names of units according as they passed from his hands or came into them and became available, he prayed specifically every night before retiring to bed that the task might not be cast upon his shoulders. He prized very much his universal popularity in his command, and he could not bear to think of how the eyes of the army would regard him as he put upon them a strain so appalling and such unbearable sufferings. He had, moreover, put that aspect of the matter very strongly in a memorandum that he had prepared in answer to a request from the home government for a scheme by which an evacuation might be effected. But he considered that the civilian element in the government was so entirely indifferent to the sufferings of the men engaged in these operations, and was so completely ignorant of what are military exigencies, that the words he had devoted to that department of the subject were merely wasted. . . .

So everything pushed him into writing confidentially to the Secretary of State for War a communication that he knew must be singularly distasteful to a number of the gentlemen who would peruse it. He chuckled indeed as he wrote, the open door behind him and the sunlight pouring in on his radiant figure. He said:

"Sit down, Tietjens. Levin, I shall not want you for ten minutes," without raising his head, and went on writing. It annoyed him that, from the corner of his eye, he could see that Tietjens was still standing, and he said rather irritably: "Sit down, sit down. . . ."

He wrote:

"It is pretty generally held here by the native population that the present very serious derangement of traffic, if not actively promoted, is at least winked at by the government of this country. It is, that is to say, intended to give us a taste of what would happen if I took any measures here for returning any large body of men to the home country or elsewhere, and it is said also to be a demonstration in favour of a single command—a measure which is here regarded by a great weight of instructed opinion as indispensable to the speedy and successful conclusion of hostilities. . . ."

The general paused over that sentence. It came very near the quick. For himself, he was absolutely in favour of a single command, and in his opinion, too, it was indispensable to any sort of conclusion of hostilities at all. The whole of military history, in so far as it concerned allied operations of any sort—from the campaigns of Xerxes and operations during the wars of the Greeks and Romans, to the campaigns of Marlborough and Napoleon and the Prussian operations of 1866 and 1870—pointed to the conclusion that a relatively small force acting homogeneously was, to the nth power again, more effective than vastly superior forces of allies acting only imperfectly in accord or not in accord at all. Modern developments in arms had made no shade at all of difference to strategy and had made differences merely of time and numbers to tactics. To-day, as in the days of the Greek Wars of the Allies, success depended on apt timing of the arrival of forces at given points, and it made no difference whether your lethal weapons acted from a distance of thirty miles or were held and operated by hand; whether you dealt death from above or below the surface of the ground, through the air by dropped missiles or by mephitic and torturing vapours. What won combats, campaigns and, in the end, wars was the brain which timed the arrival of forces at given points—and that must be one brain which could command their presence at these points, not a half-dozen authorities requesting each other to perform operations which might or might not fall in with the ideas or the prejudices of any one or other of the half-dozen. . . .

Levin came in noiselessly, slid a memorandum slip on to the blanket beside the paper on which the general was writing. The general read: "T. agrees completely, sir, with your diagnosis of the facts, except that he is much more ready to accept General O'H.'s acts as reasonable. He places himself entirely in your hands."

The general heaved an immense sigh of relief. The sunlight streaming in became very bright. He had had a real sinking at the heart when Tietjens had boggled for a second over putting on his belt. An officer may not demand or insist on a court martial. But he, Campion, could not in decency have refused Tietjens his court martial if he stood out for it. He had a right to clear his character publicly. It would have been impossible to refuse him. Then the fat would have been in the fire. For, knowing O'Hara through pretty nearly twenty-five years—or it must be thirty!—of service, Campion was pretty certain that O'Hara had made a drunken beast of himself. Yet he was very attached to O'Hara—one of the old type of rough-diamond generals who swore your head off, but were damn capable men! . . . It was a tremendous relief.

He said sharply:

"Sit down, can't you, Tietjens! You irritate me by standing there!" He said to himself: "An obstinate fellow . . . Why, he's gone!" and his mind and eyes being occupied by the sentence he had last written, the sense of irritation remained with him. He reread the closing clause: ". . . a single command—a measure which is here regarded by a great weight of instructed opinion as indispensable to the speedy and successful conclusion of hostilities. . . ."

He looked at this, whistling beneath his breath. It was pretty thick. He was not asked for his opinion as to the single command: yet he decidedly wanted to get it in and was pretty well prepared to stand the consequences. The consequences might be something pretty bad: he might be sent home. That was quite possible. That, even, was better than what was happening to poor Puffles, who was being starved of men. He had been at Sandhurst with Puffles, and they had got their commissions on the same day to the same regiment. A damn good soldier, but too hot-tempered. He was making an extraordinarily good thing of it in spite of his shortage of men, which was the talk of the army. But it must be damn agonizing for him, and a very improper strain on his men. One day—as soon as the weather broke—the enemy *must* break through. Then he, Puffles, would be sent home. That was what the fellows at Westminster and in Downing Street wanted. Puffles had been a great deal too free with his tongue. They would not send him home before he had a disaster because, unless he were in disgrace, he would be a thorn in their sides: whereas if he were disgraced no one much would listen to him. It was smart practice! . . . *Sharp* practice!

He tossed the sheet on which he had been writing across the table and said to Tietjens:

"Look at that, will you?" In the centre of the hut Tietjens was sitting bulkily on a bully-beef case that had been brought in ceremoniously by a runner. "He *does* look beastly shabby," the general said. "There are three . . . four grease stains on his tunic. He ought to get his hair cut!" He added:

"It's a perfectly damnable business. No one but this fellow would have got into it. He's a fire-brand. That's what he is. A regular fire-brand!"

Tietjens' troubles had really shaken the general not a little. He was left up in the air. He had lived the greater part of his life with his sister, Lady Claudine Sandbach, and the greater part of the remainder of his life at Groby, at any rate after he came home from India and during the reign of Tietjens' father. He had idolized Tietjens' mother, who was a saint! What indeed there had been of the idyllic in his life had really all passed at Groby, if he came to think of it. India was not so bad, but one had to be young to enjoy that. . . .

Indeed, only the day before yesterday he had been thinking that if this letter that he was thinking out did result in his being sent back, he should propose to stand for the half of the Cleveland Parliamentary division in which Groby stood. What with the Groby influence and his nephew's in the country districts, though Castlemaine had not much land left up there, and with Sandbach's interest in the ironworking districts, he would have an admirable chance of getting in. Then he would make himself a thorn in the side of certain persons.

He had thought of quartering himself on Groby. It would have been easy to get Tietjens out of the army and they could all—he, Tietjens and Sylvia—live together. It would have been his ideal of a home and of an occupation. . . .

For, of course, he was getting old for soldiering: unless he got a fighting army there was not much more to it as a career for a man of sixty. If he *did* get an army he was pretty certain of a peerage, and hefty political work could still be done in the Lords. He would have a good claim on India and that meant dying a field-marshal.

On the other hand, the only command that was at all likely to be going—except for deaths, and the health rate amongst army commanders was pretty high!—was poor Puffles'. And that would be no pleasant command—with the men all hammered to pieces. He decided to put the whole thing to Tietjens. Tietjens, like a meal-sack, was looking at him over the draft of the letter that he had just finished reading. The general said:

"Well?"

Tietjens said:

"It's splendid, sir, to see you putting the matter so strongly. It must be put strongly or we're lost."

The general said:

"You think that?"

Tietjens said:

"I'm sure of it, sir. . . . But unless you are prepared to throw up your command and take to politics . . ."

The general exclaimed:

"You're a most extraordinary fellow. . . . That was exactly what I was thinking about: this very minute."

"It's not so extraordinary," Tietjens said. "A really active general thinking as you do is very badly needed in the House. As your brother-in-law is to have a peerage whenever he asks for it, West Cleveland will be vacant at any moment, and with his influence and Lord Castlemaine's—your nephew's not got much land, but the name is immensely respected in the country districts. . . . And, of course, using Groby for your headquarters. . . ."

The general said:

"That's pretty well botched, isn't it?"

Tietjens said without moving a muscle:

"Why, no, sir. Sylvia is to have Groby, and you would naturally make it your headquarters. . . . You've still got your hunters there. . . ."

The general said:

"Sylvia is really to have Groby. . . . Good God!"

Tietjens said:

"So it was no great conjuring trick, sir, to see that you might not mind. . . ."

The general said:

"Upon my soul, I'd as soon give up my chance of Heaven . . . no, not Heaven, but India . . . as give up Groby."

"You've got," Tietjens said, "an admirable chance of India. . . . The point is: Which way? If they give you the sixteenth section . . ."

"I hate," the general said, "to think of waiting for poor Puffles' shoes. I was at Sandhurst with him. . . ."

"It's a question, sir," Tietjens said, "of which is the best way. For the country and yourself. I suppose if one were a general one would like to have commanded an army on the Western Front. . . ."

The general said:

"I don't know. . . . It's the logical end of a career. . . . But I don't feel that my career is ending. . . . I'm as sound as a roach. And in ten years' time what difference will it make?"

"One would like," Tietjens said, "to see you doing it. . . ."

The general said:

"No one will know whether I commanded a fighting army or this damned Whiteley's outfitting store. . . ."

Tietjens said:

"I know that, sir. . . . But the sixteenth section will desperately need a good man if General Perry is sent home. And particularly a general who has the confidence of all ranks . . . It will be a wonderful position. You will have every man that's now on the Western Front at your back after the war. It's a certain peerage. . . . It's certainly a sounder proposition than that of a free lance—which is what you'd be—in the House of Commons."

The general said:

"Then what am I to do with my letter? It's a damn good letter. I don't like wasting letters."

Tietjens said:

"You want it to show through that you back the single command for all you are worth, yet you don't want them to put their finger on your definitely saying so yourself?"

The general said:

". . . That's it. That's just what I do want. . . ." He added: "I suppose you take my view of the whole matter. The government's pretence of evacuating the Western Front in favour of the Middle East is probably only a put-up job to frighten our allies into giving up the single command. Just as this railway strike is a counterdemonstration by way of showing what would happen to us if we did begin to evacuate. . . ."

Tietjens said:

"It looks like that. . . . I'm not, of course, in the confidence of the Cabinet. I'm not even in contact with them as I used to be. . . . But I should put it that the section of the Cabinet that is in favour of the Eastern expedition is very small. It's said to be a one-man party—with hangers-on —but arguing him out of it has caused all this delay. That's how I see it."

The general exclaimed:

But, good God! . . . How is such a thing possible? That man must walk along his corridors with the blood of a million—I mean it, of a million—men round his head. He could not stand up under it. . . . That fellow is prolonging the war indefinitely by delaying us now. And men being killed all the time! . . . I can't. . . ." He stood up and paced, stamping up and down the hut. . . . "At Bonderstrom," he said, "I had half a company wiped out under me. . . . By my own fault, I admit. I had wrong information. . . ." He stopped and said: "Good God! . . . Good God! . . . I can see it now. . . . And it's unbearable. After eighteen years. I was a brigadier then. It was your own regiment—the Glamorganshires. . . . They were crowded into a little nullah and shelled to extinction. . . . I could see it going on and we could not get on to the Boer guns with ours to stop 'em. . . . That's hell," he said, "that's the real hell. . . . I never inspected the Glamorganshires after that for the whole war. I could not bear the thought of facing their eyes. . . . Buller was the same. . . . Buller was worse than I. . . . He never held up his head again after. . . ."

Tietjens said:

"If you would not mind, sir, not going on. . . ."

The general stamped to a halt in his stride. He said:

"Eh? . . . What's that? What's the matter with you?"

Tietjens said:

"I had a man killed on me last night. In this very hut; where I'm sitting is the exact spot. It makes me . . . It's a sort of . . . complex, they call it now. . . ."

The general exclaimed:

"Good God! I beg your pardon, my dear boy. . . . I ought not to have . . . I have never behaved like that before another soul in the world. . . . Not to Buller . . . not to Gatacre, and they were my closest friends. . . . Even after Spion Kop I never . . ." He broke off and said: "But those old memories won't interest you. . . ." He said: "I've such an absolute belief in your trustworthiness. I *know* you won't betray what you've seen. . . . What I've just said . . ." He paused and tried to adopt the air of the listening magpie. He said: "I was called Butcher Campion in South Africa, just as Gatacre was called Backacher. I don't want to be called anything else because I've made an ass of myself before you. . . . No, damn it all, not an ass. I was immensely attached to your sainted mother. . . ." He said: "It's the proudest tribute any commander of men can have. . . . To be called Butcher and have your men follow you in spite of it. It shows confidence, and it gives you, as commander, confidence! . . . One has to be prepared to lose men in hundreds at the right minute in order to avoid losing them in tens of thousands at the wrong! . . ." He said: "Successful military operations consist not in taking or retaining positions, but in taking or retaining them with a minimum sacrifice of effectives. . . . I wish to God you civilians would get that into your heads. The men have it. They know that

I will use them ruthlessly—but that I will not waste one life. . . ." He exclaimed: "Damn it, if I had ever thought I should have such troubles, in your father's days! . . ." He said: "Let's get back to what we were talking about. . . . My memorandum to the secretary . . ." He burst out: "My God! . . . *What* can that fellow think when he reads Shakespeare's 'When all those heads, legs, arms, joined together on the Last Day shall . . .' How does it run? Henry V's address to his soldiers . . . 'Every subject's body is the king's . . . but every subject's soul is his own. . . . And there is no king, be his cause ever so just'—my God! my God!— 'as can try it out with all unspotted soldiers. . . .' Have you ever thought of that?"

Alarm overcame Tietjens. The general was certainly in disorder. But over what? There was not time to think. Campion was certainly dreadfully overworked. . . . He exclaimed:

"Sir, hadn't you better? . . ." He said: "If we could get back to your memorandum . . . I am quite prepared to write a report to the effect of your sentence as to the French civilian population's attitude. That would throw the onus on me. . . ."

The general said agitatedly:

"No! No! . . . You've got quite enough on your back as it is. Your confidential report states that you are suspected of having too great common interests with the French. That's what makes the whole position so impossible. . . . I'll get Thurston to write something. He's a good man, Thurston. Reliable . . ." Tietjens shuddered a little. The general went on astonishingly:

> " 'But at my back I always hear
> Time's winged chariot hurrying near:
> And yonder all before me lie
> Deserts of vast eternity!'

That's a general's life in this accursed war. . . . You think all generals are illiterate fools. But I have spent a great deal of time in reading, though I never read anything written later than the seventeenth century."

Tietjens said:

"I know, sir. . . . You made me read Clarendon's *History of the Great Rebellion* when I was twelve."

The general said:

"In case we . . . I shouldn't like . . . In short . . ." He swallowed: it was singular to see him swallow. He was lamentably thin when you looked at the man and not the uniform.

Tietjens thought:

"What's he nervous about? He's been nervous all the morning."

The general said:

"I am trying to say—it's not much in my line—that in case we never met again, I do not wish you to think me an ignoramus."

Tietjens thought:

"He's not ill . . . and he can't think me so ill that I'm likely to die. . . . A fellow like that doesn't really know how to express himself. He's trying to be kind and he doesn't know how to. . . ."

The general had paused. He began to say:

"But there are finer things in Marvell than that. . . ."

Tietjens thought:

"He's trying to gain time. . . . Why on earth should he? . . . What is this all about?" His mind slipped a notch. The general was looking at his finger-nails on the blanket. He said:

"There's, for instance:

" 'The grave's a fine and secret place
   But none I think do there embrace. . . .' "

At those words it came to Tietjens suddenly to think of Sylvia, with the merest film of clothing on her long, shining limbs. . . . She was working a powder-puff under her armpits in a brilliant illumination from two electric lights, one on each side of her dressing-table. She was looking at him in the glass with the corners of her lips just moving. A little curled . . . He said to himself:

"One is going to that fine and secret place. . . . Why not have?" She had emanated a perfume founded on sandal-wood. As she worked her swan's-down powder-puff over those intimate regions he could hear her humming. Maliciously! It was then that he had observed the handle of the door moving minutely. She had incredible arms, stretched out amongst a wilderness of besilvered cosmetics. Extraordinarily lascivious! Yet clean! Her gilded sheath gown was about her hips on the chair. . . .

Well! She had pulled the strings of one too many shower-baths!

Shining, radiating glory but still shrivelled so that he reminded Tietjens of an old apple inside a damascened helmet, the general had seated himself once more on the bully-beef case before the blanketed table. He fingered his very large, golden fountain-pen. He said:

"Captain Tietjens, I should be glad of your careful attention!"

Tietjens said:

"Sir!" His heart stopped.

The general said that that afternoon Tietjens would receive a movement order. He said stiffly that he must not regard this new movement order as a disgrace. It was promotion. He, Major-General Campion, was requesting the colonel commanding the depot to inscribe the highest possible testimonial in his, Tietjens', small book. He, Tietjens, had exhibited the most extraordinary talent for finding solutions for difficult problems. The colonel was to write that! In addition, he, General Campion, was requesting his friend General Perry, commanding the sixteenth section . . .

Tietjens thought:

"Good God. I am being sent up the line. He's sending me to Perry's army. . . . That's certain death!"

. . . To give Tietjens the appointment of second in command of the VIth Battalion of his regiment!

Tietjens said, but he did not know where the words came from:

"Colonel Partridge will not like that. He's praying for McKechnie to come back!"

To himself he said:

"I shall fight this monstrous treatment of myself to my last breath."

The general suddenly called out:

"There you are. . . . There is another of your infernal worries. . . ."

He put a strong check on himself and, dryly, like the very great speaking to the very unimportant, asked:

"What's your medical category?"

Tietjens said:

"Permanent base, sir. My chest's rotten!"

The general said:

"I should forget that if I were you. . . . The second in command of a battalion has nothing to do but sit about in arm-chairs waiting for the colonel to be killed." He added: "It's the best I can do for you. . . . I've thought it out very carefully. It's the best I can do for you."

Tietjens said:

"I shall, of course, forget my category, sir. . . ."

Of course he would never fight any treatment of himself! . . .

There it was, then: the natural catastrophe! As when, under thunder, a dam breaks. His mind was battling with the waters. What would it pick out as the main terror? The mud: the noise: dread always at the back of the mind? Or the worry! The worry! Your eyebrows always had a slight tension on them. . . . Like eye-strain!

The general had begun, soberly:

"You will recognize that there is nothing else that I can do."

His answering:

"I recognize, naturally, sir, that there is nothing else that you can do. . . ." seemed rather to irritate the general. He wanted opposition: he *wanted* Tietjens to argue the matter. He was the Roman father counselling suicide to his son: but he wanted Tietjens to expostulate. So that he, General Campion, might absolutely prove that he, Tietjens, was a disgraced individual. . . . It could not be done. Tietjens was not going to give him the opportunity. The general said:

"You will understand that I can't—no commander could! —have such things happening in my command. . . ."

Tietjens said:

"I must accept that if you say it, sir."

The general looked at him under his eyebrows. He said:

"I have already told you that this is promotion. I have been much impressed by the way you have handled this command. You are, of course, no soldier, but you will make an admirable officer for the militia; that is all that our troops now are. . . ." He said: "I will emphasize what I am saying. . . . No officer could—without being militarily in the wrong —have a private life that is as incomprehensible and embarrassing as yours. . . ."

Tietjens said:

"He's hit it! . . ."

The general said:

"An officer's private life and his life on parade are as strategy to tactics. . . . I don't want, if I can avoid it, to go into your private affairs. It's extremely embarrassing. . . . But let me put it to you that . . . I wish to be delicate. But you are a man of the world! . . . Your wife is an extremely beautiful woman. . . . There has been a scandal . . . I admit not of your making. . . . But if, on the top of that, I appeared to show favouritism to you . . ."

Tietjens said:

"You need not go on, sir. . . . I understand. . . ." He tried to remember what the brooding and odious McKechnie had said . . . only two nights ago. . . . He couldn't remember. . . . . It was certainly a suggestion that Sylvia was the general's mistress. It had then, he remembered, seemed fantastic. . . . Well, what else *could* they think? He said to himself: "It absolutely blocks out my staying here!" He said aloud: "Of course it's my own fault. If a man so handles his women-folk that they get out of hand, he has only himself to blame."

The general was going on. He pointed out that one of his predecessors had lost that very command on account of scandals about women. He had turned the place into a damned harem! . . .

He burst out, looking at Tietjens with a peculiar goggle-eyed intentness:

"If you think I'd care about losing my command over Sylvia or any other damned Society woman . . ." He said: "I beg your pardon. . . ." and continued reasonably:

"It's the men that have to be considered. They think—and they've every right to think it if they wish to—that a man who's a wrong 'un over women isn't the man they can trust their lives in the hands of. . . ." He added: "And they're probably right. . . . A man who's a real wrong 'un . . . I don't mean who sets up a gal in a tea-shop. . . . But one who sells his wife or . . . At any rate, in *our* army . . . The French may be different! . . . Well, a man like that usually has a yellow streak when it comes to fighting. . . . Mind, I'm not saying always. . . . Usually . . . There was a fellow called . . ."

He went off into an anecdote. . . .

Tietjens recognized the pathos of his trying to get away from the agonizing present moment, back to an India where it was all real soldiering and good leather and parades that had been parades. But he did not feel called upon to follow. He could not follow. He was going up the line. . . .

He occupied himself with his mind. What was it going to do? He cast back along his military history: What had his mind done in similar moments before? . . . But there had never been a similar moment! There had been the sinister or repulsive businesses of going up, getting over, standing to—even of the casualty clearing-station! . . . But he had always been physically keener; he had never been so depressed or overwhelmed.

He said to the general:

"I recognize that I cannot stop in this command. I regret it, for I have enjoyed having this unit. . . . But does it necessarily mean the Sixth Battalion?"

He wondered what was his own motive at the moment.

Why had he asked the general that? . . . The thing presented itself as pictures: getting down bulkily from a high French train at dawn. The light picked out for you the white of large hunks of bread—half-loaves—being handed out to troops themselves duskily invisible. . . . The ovals of light on the hats of English troops: they were mostly West Country men. They did not seem to want the bread much. . . . A long ridge of light above a wooded bank: then suddenly, pervasively: a sound! . . . For all the world as, sheltering from rain in a cottager's wash-house on the moors, you hear the cottager's clothes boiling in a copper . . . Bubble . . . bubble . . . bubbubbub . . . bubble . . . Not terribly loud—but terribly demanding attention! . . . The Great Strafe! . . .

The general had said:

"If I could think of anything else to do with you, I'd do it. . . . But all the extraordinary rows you've got into . . . They block me everywhere. . . . Do you realize that I have requested General O'Hara to suspend his functions until now? . . ."

It was amazing to Tietjens how the general mistrusted his subordinates—as well as how he trusted them! . . . It was probably that that made him so successful an officer. Be worked for by men that you trust: but distrust them all the time—along certain lines of frailty: liquor, women, money! . . . Well, he had long knowledge of men!

He said:

"I admit, sir, that I misjudged General O'Hara. I have said as much to Colonel Levin and explained why."

The general said with a gloating irony:

"A damn pretty pass to come to . . . You put a general officer under arrest. . . . Then you say you had misjudged him! . . . I am not saying you were not performing a duty. . . ." He went on to recount the classical case of a subaltern cited in King's Regulations, temp. William IV, who was court-martialled and broken for not putting under arrest his colonel, who came drunk on to parade. . . . He was exhibiting his sensuous delight in misplaced erudition.

Tietjens heard himself say with great slowness:

"I absolutely deny, sir, that I put General O'Hara under arrest! I have gone into the matter very minutely with Colonel Levin."

The general burst out:

"By God! I had taken that woman to be a saint. . . . I swear she is a saint. . . ."

Tietjens said:

"There is no accusation against Mrs. Tietjens, sir!"

The general said:

"By God, there is!"

Tietjens said:

"I am prepared to take all the blame, sir."

The general said:

"You shan't. . . . I am determined to get to the bottom of all this. . . . You have treated your wife damn badly. . . . You admit to that. . . ."

Tietjens said:

"With great want of consideration, sir . . ."

The general said:

"You have been living practically on terms of separation from her for a number of years? You don't deny that that was on account of your own misbehaviour. For how many years?"

Tietjens said:

"I don't know, sir. . . . Six or seven!"

The general said sharply:

"Think, then. . . . It began when you admitted to me that you had been sold up because you kept a girl in a tobacco-shop? That was at Rye in 1912. . . ."

Tietjens said:

"We have not been on terms since 1912, sir."

The general said:

"But why? . . . She's a most beautiful woman. She's adorable. What could you want better? . . . She's the mother of your child. . . ."

Tietjens said:

"Is it necessary to go into all this, sir? . . . Our differences were caused by . . . by differences of temperament. She, as you say, is a beautiful and reckless woman. . . . Reckless in an admirable way. I, on the other hand . . ."

The general exclaimed:

"Yes! That's just it. . . . What the hell are you? . . . You're not a soldier. You've got the makings of a damn good soldier. You amaze me at times. Yet you're a disaster; you are a disaster to everyone who has to do with you. You are as conceited as a hog; you are as obstinate as a bullock. . . . You drive me mad. . . . And you have ruined the life of that beautiful woman. . . . For I maintain she once had the disposition of a saint. . . . Now: I'm waiting for your explanation!"

Tietjens said:

"In civilian life, sir, I was a statistician. Second secretary to the Department of Statistics . . ."

The general exclaimed convictingly:

"And they've thrown you out of that! Because of the mysterious rows you made . . ."

Tietjens said:

"Because, sir, I was in favour of the single command . . ."

The general began a long wrangle: "But why were you? What the hell had it got to do with you?" Couldn't Tietjens have given the department the statistics they wanted—even if it meant faking them? What was discipline for if subordinates were to act on their consciences? The home government had wanted statistics faked in order to dish the allies. . . . Well . . . Was Tietjens French or English? Every damn thing Tietjens did . . . every *damn* thing . . . made it more impossible to do anything for him! With his attainments he ought to be attached to the staff of the French commander-in-chief. But that was forbidden in his, Tietjens', confidential report. There was an underlined note in it to that effect. Where else, then, in heaven's name, could Tietjens be sent to? He looked at Tietjens with intent blue eyes:

"Where else, in God's name . . . I am not using the Almighty's name blasphemously . . . *can* you be sent to? I *know* it's probably death to send you up the line—in your condition of health. And to poor Perry's army. The Germans will be through it the minute the weather breaks."

He began again: "You understand: I'm not the War Office. I can't send any officer anywhere. I can't send you to Malta or India. Or to other commands in France. I can send you home—in disgrace. I can send you to your own battalion. On promotion! . . . Do you understand my situation? . . . I have no alternative."

Tietjens said:

"Not altogether, sir."

The general swallowed and wavered from side to side. He said:

"For God's sake, try to. . . . I am genuinely concerned for you. I won't—I'm damned if I will!—let it appear that you're disgraced. . . . If you were McKechnie himself I wouldn't! The only really good jobs I've got to give away are on my own staff. I can't have you there. Because of the men. At the same time . . ."

He paused and said with a ponderous shyness:

"I believe there's a God. . . . I believe that, though wrong may flourish, right will triumph in the end! . . . If a man is innocent, his innocence will one day appear. . . . In a humble way I want to . . . help Providence. . . . I want someone to be able one day to say: 'General Campion, who knew the ins and outs of the affair . . .' promoted you! In the middle of it. . . ." He said: "It isn't much. But it's not nepotism. I would do as much for any man in your position."

Tietjens said:

"It's at least the act of a Christian gentleman!"

A certain lack-lustre joy appeared in the general's eyes. He said:

"I'm not used to this sort of situation. . . . I hope I've always tried to help my junior officers. . . . But a case like this . . ." He said:

"Damn it. . . . The general commanding the Ninth French Army is an intimate friend of mine. . . . But in face of your confidential report—I *can't* ask him to ask for you. That's blocked!"

Tietjens said:

"I do not propose, sir, at any rate in your eyes, to pass as putting the interests of any power before those of my own country. If you examine my confidential report you will find that the unfavourable insertions are initialled *G. D.* . . . They are the initials of a Major Drake. . . ."

The general said bewilderedly:

"Drake . . . Drake . . . I've heard the name."

Tietjens said:

"It doesn't matter, sir. . . . Major Drake's a gentleman who doesn't like me. . . ."

The general said:

"There are so many. You don't try to make yourself popular, I must say!"

Tietjens said to himself:

"The old fellow feels it! . . . But he can hardly expect me to tell him that Sylvia thinks Drake was the father of my own son and desires my ruin!" But of course the old man *would* feel it. He, Tietjens, and his wife, Sylvia, were as near a son and daughter as the old man had. The obvious answer to make to the old man's query as to where he, Tietjens, ought to be sent was to remind him that his brother, Mark, had had an order put through to the effect that Tietjens was to be put in command of divisional transport. . . . *Could* he remind the old man of that? Was it a thing one could do?

Yet the idea of commanding divisional transport was like a vision of paradise to Tietjens. For two reasons: it was relatively safe, being concerned with a lot of horses . . . and the knowledge that he had that employment would put Valentine Wannop's mind at rest.

Paradise! . . . But *could* one wangle out of a hard into a soft job? Some other poor devil very likely wanted it. On the other hand—think of Valentine Wannop! He imagined her torture of mind, wandering about London, thinking of him in the very worst spot of a doomed army. She would get to hear of that. Sylvia would tell her! He would bet Sylvia would ring her up and tell her. Imagine, then, writing to Mark to say that he was with the transport! Mark would pass it on to the girl within half a minute. Why . . . he, Tietjens, would wire. He imagined himself scribbling the wire while the general talked and giving it to an orderly the moment the talk was over. . . . But *could* he put the idea into the old man's head? *Is* it done? . . . Would, say . . . say, an Anglican saint do it?

And then . . . Was he up to the job? What about the accursed obsession of 09 Morgan that intermittently jumped on him? All the while he had been riding Schomburg the day before, 09 Morgan had seemed to be just before the coffin-headed brute's off-shoulder. The animal must fall! . . . He had had the passionate impulse to pull up the horse. And all the time a dreadful depression! A weight! In the hotel last night he had nearly fainted over the thought that Morgan might have been the man whose life he had spared at Noircourt. . . . It was getting to be a serious matter! It might mean that there was a crack in his, Tietjens', brain. A lesion! If that was to go on . . . 09 Morgan, dirty as he always was, and with the mystified eyes of the subject races on his face, rising up before his horse's off-shoulder! But alive, not with half his head cut away . . . If that was to go on he would not be fit to deal with transport, which meant a great deal of riding.

But he would chance that. . . . Besides, some damn fool of a literary civilian had been writing passionate letters to the papers insisting that all horses and mules must be abolished in the army. . . . Because of their pestilence-spreading dung! . . . It might be decreed by A.C.I. that no more horses were to be used! . . . Imagine taking battalion supplies down by night with motor lorries, which was what that genius desired to see done! . . .

He remembered once or twice—it must have been in September, '16—having had the job of taking battalion transport down from Locre to B.H.Q., which were in the château of Kemmel village. . . . You muffled every bit of metal you could think of: bits, trace-chains, axles . . . and *yet*, whilst you hardly breathed, in the thick darkness some damn thing would always chink and jolt: beef tins made a noise of old iron. . . . And *bang*, after the long whine would come the

German shell, registered exactly on to the corner of the road where it went down by the shoulder of the hill: where the placards were ordering you not to go more than two men together. . . . Imagine doing it with lorries, that could be heard five miles away! . . . The battalion would go pretty short of rations! . . . The same anti-chevaline genius had emitted the sentiment that he had rather the Allies lost the war than that cavalry should distinguish themselves in any engagement! . . . A wonderful passion for the extermination of dung! . . . Or perhaps this hatred of the horse was social. . . . Because the cavalry wear long moustaches dripping with Macassar oil and breakfast off caviar, chocolate and Pommery Greno, they must be abolished! . . . Something like that . . . He exclaimed: "By God! How my mind wanders! How long will it go on?" He said: "I am at the end of my tether." He had missed what the general had said for some time.

The general said:

"Well. Has he?"

Tietjens said:

"I didn't catch, sir!"

"Are you deaf?" the general asked. "I'm sure I speak plain enough. You've just said there are no horses attached to this camp. I asked you if there is not a horse for the colonel commanding the depot. . . . A German horse, I understand!"

Tietjens said to himself:

"Great heavens! I've been talking to him. What in the world about?" It was as if his mind were falling off a hillside. He said:

"Yes, sir . . . Schomburg. But as that's a German prisoner, captured on the Marne, it is not on our strength. It is the private property of the colonel. I ride it myself. . . ."

The general exclaimed dryly:

"You *would*. . . ." He added more dryly still: "Are you aware that there is a hell of a strafe put in against you by an R.A.S.C. second-lieutenant called Hotchkiss? . . ."

Tietjens said quickly:

"If it's over Schomburg, sir . . . it's a wash-out. Lieutenant Hotchkiss has no more right to give orders about him than as to where I shall sleep. . . . And I would rather die than subject any horse for which I am responsible to the damnable torture Hotchkiss and that swine Lord Beichan want to inflict on service horses. . . ."

The general said maleficently:

"It looks as if you damn well will die on that account!" He added: "You're perfectly right to object to wrong treat-

ment of horses. But in this case your objection blocks the
only other job open to you." He quietened himself a little.
"You are probably not aware," he went on, "that your
brother, Mark . . ."

Tietjens said:

"Yes, I'm aware. . . ."

The general said: "Do you know that the Nineteenth Division, to which your brother wants you sent, is attached to
Fourth Army now—and it's Fourth Army horses that Hotchkiss is to play with? . . . How could I send you there to be
under his orders?"

Tietjens said:

"That's perfectly correct, sir. There is nothing else that you
can do. . . ." He was finished. There was now nothing left
but to find out how his mind was going to take it. He wished
they could go to his cook-houses!

The general said:

"What was I saying? . . . I'm dreadfully tired. . . . No one
could stand this. . . ." He drew from inside his tunic a lapis-
lazuli-coloured, small, be-coroneted note-case and selected
from it a folded paper that he first looked at and then slipped
between his belt and his tunic. He said: "On top of all the
responsibility I have to bear!" He asked: "Has it occurred to
you that if I'm of any service to the country, your taking
up my energy—*sapping* my energy over your affairs!—is aid-
ing your country's enemies? . . . I can only afford four hours'
sleep as it is. . . . I've got some questions to ask you. . . ."
He referred to the slip of paper from his belt, folded it again
and again slipped it into his belt.

Tietjens' mind missed a notch again. . . . It *was* the fear
of the mud that was going to obsess him. Yet, curiously, he
had never been under heavy fire in mud. . . . You would
think that that would not have obsessed him. But in his
ear he had just heard uttered in a whisper of intense weariness the words: *Es ist nicht zu ertragen; es ist das dass uns
verloren hat* . . . words in German, of utter despair, meaning: It is unbearable: it is that that has ruined us. . . . The
mud! . . . He had heard those words, standing amidst volcano craters of mud, amongst ravines, monstrosities of slime,
cliffs and distances, all of slime. . . . He had been going, for
curiosity or instruction, from Verdun, where he had been
attached to the French—on a holiday afternoon when nothing was doing—with a guide, to visit one of the outlying
forts. . . . Deaumont? . . . No, Douaumont. . . . Taken from
the enemy about a week before . . . When would that be? He

had lost all sense of chronology. . . . In November . . . A beginning of some November . . . With a miracle of sunshine: not a cloud: the mud towering up shut you in intimately with a sky that ached for limpidity. . . . And the slime had moved . . . following a French bombardier who was strolling along eating nuts, disreputably, his shoulders rolling. . . . *Déserteurs* . . . The moving slime was German deserters. . . . You could not see them: the leader of them— an officer!—had his glasses so thick with mud that you could not see the colour of his eyes, and his half-dozen decorations were like the beginnings of swallows' nests, his beard like stalactites. . . . Of the other men you could only see the eyes—extraordinarily vivid: mostly blue like the sky! . . . Deserters! Led by an officer! Of the Hamburg Regiment! As if an officer of the Buffs had gone over! . . . It was incredible. . . . And that was what the officer had said as he passed: not shamefacedly, but without any humanity left in him. . . . *Done!* . . . Those moving saurians compacted of slime kept on passing him afterwards, all the afternoon. . . . And he could not help picturing their immediate antecedents for two months. . . . In advanced pill-boxes . . . No, they didn't have pill-boxes then. . . . In advanced pockets of mud, in dreadful solitude amongst those ravines . . . suspended in eternity, at the last day of the world. And it had horribly shocked him to hear again the German language: a rather soft voice, a little suety. . . . Like an obscene whisper . . . The voice obviously of the damned: Hell could hold nothing curious for those poor beasts. . . . His French guide had said sardonically: *"On dirait l'Inferno de Dante! . . ."* Well, those Germans were getting back on him. They were now to become an obsession! A complex, they said now-a-days. . . . The general said coolly:

"I presume you refuse to answer?"

That shook him cruelly.

He said desperately:

"I had to end what I took to be an unbearable position for both parties. In the interests of my son!" Why in the world had he said that? . . . He was going to be sick. It came back to him that the general had been talking of his separation from Sylvia. Last night that had happened. He said: "I may have been right: I may have been wrong. . . ."

The general said icily:

"If you don't choose to go into it . . ."

Tietjens said:

"I would prefer not to. . . ."

The general said:

"There is no end to this. . . . But there are questions it's my duty to ask. . . . If you do not wish to go into your marital relations, I cannot force you. . . . But, damn it, are you sane? Are you responsible? Do you intend to get Miss Wannop to live with you before the war is over? Is she, perhaps, here, in this town, now? Is that your reason for separating from Sylvia? Now, of all times in the world!"

Tietjens said:

"No, sir. I ask you to believe that I have absolutely no relations with that young lady. None! I have no intention of having any. None! . . ."

The general said:

"I believe that!"

"Circumstances last night," Tietjens said, "convinced me suddenly, there, on the spot, that I had been wronging my wife. . . . I had been putting a strain on the lady that was unwarrantable. It humiliates me to have to say it! I had taken a certain course for the sake of the future of our child. But it was an atrociously wrong course. We ought to have separated years ago. It has led to the lady's pulling the strings of all these shower-baths. . . ."

The general said:

"Pulling the . . ."

Tietjens said:

"It expresses it, sir. . . . Last night was nothing but pulling the string of a shower-bath. Perfectly justifiably. I maintain that it was perfectly justifiable."

The general said:

"Then why have you given her Groby? . . . You're not a little soft, are you? . . . You don't imagine you've . . . say, got a mission? Or that you're another person? . . . That you have to . . . to forgive . . ." He took off his pretty hat and wiped his forehead with a tiny cambric handkerchief. He said: "Your poor mother was a little . . ."

He said suddenly:

"To-night when you are coming to my dinner . . . I hope you'll be decent. Why do you so neglect your personal appearance? Your tunic is a disgusting spectacle. . . ."

Tietjens said:

"I had a better tunic, sir . . . but it has been ruined by the blood of the man who was killed here last night. . . ."

The general said:

"You don't say you have only two tunics? . . . Have you no mess clothes?"

Tietjens said:

"Yes, sir, I've my blue things. I shall be all right for to-night. . . . But almost everything else I possessed was stolen from my kit when I was in hospital. . . . Even Sylvia's two pair of sheets . . ."

"But hang it all," the general exclaimed, "you don't mean to say you've spaffled all your father left you?"

Tietjens said:

"I thought fit to refuse what my father left me owing to the way it was left. . . ."

The general said:

"But, good God! . . . Read that!" He tossed the small sheet of paper at which he had been looking across the table. It fell face downwards. Tietjens read, in the minute handwriting of the general's:

"Colonel's horse: Sheets: Jesus Christ: Wannop girl: Socialism?"

The general said irritably:

"The other side . . . the other side . . ."

The other side of the paper displayed the words in large capitals: WORKERS OF THE WORLD, a woodcut of a sickle and some other objects. Then high treason for a page.

The general said:

"Have you ever seen anything like that before? Do you know what it is?"

Tietjens answered:

"Yes, sir. I sent that to you. To your intelligence . . ."

The general thumped both his fists violently on the army blanket:

"You . . ." he said. "It's incomprehensible. . . . It's incredible. . . ."

Tietjens said:

"No, sir. . . . You sent out an order asking commanders of units to ascertain what attempts were being made by socialists to undermine the discipline of their other ranks. . . . I naturally asked my sergeant-major, and he produced this sheet, which one of the men had given to him as a curiosity. It had been handed to the man in the street in London. You can see my initials on the top of the sheet!"

The general said:

"You . . . you'll excuse me, but you're not a socialist yourself? . . ."

Tietjens said:

"I knew you were working round to that, sir: But I've

no politics that did not disappear in the eighteenth century. You, sir, prefer the seventeenth!"

"Another shower-bath, I suppose," the general said.

"Of course," Tietjens said, "if it's Sylvia that called me a socialist, it's not astonishing. I'm a Tory of such an extinct type that she might take me for anything. The last megatherium. She's absolutely to be excused. . . ."

The general was not listening. He said:

"What was wrong with the way your father left his money to you? . . ."

"My father," Tietjens said—the general saw his jaw stiffen—"committed suicide because a fellow called Ruggles told him that I was . . . what the French call *maquereau*. . . . I can't think of the English word. My father's suicide was not an act that can be condoned. A gentleman does not commit suicide when he has descendants. It might influence my boy's life very disastrously. . . ."

The general said:

"I can't . . . I *can't* get to the bottom of all this. . . . What in the world did Ruggles want to go and tell your father that for? . . . What are you going to do for a living after the war? They won't take you back into your office, will they?"

Tietjens said:

"No, sir. The department will not take me back. Everyone who has served in this war will be a marked man for a long time after it is over. That's proper enough. *We're* having our fun now."

The general said:

"You say the wildest things."

Tietjens answered:

"You generally find the things I say come true, sir. Could we get this over? Ruggles told my father what he did because it is not a good thing to belong to the seventeenth or eighteenth centuries in the twentieth. Or really because it is not good to have taken one's public school's ethical system seriously. I am really, sir, the English public-school boy. That's an eighteenth-century product. What with the love of truth that—God help me!—they rammed into me at Clifton and the belief Arnold forced upon Rugby that the vilest of sins— the vilest of all sins—is to peach to the head master! That's me, sir. Other men get over their schooling. I never have. I remain adolescent. These things are obsessions with me. Complexes, sir!"

The general said:

"All this seems to be very wild. . . . What's this about peaching to a head master?"

Tietjens said:

"For a swan-song, it's not wild, sir. You're asking for a swan-song. I am to go up into the line so that the morals of the troops in your command may not be contaminated by the contemplation of my marital infelicities."

The general said:

"You don't want to go back to England, do you?"

Tietjens exclaimed:

"Certainly not! Very certainly not! I can never go home. I have to go underground somewhere. If I went back to England there would be nothing for me but going underground by suicide."

The general said:

"You see all that? I can give you testimonials. . . ."

Tietjens asked:

"Who couldn't see that it's impossible?"

The general said:

"But . . . suicide! You won't do that. As you said: think of your son."

Tietjens said:

"No, sir. I shan't do that. But you see how bad for one's descendants suicide is. That is why I do not forgive my father. Before he did it I should never have contemplated the idea. Now I have contemplated it. That's a weakening of the moral fibre. It's contemplating a fallacy as a possibility. For suicide is no remedy for a twisted situation of a psychological kind. It is for bankruptcy. Or for military disaster. For the man of action, not for the thinker. Creditors' meetings wipe the one out. Military operations sweep on. But my problem will remain the same whether I'm here or not. For it's insoluble. It's the whole problem of the relations of the sexes."

The general said:

"Good God! . . ."

Tietjens said:

"No, sir, I've not gone off my chump. That's my problem! . . . But I'm a fool to talk so much. . . . It's because I don't know what to say."

The general sat staring at the table-cloth: his face was suffused with blood. He had the appearance of a man in monstrous ill humour. He said:

"You had better say what you want to say. What the devil do you mean? . . . What's this all about? . . ."

Tietjens said:

"I'm enormously sorry, sir. It's difficult to make myself plain."

The general said:

"Neither of us do. What is language for? What the *hell* is language for? We go round and round. I suppose I'm an old fool who cannot understand your modern ways. . . . But you're not modern. I'll do you *that* justice. . . . That beastly little McKechnie is modern. . . . I shall ram him into your divisional-transport job so that he won't incommode you in your battalion. . . . Do you understand what the little beast did? He got leave to go and get a divorce. And then did not get a divorce. *That's* modernism. He said he had scruples. I understand that he and his wife and . . . some dirty other fellow . . . slept three in a bed. That's modern scruples. . . ."

Tietjens said:

"No, sir, it's not really. . . . But what is a man to do if his wife is unfaithful to him?"

The general said as if it were an insult:

"Divorce the harlot! Or live with her! . . ." Only a beast, he went on, would expect a woman to live all her life alone in a cock-loft! She's bound to die. Or go on the streets . . . What sort of a fellow wouldn't see that? Was there any sort of beast who'd expect a woman to live . . . with a man beside her? . . . Why, she'd . . . she'd be bound to . . . He'd have to take the consequences of whatever happened. The general repeated: "Whatever happened! If she pulled all the strings of all the shower-baths in the world!"

Tietjens said:

"Still, sir . . . there are . . . there used to be . . . in families of . . . position . . . a certain . . ." He stopped.

The general said:

"Well . . ."

Tietjens said:

"On the part of the man . . . a certain . . . Call it . . . parade!"

The general said:

"Then there had better be no more parades. . . ." He said: "Damn it! . . . Beside us, all women are saints. . . . Think of what child-bearing is. I know the world. . . . Who would stand that? . . . You? . . . I . . . I'd rather be the last poor devil in Perry's lines!"

He looked at Tietjens with a sort of injurious cunning:

"Why *don't* you divorce?" he asked.

Panic came over Tietjens. He knew it would be his last panic of that interview. No brain could stand more. Fragments of scenes of fighting, voices, names, went before his eyes and ears. Elaborate problems . . . The whole map of the embattled world ran out in front of him—as large as a field. An embossed map in greenish *papier mâché*—a ten-acre field of embossed *papier mâché*: with the blood of O9 Morgan blurring luminously over it. Years before . . . How many months? . . . Nineteen, to be exact, he had sat on some tobacco-plants on the Mont de Kats. . . . No, the Montagne Noire. In Belgium . . . What had he been doing? . . . Trying to get the lie of the land . . . No . . . Waiting to point out positions to some fat home general who had never come. The Belgian proprietor of the tobacco-plants had arrived and had screamed his head off over the damaged plants. . . .

But, up there you saw the whole war. . . . Infinite miles away, over the sullied land that the enemy forces held: into Germany proper. Presumably you could breathe in Germany proper. . . . Over your right shoulder you could see a stump of a tooth. The Cloth Hall at Ypres: at an angle of 50° below . . . Dark lines behind it . . . The German trenches before Wytschaete! . . .

That was before the great mines had blown Wytschaete to hell. . . .

But—every half-minute by his wrist-watch—white puffs of cotton-wool existed on the dark lines—the German trenches before Wytschaete. Our artillery practice . . . Good shooting. Jolly good shooting!

Miles and miles away to the left . . . beneath the haze of light that, on a clouded day, the sea threw off, a shaft of sunlight fell, and was reflected in a grey blur. . . . It was the glass roofs of a great aeroplane shelter!

A great plane, the largest he had then seen, was moving over, behind his back, with four little planes as an escort. . . . Over the vast slag-heaps by Béthune. . . . High, purplish-blue heaps, like the steam domes of engines or the breasts of women . . . Bluish-purple. More blue than purple . . . Like all Franco-Belgian Gobelins tapestry . . . And all quiet . . . Under the vast pall of quiet cloud!

There were shells dropping in Poperinge. . . . Five miles out, under his nose . . . The shells dropped. White vapour rose and ran away in plumes. . . . What sort of shells? . . . There were twenty different kinds of shells. . . .

The Huns were shelling Poperinge! A senseless cruelty. It

was five miles behind the line! Prussian brutality . . . There were two girls who kept a tea-shop in Poperinge. . . . High-coloured . . . General Plumer had liked them . . . a fine old general. . . . The shells had killed them both. . . . Any man might have slept with either of them with pleasure and profit. . . . Six thousand of H.M. officers must have thought the same about those high-coloured girls. Good girls! . . . But the Hun shells got them. . . . What sort of fate was that? . . . To be desired by six thousand men and smashed into little gobbets of flesh by Hun shells?

It appeared to be mere Prussianism—the senseless cruelty of the Hun!—to shell Poperinge. An innocent town with a tea-shop five miles behind Ypres . . . Little noiseless plumes of smoke rising under the quiet blanketing of the pale maroon skies, with the haze from the aeroplane shelters, and the great aeroplanes over the Béthune slag-heaps . . . What a dreadful name—Béthune . . .

Probably, however, the Germans had heard that we were massing men in Poperinge. It was reasonable to shell a town where men were being assembled. . . . Or we might have been shelling one of their towns with an army H.Q. in it. So they shelled Poperinge in the silent grey day. . . .

That was according to the rules of the service. . . . General Campion, accepting with equanimity what German aeroplanes did to the hospitals, camps, stables, brothels, theatres, boulevards, chocolate stalls and hotels of his town, would have been vastly outraged if Hun planes had dropped bombs on his private lodgings. . . . The rules of war! . . . You spare, mutually, each other's headquarters and blow to pieces girls that are desired by six thousand men apiece. . . .

That had been nineteen months before! . . . Now, having lost so much emotion, he saw the embattled world as a map. . . . An embossed map of greenish *papier mâché*. The blood of O9 Morgan was blurring luminously over it. At the extreme horizon was territory labelled *White Ruthenians!* Who the devil were *those* poor wretches?

He exclaimed to himself: "By heavens! Is this epilepsy?" He prayed: "Blessed saints, get me spared that!" He exclaimed: "No, it isn't! . . . I've complete control of my mind. My uppermost mind." He said to the general:

"I can't divorce, sir. I've no grounds."

The general said:

"Don't lie. You know what Thurston knows. Do you mean that you have been guilty of contributory misconduct? . . . Whatever it is? And can't divorce! I don't believe it."

Tietjens said to himself:

"*Why* the devil am I so anxious to shield that whore? It's not reasonable. It is an obsession!"

White Ruthenians are miserable people to the south of Lithuania. You don't know whether they incline to the Germans or to the Poles. The Germans don't even know. . . . The Germans were beginning to take their people out of the line where we were weak: they were going to give them proper infantry training. That gave him, Tietjens, a chance. They would not come over strong for at least two months. It meant, though, a great offensive in the spring. Those fellows had sense. In the poor, beastly trenches the Tommies knew nothing but how to chuck bombs. Both sides did that. But the Germans were going to cure it! Stood chucking bombs at each other from forty yards. The rifle was obsolete! Ha! Ha! Obsolete! . . . The civilian psychology!

The general said:

"No! I don't believe it. I know you did not keep any girl in any tobacco-shop. I remember every word you said at Rye in 1912. I wasn't sure then. I am now. You tried to let me think it. You had shut up your house because of your wife's misbehaviour. You let me believe you had been sold up. You weren't sold up at all."

. . . *Why* should it be the civilian psychology to chuckle with delight, uproariously, when the imbecile idea was promulgated that the rifle was obsolete? *Why* should public opinion force on the War Office a training-camp course that completely cut out any thorough instruction in the rifle and communication drill? It was queer. . . . It was, of course, disastrous. Queer. Not altogether mean. Pathetic, too . . .

"Love of truth!" the general said. "Doesn't that include a hatred for white lies? No; I suppose it doesn't, or your servants could not say you were not at home. . . ."

". . . Pathetic!" Tietjens said to himself. Naturally the civilian population wanted soldiers to be made to look like fools: and to be done in. They wanted the war won by men who would at the end be either humiliated or dead. Or both. Except, naturally, their own cousins or fiancées' relatives. That was what it came to. That was what it meant when important gentlemen said that they had rather the war were lost than that cavalry should gain any distinction in it! . . . But it was partly the simple, pathetic illusion of the day that great things could only be done by new inventions. You extinguished the horse, invented something very simple and became God! That is the real pathetic fallacy. You fill a flower-pot with gunpowder and chuck it in the other fellow's face, and heigh presto! the war is won. *All* the soldiers fall down dead! And You: you, who forced the idea on the reluctant military, are the Man that Won the War. You deserve all the women in the world. And . . . you get them! Once the cavalry are out of the way! . . .

The general was using the words:

"Head master!" It brought Tietjens completely back.

He said collectedly:

"Really, sir, why this strafe of yours is so terribly long is that it embraces the whole of life."

The general said:

"You're not going to drag a red herring across the trail. . . . I say you regarded me as a head master in 1912. Now I am your commanding officer—which is the same thing. You must not peach to me. That's what you call the Arnold of Rugby touch. . . . But who was it said: *Magna est veritas et prev . . . prev* something?"

Tietjens said:

"I don't remember, sir."

The general said:

"What was the secret grief your mother had? In 1912? She died of it. She wrote to me just before her death and said she had great troubles. And begged me to look after you, very specially! Why did she do that?" He paused and meditated. He asked: "How do you define Anglican sainthood? The other fellows have canonizations, all ship-shape like Sandhurst examinations. But us Anglicans . . . I've heard fifty persons say your mother was a saint. She was. But why?"

Tietjens said:

"It's the quality of harmony, sir. The quality of being in harmony with your own soul. God having given you your own soul, you are then in harmony with Heaven."

The general said:

"Ah, that's beyond me. . . . I suppose you will refuse any money I leave you in my will?"

Tietjens said:

"Why, no, sir."

The general said:

"But you refused your father's money. Because he believed things against you. What's the difference?"

Tietjens said:

"One's friends ought to believe that one is a gentleman. Automatically. That is what makes one and them in harmony. Probably your friends are your friends because they look at situations automatically as you look at them. . . . Mr. Ruggles knew that I was hard up. He envisaged the situation. If he were hard up, what would he do? Make a living out of the immoral earnings of women . . . That, translated into the government circles in which he lives, means selling your wife or mistress. Naturally he believed that I was the sort of fellow to sell my wife. So that's what he told my father. The point is, my father should not have believed him."

"But I . . ." the general said.

Tietjens said:

"You never believed anything against me, sir."

The general said:

"I know I've damn well worried myself to death over you. . . ."

Tietjens was sentimentally at rest, still with wet eyes. He was walking near Salisbury in a grove, regarding long pastures and plough-lands running to dark, high elms from which, embowered—embowered was the word!—peeped the spire of George Herbert's church. . . . One ought to be a seventeenth-century parson at the time of the renaissance of Anglican saintliness . . . who wrote, perhaps, poems. No, not poems. Prose. The statelier vehicle!

That was home-sickness! . . . He himself was never to go home!

The general said:

"Look here. . . . Your father . . . I'm concerned about your father. . . . Didn't Sylvia perhaps tell him some of the things that distressed him?"

Tietjens said distinctly:

"No, sir. That responsibility cannot be put on to Sylvia. My father chose to believe things that were said against me by a perfect—or a nearly perfect—stranger. . . ." He added: "As a matter of fact, Sylvia and my father were not on any sort of terms. I don't believe they exchanged two words for the last five years of my father's life."

The general's eyes were fixed with an extreme hardness on Tietjens'. He watched Tietjens' face, beginning with the edges round the nostrils, go chalk-white. He said: "He knows he's given his wife away! . . . Good God!" With his face colourless, Tietjens' eyes of porcelain-blue stuck out extraordinarily. The general thought: "What an ugly fellow! His face is all crooked!" They remained looking at each other.

In the silence the voices of men talking over the game of house came as a murmur to them. A rudimentary card game monstrously in favour of the dealer. When you heard voices going on like that you knew they were playing house. . . . So they had had their dinners.

The general said:

"It isn't Sunday, is it?"

Tietjens said:

"No, sir; Thursday, the seventeenth, I think, of January . . ."

The general said:

"Stupid of me . . ."

The men's voices had reminded him of church-bells on a Sunday. And of his youth . . . He was sitting beside Mrs. Tietjens' hammock under the great cedar at the corner of the stone house at Groby. The wind being from the east-north-east, the bells of Middlesbrough came to them faintly. Mrs. Tietjens was thirty; he himself thirty; Tietjens—the father—thirty-five or so. A most powerful, quiet man. A wonderful landowner. Like his predecessors for generations. It was not from him that this fellow got his . . . his . . . his what? . . . Was it mysticism? . . . Another word! He himself home on leave from India: his head full of polo. Talking for hours about points in ponies with Tietjens' father, who was a wonderful hand with a horse . . . But this fellow was much more wonderful! . . . Well, he got that from the sire, not the dam! . . . He and Tietjens continued to look at each other. It was as if they were hypnotized. The men's voices went on in a mournful cadence. The general supposed that he too must be pale. He said to himself: "This fellow's mother died of a broken heart in 1912. The father committed suicide five years after. He had not spoken to the son's wife for four or five years! That takes us back to 1912. . . . Then, when I strafed him in Rye, the wife was in France with Perowne."

He looked down at the blanket on the table. He intended again to look up at Tietjens' eyes with ostentatious care. That was his technique with men. He was a successful general because he knew men. He knew that all men will go to hell over three things: alcohol, money . . . and sex. This fellow apparently hadn't. Better for him if he had! He thought:

"It's all gone . . . Mother! Father! Groby! This fellow's down and out. It's a bit thick."

He thought:

"But he's right to do as he is doing."

He prepared to look at Tietjens. . . . He stretched out a sudden, ineffectual hand. Sitting on his beef case, his hands on his knees, Tietjens had lurched. A sudden lurch —as an old house lurches when it is hit by an H.E. shell. It stopped at that. Then he righted himself. He continued to stare direct at the general. The general looked carefully back. He said—very carefully too:

"In case I decide to contest West Cleveland, it is your wish that I should make Groby my headquarters?"

Tietjens said:

"I beg, sir, that you will!"

It was as if they both heaved an enormous sigh of relief. The general said:

"Then I need not keep you. . . ."

Tietjens stood on his feet, wanly, but with his heels together.

The general also rose, settling his belt. He said:

". . . You can fall out."

Tietjens said:

"My cook-houses, sir . . . Sergeant Cook Case will be very disappointed. . . . He told me that you couldn't find anything wrong if I gave him ten minutes to prepare. . . ."

The general said:

"Case . . . Case . . . Case was in the drums when we were at Delhi. He ought to be at least quartermaster by now. . . . But he had a woman he called his sister. . . ."

Tietjens said:

"He still sends money to his sister."

The general said:

". . . He went absent over her when he was coloursergeant, and was reduced to the ranks. . . . Twenty years ago that must be! . . . Yes, I'll see your dinners!"

In the cook-house, brilliantly accompanied by Colonel Levin, the cook-house spotless with limed walls and mirrors that were the tops of camp-cookers, the general, Tietjens at his side, walked between goggle-eyed men in white who stood to attention holding ladles. Their eyes bulged, but the corners of their lips curved because they liked the general and his beautifully unconcerned companions. The cookhouse was like a cathedral's nave, aisles being divided off by the pipes of stoves. The floor was of coke-brise shining under French polish and turpentine.

The building paused, as when a godhead descends. In breathless focusing of eyes the godhead, frail and shining, walked with short steps up to a high priest who had a walrus moustache and, with seven medals on his Sunday tunic, gazed away into eternity. The general tapped the sergeant's good-conduct ribbon with the heel of his crop. All stretched ears heard him say:

"How's your sister, Case? . . ."

Gazing away, the sergeant said:

"I'm thinking of making her Mrs. Case. . . ."

Slightly leaving him, in the direction of high, var-nished, pitch-pine panels, the general said:

"I'll recommend you for a quartermaster's commission any day you wish. . . . Do you remember Sir Garnet inspecting field-kitchens at Quetta?"

All the white tubular beings with global eyes resembled the pierrots of a child's Christmas nightmare. The general said: "Stand at ease, men. . . . Stand easy!" They moved as white objects move in a childish dream. It was all child-ish. Their eyes rolled.

Sergeant Case gazed away into infinite distance.

"My sister would not like it, sir," he said. "I'm better off as a first-class warrant-officer!"

With his light step the shining general went swiftly to the varnished panels in the eastern aisle of the cathedral. The white figure beside them became instantly tubular, motion-less and global-eyed. On the panels were painted: TEA! SUGAR! SALT! CURRY PDR! FLOUR! PEPPER!

The general tapped with the heel of his crop on the locker-panel labelled PEPPER: the top, right-hand locker-panel. He said to the tubular, global-eyed white figure be-side it: "Open that, will you, my man? . . ."

To Tietjens this was like the sudden bursting out of the regimental quick step, as after a funeral with military hon-ours the band and drums march away, back to barracks.

AFTERWORD

I ~

Ford Madox Ford's *Parade's End* is a tetralogy, a sequence of four novels that, though they can be read separately, are closely connected and need to be read together if their full meaning is to be appreciated. Apart from some nonfiction—notably the tribute to Conrad that Ford wrote in a burst of feeling immediately after hearing of Conrad's death, in the autumn of 1924—Ford worked steadily on these novels, so that within a span of four years the whole tetralogy had been published, *Some Do Not . . .* in 1924, *No More Parades* in 1925, *A Man Could Stand Up—* in 1926, and *Last Post* in 1928.

Thus these novels represent a single, coherent act of imagination and a single, nearly continuous act of composition. As such they constitute a large vision of a crucial period of history, from the moment when the "Victorian Compromise" collapsed—Ford believed the Boer War marked the beginning of that collapse—until the civilization that embodied it was finally destroyed by the First World War, when last post (the equivalent of the American taps) sounded at the funeral of a civilization and men who hoped to go on living had to turn away from its grave, with whatever regrets for that buried Land of Hope and Glory (and Ford, like Christopher Tietjens, felt many), knowing that its "parades," however graceful, were now so irrelevant to the inner reality of life that no one could any longer perform them. This was Parade's End.

It is this that Christopher Tietjens, Ford's central character, has in mind as he sits in the military hut near Rouen in November of 1917 listening to the shells bursting and talking to a brave but now half-mad young officer named McKechnie.

"At the beginning of the war," Tietjens said, "I had to look in on the War Office, and in a room I found a fellow. . . . What do you think he was doing . . . what the hell do you think he was doing? He was devising the ceremonial for the disbanding of a Kitchener battalion. You can't say we were not prepared in one matter at least. . . . Well, the end of the show was to be: the adjutant would stand the battalion at ease: the band would play 'Land of Hope and Glory,' and then the adjutant would say: *There will be no more parades.* . . . Don't you see how symbolical it was: the band playing 'Land of Hope and Glory,' and then the adjutant saying *There will be no more parades?* . . . For there won't. There won't, there damn well won't. . . . No more Hope, no more Glory, no more parades for you and me any more. Nor for the country . . . Nor for the world, I dare say . . . None . . . Gone . . . Napoo finny! No . . . more . . . parades!" (pp. 310–11)

2 ～

The cultural and social revolution that came to its climax in the First World War has underlain contemporary literature for nearly half a century now. It is the basis for the almost schizoid private dilemmas of Mr. Eliot's Prufrock and his Gerontion as much as it is—more obviously—for the political indignation of war novels like Hemingway's and the social preoccupations of sagas like Galsworthy's and Arnold Bennett's. *Parade's End* is the most inclusive work in English to take this revolution for its subject because it succeeds in unifying something of the realities of all these kinds of fiction.

For reasons that are deeply rooted in Ford's temperament and in the late-Victorian world he grew up in, Ford moved slowly through his early career as a novelist toward this role of "the contemporary historian in fiction," as Paul Wiley calls it. His first real success as a writer was the three related historical novels about Catherine Howard and Henry VIII now called *The Fifth Queen* (1906–1908). They are not Ford's only historical novels. In 1913, just two years before his first great novel, *The Good Soldier*, he published a medieval story called *The Young Lovell*, and two years before that a book contrasting medieval and modern life called *Ladies Whose Bright Eyes*.

The form of these books is that of the conventional historical romance of the Edwardian period, but Ford was trying to write something different from the conventional romance even then. The contemporary he most admired was Conrad, and the Conrad he admired was the author of *Under Western Eyes, Nostromo,* and *The Secret Agent*— that is, the Conrad who was a "contemporary historian in fiction." For their conception of this kind of novel, Ford and Conrad, Ford says (though truly it may have been only Ford who did so), looked to the Flaubert of *Salammbô, La Tentation de Saint-Antoine,* and above all *L'Education sentimentale*—that is, the Flaubert who tried to re-create the past in such a way as to make it both historically precise and relevant to the present or to describe the present—in both its public and its private aspects—as if it were history.

As early as 1901 Ford produced an odd novel—*The Inheritors*—that tries but fails to realize this simultaneously private and public sense of history. Conrad collaborated with him on it, but was so little interested in it that he never took it seriously. "I set myself to look upon the thing as a sort of skit upon the sort of political (?!) novel, fools of the N[ew] S[tatesman] sort do write," he wrote Edward Garnett. "This in my heart of hearts. And poor H[ueffer] was dead in earnest! Oh Lord. How he worked! There is not a chapter I haven't made him write twice— most of them three times over." Conrad may—for Garnett's benefit—be acting somewhat more superior to Ford and his novel than he really was. But at best these are not the words of a man who understood what Ford was trying—with however little success—to do in *The Inheritors*.

Ford grew up among the Pre-Raphaelites—his mother was a daughter of the Pre-Raphaelite painter Ford Madox Brown —and one of his lifelong preoccupations was an attempt to see, from the perspective of the modern world, what the late-Victorian world was like. He devoted four books to it, just as he came back again and again, in books like *Return to Yesterday* (1931) and *Portraits from Life* (1937), to the world and the writers he had known in his young manhood. These books are all, as Ford always took care to point out, more nearly works of fiction than of fact. Ford was always trying to *see* the past—"above all to make you see," as Conrad put it in a phrase Ford never forgot.

To make you see meant to Ford an intense sensory impression, but that sensory impression was important to him primarily because it was the best way to make clear the inner reality of an event. "For technical facts as facts," as he once put it, "I have no respect whatever. Normally I rather despise myself for playing for factual accuracy in a novel." There is perhaps a little swagger about this statement, but it is essentially correct. The "fixities and definites" of the literally possible, of the imaginatively dead fact, he was unconcerned with; what mattered to him was the probable fact that revealed inner meaning with a burst of illumination. In short, he was, in these books as well as in his novels, the contemporary historian in fiction.

One result of Ford's intimate knowledge of the late Victorians was that he very early felt a deep dislike of the gross sensuality dressed up in high-sounding language that was one aspect of the aesthetic movement. It seemed to him one of the seriously corrupting—if sometimes sincerely maintained—hypocrisies of the age; the other major hypocrisy of this kind, he thought, was the crude imperialism dressed up in the high-sounding language of the white man's burden that emerged during the Boer War.

Early in *Some Do Not . . .* Christopher Tietjens makes a slashing attack on Rossetti, the poet whom Vincent Macmaster, the earnest social climber of *Parade's End,* writes his monograph about and the guiding light of Macmaster's grandiloquent and grubbily *sub-rosa* love affair with Edith Ethel Duchemin. This attack on Rossetti precisely expresses Ford's feelings.

"I tell you it revolts me to think of that obese, oily man who never took a bath, in a grease-spotted dressing-gown and the underclothes he's slept in, standing beside a five-shilling model with crimped hair or some Mrs. W. Three Stars ['She had three lilies in her hand,/ And the stars in her hair were seven,' as Rossetti's 'Blessed Damozel' says], gazing into a mirror that reflects their fetid selves and gilt sunfish and drop chandeliers and plates sickening with cold bacon fat and gurgling about passion." (pp. 22–23.)

This judgment governs the treatment of sexual attitudes throughout *Parade's End,* and sexual attitudes are close to the center of Ford's conception of the moral position and personal conduct of his characters.

On the other hand, Ford learned from Pre-Raphaelites he admired, Holman Hunt and Millais and his beloved grandfather, what he believed to be the true vocation of the artist: an absolute dedication to the artist's insight and to its expression. Ford thus came early—and thanks to these late Victorians—to a conviction that the historical dimension of experience is essential and that experience itself is an insight into the quality of events rather than a mere recognition of its facts. He was thus prepared to share with his friend Ezra Pound the twentieth century's then only half-understood need for a literary form that would enable writers to represent the appearance of their age in such a way as to reveal the inner quality that was for them its informing reality. Finding that form was very difficult, and it is one of the obscuring misfortunes of literary history that Ford, with the innocent vanity of his desire to appear omniscient, and Pound, with the bumptious air of self-assurance he assumed for propaganda purposes in his criticism, concealed from us how difficult it was for them.

They meant to make us inheritors, to make the accumulated wisdom of our culture part of the contemporary knowledge of experience. They thought the only way to do that was to bring back to life those moments of the past when it had been alive, to make history an immediate and defining personal experience in the present. In what may well be Pound's finest poetry, the *Draft of Thirty Cantos*—passionate, personal, even autobiographical treatment of contemporary life though it is—he spends much time on the minute, significant details of Sigismundo Malatesta's Italian Renaissance life, and more on those forms originally created by our even earlier ancestors and revivified in the Renaissance, the gods of classical mythology. We too, Pound says at the end of the second canto, perhaps more in hope than in real belief,

> have heard the fauns chiding Proteus
>
> in the smell of hay under the olive-trees,
> And the frogs singing against the fauns
> in the half-light.
> And . . .

It was a similar vision of the past, with all its concrete particulars brought to life by the vitality of their inner reality, that Ford was struggling to realize in his early historical novels, which dealt with realistic medieval young men seduced by la belle dame (*The Young Lovell*) and heroically idealistic believers in the old religion and the new learning in the power-hungry world of Henry VIII (*The Fifth Queen*). Ford's ultimate object was, like Pound's, to create contemporary history as fiction. In the *Cantos* and *Parade's End* they both did so, for whatever the limitations of these works, they are the largest twentieth-century English literature has yet produced on this fundamental subject.

3 ~

We do not know much about the personal struggle Pound went through to achieve the complete commitment of the *Cantos*, though there are occasional glimpses of it behind his wry envy of more immediately successful poets, as when he wrote Eliot after first reading *The Waste Land*, "Complimenti, you bitch. I am wracked by the seven jealousies. . . ." But we do know something of Ford's struggle because he has described in *It Was the Nightingale* how he came to write *Parade's End*. All his life Ford was a man wholly dedicated to writing—an old man, as he once said in paraphrase of Hokusai, mad about writing; yet, as Stella Bowen tells us in her book about her life with Ford, *Drawn from Life*, he was never quite confident of his talent. As a result he felt a need for the moral support of recognition and praise that is like vanity; whenever he felt deprived of it, he was in danger of a nervous breakdown, of which he had several in his life.

Immediately after the war he felt most acutely deprived of it. He had spent three and a half years in the army, away from writing and the literary world of London, which during the war years had, he felt, developed a virulent, guilty hatred of all fighting soldiers. No doubt he exaggerated this feeling, as perhaps he overestimated, out of his need for it, the reputation as a writer he thought he had lost. In any event he felt his obscurity in postwar England acutely and never forgot how, at his first postwar literary party, a home-front critic said to him, "You used to write, didn't you?" His instinct was to give up writing and flee from London to take up the life of a small producer at Red Ford in West Sussex.

> Beneath the sagging roof
> The stylist has taken shelter,
> Unpaid, uncelebrated. . . .
>
> The haven from sophistications and contentions
> Leaks through its thatch;

He offers succulent cooking;
The door has a creaking latch,

as Pound put it in *Mauberley*.

Ford had another reason for giving up writing. One of the queer things about Ford's career is that despite his evident talent, it was not until he was forty-two, about to join the army and convinced he would never have a chance to write another book, that he committed all his resources to a novel, *The Good Soldier*. Up to then he had rather exercised his talent than put his whole imagination into a book. Clearly, total commitment was difficult for him.

Total commitment is always dangerous for a writer; it shakes him to the roots of his being, and perhaps Ford in some way understood that with his shaky psyche it might be disastrous for him. Certainly immediately after the war —for he had been shell-shocked—it was dangerous for him. During the last months of the war and immediately after, he had written a queer, shaken book called *No Enemy*, which was so personal that he did not publish it for ten years; three years later he tried out in a limited way some of the insights of *Parade's End* in *The Marsden Case* (1923). But both of these books are tentative. It must have taken great courage to commit himself completely, as he did in *Parade's End*: it was taking his psychic life in his hands, and he must have known it.

Once you see that, you see the pathos beneath the air of humorous self-regard with which Ford describes, in *It Was the Nightingale,* how more and more Americans sought him out at Red Ford until what he calls the Middle West "gave me the final tilt toward Literature and away, alas apparently forever, from hogs!"—and then goes on to show how *Parade's End* grew in his mind until

one day I sat down [in Harold Munro's villa at Cap Ferrat] at Munro's grandfather's campaign-secrétaire—it had been on the field of Waterloo—I took up a pen: saluted St. Anthony who looked down on me, in sheer gratitude for his letting me find my pen at all and I wrote my first sentence. . . . It ran:
"The two young men—they were of the English public-official class—sat in the perfectly appointed railway carriage."

He was forty-nine years old.

4 ~

The idea of writing *Parade's End* came into Ford's mind when a casual meeting with Sir Edward Elgar, the composer of "Land of Hope and Glory," reminded him simultaneously of Henry James (at whose house Ford had met Elgar) and of the war; "and for the rest of the day and for several days more I lost myself in working out an imaginary war novel on the lines of 'What Maisie Knew.'" In the foreground of *What Maisie Knew*, its primary reality and the determinant of its form, is the vivid, limited child's consciousness of Maisie; reflected there, with the human shape of the child's candid mind but without the adult mind's distorting moral sophistications, we see the intrigue that is going on around Maisie and, more faintly, as if by a double reflection, the attitudes of the whole society, which are implied by the conduct of the adults involved in this intrigue. "The one presented register of the whole complexity," as James put it in his preface, "would be the play of the child's confused and obscure notation of it."

Ford does not take over this method of presentation wholesale; it would have been impossible to handle the history of a whole decade in this way, and in any event Ford was temperamentally averse to so rigid a form, since for him both the event and the perception of it in the character's mind had meaning. What he needed was a form that would simultaneously present events so as to reveal their inner significance and the consciousness of an involved but alienated intelligence that would reveal the psychological dimension of his history.

The first purpose he fulfilled by composing the carefully selected scenes—they are few and long in *Parade's End*—according to the method he had first worked out in *The Good Soldier*, the method for treating what he called The Affair, "the slowing down of time, the multiple points of view, the worrying over minute details of etiquette and conduct, the ironic confrontation of outward appearance and inward reality, and the involvement of more and more coincidences in the pattern of meaning [until] comment and scene are so closely interwoven that they merge." (This summary of Ford's technical devices is Mr. R. W. Lid's.) This method of presenting events owes a good deal to both James and Conrad, as Ford was always anxious to point out, though it is not the method of either. In effect what Ford has done is to transfer James's way of dramatizing his central intelligence's gradual discovery of the meaning of events to the author himself and then to intensify this drama of meaning by using the time shift and other devices he and Conrad had worked out during their collaboration.

Similarly he combined devices used by James and Conrad for representing the private, psychological history of a central character. For at the center of Ford's composition is a dominant, though not exclusive, point of view, the mind of Christopher Tietjens. Christopher is not in any simple sense Ford; he is rather a kind of objective correlative for Ford's total impression of the private history of his time, to which, inevitably, Ford's own private experience contributed a good many details. He is a morally tough, intellectually brilliant, old-fashioned Tory from Yorkshire, whose attitude Ford clearly thinks is ludicrously—but by no means discreditably —out of accord with the times, a brilliant innocent with a simple, almost childlike, though exceedingly tenacious moral nature and a shamefaced, secret longing to be an Anglican saint.

In all these ways Christopher is modeled on a man named Arthur Marwood, whom Ford had known in Winchelsea before the war. This "heavy Yorkshire squire with his dark hair startlingly silver in places, his keen blue eyes, his florid complexion, his immense, expressive hands and his great shapelessness" gave Ford a point of view not his own from which to show the effects of the events he is describing on a fine mind of great integrity. If such a mind is forced by the pressure of events to change, then no one can doubt the need for such change. For Christopher is not just a reflector; like James's Lambert Strether, he is forced by the pressure of events to change radically. He is, indeed, the one person who sees quite clearly that the revolution of his time has been so great that he must transform his whole conception of how to live or he will die—as his brother and double, Mark, in fact does. Christopher thus becomes a detailed, dramatic example of the change in attitude that constitutes the internal, psychological aspect of the revolution Ford is describing.

The events of the novel represent the gradual splitting apart of the appearances and the reality of Edwardian social life, the irrelevance to life of its dazzling parade, whether of official life, as represented by "General Lord Edward Campion, G.C.B., K.C.M.G. (MILITARY), D.S.O., etc. . . . radiating glory and composing a confidential memorandum to the Secretary of State for War," or of the personal life, as represented by Sylvia sitting before her dressing table in the hotel room in Rouen "with the merest film of clothing on her long, shining limbs," "her gilded sheath gown . . . about her hips on the chair." In the same way the representation of Christopher's consciousness shows us the gradual splitting apart of the Edwardian ideal of conduct and the inner reality of self, whether with respect to public duty or private conduct.

Just, too, as the reality of Edwardian social life slowly emerges for us from beneath the once meaningful but now insignificant parade of social life, so the reality of Christopher's self slowly emerges from what Ford calls his "under self" onto the surface of his consciousness. This is the pervasive, controlling insight of *Parade's End*. What is wrong with this world is that the life of the mind and feelings no longer is expressed by the customary modes of conduct, by the mannered social ritual of Edwardian life; what people think and feel has either to be suppressed or expressed clandestinely at the same time that the orderly social ritual has become a parade without meaning, beautiful but dead.

At the beginning of *Some Do Not . . .*, while the routine of Edwardian life is still apparently intact, the alienated life beneath shows only in shockingly distorted glimpses—in the sexual madness of Duchemin and the aesthetic self-deception of Edith Ethel, in the vulgarity of the city men while drinking in the golf house or chasing suffragettes across the links, in the high-minded cheating of Macmaster, the ignorant recklessness of General Campion, the spontaneous sexual cruelty of Sylvia. With the outbreak of the war these evils erupt violently, reducing the political order to chaos, destroying the social parade of the "best" people, making the orderly individual life impossible. This is a world where

> History has many cunning passages, contrived corridors
> And issues, deceives with whispering ambitions,
> Guides us by vanities,

so that

Neither fear nor courage saves us. Unnatural vices
Are fathered by our heroism. Virtues
Are forced upon us by our impudent crimes.

"War time England," as Ford put it succinctly in *It Was the Nightingale*, was "like a lunatic asylum."

This insight, so consistently realized in *Parade's End*, is first expressed in *The Good Soldier* (1915). There the narrator, looking back, with full knowledge of the tragedy, at the life he and his wife had led with the Ashburnhams at Nauheim, thinks:

Permanence? Stability! I can't believe it's gone. I can't believe that long, tranquil life, which was just stepping a minuet, vanished. . . . No indeed, it can't be gone. You can't kill a minuet de la cour. You may shut up the music-book, close the harpsichord; in the cupboards and presses the rats may destroy the white satin favours. The mob may sack Versailles; the Trianon may fall, but surely the minuet—the minuet itself is dancing itself away into the furthest stars, even as our minuet of the Hessian bathing places must be stepping itself still. . . . No, by God, it is false! It wasn't a minuet that we stepped; it was a prison—a prison full of screaming hysterics, tied down so that they might not outsound the rolling of our carriage wheels as we went along the shaded avenues of the Taunus Wald.

The almost unbearable truth is, of course, that it is both. These people are conducting their lives—sometimes by difficult and even heroic acts of self-discipline—by a code of graceful manners that is in fact merely a pretense because the inner reality of their natures has grown completely out of accord with it, so that to live its ritual is no longer to fulfill one's nature but to frustrate it to the point of madness. The one character in *The Good Soldier* who might have lived happily in a world that really practiced this code was Edward Ashburnham, the good soldier of the title. He longs to devote himself publicly to his tenantry like a feudal lord and to devote himself privately to his ideal woman like a feudal knight. But, like Christopher Tietjens, he is misunderstood and maligned by a society that does not really live at all by its professed code but only uses it for other purposes. It therefore finds incomprehensible, even wicked, anyone who really does live by that code.

The essential tragedy of *The Good Soldier* is the widening abyss between the unconscious life of the "under self" in men and their conscious commitment to an inherited code

of conduct. It is this same split that brings Christopher
Tietjens to the edge of madness; he is saved only by a
heroic act of renunciation, when he gives up his lifelong
commitment to the role of the Yorkshire Tory Younger Son
and starts over again, from scratch, to try to live in a
way that accords with his real nature.

By the second novel of *Parade's End, No More Parades,*
Christopher's conscious mind and his real but suppressed
self have been forced so far apart that he has fallen into
the habit of deliberately waiting in his conscious mind to
see what his real self is going to think and feel. More and
more, as *No More Parades* moves toward its climax, he puz-
zles over his own intentions: "He occupied himself with his
mind. What was it going to do? He cast back along his military history: What had his mind done in similar moments
before? . . ." (p. 483). "It is bad when the mind takes charge
like that," he thinks later, in *A Man Could Stand Up—*
(p. 50).

Precisely because Christopher has lived with such heroic
literalness by the ostensible standards of conduct of Edwardian society, has devoted himself so uncompromisingly
to his public duties as a soldier and his private duties as a
husband, he has created a mess and a scandal such as only
saints are capable of producing, and at the end of *No
More Parades* General Campion decides he has no recourse
but to relieve Christopher of his base command and send him
to the front. As it turns out, this development brings to an
end Christopher's effort to conform to his society's code,
though his conscious mind does not fully take in the consequences of this decision of his "under self" until, in *A Man
Could Stand Up—,* he finally recognizes consciously his
conviction that Edwardian society is finished and that he
loves Valentine Wannop; only then does he determine to act
on the desires of his real self and to give up altogether
his efforts to realize the ideal of his society.

Nevertheless, the climax of *No More Parades* is Christopher's recognition that the Edwardian world is done for,
so that while he watches the outwardly dazzling military
figure of General Campion inspecting his unit's cookhouses,
"to Tietjens this was like the sudden bursting out of the
regimental quick step, as after a funeral with military hon-
ours the band and drums march away, back to barracks"—
for the last time so far as Christopher is concerned. The
decisive change in Christopher's conception of experience
and in the conduct of his life consequent on that change

thus occurs precisely in the middle of *Parade's End*, at the very end of *No More Parades*. The third and fourth novels of *Parade's End*, *A Man Could Stand Up—* and *Last Post*, will show us the consequences of that change, both for the Edwardian world and for Christopher's private life.

ARTHUR MIZENER

A NOTE ON THE TEXT

This Signet Classic edition reprints the first editions of *Some Do Not . . .* (1924) and *No More Parades* (1925), published by Gerald Duckworth & Co., Ltd., London.

Punctuation and spelling have largely been brought into conformity with current British usage, and obvious typographical errors have been corrected.

SELECTED BIBLIOGRAPHY

OTHER WORKS BY FORD MADOX FORD

The Fifth Queen, 1906 Novel
Privy Seal, 1907 Novel
The Fifth Queen Crowned, 1908 Novel
Ancient Lights and Certain New Reflections,
    1910 Memoirs
The Young Lovell: A Romance, 1913
Henry James: A Critical Study, 1913
The Good Soldier, 1915 Novel
Joseph Conrad: A Personal Remembrance,
    1924
No Enemy: A Tale of Reconstruction, 1929
    Novel
Return to Yesterday, 1931 Memoirs
It Was the Nightingale, 1933 Memoirs
Ladies Whose Bright Eyes: A Romance, 1935
Provence: From Minstrels to the Machine, 1935
The Great Trade Route, 1937 Novel
Portraits from Life, 1937 Memoirs

BIOGRAPHY AND CRITICISM

Bowen, Stella. *Drawn from Life*. New York and London: William Collins Sons & Co., Ltd., 1941.

Cassell, R. A. *Ford Madox Ford*. Baltimore: Johns Hopkins Press, 1962.

Goldring, Douglas. *Trained for Genius*. New York: E. P. Dutton & Co., Inc., 1949.

Hunt, Violet. *I Have This to Say: The Story of My Flurried Years*. New York: Boni & Liveright, 1926.

Lid, R. W. *Ford Madox Ford: The Essence of His Art*. In preparation, to be published by the University of California Press, Berkeley.

Meixner, J. A. *Ford Madox Ford's Novels*. Minneapolis: University of Minnesota Press, 1962.

Ohmann, Carol. *Ford Madox Ford: From Apprentice to Craftsman.* Middletown, Conn.: Wesleyan University Press, 1964.

Wiley, P. L. *Novelist of Three Worlds: Ford Madox Ford.* Syracuse, N.Y.: Syracuse University Press, 1962.